NON SANS DROICT.

William Shakespeare

LOVE'S LABOR'S LOST

THE TWO GENTLEMEN OF VERONA

THE MERRY WIVES OF WINDSOR

With New Dramatic Criticism
and an Updated Bibliography

The Signet Classic Shakespeare
GENERAL EDITOR: SYLVAN BARNET

A SIGNET CLASSIC

SIGNET CLASSIC
Published by the Penguin Group
Penguin Books USA Inc., 375 Hudson Street,
New York, New York 10014, U.S.A.
Penguin Books Ltd, 27 Wrights Lane,
London W8 5TZ, England
Penguin Books Australia Ltd, Ringwood,
Victoria, Australia
Penguin Books Canada Ltd, 10 Alcorn Avenue,
Toronto, Ontario, Canada M4V 3B2
Penguin Books (N.Z.) Ltd, 182–190 Wairau Road,
Auckland 10, New Zealand

Penguin Books Ltd, Registered Offices:
Harmondsworth, Middlesex, England

Published by Signet Classic, an imprint of New American Library,
a division of Penguin Books USA Inc.

11 10 9 8 7 6 5 4 3

Ⓒ REGISTERED TRADEMARK—MARCA REGISTRADA

Library of Congress Catalog Card Number: 85-63516

Printed in the United States of America

Shakespeare: Prefatory Remarks

Between the record of his baptism in Stratford on 26 April 1564 and the record of his burial in Stratford on 25 April 1616, some forty documents name Shakespeare, and many others name his parents, his children, and his grandchildren. More facts are known about William Shakespeare than about any other playwright of the period except Ben Jonson. The facts should, however, be distinguished from the legends. The latter, inevitably more engaging and better known, tell us that the Stratford boy killed a calf in high style, poached deer and rabbits, and was forced to flee to London, where he held horses outside a playhouse. These traditions are only traditions; they may be true, but no evidence supports them, and it is well to stick to the facts.

Mary Arden, the dramatist's mother, was the daughter of a substantial landowner; about 1557 she married John Shakespeare, who was a glove-maker and trader in various farm commodities. In 1557 John Shakespeare was a member of the Council (the governing body of Stratford), in 1558 a constable of the borough, in 1561 one of the two town chamberlains, in 1565 an alderman (entitling him to the appellation "Mr."), in 1568 high bailiff—the town's highest political office, equivalent to mayor. After 1577, for an unknown reason he drops out of local politics. The birthday of William Shakespeare, the eldest son of this locally prominent man, is unrecorded; but the Stratford parish register records that the infant was baptized on 26 April 1564. (It is quite possible that he was born on 23 April, but this date has probably been assigned by tradition because it is the date on which, fifty-two years later, he died.) The attendance records of the Stratford grammar school of the period are not extant, but it is reasonable to assume that the son of a local official attended the school and received substantial training in Latin. The masters of the school from Shakespeare's seventh to fifteenth years held Oxford degrees; the Elizabethan curriculum excluded mathematics and the natural sciences but taught a good deal of Latin rhetoric, logic, and literature. On 27 November 1582 a marriage license was issued to Shakespeare and Anne Hathaway, eight years his senior. The couple had a child in May, 1583. Perhaps the marriage was necessary, but perhaps the couple had earlier engaged in a formal "troth plight" which would render their children legitimate even if no further ceremony were performed. In 1585 Anne Hathaway bore Shakespeare twins.

That Shakespeare was born is excellent; that he married and had children is pleasant; but that we know nothing about his departure from Stratford to London, or about the beginning of his theatrical career, is lamentable and must be admitted. We would gladly sacrifice details about his children's baptism for details about his earliest days on the stage. Perhaps the poaching episode is true (but it is first reported almost a century after Shakespeare's death), or perhaps he first left Stratford to be a schoolteacher, as another tradition holds; perhaps he was moved by

> Such wind as scatters young men through the world,
> To seek their fortunes further than at home
> Where small experience grows.

In 1592, thanks to the cantankerousness of Robert Greene, a rival playwright and a pamphleteer, we have our first reference, a snarling one, to Shakespeare as an actor and playwright. Greene warns those of his own educated friends who wrote for the theater against an actor who has presumed to turn playwright:

> There is an upstart crow, beautified with our feathers, that with his *tiger's heart wrapped in a player's hide* supposes he is as well able to bombast out a blank verse as the best of you, and being an absolute Johannes-factotum is in his own conceit the only Shake-scene in a country.

The reference to the player, as well as the allusion to Aesop's crow (who strutted in borrowed plumage, as an actor struts in fine words not his own), makes it clear that by this date Shakespeare had both acted and written. That Shakespeare is meant is indicated not only by "Shake-scene" but by the parody of a line from one of Shakespeare's plays, *3 Henry VI:* "O, tiger's heart wrapped in a woman's hide." If Shakespeare in 1592 was prominent enough to be attacked by an envious dramatist, he probably had served an apprenticeship in the theater for at least a few years.

In any case, by 1592 Shakespeare had acted and written, and there are a number of subsequent references to him as an actor: documents indicate that in 1598 he is a "principal comedian," in 1603 a "principal tragedian," in 1608 he is one of the "men players." The profession of actor was not for a gentleman, and it occasionally drew the scorn of university men who resented writing speeches for persons less educated than themselves, but it was respectable enough: players, if prosperous, were in effect members of the bourgeoisie, and there is nothing to suggest that Stratford considered William Shakespeare less than a solid citizen. When, in 1596, the Shakespeares were granted a coat of arms, the grant was made to Shakespeare's father, but probably William Shakespeare (who the next year bought the second-largest house in town) had arranged the matter on his own behalf. In subsequent transactions he is occasionally styled a gentleman.

Although in 1593 and 1594 Shakespeare published two narrative poems dedicated to the Earl of Southampton, *Venus and Adonis* and *The Rape of Lucrece,* and may well have written most or all of his sonnets in the middle nineties, Shakespeare's literary activity seems to have been almost entirely devoted to the theater. (It may be significant that the two narrative poems were written in years when the plague closed the theaters for several months.) In 1594 he was a charter member of a theatrical company called the Chamberlain's Men (which in 1603 changed its name to the King's Men); until he retired to Stratford (about 1611, apparently), he was with this remarkably stable company. From 1599 the company acted primarily at the Globe Theatre, in which Shakespeare held a one-tenth interest. Other Elizabethan dramatists are known to have acted, but no other is known also to have been entitled to a share in the profits of the playhouse.

Shakespeare's first eight published plays did not have his name on them, but this is not remarkable; the most popular play of the sixteenth century, Thomas Kyd's *The Spanish Tragedy*, went through many editions without naming Kyd, and Kyd's authorship is known only because a book on the profession of acting happens to quote (and attribute to Kyd) some lines on the interest of Roman emperors in the drama. What is remarkable is that after 1598 Shakespeare's name commonly appears on printed plays—some of which are not his. Another indication of his popularity comes from Francis Meres, author of *Palladis Tamia: Wit's Treasury* (1598): in this anthology of snippets accompanied by an essay on literature, many playwrights are mentioned, but Shakespeare's name occurs more often than any other, and Shakespeare is the only playwright whose plays are listed.

From his acting, playwriting, and share in a theater, Shakespeare seems to have made considerable money. He put it to work, making substantial investments in Stratford real estate. When he made his will (less than a month before he died), he sought to leave his property intact to his descendants. Of small bequests to relatives and to friends (including three actors, Richard Burbage, John Heminges, and Henry Condell), that to his wife of the second-best bed has provoked the most comment; perhaps it was the bed the couple had slept in, the best being reserved for visitors. In any case, had Shakespeare not excepted it, the bed would have gone (with the rest of his household possessions) to his daughter and her husband. On 25 April 1616 he was buried within the chancel of the church at Stratford. An unattractive monument to his memory, placed on a wall near the grave, says he died on 23 April. Over the grave itself are the lines, perhaps by Shakespeare, that (more than his literary fame) have kept his bones undisturbed in the crowded burial ground where old bones were often dislodged to make way for new:

> Good friend, for Jesus' sake forbear
> To dig the dust enclosed here.
> Blessed be the man that spares these stones
> And cursed be he that moves my bones.

Thirty-seven plays, as well as some nondramatic poems, are held to constitute the Shakespeare canon. The dates of composition of most of the works are highly uncertain, but there is often evidence of a *terminus a quo* (starting point) and/or a *terminus ad quem* (terminal point) that provides a framework for intelligent guessing. For example, *Richard II* cannot be earlier than 1595, the publication date of some material to which it is indebted; *The Merchant of Venice* cannot be later than 1598, the year Francis Meres mentioned it. Sometimes arguments for a date hang on an alleged topical allusion, such as the lines about the unseasonable weather in *A Midsummer Night's Dream*, II.i.81–87, but such an allusion (if indeed it is an allusion) can be variously interpreted, and in any case there is always the possibility that a topical allusion was inserted during a revision, years after the composition of a play. Dates are often attributed on the basis of style, and although conjectures about style usually rest on other conjectures, sooner or later one must rely on one's literary sense. There is no real proof, for example, that *Othello* is not as early as *Romeo and Juliet*, but one feels *Othello* is later, and because the first record of its performance is 1604, one is glad enough to set its composition at that date and not push it back into Shakespeare's early years.

The following chronology, then, is as much indebted to informed guesswork and sensitivity as it is to fact. The dates, necessarily imprecise, indicate something like a scholarly consensus.

PLAYS

1588–93	The Comedy of Errors
1588–94	Love's Labor's Lost
1590–91	2 Henry VI
1590–91	3 Henry VI
1591–92	1 Henry VI
1592–93	Richard III
1592–94	Titus Andronicus
1593–94	The Taming of the Shrew
1593–95	The Two Gentlemen of Verona
1594–96	Romeo and Juliet
1595	Richard II
1594–96	A Midsummer Night's Dream
1596–97	King John
1596–97	The Merchant of Venice
1597	1 Henry IV
1597–98	2 Henry IV
1598–1600	Much Ado About Nothing
1598–99	Henry V
1599	Julius Caesar
1599–1600	As You Like It
1599–1600	Twelfth Night
1600–01	Hamlet
1597–1601	The Merry Wives of Windsor
1601–02	Troilus and Cressida
1602–04	All's Well That Ends Well
1603–04	Othello
1604	Measure for Measure
1605–06	King Lear
1605–06	Macbeth
1606–07	Antony and Cleopatra
1605–08	Timon of Athens
1607–09	Coriolanus
1608–09	Pericles

1609–10   *Cymbeline*
1610–11   *The Winter's Tale*
1611   *The Tempest*
1612–13   *Henry VIII*

POEMS

1592   *Venus and Adonis*
1593–94   *The Rape of Lucrece*
1593–1600 *Sonnets*
1600–01   *The Phoenix and the Turtle*

Shakespeare's Theater

In Shakespeare's infancy, Elizabethan actors performed wherever they could—in great halls, at court, in the courtyards of inns. The innyards must have made rather unsatisfactory theaters: on some days they were unavailable because carters bringing goods to London used them as depots; when available, they had to be rented from the innkeeper; perhaps most important, London inns were subject to the Common Council of London, which was not well disposed toward theatricals. In 1574 the Common Council required that plays and playing places in London be licensed. It asserted that

sundry great disorders and inconveniences have been found to ensue to this city by the inordinate haunting of great multitudes of people, specially youth, to plays, interludes, and shows, namely occasion of frays and quarrels, evil practices of incontinency in great inns having chambers and secret places adjoining to their open stages and galleries,

and ordered that innkeepers who wished licenses to hold performances put up a bond and make contributions to the poor.

The requirement that plays and innyard theaters be licensed, along with the other drawbacks of playing at inns, probably drove James Burbage (a carpenter-turned-actor) to rent in 1576 a plot of land northeast of the city walls and to build here—on property outside the jurisdiction of the city—England's first permanent construction designed for plays. He called it simply the Theatre. About all that is known of its construction is that it was wood. It soon had imitators, the most famous being the Globe (1599), built across the Thames (again outside the city's jurisdiction), out of timbers of the Theatre, which had been dismantled when Burbage's lease ran out.

There are three important sources of information about the structure of Elizabethan playhouses—drawings, a contract, and stage directions in plays. Of drawings, only the so-called De Witt drawing (c. 1596) of the Swan— really a friend's copy of De Witt's drawing—is of much significance. It shows a building of three tiers, with a stage jutting from a wall into the yard or center of the building. The tiers are roofed, and part of the stage is covered by a roof that projects from the rear and is supported at its front on two posts, but the groundlings, who paid a penny to stand in front of the stage, were exposed to the sky. (Performances in such a playhouse were held only in the daytime; artificial illumination was not used.) At the rear of the stage are two doors; above the stage is a gallery. The second major source of information, the contract for the Fortune, specifies that although the Globe is to be the model, the Fortune is to be square, eighty feet outside and fifty-five inside. The stage is to be forty-three feet broad, and is to extend into the middle of the yard (i.e., it is twenty-seven and a half feet deep). For patrons willing to pay more than the general admission charged of the groundlings, there were to be three galleries provided with seats. From the third chief source, stage directions, one learns that entrance to the stage was by doors, presumably spaced widely apart at the rear ("Enter one citizen at one door, and another at the other"), and that in addition to the platform stage there was occasionally some sort of curtained booth or alcove allowing for "discovery" scenes, and some sort of playing space "aloft" or "above" to represent (for example) the top of a city's walls or a room above the street. Doubtless each theater had its own peculiarities, but perhaps we can talk about a "typical" Elizabethan theater if we realize that no theater need exactly have fit the description, just as no father is the typical father with 3.7 children. This hypothetical theater is wooden, round or polygonal (in *Henry V* Shakespeare calls it a "wooden *O*"), capable of holding some eight hundred spectators standing in the yard around the projecting elevated stage and some fifteen hundred additional spectators seated in the three roofed galleries. The stage, protected by a "shadow" or "heavens" or roof, is entered by two doors; behind the doors is the "tiring house" (attiring house, i.e., dressing room), and above the doors is some sort of gallery that may sometimes hold spectators but that can be used (for example) as the bedroom from which Romeo—according to a stage direction in one text—"goeth down." Some evidence suggests that a throne can be lowered onto the platform stage, perhaps from the "shadow"; certainly characters can descend from the stage through a trap or traps into the cellar or "hell." Sometimes this space beneath the platform accommodates a sound-effects man or musician (in *Antony and Cleopatra* "music of the hautboys is under the stage") or an actor (in *Hamlet* the "Ghost cries under the stage"). Most characters simply walk on and off, but because there is no curtain in front of the platform, corpses will have to be carried off (Hamlet must lug Polonius' guts into the neighbor room), or will have to fall at the rear, where the curtain on the alcove or booth can be drawn to conceal them.

Such may have been the so-called "public theater." Another kind of theater, called the "private theater" because its much greater admission charge limited its audience' to the wealthy or the prodigal, must be briefly mentioned. The private theater was basically a large room, entirely roofed and therefore artificially illuminated, with a stage at one end. In 1576 one such theater was established in Blackfriars, a Dominican priory in London that had been suppressed in 1538 and confiscated by the Crown and thus was not under the city's jurisdiction. All the actors in the Blackfriars theater were boys about eight to thirteen years old (in the public theaters similar boys played female parts; a boy Lady Macbeth played to a man Macbeth). This private theater had a precarious existence, and ceased operations in 1584. In 1596 James Burbage, who had already made theatrical history by building the Theatre, began to construct a second Blackfriars theater. He died in 1597, and for several years this second Blackfriars theater was used by a troupe of boys, but in 1608 two of Burbage's sons and five other actors (including Shakespeare) became joint operators of the theater, using it in the winter when the open-air Globe was unsuitable. Perhaps such a smaller theater, roofed, artificially illuminated, and with a tradition of a courtly audience, exerted an influence on Shakespeare's late plays.

Performances in the private theaters may well have had intermissions during which music was played, but in the public theaters the action was probably uninterrupted, flowing from scene to scene almost without a break. Actors would enter, speak, exit, and others would immediately enter and establish (if necessary) the new locale by a few properties and by words and gestures. Here are some samples of Shakespeare's scene painting:

This is Illyria, lady.

Well, this is the Forest of Arden.

This castle hath a pleasant seat; the air
Nimbly and sweetly recommends itself
Unto our gentle senses.

On the other hand, it is a mistake to conceive of the Elizabethan stage as bare. Although Shakespeare's Chorus in *Henry V* calls the stage an "unworthy scaffold" and urges the spectators to "eke out our performance with your mind," there was considerable spectacle. The last act of *Macbeth,* for example, has five stage directions calling for "drum and colors," and another sort of appeal to the eye is indicated by the stage direction "Enter Mac-

duff, with Macbeth's head." Some scenery and properties
may have been substantial; doubtless a throne was used,
and in one play of the period we encounter this direction:
"Hector takes up a great piece of rock and casts at Ajax,
who tears up a young tree by the roots and assails
Hector." The matter is of some importance, and will be
glanced at again in the next section.

The Texts of Shakespeare

Though eighteen of his plays were published during
his lifetime, Shakespeare seems never to have supervised
their publication. There is nothing unusual here; when a
playwright sold a play to a theatrical company he sur-
rendered his ownership of it. Normally a company would
not publish the play, because to publish it meant to allow
competitors to acquire the piece. Some plays, however,
did get published: apparently treacherous actors sometimes pieced together a play for a publisher, sometimes
a company in need of money sold a play, and sometimes a
company allowed a play to be published that no longer
drew audiences. That Shakespeare did not concern himself with publication, then, is scarcely remarkable; of his
contemporaries only Ben Jonson carefully supervised the
publication of his own plays. In 1623, seven years after
Shakespeare's death, John Heminges and Henry Condell
(two senior members of Shakespeare's company, who had
performed with him for about twenty years) collected his
plays—published and unpublished—into a large volume,
commonly called the First Folio. (A folio is a volume
consisting of sheets that have been folded once, each sheet
thus making two leaves, or four pages. The eighteen plays
published during Shakespeare's lifetime had been issued
one play per volume in small books called quartos. Each
sheet in a quarto had been folded twice, making four
leaves, or eight pages.) The First Folio contains thirty-six
plays; a thirty-seventh, *Pericles*, though not in the Folio
is regarded as canonical. Heminges and Condell suggest
in an address "To the great variety of readers" that the

republished plays are presented in better form than in the quartos: "Before you were abused with diverse stolen and surreptitious copies, maimed and deformed by the frauds and stealths of injurious impostors that exposed them; even those, are now offered to your view cured and perfect of their limbs, and all the rest absolute in their numbers, as he [i.e., Shakespeare] conceived them."

Whoever was assigned to prepare the texts for publication in the First Folio seems to have taken his job seriously and yet not to have performed it with uniform care. The sources of the texts seem to have been, in general, good unpublished copies or the best published copies. The first play in the collection, *The Tempest,* is divided into acts and scenes, has unusually full stage directions and descriptions of spectacle, and concludes with a list of the characters, but the editor was not able (or willing) to present all of the succeeding texts so fully dressed. Later texts occasionally show signs of carelessness: in one scene of *Much Ado About Nothing* the names of actors, instead of characters, appear as speech prefixes, as they had in the quarto, which the Folio reprints; proofreading throughout the Folio is spotty and apparently was done without reference to the printer's copy; the pagination of *Hamlet* jumps from 156 to 257.

A modern editor of Shakespeare must first select his copy; no problem if the play exists only in the Folio, but a considerable problem if the relationship between a quarto and the Folio—or an early quarto and a later one—is unclear. When an editor has chosen what seems to him to be the most authoritative text or texts for his copy, he has not done with making decisions. First of all, he must reckon with Elizabethan spelling. If he is not producing a facsimile, he probably modernizes it, but ought he to preserve the old form of words that apparently were pronounced quite unlike their modern forms—"lanthorn," "alablaster"? If he preserves these forms, is he really preserving Shakespeare's forms or perhaps those of a compositor in the printing house? What is one to do when one finds "lanthorn" and "lantern" in adjacent lines? (The editors of this series in general, but not

invariably, assume that words should be spelled in their
modern form.) Elizabethan punctuation, too, presents
problems. For example in the First Folio, the only text for
the play, Macbeth rejects his wife's idea that he can wash
the blood from his hand:

> no: this my Hand will rather
> The multitudinous Seas incarnadine,
> Making the Greene one, Red.

Obviously an editor will remove the superfluous capitals,
and he will probably alter the spelling to "incarnadine,"
but will he leave the comma before "red," letting Macbeth speak of the sea as "the green one," or will he (like
most modern editors) remove the comma and thus have
Macbeth say that his hand will make the ocean *uniformly*
red?

An editor will sometimes have to change more than
spelling or punctuation. Macbeth says to his wife:

> I dare do all that may become a man,
> Who dares no more, is none.

For two centuries editors have agreed that the second
line is unsatisfactory, and have emended "no" to "do":
"Who dares do more is none." But when in the same
play Ross says that fearful persons

> floate vpon a wilde and violent Sea
> Each way, and moue,

need "move" be emended to "none," as it often is, on the
hunch that the compositor misread the manuscript? The
editors of the Signet Classic Shakespeare have restrained
themselves from making abundant emendations. In their
minds they hear Dr. Johnson on the dangers of emend-
ing: "I have adopted the Roman sentiment, that it is more
honorable to save a citizen than to kill an enemy." Some
departures (in addition to spelling, punctuation, and
lineation) from the copy text have of course been made,

but the original readings are listed in a note following the play, so that the reader can evaluate them for himself.

The editors of the Signet Classic Shakespeare, following tradition, have added line numbers and in many cases act and scene divisions as well as indications of locale at the beginning of scenes. The Folio divided most of the plays into acts and some into scenes. Early eighteenth-century editors increased the divisions. These divisions, which provide a convenient way of referring to passages in the plays, have been retained, but when not in the text chosen as the basis for the Signet Classic text they are enclosed in square brackets [   ] to indicate that they are editorial additions. Similarly, although no play of Shakespeare's published during his lifetime was equipped with indications of locale at the heads of scene divisions, locales have here been added in square brackets for the convenience of the reader, who lacks the information afforded to spectators by costumes, properties, and gestures. The spectator can tell at a glance he is in the throne room, but without an editorial indication the reader may be puzzled for a while. It should be mentioned, incidentally, that there are a few authentic stage directions—perhaps Shakespeare's, perhaps a prompter's—that suggest locales: for example, "Enter Brutus in his orchard," and "They go up into the Senate house." It is hoped that the bracketed additions provide the reader with the sort of help provided in these two authentic directions, but it is equally hoped that the reader will remember that the stage was not loaded with scenery.

No editor during the course of his work can fail to recollect some words Heminges and Condell prefixed to the Folio:

> It had been a thing, we confess, worthy to have been wished, that the author himself had lived to have set forth and overseen his own writings. But since it hath been ordained otherwise, and he by death departed from that right, we pray you do not envy his friends the office of their care and pain to have collected and published them.

Nor can an editor, after he has done his best, forget Heminges and Condell's final words: "And so we leave you to other of his friends, whom if you need can be your guides. If you need them not, you can lead yourselves, and others. And such readers we wish him."

SYLVAN BARNET
Tufts University

William Shakespeare

LOVE'S
LABOR'S LOST

Edited by John Arthos

Contents

Introduction

Love's Labor's Lost is one of Shakespeare's earliest and happiest comedies. It is excellently formed, moving easily towards its conclusion in a masque and a song, at the end recapitulating in all the stage's beauty the courting warfare of the young noblemen and ladies that has made up the chief part of the play, the sparrings and the surrenders and the victories. The play makes the point the theater seems to live to make, that sooner or later love conquers all, and although the title tells us that love's labor is lost, this we know is joking: the happy outcome is certain, and love and long life—as we learn at the end from what G. L. Kittredge called one of the best songs in the world —define the happy prospect.

In this Boccaccio-like setting another comic action plays its part, a comedy about the falsely learned and the grotesquely loving, partly contrasting with and partly parallel to the main story. The king and his lords, moved by the love of philosophy and virtue, have fallen into a most unphilosophical absurdity in supposing that the claims of love can easily be put aside. The foolish scholars light up the folly of the wise ones in still other ways, even as their own courting is mocked by the lovemaking of the others. As in so many of the later plays, it is all there—the multiple plot, the ranging between high and low minds, and love's challenge to every power in the world. All there, and as fluent in its display as in a dance.

The date of the play's composition must be guessed. The 1598 quarto title page mentions a performance of the play before her Highness "this last Christmas," and it adds the phrase, "Newly corrected and augmented."

This, taken along with the evidence of revisions in the text, and with the known dates of certain historical occurrences, leads to pretty substantial arguments for the composition of the play in 1593 or 1594. It should be said, however, that in the past the play was thought to be earlier than this; Coleridge, for example, believed it to be Shakespeare's first play because he thought Shakespeare was bringing into it part of the life he had just left, exploiting his experience as a schoolmaster while the memory of it was still fresh to him. This might push the writing back as far as 1589. More recently Alfred Harbage* has returned to a similar line of reasoning. Likenesses to Lyly's plays in the 1580's and certain considerations making for the possibility that the play was produced by child actors in either a private or public theater, lead him to suggest 1589 or even earlier as the time of performance.

The arguments for a later date point to a general friendliness in England for Henry of Navarre until he reverted to the Church of Rome in July 1593; the beginning of the investigation in 1594 into the atheism of men associated with Sir Walter Raleigh, a group perhaps identified in the play (in IV.iii.254) as "the school of night"; the use of language that suggests the *Venus and Adonis* of 1593, the *Lucrece* of 1594, and sonnets of presumably the same period. And, of course, a number of topical allusions.†

The occasion of the play's first production is not known, but it was surely meant for a private performance —the house of the Earl of Southampton has been suggested—perhaps in 1593. As such it would have been part of festivities in which music and dancing would naturally be called for. The first printed text of the play alludes to a performance before the Queen at Christmas, either in 1597 or 1598, and the play's immediately suc-

---

* *"Love's Labor's Lost* and the Early Shakespeare," *Philological Quarterly*, XLI (1962), 18–36.
† The basic discussion of the play's composition is in Rupert Taylor, *The Date of "Love's Labor's Lost"* (New York: AMS Press, 1966).

ceeding stage history establishes the special suitability of
the work for a courtly audience. The substance of the
play also makes this clear enough—the initiating idea of
learned gentlemen in the company of their monarch retiring from the life of power, the better to perfect their
lives; the abjuring the society of women in serious as
well as fantastic aspiration, following the directions of
the most fashionable writers out of Italy; the mockery of
literary men and most particularly of courtiers with ambitions in literature; the battles between the sexes conducted with the most elaborate and sensitive protocol. In
large and small matters alike the play seems to be taking
something directly out of the life of the court of Elizabeth
(wisely enough under another name), making what it
takes into something more than life-size. It gives the audience of lords and ladies a mirror in which they will see
themselves in all the wit, imagining, beauty and fun they
are absorbed in.

The idea of nobility sets the tone for it all. It begins in
the king's first speech, it is taken up more than once by
the princess, and, ironically, it is finally triumphant in
Berowne, the railer at both love and philosophy, so dan-
gerously close in his disposition to the discarding of all
values, himself in the end the defender of an aspiration
as passionately felt as it is truly thought.

When the king speaks of retiring to the learned academy, we feel the genuine love of learning and of virtue in
his words:

> Navarre shall be the wonder of the world;
> Our court shall be a little academe,
> Still and contemplative in living art.

(I.i.12–14)

And the chief critic of the idea is no philistine. He is
high-spirited and he is tired of going to school, but he
has his wisdom, too, and we judge he has the experience
to support it:

> So study evermore is overshot.

> While it doth study to have what it would,
> It doth forget to do the thing it should.

(I.i.141–43)

And so we immediately perceive that in the conflicts that
are to rage in the play the sparks of thought will be flying
everywhere. The issue is to be granted its proper dignity,
whatever the comic emphasis, and in the end love will
be allowed to break up the academy not only because it
is strong but because it may claim a special worth, and
because the temper of these noble persons is deeply
founded in the cultivation of the best of everything the
world offers.

The princess' first scene gives us so beautiful a picture
of a woman that it carries all before it as if it were the
very praise of womankind. The first words to tell us this
come from one of her lords, advising her on her approach
to the king:

> Be now as prodigal of all dear grace
> As Nature was in making graces dear
> When she did starve the general world beside,
> And prodigally gave them all to you.

(II.i.9–12)

On the other side, the king is acknowledged as "the sole
inheritor/Of all perfections that a man may owe" (II.i.
5–6). The bounty of the woman and the perfection of the
man, these are the qualities that set the tone, and these
are the persons to lead the dancing interplay, the parry-
ings and the reversals and the resolutions that are to
come. They themselves are the matter of love's labors,
the union of nobility and bounty, like some splendid fore-
shadowing of the masque of Ceres in *The Tempest*.

Nature has its austerity, and love has its temperance,
and the princess' chiding of the busy old lord Boyet for
his flattery is a still more telling criticism of the affectations and grossness of another kind of courtly love—

> my beauty, though but mean,

Needs not the painted flourish of your praise.

(II.i.13–14)

Armado with his affectations brought from Spain and Italy, and the courtiers with their sonnets, are abusing "the heart's still rhetoric" (II.i.229). False speaking conforms to warped natures, and the play never loses sight of the idea of inherent excellence in manhood and womanhood and of the importance of true expression in love. Whatever the follies of the great as well as lesser characters, and whatever the ironies whereby nobility and the taking of oaths are made to seem like tinder before the fires of love, the decorum of the truly courtly prevails as the basis of the play's beauty.

The comic ideas also are as alive with intellectuality as the play's most serious affirmations. When the ladies call to mind and comment on the lords who accompany the king—men in the past they had encountered only briefly—praising them as it appears they deserve to be praised, we discover that all of them are in love before they know it. The audience enters into a kind of conspiracy with Shakespeare, schooled, as we are certain he was, by literature and the conventions of the stage, agreeing in advance that the great and noble always love the beautiful, and the beautiful the brave. Since this is the stage, we know that all these must be paired no matter what the claims of study. And so, won not only by the beauty and youth but by the wit of the ladies, we anticipate with pleasure the defeat of the men. We have seen the signs of love in the first words of each of the women as she sizes up her choice, and while we know enough of the men to know they will put up a kind of fight, we cannot be sorry at the prospect of a surrender they themselves will not regret.

The intermingling of the two plots is as expert as the rest. After the king has announced the program he means to follow and Berowne has had his say about it, we meet a clown, Costard, and a fop, Armado. They are showing off, and Shakespeare mocks both the clown's wenching

and the fop's romancing. The scene is dramatically fo-
cussed when the two confront each other in the presence
of the one they are both taken with, the country maid,
Jaquenetta. Costard, who has been misbehaving, is put
into the custody of Armado, who is to guarantee his good
behavior. The contrast is in itself pleasing—the fool who
from time to time blunders into sense, and the most affected of courtiers who is yet not all fool. And in their
folly as in their sense we see that they are being made
to pose different versions of the questions the other characters are also asking—what has learning to do with love?
and what has love to do with learning? As the plots proceed, the various lovers fall into many absurdities, but
the questions themselves continually receive thoughtful
answers, or thoughtful mockery. The varieties of the questioning, from such different kinds of lovers, require and
get complex and significant answers, and the confusions
of Costard and Armado prepare for the resolution Berowne will finally discover.

Meanwhile, the lords about the king are made to show
their folly. One after another, subdued to his lady, takes
to poetry, and one after another passes across the stage,
sonnet in hand, or under his hat, or tucked into his belt—
a snow of sonnets. The mockery is so lavish it adds the
beauty of a pageant to the absurdity. The noble lords
demean themselves in becoming poets, and they glory in
their humiliation since they imagine it is pleasing to the
ladies. This is indeed what the ladies require of those they
favor, but they also require more than words. They require, as Rosaline says of her own lover,

> That he should be my fool, and I his fate.
>
> (V.ii.68)

The play will spell this out. Subjecting themselves to such
cruel and whimsical tyrants, the men become as funny
as Armado and Moth. Shakespeare lays it on with a
trowel—

> To see a king transformèd to a gnat!

> To see great Hercules whipping a gig,
> And profound Solomon to tune a jig,
> And Nestor play at push-pin with the boys,
> And critic Timon laugh at idle toys!
>
> (IV.iii.165–69)

At the end they will endure still greater transformations, but already they are well schooled in the doctrine that love is madness, and that that madness redeems all. As the song jubilantly declares of one lady:

> Thou for whom Jove would swear
> Juno but an Ethiop were.
>
> (IV.iii.116–17)

The beautiful lyric is part of the singing of the whole play, the beauty love worships is the beauty the play is celebrating. All the changes it is ringing on the courting of high and low, on absurdity and exaggeration, on grossness and refinement, are subdued to the grave and splendid beauty that conquers even Jove.

The secondary plot continues the mockery of false ideas of learning and it also brings before us the sight of other kinds of lovemaking. The most obvious point to the mockery of pedantry is as an abuse of what the academy stands for. Holofernes, the walking dictionary, may represent John Florio, or Thomas Harriot. The name Armado brings the Spanish Armada to mind, and so it has been argued that Armado is a portrayal of Sir Walter Raleigh, the man who defeated the Armada. (If this were to be substantiated, it might strengthen the argument of those who think the play was produced shortly after the defeat of the Armada in 1588). Or the character may be thought to represent a quite different person, the arrogant and tedious Gabriel Harvey. Moth may be Thomas Nashe. But however much the possibility of such identifications cause the characters to jump out of their parts, the parts they do play are plainly so much more interesting to the audience for the comments they provide on the characters in the main action. The characters of the minor plot are strangers to the nobility of the others, and in their ambitions and pretensions they are illustrating not only the follies of the court but its essential superiority. The king values learning because it serves the noblest purposes in life; the ideas of the pedants are ignoble. For them it is always the letter at the expense of the spirit, and pride in learning at the expense of its good use.

The point is also being made that the abuse of learning is like the stupidity of affectation in love. The true power of love as well as the true worth of learning is lost upon the low characters, not only in their grossness but in their false refinement too. In the fun Shakespeare is making of them he strikes at everyone, but most of all he means to preserve our esteem for the truer men. They want glory for learning, for the academy, glory that will outlast death, because they want learning to be a light for those who will come after them. It is such men, no mere inkpots, who are love's true targets. In different ways, then, both plots are reinforcing the teaching that love belongs properly to the gentle heart.

Heightening and enrichening this doctrine is the idea of the divinity of love. Character after character speaks of love as if it were a presence as well as a power. The play's title names love as the power at work in the play, and in every turn of the story we are shown events as if they were indeed the manipulations of a god—Eros, although unseen, yet surely directing and effecting all, showing his strength and enforcing his laws. As much as in *All's Well that Ends Well*, those who strive against him strive in vain.

Love's "labor" is a bringing to birth. The remembrances of ancient meetings come fast upon the courtiers and the ladies:

> Did not I dance with you in Brabant once?
> (II.i.114)

and in one after the other the seed burgeons. Part of the poetry as well as the comedy is that this growing of love goes on as it were in isolation. Cutting themselves off from so much of society, from the cares of power as well as from the entanglements with women, the lords are the more defenseless in their idleness. The king himself, treating of the matter the princess has come to negotiate on behalf of her sick father, even as he begins to talk of business finds that his heart is moved. Boyet notes this instantly:

> Why, all his behaviors did make their retire
> To the court of his eye, peeping thorough desire.
> His heart, like an agate with your print impressed,
> Proud with his form, in his eye pride expressed.
>
> (II.i.234–37)

Already love is at work, in the highest as in the lowest, sometimes beautifully and sometimes grotesquely, but always irresistibly.

This leads to the truly inspired idea in the extraordinary, not to say unlikely, happenings presumably only to be accounted for by a god's workings—that all the lovers should from the beginning have had no doubt who were to be their partners. In the masquing, the ladies switched their lords' favors in order to trick their lovers into another perjury, like Portia and Nerissa in *The Merchant of Venice*, merry in forging other chains for their slaves. So this time the lords will swear again, but to the wrong partners—as if another Puck were at work—and the ladies can mock the men until, as Berowne says, they are "dry-beaten" (V.ii.264)—the very blood leaves their faces. They are driven off, and it is no comfort to them to learn finally that they have now forsworn themselves twice. Shakespeare has had his fun with the idea of inexorable destiny in love at first sight, and he makes more fun of it still by asking another question: What is it that love sees?

Love's working and love's presence—a very god—come into full sight in Berowne's great speech, wherein the railer at love and wisdom, himself now enslaved, mocks himself:

> O, and I, forsooth, in love!
> I, that have been love's whip,
> A very beadle to a humorous sigh,

> A critic, nay, a night-watch constable,
> A domineering pedant o'er the boy,
> Than whom no mortal so magnificent!
> This wimpled, whining, purblind, wayward boy,
> This senior-junior, giant-dwarf, Dan Cupid,
> Regent of love rhymes, lord of folded arms,
> Th' anointed sovereign of sighs and groans . . .
> And I to be a corporal of his field!
>
> (III.i.175–89)

To make it worse, he is in love with the one he says is the least beautiful of the ladies, the most wanton, the one who would escape a guardian with a hundred eyes. But he accepts his fate.

> Some men must love my lady, and some Joan.
>
> (III.i.207)

This time Touchstone is a gentleman, and so somewhat more love's fool. But finally he will say more in praise of love than any other will, and however light in touch his words substantiate what the others must now acknowledge:

> From women's eyes this doctrine I derive. . . .
> They are the books, the arts, the academes,
> That show, contain, and nourish all the world;
> Else none at all in aught proves excellent.
>
> (IV.iii.349–53)

With this conclusion the play moves towards its end. The haughty must change their tactics. There is the call to arms and the embrace of battle:

> Advance your standards, and upon them, lords!
>
> (IV.iii.366)

And so they dance, recapitulating in their motions the warring that has made the play, the advances and retreats, the defeats and victories, the strivings, and capitulations, and the final treaties.

For the play's last words there is a song sung by allegorical personages, Spring and Winter, fantastic figures out of the world of musical entertainment and Renaissance allegory. It speaks of flowers and countrymaids and ploughmen, of love and marriage and cuckoldry, of spring and winter, of idleness and of hard work, of nature when it is kind and when it is cruel, of life by the hearth. It is a song about love making peace with life, with things as they are. It provides the most brilliant of comments on all that has been fanciful in the beauty of the play and in the ideas of these fine people. In the perfection and balance of the contrast with all that has gone before, this song sung by the personifications of time is the true culmination of the play, the marriage of sophistication and reality, of the stage and its glory and the strength of love's endurance outside it. The song celebrates the poetry of life as it is, and it is one of Shakespeare's most glorious inspirations that he has it sung by the deities of "curds and flowers," magnificently adorned, without doubt, as the Renaissance imagined gods would be.

The song follows the princess' farewell as she and the ladies leave Navarre, postponing the marriages. The lords are meanwhile to prove themselves by the most strenuous and demanding discipline, for the courtship has been

> A time, methinks, too short,
> To make a world-without-end bargain in.
> (V.ii.789-90)

The words of wisdom are indeed harsh after the music of the god of poetry, as the comment that ends the play says, words that may be given to Armado. They are words that sustain us as the play sustains us, and as the marvelous song does. And the reflection to which the last scene leads us is that love, like learning, is but a part of life, and what the whole of it is there is no one to say— there is only the testing, and good hope.

JOHN ARTHOS
University of Michigan

Love's
Labor's Lost

Love's Labor's Lost

[ACT I

Scene I. *The park of the King of Navarre.*]

*Enter Ferdinand King of Navarre, Berowne, Long-
aville, and Dumaine.*

King. Let fame, that all hunt after in their lives,
Live regist'red upon our brazen tombs
And then grace us in the disgrace°¹ of death,
When, spite of cormorant° devouring time,
Th' endeavor of this present breath may buy   5
That honor which shall bate° his scythe's keen edge
And make us heirs of all eternity.
Therefore, brave conquerors—for so you are
That war against your own affections
And the huge army of the world's desires—   10
Our late edict shall strongly stand in force:
Navarre shall be the wonder of the world;
Our court shall be a little academe,°
Still and contemplative in living art.°

1 The degree sign (°) indicates a footnote, which is keyed to the
text by line number. Text references are printed in **boldface** type;
the annotation follows in roman type.   I.i.3 **disgrace** degradation
4 **cormorant** ravenous   6 **bate** make dull   13 **academe** academy
14 **Still ... art** continually studying the art of living

37

15 You three, Berowne, Dumaine, and Longaville,
    Have sworn for three years' term to live with me,
    My fellow scholars, and to keep those statutes
    That are recorded in this schedule here.
    Your oaths are passed; and now subscribe your
        names,
20 That his own hand may strike his honor down
    That violates the smallest branch herein.
    If you are armed° to do as sworn to do,
    Subscribe to your deep oaths, and keep it too.

Longaville. I am resolved. 'Tis but a three years' fast.
25 The mind shall banquet though the body pine.
    Fat paunches have lean pates, and dainty bits
    Make rich the ribs, but bankrout° quite the wits.

Dumaine. My loving lord, Dumaine is mortified.°
    The grosser manner of these world's delights
30 He throws upon the gross world's baser slaves.
    To love, to wealth, to pomp, I pine and die,
    With all these living in philosophy.

Berowne. I can but say their protestation over°—
    So much, dear liege, I have already sworn,
35 That is, to live and study here three years.
    But there are other strict observances:
    As not to see a woman in that term—
    Which I hope well is not enrollèd there;
    And one day in a week to touch no food,
40 And but one meal on every day beside—
    The which I hope is not enrollèd there;
    And then to sleep but three hours in the night,
    And not be seen to wink of° all the day
    (When I was wont to think no harm all night
45 And make a dark night too of half the day)—
    Which I hope well is not enrollèd there.
    O, these are barren tasks, too hard to keep,
    Not to see ladies, study, fast, not sleep!

---

22 **armed** resolved   27 **bankrout** bankrupt   28 **mortified** dead to
worldly pleasures   33 **say their protestation over** repeat their solemn
declarations   43 **wink of** close the eyes during

King. Your oath is passed, to pass away from these.

Berowne. Let me say no, my liege, and if° you please.   50
  I only swore to study with your Grace
  And stay here in your court for three years' space.

Longaville. You swore to that, Berowne, and to the
    rest.

Berowne. By yea and nay,° sir, then I swore in jest.
  What is the end of study, let me know?   55

King. Why, that to know which else we should not
    know.

Berowne. Things hid and barred, you mean, from
    common sense?

King. Ay, that is study's godlike recompense.

Berowne. Come on then, I will swear to study so,
  To know the thing I am forbid to know: 60
  As thus—to study where I well may dine
  When I to feast expressly am forbid;
  Or study where to meet some mistress fine
  When mistresses from common sense are hid;
  Or having sworn too hard-a-keeping oath,   65
  Study to break it and not break my troth.°
  If study's gain be thus, and this be so,
  Study knows that which yet it doth not know.
  Swear me to this, and I will ne'er say no.

King. These be the stops° that hinder study quite   70
  And train° our intellects to vain delight.

Berowne. Why, all delights are vain, but that most
    vain
  Which, with pain purchased, doth inherit pain:
  As, painfully to pore upon a book,
  To seek the light of truth, while truth the while   75
  Doth falsely° blind the eyesight of his look.

---

50 and if if   54 By yea and nay in all earnestness   66 troth faith
70 stops obstructions   71 train entice   76 falsely treacherously

Light seeking light doth light of light beguile;°
So, ere you find where light in darkness lies,
Your light grows dark by losing of your eyes.
80 Study me how to please the eye indeed
By fixing it upon a fairer eye,
Who dazzling so, that eye shall be his heed°
And give him light that it was blinded by.
Study is like the heaven's glorious sun,
85 That will not be deep-searched with saucy looks.
Small have continual plodders ever won
Save base authority from others' books.
These earthly godfathers° of heaven's lights,
That give a name to every fixèd star
90 Have no more profit of their shining nights
Than those that walk and wot° not what they are.
Too much to know is to know nought but fame;°
And every godfather can give a name.

King. How well he's read to reason against reading!

Dumaine. Proceeded° well, to stop all good proceed-
95 ing!

Longaville. He weeds the corn,° and still lets grow the
weeding.°

Berowne. The spring is near, when green geese° are
a-breeding.

Dumaine. How follows that?

Berowne.   Fit in his place and time.

Dumaine. In reason nothing.

Berowne.   Something then in rhyme.

100 *King.* Berowne is like an envious sneaping° frost
That bites the first-born infants of the spring.

---

77 **Light . . . beguile** i.e., eyes in seeking truth lose their sight in too
much seeking   82 **heed** protector   88 **earthly godfathers** i.e., as-
tronomers   91 **wot** know   92 **fame** report   95 **Proceeded** took a
degree at the university   96 **corn** wheat   96 **weeding** weeds   97
green geese geese born the previous autumn   100 **sneaping** nipping
(Berowne's "rhyme" is taken as "rime" or frost)

Berowne. Well, say I am! Why should proud summer
 boast
  Before the birds have any cause to sing?
  Why should I joy in an abortive birth?
  At Christmas I no more desire a rose   *105*
  Than wish a snow in May's new-fangled shows,
  But like of each thing that in season grows.
  So you—to study now it is too late—
  Climb o'er the house to unlock the little gate.

King. Well, sit you out. Go home, Berowne. Adieu.   *110*

Berowne. No, my good lord, I have sworn to stay with
 you;
  And though I have for barbarism° spoke more
  Than for that angel knowledge you can say,
  Yet confident I'll keep what I have swore,
  And bide the penance of each three years' day.°   *115*
  Give me the paper, let me read the same,
  And to the strictest decrees I'll write my name.

King. How well this yielding rescues thee from shame!

Berowne. [*Reads*] "Item. That no woman shall come
  within a mile of my court—" Hath this been pro-   *120*
  claimed?

Longaville. Four days ago.

Berowne. Let's see the penalty. [*Reads*] "—on pain of
  losing her tongue." Who devised this penalty?

Longaville. Marry,° that did I.

Berowne.   Sweet lord, and why?   *125*

Longaville. To fright them hence with that dread penalty.

Berowne. A dangerous law against gentility!°
  [*Reads*] "Item. If any man be seen to talk with a
  woman within the term of three years, he shall

112 barbarism philistinism   115 each three years' day each day of
the three years   125 Marry By Mary (mild oath)   127 gentility
good manners

130   endure such public shame as the rest of the court
    can possibly devise."
    This article, my liege, yourself must break;
    For well you know here comes in embassy
    The French king's daughter with yourself to speak,
135   A maid of grace and complete majesty,
    About surrender up of Aquitaine
    To her decrepit, sick, and bed-rid father.
    Therefore this article is made in vain,
    Or vainly comes th' admirèd princess hither.

140 *King.* What say you, lords? Why, this was quite forgot.

Berowne. So study evermore is overshot.°
    While it doth study to have what it would,
    It doth forget to do the thing it should;
    And when it hath the thing it hunteth most,
145   'Tis won as towns with fire°—so won, so lost.

King. We must of force° dispense with this decree.
    She must lie° here on mere° necessity.

Berowne. Necessity will make us all forsworn
    Three thousand times within this three years' space:
150   For every man with his affects° is born,
    Not by might mast'red, but by special grace.
    If I break faith, this word shall speak for me,
    I am forsworn "on mere necessity."
    So to the laws at large I write my name;
                                 [*Subscribes.*]
155   And he that breaks them in the least degree
    Stands in attainder of° eternal shame.
    Suggestions° are to other as to me,
    But I believe, although I seem so loath,°
    I am the last that will last keep his oath.
160   But is there no quick recreation granted?

King. Ay, that there is. Our court, you know, is
    haunted

141 overshot wide of the mark   145 won as towns with fire destroyed
in being won   146 of force of necessity   147 lie lodge   147 mere
simple   150 affects passions   156 in attainder of to be condemned
to   157 Suggestions temptations   158 loath reluctant

With a refinèd traveler of Spain,
A man in all the world's new fashion planted,
That hath a mint of phrases in his brain;
One who the music of his own vain tongue   165
Doth ravish like enchanting harmony;
A man of complements,° whom right and wrong
Have chose as umpire of their mutiny.
This child of fancy, that Armado hight,°
For interim° to our studies shall relate   170
In high-born words the worth of many a knight
From tawny Spain, lost in the world's debate.
How you delight, my lords, I know not, I,
But, I protest, I love to hear him lie,
And I will use him for my minstrelsy.°   175

Berowne. Armado is a most illustrious wight,
A man of fire-new° words, fashion's own knight.

Longaville. Costard the swain° and he shall be our
     sport;
And so to study three years is but short.

*Enter [Dull,] a Constable, with Costard, [a Clown,]
     with a letter.*

Dull. Which is the duke's own person?   180

Berowne. This, fellow. What wouldst?

Dull. I myself reprehend° his own person, for I am
his Grace's farborough.° But I would see his own
person in flesh and blood.

Berowne. This is he.   185

Dull. Signior Arm—Arm—commends you. There's
villainy abroad. This letter will tell you more.

Costard. Sir, the contempts° thereof are as touching
me.

167 complements formal manners   169 hight is named   170 interim interruption   175 minstrelsy court entertainer   177 fire-new fresh from the mint   178 swain countryman   182 reprehend (Dull means to say, "represent")   183 farborough petty constable   188 contempts (Costard means the "contents" of the letter)

190 *King.* A letter from the magnificent Armado.

Berowne. How low soever the matter, I hope in God for high words.

Longaville. A high hope for a low heaven. God grant us patience!

195 *Berowne.* To hear, or forbear hearing?

Longaville. To hear meekly, sir, and to laugh moderately, or to forbear both.

Berowne. Well, sir, be it as the style shall give us cause to climb in the merriness.

200 *Costard.* The matter is to me, sir, as concerning Jaquenetta. The manner of it is, I was taken with the manner.°

Berowne. In what manner?

Costard. In manner and form following, sir—all those
205 three: I was seen with her in the manor-house, sitting with her upon the form,° and taken following her into the park; which, put together, is, in manner and form, following. Now, sir, for the manner— it is the manner of a man to speak to a woman.
210 For the form—in some form.

Berowne. For the following, sir?

Costard. As it shall follow in my correction,° and God defend the right!

King. Will you hear this letter with attention?

215 *Berowne.* As we would hear an oracle.

Costard. Such is the simplicity of man to hearken after the flesh.

King. [*Reads*] "Great deputy, the welkin's vicegerent,° and sole dominator of Navarre, my soul's earth's
220 God, and body's fost'ring patron—"

201–02 **with the manner** in the act   206 **form** bench   212 **correction** punishment   218 **welkin's vicegerent** deputy-ruler of heaven

Costard. Not a word of Costard yet.

King. "So it is—"

Costard. It may be so; but if he say it is so, he is, in telling true, but so.°

King. Peace!　225

Costard. Be to me and every man that dares not fight.

King. No words!

Costard. Of other men's secrets, I beseech you.

King. [*Reads*] "So it is, besieged with sable-colored melancholy, I did commend the black-oppressing 230 humor° to the most wholesome physic° of thy health-giving air; and, as I am a gentleman, betook myself to walk. The time When? About the sixth hour; when beasts most graze, birds best peck, and men sit down to that nourishment which is 235 called supper. So much for the time When. Now for the ground Which? Which, I mean, I walked upon. It is ycleped° thy park. Then for the place Where? Where, I mean, I did encounter that obscene and most preposterous event, that draweth 240 from my snow-white pen° the ebon-colored ink, which here thou viewest, beholdest, surveyest, or seest. But to the place Where? It standeth north-north-east and by east from the west corner of thy curious-knotted° garden. There did I see that low- 245 spirited swain, that base minnow of thy mirth—"

Costard. Me?

King. "that unlettered° small-knowing soul—"

Costard. Me?

King. "that shallow vassal°—"　250

224 but so not worth much　230–31 black-oppressing humor fluid in the body that causes melancholy　231 physic treatment　238 ycleped called　241 snow-white pen goose-quill　245 curious-knotted flower beds and paths in intricate patterns　248 unlettered illiterate 250 vassal underling

Costard. Still me!

King. "which, as I remember, hight° Costard—"

Costard. O me!

King. "sorted and consorted, contrary to thy estab-
255   lished proclaimed edict and continent canon,°
which with—O, with—but with this I passion to
say wherewith—"

Costard. With a wench.

King. "with a child of our grandmother Eve, a female;
260   or, for thy more sweet understanding, a woman.
Him I (as my ever-esteemed duty pricks° me on)
have sent to thee, to receive the meed° of punishment, by thy sweet Grace's officer, Anthony Dull,
a man of good repute, carriage, bearing, and esti-
265   mation."

Dull. Me, an 't shall please you: I am Anthony Dull.

King. "For Jaquenetta (so is the weaker vessel°
called), which I apprehended with the aforesaid
swain, I keep her as a vessel of thy law's fury, and
270   shall, at the least of thy sweet notice,° bring her
to trial. Thine in all compliments of devoted and
heart-burning heat of duty,

Don Adriano de Armado."

Berowne. This is not so well as I looked for, but the
275   best that ever ⸆ heard.

King. Ay, the best for the worst. But, sirrah,° what
say you to this?

Costard. Sir, I confess the wench.

King. Did you hear the proclamation?

---

252 **hight** called   255 **continent canon** the decree restraining the
members of the Academy   261 **pricks** spurs   262 **meed** reward
267 **weaker vessel** (general phrase for "womankind")   270 **at the
least . . . notice** at the slightest indication of thy concern   276 **sirrah**
(term of address used to an inferior)

Costard. I do confess much of the hearing it, but little *280*
of the marking of it.

King. It was proclaimed a year's imprisonment to be
taken with a wench.

Costard. I was taken with none, sir; I was taken with
a damsel. *285*

King. Well, it was proclaimed "damsel."

Costard. This was no damsel neither, sir, she was a
virgin.

King. It is so varied° too, for it was proclaimed
"virgin." *290*

Costard. If it were, I deny her virginity. I was taken
with a maid.

King. This maid will not serve your turn, sir.

Costard. This maid will serve my turn,° sir.

King. Sir, I will pronounce your sentence: you shall *295*
fast a week with bran and water.

Costard. I had rather pray a month with mutton and
porridge.

King. And Don Armado shall be your keeper.
My Lord Berowne, see him delivered o'er. *300*
And go we, lords, to put in practice that
Which each to other hath so strongly sworn.
        [*Exeunt King, Longuville, and Dumaine.*]

Berowne. I'll lay° my head to any good man's hat,
These oaths and laws will prove an idle scorn.
Sirrah, come on. *305*

Costard. I suffer for the truth, sir, for true it is I was
taken with Jaquenetta, and Jaquenetta is a true°
girl. And therefore welcome the sour cup of prosperity! Affliction may one day smile again, and till
then sit thee down, sorrow!   *Exeunt.* *310*

---

289 **varied** distinguished   294 **turn** (Costard uses the word in a
bawdy sense)   303 **lay** bet   307 **true** honest

[Scene II. *The park.*]

Enter Armado and Moth,° his Page.

Armado. Boy, what sign is it when a man of great
spirit grows melancholy?

Moth. A great sign, sir, that he will look sad.

Armado. Why, sadness is one and the selfsame thing,
5   dear imp.

Moth. No, no, O Lord, sir, no!

Armado. How canst thou part° sadness and melancholy, my tender juvenal?°

Moth. By a familiar demonstration of the working,
10   my tough signor.°

Armado. Why tough signor? Why tough signor?

Moth. Why tender juvenal? Why tender juvenal?

Armado. I spoke it, tender juvenal, as a congruent
epitheton° appertaining to thy young days, which
15   we may nominate tender.

Moth. And I, tough signor, as an appertinent title to
your old time, which we may name tough.

Armado. Pretty and apt.

Moth. How mean you, sir? I pretty, and my saying
20   apt? Or I apt and my saying pretty?

I.ii.s.d. **Moth** (probably pronounced, and with the meaning of,
"mote," i.e., speck)   7 **part** distinguish between   8 **juvenal** youth
(it may also signify *Juvenal*, the Roman satirist, and allude to the
nickname of Thomas Nashe, Elizabethan writer)   10 **signor** (with
a pun on "senior")   13–14 **congruent epitheton** appropriate ad-
jective

Armado. Thou pretty, because little.

Moth. Little pretty, because little. Wherefore apt?

Armado. And therefore apt because quick.

Moth. Speak you this in my praise, master?

Armado. In thy condign° praise.   25

Moth. I will praise an eel with the same praise.

Armado. What, that an eel is ingenious?

Moth. That an eel is quick.

Armado. I do say thou art quick in answers. Thou
heat'st my blood.   30

Moth. I am answered, sir.

Armado. I love not to be crossed.

Moth. [*Aside*] He speaks the mere contrary—crosses°
love not him.

Armado. I have promised to study three years with   35
the duke.

Moth. You may do it in an hour, sir.

Armado. Impossible.

Moth. How many is one thrice told?

Armado. I am ill at reck'ning—it fitteth the spirit of   40
a tapster.°

Moth. You are a gentleman and a gamester, sir.

Armado. I confess both. They are both the varnish°
of a complete man.

Moth. Then I am sure you know how much the gross   45
sum of deuce-ace amounts to.

Armado. It doth amount to one more than two.

---

25 **condign** well-deserved   33 **crosses** coins (so named for the
crosses engraved on them)   41 **tapster** bartender   43 **varnish** outward gloss

Moth. Which the base vulgar do call three.

Armado. True.

50 *Moth.* Why, sir, is this such a piece of study? Now
here is three studied ere ye'll thrice wink; and how
easy it is to put "years" to the word "three," and
study three years in two words, the dancing horse°
will tell you.

55 *Armado.* A most fine figure.°

Moth. [*Aside*] To prove you a cipher.

Armado. I will hereupon confess I am in love, and
as it is base for a soldier to love, so am I in love
with a base wench. If drawing my sword against
60 the humor° of affection would deliver me from the
reprobate thought of it, I would take Desire prisoner and ransom him to any French courtier for
a new devised cursy.° I think scorn° to sigh: methinks I should outswear° Cupid. Comfort me, boy.
65 What great men have been in love?

Moth. Hercules, master.

Armado. Most sweet Hercules! More authority, dear
boy, name more; and, sweet my child, let them
be men of good repute and carriage.

70 *Moth.* Samson, master—he was a man of good carriage, great carriage, for he carried the town-gates
on his back like a porter, and he was in love.

Armado. O well-knit Samson, strong-jointed Samson!
I do excel thee in my rapier as much as thou didst
75 me in carrying gates. I am in love too. Who was
Samson's love, my dear Moth?

Moth. A woman, master.

---

53 **dancing horse** (a performing horse well-known for beating out
numbers) 55 **figure** figure of speech 60 **humor** innate disposition 63 **new devised cursy** novel mannerism 63 **think scorn** disdain 64 **outswear** forswear

Armado. Of what complexion?°

Moth. Of all the four,° or the three, or the two, or
one of the four.   80

Armado. Tell me precisely of what complexion.

Moth. Of the sea-water green, sir.

Armado. Is that one of the four complexions?

Moth. As I have read, sir, and the best of them too.

Armado. Green° indeed is the color of lovers. But to   85
have a love of that color, methinks Samson had
small reason for it. He surely affected her for her
wit.°

Moth. It was so, sir, for she had a green wit.

Armado. My love is most immaculate white and red.   90

Moth. Most maculate° thoughts, master, are masked
under such colors.

Armado. Define, define, well-educated infant.

Moth. My father's wit, and my mother's tongue, assist
me!   95

Armado. Sweet invocation of a child, most pretty and
pathetical.

Moth. If she be made of white and red,
    Her faults will ne'er be known,
For blushing cheeks by faults are bred,   100
    And fears by pale white shown.
Then if she fear or be to blame,
    By this you shall not know,
For still her cheeks possess the same
    Which native° she doth owe.°   105
A dangerous rhyme, master, against the reason of
white and red.

---

78 **complexion** disposition   79 **all the four** (the four humors or
fluids of the body: blood, phlegm, bile, black bile)   85 **Green** (im-
mature)   88 **wit** mind   91 **maculate** spotted   105 **native** by nature
105 **owe** possess

Armado. Is there not a ballet,° boy, of the King and
the Beggar?

110 *Moth.* The world was very guilty of such a ballet
some three ages since. But I think now 'tis not to
be found, or if it were, it would neither serve for
the writing nor the tune.

Armado. I will have that subject newly writ o'er, that
115 I may example my digression° by some mighty
precedent. Boy, I do love that country girl that I
took in the park with the rational hind,° Costard.
She deserves well.

Moth. [*Aside*] To be whipped—and yet a better love
120 than my master.

Armado. Sing, boy. My spirit grows heavy in love.

Moth. And that's great marvel, loving a light wench.

Armado. I say, sing.

Moth. Forbear till this company be past.

    Enter [Costard, the] Clown, [Dull, the]
      Constable, and [Jaquenetta, a] Wench.

125 *Dull.* Sir, the duke's pleasure is that you keep Costard
safe, and you must suffer him to take no delight
nor no penance,° but 'a° must fast three days a
week. For this damsel, I must keep her at the park
—she is allowed for the day-woman.° Fare you
130 well.

Armado. I do betray myself with blushing. Maid!

Jaquenetta. Man?

Armado. I will visit thee at the lodge.

Jaquenetta. That's hereby.

108 **ballet** ballad   115 **digression** (Armado means to say, "transgression")   117 **rational hind** intelligent yokel   127 **penance** (perhaps Dull means to say "pleasance," meaning pleasure)   127 **'a** he
129 **allowed for the day-woman** admitted as the dairy maid

Armado. I know where it is situate.   *135*

Jaquenetta. Lord, how wise you are!

Armado. I will tell thee wonders.

Jaquenetta. With that face?

Armado. I love thee.

Jaquenetta. So I heard you say.   *140*

Armado. And so farewell.

Jaquenetta. Fair weather after you!

Dull. Come, Jaquenetta, away!
                              Exeunt [Dull and Jaquenetta].

Armado. Villain, thou shalt fast for thy offenses ere
  thou be pardoned.   *145*

Costard. Well, sir, I hope when I do it I shall do it
  on a full stomach.°

Armado. Thou shalt be heavily punished.

Costard. I am more bound to you than your fellows,°
  for they are but lightly rewarded.   *150*

Armado. Take away this villain. Shut him up.

Moth. Come, you transgressing slave, away!

Costard. Let me not be pent up, sir. I will fast, being
  loose.

Moth. No, sir, that were fast and loose.° Thou shalt   *155*
  to prison.

Costard. Well, if ever I do see the merry days of desolation that I have seen, some shall see.

Moth. What shall some see?

Costard. Nay, nothing, Master Moth, but what they   *160*
  look upon. It is not for prisoners to be too silent

___

147 on a full stomach bravely   149 fellows servants   155 fast and
loose not playing fairly

in their words,° and therefore I will say nothing. I
thank God I have as little patience as another man,
and therefore I can be quiet.   *Exit [with Moth].*

165   *Armado.* I do affect° the very ground (which is base)
where her shoe (which is baser) guided by her foot
(which is basest) doth tread. I shall be forsworn
(which is a great argument of falsehood) if I love.
And how can that be true love which is falsely at-
170   tempted? Love is a familiar;° Love is a devil. There
is no evil angel but Love. Yet was Samson so
tempted, and he had an excellent strength; yet was
Solomon so seduced, and he had a very good wit.
Cupid's butt-shaft° is too hard for Hercules' club,
175   and therefore too much odds for a Spaniard's
rapier. The first and second cause° will not serve
my turn; the *passado*° he respects not, the *duello*°
he regards not. His disgrace is to be called boy, but
his glory is to subdue men. Adieu, valor; rust, ra-
180   pier; be still, drum; for your manager is in love;
yea, he loveth. Assist me some extemporal god of
rhyme,° for I am sure I shall turn sonnet.° Devise,
wit; write, pen; for I am for whole volumes in folio.
                                                    Exit.

162 words (probably with pun on wards = cells)   165 affect love
170 familiar   attendant   spirit   174 butt-shaft   unbarbed   arrow
176 first and second cause (referring to rules governing the conduct
of a duel)   177 passado forward thrust   177 duello correct way
of dueling   181–82 extemporal god of rhyme god of rhymes written on the spur of the moment   182 turn sonnet compose a sonnet

[ACT II

Scene I. *The park.*]

*Enter the Princess of France, with three attending
Ladies [Maria, Katharine, Rosaline] and three
Lords, [one named Boyet].*

Boyet. Now, madam, summon up your dearest
    spirits.°
  Consider who the king your father sends,
  To whom he sends, and what's his embassy:
  Yourself, held precious in the world's esteem,
  To parley with the sole inheritor°   5
  Of all perfections that a man may owe,°
  Matchless Navarre; the plea of no less weight
  Than Aquitaine, a dowry for a queen.
  Be now as prodigal of all dear grace
  As Nature was in making graces dear°   10
  When she did starve the general world beside,
  And prodigally gave them all to you.

Princess. Good Lord Boyet, my beauty, though but
    mean,
  Needs not the painted flourish° of your praise.
  Beauty is bought by judgment of the eye,   15
  Not utt'red by base sale of chapmen's tongues.°

II.i.1 **dearest spirits** best intelligence 5 **inheritor** possessor 6 **owe**
own 10 **graces dear** beauty scarce 14 **painted flourish** elaborate
ornament 16 **utt'red ... tongues** put up for sale by hucksters

I am less proud to hear you tell my worth
Than you much willing to be counted wise
In spending your wit in the praise of mine.
20 But now to task the tasker:° good Boyet,
You are not ignorant all-telling fame
Doth noise abroad Navarre hath made a vow,
Till painful study shall outwear three years,
No woman may approach his silent court.
25 Therefore to's seemeth it a needful course,
Before we enter his forbidden gates,
To know his pleasure; and in that behalf,
Bold of your worthiness,° we single you
As our best-moving° fair solicitor.
30 Tell him the daughter of the king of France,
On serious business, craving quick dispatch,
Importunes personal conference with his Grace.
Haste, signify so much while we attend
Like humble-visaged suitors his high will.

35 *Boyet.* Proud of employment, willingly I go.
                              Exit Boyet.

Princess. All pride is willing pride, and yours is so.
Who are the votaries,° my loving lords,
That are vow-fellows with this virtuous duke?

Lord. Longaville is one.

Princess.   Know you the man?

40 *Maria.* I know him, madam. At a marriage feast
Between Lord Perigort and the beauteous heir
Of Jacques Falconbridge solemnizèd
In Normandy saw I this Longaville.
A man of sovereign parts° he is esteemed,
45 Well fitted in arts, glorious in arms.
Nothing becomes him ill that he would well.°
The only soil of his fair virtue's gloss—

20 **task the tasker** set a task to the one who sets tasks   28 **Bold of
your worthiness** confident of your worth   29 **best-moving** most
persuasive   37 **votaries** those who have sworn a vow   44 **sovereign
parts** lordly qualities   46 **Nothing . . . well** nothing that he values
is unbecoming to him

If virtue's gloss will stain with any soil—
Is a sharp wit matched with too blunt a will,
Whose edge hath power to cut, whose will still wills   50
It should none spare that come within his power.

Princess. Some merry mocking lord, belike—is 't so?

Maria. They say so most that most his humors know.

Princess. Such short-lived wits do wither as they grow.
Who are the rest?   55

Katharine. The young Dumaine, a well-accomplished
   youth,
Of all that virtue love for virtue loved;
Most power to do most harm, least knowing ill,
For he hath wit to make an ill shape good,
And shape to win grace though he had no wit.   60
I saw him at the Duke Alençon's once;
And much too little° of that good I saw
Is my report to° his great worthiness.

Rosaline. Another of these students at that time
Was there with him, if I have heard a truth.   65
Berowne they call him; but a merrier man,
Within the limit of becoming mirth,
I never spent an hour's talk withal.°
His eye begets occasion° for his wit;
For every object that the one doth catch   70
The other turns to a mirth-moving jest,
Which his fair tongue (conceit's expositor°)
Delivers in such apt and gracious words,
That agèd ears play truant at his tales,
And younger hearings are quite ravishèd,   75
So sweet and voluble is his discourse.

Princess. God bless my ladies! Are they all in love,
That every one her own hath garnishèd
With such bedecking ornaments of praise?

---

62 **much too little** far short   63 **to** compared to   68 **withal** with
69 **begets occasion** finds opportunity   72 **conceit's expositor** one
who explains an ingenious notion

Lord. Here comes Boyet.

Enter Boyet.

80 *Princess.*   Now, what admittance,° lord?

Boyet. Navarre had notice of your fair approach;
And he and his competitors° in oath
Were all addressed° to meet you, gentle lady,
Before I came. Marry, thus much I have learnt;
85 He rather means to lodge you in the field,
Like one that comes here to besiege his court,
Than seek a dispensation for his oath
To let you enter his unpeopled house.
                              [*The Ladies mask.*]

*Enter Navarre, Longaville, Dumaine, and
Berowne, [with Attendants].*

Here comes Navarre.

90 *King.* Fair princess, welcome to the court of Navarre.

Princess. "Fair" I give you back again; and "welcome" I have not yet. The roof of this court is too
high to be yours, and welcome to the wide fields
too base to be mine.

95 *King.* You shall be welcome, madam, to my court.

Princess. I will be welcome, then. Conduct me thither.

King. Hear me, dear lady—I have sworn an oath.

Princess. Our Lady help my lord! He'll be forsworn.

King. Not for the world, fair madam, by my will.

Princess. Why, will shall break it, will, and nothing
100   else.

King. Your ladyship is ignorant what it is.

80 admittance permission to enter   82 competitors partners   83 ad-
dressed ready

Princess. Were my lord so, his ignorance were wise,
  Where now his knowledge must prove ignorance.
  I hear your Grace hath sworn out house-keeping.°
  'Tis deadly sin to keep that oath, my lord,   *105*
  And sin to break it.
  But pardon me, I am too sudden-bold;
  To teach a teacher ill beseemeth me.
  Vouchsafe to read the purpose of my coming,
  And suddenly resolve me° in my suit.   *110*
                              [*Gives a paper.*]

King. Madam, I will, if suddenly I may.

Princess. You will the sooner that I were away,
  For you'll prove perjured if you make me stay.

Berowne. Did not I dance with you in Brabant once?

Rosaline. Did not I dance with you in Brabant once?   *115*

Berowne. I know you did.

Rosaline.   How needless was it then
  To ask the question!

Berowne.   You must not be so quick.

Rosaline. 'Tis long° of you that spur me with such
  questions.

Berowne. Your wit's too hot, it speeds too fast, 'twill
  tire.

Rosaline. Not till it leave the rider in the mire.   *120*

Berowne. What time o' day?

Rosaline. The hour that fools should ask.

Berowne. Now fair befall° your mask!

Rosaline. Fair fall the face it covers!

Berowne. And send you many lovers!   *125*

---

104 **sworn out house-keeping** sworn not to keep house or offer hospitality   110 **suddenly resolve me** quickly give me a decision
118 **long** because   123 **fair befall** good luck to

Rosaline. Amen, so you be none.

Berowne. Nay, then will I be gone.

King. Madam, your father here doth intimate°
    The payment of a hundred thousand crowns,
130   Being but the one half of an entire sum
    Disbursèd by my father in his wars.
    But say that he, or we (as neither have),
    Received that sum, yet there remains unpaid
    A hundred thousand more, in surety of the which,
135   One part of Aquitaine is bound to us,
    Although not valued to the money's worth.
    If then the king your father will restore
    But that one half which is unsatisfied,
    We will give up our right in Aquitaine,
140   And hold fair friendship with his Majesty.
    But that, it seems, he little purposeth,
    For here he doth demand to have repaid
    A hundred thousand crowns; and not demands,
    On payment of a hundred thousand crowns,
145   To have his title live in Aquitaine;
    Which we much rather had depart withal,°
    And have the money by our father lent,
    Than Aquitaine, so gelded° as it is.
    Dear princess, were not his requests so far
150   From reason's yielding, your fair self should make
    A yielding 'gainst some reason in my breast,
    And go well satisfied to France again.

Princess. You do the king my father too much wrong,
    And wrong the reputation of your name,
155   In so unseeming° to confess receipt
    Of that which hath so faithfully been paid.

King. I do protest I never heard of it;
    And if you prove it, I'll repay it back
    Or yield up Aquitaine.

---

128 **intimate** make known   146 **depart withal** give up   148 **gelded**
cut up   155 **unseeming** not appearing

Princess.   We arrest your word.°
  Boyet, you can produce acquittances°   160
  For such a sum from special officers
  Of Charles his father.

King.   Satisfy me so.

Boyet. So please your Grace, the packet° is not come
  Where that and other specialties° are bound.
  Tomorrow you shall have a sight of them.   165

King. It shall suffice me—at which interview
  All liberal reason I will yield unto.
  Meantime, receive such welcome at my hand
  As honor (without breach of honor) may
  Make tender of° to thy true worthiness.   170
  You may not come, fair princess, within my gates;
  But here without you shall be so received
  As you shall deem yourself lodged in my heart,
  Though so denied fair harbor in my house.
  Your own good thoughts excuse me, and farewell. 175
  Tomorrow shall we visit you again.

Princess. Sweet health and fair desires consort° your
  Grace.

King. Thy own wish wish I thee in every place.
                   Exit [King and his Train].

Berowne. Lady, I will commend you to mine own
  heart.   180

Rosaline. Pray you, do my commendations, I would
  be glad to see it.

Berowne. I would you heard it groan.

Rosaline. Is the fool sick?

Berowne. Sick at the heart.   185

Rosaline. Alack, let it blood!°

---

159 **arrest your word** take your word as security   160 **acquittances**
receipts   163 **packet** package   164 **specialties** particular legal documents   170 **Make tender of** offer   177 **consort** accompany   186 **let
it blood** bleed him

Berowne. Would that do it good?

Rosaline. My physic says ay.

Berowne. Will you prick 't with your eye?

190 *Rosaline.* No point,° with my knife.

Berowne. Now, God save thy life!

Rosaline. And yours from long living!

Berowne. I cannot stay thanksgiving.°   *Exit.*

Enter Dumaine.

Dumaine, Sir, I pray you a word. What lady is that same?

195 *Boyet.* The heir of Alençon, Katharine her name.

Dumaine. A gallant lady. Monsieur, fare you well.
          Exit.

[Enter Longaville.]

Longaville. I beseech you a word. What is she in the white?

Boyet. A woman sometimes, and° you saw her in the light.

Longaville. Perchance light in the light.° I desire her name.

Boyet. She hath but one for herself. To desire that
200   were a shame.

Longaville. Pray you, sir, whose daughter?

Boyet. Her mother's, I have heard.

Longaville. God's blessing on your beard!

---

190 **No point** not at all   193 **stay thanksgiving** stay long enough to
give you proper thanks (for your unkind remark)   198 **and** if
199 **light in the light** wanton if rightly perceived

Boyet. Good sir, be not offended.
  She is an heir of Falconbridge.   205

Longaville. Nay, my choler° is ended.
  She is a most sweet lady.

Boyet. Not unlike, sir; that may be.
                              Exit Longaville.

                  Enter Berowne.

Berowne. What's her name in the cap?

Boyet. Rosaline, by good hap.

Berowne. Is she wedded or no?

Boyet. To her will, sir, or so.°

Berowne. O, you are welcome, sir! Adieu.

Boyet. Farewell to me, sir, and welcome to you.
                              Exit Berowne.

Maria. That last is Berowne, the merry madcap lord.   215
  Not a word with him but a jest.

Boyet.   And every jest but a word.

Princess. It was well done of you to take him at his
  word.

Boyet. I was as willing to grapple as he was to board.

Katharine. Two hot sheeps, marry!

Boyet.   And wherefore not ships?
  No sheep, sweet lamb, unless we feed on your lips.   220

Katharine. You sheep, and I pasture. Shall that finish
  the jest?

Boyet. So you grant pasture for me.
                              [*Offers to kiss her.*]

206 choler wrath   212 or so something like that

Katharine.　　　　　　　　　　　Not so, gentle beast.
　My lips are no common,° though several° they be.

Boyet. Belonging to whom?

Katharine.　　　　　　　　　　To my fortunes and me.

Princess. Good wits will be jangling; but, gentles,
225　　agree.
　This civil war of wits were much better used
　On Navarre and his book-men, for here 'tis abused.

Boyet. If my observation (which very seldom lies)
　By the heart's still rhetoric disclosèd with eyes
230　Deceive me not now, Navarre is infected.

Princess. With what?

Boyet. With that which we lovers entitle "affected."°

Princess. Your reason?

Boyet. Why, all his behaviors° did make their retire
235　To the court° of his eye, peeping thorough desire.
　His heart, like an agate° with your print im-
　　pressed,°
　Proud with his form, in his eye pride expressed.
　His tongue, all impatient to speak and not see,°
　Did stumble with haste in his eyesight to be;
240　All senses to that sense did make their repair,
　To feel only looking on fairest of fair.°
　Methought all his senses were locked in his eye,
　As jewels in crystal for some prince to buy;
　Who, tend'ring° their own worth from where they
　　were glassed,°
245　Did point° you to buy them, along as you passed.

223 **no common** i.e., not like pasture held in common　223 **several** two (the word also, in this context, signifies "private property") 232 **affected** impassioned　234 **behaviors** expression of his feelings 235 **court** watch-post　236 **agate** (stone used for the engraving of images)　236 **impressed** imprinted　238 **His tongue . . . see** his tongue, vexed at having the power of speaking without having the power of seeing　241 **To feel . . . fair** (sight is translated into feeling in regarding her)　244 **tend'ring** offering　244 **glassed** enclosed in glass　245 **point** urge

His face's own margent did quote such amazes
That all eyes saw his eyes enchanted with gazes.°
I'll give you Aquitaine, and all that is his,
And° you give him for my sake but one loving kiss.

Princess. Come to our pavilion. Boyet is disposed.   250

Boyet. But to speak that in words which his eye hath
    disclosed.
I only have made a mouth of his eye
By adding a tongue which I know will not lie.

Rosaline. Thou art an old love-monger, and speakest
    skillfully.

Maria. He is Cupid's grandfather, and learns news of
    him.   255

Katharine. Then was Venus like her mother, for her
    father is but grim.

Boyet. Do you hear, my mad wenches?

Rosaline.   No.

Boyet.   What then? Do you see?

Rosaline. Ay, our way to be gone.

Boyet.   You are too hard for me.
                            Exeunt omnes.°

[ACT III

Scene I. *The park.*]

Enter [Armado, the] Braggart, and [Moth,] his Boy.

Armado. Warble, child, make passionate my sense of
hearing.

Moth. [*Sings*] Concolinel.°

Armado. Sweet air! Go, tenderness of years,° take
5   this key, give enlargement° to the swain, bring him
festinately° hither. I must employ him in a letter
to my love.

Moth. Master, will you win your love with a French
brawl?°

10 *Armado.* How meanest thou? Brawling in French?

Moth. No, my complete master; but to jig off a tune
at the tongue's end, canary to it° with your feet,
humor it with turning up your eyelids, sigh a note
and sing a note, sometime through the throat as if
15   you swallowed love with singing love, sometime
through the nose as if you snuffed up love by smelling love, with your hat penthouse-like o'er the shop

III.i.3 **Concolinel** (perhaps the name of a song) 4 **tenderness of
years** (affected talk for "young fellow") 5 **enlargement** freedom
6 **festinately** quickly 8–9 **French brawl** French dance 12 **canary
to it** dance in a lively way

of your eyes, with your arms crossed° on your
thin-belly doublet° like a rabbit on a spit, or your
hands in your pocket like a man after the old paint-　20
ing; and keep not too long in one tune, but a snip°
and away. These are complements,° these are humors, these betray nice wenches (that would be
betrayed without these), and make them men of
note—do you note me?—that most are affected　25
to° these.

Armado. How hast thou purchased this experience?

Moth. By my penny of observation.

Armado. But O—but O—

Moth. "The hobby-horse is forgot."°　　　30

Armado. Call'st thou my love "hobby-horse"?

Moth. No, master. The hobby-horse is but a colt, and
your love perhaps a hackney.° But have you forgot your love?

Armado. Almost I had.　　　35

Moth. Negligent student, learn her by heart.

Armado. By heart, and in heart, boy.

Moth. And out of heart, master. All those three I will
prove.

Armado. What wilt thou prove?　　　40

Moth. A man, if I live; and this, by, in, and without,
upon the instant. By heart you love her, because
your heart cannot come by her; in heart you love
her, because your heart is in love with her; and
out of heart you love her, being out of heart that　45
you cannot enjoy her.

18 **arms crossed** (a sign of melancholy)　19 **thin-belly doublet**
garment unpadded in the lower part (across your thin belly)　21 **snip**
snatch　22 **complements** accompaniments　25–26 **affected to** taken
with　30 **"The hobby-horse is forgot"** (perhaps a phrase from an
old song)　32–33 **hobby-horse, colt, hackney** (slang words for
"whore")

Armado. I am all these three.

Moth. [*Aside*] And three times as much more, and yet nothing at all.

50 *Armado.* Fetch hither the swain. He must carry me a letter.

Moth. A message well sympathized°—a horse to be ambassador for an ass.

Armado. Ha, ha, what sayest thou?

55 *Moth.* Marry, sir, you must send the ass upon the horse, for he is very slow-gaited. But I go.

Armado. The way is but short. Away!

Moth. As swift as lead, sir.

Armado. The meaning, pretty ingenious?
60   Is not lead a metal heavy, dull, and slow?

Moth. Minime,° honest master; or rather, master, no.

Armado. I say, lead is slow.

Moth.   You are too swift, sir, to say so.
   Is that lead slow which is fired from a gun?

Armado. Sweet smoke of rhetoric!
65   He reputes me a cannon; and the bullet, that's he:
   I shoot thee at the swain.

Moth.   Thump, then, and I flee.
                                   [*Exit.*]

Armado. A most acute juvenal,° voluble and free of grace!
   By thy favor, sweet welkin,° I must sigh in thy face:
   Most rude melancholy, valor gives thee place.°
70   My herald is returned.

---

52 **well sympathized** in proper accord   61 **Minime** by no means
(Latin)   67 **juvenal** (in two senses) young fellow, satirist   68 **welkin**
heaven   69 **gives thee place** gives place to you

Enter [Moth, the] Page and [Costard, the] Clown.

Moth. A wonder, master! Here's a costard° broken
    in a shin.

Armado. Some enigma, some riddle. Come, thy
    l'envoy°—begin.

Costard. No egma, no riddle, no l'envoy; no salve°
    in the mail,° sir. O, sir, plantain,° a plain plantain.
    No l'envoy, no l'envoy, no salve, sir, but a plantain.   *73*

Armado. By virtue, thou enforcest laughter; thy silly
    thought, my spleen;° the heaving of my lungs pro-
    vokes me to ridiculous smiling. O, pardon me, my
    stars! Doth the inconsiderate° take salve for
    l'envoy, and the word l'envoy for a salve?   *80*

Moth. Do the wise think them other? Is not l'envoy
    a salve?

Armado. No, page; it is an epilogue, or discourse to
    make plain
    Some obscure precedence° that hath tofore been
    sain.°
    I will example it: *85*
        The fox, the ape, and the humble-bee
        Were still at odds, being but three.
    There's the moral. Now the l'envoy.

Moth. I will add the l'envoy. Say the moral again.

Armado. The fox, the ape, and the humble-bee   *90*
        Were still at odds, being but three.

Moth.   Until the goose came out of door,
        And stayed the odds by adding four.°

---

71 **costard** apple, or head   72 **l'envoy** words ending a composition
by way of leave-taking   73 **salve** (with a pun on *salve,* the Latin
word for salute)   74 **mail** bag, container   74 **plantain** tree whose
leaves were used for healing   77 **spleen** mirth   79 **inconsiderate**
unthinking   84 **precedence** preceding statement   84 **tofore been
sain** been said before   93 **stayed . . . four** turned them into evens
by adding a fourth

Now will I begin your moral, and do you follow
95 with my l'envoy.
>   The fox, the ape, and the humble-bee
>   Were still at odds, being but three.

Armado. Until the goose came out of door,
>   Staying the odds by adding four.

100 *Moth.* A good l'envoy, ending in the goose. Would
you desire more?

Costard. The boy hath sold him a bargain,° a goose
—that's flat.
Sir, your pennyworth is good, and° your goose be
fat.
To sell a bargain well is as cunning as fast and
loose.°
105 Let me see: a fat l'envoy—ay, that's a fat goose.

Armado. Come hither, come hither. How did this
argument begin?

Moth. By saying that a costard was broken in a shin.
Then called you for the l'envoy.

Costard. True, and I for a plantain; thus came your
argument in;
Then the boy's fat l'envoy, the goose that you
110 bought,
And he ended the market.

Armado. But tell me, how was there a costard broken
in a shin?

Moth. I will tell you sensibly.°

115 *Costard.* Thou hast no feeling of it, Moth. I will speak
that l'envoy:
I, Costard, running out, that was safely within,
Fell over the threshold and broke my shin.

Armado. We will talk no more of this matter.

120 *Costard.* Till there be more matter° in the shin.

102 **sold him a bargain** made a fool of him   103 **and** if   104 **fast
and loose** cheating   114 **sensibly** with feeling   120 **matter** pus

Armado. Sirrah Costard, I will enfranchise° thee.

Costard. O, marry me to one Frances! I smell some
l'envoy, some goose, in this.

Armado. By my sweet soul, I mean setting thee at
liberty, enfreedoming thy person. Thou wert im-   *125*
mured, restrained, captivated, bound.

Costard. True, true, and now you will be my purga-
tion and let me loose.

Armado. I give thee thy liberty, set thee from dur-
ance, and in lieu thereof, impose on thee nothing   *130*
but this. [*Gives a letter.*] Bear this significant° to
the country maid Jaquenetta. [*Gives a coin.*] There
is remuneration; for the best ward° of mine honor
is rewarding my dependents. Moth, follow.

Moth. Like the sequel, I. Signior Costard, adieu.   *135*
                    Exit [Armado, followed by Moth].

Costard. My sweet ounce of man's flesh, my incony°
Jew!—Now will I look to his remuneration. Remuneration? O that's the Latin word for three farthings. Three farthings—remuneration. "What's the
price of this inkle?"° "One penny." "No, I'll give   *140*
you a remuneration." Why, it carries it! Remuneration! Why, it is a fairer name than French
crown.° I will never buy and sell out of this word.

                    Enter Berowne.

Berowne. O my good knave Costard, exceedingly well
met.   *145*

Costard. Pray you, sir, how much carnation° ribbon
may a man buy for a remuneration?

Berowne. O, what is a remuneration?

---

121 **enfranchise** set free   131 **significant** letter   133 **ward** protection
136 **incony** darling   140 **inkle** band of linen   142–43 French crown
(in two senses: a coin, and the baldness caused by syphilis, the so-
called "French disease")   146 **carnation** flesh-colored

Costard. Marry, sir, halfpenny farthing.

150 *Berowne.* O, why then, three-farthing-worth of silk.

Costard. I thank your worship. God be wi' you!

Berowne. O stay, slave, I must employ thee.
    As thou wilt win my favor, good my knave,
    Do one thing for me that I shall entreat.

155 *Costard.* When would you have it done, sir?

Berowne. O, this afternoon.

Costard. Well, I will do it, sir. Fare you well.

Berowne. O, thou knowest not what it is.

Costard. I shall know, sir, when I have done it.

160 *Berowne.* Why, villain, thou must know first.

Costard. I will come to your worship tomorrow morn-
    ing.

Berowne. It must be done this afternoon. Hark, slave,
    it is but this:
165 The princess comes to hunt here in the park,
    And in her train there is a gentle lady;
    When tongues speak sweetly, then they name her
        name,
    And Rosaline they call her. Ask for her,
    And to her white hand see thou do commend
    This sealed-up counsel. [*Gives him a letter and a*
170   *shilling.*] There's thy guerdon.° Go.

Costard. Gardon, O sweet gardon! Better than re-
    muneration—a 'leven-pence farthing better. Most
    sweet gardon! I will do it, sir, in print.° Gardon!
    Remuneration!   *Exit.*

175 *Berowne.* O, and I, forsooth, in love!
    I, that have been love's whip,
    A very beadle° to a humorous sigh,

---

170 guerdon reward   173 in print most carefully   177 beadle parish constable

A critic, nay, a night-watch constable,
A domineering pedant o'er the boy, *Cupid*
Than whom no mortal so magnificent!   180
This wimpled,° whining, purblind,° wayward boy,
This senior-junior, giant-dwarf, Dan° Cupid,
Regent of love-rhymes, lord of folded arms,
Th' anointed sovereign of sighs and groans,
Liege° of all loiterers and malcontents,   185
Dread prince of plackets,° king of codpieces,°
Sole imperator and great general
Of trotting paritors°—O my little heart!—
And I to be a corporal of his field,°
And wear his colors like a tumbler's° hoop!   190
What? I love? I sue? I seek a wife?
A woman that is like a German clock,
Still a-repairing, ever out of frame,°
And never going aright, being a watch,
But being watched that it may still go right!   195
Nay, to be perjured, which is worst of all;
And, among three, to love the worst of all,
A whitely° wanton with a velvet brow,
With two pitch balls stuck in her face for eyes.
Ay, and, by heaven, one that will do the deed,°   200
Though Argus° were her eunuch and her guard!
And I to sigh for her, to watch for her,
To pray for her! Go to, it is a plague
That Cupid will impose for my neglect
Of his almighty dreadful little might.   205
Well, I will love, write, sigh, pray, sue, groan.
Some men must love my lady, and some Joan.
                                              [*Exit.*]

---

181 **wimpled** covered with a muffler   181 **purblind** completely blind
182 **Dan** ("don," a derivation of *dominus*, lord)   185 **Liege** lord
186 **plackets** slits in petticoats (vulgar term for women)   186 **codpieces** cloth covering the opening in men's breeches   188 **paritors**
(officers of the Ecclesiastical Court who serve summonses for certain, often sexual, offenses)   189 **corporal of his field** aide to a
general   190 **tumbler's** acrobat's   193 **frame** order   198 **whitely**
pale   200 **do the deed** perform the act of coition   201 **Argus** (ancient mythological being with a hundred eyes)

[ACT IV

Scene I. *The park.*]

*Enter the Princess, a Forester, her Ladies,
and her Lords.*

Princess. Was that the king, that spurred his horse so
    hard
  Against the steep uprising of the hill?

Forester. I know not, but I think it was not he.

Princess. Whoe'er 'a° was, 'a showed a mounting
    mind.°
5   Well, lords, today we shall have our dispatch;
  On Saturday we will return to France.
  Then, forester, my friend, where is the bush
  That we must stand and play the murderer in?

Forester. Hereby, upon the edge of yonder coppice,°
10   A stand where you may make the fairest shoot.

Princess. I thank my beauty, I am fair that shoot,
  And thereupon thou speak'st the fairest shoot.

Forester. Pardon me, madam, for I meant not so.

Princess. What, what? First praise me, and again say
    no?
15   O short-lived pride! Not fair? Alack for woe!

Forester. Yes, madam, fair.

IV.i.4 'a he   4 mounting mind lofty spirit (with pun on "mountain")
9 coppice undergrowth of small trees

74

Princess.   Nay, never paint° me now!
  Where fair is not, praise cannot mend the brow.°
  Here, good my glass,° take this for telling true—
                                [*giving him money*]
  Fair payment for foul words is more than due.

Forester. Nothing but fair is that which you inherit.   20

Princess. See, see—my beauty will be saved by
      merit!°
  O heresy in fair,° fit for these days!
  A giving hand, though foul, shall have fair praise.
  But come, the bow! Now mercy goes to kill,°
  And shooting well is then accounted ill.   25
  Thus will I save my credit in the shoot:
  Not wounding, pity would not let me do 't;
  If wounding, then it was to show my skill,
  That more for praise than purpose meant to kill.
  And out of question so it is sometimes,   30
  Glory° grows guilty of detested crimes,
  When, for fame's sake, for praise, an outward part,
  We bend to that the working of the heart;
  As I for praise alone now seek to spill
  The poor deer's blood that my heart means no ill.   35

Boyet. Do not curst° wives hold that self-sovereignty
  Only for praise sake, when they strive to be
  Lords o'er their lords?

Princess. Only for praise, and praise we may afford
  To any lady that subdues a lord.   40

                  Enter [Costard, the] Clown.

Boyet. Here comes a member of the commonwealth.°

16 paint flatter   17 mend the brow make the brow more beautiful
18 good my glass my fine mirror   21 saved by merit saved by what
I truly deserve   22 heresy in fair heresy with respect to beauty
24 mercy goes to kill (the merciful huntsman goes forth to kill—
instead of leaving the prey wounded—but such killing is not well
regarded)   31 Glory i.e., ambition for glory   36 curst peevish
41 member of the commonwealth i.e., one of our group

Costard. God dig-you-den° all! Pray you, which is
the head lady?

Princess. Thou shalt know her, fellow, by the rest
45   that have no heads.

Costard. Which is the greatest lady, the highest?

Princess. The thickest and the tallest.

Costard. The thickest and the tallest—it is so. Truth
is truth.
And° your waist, mistress, were as slender as my
50   wit,
One o' these maids' girdles for your waist should
be fit.
Are not you the chief woman? You are the thickest
here.

Princess. What's your will, sir? What's your will?

Costard. I have a letter from Monsieur Berowne to
one Lady Rosaline.

Princess. O thy letter, thy letter! He's a good friend
55   of mine.
Stand aside, good bearer. Boyet, you can carve°—
Break up this capon.°

Boyet.   I am bound to serve.
This letter is mistook; it importeth° none here.
It is writ to Jaquenetta.

Princess.   We will read it, I swear.
Break the neck° of the wax, and every one give
60   ear.

Boyet. (Reads) "By heaven, that thou art fair is
most infallible; true that thou art beauteous; truth
itself that thou art lovely. More fairer than fair,
beautiful than beauteous, truer than truth itself,

---

42 **God dig-you-den** God give you good evening   50 **And** if   56
carve (with pun on the sense "flirt")   57 **Break up this capon** (1)
carve this chicken (2) open this love-letter   58 **importeth** concerns
60 **Break the neck** (still referring to the capon)

have commiseration on thy heroical vassal. The　65
magnanimous and most illustrate° king Cophetua
set eye upon the pernicious and indubitate° beggar
Zenelophon,° and he it was that might rightly say
veni, vidi, vici; which to annothanize° in the vulgar
(O base and obscure vulgar!) *videlicet,°* he came,　70
saw, and overcame. He came, one; saw, two;
overcame, three. Who came? The king. Why did
he come? To see. Why did he see? To overcome.
To whom came he? To the beggar. What saw he?
The beggar. Who overcame he? The beggar. The　75
conclusion is victory. On whose side? The king's.
The captive is enriched. On whose side? The beggar's. The catastrophe is a nuptial. On whose side?
The king's. No—on both in one, or one in both.
I am the king, for so stands the comparison, thou　80
the beggar, for so witnesseth thy lowliness. Shall
I command thy love? I may. Shall I enforce thy
love? I could. Shall I entreat thy love? I will. What
shalt thou exchange for rags? Robes. For tittles?°
Titles. For thyself? Me. Thus, expecting thy reply,　85
I profane my lips on thy foot, my eyes on thy picture, and my heart on thy every part.

　　Thine in the dearest design of industry,°
　　　　　　　　　　Don Adriano de Armado.
Thus dost thou hear the Nemean lion° roar　　90
　'Gainst thee, thou lamb, that standest as his prey.
Submissive fall his princely feet before,
　And he from forage° will incline to play.
But if thou strive, poor soul, what art thou then?
Food for his rage, repasture° for his den."　　95

Princess. What plume of feathers is he that indited°
　　this letter?

66 **illustrate** illustrious　67 **indubitate** undoubted　68 **Zenelophon**
(character in the ballad of King Cophetua and the Beggar)　69 **an-
nothanize** anatomize (or a mock-Latin word to mean "annotate")
70 **videlicet** namely (Latin)　84 **tittles** small jottings in ink　88 **industry** faithful service　90 **Nemean lion** (lion killed by Hercules)
93 **from forage** turning away from feeding　95 **repasture** food
96 **indited** wrote

What vane?° What weathercock?° Did you ever
hear better?

Boyet. I am much deceived but I remember the style.

Princess. Else your memory is bad, going o'er it ere-
while.

Boyet. This Armado is a Spaniard that keeps here in
100   court;
A phantasime,° a Monarcho,° and one that makes
sport
To the prince and his book-mates.

Princess.   Thou fellow, a word.
Who gave thee this letter?

Costard.   I told you—my lord.

Princess. To whom shouldst thou give it?

Costard.   From my lord to my lady.

105 *Princess.* From which lord to which lady?

Costard. From my lord Berowne, a good master of
mine,
To a lady of France that he called Rosaline.

Princess. Thou hast mistaken° his letter. Come, lords,
away.
Here, sweet, put up this; 'twill be thine another day.
     [*Exeunt Princess and Train. Boyet remains.*]

Boyet. Who is the suitor?° Who is the suitor?

110 *Rosaline.*   Shall I teach you to know?

Boyet. Ay, my continent° of beauty.

Rosaline.   Why, she that bears the bow.
Finely put off!°

97 vane weather-vane   97 weather-cock ostentatious thing   101
phantasime person of wild imaginings   101 Monarcho (nickname of
a crazy Italian at the court of Elizabeth)   108 mistaken taken to
the wrong person   110 suitor (pronounced "shooter")   111 continent container   112 put off repulsed

Boyet. My lady goes to kill horns, but, if thou marry,
Hang me by the neck if horns that year miscarry.°
Finely put on!°   115

Rosaline. Well then, I am the shooter.

Boyet.   And who is your deer?

Rosaline. If we choose by the horns, yourself. Come
not near.
Finely put on indeed!

Maria. You still wrangle with her, Boyet, and she
strikes at the brow.°

Boyet. But she herself is hit lower. Have I hit her
now?   120

Rosaline. Shall I come upon thee with an old saying
that was a man when King Pepin of France was a
little boy, as touching the hit it?°

Boyet. So I may answer thee with one as old, that was
a woman when Queen Guinever of Britain was a   125
little wench, as touching the hit it.

Rosaline. "Thou canst not hit it, hit it, hit it,
Thou canst not hit it, my good man.

Boyet.   "And° I cannot, cannot, cannot,
And I cannot, another can."   130
                    Exit [Rosaline with Katharine].

Costard. By my troth, most pleasant, how both did
fit it!

Maria. A mark marvelous well shot, for they both did
hit it.

Boyet. A mark! O, mark but that mark!° A mark,
says my lady!

---

114 **if horns that year miscarry** i.e., if someone is not made a
cuckold   115 **put on** lay on, as a blow   119 **strikes at the brow**
takes careful aim (with an allusion to the cuckold's horns)   123 **hit
it** name of a dance tune (leading to pun on the sense of *hit* = to
copulate)   129 **And if**   133 **mark** (1) target (2) pudend

Let the mark have a prick° in 't, to mete° at if it
may be.

Maria. Wide o' the bow hand!° I' faith, your hand
135 is out.

Costard. Indeed 'a must shoot nearer, or he'll ne'er
hit the clout.°

Boyet. And if my hand be out, then belike your hand
is in.

Costard. Then will she get the upshoot° by cleaving
the pin.°

Maria. Come, come, you talk greasily;° your lips grow
foul.

Costard. She's too hard for you at pricks, sir. Chal-
140 lenge her to bowl.

Boyet. I fear too much rubbing.° Good night, my
good owl.

                    [*Exeunt Boyet and Maria.*]

Costard. By my soul, a swain,° a most simple clown!
Lord, lord, how the ladies and I have put him
down!
O' my troth,° most sweet jests, most incony° vul-
gar wit.
When it comes so smoothly off, so obscenely as it
145 were, so fit!
Armado to th' one side—O, a most dainty man!
To see him walk before a lady, and to bear her fan!
To see him kiss his hand, and how most sweetly
'a will swear!

134 prick mark within the target (with additional bawdy suggestion)
134 mete aim   135 Wide o' the bow hand far from the target on
the bow-hand side   136 clout nail in the center of the target
138 upshoot best shot   138 cleaving the pin (1) striking the center
of the target (2) causing emission in the male   139 greasily in-
decently   141 rubbing (bowling balls striking each other; with
sexual innuendo)   142 swain herdsman   144 O' my troth by my
faith   144 incony fine

And his page o' t' other side, that handful of wit,
Ah, heavens, it is a most pathetical nit!°   150

                                        Shout within.
Sola,° sola!   [*Exit.*]

[Scene II. *The park.*]

Enter Dull, Holofernes the Pedant, and Nathaniel.

Nathaniel. Very reverend sport, truly, and done in
the testimony° of a good conscience.

Holofernes. The deer was, as you know, *sanguis,* in
blood; ripe as the pomewater,° who now hangeth
like a jewel in the ear of *coelo,* the sky, the welkin,   5
the heaven; and anon falleth like a crab° on the
face of *terra,* the soil, the land, the earth.

Nathaniel. Truly, Master Holofernes, the epithets are
sweetly varied, like a scholar at the least. But sir,
I assure ye it was a buck of the first head.°   10

Holofernes. Sir Nathaniel, *haud credo.*°

Dull. 'Twas not a *haud credo,* 'twas a pricket.°

Holofernes. Most barbarous intimation!° Yet a kind
of insinuation, as it were, *in via,* in way, of expli-
cation;° *facere,*° as it were, replication,° or rather,   15
ostentare, to show, as it were, his inclination—after
his undressed, unpolished, uneducated, unpruned,
untrained, or, rather, unlettered, or, ratherest, un-

150 **nit** small thing (louse)   151 **Sola** (a hunting cry)   IV.ii.2 **testi-
mony** approval   4 **pomewater** (variety of a sweet apple)   6 **crab**
crab apple   10 **buck of the first head** full-grown buck   11 **haud
credo** I do not believe it (Latin; in the next line, Dull apparently
takes the words as *old gray doe*)   12 **pricket** two-year old red deer
13 **intimation** (a pedantic substitute for "insinuation")   14–15 **ex-
plication** explanation   15 **facere** to make   15 **replication** unfolding, revelation

confirmed fashion—to insert again my *haud credo*
20 for a deer.

Dull. I said the deer was not a *haud credo,* 'twas a
pricket.

Holofernes. Twice sod° simplicity, *bis coctus!*°
O thou monster Ignorance, how deformed dost
thou look!

Nathaniel. Sir, he hath never fed of the dainties that
25   are bred in a book.
He hath not eat paper, as it were, he hath not
drunk ink. His intellect is not replenished. He is
only an animal, only sensible in the duller parts.
And such barren plants are set before us that we
thankful should be,
Which we of taste and feeling are, for those parts
30   that do fructify° in us more than he.
For as it would ill become me to be vain, indiscreet, or a fool,
So were there a patch° set on learning, to see him
in a school.
But, *omne bene,*° say I, being of an old father's
mind,
Many can brook° the weather that love not the
wind.

Dull. You two are book-men. Can you tell me by
35   your wit
What was a month old at Cain's birth that's not
five weeks old as yet?

Holofernes. Dictynna,° goodman Dull. Dictynna,
goodman Dull.

Dull. What is Dictynna?

Nathaniel. A title to Phoebe, to Luna, to the moon.

___

23 **Twice sod** soaked twice (again and again)   23 **bis coctus** cooked
twice   30 **fructify** bear fruit   32 **patch** fool   33 **omne bene** all is
well   34 **brook** endure   37 **Dictynna** Diana, the moon

Holofernes. The moon was a month old when Adam
    was no more,   *40*
    And raught° not to five weeks when he came to
    fivescore.
    Th' allusion holds in the exchange.°

Dull. 'Tis true indeed; the collusion° holds in the ex-
    change.

Holofernes. God comfort thy capacity! I say th' allu-   *45*
    sion holds in the exchange.

Dull. And I say the pollusion holds in the exchange,
    for the moon is never but a month old; and I say
    beside that 'twas a pricket that the princess killed.

Holofernes. Sir Nathaniel, will you hear an extempo-   *50*
    ral° epitaph on the death of the deer? And, to
    humor the ignorant, I call the deer the princess
    killed, a pricket.

Nathaniel. Perge,° good Master Holofernes, *perge,* so
    it shall please you to abrogate scurrility.°   *55*

Holofernes. I will something affect the letter° for it
    argues facility.
    The preyful° princess pierced and pricked a pretty
    pleasing pricket;
    Some say a sore,° but not a sore till now made sore
    with shooting.
    The dogs did yell. Put L° to sore, then sorel° jumps
    from thicket;
    Or pricket, sore, or else sorel. The people fall a
    hooting.   *60*
    If sore be sore, then L to sore makes fifty sores—
    o' sorel.

---

41 **raught** attained   42 **Th' allusion . . . exchange** (the riddle serves
for Adam as well as for Cain)   43 **collusion** (a pedantic misunderstanding)   50–51 **extemporal** on the spur of the moment   54 **Perge**
continue   55 **abrogate scurrility** put aside foul talk   56 **affect the
letter** alliterate   57 **preyful** killing much prey   58 **sore** four-year
old buck   59 **L** (the Roman numeral fifty) · 59 **sorel** young buck

Of one sore I an hundred make by adding but one
more L.

Nathaniel. A rare talent!°

Dull. If a talent be a claw, look how he claws° him
65   with a talent.

Holofernes. This is a gift that I have, simple, simple;
a foolish extravagant spirit, full of forms, figures,
shapes, objects, ideas, apprehensions, motions, rev-
olutions. These are begot in the ventricle° of mem-
70   ory, nourished in the womb of *pia mater,*° and delivered upon the mellowing of occasion.° But the
gift is good in those in whom it is acute, and I am
thankful for it.

Nathaniel. Sir, I praise the Lord for you, and so may
75   my parishioners, for their sons are well tutored by
you, and their daughters profit very greatly under
you. You are a good member of the commonwealth.

Holofernes. Mehercle,° if their sons be ingenious, they
shall want no instruction; if their daughters be ca-
80   pable, I will put it to them. But *vir sapit qui pauca
loquitur.*° A soul feminine saluteth us.

Enter Jaquenetta and [Costard,] the Clown.

Jaquenetta. God give you good morrow, Master Parson.

Holofernes. Master Parson, *quasi*° pierce-one? And if
85   one should be pierced, which is the one?

Costard. Marry, Master Schoolmaster, he that is likest
to a hogshead.°

Holofernes. Of piercing a hogshead!° A good luster

---

63 **talent** talon   64 **claws** flatters   69 **ventricle** part of the brain
containing the memory   70 **pia mater** membrane enclosing the
brain   71 **mellowing of occasion** fit time   78 **Mehercle** By Hercules
80–81 **vir . . . loquitur** "the man is wise who speaks little"   84 **quasi**
as if   87 **hogshead** fathead   88 **piercing a hogshead** getting drunk

of conceit° in a turf° of earth, fire enough for a
flint, pearl enough for a swine. 'Tis pretty; it is well.   *90*

Jaquenetta. Good Master Parson, be so good as read
me this letter. It was given me by Costard, and
sent me from Don Armado. I beseech you read it.

*Holofernes. Fauste, precor, gelida quando pecus omne
sub umbra ruminat,°* and so forth. Ah, good old   *95*
Mantuan. I may speak of thee as the traveler doth
of Venice:
    Venetia, Venetia,
    Chi non ti vede, non ti pretia.°
Old Mantuan, old Mantuan! Who understandeth   *100*
thee not, loves thee not. *Ut, re, sol, la, mi, fa.* Under pardon, sir, what are the contents? Or, rather,
as Horace says in his—What, my soul, verses?

Nathaniel. Ay, sir, and very learned.

Holofernes. Let me hear a staff,° a stanze, a verse.   *105*
Lege, domine.°

[*Nathaniel reads.*] "If love make me forsworn, how
    shall I swear to love?
    Ah, never faith could hold if not to beauty
      vowed!
Though to myself forsworn, to thee I'll faithful
      prove;
    Those thoughts to me were oaks, to thee like
      osiers bowed.   *110*
Study his bias leaves° and makes his book thine
      eyes,
    Where all those pleasures live that art would
      comprehend.
If knowledge be the mark, to know thee shall suf-
      fice:

88–89 **luster of conceit** brilliant idea   89 **turf** clod   94–95 **Fauste
. . . ruminat** "I pray thee, Faustus, when all the cattle ruminate
beneath the cool shade" (a quotation from a Latin poem by Mantuan, an Italian Renaissance poet)   98–99 **Venetia . . . pretia** "Venice, Venice, only those who do not see thee do not value thee"
(Italian)   105 **staff** stanza   106 **Lege, domine** read, master   111
Study his bias leaves (the student leaves his favorite studies)

    Well learnèd is that tongue that well can thee
        commend,
  All ignorant that soul that sees thee without won-
115   der;
    Which is to me some praise, that I thy parts
        admire.
  Thy eye Jove's lightning bears, thy voice his dread-
      ful thunder,
    Which, not to anger bent, is music and sweet fire.
  Celestial as thou art, O pardon love this wrong,
  That sings heaven's praise with such an earthly
120   tongue!"

Holofernes. You find not the apostrophus,° and so
miss the accent. Let me supervise the canzonet.°
Here are only numbers ratified;° but, for the ele-
gancy, facility, and golden cadence of poesy, *caret.*°
125 Ovidius Naso was the man; and why indeed
"Naso"° but for smelling out the odoriferous flowers of fancy, the jerks of invention?° *Imitari*° is
nothing. So doth the hound his master, the ape his
keeper, the tired horse his rider. But, damosella
130 virgin, was this directed to you?

Jaquenetta. Ay, sir, from one Monsieur Berowne, one
of the strange° queen's lords.

Holofernes. I will overglance the superscript.° "To
the snow-white hand of the most beauteous Lady
135 Rosaline." I will look again on the intellect° of the
letter for the nomination° of the party writing to
the person written unto. "Your ladyship's, in all
desired employment, Berowne." Sir Nathaniel, this
Berowne is one of the votaries° with the king; and
140 here he hath framed° a letter to a sequent° of the

---

121 apostrophus (mark of punctuation taking the place of a vowel)
122 canzonet song   123 numbers ratified rhythm regularized   124
caret it is deficient   126 Naso nose   127 jerks of invention clever
strokes of wit   127 Imitari to imitate   132 strange foreign   133
superscript address   135 intellect purport   136 nomination name
139 votaries persons who have taken a vow   140 framed devised
140 sequent follower

stranger queen's, which accidentally, or by the way
of progression,° hath miscarried. Trip and go,° my
sweet, deliver this paper into the royal hand of the
king; it may concern much. Stay not thy compliment;° I forgive thy duty. Adieu.   145

Jaquenetta. Good Costard, go with me. Sir, God save
your life.

Costard. Have with thee, my girl.
                          Exit [with Jaquenetta].

Nathaniel. Sir, you have done this in the fear of God
very religiously; and as a certain father saith—   150

Holofernes. Sir, tell not me of the father, I do fear
colorable colors.° But to return to the verses—did
they please you, Sir Nathaniel?

Nathaniel. Marvelous well for the pen.°

Holofernes. I do dine today at the father's of a certain   155
pupil of mine, where, if before repast it shall please
you to gratify the table with a grace, I will, on my
privilege I have with the parents of the foresaid
child or pupil, undertake your *ben venuto;*° where
I will prove those verses to be very unlearned,   160
neither savoring of poetry, wit, nor invention. I beseech your society.

Nathaniel. And thank you too, for society (saith the
text) is the happiness of life.

Holofernes. And, certes,° the text most infallibly con-   165
cludes it. [*To Dull*] Sir, I do invite you too; you
shall not say me nay. *Pauca verba.*° Away! The
gentles are at their game, and we will to our recreation.   *Exeunt.*

141–42 by the way of progression on its way   142 Trip and go
(phrase used of a morris dance)   144–45 Stay not thy compliment
do not wait on ceremony   152 colorable colors plausible excuses
154 pen penmanship, or style of writing   159 ben venuto welcome
(Italian)   165 certes certainly   167 Pauca verba few words

[Scene III. *The park.*]

Enter Berowne with a paper in his hand, alone.

Berowne. The king he is hunting the deer; I am cours-
ing° myself. They have pitched a toil;° I am toiling
in a pitch—pitch that defiles. Defile—a foul word!
Well, set thee down, sorrow, for so they say the
5   fool said, and so say I, and I the fool. Well proved,
wit! By the Lord, this love is as mad as Ajax:°
it kills sheep; it kills me—I a sheep. Well proved
again o' my side! I will not love; if I do, hang me!
I' faith, I will not. O but her eye! By this light, but
10 for her eye, I would not love her—yes, for her two
eyes. Well, I do nothing in the world but lie, and
lie in my throat. By heaven, I do love, and it hath
taught me to rhyme, and to be melancholy; and here
is part of my rhyme, and here my melancholy. Well,
15 she hath one o' my sonnets already. The clown
bore it, the fool sent it, and the lady hath it—
sweet clown, sweeter fool, sweetest lady! By the
world, I would not care a pin if the other three
were in. Here comes one with a paper. God give
20 him grace to groan!   *He stands aside.*

The King ent'reth [with a paper].

King. Ay me!

Berowne. [*Aside*] Shot, by heaven! Proceed, sweet
Cupid. Thou hast thumped him with thy bird-bolt°
under the left pap.° In faith, secrets!

IV.iii.1–2 **coursing** chasing   2 **pitched a toil** set a snare   6 **Ajax**
(ancient Greek warrior who, going mad, killed sheep, believing
them his enemies)   23 **bird-bolt** arrow for shooting birds   24 **pap**
breast

King. [*Reads*] "So sweet a kiss the golden sun gives
    not   25
    To those fresh morning drops upon the rose,
As thy eye-beams when their fresh rays have smote
    The night of dew that on my cheeks down flows.
Nor shines the silver moon one half so bright
    Through the transparent bosom of the deep   30
As doth thy face, through tears of mine, give light.
    Thou shin'st in every tear that I do weep;
No drop but as a coach doth carry thee.
    So ridest thou triumphing in my woe.
Do but behold the tears that swell in me,   35
    And they thy glory through my grief will show.
But do not love thyself—then thou will keep
My tears for glasses° and still make me weep.
O queen of queens, how far dost thou excel
No thought can think, nor tongue of mortal tell!"   40
How shall she know my griefs? I'll drop the paper.
Sweet leaves, shade folly. Who is he comes here?

Enter Longaville [*with a paper*]. *The King steps aside.*

What, Longaville, and reading! Listen, ear.

Berowne. Now, in thy likeness, one more fool appear!

Longaville. Ay me, I am forsworn.   45

Berowne. Why, he comes in like a perjure,° wearing
    papers.°

King. In love, I hope—sweet fellowship in shame!

Berowne. One drunkard loves another of the name.

Longaville. Am I the first that have been perjured so?   50

Berowne. I could put thee in comfort—not by two
    that I know.

---

38 **glasses** mirrors   46 **perjure** perjurer   46 **wearing papers** (a punishment for perjury, to wear a paper on the head as a public shame; presumably Longaville has a sonnet in his hatband)

Thou makest the triumviry,° the corner-cap° of
society,
The shape of Love's Tyburn,° that hangs up simplicity.

Longaville. I fear these stubborn lines lack power to
move.
55   O sweet Maria, empress of my love!
These numbers will I tear, and write in prose.

Berowne. O, rhymes are guards° on wanton Cupid's
hose;
Disfigure not his shop.°

Longaville.   This same shall go.

He reads the sonnet.

"Did not the heavenly rhetoric of thine eye,
60   'Gainst whom the world cannot hold argument,
Persuade my heart to this false perjury?
     Vows for thee broke deserve not punishment.
A woman I forswore, but I will prove,
     Thou being a goddess, I forswore not thee.
65   My vow was earthly, thou a heavenly love;
     Thy grace, being gained, cures all disgrace in me.
Vows are but breath, and breath a vapor is;
     Then thou, fair sun, which on my earth dost
     shine,
Exhal'st this vapor-vow; in thee it is.
70   If broken then, it is no fault of mine;
If by me broke, what fool is not so wise
To lose an oath to win a paradise?"

Berowne. This is the liver-vein,° which makes flesh a
deity,
A green goose° a goddess. Pure, pure idolatry.

---

52 **triumviry** triumvirate   52 **corner-cap** cap with corners (worn
by divines, judges, and scholars)   53 **Tyburn** place of execution
(the triangular-shaped gallows bears a resemblance to a corner-cap)
57 **guards** ornaments   58 **shop** organ of generation, or codpiece
73 **liver-vein** vein coming from the liver (the place of the origin of
love)   74 **green goose** goose born the previous autumn (and so, a
young girl)

God amend us, God amend! We are much out o'
th' way.°   75

Enter Dumaine [with a paper].

Longaville. By whom shall I send this?—Company?
Stay.   [*Steps aside.*]

Berowne. All hid,° all hid—an old infant play.
Like a demi-god here sit I in the sky,
And wretched fools' secrets heedfully o'er-eye.
More sacks to the mill°—O heavens, I have my
wish!   80
Dumaine transformed! Four woodcocks° in a dish!

Dumaine. O most divine Kate!

Berowne. O most profane coxcomb!

Dumaine. By heaven, the wonder in a mortal eye!

Berowne. By earth, she is not, Corporal.° There you
lie!   85

Dumaine. Her amber hairs for foul hath amber
quoted.°

Berowne. An amber-colored raven was well noted.

Dumaine. As upright as the cedar.

Berowne.   Stoop,° I say—
Her shoulder is with child.°

Dumaine.   As fair as day.

Berowne. Ay, as some days; but then no sun must
shine.   90

Dumaine. O that I had my wish!

---

75 **out o' th' way** on the wrong track   77 **All hid** (formula from a
child's game)   80 **More sacks to the mill** more yet to do   81 **wood-
cocks** silly birds   85 **Corporal** officer (with a pun on the word for
bodily, human)   86 **Her amber . . . quoted** her amber-colored hair
made amber look ugly by contrast   88 **Stoop** stooped   89 **with
child** i.e., rounded

Longaville.   And I had mine!

King. And I mine too, good Lord!

Berowne. Amen, so I had mine! Is not that a good
    word?

Dumaine. I would forget her, but a fever she
95   Reigns in my blood, and will rememb'red be.

Berowne. A fever in your blood? Why, then incision
    Would let her out in saucers. Sweet misprision!°

Dumaine. Once more I'll read the ode that I have writ.

Berowne. Once more I'll mark how love can vary wit.

        Dumaine reads his sonnet.

100 *Dumaine.* "On a day—alack the day!—
        Love, whose month is ever May,
        Spied a blossom passing fair
        Playing in the wanton air.
        Through the velvet leaves the wind,
105   All unseen, can passage find;
        That the lover, sick to death,
        Wished himself the heaven's breath.
        Air, quoth he, thy cheeks may blow;
        Air, would I might triumph so!
110   But, alack, my hand is sworn
        Ne'er to pluck thee from thy thorn.
        Vow, alack, for youth unmeet,
        Youth so apt to pluck a sweet!
        Do not call it sin in me,
115   That I am forsworn for thee;
        Thou for whom Jove would swear
        Juno but an Ethiop° were,
        And deny himself for Jove,
        Turning mortal for thy love."
120   This will I send, and something else more plain,
    That shall express my true love's fasting pain.°

---

97 **misprision** mistake   117 Ethiop black person   121 fasting pain
pain caused by deprivation

O, would the king, Berowne, and Longaville
Were lovers too! Ill, to example ill,
Would from my forehead wipe a perjured note,°
For none offend where all alike do dote.   125

Longaville. [*Advancing*] Dumaine, thy love is far from
    charity,
That in love's grief desir'st society.
You may look pale, but I should blush, I know,
To be o'erheard and taken napping so.

King. [*Advancing*] Come, sir, you blush! As his your
    case is such;   130
You chide at him, offending twice as much.
You do not love Maria! Longaville
Did never sonnet for her sake compile,
Nor never lay his wreathèd arms athwart
His loving bosom to keep down his heart.   135
I have been closely shrouded in this bush,
And marked you both, and for you both did blush.
I heard your guilty rhymes, observed your fashion,
Saw sighs reek° from you, noted well your passion.
"Ay me!" says one; "O Jove!" the other cries.   140
One, her hairs were gold; crystal, the other's eyes.
[*To Longaville*] You would for paradise break faith
    and troth,
[*To Dumaine*] And Jove, for your love, would in-
    fringe an oath.
What will Berowne say when that he shall hear
Faith infringèd, which such zeal did swear?   145
How will he scorn, how will he spend his wit!
How will he triumph, leap and laugh at it!
For all the wealth that ever I did see,
I would not have him know so much by me.°

Berowne. [*Advancing*] Now step I forth to whip hy-
    pocrisy.   150
Ah, good my liege, I pray thee pardon me.
Good heart, what grace hast thou, thus to reprove

123–24 Ill . . . note wickedness, not liking to make itself an example,
would remove from me the papers I bear as the punishment for
perjury   139 reek exhale   149 by me concerning me

These worms for loving, that art most in love?
Your eyes do make no coaches;° in your tears
155 There is no certain princess that appears.
You'll not be perjured, 'tis a hateful thing.
Tush, none but minstrels like of sonneting!
But are you not ashamed? Nay, are you not,
All three of you, to be thus much o'ershot?°
160 You found his mote, the king your mote did see;
But I a beam° do find in each of three.
O what a scene of fool'ry have I seen,
Of sighs, of groans, of sorrow, and of teen!°
O me, with what strict patience have I sat,
165 To see a king transformèd to a gnat!
To see great Hercules whipping a gig,°
And profound Solomon to tune a jig,
And Nestor° play at push-pin° with the boys,
And critic Timon° laugh at idle toys!
170 Where lies thy grief? O, tell me, good Dumaine.
And, gentle Longaville, where lies thy pain?
And where my liege's? All about the breast.
A caudle,° ho!

King.   Too bitter is thy jest.
Are we betrayed thus to thy over-view?

175 *Berowne.* Not you by me, but I betrayed to you;
I that am honest, I that hold it sin
To break the vow I am engagèd in,
I am betrayed by keeping company
With men like you, men of inconstancy.
180 When shall you see me write a thing in rhyme?
Or groan for Joan? Or spend a minute's time
In pruning° me? When shall you hear that I
Will praise a hand, a foot, a face, an eye,
A gait, a state, a brow, a breast, a waist,
A leg, a limb—

154 **coaches** (for love to ride in—as in line 33)   159 **o'ershot** wide
of the mark   160–61 **mote . . . beam** (the contrast is between small
and large faults; see Matthew 7:3-5; Luke 6:41-42)   163 **teen** grief
166 **gig** top   168 **Nestor** ancient Greek sage   168 **push-pin** child's
game   169 **critic Timon** Greek misanthrope   173 **caudle** healing
drink for an invalid   182 **pruning** preening

King.   Soft!° Whither away so fast?   185
  A true° man or a thief, that gallops so?

Berowne. I post° from love. Good lover, let me go.

   Enter Jaquenetta and [Costard, the] Clown.

Jaquenetta. God bless the king!

King.   What present hast thou there?

Costard. Some certain treason.

King.   What makes° treason here?

Costard. Nay, it makes nothing, sir.

King.   If it mar nothing neither,   190
  The treason and you go in peace away together.

Jaquenetta. I beseech your Grace let this letter be read.
  Our parson misdoubts° it; 'twas treason, he said.

King. Berowne, read it over.
                He [Berowne] reads the letter.
  Where hadst thou it?

Jaquenetta. Of Costard.

King. Where hadst thou it?   195

Costard. Of Dun Adramadio, Dun Adramadio.
                [Berowne tears the letter.]

King. How now, what is in you? Why dost thou tear it?

Berowne. A toy, my liege, a toy. Your Grace needs
  not fear it.   200

Longaville. It did move him to passion, and therefore
  let's hear it.

Dumaine. [*Gathering up the pieces*] It is Berowne's
  writing, and here is his name.

185 **Soft** wait a minute (an exclamation)   186 **true** honest   187 **post**
ride in haste   189 **makes** does   193 **misdoubts** mistrusts

Berowne. [*To Costard*] Ah, you whoreson loggerhead,° you were born to do me shame!
   Guilty, my lord, guilty. I confess, I confess.

203 *King.* What?

Berowne. That you three fools lacked me fool to make
   up the mess.°
   He, he, and you—and you, my liege, and I,
   Are pick-purses in love, and we deserve to die.
   O dismiss this audience, and I shall tell you more.

Dumaine. Now the number is even.

210 *Berowne.*   True, true, we are four.
   Will these turtles° be gone?

King.   Hence, sirs, away!

Costard. Walk aside the true folk, and let the traitors
   stay.   [*Exeunt Costard and Jaquenetta.*]

Berowne. Sweet lords, sweet lovers, O let us embrace!
   As true we are as flesh and blood can be.
215 The sea will ebb and flow, heaven show his face;
   Young blood doth not obey an old decree.
   We cannot cross° the cause why we were born;
   Therefore of all hands must we be forsworn.

King. What, did these rent° lines show some love of
   thine?

Berowne. Did they? quoth you. Who sees the heavenly
220   Rosaline,
   That, like a rude and savage man of Inde
   At the first op'ning of the gorgeous East,
   Bows not his vassal head and, strooken blind,
   Kisses the base ground with obedient breast?
225 What peremptory° eagle-sighted eye
   Dares look upon the heaven of her brow
   That is not blinded by her majesty?

203 whoreson loggerhead rascally blockhead 206 mess party of
four at table 211 turtles turtledoves, lovers 217 cross thwart
219 rent damaged 225 peremptory resolute

King. What zeal, what fury, hath inspired thee now?
My love, her mistress, is a gracious moon;
She, an attending star, scarce seen a light.   230

Berowne. My eyes are then no eyes, nor I Berowne.
O, but for my love, day would turn to night!
Of all complexions the culled sovereignty°
Do meet, as at a fair, in her fair cheek,
Where several worthies° make one dignity,   235
Where nothing wants° that want itself doth seek.
Lend me the flourish° of all gentle tongues—
Fie, painted rhetoric!° O, she needs it not!
To things of sale° a seller's praise belongs:
She passes praise; then praise too short doth blot.   240
A withered hermit, five-score winters worn,
Might shake off fifty, looking in her eye.
Beauty doth varnish° age as if new-born,
And gives the crutch the cradle's infancy.
O, 'tis the sun that maketh all things shine.   245

King. By heaven, thy love is black as ebony!

Berowne. Is ebony like her? O wood divine!
A wife of such wood were felicity.
O, who can give an oath? Where is a book?
That I may swear beauty doth beauty lack   250
If that she learn not of her eye to look.
No face is fair that is not full so black.

King. O paradox! Black is the badge of hell,
The hue of dungeons, and the school of night;°
And beauty's crest becomes the heavens well.°   255

Berowne. Devils soonest tempt, resembling spirits of
light.

233 **culled sovereignty** chosen as the best   235 **worthies** good qualities   236 **wants** lacks   237 **flourish** adornment   238 **painted** rhetoric extravagant speech   239 **of sale** for sale   243 **varnish** lend
freshness   254 **school of night** (some editors emend "school" to
"suit" or to "shade," but perhaps the term means a place for learning dark things)   255 **beauty's . . . well** true beauty, which is bright,
is heavenly, but if blackness is taken as the sign of beauty, it would
be ironic to link beauty with heaven, which is the source of light

O, if in black my lady's brows be decked,
It mourns that painting and usurping° hair
Should ravish doters with a false aspect;°
260 And therefore is she born to make black fair.
Her favor° turns the fashion of the days,
For native blood° is counted painting now;
And therefore red that would avoid dispraise
Paints itself black to imitate her brow.

Dumaine. To look like her are chimney-sweepers
265   black.

Longaville. And since her time are colliers° counted
bright.

King. And Ethiops of their sweet complexion crack.°

Dumaine. Dark needs no candles now, for dark is
light.

Berowne. Your mistresses dare never come in rain,
270   For fear their colors should be washed away.

King. 'Twere good yours did; for, sir, to tell you plain,
I'll find a fairer face not washed today.

Berowne. I'll prove her fair or talk till doomsday here.

King. No devil will fright thee then so much as she.

275 *Dumaine.* I never knew man hold vile stuff so dear.

Longaville. Look, here's thy love; [*showing his shoe*]
my foot° and her face see.

Berowne. O, if the streets were pavèd with thine eyes,
Her feet were much too dainty for such tread.

Dumaine. O vile! Then, as she goes, what upward lies
280   The street should see as she walked overhead.

King. But what of this? Are we not all in love?

---

258 **usurping false** 259 **aspect** appearance 261 **favor** complexion
262 **native blood** naturally red complexion 266 **colliers** coal-men
267 **crack** boast 276 **my foot** (he is wearing black shoes)

Berowne. O, nothing so sure, and thereby all forsworn.

King. Then leave this chat, and, good Berowne, now prove
Our loving lawful and our faith not torn.

Dumaine. Ay marry, there, some flattery for this evil!   285

Longaville. O, some authority how to proceed!
Some tricks, some quillets,° how to cheat the devil!

Dumaine. Some salve for perjury.

Berowne.   O, 'tis more than need!
Have at you, then, affection's men-at-arms!°
Consider what you first did swear unto.   290
To fast, to study, and to see no woman—
Flat treason 'gainst the kingly state of youth.
Say, can you fast? Your stomachs are too young,
And abstinence engenders maladies.
[And where that° you have vowed to study, lords,   295
In that each of you have forsworn his book,
Can you still dream and pore and thereon look?
For when would you, my lord, or you, or you,
Have found the ground of study's excellence
Without the beauty of a woman's face?   300
From women's eyes this doctrine I derive:
They are the ground, the books, the academes,°
From whence doth spring the true Promethean
fire.°
Why, universal plodding poisons° up
The nimble spirits in the arteries,   305
As motion and long-during° action tires
The sinewy vigor of the traveler.
Now for not looking on a woman's face,

---

287 **quillets** subtleties   289 **affection's men-at-arms** love's warriors
295 **where that** whereas (after writing lines 295–316, here bracketed,
Shakespeare apparently decided he could do better, and rewrote the
passage in the ensuing lines, but the printer mistakenly printed
both versions)   302 **academes** academies   303 **Promethean fire** fire
stolen from heaven by Prometheus   304 **poisons** (some editors
emend to *prisons*)   306 **long-during** long-lasting

You have in that forsworn the use of eyes,
310   And study too, the causer of your vow;
For where is any author in the world
Teaches such beauty as a woman's eye?
Learning is but an adjunct to ourself,
And where we are our learning likewise is.
315   Then when ourselves we see in ladies' eyes,
Do we not likewise see our learning there?]
O, we have made a vow to study, lords,
And in that vow we have forsworn our books;
For when would you, my liege, or you, or you,
320   In leaden contemplation have found out
Such fiery numbers° as the prompting eyes
Of beauty's tutors have enriched you with?
Other slow arts entirely keep the brain,
And therefore, finding barren practisers,
325   Scarce show a harvest of their heavy toil;
But love, first learnèd in a lady's eyes,
Lives not alone immurèd in the brain,
But with the motion of all elements,°
Courses as swift as thought in every power,
330   And gives to every power a double power
Above their functions and their offices.
It adds a precious seeing to the eye:
A lover's eyes will gaze an eagle blind.
A lover's ear will hear the lowest sound,
335   When the suspicious head of theft° is stopped.
Love's feeling is more soft and sensible
Than are the tender horns of cockled° snails.
Love's tongue proves dainty Bacchus gross in taste.
For valor, is not Love a Hercules,
340   Still climbing trees in the Hesperides?°
Subtle as Sphinx; as sweet and musical
As bright Apollo's lute, strung with his hair.
And when Love speaks, the voice of all the gods

321 fiery numbers passionate verses   **328 with the motion of all elements** i.e., with the force of all the components of the universe   **335 the suspicious head of theft** i.e., a thief's hearing, suspicious of every sound   **337 cockled** in shells   **340 Hesperides** (garden where Hercules picked the golden apples)

Make heaven drowsy with the harmony.
Never durst poet touch a pen to write   345
Until his ink were temp'red with Love's sighs.
O, then his lines would ravish savage ears
And plant in tyrants mild humility.
From women's eyes this doctrine I derive.
They sparkle still the right Promethean fire;   350
They are the books, the arts, the academes,
That show, contain, and nourish all the world;
Else none at all in aught proves excellent.
Then fools you were these women to forswear,
Or, keeping what is sworn, you will prove fools.   355
For wisdom's sake, a word that all men love,
Or for love's sake, a word that loves all men,
Or for men's sake, the authors of these women,
Or women's sake, by whom we men are men—
Let us once lose our oaths to find ourselves,   360
Or else we lose ourselves to keep our oaths.
It is religion to be thus forsworn,
For charity itself fulfils the law,°
And who can sever love from charity?

King. Saint Cupid then! And, soldiers, to the field!   365

Berowne. Advance your standards, and upon them,
    lords!
Pell-mell, down with them! But be first advised,
In conflict that you get the sun of them.°

Longaville. Now to plain-dealing. Lay these glozes°
    by.
Shall we resolve to woo these girls of France?   370

King. And win them too! Therefore let us devise
Some entertainment for them in their tents.

Berowne. First from the park let us conduct them
    thither;
Then homeward every man attach the hand

363 charity . . . law (Romans 13:8: "he that loveth another hath fulfilled the law")   368 get the sun of them approach when the sun
is in their eyes   369 glozes trivial comments

375   Of his fair mistress. In the afternoon
We will with some strange pastime solace them,
Such as the shortness of the time can shape;
For revels, dances, masks, and merry hours
Forerun fair Love, strewing her way with flowers.

380   *King.* Away, away! No time shall be omitted
That will be time,° and may by us be fitted.

Berowne. Allons!° Allons! Sowed cockle reaped no
corn,°
And justice always whirls in equal measure.
Light wenches may prove plagues to men forsworn;
385   If so, our copper buys no better treasure.   [*Exeunt.*]

381 be time come to pass   382 Allons let's go (French)   382 Sowed
... corn if weeds are sown, wheat is not reaped

[ACT V

Scene I. *The park.*]

*Enter [Holofernes,] the Pedant, [Nathaniel,] the
Curate, and Dull, [the Constable].*

Holofernes. Satis quid sufficit.°

Nathaniel. I praise God for you, sir. Your reasons°
at dinner have been sharp and sententious,° pleasant without scurrility, witty without affection,° au-
dacious without impudency, learned without   5
opinion,° and strange without heresy. I did converse this *quondam*° day with a companion of the
king's, who is intituled, nominated, or called, Don
Adriano de Armado.

Holofernes. Novi hominem tanquam te.° His humor   10
is lofty, his discourse peremptory,° his tongue
filed,° his eye ambitious, his gait majestical, and
his general behavior vain, ridiculous, and thrasonical.° He is too picked,° too spruce, too affected, too odd, as it were, too peregrinate,° as I   15
may call it.

V.i.1 **Satis quid sufficit** enough is as good as a feast 2 **reasons**
discourses 3 **sententious** full of meaning 4 **affection** affectation
6 **opinion** dogmatism 7 **quondam** former 10 **Novi hominem tanquam te** I know the man as well as I know you 11 **peremptory**
decisive 12 **filed** polished 13–14 **thrasonical** boastful 14 **picked**
refined 15 **peregrinate** foreign in manner

103

Nathaniel. A most singular and choice epithet.

                 Draw out his table-book.°

Holofernes. He draweth out the thread of his ver-
bosity finer than the staple° of his argument. I
20   abhor such fanatical phantasimes,° such insociable°
and point-devise° companions; such rackers° of
orthography as to speak "dout" fine when he
should say "doubt," "det" when he should pronounce "debt"—d, e, b, t, not d, e, t. He clepeth°
25   a calf "cauf," half "hauf," neighbor *vocatur°*
"nebor," neigh abbreviated "ne." This is abhomina-
ble, which he would call "abominable." It insinuateth me of insanie.° *Ne intelligis, domine?°* To
make frantic, lunatic.

30 *Nathaniel. Laus Deo bone intelligo.°*

Holofernes. Bone?° Bone for bene! Priscian° a little
scratched;° 'twill serve.

       *Enter [Armado, the] Braggart, [Moth, the] Boy,
               [and Costard, the Clown].*

Nathaniel. Videsne quis venit?°

Holofernes. Video, et gaudeo.°

33 *Armado.* [*To Moth*] Chirrah!°

Holofernes. Quare° "chirrah," not "sirrah"?

Armado. Men of peace, well encount'red.

---

17 s.d. table-book tablet (stage directions are often, as here, in the
imperative)   **19 staple** fiber   **20 phantasimes** wild imaginers   **20
insociable** impossible to associate with   **21 point-devise** perfectly
correct   **21 rackers** torturers   **24 clepeth** calls   **25 vocatur** is called
27–28 insinuateth me of insanie suggests insanity to me   **28 Ne intelligis, domine** do you not understand, sir?   **30 Laus Deo bone
intelligo** praise be to God, I well understand   **31 Bone** (probably
a mixture of Latin *bene* and French *bon*)   **31 Priscian** Latin gram-
marian of sixth century A.D.   **32 scratched** damaged   **33 Videsne quis
venit?** do you see who is coming?   **34 Video, et gaudeo** I see, and
I rejoice   **35 Chirrah** (dialect form for "sirrah")   **36 Quare** why?

Holofernes. Most military sir, salutation.

Moth. [*Aside to Costard*] They have been at a great
feast of languages and stol'n the scraps.   *40*

Costard. O, they have lived long on the alms-basket°
of words. I marvel thy master hath not eaten thee
for a word; for thou art not so long by the head
as *honorificabilitudinitatibus*.° Thou art easier swallowed than a flapdragon.°   *45*

Moth. Peace! The peal° begins.

Armado. Monsieur, are you not lett'red?°

Moth. Yes, yes! He teaches boys the hornbook.°
What is a, b, spelled backward with the horn on
his head?   *50*

Holofernes. Ba, *pueritia*,° with a horn added.

Moth. Ba, most silly sheep with a horn. You hear his
learning.

Holofernes. Quis,° *quis*, thou consonant?

Moth. The last of the five vowels, if you repeat them;   *55*
or the fifth, if I.

Holofernes. I will repeat them: a, e, i—

Moth. The sheep. The other two concludes it—o, u.

Armado. Now, by the salt wave of the Mediterranean,
a sweet touch, a quick venew° of wit! Snip, snap,   *60*
quick and home! It rejoiceth my intellect. True wit!

Moth. Offered by a child to an old man—which is
wit-old.°

---

41 alms-basket (basket used at feasts to collect scraps from the table
for the poor)   44 honorificabilitudinitatibus (Latin tongue-twister,
thought to be the longest word known)   45 flapdragon (burning
raisin or plum floating in liquor, and so drunk)   46 peal (of bells)
47 lett'red man of letters   48 hornbook (parchment with alphabet
and numbers, covered with transparent horn, for teaching spelling
and counting)   51 pueritia childishness   54 Quis what?   60 venew
thrust   63 wit-old i.e., mentally feeble (with pun on *wittol* = cuckold)

Holofernes. What is the figure?° What is the figure?

65 *Moth.* Horns.

Holofernes. Thou disputes like an infant. Go whip
thy gig.°

Moth. Lend me your horn to make one, and I will
whip about your infamy *manu cita.*° A gig of a
70   cuckold's horn.

Costard. And° I had but one penny in the world,
thou shouldst have it to buy gingerbread. Hold,
there is the very remuneration I had of thy master,
thou halfpenny purse of wit, thou pigeon-egg of
75   discretion. O, and the heavens were so pleased
that thou wert but my bastard, what a joyful father
wouldest thou make me! Go to, thou hast it *ad*
dunghill,° at the fingers' ends, as they say.

Holofernes. O, I smell false Latin! "Dunghill" for
80   *unguem.*

Armado. Arts-man,° preambulate.° We will be singled from the barbarous. Do you not educate youth
at the charge-house° on the top of the mountain?

Holofernes. Or *mons,* the hill.

85 *Armado.* At your sweet pleasure, for the mountain.

Holofernes. I do, *sans question.*

Armado. Sir, it is the king's most sweet pleasure and
affection to congratulate the princess at her pavilion
in the posteriors° of this day, which the rude mul-
90   titude call the afternoon.

Holofernes. The posterior of the day, most generous

---

64 **figure** figure of speech   67 **gig** top   69 **manu cita** with a swift
hand   71 **And** if   77–78 **ad dunghill** (perhaps a schoolboy's corruption of the proverb "ad unguem," to the fingernail, meaning "precisely")   81 **Arts-man** learned man   81 **preambulate** walk forth
83 **charge-house** school (perhaps an allusion to a specific school on
a hill, mentioned by Erasmus)   89 **posteriors** hind parts

sir, is liable, congruent, and measurable° for the
afternoon. The word is well culled, chose, sweet
and apt, I do assure you, sir, I do assure.

Armado. Sir, the king is a noble gentleman, and my   95
familiar,° I do assure ye, very good friend. For
what is inward° between us, let it pass. I do beseech thee, remember thy courtesy.° I beseech thee
apparel thy head. And among other importunate
and most serious designs, and of great import in-   100
deed, too—but let that pass; for I must tell thee,
it will please his Grace, by the world, sometime to
lean upon my poor shoulder, and with his royal
finger thus dally with my excrement,° with my
mustachio—but, sweet heart, let that pass. By the   105
world, I recount no fable! Some certain special
honors it pleaseth his greatness to impart to Armado, a soldier, a man of travel, that hath seen
the world—but let that pass. The very all of all
is (but, sweet heart, I do implore secrecy) that the   110
king would have me present the princess (sweet
chuck) with some delightful ostentation, or show,
or pageant, or antic,° or fire-work. Now, understanding that the curate and your sweet self are
good at such eruptions and sudden breaking out   115
of mirth, as it were, I have acquainted you withal,
to the end to crave your assistance.

Holofernes. Sir, you shall present before her the Nine
Worthies.° Sir Nathaniel, as concerning some entertainment of time, some show in the posterior of   120
this day, to be rend'red by our assistance, the king's
command, and this most gallant, illustrate, and

92 **liable, congruent, measurable** (all synonyms for "suitable")   96
familiar close friend   97 **inward** private   98 **remember thy courtesy**
(possibly: remove your hat when the king's name is mentioned)
104 **excrement** that which grows out (such as hair, nails, feathers)
113 **antic** fanciful pageant   118–19 **Nine Worthies** (traditionally,
Hector, Caesar, Joshua, David, Judas Maccabaeus, Alexander, King
Arthur, Charlemagne, Godfrey of Boulogne; here Hercules and
Pompey are included)

learned gentleman, before the princess—I say, none so fit as to present the Nine Worthies.

125 *Nathaniel.* Where will you find men worthy enough to present them?

Holofernes. Joshua, yourself; myself; and this gallant gentleman, Judas Maccabaeus; this swain, because of his great limb or joint, shall pass° Pompey the
130 Great; the page, Hercules—

Armado. Pardon, sir—error! He is not quantity enough for that Worthy's thumb; he is not so big as the end of his club.

Holofernes. Shall I have audience?° He shall present
135 Hercules in minority.° His enter and exit shall be strangling a snake; and I will have an apology° for that purpose.

Moth. An excellent device! So if any of the audience hiss, you may cry, "Well done, Hercules! Now
140 thou crushest the snake!" That is the way to make an offense gracious, though few have the grace to do it.

Armado. For the rest of the Worthies?

Holofernes. I will play three myself.

145 *Moth.* Thrice-worthy gentleman!

Armado. Shall I tell you a thing?

Holofernes. We attend.

Armado. We will have, if this fadge° not, an antic. I beseech you, follow.

150 *Holofernes. Via,°* goodman Dull! Thou hast spoken no word all this while.

Dull. Nor understood none neither, sir.

---

129 pass represent   134 have audience be heard   135 minority early youth   136 apology justification   148 fadge succeed   150 Via come on (Italian)

Holofernes. *Allons,* we will employ thee.

Dull. I'll make one in a dance, or so; or I will play
　　on the tabor° to the Worthies, and let them dance   155
　　the hay.°

Holofernes. Most dull, honest Dull! To our sport,
　　away!   *Exeunt.*

[Scene II. *The park.*]

*Enter the Ladies [the Princess, Katharine,
Rosaline, and Maria].*

Princess. Sweet hearts, we shall be rich ere we depart
　　If fairings° come thus plentifully in.
　　A lady walled about with diamonds!
　　Look you what I have from the loving king.

Rosaline. Madam, came nothing else along with that?   5

Princess. Nothing but this? Yes, as much love in
　　rhyme
　　As would be crammed up in a sheet of paper,
　　Writ o' both sides the leaf, margent° and all,
　　That he was fain° to seal on Cupid's name.

Rosaline. That was the way to make his godhead
　　wax,°   10
　　For he hath been five thousand year a boy.

Katharine. Ay, and a shrowd° unhappy gallows° too.

Rosaline. You'll ne'er be friends with him: 'a killed
　　your sister.

155 tabor small drum   156 hay country dance   V.ii.2 fairings presents   8 margent margin   9 fain eager   10 wax grow (and with a
pun on sealing-wax)   12 shrowd accursed   12 gallows one fit to be
hanged

Katharine. He made her melancholy, sad, and heavy;
15   And so she died. Had she been light, like you,
Of such a merry, nimble, stirring spirit,
She might ha' been a grandam ere she died.
And so may you, for a light heart lives long.

Rosaline. What's your dark meaning, mouse, of this
light word?

20   *Katharine.* A light condition in a beauty dark.

Rosaline. We need more light to find your meaning
out.

Katharine. You'll mar the light by taking it in snuff,°
Therefore, I'll darkly end the argument.

Rosaline. Look what° you do, you do it still i' th'
dark.

25   *Katharine.* So do not you, for you are a light wench.

Rosaline. Indeed I weigh° not you, and therefore
light.

Katharine. You weigh me not? O, that's you care not
for me!

Rosaline. Great reason, for past care is still past cure.

Princess. Well bandied° both! A set of wit well
played.
30   But Rosaline, you have a favor too—
Who sent it? And what is it?

Rosaline.   I would you knew.
And if my face were but as fair as yours,
My favor were as great. Be witness this.
Nay, I have verses too, I thank Berowne;
35   The numbers° true, and, were the numb'ring° too,
I were the fairest goddess on the ground.

---

22 **taking it in snuff** being annoyed   24 **Look what** whatever   26
weigh value at a certain rate   29 **bandied** hit back and forth (figure
from tennis)   35 **numbers** meter   35 **numb'ring** estimate

I am compared to twenty thousand fairs.°
O, he hath drawn my picture in his letter!

Princess. Anything like?

Rosaline. Much in the letters, nothing in the praise.   40

Princess. Beauteous as ink—a good conclusion.

Katharine. Fair as a text B in a copy-book.

Rosaline. 'Ware° pencils, ho! Let me not die your debtor,
My red dominical,° my golden letter.
O, that your face were not so full of O's!°   45

Princess. A pox of° that jest, and I beshrow all shrows!°
But Katharine, what was sent to you from fair Dumaine?

Katharine. Madam, this glove.

Princess.   Did he not send you twain?

Katharine. Yes, madam; and moreover,
Some thousand verses of a faithful lover.   50
A huge translation of hypocrisy,
Vilely compiled, profound simplicity.°

Maria. This, and these pearls, to me sent Longaville.
The letter is too long by half a mile.

Princess. I think no less. Dost thou not wish in heart   55
The chain were longer and the letter short?

Maria. Ay, or I would these hands might never part.

Princess. We are wise girls to mock our lovers so.

Rosaline. They are worse fools to purchase mocking so.

---

37 **fairs** beautiful women   43 **'Ware** beware   44 **red dominical** red S (for Sunday, the Lord's Day)   45 **O's** smallpox scars   46 **A pox of** may a plague strike   46 **beshrow all shrows** curse all shrews
52 **simplicity** simple-mindedness

60　That same Berowne I'll torture ere I go.
　　O that I knew he were but in by th' week!°
　　How I would make him fawn, and beg, and seek,
　　And wait the season, and observe the times,
　　And spend his prodigal wits in bootless rhymes,
65　And shape his service wholly to my hests,°
　　And make him proud to make me proud that jests!
　　So pertaunt-like° would I o'ersway his state°
　　That he should be my fool, and I his fate.

Princess. None are so surely caught, when they are
　　catched,
70　As wit turned fool. Folly, in wisdom hatched,
　　Hath wisdom's warrant and the help of school
　　And wit's own grace to grace a learnèd fool.

Rosaline. The blood of youth burns not with such
　　excess
　　As gravity's revolt to wantonness.

75　*Maria.* Folly in fools bears not so strong a note
　　As fool'ry in the wise when wit doth dote;
　　Since all the power thereof it doth apply
　　To prove, by wit, worth in simplicity.

Enter Boyet.

Princess. Here comes Boyet, and mirth is in his face.

Boyet. O, I am stabbed with laughter! Where's her
80　Grace?

Princess. Thy news, Boyet?

Boyet.　　　　　　　　Prepare, madam, prepare!
　　Arm, wenches, arm! Encounters mounted are
　　Against your peace. Love doth approach disguised,
　　Armèd in arguments; you'll be surprised.
85　Muster your wits; stand in your own defense,
　　Or hide your heads like cowards and fly hence.

61 in by th' week trapped　65 hests commands　67 pertaunt-like
(like a winning hand [*Pair-taunt*] in a certain card game)　67 o'ersway his state overrule his power

Princess. Saint Denis° to Saint Cupid! What are they
  That charge their breath against us? Say, scout, say.

Boyet. Under the cool shade of a sycamore
  I thought to close mine eyes some half an hour,   *90*
  When, lo, to interrupt my purposed rest,
  Toward that shade I might behold addrest°
  The king and his companions! Warily
  I stole into a neighbor thicket by,
  And overheard what you shall overhear—   *95*
  That, by and by, disguised they will be here.
  Their herald is a pretty knavish page
  That well by heart hath conned his embassage.°
  Action and accent did they teach him there:
  "Thus must thou speak, and thus thy body bear."   *100*
  And ever and anon they made a doubt°
  Presence majestical would put him out;
  "For," quoth the king, "an angel shalt thou see,
  Yet fear not thou, but speak audaciously."
  The boy replied, "An angel is not evil;   *105*
  I should have feared her had she been a devil."
  With that all laughed and clapped him on the
    shoulder,
  Making the bold wag by their praises bolder.
  One rubbed his elbow thus, and fleered,° and swore
  A better speech was never spoke before.   *110*
  Another, with his finger and his thumb,
  Cried "*Via*, we will do 't, come what will come!"
  The third he capered and cried, "All goes well!"
  The fourth turned on the toe,° and down he fell.
  With that they all did tumble on the ground   *115*
  With such a zealous laughter, so profound,
  That in this spleen° ridiculous appears,
  To check their folly, passion's solemn tears.

Princess. But what, but what? Come they to visit us?

Boyet. They do, they do, and are apparelled thus—   *120*

87 **Saint Denis** patron saint of France   92 **addrest** approaching
98 **conned his embassage** learned his commission   101 **made a doubt**
expressed a fear   109 **fleered** grinned   114 **turned on the toe** turned
quickly to leave   117 **spleen** excess of mirth

Like Muscovites or Russians, as I guess.
Their purpose is to parley,° court and dance,
And every one his love-feat° will advance
Unto his several mistress, which they'll know
125 By favors several which they did bestow.

Princess. And will they so? The gallants shall be
    tasked;°
For, ladies, we will every one be masked,
And not a man of them shall have the grace,
Despite of suit,° to see a lady's face.
130 Hold, Rosaline, this favor thou shalt wear,
And then the king will court thee for his dear.
Hold, take thou this, my sweet, and give me thine;
So shall Berowne take me for Rosaline.
And change you favors too; so shall your loves
135 Woo contrary, deceived by these removes.°

Rosaline. Come on, then; wear the favors most in
    sight.°

Katharine. But in this changing what is your intent?

Princess. The effect of my intent is to cross° theirs.
They do it but in mockery merriment,
140 And mock for mock is only my intent.
Their several counsels they unbosom° shall
To loves mistook and so be mocked withal
Upon the next occasion that we meet,
With visages displayed, to talk and greet.

145 *Rosaline.* But shall we dance if they desire us to 't?

Princess. No, to the death° we will not move a foot,
Nor to their penned speech render we no grace,
But while 'tis spoke each turn away her face.

Boyet. Why, that contempt will kill the speaker's
    heart,
150 And quite divorce his memory from his part.

122 **parley** hold a conference   123 **love-feat** exploit prompted by
love   126 **tasked** tested   129 **Despite of suit** in spite of his pleading
135 **removes** changes   136 **most in sight** conspicuously   138 **cross**
thwart   141 **unbosom** confide   146 **to the death** as long as we live

Princess. Therefore I do it, and I make no doubt
 The rest will e'er come in if he be out.
 There's no such sport as sport by sport o'erthrown,
 To make theirs ours, and ours none but our own.
 So shall we stay, mocking intended game,°   *155*
 And they, well mocked, depart away with shame.
          Sound trumpet.

Boyet. The trumpet sounds. Be masked—the maskers
 come.
          [*The Ladies mask.*]

*Enter Blackamoors with music; [Moth,] the Boy,
with a speech, and [the King, Berowne, and] the
rest of the Lords [in Russian dress and] disguised.*

Moth. "All hail, the richest beauties on the earth!"

Boyet. Beauties no richer than rich taffeta.

Moth. "A holy parcel of the fairest dames,   *160*
    The Ladies turn their backs to him.
 That ever turned their backs to mortal views!"

Berowne. "Their eyes," villain, "their eyes!"

Moth. "That ever turned their eyes to mortal views!
 Out—"

Boyet. True. "Out" indeed!   *165*

Moth. "Out of your favors, heavenly spirits, vouchsafe
 Not to behold"—

Berowne. "Once to behold," rogue!

Moth. "Once to behold with your sun-beamèd eyes,
 —with your sun-beamèd eyes"—   *170*

Boyet. They will not answer to that epithet.
 You were best call it "daughter-beamèd eyes."

Moth. They do not mark me, and that brings° me out.

155 game sport   173 brings puts

Berowne. Is this your perfectness? Be gone, you rogue!
[*Exit Moth.*]

Rosaline. What would these strangers? Know their
175   minds, Boyet.
If they do speak our language, 'tis our will
That some plain man recount their purposes.
Know what they would.

Boyet. What would you with the Princess?

180 *Berowne.* Nothing but peace and gentle visitation.

Rosaline. What would they, say they?

Boyet. Nothing but peace and gentle visitation.

Rosaline. Why, that they have, and bid them so be
gone.

Boyet. She says you have it and you may be gone.

185 *King.* Say to her, we have measured many miles,
To tread a measure with her on this grass.

Boyet. They say that they have measured many a mile,
To tread a measure° with you on this grass.

Rosaline. It is not so. Ask them how many inches
190   Is in one mile. If they have measured many,
The measure then of one is eas'ly told.

Boyet. If to come hither you have measured miles,
And many miles, the princess bids you tell
How many inches doth fill up one mile.

195 *Berowne.* Tell her we measure them by weary steps.

Boyet. She hears herself.

Rosaline.   How many weary steps,
Of many weary miles you have o'ergone,
Are numb'red in the travel of one mile?

Berowne. We number nothing that we spend for you.
200   Our duty is so rich, so infinite,

188 **measure** stately dance

That we may do it still without accompt.°
Vouchsafe to show the sunshine of your face,
That we like savages may worship it.

Rosaline. My face is but a moon, and clouded too.

King. Blessèd are clouds, to do as such clouds do.   205
    Vouchsafe, bright moon, and these thy stars, to
      shine
    (Those clouds removed) upon our watery eyne.°

Rosaline. O vain petitioner, beg a greater matter!
    Thou now requests but moonshine in the water.°

King. Then in our measure do but vouchsafe one
      change.°   210
    Thou bid'st me beg; this begging is not strange.°

Rosaline. Play, music then. Nay, you must do it soon.
                              [*The musicians play.*]
    Not yet? No dance! Thus change I like the moon.

King. Will you not dance? How come you thus es-
      trangèd?

Rosaline. You took the moon at full, but now she's
      changèd.   215

King. Yet still she is the moon, and I the man.
    The music plays; vouchsafe some motion to it.

Rosaline. Our ears vouchsafe it.

King.   But your legs should do it.

Rosaline. Since you are strangers and come here by
      chance,
    We'll not be nice.° Take hands. We will not dance.   220

King. Why take we hands then?

Rosaline.   Only to part friends.
    Curtsy, sweet hearts. And so the measure ends.

---

201 **accompt** reckoning   207 **eyne** eyes   209 **moonshine in the water**
a mere nothing   210 **change** round of dancing   211 **not strange** not
unsuitably foreign   220 **nice** fastidious

King. More measure of this measure! Be not nice.

Rosaline. We can afford no more at such a price.

225 *King.* Price you yourselves. What buys your company?

Rosaline. Your absence only.

King.   That can never be.

Rosaline. Then cannot we be bought; and so adieu—
    Twice to your visor,° and half once to you.

King. If you deny to dance, let's hold more chat.

Rosaline. In private then.

230 *King.*   I am best pleased with that.
                         [*They converse apart.*]

Berowne. White-handed mistress, one sweet word with
    thee.

Princess. Honey, and milk, and sugar—there is three.

Berowne. Nay then, two treys,° an if° you grow so
    nice,
    Metheglin,° wort,° and malmsey.° Well run, dice!
    There's half a dozen sweets.

235 *Princess.*   Seventh sweet, adieu.
    Since you can cog,° I'll play no more with you.

Berowne. One word in secret.

Princess.   Let it not be sweet.

Berowne. Thou grievest my gall.°

Princess.   Gall! Bitter.

Berowne.   Therefore meet.°
                         [*They converse apart.*]

228 **visor** mask   233 **treys** threes (at dice)   233 **an if** if   234 **Me-
theglin** drink mixed with honey   234 **wort** unfermented beer   234
malmsey a Mediterranean wine   236 **cog** cheat   238 **gall** sore spot
238 **meet** fitting

Dumaine. Will you vouchsafe with me to change° a
    word?

Maria. Name it.

Dumaine.   Fair lady—

Maria.   Say you so? Fair lord.   240
    Take that for your "fair lady."

Dumaine.   Please it you,
    As much in private, and I'll bid adieu.
                      [They converse apart.]

Katharine. What, was your vizard° made without a
    tongue?

Longaville. I know the reason, lady, why you ask.

Katharine. O for your reason! Quickly, sir, I long.   243

Longaville. You have a double tongue° within your
    mask
    And would afford my speechless vizard half.

Katharine. "Veal,"° quoth the Dutchman. Is not
    "veal" a calf?

Longaville. A calf, fair lady?

Katharine.   No, a fair lord calf.

Longaville. Let's part the word.

Katharine.   No, I'll not be your half.   250
    Take all and wean it, it may prove an ox.

Longaville. Look how you butt yourself in these sharp
    mocks.
    Will you give horns,° chaste lady? Do not so.

Katharine. Then die a calf before your horns do grow.

Longaville. One word in private with you ere I die.   253

---

239 **change** exchange   243 **vizard** mask   246 **double tongue** (an inner projection or tongue held in the mouth to keep the mask in place)
248 **Veal** (Dutch or German pronunciation of "well")   253 **give
horns** prove unfaithful

Katharine. Bleat softly then. The butcher hears you
    cry.   [*They converse apart.*]

Boyet. The tongues of mocking wenches are as keen
    As is the razor's edge invisible,
    Cutting a smaller hair than may be seen,
260   Above the sense° of sense; so sensible
    Seemeth their conference,° their conceits° have
      wings
    Fleeter than arrows, bullets, wind, thought, swifter
      things.

Rosaline. Not one word more, my maids, break off,
    break off.

Berowne. By heaven, all dry-beaten° with pure scoff!

265 *King.* Farewell, mad wenches. You have simple wits.
      Exeunt [*King, Lords, and Blackamoors*].

Princess. Twenty adieus, my frozen Muscovits.
    Are these the breed of wits so wondered at?

Boyet. Tapers they are, with your sweet breaths
    puffed out.

Rosaline. Well-liking° wits they have; gross, gross;
    fat, fat.

270 *Princess.* O poverty in wit, kingly-poor flout!°
    Will they not, think you, hang themselves tonight?
    Or ever but in vizards show their faces?
    This pert Berowne was out of count'nance quite.

Rosaline. They were all in lamentable cases.°
275   The king was weeping-ripe° for a good word.

Princess. Berowne did swear himself out of all suit.°

Maria. Dumaine was at my service, and his sword.
    "No point,"° quoth I; my servant straight was mute.

260 **Above the sense** above the reach   261 **conference** conferring
261 **conceits** witticisms   264 **dry-beaten** beaten with blood being
drawn   269 **Well-liking** plump, sleek   270 **kingly-poor** flout a poor
jest for a king   274 **cases** (with pun on the sense "masks" or "costumes")   275 **weeping-ripe** about to weep   276 **out of all suit** beyond all reasonableness   278 **No point** not at all

Katharine. Lord Longaville said I came o'er his heart;
  And trow° you what he called me?

Princess.   Qualm,° perhaps.   *280*

Katharine. Yes, in good faith.

Princess.   Go, sickness as thou art!

Rosaline. Well, better wits have worn plain statute-
  caps.°
  But will you hear? The king is my love sworn.

Princess. And quick Berowne hath plighted faith to
  me.

Katharine. And Longaville was for my service born.   *285*

Maria. Dumaine is mine as sure as bark on tree.

Boyet. Madam, and pretty mistresses, give ear.
  Immediately they will again be here
  In their own shapes, for it can never be
  They will digest this harsh indignity.   *290*

Princess. Will they return?

Boyet.   They will, they will, God knows,
  And leap for joy though they are lame with blows.
  Therefore change° favors, and when they repair,°
  Blow° like sweet roses in this summer air.

Princess. How blow? How blow? Speak to be understood.   *295*

Boyet. Fair ladies masked are roses in their bud;
  Dismasked, their damask° sweet commixture shown,
  Are angels vailing° clouds, or roses blown.

Princess. Avaunt, perplexity!° What shall we do
  If they return in their own shapes to woo?   *300*

---

280 **trow** know   280 **Qualm** sudden sickness   282 **statute-caps** caps
apprentices were required to wear   293 **change** exchange   293 **repair** come again   294 **blow** blossom   297 **damask** red and white
(like the Damascus rose)   298 **vailing** letting fall   299 **Avaunt, perplexity** away, confusion

Rosaline. Good madam, if by me you'll be advised,
     Let's mock them still, as well known as disguised.
     Let us complain to them what fools were here,
     Disguised like Muscovites in shapeless gear;°
305 And wonder what they were, and to what end
     Their shallow shows and prologue vilely penned,
     And their rough carriage so ridiculous,
     Should be presented at our tent to us.

Boyet. Ladies, withdraw. The gallants are at hand.

310 *Princess.* Whip to our tents, as roes run o'er land.
               Exeunt [*Princess and Ladies*].

     Enter the King and the rest: [*Berowne, Longaville,
     and Dumaine, all in their proper habits*].

King. Fair sir, God save you. Where's the princess?

Boyet. Gone to her tent. Please it your Majesty
     Command me any service to her thither?

King. That she vouchsafe me audience for one word.

315 *Boyet.* I will; and so will she, I know, my lord.   *Exit.*

Berowne. This fellow pecks up wit, as pigeons peas,
     And utters it again when God doth please.
     He is wit's pedlar, and retails his wares
     At wakes° and wassails,° meetings, markets, fairs;
320 And we that sell by gross, the Lord doth know,
     Have not the grace to grace it with such show.
     This gallant pins the wenches° on his sleeve.
     Had he been Adam, he had tempted Eve.
     'A can carve° too, and lisp. Why, this is he
325 That kissed his hand away in courtesy.
     This is the ape of form,° Monsieur the Nice,°
     That, when he plays at tables,° chides the dice
     In honorable terms. Nay, he can sing

---

304 **gear** outfit   319 **wakes** vigils and feastings   319 **wassails** revelry
322 **pins the wenches wears** maidens' favors   324 **carve** make gestures of courtship   326 **form** etiquette   326 **Nice** exquisite   327 **at
tables** backgammon

A mean° most meanly; and in ushering
Mend° him who can. The ladies call him sweet.   *330*
The stairs, as he treads on them, kiss his feet.
This is the flow'r that smiles on every one,
To show his teeth as white as whalës-bone;
And consciences that will not die in debt
Pay him the due of "honey-tongued Boyet."   *335*

King. A blister on his sweet tongue, with my heart,
   That put Armado's page out of his part!

   Enter [the Princess and] the Ladies [with Boyet].

Berowne. See where it comes! Behavior, what wert
   thou
   Till this madman showed thee, and what art thou
   now?

King. All hail, sweet madam, and fair time of day.   *340*

Princess. "Fair" in "all hail"° is foul, as I conceive.

King. Construe my speeches better, if you may.

Princess. Then wish me better, I will give you leave.

King. We came to visit you, and purpose now
   To lead you to our court. Vouchsafe it then.   *345*

Princess. This field shall hold me, and so hold your
   vow.
   Nor God nor I delights in perjured men.

King. Rebuke me not for that which you provoke.
   The virtue° of your eye must break my oath.

Princess. You nickname° virtue. "Vice" you should
   have spoke;   *350*
   For virtue's office never breaks men's troth.
   Now, by my maiden honor, yet as pure
   As the unsullied lily, I protest,

---

329 **mean** intermediate part   330 **Mend** surpass   341 **hail** (with a
pun on hail meaning "sleet")   349 **virtue** power   350 **nickname**
name by mistake

A world of torments though I should endure,
355   I would not yield to be your house's guest,
So much I hate a breaking cause° to be
Of heavenly oaths, vowed with integrity.

King. O, you have lived in desolation here,
  Unseen, unvisited, much to our shame.

360 *Princess.* Not so, my lord. It is not so, I swear.
  We have had pastimes here and pleasant game.
  A mess° of Russians left us but of late.

King. How, madam? Russians?

Princess.   Ay, in truth, my lord;
  Trim gallants, full of courtship and of state.

365 *Rosaline.* Madam, speak true. It is not so, my lord.
  My lady, to the manner of the days,°
  In courtesy gives undeserving praise.
  We four indeed confronted were with four
  In Russian habit.° Here they stayed an hour
370   And talked apace; and in that hour, my lord,
  They did not bless us with one happy° word.
  I dare not call them fools, but this I think,
  When they are thirsty, fools would fain have drink.

Berowne. This jest is dry to me. Gentle sweet,
375   Your wit makes wise things foolish. When we greet
  With eyes best seeing heaven's fiery eye,°
  By light we lose light. Your capacity
  Is of that nature that to your huge store
  Wise things seem foolish and rich things but poor.

Rosaline. This proves you wise and rich, for in my
380   eye—

Berowne. I am a fool, and full of poverty.

Rosaline. But that you take what doth to you belong,
  It were a fault to snatch words from my tongue.

---

356 **breaking cause** cause for breaking off   362 **mess** group of four
366 **to the manner of the days** according to the fashion of the time
369 **habit** dress   371 **happy** appropriate   376 **heaven's fiery eye** the
sun

Berowne. O, I am yours, and all that I possess.

Rosaline. All the fool mine?

Berowne.   I cannot give you less.   385

Rosaline. Which of the vizards was it that you wore?

Berowne. Where, when, what vizard? Why demand
you this?

Rosaline. There, then, that vizard, that superfluous
case°
That hid the worse, and showed the better face.

King. We were descried. They'll mock us now downright.   390

Dumaine. Let us confess, and turn it to a jest.

Princess. Amazed, my lord? Why looks your Highness sad?

Rosaline. Help! Hold his brows! He'll sound.° Why
look you pale?
Seasick, I think, coming from Muscovy.

Berowne. Thus pour the stars down plagues for per-
jury.   395
Can any face of brass° hold longer out?
Here stand I, lady, dart thy skill at me.
Bruise me with scorn, confound me with a flout,
Thrust thy sharp wit quite through my ignorance,
Cut me to pieces with thy keen conceit,°   400
And I will wish thee never more to dance,
Nor never more in Russian habit wait.
O, never will I trust to speeches penned,
Nor to the motion of a schoolboy's tongue,
Nor never come in vizard to my friend,   405
Nor woo in rhyme, like a blind harper's song!
Taffeta phrases,° silken terms precise,
Three-piled° hyperboles, spruce affectation,

---

388 **case** covering   393 **sound** swoon   396 **face of brass** brazen
manner   400 **conceit** imagination   407 **Taffeta phrases** fine speech
408 **Three-piled** (the finest weight velvet)

Figures° pedantical—these summer flies
410 Have blown° me full of maggot ostentation.
I do forswear them; and I here protest
By this white glove (how white the hand, God
    knows!)
Henceforth my wooing mind shall be expressed
In russet° yeas and honest kersey° noes.
415 And to begin, wench—so God help me, law!—
My love to thee is sound, sans° crack or flaw.

Rosaline. Sans "sans," I pray you.

Berowne.   Yet I have a trick°
Of the old rage. Bear with me, I am sick.
I'll leave it by degrees. Soft, let us see—
420 Write "Lord have mercy on us"° on those three.
They are infected, in their hearts it lies;
They have the plague, and caught it of your eyes.
These lords are visited;° you are not free,°
For the Lord's tokens° on you do I see.

425 *Princess.* No, they are free that gave these tokens to us.

Berowne. Our states° are forfeit. Seek not to undo us.

Rosaline. It is not so, for how can this be true,
That you stand forfeit, being those that sue?

Berowne. Peace! for I will not have to do with you.

430 *Rosaline.* Nor shall not if I do as I intend.

Berowne. Speak for yourselves. My wit is at an end.

King. Teach us, sweet madam, for our rude transgres-
    sion
Some fair excuse.

Princess.   The fairest is confession.
Were not you here but even now disguised?

409 **Figures** figures of speech   410 **blown** filled   414 **russet** (characteristic red-brown color of peasants' clothes)   414 **kersey** plain
wool cloth   416 **sans** without   417 **trick** trace   420 **Lord have
mercy on us** (inscription posted on the doors of houses harboring the
plague)   423 **visited** attacked by plague   423 **free** free of infection
424 **the Lord's tokens** plague spots   426 **states** estates

King. Madam, I was.

Princess.   And were you well advised?   435

King. I was, fair madam.

Princess.   When you then were here,
What did you whisper in your lady's ear?

King. That more than all the world I did respect her.

Princess. When she shall challenge this, you will reject her.

King. Upon mine honor, no.

Princess.   Peace, peace, forbear!   440
Your oath once broke, you force not° to forswear.

King. Despise me when I break this oath of mine.

Princess. I will, and therefore keep it. Rosaline,
What did the Russian whisper in your ear?

Rosaline. Madame, he swore that he did hold me dear   445
As precious eyesight, and did value me
Above this world; adding thereto, moreover,
That he would wed me or else die my lover.

Princess. God give thee joy of him. The noble lord
Most honorably doth uphold his word.   450

King. What mean you, madam? By my life, my troth,
I never swore this lady such an oath.

Rosaline. By heaven you did! And to confirm it plain,
You gave me this, but take it, sir, again.

King. My faith and this the princess I did give.   455
I knew her by this jewel on her sleeve.

Princess. Pardon me, sir, this jewel did she wear,
And Lord Berowne, I thank him, is my dear.
What! Will you have me, or your pearl again?

Berowne. Neither of either, I remit both twain.   460
I see the trick on 't. Here was a consent,

441 force not do not think it wrong

Knowing aforehand of our merriment,
To dash° it like a Christmas comedy.
Some carry-tale, some please-man,° some slight
zany,°
Some mumble-news,° some trencher-knight,° some
465   Dick°
That smiles his cheek in years,° and knows the trick
To make my lady laugh when she's disposed,
Told our intents before; which once disclosed,
The ladies did change favors, and then we,
470   Following the signs, wooed but the sign of she.
Now, to our perjury to add more terror,
We are again forsworn, in will and error.
Much upon this 'tis.° [*To Boyet*] And might not you
Forestall our sport, to make us thus untrue?
475   Do not you know my lady's foot by th' squier,°
And laugh upon the apple of her eye?°
And stand between her back, sir, and the fire,
Holding a trencher,° jesting merrily?
You put our page out.° Go, you are allowed.°
480   Die when you will, a smock° shall be your shroud.
You leer upon me, do you? There's an eye
Wounds like a leaden sword.

Boyet.   Full merrily
Hath this brave manage,° this career,° been run.

Berowne. Lo, he is tilting straight.° Peace! I have
done.

Enter [Costard, the] Clown.

485   Welcome, pure wit! Thou part'st a fair fray.

463 dash ridicule   464 please-man toady   464 zany buffoon   465
mumble-news prattler   465 trencher-knight brave man at the table
465 Dick fellow   466 smiles his cheek in years laughs his face into
wrinkles   473 Much upon this 'tis it is very much like this   475 by
th' squier by the rule (that is, have her measure)   476 laugh . . .
eye laugh, looking closely into her eyes   478 trencher wooden plate
479 put our page out take him out of his part   479 allowed permitted (licensed, like a court fool)   480 smock woman's garment
483 manage display of horsemanship   483 career charge   484 tilting straight already jousting

Costard. O Lord, sir, they would know
Whether the three Worthies shall come in or no.

Berowne. What, are there but three?

Costard.   No, sir, but it is vara° fine,
For every one pursents° three.

Berowne.   And three times thrice is nine.

Costard. Not so, sir, under correction, sir, I hope, it
    is not so.   490
You cannot beg us,° sir, I can assure you, sir; we
    know what we know.
I hope, sir, three times thrice, sir—

Berowne.   Is not nine?

Costard. Under correction, sir, we know whereuntil it
    doth amount.

Berowne. By Jove, I always took three threes for nine. 495

Costard. O Lord, sir, it were pity you should get your
    living by reck'ning, sir.

Berowne. How much is it?

Costard. O Lord, sir, the parties themselves, the ac-
    tors, sir, will show whereuntil it doth amount. For 500
    mine own part, I am, as they say, but to parfect°
    one man in one poor man—Pompion° the Great,
    sir.

Berowne. Art thou one of the Worthies?

Costard. It pleased them to think me worthy of Pom- 505
    pey the Great. For mine own part, I know not the
    degree° of the Worthy, but I am to stand for him.

Berowne. Go, bid them prepare.

Costard. We will turn it finely off, sir; we will take
    some care.   *Exit.*

488 **vara** (northern pronunciation of "very")   489 **pursents** represents   491 **beg us** prove us fools   501 **parfect** play the part of
502 **Pompion** pumpkin (for Pompey)   507 **degree** rank

King. Berowne, they will shame us. Let them not ap-
510   proach.

Berowne. We are shame-proof, my lord; and 'tis some
policy°
To have one show worse than the king's and his
company.

King. I say they shall not come.

Princess. Nay, my good lord, let me o'errule you now.
515   That sport best pleases that doth least know how,
Where zeal strives to content, and the contents
Dies in the zeal of that which it presents.°
Their form confounded makes most form in mirth°
When great things laboring perish in their birth.

520   *Berowne.* A right description of our sport, my lord.

Enter [Armado, the] Braggart.

Armado. Anointed, I implore so much expense of thy
royal sweet breath as will utter a brace° of words.
[*Converses apart with the King, and delivers
a paper to him.*]

Princess. Doth this man serve God?

Berowne. Why ask you?

525   *Princess.* 'A speaks not like a man of God his making.

Armado. That is all one, my fair, sweet, honey monarch; for, I protest, the schoolmaster is exceeding
fantastical; too-too vain, too-too vain; but we will
put it, as they say, to *fortuna de la guerra.*° I wish
530   you the peace of mind, most royal couplement!°
Exit.

King. Here is like to be a good presence of Worthies.

---

511 **policy** crafty device   516–17 **contents . . . presents** i.e., the
substance is destroyed by the excessive zeal in presenting it   518
Their form . . . mirth i.e., art that is confused is most laughable
entertainment   522 **brace** pair   529 **fortuna de la guerra** fortune
of war (Italian)   530 **couplement** pair

He presents Hector of Troy; the swain, Pompey the
Great; the parish curate, Alexander; Armado's page,
Hercules; the pedant, Judas Maccabaeus:
And if these four Worthies in their first show thrive,   *535*
These four will change habits° and present the
    other five.

Berowne. There is five in the first show.

King. You are deceivèd, 'tis not so.

Berowne. The pedant, the braggart, the hedge-priest,°
    the fool, and the boy—   *540*
Abate throw at novum,° and the whole world again
Cannot pick out five such, take each one in his
    vein.°

King. The ship is under sail, and here she comes
    amain.°

       Enter [Costard, for] Pompey.

Costard. "I Pompey am—"

Berowne.   You lie, you are not he!

Costard. "I Pompey am—"

Boyet.   With libbard's head° on knee.   *545*

Berowne. Well said, old mocker. I must needs be
    friends with thee.

Costard. "I Pompey am, Pompey surnamed the Big—"

Dumaine. The "Great."

Costard. It is "Great," sir—"Pompey surnamed the
    Great,
That oft in field, with targe° and shield, did make
    my foe to sweat,   *550*
And traveling along this coast I here am come by
    chance,

536 **habits** costumes   539 **hedge-priest** unlearned priest   541 **Abate
throw at novum** except for the throw at nine (in a game of dice)
542 **vein** characteristic way   543 **amain** swiftly   545 **libbard's head**
heraldic painting of leopard   550 **targe** shield

And lay my arms before the legs of this sweet lass
   of France."
If your ladyship would say, "Thanks, Pompey," I
had done.

555 *Princess.* Great thanks, great Pompey.

Costard. 'Tis not so much worth, but I hope I was
perfect. I made a little fault in "Great."

Berowne. My hat to a halfpenny, Pompey proves the
best Worthy.

Enter [Nathaniel, the] Curate, for Alexander.

Nathaniel. "When in the world I lived, I was the
560   world's commander;
By east, west, north, and south, I spread my con-
   quering might;
My scutcheon° plain declares that I am Alisander—"

Boyet. Your nose says, no, you are not; for it stands
too right.°

Berowne. Your nose smells "no" in this, most tender-
smelling knight.

Princess. The conqueror is dismayed. Proceed, good
563   Alexander.

Nathaniel. "When in the world I lived, I was the
world's commander—"

Boyet. Most true, 'tis right—you were so, Alisander.

Berowne. Pompey the Great—

Costard. Your servant, and Costard.

570 *Berowne.* Take away the conqueror, take away Alisander.

Costard. [*To Nathaniel*] O, sir, you have overthrown

562 **scutcheon** coat of arms   563 **right** straight (Alexander's neck
was a little awry)

Alisander the conqueror! You will be scraped out
of the painted cloth° for this. Your lion that holds
his pole-ax° sitting on a close-stool° will be given   575
to Ajax.° He will be the ninth Worthy. A conqueror, and afeard to speak? Run away for shame,
Alisander. [*Nathaniel stands aside.*] There, an 't°
shall please you, a foolish mild man; an honest
man, look you, and soon dashed. He is a marvelous   580
good neighbor, faith, and a very good bowler; but
for Alisander—alas! you see how 'tis—a little o'erparted.° But there are Worthies a-coming will speak
their mind in some other sort.

Princess. Stand aside, good Pompey.   585
                        [*Costard stands aside.*]

Enter [*Holofernes, the*] *Pedant, for Judas, and*
        [*Moth,*] *the Boy, for Hercules.*

Holofernes. "Great Hercules is presented by this imp,°
    Whose club killed Cerberus, that three-headed
        canus;°
And when he was a babe, a child, a shrimp,
Thus did he strangle serpents in his *manus.*°
Quoniam° he seemeth in minority,°   590
Ergo° I come with this apology."
Keep some state° in thy exit, and vanish.
                        Exit Boy [*to one side*].
    "Judas I am—"

Dumaine. A Judas?

Holofernes. Not Iscariot, sir.   595
    "Judas I am, ycleped° Maccabaeus."°

Dumaine. Judas Maccabaeus clipt° is plain Judas.

---

574 **painted cloth** wall-hanging   575 **pole-ax** battle-ax (and penis)
575 **close-stool** commode   576 **Ajax** Greek warrior (with a pun on
"jakes," privy)   578 **an't** if it   582–83 **o'erparted** having too difficult a part   586 **imp** child   587 **canus** (from Latin *canis*) dog
589 **manus** hand   590 **Quoniam** since   590 **in minority** under age
591 **Ergo** therefore   592 **state** dignity   596 **ycleped** called   596
Maccabaeus Hebrew warrior   597 **clipt** (1) cut (2) embraced

Berowne. A kissing traitor. How, art thou proved Judas?

600 *Holofernes.* "Judas I am—"

Dumaine. The more shame for you, Judas.

Holofernes. What mean you, sir?

Boyet. To make Judas hang himself.

Holofernes. Begin, sir; you are my elder.

605 *Berowne.* Well followed: Judas was hanged on an elder.°

Holofernes. I will not be put out of countenance.

Berowne. Because thou hast no face.

Holofernes. What is this?

610 *Boyet.* A cittern-head.°

Dumaine. The head of a bodkin.°

Berowne. A death's face in a ring.°

Longaville. The face of an old Roman coin, scarce seen.

615 *Boyet.* The pommel of Caesar's falchion.°

Dumaine. The carved-bone face on a flask.

Berowne. Saint George's half-cheek° in a brooch.

Dumaine. Ay, and in a brooch of lead.°

Berowne. Ay, and worn in the cap of a toothdrawer.
620   And now forward, for we have put thee in countenance.

Holofernes. You have put me out of countenance.°

---

606 **elder** a kind of tree   610 **cittern-head** head of a stringed musical instrument   611 **bodkin** long hairpin   612 **death's face in a ring** finger ring with the carving of a skull   615 **falchion** sword   617 **half-cheek** profile   618 **brooch of lead** ornament worn in cap as badge of dentist's trade   622 **out of countenance** disconcerted

Berowne. False. We have given thee faces.

Holofernes. But you have outfaced them all.

Berowne. And° thou wert a lion, we would do so.   625

Boyet. Therefore as he is an ass, let him go.
And so adieu, sweet Jude. Nay, why dost thou stay?

Dumaine. For the latter end of his name.

Berowne. For the ass to the Jude? Give it him. Jud-as,
away!

Holofernes. This is not generous, not gentle, not humble.   630

Boyet. A light for Monsieur Judas! It grows dark, he
may stumble.   [*Holofernes stands aside.*]

Princess. Alas, poor Maccabaeus, how hath he been
baited!°

Enter [Armado, the] Braggart, [for Hector].

Berowne. Hide thy head, Achilles! Here comes Hec-
tor° in arms.

Dumaine. Though my mocks come home by me, I   635
will now be merry.

King. Hector was but a Troyan in respect of this.

Boyet. But is this Hector?

King. I think Hector was not so clean-timbered.°

Longaville. His leg is too big for Hector's.   640

Dumaine. More calf, certain.

Boyet. No; he is best indued in the small.°

Berowne. This cannot be Hector.

Dumaine. He's a god or a painter; for he makes faces.

625 **And if**   632 **baited** tormented   633–34 **Achilles . . . Hector**
(the Greek and Trojan champions)   639 **clean-timbered** clean-
limbed   642 **small** lower part of the leg

Armado. "The armipotent° Mars, of lances the al-
645   mighty,
   Gave Hector a gift—"

Dumaine. A gilt nutmeg.°

Berowne. A lemon.

Longaville. Stuck with cloves.

650 *Dumaine.* No, cloven.

Armado. Peace!
   "The armipotent Mars, of lances the almighty,
   Gave Hector a gift, the heir of Ilion;
   A man so breathed° that certain he would fight, yea
655 From morn till night, out of his pavilion.°
   I am that flower—"

Dumaine.   That mint.

Longaville.   That columbine.

Armado. Sweet Lord Longaville, rein thy tongue.

Longaville. I must rather give it the rein, for it runs
   against Hector.

660 *Dumaine.* Ay, and Hector's a greyhound.

Armado. The sweet war-man is dead and rotten.
   Sweet chucks, beat not the bones of the buried.
   When he breathed, he was a man. But I will forward with my device. [*To the Princess*] Sweet roy-
665 alty, bestow on me the sense of hearing.
           Berowne steps forth [*to whisper to Costard*].

Princess. Speak, brave Hector; we are much delighted.

Armado. I do adore thy sweet Grace's slipper.

Boyet. [*Aside to Dumaine*] Loves her by the foot.

Dumaine. [*Aside to Boyet*] He may not by the yard.°

---

645 armipotent powerful in arms   647 gilt nutmeg (with special
icing)   654 breathed well-exercised   655 pavilion tent for a champion at a tournament   669 yard (slang word for male organ)

Armado. "This Hector far surmounted Hannibal—"   670
The party is gone.°

Costard. Fellow Hector, she is gone.° She is two
months on her way.

Armado. What meanest thou?

Costard. Faith, unless you play the honest Troyan,   675
the poor wench is cast away. She's quick;° the child
brags in her belly already. 'Tis yours.

Armado. Dost thou infamonize° me among potentates? Thou shalt die.

Costard. Then shall Hector be whipped for Jaquenetta   680
that is quick by him, and hanged for Pompey that
is dead by him.

Dumaine. Most rare Pompey!

Boyet. Renowned Pompey!

Berowne. Greater than great. Great, great, great Pom-   685
pey! Pompey the Huge!

Dumaine. Hector trembles.

Berowne. Pompey is moved. More Ates,° more Ates!
Stir them on, stir them on!

Dumaine. Hector will challenge him.   690

Berowne. Ay, if 'a have no more man's blood in his
belly than will sup a flea.

Armado. By the North Pole, I do challenge thee.

Costard. I will not fight with a pole, like a northern
man. I'll slash; I'll do it by the sword. I bepray   695
you, let me borrow my arms again.

Dumaine. Room for the incensed Worthies!

Costard. I'll do it in my shirt.

671 The party is gone (referring to Hector)   672 she is gone she is
pregnant   676 quick pregnant   678 infamonize defame   688 Ates
goddess of mischief

Dumaine. Most resolute Pompey!

700 *Moth.* Master, let me take you a buttonhole lower.° Do you not see, Pompey is uncasing° for the combat? What mean you? You will lose your reputation.

Armado. Gentlemen and soldiers, pardon me. I will
705 not combat in my shirt.

Dumaine. You may not deny it. Pompey hath made the challenge.

Armado. Sweet bloods, I both may and will.

Berowne. What reason have you for 't?

710 *Armado.* The naked truth of it is, I have no shirt. I go woolward° for penance.

Boyet. True, and it was enjoined° him in Rome for want of linen; since when, I'll be sworn he wore none but a dishclout of Jaquenetta's, and that 'a
715 wears next his heart for a favor.

Enter a Messenger, Monsieur Marcade.

Marcade. God save you, madam.

Princess. Welcome, Marcade,
But that thou interrupt'st our merriment.

Marcade. I am sorry, madam, for the news I bring
720 Is heavy in my tongue. The king your father—

Princess. Dead, for my life!

Marcade. Even so. My tale is told.

Berowne. Worthies, away! The scene begins to cloud.

Armado. For mine own part, I breathe free breath.

---

700 **take you a buttonhole lower** take you down a peg   701 **uncasing** removing his coat   711 **go woolward** wearing wool next to the skin
712 **enjoined** commanded

I have seen the day of wrong through the little hole   *725*
of discretion, and I will right myself like a soldier.
                                        Exeunt Worthies.

King. How fares your Majesty?

Princess. Boyet, prepare. I will away tonight.

King. Madam, not so. I do beseech you, stay.

Princess. Prepare, I say. I thank you, gracious lords,   *730*
For all your fair endeavors, and entreat
Out of a new-sad soul that you vouchsafe
In your rich wisdom to excuse, or hide
The liberal opposition of our spirits,
If over-boldly we have borne ourselves   *735*
In the converse of breath.° Your gentleness
Was guilty of it. Farewell, worthy lord.
A heavy heart bears not a humble° tongue.
Excuse me so, coming too short of thanks
For my great suit so easily obtained.   *740*

King. The extreme parts of time extremely forms
All causes to the purpose of his speed,°
And often at his very loose° decides
That which long process could not arbitrate.
And though the mourning brow of progeny•   *745*
Forbid the smiling courtesy of love
The holy suit which fain it would convince,°
Yet, since love's argument was first on foot,
Let not the cloud of sorrow justle it
From what it purposed; since to wail friends lost   *750*
Is not by much so wholesome-profitable
As to rejoice at friends but newly found.

Princess. I understand you not. My griefs are double.

Berowne. Honest plain words best pierce the ear of
        grief;
And by these badges° understand the king.   *755*

736 **converse of breath** conversation   738 **humble** i.e., civil, tactful
741–42 **The extreme . . . speed** time, as it runs out, directs everything
towards its conclusion   743 **at his very loose** in the act of letting go
745 **progeny** descendants   747 **convince** prove   755 **badges** tokens

For your fair sakes have we neglected time,
Played foul play with our oaths. Your beauty, ladies,
Hath much deformed us, fashioning our humors
Even to the opposèd end of our intents;
760 And what in us hath seemed ridiculous—
As love is full of unbefitting strains,
All wanton as a child, skipping and vain,
Formed by the eye and therefore, like the eye,
Full of straying shapes, of habits and of forms,
765 Varying in subjects as the eye doth roll
To every varied object in his glance;
Which parti-coated° presence of loose love
Put on by us, if, in your heavenly eyes,
Have misbecomed our oaths and gravities,
770 Those heavenly eyes that look into these faults
Suggested° us to make. Therefore, ladies,
Our love being yours, the error that love makes
Is likewise yours. We to ourselves prove false,
By being once false forever to be true
775 To those that make us both—fair ladies, you.
And even that falsehood, in itself a sin,
Thus purifies itself and turns to grace.

Princess. We have received your letters, full of love;
Your favors, the ambassadors of love;
780 And in our maiden council rated° them
At courtship, pleasant jest, and courtesy,
As bombast° and as lining to the time.
But more devout than this in our respects
Have we not been, and therefore met your loves
785 In their own fashion, like a merriment.

Dumaine. Our letters, madam, showed much more than jest.

Longaville. So did our looks.

Rosaline.   We did not quote° them so.

---

767 parti-coated fool's motley   771 Suggested tempted   780 rated
valued   782 bombast padding   787 quote regard

King. Now, at the latest minute of the hour
  Grant us your loves.

Princess.   A time, methinks, too short
  To make a world-without-end bargain in.   790
  No, no, my lord, your Grace is perjured much,
  Full of dear guiltiness; and therefore this—
  If for my love (as there is no such cause)
  You will do aught, this shall you do for me:
  Your oath I will not trust, but go with speed   795
  To some forlorn and naked hermitage,
  Remote from all the pleasures of the world;
  There stay until the twelve celestial signs°
  Have brought about the annual reckoning.
  If this austere insociable life   800
  Change not your offer made in heat of blood—
  If frosts and fasts, hard lodging and thin weeds,°
  Nip not the gaudy blossoms of your love,
  But that it bear this trial, and last love—
  Then, at the expiration of the year,   805
  Come challenge me, challenge me by these deserts,
  And, by this virgin palm now kissing thine,
  I will be thine; and till that instant, shut
  My woeful self up in a mourning house,
  Raining the tears of lamentation   810
  For the remembrance of my father's death.
  If this thou do deny, let our hands part,
  Neither entitled in the other's heart.

King. If this, or more than this, I would deny,
  To flatter up° these powers of mine with rest,   815
  The sudden hand of death close up mine eye!
  Hence hermit then—my heart is in thy breast.

[*Berowne.* And what to me, my love? and what to me?

Rosaline. You must be purgèd, too, your sins are
  rank,
  You are attaint° with faults and perjury;   820

798 twelve celestial signs (of the Zodiac)   802 weeds garments 815
flatter up pamper   820 attaint charged

Therefore, if you my favor mean to get,
A twelvemonth shall you spend, and never rest,
But seek the weary beds of people sick.]°

Dumaine. But what to me, my love? But what to me?
825   A wife?

Katharine.   A beard, fair health, and honesty;
With three-fold love I wish you all these three.

Dumaine. O, shall I say "I thank you, gentle wife"?

Katharine. Not so, my lord. A twelvemonth and a day
I'll mark no words that smooth-faced wooers say.
830   Come when the king doth to my lady come;
Then, if I have much love, I'll give you some.

Dumaine. I'll serve thee true and faithfully till then.

Katharine. Yet swear not, lest ye be forsworn again.

Longaville. What says Maria?

Maria.   At the twelvemonth's end
835   I'll change my black gown for a faithful friend.

Longaville. I'll stay with patience, but the time is long.

Maria. The liker° you! Few taller are so young.

Berowne. Studies my lady? Mistress, look on me.
Behold the window of my heart, mine eye,
840   What humble suit attends thy answer there.
Impose some service on me for thy love.

Rosaline. Oft have I heard of you, my Lord Berowne,
Before I saw you, and the world's large tongue
Proclaims you for a man replete with mocks,
845   Full of comparisons and wounding flouts,°
Which you on all estates° will execute
That lie within the mercy of your wit.

818–23 (lines 824–35) duplicate this passage in an expanded form;
probably Shakespeare failed to indicate clearly that these six lines
had been superseded)   837 **liker** more like   845 **wounding flouts**
painful jokes   846 **all estates** men of all kinds

To weed this wormwood° from your fructful° brain,
And therewithal to win me, if you please,
Without the which I am not to be won,   850
You shall this twelvemonth term from day to day
Visit the speechless sick, and still° converse
With groaning wretches; and your task shall be
With all the fierce endeavor of your wit
To enforce the painèd impotent to smile.   855

Berowne. To move wild laughter in the throat of
    death?
  It cannot be; it is impossible;
  Mirth cannot move a soul in agony.

Rosaline. Why, that's the way to choke a gibing spirit,
  Whose influence is begot of that loose grace   860
  Which shallow laughing hearers give to fools.
  A jest's prosperity lies in the ear
  Of him that hears it, never in the tongue
  Of him that makes it. Then, if sickly ears,
  Deafed with the clamors of their own dear groans,   865
  Will hear your idle scorns, continue then,
  And I will have you and that fault withal;
  But if they will not, throw away that spirit,
  And I shall find you empty of that fault,
  Right joyful of your reformation.   870

Berowne. A twelvemonth? Well, befall what will be-
    fall,
  I'll jest a twelvemonth in an hospital.

Princess. [*To the King*] Ay, sweet my lord, and so I
    take my leave.

King. No, madam, we will bring you on your way.

Berowne. Our wooing doth not end like an old play;   875
  Jack hath not Jill. These ladies' courtesy
  Might well have made our sport a comedy.

---

848 **wormwood** bitterness   848 **fructful** fruitful   852 **still** always

King. Come, sir, it wants a twelvemonth and a day,
And then 'twill end.

Berowne.   That's too long for a play.

Enter [Armado, the] Braggart.

880 *Armado.* Sweet Majesty, vouchsafe me—

Princess. Was not that Hector?

Dumaine. The worthy knight of Troy.

Armado. I will kiss thy royal finger, and take leave.
I am a votary;° I have vowed to Jaquenetta to hold
885 the plough for her sweet love three year. But, most
esteemed greatness, will you hear the dialogue that
the two learned men have compiled in praise of the
owl and the cuckoo? It should have followed in
the end of our show.

890 *King.* Call them forth quickly; we will do so.

Armado. Holla! Approach.

Enter all.

This side is *Hiems,* Winter; this *Ver,* the Spring;
the one maintained by the owl, th' other by the
cuckoo. *Ver,* begin.

The Song.

895 [*Spring.*]   When daisies pied° and violets blue
                And lady-smocks° all silver-white
            And cuckoo-buds° of yellow hue
                Do paint the meadows with delight,

---

884 **votary** sworn follower   895 **pied** parti-colored   896 **lady-smocks**
water-cresses, or cuckoo flowers   897 **cuckoo-buds** crowfoot, or
buttercup

The cuckoo then, on every tree,
Mocks married men; for thus sings he,　　900
　　　　　　"Cuckoo!

Cuckoo, cuckoo!" O word of fear,
Unpleasing to a married ear!
When shepherds pipe on oaten straws,
　　And merry larks are ploughmen's
　　　　　　clocks,　　905
When turtles tread,° and rooks, and daws,
　　And maidens bleach their summer
　　　　　　smocks,
The cuckoo then, on every tree,
Mocks married men; for thus sings he,
　　　　　　"Cuckoo!　　910

Cuckoo, cuckoo!" O word of fear,
Unpleasing to a married ear!

Winter.　When icicles hang by the wall,
　　And Dick the shepherd blows his nail,°
And Tom bears logs into the hall,　　915
　　And milk comes frozen home in pail,
When blood is nipped, and ways be foul,
Then nightly sings the staring owl,
　　　　　　"Tu-whit,

Tu-who!" a merry note,　　920
While greasy Joan doth keel° the pot.

When all aloud the wind doth blow,
　　And coughing drowns the parson's
　　　　　　saw,°
And birds sit brooding in the snow,
　　And Marian's nose looks red and raw,　　925
When roasted crabs° hiss in the bowl,
Then nightly sings the staring owl,
　　　　　　"Tu-whit,

---

906 **turtles tread** turtledoves mate　914 **blows his nail** blows on his
fingernails to warm them (and so, waiting patiently)　921 **keel** cool,
by stirring or skimming　923 **saw** wise saying　926 **crabs** crab
apples

Tu-who!" a merry note,
930   While greasy Joan doth keel the pot.

[*Armado.*] The words of Mercury are harsh after the
songs of Apollo.° [You that way, we this way.
Exeunt omnes.]

FINIS

931–32 **The words . . . Apollo** i.e., let us end with the songs, because
clever words of the god Mercury would come harshly after the songs
of Apollo, the god of poetry

Textual Note

This edition is based upon the quarto of 1598, which, it is generally agreed, was printed from a manuscript in Shakespeare's own hand. The title page reads: "A / Pleasant / Conceited Comedie / Called, / Loues labors lost. / As it was presented before her Highnes / this last Christmas. / Newly corrected and augmented / By W. Shakespere. / Imprinted at London by W. W. / for Cutbert Burby. / 1598."

Although here there may be a reference to a previous printing, there is no trace of an earlier edition. "Newly corrected and augmented" probably refers to revisions in the manuscript, some of which, as it happens, may be detected in examining the printed text. (See footnotes at IV.iii.295 and V.ii.818–23.)

The printing of the 1623 Folio is based upon the quarto. It corrects some errors of the quarto and adds a number of its own. It provides act divisions (mistakenly heading the fifth act "Actus Quartus"), but the scene divisions as well as the list of the names of the persons in the play are the contributions of later editors.

Apart from a considerable number of misreadings the most noteworthy confusions in the quarto are in the speech headings. It is not merely that occasionally *Nathaniel* stands for *Holofernes,* that the *King* is sometimes *Navarre* and sometimes *Ferdinand* in the early part of the second act, and that in the same part of the play Rosaline and Katharine are confused. In the next act the character previously identified as Armado becomes

"Braggart," Moth, the Page, becomes "Boy," Holofernes becomes "Pedant," Costard becomes "Clown." Later Sir Nathaniel becomes "Curate" and "Constable" becomes "Dull." The use of the generic names to take the place of the individual ones may be evidence of Shakespeare's revisions. In the present edition the speech headings have been made consistent, but the later substitutions are made evident by the supplementary stage directions indicating the entrances of the various characters.

The revision of the manuscript has left a couple of other obvious confusions. Berowne's speech in Act IV, Scene iii contains lines that belong to an earlier version, and some of these should have been canceled. If lines 295–316 were omitted, the speech would continue connectedly and without obvious repetitions. It also seems that the exchange between Berowne and Rosaline in Act V, Scene ii, lines 818–23, was meant to be struck out. In the present edition these passages are retained, but enclosed in square brackets.

The text of this edition is based upon the Heber-Daniel copy of the quarto in the British Museum; the spelling and punctuation have been modernized, obvious misspellings and wrong speech headings corrected, and the quotations from foreign languages regularized. Other departures from the quarto text are listed below: the adopted reading is given first, in italics, followed immediately by the quarto reading in roman letters.

I.i.24 *three* thee 31 *pomp* pome 62 *feast* fast 104 *an* any 114 *swore* sworne 127–31 [Q gives to Longaville] 127 *gentility* gentletie 130 *public* publibue 131 *possibly* possible 218 *welkin's vicegerent* welkis Vizgerent 240 *preposterous* propostrous 276 *worst* wost 289 *King* Ber. 308–09 *prosperity* prosperie

I.ii.14 *epitheton* apethaton 100 *blushing* blush-in 143 *Dull* Clo.

II.i.32 *Importunes* Importuous 34 *visaged* visage 44 *parts* peerelsse 88 *unpeopled* vnpeeled 115–26 [the lines here given to Rosaline are in Q given to Katharine] 130 *half of an* halfe of, of an 140 *friendship* faiendship 142 *demand* pemaund 144 *On* One 179 *mine own* my none 195 *Katharine* Rosalin 210 *Rosaline* Katherin 221 [Q gives to La.] 222–23 [Q gives to Lad.] 224 [Q gives to La.] 236 *agate* Agot 246 *quote* coate 254 [Q gives to

Lad.] 255 [Q gives to *Lad.* 2] 256 [Q gives to *Lad.* 3] 257 [Q gives to *Lad.*] 258 [Q gives to *Lad.*]

III.i.14 *throat as if* throate, if 16 *through the nose* through: nose 19 *thin-belly* thinbellies 25 *note me?—that* note men that 28 *penny* penne 67 *voluble* volable 74 *the mail* thee male 74 *plain* pline 136 *ounce* ouce 139 *remuneration* remuration 140 *One penny* i.d. 177 *beadle* Bedell 178 *critic* Crietick 182 *senior-junior* signior Iunios 186 *plackets* Placcats 188 *paritors* Parrators 192 *German clock* Iermane Cloake 198 *whitely* whitly 206 *sue* shue

IV.i.6 *On* Ore 33 *heart* hart 71 *saw . . . saw* See . . . see 72 *over-came* couercame 76 *king's* King 110 *suitor . . . suitor* shooter . . . shooter 122 *Pepin* Pippen 125 *Guinever* Guinouer 132 *hit it* hit 134 *mete* meate 136 *ne'er* neare 138 *pin* is in 140 *too* to 146 *to th' one* ath toothen 149 *o' t' other* another 150 *a most* most 150 s.d. *Shout* Shoot 151 *Exit* Exeunt

IV.ii.5 *coelo* Celo 8 *epithets* epythithes 30 *we of taste* we taste 31 *indiscreet* indistreell 37 *Dictynna . . . Dictynna* Dictisima . . . dictisima 38 *Dictynna* dictima 52 *ignorant, I* call ignorault cald 55 *scurrility* squirilitie 57 *preyful* prayfull 61 *sores o' sorel* sores o sorell 66–150 [all speech prefixes of Holofernes and Nathaniel are reversed in Q, except at 107] 70 *pia mater* primater 72 *those in whom* those whom 78 *ingenious* ingenous 80 *sapit* sapis 84 *pierce-one* Person 86 *likest* liklest 94–95 *Fauste . . . ruminat* Facile precor gellida, quando pecas omnia sub vmbra ruminat 98–99 *Venetia . . . pretia* vemchie, vencha, que non te vnde, que non te perreche 122 *canzonet* cangenet 136 *writing* written 138 *Sir Nathaniel* Ped. Sir Holofernes 159 *ben* bien

IV.iii.13,14 *melancholy* mallicholie 48 *King* Long 52 *triumviry* triumpherie 74 *idolatry* ydotarie 86 *quoted* coted 92 *And I mine* And mine 98 *ode* Odo 107 *Wished* Wish 111 *thorn* throne 129 *o'erheard* ore-hard 154 *coaches* couches 160 *mote . . . mote* Moth . . . Moth 179 *men like you, men* men like men 181 *Joan* Ione 247 *wood* word 258 *painting and usurping* painting vsurping 259 *doters* dooters 312 *woman's* womas 315–16 [between these lines Q has: With our selues] 322 *beauty's* beautis 358 *authors* authour 360 *Let us* Lets vs 382 *Allons! Allons!* Alone alone 384 *forsworn* forsorne

V.i.10 *hominem* hominum 28 *insanie* infamie 30 *bone* bene 31 *Bone? Bone for bene! Priscian* Bome boon for boon prescian 34 *gaudeo* gaudio 36 *Quare* Quari 51 *pueritia* puericia 52 *silly* seely 59 *wave* wane 59 *Mediterranean* meditaranium 60 *venew* vene we 69 *manu* vnū 78 *dunghill* dungil 79 *Dunghill* dunghel 99 *importunate* importunt 110 *secrecy* secretie 119 *Nathaniel* Holofernes 121 *rend'red* rended 153 *Allons* Alone

V.ii.13 *ne'er* neare   17 *ha' been a grandam* a bin Grandam   43
'Ware pencils, ho! Ware pensalls, How?   53 *pearls* Pearle   65 *hests*
deuice   74 *wantonness* wantons be   80 *stabbed* stable   89 *sycamore* Siccamone   93 *Warily* warely   95 *overheard* ouer hard   96
they thy   122 *parley, court* parlee, to court   134 *too* two   148 *her*
his   152 *e'er* ere   159 [Q gives to Berowne]   163 *ever* euen   175
strangers stranges   217 [Q gives to Rosaline]   225 *Price* Prise
243–56 [Q gives "Maria" for "Katharine"]   298 *vailing* varling   300
woo woe · 310 *run* runs   324 *too* to   329 *ushering* hushering   342
Construe Consture   353 *unsullied* vnsallied   375 *wit* wits   408 *affectation* affection   461 *on't* ant   464 *zany* saine   483 *manage*
nuage   501 *they* thy   515 *least* best   529 *de la guerra* delaguar
564 *this* his   584 [Q has "Exit Curat"]   598 *proved* proud   647
gilt gift   689 *Stir them on, stir* stir them, or stir   751 *wholesome*
holdsome   779 *the ambassadors* embassadours   783 *this in our* this
our   787 *quote* cote   808 *instant* instance   813 *entitled* intiled
817 *hermit* herrite   819 *rank* rackt   825 *A wife?* [included in following speech in Q]   829 *smoothed-faced* smothfast   896–97
[these lines transposed in Q]   917 *foul* full   931–32 *The words . . .
Apollo* [printed in larger type in Q without any speech-heading; F
adds *You that way: we this way,* and heading *Brag.*]

A Note on the Sources of
Love's Labor's Lost

No source for the plot of *Love's Labor's Lost* is known to exist but it is often supposed that Shakespeare was building upon reports of historic events. The very names of Navarre and the lords,[1] the matter of property disputes involving the King of France, the existence of a learned academy favored by the French nobility, and accounts of political negotiations in which certain court ladies were involved, all these point to incidents in recent French history which were reported upon at the time. So far no record has been found of any single happening that is plainly the original of the episodes of the play. It is only in the sum of the reports of similar incidents that the idea that Shakespeare is building upon historical matters comes to seem truly likely.

The play, whether meant originally for performance at a great house, or at a children's theater, exploited these historical events presumably because they treated matters in which the audience was also interested. English court circles were also drawn to the idea of learned academies and were involved in disputes centering on Platonic theories of love. Upon reflection, the treatment of certain episodes in France would have served as comment upon the life of the court in England. Quite as naturally Shake-

---

[1] The Marshall de Biron (Berowne) and Longueville were close associates of Henry, not Ferdinand, of Navarre. The Duc de Mayenne (Dumaine?) was once his enemy but later an ally. Boyet and Marcadé are the names of historical persons.

speare could work into the main story all sorts of allusions to the life of letters and introduce subsidiary plotting to expand upon the story of the aristocratic academicians. So the play directs particular satire against specific English fashions—euphuism, for instance—as well as the universal extravagances of humanists and pedants and actors. Here, too, the references seem again and again to point to particular persons and to specific incidents, and scholars have therefore argued that Shakespeare took some of his contemporaries as models for the characters in his comic plot, and the characters that were in part borrowed from the *commedia dell'arte* from time to time present themselves in the guise of Thomas Nashe, Sir Walter Raleigh, John Florio, and perhaps others. To J. D. Wilson these matters become so important that he is convinced that the play "was written as a *topical* play." But G. L. Kittredge, and others after him, have thought it "merely whimsical" to identify Armado and Holofernes and the others in any such way.

On particular points it is seldom possible to resolve this dispute, most especially if the supposed allusions are studied primarily in the light of literary history. But the direction of much modern literary scholarship is to give precedence in the consideration of the elements of a work of art to a study of their relation to the work itself as an imaginative entity, and the effect of such an emphasis is to work in opposition to any theory that regards the work primarily as a historical record. In short, the impression of topical allusion is inescapable, but if one takes the play as substantially summed up by its title, the topicality seems to be absorbed in the imaginative and the fanciful, and in all the charm of the play's poetic and theatrical effects.

The historical documents that are most often cited in presenting analogues to certain incidents in the play are: *The Chronicles of Enguerrand de Monstrelet, 1440–1516;* Pierre de la Primaudaye, *The French Academie;* H. C. Davila, *The History of the Civil Wars of France; Gesta Grayorum: or The History of the High and Mighty Prince Henry, Prince of Purpoole . . . who Reigned and Died,*

A. D. 1594. The relevant sections can be found in the first volume of Geoffrey Bullough's *Narrative and Dramatic Sources of Shakespeare.* There are of course no documents that in any substantial way support the ascriptions of topicality.

Commentaries

WALTER PATER

from *Appreciations*

Love's Labors Lost is one of the earliest of Shakespeare's dramas, and has many of the peculiarities of his poems, which are also the work of his earlier life. The opening speech of the king on the immortality of fame —on the triumph of fame over death—and the nobler parts of Biron, display something of the monumental style of Shakespeare's sonnets, and are not without their conceits of thought and expression. This connection of *Love's Labors Lost* with Shakespeare's poems is further enforced by the actual insertion in it of three sonnets and a faultless song; which, in accordance with his practice in other plays, are inwoven into the argument of the piece and, like the golden ornaments of a fair woman, give it a peculiar air of distinction. There is merriment in it also, with choice illustrations of both wit and humor; a laughter, often exquisite, ringing, if faintly, yet as genuine laughter still, though sometimes sinking into mere

From *Appreciations* by Walter Pater. London and New York: The Macmillan Company, 1889. The essay was first published in *Macmillan's Magazine*, December, 1885.

burlesque, which has not lasted quite so well. And Shakespeare brings a serious effect out of the trifling of his
characters. A dainty lovemaking is interchanged with the
more cumbrous play: below the many artifices of Biron's
amorous speeches we may trace sometimes the "unutter-
able longing"; and the lines in which Katherine describes
the blighting through love of her younger sister are one
of the most touching things in older literature.[1] Again,
how many echoes seem awakened by those strange words,
actually said in jest!—"The sweet war-man (Hector of
Troy) is dead and rotten; sweet chucks, beat not the
bones of the buried: when he breathed, he was a man!"
—words which may remind us of Shakespeare's own
epitaph. In the last scene, an ingenious turn is given to
the action, so that the piece does not conclude after the
manner of other comedies.—

>   Our wooing doth not end like an old play;
>   Jack hath not Jill:

and Shakespeare strikes a passionate note across it at
last, in the entrance of the messenger, who announces to
the princess that the king her father is suddenly dead.

The merely dramatic interest of the piece is slight
enough; only just sufficient, indeed, to form the vehicle
of its wit and poetry. The scene—a park of the King
of Navarre—is unaltered throughout; and the unity of
the play is not so much the unity of a drama as that of a
series of pictorial groups, in which the same figures re-
appear, in different combinations but on the same background. It is as if Shakespeare had intended to bind
together, by some inventive conceit, the devices of an
ancient tapestry, and give voices to its figures. On one
side, a fair palace; on the other, the tents of the Princess
of France, who has come on an embassy from her father
to the King of Navarre; in the midst, a wide space of
smooth grass. The same personages are combined over
and over again into a series of gallant scenes: the princess, the three masked ladies, the quaint, pedantic king—

[1] Act V. Scene II.

one of those amiable kings men have never loved enough,
whose serious occupation with the things of the mind
seems, by contrast with the more usual forms of kingship,
like frivolity or play. Some of the figures are grotesque
merely, and all the male ones at least, a little fantastic.
Certain objects reappearing from scene to scene—love
letters crammed with verses to the margin, and lovers'
toys—hint obscurely at some story of intrigue. Between
these groups, on a smaller scale, come the slighter and
more homely episodes, with Sir Nathaniel the curate, the
country-maid Jaquenetta, Moth or Mote the elfin-page,
with Hiems and Ver, who recite "the dialogue that the
two learned men have compiled in praise of the owl and
the cuckoo." The ladies are lodged in tents, because the
king, like the princess of the modern poet's fancy, has
taken a vow

> To make his court a little Academe,

and for three years' space no woman may come within
a mile of it; and the play shows how this artificial attempt
was broken through. For the king and his three fellow
scholars are of course soon forsworn, and turn to writing
sonnets, each to his chosen lady. These fellow scholars
of the king—"quaint votaries of science" at first, afterwards "affection's men-at-arms"—three youthful knights,
gallant, amorous, chivalrous, but also a little affected,
sporting always a curious foppery of language, are,
throughout, the leading figures in the foreground; one of
them, in particular, being more carefully depicted than
the others, and in himself very noticeable—a portrait
with somewhat puzzling manner and expression, which
at once catches the eye irresistibly and keeps it fixed.

Play is often that about which people are most serious;
and the humorist may observe how, under all love of
playthings, there is almost always hidden an appreciation
of something really engaging and delightful. This is true
always of the toys of children: it is often true of the playthings of grown-up people, their vanities, their fopperies
even, their lighter loves; the cynic would add their pur-

suit of fame. Certainly, this is true without exception of the playthings of a past age, which to those who succeed it are always full of a pensive interest—old manners, old dresses, old houses. For what is called fashion in these matters occupies, in each age, much of the care of many of the most discerning people, furnishing them with a kind of mirror of their real inward refinements and their capacity for selection. Such modes or fashions are, at their best, an example of the artistic predominance of form over matter—of the manner of the doing of it over the thing done—and have a beauty of their own. It is so with that old euphuism of the Elizabethan age—that pride of dainty language and curious expression, which it is very easy to ridicule, which often made itself ridiculous, but which had below it a real sense of fitness and nicety; and which, as we see in this very play, and still more clearly in the sonnets, had some fascination for the young Shakespeare himself. It is this foppery of delicate language, this fashionable plaything of his time, with which Shakespeare is occupied in *Love's Labors Lost*. He shows us the manner in all its stages, passing from the grotesque and vulgar pedantry of Holofernes, through the extravagant but polished caricature of Armado, to become the peculiar characteristic of a real though still quaint poetry in Biron himself, who is still chargeable even at his best with just a little affectation. As Shakespeare laughs broadly at it in Holofernes or Armado, so he is the analyst of its curious charm in Biron; and this analysis involves a delicate raillery by Shakespeare himself at his own chosen manner.

This "foppery" of Shakespeare's day had, then, its really delightful side, a quality in no sense "affected," by which it satisfies a real instinct in our minds—the fancy so many of us have for an exquisite and curious skill in the use of words. Biron is the perfect flower of this manner:

A man of fire-new words, fashion's own knight:

—as he describes Armado, in terms which are really

applicable to himself. In him this manner blends with a true gallantry of nature and an affectionate complaisance and grace. He has at times some of its extravagance or caricature also, but the shades of expression by which he passes from this to the "golden cadence" of Shakespeare's own most characteristic verse are so fine that it is sometimes difficult to trace them. What is a vulgarity in Holofernes, and a caricature in Armado, refines itself with him into the expression of a nature truly and inwardly bent upon a form of delicate perfection, and is accompanied by a real insight into the laws which determine what is exquisite in language and their root in the nature of things. He can appreciate quite the opposite style—

In russet yeas, and honest kersey noes;

he knows the first law of pathos, that

Honest plain words best suit the ear of grief.

He delights in his own rapidity of intuition; and, in harmony with the half-sensuous philosophy of the sonnets, exalts, a little scornfully, in many memorable expressions, the judgment of the senses, above all slower, more toilsome means of knowledge, scorning some who fail to see things only because they are so clear:

So ere you find where light in darkness lies,
Your light grows dark by losing of your eyes:—

as with some German commentators on Shakespeare. Appealing always to actual sensation from men's affected theories, he might seem to despise learning, as, indeed, he has taken up his deep studies partly in sport, and demands always the profit of learning in renewed enjoyment. Yet he surprises us from time to time by intuitions which could come only from a deep experience and power of observation; and men listen to him, old and young, in spite of themselves. He is quickly impressi-

ble to the slightest clouding of the spirits in social inter-
course, and has moments of extreme seriousness: his
trial-task may well be, as Rosaline puts it—

To enforce the pained impotent to smile.

But still, through all, he is true to his chosen manner:
that gloss of dainty language is a second nature with
him; even at his best he is not without a certain artifice;
the trick of playing on words never deserts him; and
Shakespeare, in whose own genius there is an element of
this very quality, shows us in this graceful, and, as it
seems, studied, portrait, his enjoyment of it.

As happens with every true dramatist, Shakespeare is
for the most part hidden behind the persons of his creation. Yet there are certain of his characters in which we
feel that there is something of self-portraiture. And it is
not so much in his grander, more subtle and ingenious
creations that we feel this—in *Hamlet* and *King Lear*—
as in those slighter and more spontaneously developed
figures, who, while far from playing principal parts, are
yet distinguished by a peculiar happiness and delicate
ease in the drawing of them—figures which possess,
above all, that winning attractiveness which there is no
man but would willingly exercise, and which resemble
those works of art which, though not meant to be very
great or imposing, are yet wrought of the choicest material. Mercutio, in *Romeo and Juliet,* belongs to this
group of Shakespeare's characters—versatile, mercurial
people, such as make good actors, and in whom the

Nimble spirits of the arteries,

the finer but still merely animal elements of great wit,
predominate. A careful delineation of minor, yet expres-
sive traits seems to mark them out as the characters of
his predilection; and it is hard not to identify him with
these more than with others. Biron, in *Love's Labors
Lost,* is perhaps the most striking member of this group.
In this character, which is never quite in touch, never

quite on a perfect level of understanding, with the other persons of the play, we see, perhaps, a reflex of Shakespeare himself, when he has just become able to stand aside from and estimate the first period of his poetry.

NORTHROP FRYE

The Argument of Comedy

The Greeks produced two kinds of comedy, Old Comedy, represented by the eleven extant plays of Aristophanes, and New Comedy, of which the best known exponent is Menander. About two dozen New Comedies survive in the work of Plautus and Terence. Old Comedy, however, was out of date before Aristophanes himself was dead; and today, when we speak of comedy, we normally think of something that derives from the Menandrine tradition.

New Comedy unfolds from what may be described as a comic Oedipus situation. Its main theme is the successful effort of a young man to outwit an opponent and possess the girl of his choice. The opponent is usually the father (*senex*), and the psychological descent of the heroine from the mother is also sometimes hinted at. The father frequently wants the same girl, and is cheated out of her by the son, the mother thus becoming the son's ally. The girl is usually a slave or courtesan, and the plot turns on a *cognitio* or discovery of birth which makes her marriageable. Thus it turns out that she is not under an insuperable taboo after all but is an accessible object of desire, so that the plot follows the regular wish-fulfillment

From *English Institute Essays, 1948*, edited by D. A. Robertson. New York: Columbia University Press, 1949. Copyright 1949 by Columbia University Press. Reprinted by permission of the publisher.

pattern. Often the central Oedipus situation is thinly concealed by surrogates or doubles of the main characters, as when the heroine is discovered to be the hero's sister, and has to be married off to his best friend. In Congreve's *Love for Love,* to take a modern instance well within the Menandrine tradition, there are two Oedipus themes in counterpoint: the hero cheats his father out of the heroine, and his best friend violates the wife of an impotent old man who is the heroine's guardian. Whether this analysis is sound or not, New Comedy is certainly concerned with the maneuvering of a young man toward a young woman, and marriage is the tonic chord on which it ends. The normal comic resolution is the surrender of the *senex* to the hero, never the reverse. Shakespeare tried to reverse the pattern in *All's Well That Ends Well,* where the king of France forces Bertram to marry Helena, and the critics have not yet stopped making faces over it.

New Comedy has the blessing of Aristotle, who greatly preferred it to its predecessor, and it exhibits the general pattern of Aristotelian causation. It has a material cause in the young man's sexual desire, and a formal cause in the social order represented by the *senex,* with which the hero comes to terms when he gratifies his desire. It has an efficient cause in the character who brings about the final situation. In classical times this character is a tricky slave; Renaissance dramatists often use some adaptation of the medieval "vice"; modern writers generally like to pretend that nature, or at least the natural course of events, is the efficient cause. The final cause is the audience, which is expected by its applause to take part in the comic resolution. All this takes place on a single order of existence. The action of New Comedy tends to become probable rather than fantastic, and it moves toward realism and away from myth and romance. The one romantic (originally mythical) feature in it, the fact that the hero or heroine turns out to be freeborn or someone's heir, is precisely the feature that trained New Comedy audiences tire of most quickly.

The conventions of New Comedy are the conventions

of Jonson and Molière, and a fortiori of the English Restoration and the French rococo. When Ibsen started giving ironic twists to the same formulas, his startled hearers took them for portents of a social revolution. Even the old chestnut about the heroine's being really the hero's sister turns up in *Ghosts* and *Little Eyolf.* The average movie of today is a rigidly conventionalized New Comedy proceeding toward an act which, like death in Greek tragedy, takes place offstage, and is symbolized by the final embrace.

In all good New Comedy there is a social as well as an individual theme which must be sought in the general atmosphere of reconciliation that makes the final marriage possible. As the hero gets closer to the heroine and opposition is overcome, all the right-thinking people come over to his side. Thus a new social unit is formed on the stage, and the moment that this social unit crystallizes is the moment of the comic resolution. In the last scene, when the dramatist usually tries to get all his characters on the stage at once, the audience witnesses the birth of a renewed sense of social integration. In comedy as in life the regular expression of this is a festival, whether a marriage, a dance, or a feast. Old Comedy has, besides a marriage, a *komos,* the processional dance from which comedy derives its name; and the masque, which is a by-form of comedy, also ends in a dance.

This new social integration may be called, first, a kind of moral norm and, second, the pattern of a free society. We can see this more clearly if we look at the sort of characters who impede the progress of the comedy toward the hero's victory. These are always people who are in some kind of mental bondage, who are helplessly driven by ruling passions, neurotic compulsions, social rituals, and selfishness. The miser, the hypochondriac, the hypocrite, the pedant, the snob: these are humors, people who do not fully know what they are doing, who are slaves to a predictable self-imposed pattern of behavior. What we call the moral norm is, then, not morality but deliverance from moral bondage. Comedy is designed not to condemn evil, but to ridicule a lack of self-knowledge. It finds the virtues of Malvolio and Angelo as comic as the vices of Shylock.

The essential comic resolution, therefore, is an individual release which is also a social reconciliation. The normal individual is freed from the bonds of a humorous society, and a normal society is freed from the bonds imposed on it by humorous individuals. The Oedipus pattern we noted in New Comedy belongs to the individual side of this, and the sense of the ridiculousness of the humor to the social side. But all real comedy is based on the principle that these two forms of release are ultimately the same: this principle may be seen at its most concentrated in *The Tempest*. The rule holds whether the resolution is expressed in social terms, as in *The Merchant of Venice*, or in individual terms, as in Ibsen's *An Enemy of the People*.

The freer the society, the greater the variety of individuals it can tolerate, and the natural tendency of comedy is to include as many as possible in its final festival. The motto of comedy is Terence's "Nothing human is alien to me." This may be one reason for the traditional comic importance of the parasite, who has no business to be at the festival but is nevertheless there. The spirit of reconciliation which pervades the comedies of Shakespeare is not to be ascribed to a personal attitude of his own, about which we know nothing whatever, but to his impersonal concentration on the laws of comic form.

Hence the moral quality of the society presented is not the point of the comic resolution. In Jonson's *Volpone* the final assertion of the moral norm takes the form of a social revenge on Volpone, and the play ends with a great bustle of sentences to penal servitude and the galleys. One feels perhaps that the audience's sense of the moral norm does not need so much hard labor. In *The Alchemist*, when Lovewit returns to his house, the virtuous characters have proved so weak and the rascals so ingenious that the action dissolves in laughter. Whichever is morally the better ending, that of *The Alchemist* is more concentrated comedy. *Volpone* is starting to move toward

tragedy, toward the vision of a greatness which develops
hybris and catastrophe.

The same principle is even clearer in Aristophanes.
Aristophanes is the most personal of writers: his opinions
on every subject are written all over his plays, and we
have no doubt of his moral attitude. We know that he
wanted peace with Sparta and that he hated Cleon, and
when his comedy depicts the attaining of peace and the
defeat of Cleon we know that he approved and wanted his
audience to approve. But in *Ecclesiazusae* a band of
women in disguise railroad a communistic scheme through
the Assembly, which is a horrid parody of Plato's *Republic,* and proceed to inaugurate Plato's sexual com-
munism with some astonishing improvements. Presumably
Aristophanes did not applaud this, yet the comedy follows the same pattern and the same resolution. In *The
Birds* the Peisthetairos who defies Zeus and blocks out
Olympus with his Cloud-Cuckoo-Land is accorded the
same triumph that is given to the Trygaeus of the *Peace*
who flies to heaven and brings a golden age back to
Athens.

Comedy, then, may show virtue her own feature and
scorn her own image—for Hamlet's famous definition of
drama was originally a definition of comedy. It may em-
phasize the birth of an ideal society as you like it, or the
tawdriness of the sham society which is the way of the
world. There is an important parallel here with tragedy.
Tragedy, we are told, is expected to raise but not ultimately to accept the emotions of pity and terror. These
I take to be the sense of moral good and evil, respectively,
which we attach to the tragic hero. He may be as good
as Caesar, and so appeal to our pity, or as bad as Macbeth, and so appeal to terror, but the particular thing
called tragedy that happens to him does not depend on
his moral status. The tragic catharsis passes beyond moral
judgment, and while it is quite possible to construct a
moral tragedy, what tragedy gains in morality it loses in
cathartic power. The same is true of the comic catharsis,
which raises sympathy and ridicule on a moral basis, but
passes beyond both.

Many things are involved in the tragic catharsis, but one of them is a mental or imaginative form of the sacrificial ritual out of which tragedy arose. This is the ritual of the struggle, death, and rebirth of a God-Man, which is linked to the yearly triumph of spring over winter. The tragic hero is not really killed, and the audience no longer eats his body and drinks his blood, but the corresponding thing in art still takes place. The audience enters into communion with the body of the hero, becoming thereby a single body itself. Comedy grows out of the same ritual, for in the ritual the tragic story has a comic sequel. Divine men do not die: they die and rise again. The ritual pattern behind the catharsis of comedy is the resurrection that follows the death, the epiphany or manifestation of the risen hero. This is clear enough in Aristophanes, where the hero is treated as a risen God-Man, led in triumph with the divine honors of the Olympic victor, rejuvenated, or hailed as a new Zeus. In New Comedy the new human body is, as we have seen, both a hero and a social group. Aristophanes is not only closer to the ritual pattern, but contemporary with Plato; and his comedy, unlike Menander's, is Platonic and dialectic: it seeks not the entelechy of the soul but the Form of the Good, and finds it in the resurrection of the soul from the world of the cave to the sunlight. The audience gains a vision of that resurrection whether the conclusion is joyful or ironic, just as in tragedy it gains a vision of a heroic death whether the hero is morally innocent or guilty.

Two things follow from this: first, that tragedy is really implicit or uncompleted comedy; second, that comedy contains a potential tragedy within itself. With regard to the latter, Aristophanes is full of traces of the original death of the hero which preceded his resurrection in the ritual. Even in New Comedy the dramatist usually tries to bring his action as close to a tragic overthrow of the hero as he can get it, and reverses this movement as suddenly as possible. In Plautus the tricky slave is often forgiven or even freed after having been threatened with all the brutalities that a very brutal dramatist can think of, including crucifixion. Thus the resolution of New Comedy

seems to be a realistic foreshortening of a death-and-res-
urrection pattern, in which the struggle and rebirth of a
divine hero has shrunk into a marriage, the freeing of a
slave, and the triumph of a young man over an older one.

As for the conception of tragedy as implicit comedy,
we may notice how often tragedy closes on the major
chord of comedy: the Aeschylean trilogy, for instance,
proceeds to what is really a comic resolution, and so do
many tragedies of Euripides. From the point of view of
Christianity, too, tragedy is an episode in that larger
scheme of redemption and resurrection to which Dante
gave the name of *commedia*. This conception of *commedia*
enters drama with the miracle-play cycles, where such
tragedies as the Fall and the Crucifixion are episodes of a
dramatic scheme in which the divine comedy has the last
word. The sense of tragedy as a prelude to comedy is
hardly separable from anything explicitly Christian. The
serenity of the final double chorus in the St. Matthew
Passion would hardly be attainable if composer and audience did not know that there was more to the story. Nor
would the death of Samson lead to "calm of mind all
passion spent" if Samson were not a prototype of the
rising Christ.

New Comedy is thus contained, so to speak, within the
symbolic structure of Old Comedy, which in its turn is
contained within the Christian conception of *commedia*.
This sounds like a logically exhaustive classification, but
we have still not caught Shakespeare in it.

It is only in Jonson and the Restoration writers that
English comedy can be called a form of New Comedy.
The earlier tradition established by Peele and developed
by Lyly, Greene, and the masque writers, which uses
themes from romance and folklore and avoids the comedy
of manners, is the one followed by Shakespeare. These
themes are largely medieval in origin, and derive, not
from the mysteries or the moralities or the interludes,
but from a fourth dramatic tradition. This is the drama
of folk ritual, of the St. George play and the mummers'
play, of the feast of the ass and the Boy Bishop, and of
all the dramatic activity that punctuated the Christian

calendar with the rituals of an immemorial paganism. We may call this the drama of the green world, and its theme is once again the triumph of life over the waste land, the death and revival of the year impersonated by figures still human, and once divine as well.

When Shakespeare began to study Plautus and Terence, his dramatic instinct, stimulated by his predecessors, divined that there was a profounder pattern in the argument of comedy than appears in either of them. At once—for the process is beginning in *The Comedy of Errors*—he started groping toward that profounder pattern, the ritual of death and revival that also underlies Aristophanes, of which an exact equivalent lay ready to hand in the drama of the green world. This parallelism largely accounts for the resemblances to Greek ritual which Colin Still has pointed out in *The Tempest.*

The Two Gentlemen of Verona is an orthodox New Comedy except for one thing. The hero Valentine becomes captain of a band of outlaws in a forest, and all the other characters are gathered into this forest and become converted. Thus the action of the comedy begins in a world represented as a normal world, moves into the green world, goes into a metamorphosis there in which the comic resolution is achieved, and returns to the normal world. The forest in this play is the embryonic form of the fairy world of *A Midsummer Night's Dream,* the Forest of Arden in *As You Like It,* Windsor Forest in *The Merry Wives of Windsor,* and the pastoral world of the mythical sea-coasted Bohemia in *The Winter's Tale.* In all these comedies there is the same rhythmic movement from normal world to green world and back again. Nor is this second world confined to the forest comedies. In *The Merchant of Venice* the two worlds are a little harder to see, yet Venice is clearly not the same world as that of Portia's mysterious house in Belmont, where there are caskets teaching that gold and silver are corruptible goods, and from whence proceed the wonderful cosmological harmonies of the fifth act. In *The Tempest* the entire action takes place in the second world, and the same may be said of *Twelfth Night,* which, as its title implies, presents

a carnival society, not so much a green world as an ever-
green one. The second world is absent from the so-called
problem comedies, which is one of the things that makes
them problem comedies.

The green world charges the comedies with a symbolism in which the comic resolution contains a suggestion
of the old ritual pattern of the victory of summer over
winter. This is explicit in *Love's Labor's Lost*. In this very
masque-like play, the comic contest takes the form of the
medieval debate of winter and spring. In *The Merry Wives
of Windsor* there is an elaborate ritual of the defeat of
winter, known to folklorists as "carrying out Death," of
which Falstaff is the victim; and Falstaff must have felt
that, after being thrown into the water, dressed up as a
witch and beaten out of a house with curses, and finally
supplied with a beast's head and singed with candles while
he said, "Divide me like a brib'd buck, each a haunch,"
he had done about all that could reasonably be asked of
any fertility spirit.

The association of this symbolism with the death and
revival of human beings is more elusive, but still percep-
tible. The fact that the heroine often brings about the
comic resolution by disguising herself as a boy is familiar
enough. In the Hero of *Much Ado About Nothing* and the
Helena of *All's Well That Ends Well*, this theme of the
withdrawal and return of the heroine comes as close to a
death and revival as Elizabethan conventions will allow.
The Thaisa of *Pericles* and the Fidele of *Cymbeline* are
beginning to crack the conventions, and with the disappearance and revival of Hermione in *The Winter's Tale*,
who actually returns once as a ghost in a dream, the original nature-myth of Demeter and Proserpine is openly
established. The fact that the dying and reviving character
is usually female strengthens the feeling that there is
something maternal about the green world, in which the
new order of the comic resolution is nourished and
brought to birth. However, a similar theme which is
very like the rejuvenation of the *senex* so frequent in
Aristophanes occurs in the folklore motif of the healing
of the impotent king on which *All's Well That Ends Well*

is based, and this theme is probably involved in the symbolism of Prospero.

The conception of a second world bursts the boundaries of Menandrine comedy, yet it is clear that the world of Puck is no world of eternal forms or divine revelation. Shakespeare's comedy is not Aristotelian and realistic like Menander's, nor Platonic and dialectic like Aristophanes', nor Thomist and sacramental like Dante's, but a fourth kind. It is an Elizabethan kind, and is not confined either to Shakespeare or to the drama. Spenser's epic is a wonderful contrapuntal intermingling of two orders of existence, one the red and white world of English history, the other the green world of the Faerie Queene. The latter is a world of crusading virtues proceeding from the Faerie Queene's court and designed to return to that court when the destiny of the other world is fulfilled. The fact that the Faerie Queene's knights are sent out during the twelve days of the Christmas festival suggests our next point.

Shakespeare too has his green world of comedy and his red and white world of history. The story of the latter is at one point interrupted by an invasion from the comic world, when Falstaff *senex et parasitus* throws his gigantic shadow over Prince Henry, assuming on one occasion the role of his father. Clearly, if the Prince is ever to conquer France he must reassert the moral norm. The moral norm is duly reasserted, but the rejection of Falstaff is not a comic resolution. In comedy the moral norm is not morality but deliverance, and we certainly do not feel delivered from Falstaff as we feel delivered from Shylock with his absurd and vicious bond. The moral norm does not carry with it the vision of a free society: Falstaff will always keep a bit of that in his tavern.

Falstaff is a mock king, a lord of misrule, and his tavern is a Saturnalia. Yet we are reminded of the original meaning of the Saturnalia, as a rite intended to recall the golden age of Saturn. Falstaff's world is not a golden world, but as long as we remember it we cannot forget that the world of *Henry V* is an iron one. We are reminded too of another traditional denizen of the green world, Robin Hood, the outlaw who manages to suggest

a better kind of society than those who make him an outlaw can produce. The outlaws in *The Two Gentlemen of
Verona* compare themselves, in spite of the Italian setting, to Robin Hood, and in *As You Like It* Charles the
wrestler says of Duke Senior's followers: "There they live
like the old Robin Hood of England: they say many
young gentlemen flock to him every day, and fleet the
time carelessly, as they did in the golden world."

In the histories, therefore, the comic Saturnalia is a
temporary reversal of normal standards, comic "relief"
as it is called, which subsides and allows the history to
continue. In the comedies, the green world suggests an
original golden age which the normal world has usurped
and which makes us wonder if it is not the normal world
that is the real Saturnalia. In *Cymbeline* the green world
finally triumphs over a historical theme, the reason being
perhaps that in that play the incarnation of Christ, which
is contemporary with Cymbeline, takes place offstage,
and accounts for the halcyon peace with which the play
concludes. From then on in Shakespeare's plays, the
green world has it all its own way, and both in *Cymbeline*
and in *Henry VIII* there may be suggestions that Shakespeare, like Spenser, is moving toward a synthesis of the
two worlds, a wedding of Prince Arthur and the Faerie
Queene.

This world of fairies, dreams, disembodied souls, and
pastoral lovers may not be a "real" world, but, if not,
there is something equally illusory in the stumbling and
blinded follies of the "normal" world, of Theseus' Athens
with its idiotic marriage law, of Duke Frederick and his
melancholy tyranny, of Leontes and his mad jealousy, of
the Court Party with their plots and intrigues. The famous
speech of Prospero about the dream nature of reality
applies equally to Milan and the enchanted island. We
spend our lives partly in a waking world we call normal
and partly in a dream world which we create out of our
own desires. Shakespeare endows both worlds with equal
imaginative power, brings them opposite one another, and
makes each world seem unreal when seen by the light
of the other. He uses freely both the heroic triumph of

New Comedy and the ritual resurrection of its predecessor, but his distinctive comic resolution is different from either: it is a detachment of the spirit born of this reciprocal reflection of two illusory realities. We need not ask whether this brings us into a higher order of existence or not, for the question of existence is not relevant to poetry.

We have spoken of New Comedy as Aristotelian, Old Comedy as Platonic and Dante's *commedia* as Thomist, but it is difficult to suggest a philosophical spokesman for the form of Shakespeare's comedy. For Shakespeare, the subject matter of poetry is not life, or nature, or reality, or revelation, or anything else that the philosopher builds on, but poetry itself, a verbal universe. That is one reason why he is both the most elusive and the most substantial of poets.

RICHARD DAVID

from *Shakespeare's Comedies and the Modern Stage*

[A study of production problems with particular reference to *Love's Labor's Lost* at the New Theatre (1949–50) . . .]

Dr. Johnson was the last critic who dared to say that Shakespeare's most characteristic and most inspired work lay in his comedies. The Romantics, putting an exaggerated value on tragedy as in some way nearer to the heart of the matter, degraded the comedies to the status of potboilers; and even today we have hardly escaped from the Romantics' spell. We have one expounder of the comedies for every ten on the tragedies; and for a Granville-Barker to stoop to *A Midsummer Night's Dream,* or an Edith Evans to Rosalind, is exceptional.

We may not agree with Johnson that the comedies deserve more effort than the tragedies, but clearly they require more if they are to make a comparable impression on a modern audience. Tragedy is large in gesture and

From *Shakespeare Survey 4* (1951), edited by Allardyce Nicoll, 129–35. Reprinted by permission of Richard David and the Cambridge University Press.

effect, and even when its overtones are lost and the subsidiary strokes bungled, its main import can hardly be missed. Comedy depends much more on detail, on delicate adjustments of balance and of contrast; it seeks to reproduce the climate rather than the actual predicaments of real life and its method is rather allusiveness than direct presentation. Comedy has more and finer points of attachment to the world in which it is composed than has tragedy. For this reason, comedy dates the more rapidly and the more thoroughly, and after a lapse of years a tragedy based even on so fantastic a convention as Fletcher's is easier to grasp than a comedy of Jonson or Middleton, for all its firm grounding in human nature. Tragedy can be understood in the original, as it were, even by those unacquainted with the tongue; whereas comedy, to be appreciated by a modern audience, must undergo some degree of translation into modern terms.

The difficulties that face the would-be translator are broadly of two kinds. Some old comedies have remained crystal clear in intention, though the details of the action and of the language through which that intention is conveyed are now largely incomprehensible without a gloss; in others, language and action are perfectly plain and yet the point of the whole has become obscure or capable of various interpretations. These peculiar difficulties are well exemplified in two distinguished recent productions, the *Love's Labor's Lost* directed by Hugh Hunt for the Old Vic Company in the winter of 1949–50, and Peter Brook's *Measure for Measure,* with which the Stratford Memorial Theatre opened its 1950 season. Whatever may be the topical implications of *Love's Labor's Lost* its main point is plain—the gentle ragging of youthful priggishness and affectation, as measured against natural good sense and natural good feeling—and it is a point that time has not dulled. Dons and donnishness are today even more popular as butts than they were in the 1590's, and the vivacity controlled by a good heart that Shakespeare praises is a virtue that does not grow stale. On the other hand, the almost Joycean reduplication of puns and the obscure allusions of the play are a byword. *Meas-*

ure for Measure is by comparison straightforwardness
itself as far as the text goes; but the arguments as to
whether the piece is comedy or problem-play, Isabella
heroine or caricature, are unending.

Even though the intention of *Love's Labor's Lost* may
be plain enough, some skill is required in the presentation
to convey it to a modern audience. The point or moral
of the play (as of so many comedies) is a code of manners, a demonstration of what rational behavior should
be by a comparison with irrational behavior. Nathaniel
is unwittingly providing an ironic commentary on himself
and his peers when he says of Dull:

> . . . such barren plants are set before us, that we thankful
>   should be,
> Which we of taste and feeling are, for those parts that do
>   fructify in us more than he.
>
> (IV.ii.29–30)

The standards set are those of taste and feeling, aristocratic standards, and the ladies must live up to them—
the lords, too, once they have come to their senses. Moreover, the audience must be conscious throughout that
the action is enclosed in a coherent and self-contained
world defined by these standards.

The coherence of the play was admirably preserved
in the Old Vic production. The sets perfectly suggested
the self-contained world of Navarre's park, shut away
among steep hillslopes down which the hanging woods
cascaded, excluding the everyday world and blanketing
every sound that might penetrate from it. Among the
trees showed the turrets of castles and hunting lodges,
each retreat and secret corner of the domain isolated
from the others by the waters of a spreading lake that
was at the same time the means of communication between them. One may criticize the elaboration and heavi-
ness of this set. It was no doubt suggested by the back-
grounds to Elizabethan miniatures, the more extended
works of Hillyard or of Oliver; but enlarged to backcloth
scale the effect was baroque rather than renaissance, more

Jacobean than Elizabethan. It accorded well with the autumnal ending of the play, but hardly with the green goose season of its opening. The devotees are solemn enough, but their solemnity must be seen to be against nature; the landscape (if we must have one) should be a laughing landscape that mocks their sober suits and matches the frills and freshness of the ladies through whose eyes we judge them. And yet the sense of a private and self-sufficient world, so successfully achieved in this production, owed much to the swathing and insistent scenery.

The structure of the play is uncomplicated. The first three acts present the situation and the opposing parties in bold and simple colors. Act IV is a helter-skelter with everyone at cross purposes, diversified by the to and fro of the hunt and the entrances of the comics. The long last scene builds up slowly but steadily, becoming more and more fantastic and ebullient until the appearance of Marcade bursts the bubble in an instant; this is one of the greatest *coups de théâtre* in Shakespeare, and it brings, after the whirlwind of fooling that has preceded it, the still small voice of sincerity and actuality before the play dissolves in thin air and birdsong. Hugh Hunt divided the whole naturally enough into three movements, each set in a different part of the labyrinthine park. In the first the nobles of Navarre made their pact to forego female company, and rated Costard the clown for his transgression of it; at the same spot Armado wandered ashore, from a boat paddled by Moth, to meet the disquieting vision of Jaquenetta; here too the ladies of the French embassy, advancing through the forest glades, were intercepted by Navarre and his courtiers. The focus of the second movement was a rustic cottage, again by the waterside, which provided shelter for Armado's lovesick meditations, and a prison for Costard; after the hunt arranged for the entertainment of the French ladies had swept by, it served as a convenient hiding place from which the eavesdropping lords could overhear each other's confession of forbidden love, and a rendezvous for Armado and the other devisers of his pageant. The last movement (that is, the last scene of the play) opened with the ladies idling outside their pavilion; to them the masques of the Russians and of the Nine Worthies; and over the lake at their back, when the merriment was at its height, loomed the barge that brings the funereal Marcade with his news of the French King's death to cloud the scene. The management of this effect was overwhelmingly successful, as was the quiet recapitulation of the lovers' problems that follows, and the final fading of the play in trills and falling darkness. This by itself was full justification for both setting and production.

Such elaborate dressing and marshaling of the action, though foreign to Shakespeare's theater, is legitimate as the just translation of his intention into modern terms. The original audience of a coterie play or a play of manners (and *Love's Labor's Lost* is in some sense this) is specially conditioned, by the community of interests it shares with the author, to appreciate the mood of his work and accept his illusion. A modern audience, unused even to the unifying and sharpening effect of verse, may well be encouraged to draw the same sense of characteristic atmosphere from scenery and direction. In some of his efforts to this end Hunt nevertheless went outside his brief.

The play must open with a tableau of the lords signing their solemn declaration. It is tidy and elegant to balance this, at the point where the ladies are to take over the lead, with a similar tableau of the feminine party, and the last movement in the Old Vic production accordingly opened with a "still" of the ladies outside their pavilion. Shakespeare, however, has made no allowance for this, nor has he provided accompanying action. What are the ladies to do? They shall sing a song in chorus. This is "pretty and apt," but something irrelevant has been added to Shakespeare.

There were other instances of this striving to impose an extra formality on an already formal play. The second movement was rounded off—after Armado and Holofernes had completed their plans for the pageant—with a burlesque dance in which *all* the comics joined. Now it may be appropriate, as Granville-Barker has suggested, that Dull should here dance a few steps of his hay to show what he thinks is a suitable entertainment for the gentlefolk; but for Armado or Holofernes, who has just expressed his disgust at Dull's low suggestion, to take part in it is to deny their nature, and at this point of the play they must still be true to themselves. At the end, when comedy slips imperceptibly into vaudeville, let them dance their jig if you will. A more blatant, though less serious, reversal of Shakespeare's intention for the sake of spectacle occurred in the last movement, when the Russian maskers are begging the ladies for a dance. "Play music then," says the mock princess. "Nay, you must do it soon. Not yet? No dance. Thus change I like the moon." In the Old Vic production a formal dance did in fact follow the words "Play music then," and continued some time before Rosaline, resuming her broken speech, brought the measure to an end. Yet it is clear that the lords, though constantly tantalized into thinking that the ladies may dance with them, are as constantly put off. Ten lines later the King is still begging the "princess" to begin.

Such dislocations, the first of dramatic propriety, the second of literal meaning, could hardly be justified even if the added dances succeeded perfectly in reinforcing the tone or continuity of the action. Here they had the opposite effect. The movements were perfunctory, the music feeble and banal to a degree. Yet even perfectly designed music and choreography would here have been an intrusion, a formal element introduced just where the text avoids it. Shakespeare has given plenty of opportunities in this play for formality, and we have now to see the opposite error, of trying to break down a given artificiality and make the scenes of spectacle "come to life." The tableaux, or scenes of ceremony, demand some supporting cast, and no doubt Shakespeare gave his king and princess as large a train of attendants as his company could muster. The sole function of these extras, however, is to add weight and volume to the dignity of their masters, and any attempt to give depth to the scene by making individuals of them is totally un-Shakespearian. A tendency to "work up" the crowd is one of the most dangerous features of modern productions of Shakespeare. In *Love's Labor's Lost,* it is true, there was nothing to equal the horrors of Komisarjevsky's *King Lear,* in which the hundred knights, vociferously echoing their master's "Return with her?," effectively broke not only the rhythm but the mounting tension of one of Shakespeare's greatest dramatic crescendos. The interpolations which the ladies were allowed to make in Boyet's reading of Armado's love letter were exactly similar but in this context harmless; while the caperings and posturings and beard-waggings of the burlesque philosophers in Navarre's train, which were employed to "lighten" the King's first speech and his reception of the ladies' embassy, were not so much destroying Shakespeare's intention, as grossly overplaying it. The solemn performance of Navarre and his peers has indeed its anti-masque; but that is later provided by Armado, Holofernes and Nathaniel and no duplication of it is needed. It was again an overzealous striving for vigor and variety that made a pantomime of the hunting scene.

Finally, a rather different form of overemphasis. At the beginning of the last scene the ladies' lighthearted chatter about Cupid suddenly steadies as Rosaline says to Katharine:

> You'll ne'er be friends with him, 'a killed your sister.

Katharine's reply introduces the first note of seriousness into the play:

> He made her melancholy, sad, and heavy—
> And so she died: had she been light, like you,
> Of such a merry, nimble, stirring spirit,
> She might ha' been a grandam ere she died.

Hunt properly seized on this as a forecast of the serious mood of the end of the play. For a moment the sun is hidden by a forerunner of those clouds that are later to overcast the scene, and we get a premonition of love's labor *lost*. This is admirable; but the mood was unduly prolonged in the repartee that follows between the two girls, which was worked up into a real quarrel, so that the Princess' "I beshrew all shrows" had to be delivered *tutta forza* in order to quell it. This gave a change of tempo and color, and showed us a new side of Rosaline's character, a hard shrewish side; but at this stage of the play neither the action nor the character has been sufficiently developed to bear this elaboration, and the only result was to turn the audience against so viperish a heroine.

This prolonged analysis of faults has been undertaken to show how the producer with the very best intentions —of giving continuity or variety to his play—may achieve the exact opposite. In general, however, the total mood of the play—buoyant, lyrical, penetrating, extravagant— had been so firmly and truly established by both producer and actors that it could not be shattered by incidental "wrong notes." As Elizabethans and as courtiers the ladies were perhaps more convincing than the men, who had a touch of the hobbledehoy about them; but that did little harm in a play wherein the ladies must show a superiority of wit and grace throughout, for all that their task is the harder, since there is less of substance in their badinage and only an exactly calculated bravura of speech and movement can carry it off. The greater delicacy of the ladies' playing was, however, counterbalanced by Michael Redgrave's performance as Berowne. He succeeded not only in conveying the wit, the wisdom and the vitality of the man, but in making him completely sympathetic to the audience. The great set speech of act IV, Scene i—"And I forsooth in love," in which he takes the audience into his confidence, was a *tour de force*. The speech is by no means easy, for many of its terms and turns of expression are obsolete today; but by treating it simply and directly, by trusting himself to the words (and his confidence clearly grew with practice), he made its point clear and its effect captivating.

The comic performances in no way betrayed the standard set by those of the straight parts, although (as, alas, so often happens) their unnecessary business seemed to increase and to get more out of hand as the run of the play proceeded. George Benson gave us the perfect Costard; would that all players of Shakepearian clowns were as direct and bold and true to the text as this. On the other hand, the Holofernes and the Nathaniel were rather translations into modern equivalents—a Will Hay or a Groucho Marx with his stooge. This is legitimate; the Crazy Gang or the Itma comics are today the closest in line of descent to the figures of the Commedia dell'arte from whom the fantastics of *Love's Labor's Lost* derive. The only characters that were totally off key were Armado and Moth, presented as a seedy Don Quixote and a ragged urchin. Now it is of the essence of both figures that they are of the Court (Dull and Costard are quite enough to represent the bumpkins). Armado is as much an exquisite as Osric. It is part of the joke that his finery is only on the surface (he cannot afford a shirt) but his every effort goes into maintaining the *appearance* of finery, and finery it is. Moth is the cheeky page boy, a "cit" if ever there was one, and a diminutive echo of his master's finicking fashion. The humor of their interchanges, already precarious after the lapse of three and a half centuries, fades utterly if they are presented not as the lightning duels of court rapiers but as the rustic's solemn game of quarterstaff.

This brings us to the consideration of the topical jokes and private humors that make up so large a part of the dialogue, particularly between the farcical characters, and present the second and more troublesome problem to any would-be translator for the modern stage. There would seem to be four ways of dealing with this largely deadwood: (1) to cut the passage altogether; (2) to accompany it with some entirely extraneous piece of business, in the hope that this will distract attention from the words, which are "thrown away" as best may be; (3) to have the words spoken against music which will render them inaudible; (4) to try the passage straight and hope that *someone* will see, or pretend to see, the joke—at least the purists will be satisfied. The purists of course will object strongly to the first solution, but I do not see how with some passages it can be avoided if the performance of the play is to be living entertainment and not merely a (possibly edifying) ritual. Solutions two and three are clearly abominable, and though one would like always to see the direct method given a trial there are some things it cannot save. The trouble is that producers will differ in their judgment of what can be saved and what must be cut, and most of them are likely to err on the side of pessimism.

The Old Vic production used all four methods. Of the seven cruces that have notoriously baffled or divided commentators only two, the "envoy" of the fox, the ape and the humble-bee, and the play of Holofernes and Moth on "piercing a hogshead," were cut (and rightly cut) *in toto*. The "tender juvenal," the "school of night," and the "charge-house on the mountain" were all given their chance, perhaps in the belief that their ill fame was too great for them to be ignored. Armado's odd salutation —"Chirrah"—was also left in, together with the reference to an eel that so strangely annoys him on his first appearance. This proved a dangerous course, however, at least in the case of the eel, for with the disappearance of the real occasion of the joke it was necessary to drop Armado's inexplicable irritation at it ("Thou heat'st my blood") and invent a new cue for it. Moth therefore made his entrance carrying a real eel, which he might be supposed recently to have fished out of the encircling lake; and I suspect this detail conditioned the producer's whole view of Moth's (and, with him, Armado's) appearance and status, which I have already tried to show were misconceived.

Some other jokes, of which the point is known but cannot be explained without a considerable gloss, were also wisely cut: Moth's play with the four complexions, his skirmish with Holofernes over sheep and vowels, and most of the "greasy" talk between Boyet and Maria at the end of the hunting scene. There was little excuse, however, for devoting to the same extinction such simple puns as those on style, stile and climbing in the merriness, or the frequent and pertinent comments on the fantastics' inability to count; and it was surely strange, if these were to go, that such obvious interpolations as the duplicated versions of the lovers' first dialogues, and Costard's comments on a vanished entry for Armado and Moth in the hunting scene, should have been spared to puzzle us.

Of the second method of dealing with an obscure passage, the introduction of distracting business, there were three prominent examples, two of them particularly unhappy. It was perhaps allowable that Dull, in the midst of Nathaniel's wordy tirade on his insensitivity, should be discovered to be carrying, apparently without being aware of it or discommoded by it, an arrow from the hunt still firmly embedded in his posterior. This is at least a fair gloss on Nathaniel's "only sensible in the duller parts"; but the disproportionate laughter it aroused in the audience shattered the continuity of the scene and the delicate balance between its actors. The other two instances of this technique were unhappy because the jokes so painstakingly masked remain perfectly valid ones today and if allowed to make their own effect would have raised greater and more relevant amusement than their substitutes. When Jaquenetta brings Berowne's letter to Nathaniel to interpret, Holofernes is consumed with curiosity to see it but feels it would be beneath his dignity to look over the Curate's shoulder. He therefore pretends to be very much absorbed in his own thoughts, on a plane far above mere mundane affairs. He murmurs (incorrectly) a verse from Mantuan, hums the notes of the scale (again wrongly) all the time striving, under cover of this pretended abstraction, to get a glimpse of the letter. In the Old Vic production all this was thrown away to the accompaniment of a stupid piece of byplay in which Nathaniel tried surreptitiously to put his arm round the trusting Jaquenetta and found himself embracing Costard instead. This is entirely out of character for the Curate, while the Pedant's itch to meddle, sacrificed for it, is a typical and essential trait. Again, when the comics return from the dinner to which Holofernes has invited Nathaniel to witness his eloquence, the Curate is more than ever impressed by his host's superior learning. When Holofernes utters a particularly choice word Nathaniel, according to a direction in the original First Quarto text, draws out his notebook and with admiring comments records the *trouvaille*. In place of this characteristic and revealing action, Hunt made his players enter as if tipsy, and for the unction and the notebook of the toady substituted slurred syllables and some sorry business with a bottle. This is presumption.

To resort to the third way out, on the other hand, is the rankest cowardice, and it speaks well for the Old Vic production that this all too popular device was only used once, for the admittedly involved and paradoxical lines in which Boyet describes to the ladies how, Navarre having fallen in love at first sight, all his faculties are concentrated in his longing gaze. This speech was half chanted to a musical accompaniment to which Boyet's audience swayed in time. The effect was odious, but it was certainly impossible that many words should be caught, much less interpreted. It was perhaps surprising that the producer should have funked this passage when such teasers as "Light seeking light doth light of light beguile," and many of the "sets of wit," were left to take care of themselves, and did so very nicely.

JOHN ARTHOS

Love's Labor's Lost on the Stage

Love's Labor's Lost was written about 1595, but the first printing, in quarto, is dated 1598: "A Pleasant Conceited Comedie Called, Loues labors lost. As it was presented before her Highnes this last Christmas. Newly corrected and augmented By *W. Shakespere*."

A certain irony attaches to the next production of the play, which was offered as part of the Christmas festivities of 1604. The Earl of Southampton, having been imprisoned for his part in the plot of Essex against Queen Elizabeth, in celebrating his release by King James entertained the King and Queen at his house with a production of the play. There was an agreeable humor in choosing a play in which the chief male persons, men of royal and noble rank, propose to abandon life in the great world in order to pursue a celibate existence in an academy, a theme not wholly incongruous under the circumstances. The humor would have been apparent to the King, and what is topical in the play—in particular references to relations between England and France—also would have suggested matters of interest to the King.

The second quarto (1631) tells that the play was publicly acted at the Black-Friars and the Globe, but no record of these productions is known to survive. There is no mention of a performance of the play in Henslowe's and Pepys's diaries, and Genest, who surveyed all productions of Shakespeare's plays from 1642 till 1830, found no notice of *Love's Labor's Lost* in all that time.

Explanations for the neglect of the work center upon the opinion that the wordplay was so pervasive and complex that it was not stageworthy. There was also the frequent judgment that the supposed topicality was obscure and distracting. The critical reservations expressed by Hazlitt and Coleridge may also have been influential.

Madame Vestris, however, a gifted and popular actress, saw in the play the opportunity to make the most of the women's parts and put it on in the new Olympic theatre in London in 1839. Although it was praised, it held the stage for only a few days, despite what was said to have been a talented cast.

The next notices available are of productions at Sadler's Wells in 1857 and, surprisingly, at the Arch Street Theater in Philadelphia in 1858. And it was in the United States, at Augustin Daly's theater in New York—in 1873 and again in 1891—that the marvelous quality of the work was evidently understood and appreciated. The liberties Daly took with the text were considerable, yet one may judge from the prefatory remarks attached to the prompter's copy that they were as thoughtfully conceived as they were successful. For example: "The pageant is transposed to the end of the comedy, which closes with one of the sweetest of all the Shakespeare melodies and leaves its spectators with a mental vision of all the lovely spring flowers that grow on Avon's banks." *The New York Herald*'s critic was most enthusiastic:

The skill with which the sense of atmosphere and expanse was given to the forest scenes was delightful. The tableau of winter showed an ice-hung scene, in the midst of which a snow-clad figure sang the strongly picturesque lines beginning 'When icicles hang'. Spring was indicated by a Watteau tableau of great brilliancy. Cunning shepherds and shepherdesses sat on mossy elevations, fountains gurgled, arbors twined, gloomily green vistas opened, dazzling flowers and foliage spread seeming fragrance and rich growth, and over all fell a shower of changing light. The acting was respectable throughout, with special excellence in the case of Miss Dyas, whose refinement, intelligence and vivacity exhausted all the significance contained in the role of the Princess. . . . The costumes were brilliant beyond all precedent and description. From beginning to end, the comedy was placed upon the stage in the most generous and splendid style.

With such a success one might have believed the play would be entering upon a new life in the theater, but there was to be, in fact, another long dry spell before *Love's Labor's Lost* was to establish its appeal securely, and we may only conclude that the times were not yet ripe for it despite this remarkable example.

There is no record of another production before the one at the Old Vic in 1906 and another at Stratford in 1907. There were three productions at the Old Vic in the next thirty years, but Tyrone Guthrie's in 1936 was accounted a failure even with Edith Evans as Rosaline and Michael Redgrave as the King of Navarre. There were a few successes at the Open Air Theatre in Regent's Park. It was only in 1946 that Peter Brook's "landmark" production demonstrated such attractive qualities in the work that it is credited with leading the way for the more than ninety productions in the English-speaking world in the next three decades.

Brook had seen a production in French at the Odéon in Paris in 1945 in which the pictorial potentialities of the play were effectively developed. J. Dapoigny had devised settings and provided costumes with the paintings of Watteau in mind: "The style of Watteau's dresses with its broad undecorated expanses of billowing satin seemed the ideal visual correlative of the essential sweet-sad mood of the play." (It is a curious coincidence that Daly's production had brought Watteau to the mind of the New York critic.)

Still, more than a pictorial emphasis was involved,

however, in the stimulus Brook took from this production. The theories and practices of Artaud and Genet were also involved in the French adaptation, and Brook was evidently inspired by the rejection of naturalism and in particular by the refusal to be bound by the constraints imposed when adhering to normal time patterns. To begin with, this meant to Brook that a Shakespeare play should not be offered as a period piece; it should be wholly free of antiquarian appeal. He has made the point this way, in *The Empty Space*: "I dressed the character called the Constable Dull as a Victorian policeman because his name conjured up the typical figure of the London bobby. For other reasons the rest of the characters were dressed in Watteau-eighteenth-century clothes, but no one was conscious of an anachronism." He put the case in this way: the aim of drama is toward "immediacy." "A representation is the occasion when something is represented that once was, now is. For representation is not an imitation or a description of a past event, a representation denies time. It abolishes the difference between yesterday and today."

The success of Brook's production of *Love's Labor's Lost* was thus in part the success of the new drama, leading the way to other productions of the play that were to be equally free of the constraints of naturalistic imitation and as open to transformation. The example was evidently so attractive that in the years following it was a rare undertaking, such as the reputedly exquisite staging of Hugh Hunt's in 1949 at the New Theater, that aimed to capture the atmosphere of an Elizabethan production, although here, too, the pictorial emphasis Brook had made so much of was key to the success of this production, Hunt following Nicholas Hillyard rather than Watteau. He also stressed the lyrical potentialities of the work, even in the humorous exchanges, and with such emphasis on choreography as to recall the manner of masques. Hunt was profoundly obligated to the doctrine Granville-Barker enunciated in his essay on *Love's Labor's Lost*:

The actor, in fine, must think of the dialogue in terms of music; of the tune and rhythm of it as at one with the sense—sometimes outbidding the sense—in telling him what to do and how to do it, in telling him, indeed, what to *be*.

A City Center production in New York in 1953 gave the play a quasi-Oscar Wilde tone but with very turn-of-the-century furnishings—the ladies made their entrance in an ancient roadster, there was a gramophone with a great horn, a crooked croquet game, pleasing some critics but not Wolcott Gibbs and Brooks Atkinson. Brook's principles had gone astray, as they were to in several of the new ventures. What might have sustained the satirical intent of the play sometimes ended in travesty, as one may judge in Bernard Beckerman's account of the 1968 production in Stratford, Connecticut:

The academy was the retreat of a guru. Berowne, Longaville, and Dumaine were fashionable young men come to share the retreat with the Maharishi King of Navarre. Probably stimulated by the adventures of the Beatles in yoga-land, Dumaine turned out to be a rock-singer. Holofernes, in what I assume to be a parody of Mahatma Gandhi, wore silver-rimmed spectacles and a diaper-like sheet. And the ladies of France were cycle-riding, fast-moving members of the jet-set, chaperoned by a swishing Boyet chattering in a deep South drawl.

The BBC telecast in 1985 developed a similar kind of transformation, but on this occasion the television frame itself set limits on what can be done pictorially with what was originally a stage play. As the producer saw it, this limitation precluded any disposition to offer settings in the open country or in a park. The beautiful pastoral setting was obliterated, the Academy and the pavilion became, the reviewer said, "a cold-lit library, across whose chilly spaces—littered with frigid statuary and leathern tomes—tread bewigged would-be *philosophes*."

Recently the wheel seems to have come full circle in the

1984 production of the Royal Shakespeare Company, or so it seemed to Giles Gordon:

> To me, *Love's Labor's Lost* is one of the supreme glories of dramatic art, the equal of that most essential of operas, Mozart's *Cosí fan Tutte*. The wit, brio and erudition of the verbal music are marvelous to experience. The stage is washed in white leaves which, from the first entrance of the princess of France and her court, suggests spring until the end, the arrival of the Messenger of Death, when Autumn gives way to Winter and icicles hang by the wall, and Dick the shepherd blows his nail.

Pace Brook, the sequential is once again at the heart of the play, although it is only fair to observe that the costumes were nineteenth century and the setting Chekhovian.

Quite as significant as the experimenting that followed Brook's example was the increasing recognition of the excellence of the play, as theater and as poetry. It was put into the hands of the best actors and actresses—Olivier, Derek Jacobi, Joan Plowright, Ian Richardson, Paul Scofield, to single out but a few. Again and again the word "exquisite" is applied to the conceits and humor that engage the characters, to the sequences that call for dance-like movements—not only in the mask but from the very beginning, as in the San Diego production of 1962, described by Eleanor Prosser:

> The brilliant choreography of Shirlee Dodge combined with creative direction to make this the artistic triumph of the season. The high style of dance was established in the opening scenes. To the accompaniment of music from the balcony, servants scurried from the center curtains in balanced patterns, setting up an abacus, a telescope, and a globe. The dance movement and the pretty artificiality of the props (a powder-blue telescope?) against a background of crystalline trees set the stage for Navarre's foolish game.

And at the end the musical impetus was irresistible:

Accompanied solely by Don Armado on the tabor and two lonely recorders, the cast sang of the owl and the cuckoo while the lovers moved through a series of measured dances. Bernard Windt had written new music for the song, two haunting melodies in a minor key, sung first in unison, then antiphonally by the divided cast banked on each side of the stage, and then together in a round. As the singers and the song faded through the side doors and the light gradually dimmed, one by one each couple parted in the center, still in dance, until finally only Rosaline and Berowne were left—each pausing at the side door for a final look and a gentle salute of promise and yet regret, before leaving the stage to hushed darkness and the night.

And finally, as so much talent and intelligence were lavished upon a play that had been so long neglected, so the humor and the wordplay that had once been supposed to be a drawback came to be understood as wonderfully effective dramatically. No one has pointed this out better than Richard David, unless it be the actors themselves, such as Paul Scofield and Tony Church:

David Jones, it seemed to me in the 1973 production of the Royal Shakespeare Company, had seized the essential fact that Shakespeare's comic effects are almost always very strongly visual; get these visual effects right, and the words will fall into place of themselves. Take one of the simplest, Armado and Moth: the basic jest is the mere juxtaposition of the lofty, slow-moving, and solemn Spaniard with his diminutive quicksilver page. The verbal altercations between Armado and Moth are little more than elaborations of the fundamental contrast between dignity and impudence. Or take the scene where Jacquenetta asks the Parson to interpret Berowne's letter which was mistakenly delivered to her instead of to Rosaline. The schoolmaster, convinced that he is the only man present who is competent to deal with the written word, itches to be involved but has to pretend to be thinking of higher things while he edges himself into the act. His impatience, his various mumming routines to cover his real intentions, and his efforts to look over the Parson's shoulder, are *visual* comedy. . . . The essentials of these and other comic scenes were given so clear a visual projection that they were able to carry any amount of verbal superstructure.

In short, the recent history of the play upon the stage justifies the judgment made upon it as beautifully and wonderfully conceived. But it has been a rocky road, and in some aspects still is. In 1733 when Theobald completed his edition of the play he wrote in exasperation: "I have now done with this Play, which in the Main may be call'd a very bad One: and I have found it so very troublesome in the Corruptions, that, I think, I may conclude with the old religious Editors, *Deo gratias!*" As for some of the modern versions, the reception has been less than complimentary, as W. L. Godshalk summarizes: "The more recent productions of *Love's Labor's Lost*, especially those of the 1960's and 1970's, are marked by a general distrust of the play on its merits, for what it attempts to say and its ability to do so." Godshalk gives examples, and then says:

Such corruptions of the text seem to imply that the productions become, in the words of Vincent Canby, " 'such a flat denial of the original that it becomes an elaborate apology for anyone's being caught alive doing the play'." Brooks Atkinson was no more forgiving: "After a glimpse of *Love's Labor's Lost*, which opened at the City Center last evening, it is easy to see why this Shakespearean comedy had not been played since 1891."

All the same it is certain that the play now has a secure place in the repertory. Colleges and universities as well as the professional theaters are putting it on, many of the productions truly imaginative. It is increasingly understood that this comic treatment of some cultivated young bloods, as Granville-Barker spoke of them, is as rich in intellectuality as in antics, and that the gloriously beautiful song at the end has been prepared for by a sustained articulation of ideas.

William Shakespeare

THE
TWO GENTLEMEN
OF VERONA

Edited by Bertrand Evans

Contents

Introduction

Perhaps more than any other work of Shakespeare's, *The Two Gentlemen of Verona* needs to be taken for what it is: a product of its time written by a young poet-dramatist seeking his way in what was for him a new genre. So understood, it requires no defense and no apology.

The genre was romantic comedy, in the sense we mean when we mention the masterpieces that would follow in quick succession—*The Merchant of Venice, Much Ado About Nothing, As You Like It,* and *Twelfth Night.* The date of *The Two Gentlemen of Verona* is uncertain; the play may have been written as early as 1590–91, or as late as 1594–95. Most likely it was written in about 1592–93. But however late or early, within these extremes, it was for Shakespeare the first of a kind. Probably the only comedy he had written before it was *The Comedy of Errors,* a generally more satisfactory work than this, but one of an essentially different species, which gave him little practice toward the new kind that he was attempting. For the *Errors* he had a model, a good one, made by a master craftsman of Latin comedy, Plautus. Though Shakespeare injected certain romantic elements into this model, or grafted them onto it, the finished work remained rather more Plautine than Shakespearean, more a succession of farcical incidents than a pattern woven of romance elements.

And in the unlikely event that *The Two Gentlemen of Verona* followed rather than preceded *Love's Labor's*

Lost[1] and *The Taming of the Shrew*, it must yet be said that Shakespeare gained from these very little practice toward his new genre. *Love's Labor's Lost* was aimed satirically at fashionable but outlandish excesses in courtly language, manners, and ideas, and to the exploitation of these excesses the elements of romance were only incidental. The main plot of the *Shrew*, that of the taming, had no place at all for romance, in either atmosphere or action; it was hilarious farce, done in burlesque proportions. Nor did the secondary plot, that of the competition for Bianca, offer happy accommodation to the spirit and mood of romance; it turned upon a game of "supposes," in which only the attitudes of farce could be at home.

Whether before or after *Love's Labor's Lost* and *The Taming of the Shrew*, then, it was with *The Two Gentlemen of Verona* that Shakespeare found the way that led to the ultimate *Twelfth Night*. The basic stuff of romance, of course, lay around him everywhere, in prose and verse, in English, French, Spanish, and Italian, in medieval and in contemporary tellings and retellings. Long before *The Two Gentlemen of Verona* was written, the materials of romance had grown enamored of specific themes and encrusted with specific conventions. The theme of conflict between friendship and love was one that Chaucer had used and that was used again and again, in various forms of romantic tale and in various countries; indeed, Shakespeare's own sonnets play variations upon this theme, in the shadowy outline of a story that they tell of friendship between young men, of jealousy and separation occasioned by love of a third person, and finally of reconciliation. Lyly in his *Euphues*, Sidney in his *Arcadia*, less well-known contemporary romancers and translators all contributed to make the matters of romance, their themes and conventions, familiar to everyone who read or listened, familiar enough, indeed, that in any

---

[1] For an argument to the contrary, suggesting that *Love's Labors Lost* may be as early as 1588, see Alfred Harbage, "*Love's Labor's Lost* and the Early Shakespeare," *Philological Quarterly*, XLI (1962), 18–36.

"new" romance, how a friend or lover, hero or heroine would behave in a given situation might be foretold with considerable accuracy.

What Shakespeare undertook in *The Two Gentlemen of Verona* was the experimental task of adapting the materials, themes, and conventions of meandering narrative romance (or of lyric verse) to dramatic form—to create action that might be contained in two hours, characters sufficiently credible that they might be represented by corporeal actors on a stage, a "world" of sufficient density to sustain both the action and the characters. For what he attempted there was nothing like a satisfactory precedent. For *The Comedy of Errors* he had had Plautus' *Menaechmi;* for the new genre of romantic comedy, he had nothing more suitable than, say, Lyly's *Endimion,* which was useful in every way except the one way that was needed; instead of being dramatically solid, *Endimion* was as watery as the moon.

For his principal story he turned to the tale of her life told by the shepherdess Felismena, in the *Diana Enamorada* of Jorge de Montemayor, of which the relevant portions are reprinted after the text in this edition of the play. But in fact the whole reservoir of romance served him, inevitably, whether he would or no. Its conventions, intruding, have made three centuries of critics of *The Two Gentlemen* wince: How could Proteus have been so dastardly as to betray, in an instant, his beloved, his friend, and his royal host—not to mention his own honor? How could Valentine so abruptly forgive his disloyal friend all his trespasses? How could he as quickly proffer his beloved Silvia to the miscreant Proteus who only a moment before threatened to rape her? How could Silvia—the daughter of a duke—stand by without a word during this base interchange? How could Julia, after this exhibition of general dastardliness, on the second or third bounce, welcome back her errant lover?

Indeed, very nearly the sole good thing that critics have found it appropriate to say about *The Two Gentlemen of Verona* is that it was a kind of "dry run" for its great successors, anticipating in many of its details the incidents, persons, and relationships the more masterful delineation of which distinguishes the later romantic comedies. It is impossible to do other than concur—in part—with this view of the play as proving ground for the later, greater works; in fact, we have already gone somewhat beyond concurrence by flatly stating that in this play Shakespeare found the way to *Twelfth Night*. That alone should be praise enough, for it allows to *The Two Gentlemen* the same kind and degree of significance that we allow to *Julius Caesar* when we say that in it Shakespeare first worked out the basic pattern of order and relationships that we have in mind when we speak of "Shakespearean" tragedy.

It is appropriate, therefore, that we review some of the ways in which this first of the romantic comedies prepared for those to come. Perhaps it is just to say that in most cases it furnished no more than an artist's preliminary sketches for the fuller, finished portraits of character, incident, and "world" that would come after. But at the same time that we review these, we should consider whether anything contains merit and deserves praise for itself, aside from being a "first."

A good place to begin is with the heroine. Shakespeare did not invent the bright, daring girl of the comedies who, for one reason or another, casts off the outward signs of her sex and personal identity and goes a-masquerading in the world as a man; she existed already in the romances, both in those on which he directly drew for plot and in others which exercised a pervasive influence merely by existing. But in the romances she is a shadowy, pale, and bloodless abstraction that does not come alive enough to be visualized; she would never do on any stage. Shakespeare's creation, in Julia, of the flesh-and-blood heroine who set a great line going was a tremendous achievement. The world of the romantic comedies is a woman's world, and it is dominated by this recurrent figure who masquerades as a man while all of her womanliness is apparent to the audience, which is always aware of her secret. While each belongs to the line, each superlative heroine also has a life that is peculiarly her own. Portia of *The Merchant of Venice*, Rosalind of *As You Like It*, Viola of *Twelfth Night*—these can properly be likened to one another only in the common role they play, in specific recurrent situations in which they take part, and in a kind of brilliance they share that marks them as extraordinary human beings: yet this very brilliance varies markedly in its quality, showing in one as a grand and dignified capability, in another as a mischievous brightness, and in another as a gently feminine and utterly disarming subtlety.

No doubt each of these represents as much of an improvement on Julia as Julia does upon the nebulous female of the prose romances. Nearly every incident in which Julia takes part will be repeated in richer detail by one or more of the later heroines, and just because we are so busy noting the resemblances of the first version to the later ones, and mentally comparing the earlier —to its disadvantage, of course—with the later, we may overlook the peculiar charm of this first heroine herself as she plays her part. Thus in I.ii, Julia's review of the "fair resort of gentlemen" who "every day with parle encounter me" appears a puny forerunner of Portia's review, with Nerissa, of her suitors at Belmont; for one reason, in the latter version Shakespeare knew to give the witty descriptive lines to Portia, not Nerissa, whereas in this first sketch Julia merely asks the questions and it is Lucetta who furnishes the witty replies. But it is in the incident of the letter—an incident that is *not* repeated and thereby shamed by later versions—that we come suddenly upon the fresh and ingratiating charm by which Julia bursts out of the conventions among which the insipid heroines of prose romance move, and comes quite alive; no doubt, this was the first glimpse afforded by the English stage of a new and magnificent creature, the heroine of romantic comedy. The incident immediately follows the review of potential suitors. Lucetta presents a letter from Proteus, and Julia stretches to the tiptoes of indignation in upbraiding her:

> Now, by my modesty, a goodly broker!
> Dare you presume to harbor wanton lines?
> To whisper and conspire against my youth?
> Now, trust me, 'tis an office of great worth,
> And you an officer fit for the place.
> There, take the paper; see it be returned,
> Or else return no more into my sight.
>
> (I.ii.41–47)

This show of spunk is itself worth a good deal; the pale heroine of romance could never have risen to it. Yet the heroine of Shakespearean romantic comedy is not truly born until the next instant, after Lucetta has left the stage; then, thus she speaks:

> And yet I would I had o'erlooked the letter.
> It were a shame to call her back again,
> And pray her to a fault for which I chid her.
> What fool is she, that knows I am a maid,
> And would not force the letter to my view!
>
> (I.ii.50–54)

Shakespeare could definitely have stopped the incident at this; it would have been enough to establish a new institution. But he goes on: Julia calls back Lucetta, takes the letter from her, and, in a simply superb demonstration of the chastity of mind appropriate to highborn ladies in the presence of their lessers, tears it all to bits. Shakespeare could have stopped here, too; it would have been more than enough. But once more he goes on: Lucetta is again dismissed—and in an instant Julia is down on the floor, scrambling to reassemble the pieces:

> Be calm, good wind, blow not a word away
> Till I have found each letter in the letter,
> Except mine own name: that some whirlwind bear
> Unto a ragged, fearful-hanging rock,
> And throw it thence into the raging sea!
>
> (I.ii.118–22)

In later scenes Julia repeatedly breaks the way for her

great successors. In II.vii, she takes the plunge for all of them: she decides to go to Milan, to check on her—of course!—completely faithful Proteus; but not in her own identity:

> Not like a woman, for I would prevent
> The loose encounters of lascivious men.
> Gentle Lucetta, fit me with such weeds
> As may beseem some well-reputed page.
>
> (II.vii.40–43)

This was a fateful step. Soon Portia would say to Nerissa,

> I'll hold thee any wager,
> When we are both accoutred like young men,
> I'll prove the prettier fellow of the two . . .
>
> (*Merchant of Venice*, III.iv.62–64)

Rosalind would say to Celia,

> Were it not better,
> Because that I am more than common tall,
> That I did suit me all points like a man?
> A gallant curtle-ax upon my thigh,
> A boar-spear in my hand . . .
>
> (*As You Like It*, I.iii.112–16)

And Viola would say to the Captain, who fished her out of the deep,

> Conceal me what I am, and be my aid
> For such disguise as haply shall become
> The form of my intent. I'll serve this duke . . .
>
> (*Twelfth Night*, I.ii.53–55)

The parallels of this kind are numerous. Like all three of her famed successors, Julia talks with her loved one, who knows her not. Like Viola, she is sent as an envoy of love by her truelove to *his* love. Like Portia, she receives from his finger the ring that she gave him. Like Rosalind, she all but gives away her sex by swooning at a crucial time. And like all the others, she gets her love at last on terms of uncompromising surrender:

> What is in Silvia's face, but I may spy
> More fresh in Julia's with a constant eye?
> . . . .
> Bear witness, Heaven, I have my wish forever.
>
> (V.iv.114–15, 119)

In every parallel incident, she suffers from the inevitable comparison, and it is only in the rare moments when we catch her, so to speak, alone, doing something uniquely hers, not "trying out" something that her successors would perfect, that she has a chance to shine. So she does in the incident of the letter, and so, for example, she does in IV.ii, when, wearing boy's clothes and accompanied by the Host, she eavesdrops on Proteus' serenade of Silvia. Here, though the song is all Silvia's, the dramatic center is all Julia's:

Host. How do you, man? The music likes you not.

Julia. You mistake; the musician likes me not.

Host. Why, my pretty youth?

Julia. He plays false, father.

> (IV.ii.54–57)

She is great here not merely for the emotional impact of her moment of heartbreak, but for her resilience. The pallid heroine of prose romance would have crawled away to bleed in secret; but Julia asks of the Host, "Where lies Sir Proteus?" Her mind has already conceived a device by which she can keep an eye on him until such time as she can capture him for once and all.

It is almost certain that Proteus and Valentine suffer less by comparison with their successors than does Julia. This will appear a startling statement, particularly with reference to Proteus, who has a long and virtually un-deviating history of being abominated by critics. It is nevertheless essentially true, and the reason it is so is not hard to find. The fact is that the heroes of the romantic comedies—unlike the heroines, whose power to dazzle the eye and the imagination makes a beginning with Julia and at once thereafter becomes blinding—never do come to amount to very much. Proteus and Valentine, therefore, look about as good as any.

Between them, these two gentlemen define both of the emphases of which the one or the other dominates the later heroes. It is not strictly accurate to classify Shakespeare's romantic young males in two "types"—one wicked, the other stupid—but it is fair to say that each of them evinces a *tendency* in one or the other direction, and that two of them even tend toward both directions at the same time. To say that they exhibit a tendency toward wickedness or toward stupidity is not to say that they are wicked or stupid, but is to suggest that if they went somewhat farther along the road their qualities point them in, they would indeed be downright wicked or downright stupid. It should be added at once that though this view of the heroes is hardly flattering, surely none of us could seriously wish any one of the heroes changed in the slightest; each is perfect for the thing he is, perfect for the particular dramatic "world" of which he is part—and, what is most important, in each case the brilliant heroine loves the fellow either just as he stands or just as she has made him be by the end of the play.

Valentine is the simpler case, in more ways than one, and we should look at him before we deal with Proteus. Valentine looks ahead to the hero who is best represented by Orlando of *As You Like It*. The main thing to be said of this kind of hero is that there is nothing in the least "wrong" with him. He has nothing but virtues—all the virtues that anyone can name, except brilliance. He is kind, brave, loyal, generous, modest, forgiving—anything and everything as you like it; but any passing remark can make him look like a wonderful simpleton in an instant: "I found him under a tree," says Celia of Orlando, "like a dropped acorn." If Valentine is not quite up to Orlando in the kind that he is, he is nevertheless very nearly his equal, both in the sterling qualities of romantic young manhood that his kind of hero stands for and in the lack of intellectual keenness (especially around heroines) that he also stands for. Valentine is the perfect exemplar of friendship; he would never violate friendship even for love —and he is entirely true to his kind when, in the end, without needing to go through the painful process of thinking about it, he cheerfully offers Silvia—for whom he would just as cheerfully die—to Proteus. He could not do otherwise and be what he is; and because Shakespeare has been entirely clear in showing us what he is, it is we who are at fault if we so much as imagine that he should do otherwise. Valentine shares with Orlando, and not particularly with any of Shakespeare's other heroes of romantic comedy, a certain exaggeratedly heroic valor. Orlando hurls a professional wrestler to the ground, breaking his bones, and deals just as directly, and with no sweat, with a "sucked and hungry" lioness. But he best sums up all the qualities of his kind of romantic hero in a single incident and a single posture when, seeking food for old Adam, he pops into the clearing where the exiled Duke and his followers are at table, and mistaking them all for savages who have never been out of the woods, demands with drawn sword that they "Forbear, and eat no more" until his needs are served. Here, in a stroke, he is heroic on the grand scale, greathearted, nobly unselfish for his old servant—and, quite unconsciously, just a little ludicrous for having so much misjudged the situation.

With such a stroke, Shakespeare imparted a kind of flavor that transformed the romance hero, somewhat as he transformed the vapid romance heroine by adding some special feminine touches, including spunk. Bassanio of *The Merchant of Venice* exhibits the added quality very well when—of all people—he, the golden-fleece hunter, coolly reasons his way past the gold casket and the silver casket and takes the lead one; and he exhibits it again when, in the court scene, after Portia has pinned Shylock to the wall and has him quite at her mercy, he fails to perceive how completely the tables have turned and continues to rush forward, nobly generous, with bags of ducats—Portia's own—to buy off his friend. And this very way of surrounding his hero's grimly stalwart attitude with a tongue-in-cheek attitude Shakespeare first explored in Valentine, notably at his first encounter with the outlaws, upon whom he makes such a favorable impression that they invite him to be "king for our wild faction" after two minutes of conversation. Surely, this is an incident to the abruptness of which critics should take no such exception as some have; like Orlando's heroic-ludicrous posture at the Duke's banquet, and like Valentine's own quick offer to surrender Silvia to Proteus, and like Bassanio's straight-faced choice of the leaden casket, it hints of what Shakespeare did to romance to make it romantic *comedy*.

Thus the attitude of comedy within which the actions of the Valentine-Orlando kind of hero are framed is not limited to the more obvious situations in which the comic potentialities of the hero's intellectual equipment are exploited—as in the case of Valentine's penning a love note for Silvia and not understanding, while the simple Speed is appalled by his obtuseness, that her "secret nameless friend" is himself—but extends to his most heroic and high-minded moments. On both counts, Valentine is more nearly a finished portrait than a first sketch.

At least as much may be said of Proteus, first of those who represent a contrary emphasis in the heroic character. Valentine, Bassanio, Orlando are innocent and goodhearted; none of them could ever be imagined as "going bad" under any circumstances. Proteus not only could but temporarily does go bad, and so do those who follow in his line, namely, Claudio of *Much Ado About Nothing* and—stepping just over the boundary into the "dark comedies"—Bertram of *All's Well That Ends Well*.

These heroes are clearly not so much like one another as are those of the other line, who might almost be said to be interchangeable. Claudio, in particular, shares with the Valentine-Orlando hero a certain congenital unawareness of situation; but, curiously, while this appears a lovable fault in the others and endears them to us as well as to the heroines, in Claudio it is odious. A callow princox of a youth, Claudio looks from the outset like one who could mistake a situation and become nasty about it, as indeed he does. If he is "cured" in the end, when the truth of the situation has been made apparent, yet he remains the same callow princox still, and one supposes that he would be capable of dastardly conduct again tomorrow or the next day if the right set of circumstances invited him. Bertram and Claudio differ most notably in that, while each is capable of dastardly conduct, Claudio's worst exhibition of contemptible qualities is based on his initial misunderstanding of situation, whereas Bertram's involvement in such unheroic activities as illicit pursuits and outright lying is quite deliberate. If Claudio is capable of contemptible behavior only when he misunderstands, Bertram is most capable of it when he understands very well.

As a hero of his kind, therefore, not being in competition with the Valentine-Orlando kind, but compared with Claudio and Bertram, Proteus looks remarkably good. As a dramatic character he is certainly as well drawn as they are, and as a man he is hardly worse than they. Proteus is like Bertram in needing no misunderstanding of situation to start him on a wayward course. It has been remarked of Macbeth that of all Shakespeare's tragic heroes he alone knowingly embraces evil as his good, and it may as well be said of Proteus and Bertram that they alone of the comic heroes knowingly take to the crooked paths of dishonor. Bertram rejects the wife of inferior birth who was forced on him; lies to her; pursues, with the intention of corrupting, for no reason but lust, a virgin of Florence; is prevented from committing adultery only by his wife's shrewd intervention; and thereafter, confronted with his deeds, lies, slanders others, and abandons all dignity and honor in an exhibition of squirming and twisting; and after his disgraceful wallowing, he is abruptly forgiven all his trespasses and welcomed home as a worthy subject, son, and husband.

Against Bertram's record as a hero, Proteus' fairly shines. He does not choose to leave his Julia, but is sent away by his father. Neither does he choose to fall in love with Silvia, any more than Romeo chooses to fall in

love with Juliet (and many details of the play prove that
Shakespeare had Brooke's *Romeus and Juliet* in mind as
he wrote). Here, in reducing the odium of Proteus' initial
fault, Shakespeare has been characteristically shrewd, for
he has made Silvia irresistible, with both an inward and
an outward beauty. If, lest she put Julia in the shade, he
had made her only an ordinary beauty, Proteus' "three-
fold perjury" committed in pursuit of her would have been
difficult to understand and all but impossible to forgive.
But on Silvia he has lavished all his superlatives, made
her dazzling, wholly worthy of the song with which she is
serenaded in Act IV and which is itself incomparable. All
things considered, Silvia being as she is and what she is,
who can blame Proteus?

In two other ways, also, Shakespeare goes farther toward explaining and extenuating Proteus' fault than he
was to do with the faults of Claudio and Bertram. In the
first scene of the play, Proteus is shown to be both a faithful friend and a faithful lover; but also the point is made
evident that in a crisis of conflict between friendship and
love, love would claim him:

> He after honor hunts, I after love.
> He leaves his friends to dignify them more,
> I leave myself, my friends, and all, for love.
>
> (I.i.63–65)

He is love's votary; as it has been with Julia, so will it
be with Silvia when the time comes: he will leave himself,
his true friend, and all else, for love. Second, as he does
not do for Claudio and Bertram, Shakespeare does Proteus the credit of allowing him to debate the right and
wrong of his multiple perjury before he commits it, to
debate the question, in fact, twice, in II.iv. 191–213, and
in II.vi. 1–43. Claudio and Bertram, one notes, engage in
no self-debate; they directly announce their bad intentions without troubling with any such preliminaries. Even
though his decision is "wrong," Proteus at least undergoes
the formality of weighing right and wrong. It is true that
his self-debate involves no agonizing soul struggle such as

Angelo of *Measure for Measure* undergoes in a roughly comparable situation, when flesh and the spirit are at war in him; Shakespeare quite rightly keeps Proteus' "struggle" light, superficial, artificial, well within the tone and the terms appropriate to romantic comedy:

> And ev'n that pow'r which gave me first my oath
> Provokes me to this threefold perjury:
> Love bade me swear, and Love bids me forswear.
>
> (II.vi.4–6)

Surely, this is as far as a proper hero of romantic comedy dare go in soul struggle, and critics who deplore the too-easy entrance of Proteus into treachery—even as they deplore his too-easy return from it—would do well to remember that the moral ponderings of a Hamlet, an Angelo, or a Macbeth at this point would crash out of and destroy the very genre that this particular romantic hero helped to create.

But all this is not to suggest that Proteus is a blameless hero; if he were so, he would not belong with Claudio and Bertram, but with Valentine and Orlando. It is rather to insist that of the specific kind he represents, he runs true to form and measures up extremely well. Launce identifies him and his kind clearly enough: "I am but a fool, look you, and yet I have the wit to think my master is a kind of a knave." Is he any worse than that? For only a moment he seems to be, when he threatens Silvia with violence in the forest, and here perhaps Shakespeare did indeed go too far. But whether he would actually attack Silvia we neither know nor need to know; the fact is that he does not attack her, and we are quite aware that, with Valentine at hand, watching every move, there never was any real danger in the situation. He is guilty of nothing more than a thoroughly wicked intent, which is thwarted while it is only an impulse. A wicked impulse is not punishable, and in the world of romantic comedy is not even to be thought on too seriously.

Julia and Silvia, Valentine and Proteus are the most notable human fixtures in the special world of romantic comedy that was born with *The Two Gentlemen of Verona*. They are light but durable fixtures, as that world requires. If they are not wholly credible, yet they are more credible than were their forbears in the romances, and they are credible enough, palpable enough, one may say, for the world of romantic comedy, the nature of which would be altered if it were made to sustain creatures more solid. They are of a kind with this special world.

The world of romantic comedy, both as it was first drawn in this play and as it was re-created in each of the masterpieces that followed, of course includes other features besides the heroes and the heroines who invariably inhabit it. It includes, for example, clowns and fools. Speed and Launce stand rather uncertainly between the twin Dromios, the bewildered but witty slaves of *The Comedy of Errors,* before them, and the magnificent creations that came after, like Launcelot Gobbo of *The Merchant of Venice* and Touchstone of *As You Like It.* They are not as gifted as these—if Launcelot Gobbo, a great dunce, may be said to be gifted—and they talk too long with one another and with their masters. With the exception of Launce's long exhortation to his dog to be a better dog, their appearances are likely to be found tedious in both the theater and the study. But if they are not at all well and functionally fitted into the plot of the play—and the fact is that they are almost always purely interruptive—yet Shakespeare's introduction of them into romance helped to bring romantic comedy into being: the oozy world of romance needed their dryness. Their presence does not particularly help to make this incredible world more credible; but it does what is just as good—namely, helps to make the point that this world does not *have* to be perfectly credible, helps to render its very incredibility acceptable. In such a world as they inhabit, how can we reasonably balk at such a turn as the sudden redemption of Proteus or Valentine's magnanimous offer of Silvia? They are reminders that we are to keep our perspective and not consider things too seriously; annoying as they have proved for many critics, with their dreary stretches of low-grade quibbles and mental horseplay, they nevertheless serve the important perspective-giving function implied by Feste's refrain at the end of *Twelfth Night:* ". . . the rain it raineth every day."

Like the heroes and the heroines, the clowns and fools, and the incidents that take extravagant turns, the dramatic verse of *The Two Gentlemen of Verona* needs also to be taken for what it is and does within the world of romantic comedy. No passages and almost no single lines in this play (setting aside the whole of the song to Silvia) are particularly memorable. If one sets, for instance, the poetic language of Julia's interviews (in disguise) with Proteus and with Silvia beside that of Viola-Cesario's interviews with Orsino and Olivia in *Twelfth Night*—a fair comparison, involving similar characters in virtually identical situations—the contrast is obvious enough; yet it is not shocking. Here is Julia-Sebastian speaking to Silvia:

> She hath been fairer, madam, than she is.
> When she did think my master loved her well,
> She, in my judgment, was as fair as you.
> But since she did neglect her looking glass,
> And threw her sun-expelling mask away,
> The air hath starved the roses in her cheeks
> And pinched the lily-tincture of her face,
> That now she is become as black as I.
>
> (IV.iv.149–56)

And here is Viola-Cesario, telling how she-he would woo Olivia:

> Make me a willow cabin at your gate,
> And call upon my soul within the house;
> Write loyal cantons of contemnèd love
> And sing them loud even in the dead of night;
> Halloo your name to the reverberate hills
> And make the babbling gossip of the air
> Cry out "Olivia!"
>
> (*Twelfth Night* I.v.254–60)

There is a resonance, a throaty vibrance in the music of the great poetic passages of *Twelfth Night*—

> She never told her love,
> But let concealment, like a worm i' th' bud,
> Feed on her damask cheek. She pined in thought,
> And with a green and yellow melancholy
> She sat, like Patience on a monument,
> Smiling at grief.
>
> (II.iv.109–14)

—to which at best *The Two Gentlemen of Verona* never once attains, unless in the single line so much praised by Logan Pearsall Smith (*Shakespeare*, p. 74): ". . . but it is only in the *Two Gentlemen of Verona*, with the song 'Who is Silvia,' with the line:

> The uncertain glory of an April day,

and the passage about the brook that makes sweet music as it strays, that his power over words becomes a magic power, and his golden mastery of speech begins to almost blind us with its beauty."

Though it is easy to assent to the glory of this single line, no one would be likely to claim particular distinction for all the poetry of the play. What is here asserted, instead, is that the poetic language is "right" for the play, that it helps in the same way that the heroes and heroines and the extravagant incidents do to create the "world" of romantic comedy. This poetry has a good deal of chaff in it; it is sometimes glittering chaff, but chaff it is. It is light and usually frivolous; even when deep ideas are asserted, they are not asserted profoundly. The speakers habitually play along the surface of things:

Proteus. So, by your circumstance, you call me fool.

Valentine. So, by your circumstance, I fear you'll prove.

Proteus. 'Tis love you cavil at. I am not Love.

Valentine. Love is your master, for he masters you;
　And he that is so yokèd by a fool,
　Methinks, should not be chronicled for wise.

Proteus. Yet writers say, as in the sweetest bud
The eating canker dwells, so eating love
Inhabits in the finest wits of all.

Valentine. And writers say . . .

(I.i.36–45)

This is as typical an example as any of the poetic talk that fills the play, and in filling it defines its kind. It is both superficial and artificial, if one will, but "right" for the kind of world in which it is spoken and which it creates in being spoken, just as, for the same reason, the principal characters and incidents are also "right." There is an attitude of frivolity about this world which is figured forth in language, character, and incident.

Viewed thus, for what it is in part and whole, the play needs no apology, and certainly it does not deserve the harsh criticism that it has received from many who have not been content to take it for what it is. It transformed romance to romantic comedy, and it founded a great line. But, viewed as we have viewed it, it need not depend for its whole credit upon the fact that it was an important "first." It would be what it is if there were no *Twelfth Night*—indeed, it would no doubt look much better if there were no *Twelfth Night*.

BERTRAND EVANS
*University of California
Berkeley*

The
Two Gentlemen
of Verona

The Names of All the Actors

Duke [of Milan], father to Silvia
Valentine }
Proteus   } the two gentlemen
Antonio, father to Proteus
Thurio, a foolish rival to Valentine
Eglamour, agent for Silvia in her escape
Host, where Julia lodges
Outlaws, with Valentine
Speed, a clownish servant to Valentine
Launce, the like to Proteus
Panthino, servant to Antonio
Julia, beloved of Proteus
Silvia, beloved of Valentine
Lucetta, waiting woman to Julia
[Servants, Musicians

Scene: Verona; Milan; a forest]

The Two Gentlemen of Verona

ACT I

Scene I. [*Verona. An open place.*]

[Enter] Valentine [and] Proteus.

Valentine. Cease to persuade, my loving Proteus:
  Home-keeping youth have ever homely wits.
  Were't not affection chains thy tender days
  To the sweet glances of thy honored love,
  I rather would entreat thy company   5
  To see the wonders of the world abroad,
  Than, living dully sluggardized at home,
  Wear out thy youth with shapeless idleness.
  But since thou lov'st, love still, and thrive therein,
  Even as I would, when I to love begin.   10

Proteus. Wilt thou be gone? Sweet Valentine, adieu!
  Think on thy Proteus when thou haply°[1] seest
  Some rare noteworthy object in thy travel;
  Wish me partaker in thy happiness
  When thou dost meet good hap;° and in thy danger, 15

---

[1] The degree sign (°) indicates a footnote, which is keyed to the text by line number. Text references are printed in *italic* type; the annotation follows in roman type.

I.i.12 *haply* by chance   **15** *hap* luck

43

If ever danger do environ thee,
Commend thy grievance to my holy prayers,
For I will be thy beadsman,° Valentine.

Valentine. And on a love-book° pray for my success?

20 *Proteus.* Upon some book I love I'll pray for thee.

Valentine. That's on some shallow story of deep love:
How young Leander° crossed the Hellespont.

Proteus. That's a deep story of a deeper love,
For he was more than over shoes in love.

25 *Valentine.* 'Tis true, for you are over boots in love,
And yet you never swum the Hellespont.

Proteus. Over the boots? Nay, give me not the boots.°

Valentine. No, I will not, for it boots° thee not.

Proteus.   What?

Valentine. To be in love—where scorn is bought with groans,
Coy looks with heartsore sighs, one fading mo-
30 ment's mirth
With twenty watchful, weary, tedious nights;
If haply won, perhaps a hapless° gain;
If lost, why then a grievous labor won;
However,° but a folly bought with wit,
35 Or else a wit by folly vanquishèd.

Proteus. So, by your circumstance,° you call me fool.

Valentine. So, by your circumstance, I fear you'll prove.

Proteus. 'Tis love you cavil at. I am not Love.

Valentine. Love is your master, for he masters you;

18 *beadsman* one who contracts to pray in behalf of another   19
love-book i.e., instead of a prayer book   22 *Leander* (legendary
Greek youth who nightly swam the Hellespont to visit his beloved
Hero and, one night, was drowned)   27 *give me not the boots* i.e.,
don't jest with me   28 *boots* benefits (with pun on preceding line)
32 *hapless* luckless   34 *However* in either case   36 *by your circumstance* i.e., by your argument (in the next line the same phrase
means "in your condition [of love]")

    And he that is so yokèd by a fool,   40
    Methinks, should not be chronicled° for wise.

Proteus. Yet writers say, as in the sweetest bud
    The eating canker° dwells, so eating love
    Inhabits in the finest wits of all.

Valentine. And writers say, as the most forward° bud   45
    Is eaten by the canker ere it blow,°
    Even so by love the young and tender wit
    Is turned to folly, blasting° in the bud,
    Losing his verdure even in the prime,°
    And all the fair effects of future hopes.   50
    But wherefore waste I time to counsel thee,
    That art a votary to fond desire?
    Once more adieu! My father at the road°
    Expects my coming, there to see me shipped.

Proteus. And thither will I bring° thee, Valentine.   55

Valentine. Sweet Proteus, no; now let us take our
    leave.
    To Milan let me hear from thee by letters
    Of thy success° in love, and what news else
    Betideth here in absence of thy friend,
    And I likewise will visit thee with mine.   60

Proteus. All happiness bechance to thee in Milan!

Valentine. As much to you at home! And so, farewell.
                                       Exit.

Proteus. He after honor hunts, I after love.
    He leaves his friends to dignify them more,
    I leave myself, my friends, and all, for love.   65
    Thou, Julia, thou hast metamorphized me,
    Made me neglect my studies, lose my time,
    War with good counsel, set the world at nought,
    Made wit with musing weak, heart sick with
    thought.

---

41 *chronicled* written down   **43** *canker* cankerworm   **45** *most forward* earliest   **46** *blow* bloom   **48** *blasting* withering   **49** *prime* spring   **53** *road* harbor   **55** *bring* accompany   **58** *success* fortune (good or bad)

[Enter Speed.]

70 *Speed.* Sir Proteus, save you!° Saw you my master?

Proteus. But now he parted hence, to embark for Milan.

Speed. Twenty to one, then, he is shipped already,
And I have played the sheep° in losing him.

Proteus. Indeed, a sheep doth very often stray,
75 And if° the shepherd be awhile away.

Speed. You conclude that my master is a shepherd, then, and I a sheep?

Proteus. I do.

Speed. Why then, my horns are his horns,° whether I
80 wake or sleep.

Proteus. A silly answer, and fitting well a sheep.

Speed. This proves me still a sheep.

Proteus. True, and thy master a shepherd.

Speed. Nay, that I can deny by a circumstance.°

85 *Proteus.* It shall go hard but I'll prove it by another.

Speed. The shepherd seeks the sheep, and not the sheep the shepherd; but I seek my master, and my master seeks not me. Therefore I am no sheep.

Proteus. The sheep for fodder follow the shepherd;
90 the shepherd for food follows not the sheep; thou for wages followest thy master, thy master for wages follows not thee. Therefore thou art a sheep.

Speed. Such another proof will make me cry "baa."

Proteus. But, dost thou hear? Gav'st thou my letter to
95 Julia?

---

70 *save you* (a greeting)   73 *sheep* (pun on "ship")   75 *And if* if
79 *my horns are his horns* i.e., my (sheep's) horns belong to him
(making him a cuckold)   84 *circumstance* logical proof

Speed. Ay, sir: I, a lost mutton, gave your letter to her, a laced mutton,° and she, a laced mutton, gave me, a lost mutton, nothing for my labor.

Proteus. Here's too small a pasture for such store of muttons.   *100*

Speed. If the ground be overcharged,° you were best stick° her.

Proteus. Nay, in that you are astray; 'twere best pound° you.

Speed. Nay, sir, less than a pound shall serve me for   *105* carrying your letter.

Proteus. You mistake. I mean the pound—a pinfold.

Speed. From a pound to a pin? Fold it over and over, 'Tis threefold too little for carrying a letter to your lover.

Proteus. But what said she?   *110*

Speed. [*Nodding*] Ay.

Proteus. Nod—ay. Why, that's noddy.°

Speed. You mistook, sir. I say she did nod; and you ask me if she did nod, and I say, "Ay."

Proteus. And that set together is noddy.   *115*

Speed. Now you have taken the pains to set it together, take it for your pains.

Proteus. No, no. You shall have it for bearing the letter.

Speed. Well, I perceive I must be fain to bear with   *120* you.

Proteus. Why, sir, how do you bear with me?

96-97 *lost mutton . . . laced mutton* i.e., lost sheep and laced courtesan (probably "lost" and "laced" were similarly pronounced) 101 *overcharged* overgrazed   102 *stick* stab (slaughter)   104 *pound* impound (with pun)   112 *noddy* fool

Speed. Marry,° sir, the letter, very orderly; having
nothing but the word "noddy" for my pains.

125 *Proteus.* Beshrew° me, but you have a quick wit.

Speed. And yet it cannot overtake your slow purse.

Proteus. Come, come, open the matter in brief. What
said she?

Speed. Open your purse, that the money and the mat-
130 ter may be both at once delivered.

Proteus. Well, sir, here is for your pains. What said
she?

Speed. Truly, sir, I think you'll hardly win her.

Proteus. Why, couldst thou perceive so much from
135 her?

Speed. Sir, I could perceive nothing at all from her;
no, not so much as a ducat for delivering your letter.
And being so hard to me that brought your mind,
I fear she'll prove as hard to you in telling your
140 mind. Give her no token but stones;° for she's as
hard as steel.

Proteus. What said she? Nothing?

Speed. No, not so much as "Take this for thy pains."
To testify your bounty, I thank you, you have tes-
145 terned me;° in requital whereof, henceforth carry
your letters yourself. And so, sir, I'll commend you
to my master.

Proteus. Go, go, be gone, to save your ship from wrack,
Which cannot perish, having thee aboard,
150 Being destined to a drier death on shore.°
                                     [Exit Speed.]

---

123 *Marry* by the Virgin Mary (a casual oath)   125 *Beshrew* curse
(used casually)   140 *stones* (in addition to punning on its meanings
of "jewels" and "worthless gifts," Speed may be punning on another
meaning, "testicles")   144–45 *testerned me* i.e., given me a testern
(sixpence)   150 *Being destined . . . shore* i.e., being destined to hang

I must go send some better messenger;
I fear my Julia would not deign my lines,
Receiving them from such a worthless post.°   *Exit.*

Scene II. [*Verona. Julia's house.*]

Enter Julia and Lucetta.

Julia. But say, Lucetta, now we are alone,
  Wouldst thou, then, counsel me to fall in love?

Lucetta. Ay, madam; so you stumble not unheedfully.

Julia. Of all the fair resort of gentlemen°
  That every day with parle° encounter me,   5
  In thy opinion which is worthiest love?

Lucetta. Please you repeat their names, I'll show my
    mind
  According to my shallow simple skill.

Julia. What think'st thou of the fair Sir Eglamour?

Lucetta. As of a knight well spoken, neat, and fine;   10
  But, were I you, he never should be mine.

Julia. What think'st thou of the rich Mercatio?

Lucetta. Well of his wealth; but of himself, so so.

Julia. What think'st thou of the gentle Proteus?

Lucetta. Lord, Lord! To see what folly reigns in us!   15

Julia. How now! What means this passion° at his
    name?

Lucetta. Pardon, dear madam; 'tis a passing° shame
  That I, unworthy body as I am,
  Should censure° thus on lovely gentlemen.

153 *post* messenger I.ii.4 *resort of gentlemen* crowd of suitors 5
parle parley 16 *passion* emotion 17 *passing* surpassing 19 *censure* pass judgment

20 *Julia.* Why not on Proteus, as of all the rest?

Lucetta. Then thus: of many good I think him best.

Julia. Your reason?

Lucetta. I have no other but a woman's reason:
   I think him so because I think him so.

25 *Julia.* And wouldst thou have me cast my love on him?

Lucetta. Ay, if you thought your love not cast away.

Julia. Why, he, of all the rest, hath never moved° me.

Lucetta. Yet he, of all the rest, I think, best loves ye.

Julia. His little speaking shows his love but small.

30 *Lucetta.* Fire that's closest kept burns most of all.

Julia. They do not love that do not show their love.

Lucetta. O, they love least that let men know their love.

Julia. I would I knew his mind.

Lucetta. Peruse this paper, madam.

35 *Julia.* "To Julia."—Say, from whom?

Lucetta. That the contents will show.

Julia. Say, say, who gave it thee?

Lucetta. Sir Valentine's page; and sent, I think, from
      Proteus.
   He would have given it you; but I, being in the way,
40   Did in your name receive it. Pardon the fault, I pray.

Julia. Now, by my modesty, a goodly broker!°
   Dare you presume to harbor wanton lines?
   To whisper and conspire against my youth?
   Now, trust me, 'tis an office of great worth,
45   And you an officer fit for the place.
   There, take the paper; see it be returned,
   Or else return no more into my sight.

27 *moved* i.e., proposed to   41 *broker* go-between

Lucetta. To plead for love deserves more fee than hate.

Julia. Will ye be gone?

Lucetta.   That you may ruminate.   *Exit.*

Julia. And yet I would I had o'erlooked° the letter.   50
It were a shame to call her back again,
And pray her to° a fault for which I chid her.
What fool is she, that knows I am a maid,
And would not force the letter to my view!
Since maids, in modesty, say "no" to that   55
Which they would have the profferer construe "ay."
Fie, fie, how wayward is this foolish love,
That, like a testy° babe, will scratch the nurse,
And presently,° all humbled, kiss the rod!
How churlishly I chid Lucetta hence,   60
When willingly I would have had her here!
How angerly I taught my brow to frown,
When inward joy enforced my heart to smile!
My penance is to call Lucetta back
And ask remission for my folly past.   65
What, ho! Lucetta!

[Enter Lucetta.]

Lucetta.   What would your ladyship?

Julia. Is't near dinnertime?

Lucetta.   I would it were;
That you might kill your stomach° on your meat,
And not upon your maid.°

Julia. What is't that you took up so gingerly?   70

Lucetta. Nothing.

Julia. Why didst thou stoop, then?

Lucetta. To take a paper up that I let fall.

---

50 *o'erlooked* perused   52 *pray her to* apologize to her for   58 *testy* irritable   59 *presently* immediately   68 *kill your stomach* (1) allay your vexation (2) appease your hunger   68–69 *meat . . . maid* (pun on "mate")

Julia. And is that paper nothing?

75 *Lucetta.* Nothing concerning me.

Julia. Then let it lie for those that it concerns.

Lucetta. Madam, it will not lie where it concerns,°
Unless it have a false interpreter.

Julia. Some love of yours hath writ to you in rhyme.

80 *Lucetta.* That I might sing it, madam, to a tune.
Give me a note: your ladyship can set.°

Julia. As little by such toys° as may be possible.
Best sing it to the tune of "Light o' love."°

Lucetta. It is too heavy for so light a tune.

85 *Julia.* Heavy! Belike it hath some burden,° then?

Lucetta. Ay, and melodious were it, would you sing it.

Julia. And why not you?

Lucetta.   I cannot reach so high.

Julia. Let's see your song. [*Takes the letter.*] How now,
minion!

Lucetta. Keep tune there still, so you will sing it out:
90 And yet methinks I do not like this tune.

Julia. You do not?

Lucetta.   No, madam; 'tis too sharp.

Julia. You, minion, are too saucy.

Lucetta. Nay, now you are too flat,
And mar the concord with too harsh a descant.°
95 There wanteth but a mean° to fill your song.

Julia. The mean is drowned with your unruly bass.

---

77 *lie where it concerns* i.e., express its content falsely (with
quibble on preceding line)   81 *set* set to music   82 *toys* trifles
83 *Light o' love* a contemporary popular ditty   85 *burden* bass refrain (with pun)   94 *descant* improvised harmony   95 *wanteth but
a mean* lacks a tenor part (Proteus?)

Lucetta. Indeed, I bid the base° for Proteus.

Julia. This babble shall not henceforth trouble me.
    Here is a coil with protestation!°   [*Tears the letter.*]
    Go get you gone, and let the papers lie;   100
    You would be fing'ring them, to anger me.

Lucetta. She makes it strange;° but she would be best
    pleased
    To be so ang'red with another letter.   [*Exit.*]

Julia. Nay, would I were so ang'red with the same!
    O hateful hands, to tear such loving words!   105
    Injurious wasps, to feed on such sweet honey,
    And kill the bees, that yield it, with your stings!
    I'll kiss each several° paper for amends.
    Look, here is writ "kind Julia." Unkind Julia!
    As in revenge of thy ingratitude,   110
    I throw thy name against the bruising stones,
    Trampling contemptuously on thy disdain.
    And here is writ "love-wounded Proteus."
    Poor wounded name! My bosom, as a bed,
    Shall lodge thee, till thy wound be throughly°
    healed;   115
    And thus I search° it with a sovereign kiss.
    But twice or thrice was "Proteus" written down.
    Be calm, good wind, blow not a word away
    Till I have found each letter in the letter,
    Except mine own name: that some whirlwind bear   120
    Unto a ragged, fearful-hanging rock,
    And throw it thence into the raging sea!
    Lo, here in one line is his name twice writ,
    "Poor forlorn Proteus, passionate Proteus,
    To the sweet Julia." That I'll tear away.—   125
    And yet I will not, sith° so prettily
    He couples it to his complaining names.

97 *bid the base* (in the game of Prisoner's Base, a challenge to
a test of speed [with pun])   99 *coil with protestation* much ado
made up of lover's protestations   102 *makes it strange* i.e., pretends that it is nothing to her   108 *several* separate   115 *throughly*
thoroughly   116 *search* probe (as in cleaning a wound)   126 *sith*
since

Thus will I fold them one upon another.
Now kiss, embrace, contend, do what you will.

[Enter Lucetta.]

130 *Lucetta.* Madam,
Dinner is ready, and your father stays.

Julia. Well, let us go.

Lucetta. What, shall these papers lie like telltales here?

Julia. If you respect them, best to take them up.

135 *Lucetta.* Nay, I was taken up for laying them down;
Yet here they shall not lie, for catching cold.

Julia. I see you have a month's mind° to them.

Lucetta. Ay, madam, you may say what sights you see;
I see things too, although you judge I wink.°

140 *Julia.* Come, come; will't please you go?   *Exeunt.*

Scene III. [*Verona. Antonio's house.*]

Enter Antonio and Panthino.

Antonio. Tell me, Panthino, what sad° talk was that
Wherewith my brother held you in the cloister?

Panthino. 'Twas of his nephew Proteus, your son.

Antonio. Why, what of him?

Panthino.   He wond'red that your lordship
5   Would suffer him to spend his youth at home,
While other men, of slender reputation,°
Put forth their sons to seek preferment out:

---

137 *month's mind* i.e., lasting desire   139 *wink* have my eyes shut,
see nothing   I.iii.1 *sad* serious   6 *slender reputation* unimportant
place

Some to the wars, to try their fortune there,
Some to discover islands far away,
Some to the studious universities.   10
For any, or for all these exercises,
He said that Proteus your son was meet,°
And did request me to importune you
To let him spend his time no more at home,
Which would be great impeachment° to his age,   15
In having known no travel in his youth.

Antonio. Nor need'st thou much importune me to that
Whereon this month I have been hammering.°
I have considered well his loss of time,
And how he cannot be a perfect man,   20
Not being tried and tutored in the world.
Experience is by industry achieved,
And perfected° by the swift course of time.
Then, tell me, whither were I best to send him?

Panthino. I think your lordship is not ignorant   25
How his companion, youthful Valentine,
Attends the Emperor° in his royal court.

Antonio. I know it well.

Panthino. 'Twere good, I think, your lordship sent him
   thither.
There shall he practice tilts and tournaments,   30
Hear sweet discourse, converse with noblemen,
And be in eye of° every exercise
Worthy his youth and nobleness of birth.

Antonio. I like thy counsel; well hast thou advised.
And that thou mayst perceive how well I like it,   35
The execution of it shall make known.
Even with the speediest expedition°
I will dispatch him to the Emperor's court.

Panthino. Tomorrow, may it please you, Don Al-
   phonso,

12 *meet* fitted   15 *impeachment* detriment   18 *hammering* i.e., pondering   23 *perfected* (accented on first syllable)   27 *Emperor* i.e.,
Duke (of Milan)   32 *be in eye of* have sight of   37 *expedition*
haste

40 With other gentlemen of good esteem,
Are journeying to salute the Emperor,
And to commend their service to his will.

Antonio. Good company; with them shall Proteus go.
And—in good time! Now will we break with° him.

[*Enter Proteus.*]

45 *Proteus.* Sweet love! Sweet lines! Sweet life!
Here is her hand, the agent of her heart.
Here is her oath for love, her honor's pawn.°
O, that our fathers would applaud our loves,
To seal our happiness with their consents!
50 O heavenly Julia!

Antonio. How now! What letter are you reading there?

Proteus. May't please your lordship, 'tis a word or two
Of commendations° sent from Valentine,
Delivered by a friend that came from him.

55 *Antonio.* Lend me the letter; let me see what news.

Proteus. There is no news, my lord, but that he writes
How happily he lives, how well beloved
And daily gracèd by the Emperor,
Wishing me with him, partner of his fortune.

60 *Antonio.* And how stand you affected to his wish?

Proteus. As one relying on your lordship's will,
And not depending on his friendly wish.

Antonio. My will is something sorted° with his wish.
Muse not that I thus suddenly proceed,
65 For what I will, I will, and there an end.
I am resolved that thou shalt spend some time
With Valentinus in the Emperor's court.
What maintenance he from his friends receives,
Like exhibition° thou shalt have from me.
70 Tomorrow be in readiness to go.

44 *break with* break the news to   47 *pawn* pledge   53 *commenda-tions* greetings   63 *something sorted* somewhat in accord   69 *ex-hibition* allowance

Excuse it not,° for I am peremptory.°

Proteus. My lord, I cannot be so soon provided.
Please you, deliberate a day or two.

Antonio. Look what° thou want'st shall be sent after
thee.
No more of stay! Tomorrow thou must go.   75
Come on, Panthino; you shall be employed
To hasten on his expedition.
                    [*Exeunt Antonio and Panthino.*]

Proteus. Thus have I shunned the fire for fear of
    burning,
And drenched me in the sea, where I am drowned.
I feared to show my father Julia's letter,   80
Lest he should take exceptions to my love;
And with the vantage of mine own excuse
Hath he excepted most against my love.°
O, how this spring of love resembleth
The uncertain glory of an April day,   85
Which now shows all the beauty of the sun,
And by and by a cloud takes all away!

[*Enter Panthino.*]

Panthino. Sir Proteus, your father calls for you.
He is in haste; therefore, I pray you, go.

Proteus. Why, this it is: my heart accords thereto,   90
And yet a thousand times it answers "no."   *Exeunt.*

71 *Excuse it not* offer no excuses   71 *peremptory* determined
74 *Look what* whatever   82–83 *with the vantage . . . my love* i.e., he
took advantage of my own device (the pretended letter from Valentine) to strike the heaviest blow to my affair of love (with Julia)

ACT II

Scene I. [*Milan. The Duke's palace.*]

Enter Valentine [and] Speed.

Speed. Sir, your glove.

Valentine.   Not mine; my gloves are on.

Speed. Why, then, this may be yours, for this is but
 one.°

Valentine. Ha, let me see. Ay, give it me, it's mine.
 Sweet ornament that decks a thing divine!
5   Ah, Silvia, Silvia!

Speed. Madam Silvia! Madam Silvia!

Valentine. How now, sirrah?°

Speed. She is not within hearing, sir.

Valentine. Why, sir, who bade you call her?

10 *Speed.* Your worship, sir, or else I mistook.

Valentine. Well, you'll still° be too forward.

Speed. And yet I was last chidden for being too slow.

Valentine. Go to, sir. Tell me, do you know Madam
 Silvia?

II.i.1–2 *on . . . one* (a pun in Elizabethan speech)   7 *sirrah* (common form of address to inferiors)   11 *still* always

58

Speed. She that your worship loves?   15

Valentine. Why, how know you that I am in love?

Speed. Marry, by these special marks: first, you have
learned, like Sir Proteus, to wreathe your arms, like
a malcontent; to relish a love song, like a robin red-
breast; to walk alone, like one that had the pesti-   20
lence; to sigh, like a schoolboy that had lost his
A B C; to weep, like a young wench that had buried
her grandam; to fast, like one that takes diet; to
watch,° like one that fears robbing; to speak puling,°
like a beggar at Hallowmas.° You were wont, when   25
you laughed, to crow like a cock; when you walked,
to walk like one of the lions; when you fasted, it
was presently after dinner; when you looked sadly,
it was for want of money. And now you are meta-
morphized with a mistress, that,° when I look on   30
you, I can hardly think you my master.

Valentine. Are all these things perceived in me?

Speed. They are all perceived without ye.°

Valentine. Without me? They cannot.

Speed. Without you? Nay, that's certain, for, without°   35
you were so simple, none 'else would. But you are
so without these follies, that these follies are within
you, and shine through you like the water in an
urinal, that not an eye that sees you but is a physician to comment on your malady.   40

Valentine. But tell me, dost thou know my lady Silvia?

Speed. She that you gaze on so as she sits at supper?

Valentine. Hast thou observed that? Even she, I mean.

Speed. Why, sir, I know her not.

24 *watch* lie awake   24 *puling* whiningly   25 *at Hallowmas* on All
Saints' Day (when beggars vied for special treats)   30 *that* so
that   33 *without ye* i.e., by external signs (here begins a series
of quibbles)   35 *without* unless

45 *Valentine.* Dost thou know her by my gazing on her,
and yet know'st her not?

Speed. Is she not hard-favored,° sir?

Valentine. Not so fair, boy, as well-favored.

Speed. Sir, I know that well enough.

50 *Valentine.* What dost thou know?

Speed. That she is not so fair as, of you, well favored.

Valentine. I mean that her beauty is exquisite, but her
favor° infinite.

Speed. That's because the one is painted, and the other
55 out of all count.°

Valentine. How painted? And how out of count?

Speed. Marry, sir, so painted, to make her fair, that
no man counts of° her beauty.

Valentine. How esteem'st thou me? I account of her
60 beauty.

Speed. You never saw her since she was deformed.°

Valentine. How long hath she been deformed?

Speed. Ever since you loved her.

Valentine. I have loved her ever since I saw her; and
65 still I see her beautiful.

Speed. If you love her, you cannot see her.

Valentine. Why?

Speed. Because Love is blind. O, that you had mine
eyes; or your own eyes had the lights they were wont
70 to have when you chid at Sir Proteus for going
ungartered!°

---

47 *hard-favored* homely   53 *favor* charm, graciousness   55 *out of
all count* beyond counting   58 *counts of* takes account of   61 *deformed* i.e., distorted by your lover's view   70–71 *going ungartered*
(a sure sign that one is in love; see *As You Like It*, III.ii.371)

Valentine. What should I see then?

Speed. Your own present folly, and her passing° deformity. For he, being in love, could not see to garter his hose; and you, being in love, cannot see *75* to put on your hose.

Valentine. Belike, boy, then, you are in love; for last morning you could not see to wipe my shoes.

Speed. True, sir; I was in love with my bed. I thank you, you swinged° me for my love, which makes *80* me the bolder to chide you for yours.

Valentine. In conclusion, I stand affected to her.

Speed. I would you were set,° so your affection would cease.

Valentine. Last night she enjoined me to write some *85* lines to one she loves.

Speed. And have you?

Valentine. I have.

Speed. Are they not lamely writ?

Valentine. No, boy, but as well as I can do them. *90* Peace! Here she comes.

Speed. [*Aside*] O excellent motion! O exceeding puppet! Now will he interpret° to her.

[*Enter Silvia.*]

Valentine. Madam and mistress, a thousand good morrows. *95*

Speed. [*Aside*] O, give ye good ev'n! Here's a million of manners.

Silvia. Sir Valentine and servant,° to you two thousand.

73 *passing* surpassing, extreme   80 *swinged* beat   83 *set* seated (quibble on "stand")   92–93 *motion . . . puppet . . . interpret* (the puppeteer's voice "interprets" for the figures in the puppet play, or "motion")   98 *servant* gallant lover (i.e., alludes not to Speed but to Valentine)

Speed. [*Aside*] He should give her interest, and she
100   gives it him.

Valentine. As you enjoined me, I have writ your letter
Unto the secret nameless friend of yours,
Which I was much unwilling to proceed in,
But for my duty to your ladyship.

Silvia. I thank you, gentle servant; 'tis very clerkly°
105   done.

Valentine. Now trust me, madam, it came hardly off;
For, being ignorant to whom it goes,
I writ at random, very doubtfully.

Silvia. Perchance you think too much of so much
pains?

110 *Valentine.* No, madam; so it stead° you, I will write,
Please you command, a thousand times as much.
And yet—

Silvia. A pretty period!° Well, I guess the sequel;
And yet I will not name it; and yet I care not;
115   And yet take this again; and yet I thank you,
Meaning henceforth to trouble you no more.

Speed. [*Aside*] And yet you will; and yet another "yet."

Valentine. What means your ladyship? Do you not
like it?

Silvia. Yes, yes: the lines are very quaintly° writ;
120   But since unwillingly, take them again.
Nay, take them.

Valentine. Madam, they are for you.

Silvia. Ay, ay. You writ them, sir, at my request;
But I will none of them; they are for you;
125   I would have had them writ more movingly.

Valentine. Please you, I'll write your ladyship another.

Silvia. And when it's writ, for my sake read it over,

105 *clerkly* scholarly   110 *stead* be useful to   113 *period* full stop
119 *quaintly* ingeniously

And if it please you, so; if not, why, so.

Valentine. If it please me, madam, what then?

Silvia. Why, if it please you, take it for your labor;   130
And so, good morrow, servant.   *Exit Silvia.*

Speed. O jest unseen, inscrutable, invisible,
As a nose on a man's face, or a weathercock on a
steeple!
My master sues to her, and she hath taught her
suitor,
He being her pupil, to become her tutor.   135
O excellent device! Was there ever heard a better,
That my master, being scribe, to himself should
write the letter?

Valentine. How now, sir? What are you reasoning with
yourself?

Speed. Nay, I was rhyming; 'tis you that have the   140
reason.

Valentine. To do what?

Speed. To be a spokesman from Madam Silvia.

Valentine. To whom?

Speed. To yourself. Why, she woos you by a figure.°   145

Valentine. What figure?

Speed. By a letter, I should say.

Valentine. Why, she hath not writ to me?

Speed. What need she, when she hath made you write
to yourself? Why, do you not perceive the jest?   150

Valentine. No, believe me.

Speed. No believing you, indeed, sir. But did you
perceive her earnest?°

Valentine. She gave me none, except an angry word.

145 *by a figure* by indirect means   153 *earnest* (1) seriousness
(2) token payment

155 *Speed.* Why, she hath given you a letter.

Valentine. That's the letter I writ to her friend.

Speed. And that letter hath she delivered, and there
an end.

Valentine. I would it were no worse.

160 *Speed.* I'll warrant you, 'tis as well;
For often have you writ to her, and she, in modesty,
Or else for want of idle time, could not again reply;
Or fearing else some messenger that might her mind
discover,°
Herself hath taught her love himself to write unto
her lover.
165 All this I speak in print,° for in print I found it.
Why muse you, sir? 'Tis dinnertime.

Valentine. I have dined.

Speed. Ay, but hearken, sir; though the chameleon
Love can feed on the air,° I am one that am nour-
170 ished by my victuals, and would fain have meat. O,
be not like your mistress; be moved, be moved.
Exeunt.

Scene II. [*Verona. Julia's house.*]

Enter Proteus [*and*] *Julia.*

Proteus. Have patience, gentle Julia.

Julia. I must, where is no remedy.

Proteus. When possibly I can, I will return.

---

163 *discover* reveal   165 *speak in print* i.e., quote   168–69 *chameleon . . . the air* (the chameleon was thought to eat nothing but
air; see also II.iv.24–26 and *Hamlet* III.ii.95)

Julia. If you turn° not, you will return the sooner.
    Keep this remembrance for thy Julia's sake.   5
                            [*Giving a ring.*]

Proteus. Why, then, we'll make exchange; here, take
    you this.

Julia. And seal the bargain with a holy kiss.

Proteus. Here is my hand for my true constancy;
    And when that hour o'erslips me in the day
    Wherein I sigh not, Julia, for thy sake,   10
    The next ensuing hour some foul mischance
    Torment me for my love's forgetfulness!
    My father stays° my coming; answer not;
    The tide is now:—nay, not thy tide of tears;
    That tide will stay me longer than I should.   15
    Julia, farewell!   [*Exit Julia.*]
            What, gone without a word?
    Ay, so true love should do: it cannot speak;
    For truth hath better deeds than words to grace it.

[*Enter Panthino.*]

Panthino. Sir Proteus, you are stayed for.

Proteus. Go; I come, I come.   20
    Alas! This parting strikes poor lovers dumb. *Exeunt.*

Scene III. [*Verona. A street.*]

Enter Launce, [leading a dog].

Launce. Nay, 'twill be this hour ere I have done weep-
    ing; all the kind of the Launces have this very fault.
    I have received my proportion,° like the prodigious°

II.ii.4 *turn* i.e., change your affection (perhaps with the additional
meaning of "engage in sexual acts")   13 *stays* waits for   III.iii.3
proportion (Launce's blunder for "portion")   3 *prodigious* (blunder
for "prodigal")

son, and am going with Sir Proteus to the Imperial's
5   court. I think Crab my dog be the sourest-natured
dog that lives. My mother weeping, my father wailing, my sister crying, our maid howling, our cat
wringing her hands, and all our house in a great
perplexity, yet did not this cruel-hearted cur shed
10   one tear. He is a stone, a very pebble stone, and
has no more pity in him than a dog. A Jew would
have wept to have seen our parting. Why, my
grandam, having no eyes, look you, wept herself
blind at my parting. Nay, I'll show you the manner
15   of it. This shoe is my father; no, this left shoe is
my father. No, no, this left shoe is my mother; nay,
that cannot be so neither. Yes, it is so, it is so, it
hath the worser sole. This shoe, with the hole in it,
is my mother, and this my father; a vengeance on't!
20   There 'tis. Now, sir, this staff is my sister, for, look
you, she is as white as a lily, and as small as a
wand. This hat is Nan, our maid. I am the dog. No,
the dog is himself, and I am the dog. Oh! The dog
is me, and I am myself; ay, so, so. Now come I to
25   my father: Father, your blessing. Now should not
the shoe speak a word for weeping: now should I
kiss my father: well, he weeps on. Now come I to
my mother. Oh, that she could speak now like a
wood woman!° Well, I kiss her; why, there 'tis.
30   Here's my mother's breath up and down.° Now
come I to my sister; mark the moan she makes.
Now the dog all this while sheds not a tear, nor
speaks a word; but see how I lay the dust with my
tears.

[*Enter Panthino.*]

35 *Panthino.* Launce, away, away, aboard! Thy master is
shipped, and thou art to post after with oars. What's
the matter? Why weep'st thou, man? Away, ass!
You'll lose the tide, if you tarry any longer.

28–29 *Oh, that . . . wood woman* (Launce laments that his [wooden]
shoe is not really his mother, madly distressed [wood] as she was at
parting)   30 *up and down* identically

Launce. It is no matter if the tied were lost; for it is
the unkindest tied that ever any man tied.   40

Panthino. What's the unkindest tide?

Launce. Why, he that's tied here, Crab, my dog.

Panthino. Tut, man, I mean thou'lt lose the flood,°
and, in losing the flood, lose thy voyage, and, in
losing thy voyage, lose thy master, and, in losing   45
thy master, lose thy service, and, in losing thy service— Why dost thou stop my mouth?

Launce. For fear thou shouldst lose thy tongue.

Panthino. Where should I lose my tongue?

Launce. In thy tale.   50

Panthino. In thy tail!

Launce. Lose the tide, and the voyage, and the master,
and the service, and the tied! Why, man, if the river
were dry, I am able to fill it with my tears; if the
wind were down, I could drive the boat with my   55
sighs.

Panthino. Come, come away, man; I was sent to call
thee.

Launce. Sir, call me what thou dar'st.

Panthino. Wilt thou go?   60

Launce. Well, I will go.   *Exeunt.*

Scene IV. [*Milan. The Duke's palace.*]

Enter Valentine, Silvia, Thurio, [and] Speed.

Silvia. Servant!

Valentine. Mistress?

43 *flood* full tide

Speed. Master, Sir Thurio frowns on you.

Valentine. Ay, boy, it's for love.

5   *Speed.* Not of you.

Valentine. Of my mistress, then.

Speed. 'Twere good you knocked him.   [*Exit.*]

Silvia. Servant, you are sad.

Valentine. Indeed, madam, I seem so.

10   *Thurio.* Seem you that you are not?

Valentine. Haply I do.

Thurio. So do counterfeits.

Valentine. So do you.

Thurio. What seem I that I am not?

15   *Valentine.* Wise.

Thurio. What instance of the contrary?

Valentine. Your folly.

Thurio. And how quote° you my folly?

Valentine. I quote it in your jerkin.

20   *Thurio.* My jerkin is a doublet.°

Valentine. Well, then, I'll double your folly.

Thurio. How?

Silvia. What, angry, Sir Thurio! Do you change color?

Valentine. Give him leave, madam; he is a kind of
25   chameleon.

Thurio. That hath more mind to feed on your blood
than live in your air.

Valentine. You have said, sir.

II.iv.18 *quote* observe (pronounced "coat")   20 *doublet* close-fit-
ting jacket

Thurio. Ay, sir, and done too, for this time.

Valentine. I know it well, sir; you always end ere you   30
begin.

Silvia. A fine volley of words, gentlemen, and quickly
shot off.

Valentine. 'Tis indeed, madam; we thank the giver.

Silvia. Who is that, servant?   35

Valentine. Yourself, sweet lady; for you gave the fire.
Sir Thurio borrows his wit from your ladyship's
looks, and spends what he borrows kindly in your
company.

Thurio. Sir, if you spend word for word with me, I   40
shall make your wit bankrupt.

Valentine. I know it well, sir. You have an exchequer
of words, and, I think, no other treasure to give
your followers, for it appears by their bare° liveries
that they live by your bare words.   45

Silvia. No more, gentlemen, no more—here comes my
father.

[*Enter Duke.*]

Duke. Now, daughter Silvia, you are hard beset.
Sir Valentine, your father's in good health.
What say you to a letter from your friends   50
Of much good news?

Valentine.   My lord, I will be thankful
To any happy messenger° from thence.

Duke. Know ye Don Antonio, your countryman?

Valentine. Ay, my good lord, I know the gentleman
To be of worth, and worthy estimation,   55
And not without desert so well reputed.

Duke. Hath he not a son?

44 *bare* threadbare   52 *happy messenger* i.e., bringer of good news

Valentine. Ay, my good lord, a son that well deserves
 The honor and regard of such a father.

60 *Duke.* You know him well?

Valentine. I knew him as myself; for from our infancy
 We have conversed and spent our hours together;
 And though myself have been an idle truant,
 Omitting the sweet benefit of time
65 To clothe mine age with angel-like perfection,
 Yet hath Sir Proteus, for that's his name,
 Made use and fair advantage of his days;
 His years but young, but his experience old;
 His head unmellowed, but his judgment ripe.
70 And, in a word, for far behind his worth
 Comes all the praises that I now bestow,
 He is complete in feature and in mind
 With all good grace to grace a gentleman.

Duke. Beshrew me, sir, but if he make this good,
75 He is as worthy for an empress' love
 As meet° to be an emperor's counselor.
 Well, sir, this gentleman is come to me
 With commendation from great potentates,
 And here he means to spend his time awhile.
80 I think 'tis no unwelcome news to you.

Valentine. Should I have wished a thing, it had been he.

Duke. Welcome him, then, according to his worth.
 Silvia, I speak to you, and you, Sir Thurio;
 For Valentine, I need not cite° him to it.
85 I will send him hither to you presently. *[Exit.]*

Valentine. This is the gentleman I told your ladyship
 Had come along with me, but that his mistress
 Did hold his eyes locked in her crystal looks.

Silvia. Belike that now she hath enfranchised them,
90 Upon some other pawn for fealty.°

---

76 *meet* fitted **84** *cite* incite, urge **90** *pawn for fealty* pledge for
loyalty

Valentine. Nay, sure, I think she holds them prisoners
   still.

Silvia. Nay, then, he should be blind; and, being blind,
   How could he see his way to seek out you?

Valentine. Why, lady, Love hath twenty pair of eyes.

Thurio. They say that Love hath not an eye at all.   95

Valentine. To see such lovers, Thurio, as yourself.
   Upon a homely object Love can wink. [*Exit Thurio.*]

Silvia. Have done, have done; here comes the gentleman.

[*Enter Proteus.*]

Valentine. Welcome, dear Proteus! Mistress, I beseech
   you,
   Confirm his welcome with some special favor.   100

Silvia. His worth is warrant for his welcome hither,
   If this be he you oft have wished to hear from.

Valentine. Mistress, it is. Sweet lady, entertain° him
   To be my fellow servant to your ladyship.

Silvia. Too low a mistress for so high a servant.   105

Proteus. Not so, sweet lady, but too mean° a servant
   To have a look of such a worthy mistress.

Valentine. Leave off discourse of disability.°
   Sweet lady, entertain him for your servant.

Proteus. My duty will I boast of, nothing else.   110

Silvia. And duty never yet did want his meed.°
   Servant, you are welcome to a worthless mistress.

Proteus. I'll die on° him that says so but yourself.

Silvia. That you are welcome?

---

103 *entertain* welcome   106 *mean* low, humble   108 *Leave . . . disability* i.e., cease this modest talk   111 *want his meed* lack its reward   113 *die on* fight to the death

Proteus.   That you are worthless.

[Enter Thurio.]

Servant. Madam, my lord your father would speak
115   with you.

Silvia. I wait upon his pleasure. *[Exit Servant.]* Come,
Sir Thurio,
Go with me. Once more, new servant, welcome.
I'll leave you to confer of home affairs.
When you have done, we look to hear from you.

120 *Proteus.* We'll both attend upon your ladyship.
                         [Exeunt Silvia and Thurio.]

Valentine. Now, tell me, how do all from whence you
came?

Proteus. Your friends are well, and have them much
commended.°

Valentine. And how do yours?

Proteus.   I left them all in health.

Valentine. How does your lady? And how thrives your
love?

125 *Proteus.* My tales of love were wont to weary you;
I know you joy not in a love discourse.

Valentine. Ay, Proteus, but that life is altered now.
I have done penance for contemning Love,
Whose high imperious thoughts have punished me
130   With bitter fasts, with penitential groans,
With nightly tears, and daily heartsore sighs;
For, in revenge of my contempt of love,
Love hath chased sleep from my enthrallèd eyes,
And made them watchers of mine own heart's sor-
row.
135   O gentle Proteus, Love's a mighty lord,
And hath so humbled me, as° I confess

122 *have them much commended* i.e., themselves to you   136 *as*
that

There is no woe to° his correction,
Nor to his service no such joy on earth.
Now no discourse, except it be of love;
Now can I break my fast, dine, sup, and sleep   140
Upon the very naked name of love.

Proteus. Enough; I read your fortune in your eye.
Was this the idol that you worship so?

Valentine. Even she; and is she not a heavenly saint?

Proteus. No; but she is an earthly paragon.   145

Valentine. Call her divine.

Proteus.   I will not flatter her.

Valentine. O, flatter me, for love delights in praises.

Proteus. When I was sick, you gave me bitter pills,
And I must minister the like to you.

Valentine. Then speak the truth by her; if not divine, 150
Yet let her be a principality,
Sovereign to all the creatures on the earth.

Proteus. Except my mistress.

Valentine.   Sweet, except not any,
Except thou wilt except against° my love.

Proteus. Have I not reason to prefer mine own?   155

Valentine. And I will help thee to prefer° her too.
She shall be dignified with this high honor—
To bear my lady's train, lest the base earth
Should from her vesture chance to steal a kiss,
And, of so great a favor growing proud,   160
Disdain to root the summer-swelling flow'r,
And make rough winter everlastingly.

Proteus. Why, Valentine, what braggardism is this?

Valentine. Pardon me, Proteus. All I can is nothing

---

137 *to* like unto   154 *Except thou wilt except against* unless you
will take exception to   156 *prefer* advance

165   To her, whose worth makes other worthies nothing;
    She is alone.

Proteus.   Then let her alone.

Valentine. Not for the world. Why, man, she is mine
        own,
    And I as rich in having such a jewel
    As twenty seas, if all their sand were pearl,
170   The water nectar, and the rocks pure gold.
    Forgive me that I do not dream on° thee,
    Because thou see'st me dote upon my love.
    My foolish rival, that her father likes
    Only for his possessions are so huge,
175   Is gone with her along; and I must after,
    For love, thou know'st, is full of jealousy.

Proteus. But she loves you?

Valentine. Ay, and we are betrothed; nay, more, our
        marriage hour,
    With all the cunning manner of our flight,
180   Determined of: how I must climb her window,
    The ladder made of cords, and all the means
    Plotted and 'greed on for my happiness.
    Good Proteus, go with me to my chamber,
    In these affairs to aid me with thy counsel.

185   *Proteus.* Go on before; I shall inquire you forth.
    I must unto the road, to disembark
    Some necessaries that I needs must use,
    And then I'll presently attend you.

Valentine. Will you make haste?

190   *Proteus.* I will.   *Exit [Valentine].*
    Even as one heat another heat expels,
    Or as one nail by strength drives out another,
    So the remembrance of my former love
    Is by a newer object quite forgotten.
195   Is it mine eye, or Valentine's praise,
    Her true perfection, or my false transgression,
    That makes me reasonless° to reason thus?

171 *on* of   197 *reasonless* without justification

She is fair; and so is Julia, that I love—
That I did love, for now my love is thawed,
Which, like a waxen image 'gainst a fire,   200
Bears no impression of the thing it was.
Methinks my zeal to Valentine is cold,
And that I love him not as I was wont.
O, but I love his lady too too much!
And that's the reason I love him so little.   205
How shall I dote on her with more advice,°
That thus without advice begin to love her!
'Tis but her picture° I have yet beheld,
And that hath dazzled my reason's light;
But when I look on her perfections,   210
There is no reason° but I shall be blind.
If I can check my erring love, I will;
If not, to compass° her I'll use my skill.   *Exit.*

Scene V. [*Milan. A street.*]

Enter Speed and Launce [meeting].

Speed. Launce! By mine honesty, welcome to Padua!°

Launce. Forswear° not thyself, sweet youth; for I am
not welcome. I reckon this always—that a man is
never undone till he be hanged, nor never welcome
to a place till some certain shot° be paid, and the   5
hostess say "Welcome!"

Speed. Come on, you madcap, I'll to the alehouse with
you presently, where, for one shot of five pence,
thou shalt have five thousand welcomes. But, sirrah,
how did thy master part with Madam Julia?   10

206 *advice* careful thought   208 *picture* i.e., her visible being,
outward appearance   211 *reason* question   213 *compass* get, achieve
II.v.1 *Padua* (apparently Shakespeare forgot that his characters are
in Milan)   2 *Forswear* perjure   5 *shot* alehouse bill

Launce. Marry, after they closed in earnest,° they parted very fairly in jest.

Speed. But shall she marry him?

Launce. No.

15 *Speed.* How, then? Shall he marry her?

Launce. No, neither.

Speed. What, are they broken?

Launce. No, they are both as whole as a fish.

Speed. Why, then, how stands the matter with them?

20 *Launce.* Marry, thus: when it stands well with him, it stands well with her.

Speed. What an ass art thou! I understand thee not.

Launce. What a block art thou, that thou canst not! My staff understands me.

25 *Speed.* What thou sayest?

Launce. Ay, and what I do too. Look thee, I'll but lean, and my staff understands me.

Speed. It stands under thee, indeed.

Launce. Why, stand-under and under-stand is all one.

30 *Speed.* But tell me true, will't be a match?

Launce. Ask my dog. If he say ay, it will; if he say, no, it will; if he shake his tail and say nothing, it will.

Speed. The conclusion is, then, that it will.

35 *Launce.* Thou shalt never get such a secret from me but by a parable.°

Speed. 'Tis well that I get it so. But, Launce, how say-

---

11 *closed in earnest* (1) formally agreed (2) embraced   36 *by a parable* i.e., by indirect affirmation

est thou,° that my master is become a notable lover?

Launce. I never knew him otherwise.   40

Speed. Than how?

Launce. A notable lubber, as thou reportest him to be.

Speed. Why, thou whoreson ass, thou mistak'st me.

Launce. Why fool, I meant not thee; I meant thy master.   45

Speed. I tell thee, my master is become a hot lover.

Launce. Why, I tell thee, I care not though he burn himself in love. If thou wilt, go with me to the alehouse; if not, thou art an Hebrew, a Jew, and not worth the name of a Christian.   50

Speed. Why?

Launce. Because thou hast not so much charity in thee as to go to the ale with a Christian.° Wilt thou go?

Speed. At thy service.   *Exeunt.*   55

Scene VI. [*Milan. The Duke's palace.*]

Enter Proteus solus.°

Proteus. To leave my Julia shall I be forsworn;
To love fair Silvia shall I be forsworn;
To wrong my friend, I shall be much forsworn;
And ev'n that pow'r which gave me first my oath
Provokes me to this threefold perjury: 5

37–38 *how sayest thou* what do you think about this   53 *go to the ale with a Christian* i.e., attend a church-benefit festivity   II.vi.s.d. *solus* alone (Latin)

Love bade me swear, and Love bids me forswear.
O sweet-suggesting Love, if thou hast sinned,
Teach me, thy tempted subject, to excuse it!
At first I did adore a twinkling star,
10 But now I worship a celestial sun.
Unheedful vows may heedfully be broken;
And he wants° wit that wants resolvèd will
To learn° his wit t' exchange the bad for better.
Fie, fie, unreverend tongue! To call her bad,
15 Whose sovereignty so oft thou hast preferred
With twenty thousand soul-confirming oaths.
I cannot leave to love, and yet I do;
But there I leave to love where I should love.
Julia I lose, and Valentine I lose.
20 If I keep them, I needs must lose myself;
If I lose them, thus find I by their loss
For Valentine, myself, for Julia, Silvia.
I to myself am dearer than a friend,
For love is still most precious in itself,
25 And Silvia—witness Heaven, that made her fair!—
Shows Julia but a swarthy Ethiope.
I will forget that Julia is alive,
Rememb'ring that my love to her is dead;
And Valentine I'll hold an enemy,
30 Aiming at Silvia as a sweeter friend.
I cannot now prove constant to myself,
Without some treachery used to Valentine.
This night he meaneth with a corded ladder
To climb celestial Silvia's chamber window,
35 Myself in counsel, his competitor.°
Now presently I'll give her father notice
Of their disguising and pretended° flight;
Who, all enraged, will banish Valentine;
For Thurio, he intends, shall wed his daughter.
40 But, Valentine being gone, I'll quickly cross
By some sly trick blunt Thurio's dull proceeding.
Love, lend me wings to make my purpose swift,
As thou hast lent me wit to plot this drift!°   *Exit.*

12 *wants* lacks   13 *learn* teach   35 *competitor* accomplice   37 *pretended* intended   43 *drift* device

Scene VII. [*Verona. Julia's house.*]

Enter Julia and Lucetta.

Julia. Counsel, Lucetta; gentle girl, assist me;
And, ev'n in kind love, I do conjure thee,
Who art the table° wherein all my thoughts
Are visibly charactered and engraved,
To lesson me, and tell me some good mean,   5
How, with my honor,° I may undertake
A journey to my loving Proteus.

Lucetta. Alas, the way is wearisome and long!

Julia. A true-devoted pilgrim is not weary
To measure kingdoms with his feeble steps;   10
Much less shall she that hath Love's wings to fly—
And when the flight is made to one so dear,
Of such divine perfection, as Sir Proteus.

Lucetta. Better forbear till Proteus make return.

Julia. O, know'st thou not his looks are my soul's
food?   15
Pity the dearth that I have pinèd in
By longing for that food so long a time.
Didst thou but know the inly° touch of love,
Thou wouldst as soon go kindle fire with snow
As seek to quench the fire of love with words.   20

Lucetta. I do not seek to quench your love's hot fire,
But qualify° the fire's extreme rage,
Lest it should burn above the bounds of reason.

Julia. The more thou damm'st it up, the more it burns.
The current that with gentle murmur glides,   25
Thou know'st, being stopped, impatiently doth rage;
But when his fair course is not hinderèd,
He makes sweet music with th' enameled° stones,

II.vii.3 *table* tablet   6 *with my honor* preserving my honor   18 *inly*
inward   22 *qualify* mitigate   28 *enameled* shiny

Giving a gentle kiss to every sedge
30 He overtaketh in his pilgrimage;
And so by many winding nooks he strays,
With willing sport, to the wild ocean.
Then let me go, and hinder not my course.
I'll be as patient as a gentle stream,
33 And make a pastime of each weary step,
Till the last step have brought me to my love;
And there I'll rest, as after much turmoil
A blessèd soul doth in Elysium.

Lucetta. But in what habit° will you go along?

40 *Julia.* Not like a woman, for I would prevent
The loose encounters of lascivious men.
Gentle Lucetta, fit me with such weeds°
As may beseem some well-reputed page.

Lucetta. Why, then, your ladyship must cut your hair.

45 *Julia.* No, girl; I'll knit it up in silken strings
With twenty odd-conceited° truelove knots.
To be fantastic may become a youth
Of greater time° than I shall show to be.

Lucetta. What fashion, madam, shall I make your
breeches?

50 *Julia.* That fits as well as, "Tell me, good my lord,
What compass° will you wear your farthingale?"°
Why, ev'n what fashion thou best likes, Lucetta.

Lucetta. You must needs have them with a codpiece,°
madam.

Julia. Out, out,° Lucetta! That will be ill-favored.

55 *Lucetta.* A round hose, madam, now's not worth a pin,
Unless you have a codpiece to stick pins on.

Julia. Lucetta, as thou lov'st me, let me have

39 *habit* costume   42 *weeds* garments   46 *odd-conceited* ingeniously devised   48 *Of greater time* i.e., older   51 *compass* circumference   51 *farthingale* hooped petticoat   53 *codpiece* pocket or
bag at front of men's breeches (*round hose*, line 55), often fashion-
ably exaggerated   54 *Out, out* fie, fie

What thou think'st meet, and is most mannerly.
But tell me, wench, how will the world repute me
For undertaking so unstaid° a journey?   60
I fear me, it will make me scandalized.

Lucetta. If you think so, then stay at home, and go not.

Julia. Nay, that I will not.

Lucetta. Then never dream on infamy, but go.
If Proteus like your journey when you come,   65
No matter who's displeased when you are gone:
I fear me, he will scarce be pleased withal.°

Julia. That is the least, Lucetta, of my fear.
A thousand oaths, an ocean of his tears,
And instances of infinite° of love   70
Warrant me welcome to my Proteus.

Lucetta. All these are servants to deceitful men.

Julia. Base men, that use them to so base effect!
But truer stars did govern Proteus' birth.
His words are bonds, his oaths are oracles;   75
His love sincere, his thoughts immaculate;
His tears pure messengers sent from his heart;
His heart as far from fraud as heaven from earth.

Lucetta. Pray heav'n he prove so, when you come to
   him!

Julia. Now, as thou lov'st me, do him not that wrong, 80
To bear a hard opinion of his truth.
Only deserve my love by loving him,
And presently go with me to my chamber
To take a note of what I stand in need of
To furnish me upon my longing° journey.   85
All that is mine I leave at thy dispose,
My goods, my lands, my reputation;
Only, in lieu thereof, dispatch me hence.
Come, answer not, but to it presently!
I am impatient of my tarriance.   *Exeunt.*   90

60 *unstaid* unbecoming   67 *withal* with it   70 *infinite* infinity
85 *longing* i.e., occasioned by my longing

ACT III

Scene I. [*Milan. The Duke's palace.*]

Enter Duke, Thurio, [and] Proteus.

Duke. Sir Thurio, give us leave, I pray, awhile;
We have some secrets to confer about.

                        [*Exit Thurio.*]
Now, tell me, Proteus, what's your will with me?

Proteus. My gracious lord, that which I would discover°
5   The law of friendship bids me to conceal;
But when I call to mind your gracious favors
Done to me, undeserving as I am,
My duty pricks me on to utter that
Which else no worldly good should draw from me.
10   Know, worthy prince, Sir Valentine, my friend,
This night intends to steal away your daughter.
Myself am one made privy to the plot.
I know you have determined to bestow her
On Thurio, whom your gentle daughter hates,
15   And should she thus be stol'n away from you,
It would be much vexation to your age.
Thus, for my duty's sake, I rather chose

III.i.4 *discover* disclose

To cross my friend in his intended drift
Than, by concealing it, heap on your head
A pack of sorrows which would press you down,   20
Being unprevented, to your timeless° grave.

Duke. Proteus, I thank thee for thine honest care,
Which to requite, command me while I live.
This love of theirs myself have often seen,
Haply when they have judged me fast asleep;   25
And oftentimes have purposed to forbid
Sir Valentine her company and my court.
But, fearing lest my jealous° aim might err,
And so, unworthily disgrace the man,
A rashness that I ever yet have shunned,   30
I gave him gentle looks; thereby to find
That which thyself hast now disclosed to me.
And, that thou mayst perceive my fear of this,
Knowing that tender youth is soon suggested,°
I nightly lodge her in an upper tow'r,   35
The key whereof myself have ever kept;
And thence she cannot be conveyed away.

Proteus. Know, noble lord, they have devised a mean
How he her chamber window will ascend,
And with a corded ladder fetch her down;   40
For which the youthful lover now is gone,
And this way comes he with it presently,
Where, if it please you, you may intercept him.
But, good my lord, do it so cunningly
That my discovery be not aimèd at;°   45
For love of you, not hate unto my friend,
Hath made me publisher of this pretense.°

Duke. Upon mine honor, he shall never know
That I had any light from thee of this.

Proteus. Adieu, my lord; Sir Valentine is coming.   50
                                                [*Exit.*]

21 *timeless* untimely   28 *jealous* suspicious   34 *suggested* tempted,
prompted   45 *aimèd at* guessed   47 *pretense* intention

[Enter Valentine.]

Duke. Sir Valentine, whither away so fast?

Valentine. Please it your Grace, there is a messenger
  That stays to bear my letters to my friends,
  And I am going to deliver them.

55 *Duke.* Be they of much import?

Valentine. The tenor of them doth but signify
  My health and happy being at your court.

Duke. Nay then, no matter; stay with me awhile.
  I am to break with thee of some affairs
60 That touch me near, wherein thou must be secret.
  'Tis not unknown to thee that I have sought
  To match my friend Sir Thurio to my daughter.

Valentine. I know it well, my lord; and, sure, the
      match
  Were rich and honorable; besides, the gentleman
65 Is full of virtue, bounty, worth, and qualities
  Beseeming such a wife as your fair daughter.
  Cannot your Grace win her to fancy him?

Duke. No, trust me; she is peevish, sullen, froward,°
  Proud, disobedient, stubborn, lacking duty,
70 Neither regarding that she is my child
  Nor fearing me as if I were her father.
  And, may I say to thee, this pride of hers,
  Upon advice,° hath drawn° my love from her;
  And, where I thought the remnant of mine age
75 Should have been cherished by her childlike duty,
  I now am full resolved to take a wife,
  And turn her out to who will take her in.
  Then let her beauty be her wedding dow'r,
  For me and my possessions she esteems not.

Valentine. What would your Grace have me to do in
80   this?

68 *peevish . . . froward* obstinate . . . willful   73 *advice* consideration   73 *drawn* withdrawn

Duke. There is a lady in Verona here°
   Whom I affect; but she is nice° and coy,
   And nought esteems my agèd eloquence.
   Now, therefore, would I have thee to my tutor—
   For long agone I have forgot to court;   *85*
   Besides, the fashion of the time is changed—
   How and which way I may bestow° myself,
   To be regarded in her sun-bright eye.

Valentine. Win her with gifts, if she respect not words.
   Dumb jewels often in their silent kind°   *90*
   More than quick words do move a woman's mind.

Duke. But she did scorn a present that I sent her.

Valentine. A woman sometime scorns what best con-
     tents her.
   Send her another; never give her o'er;
   For scorn at first makes after-love the more.
   If she do frown, 'tis not in hate of you,   *95*
   But rather to beget more love in you,
   If she do chide, 'tis not to have you gone;
   For why, the fools are mad, if left alone.
   Take no repulse, whatever she doth say;   *100*
   For "get you gone," she doth not mean "away!"
   Flatter and praise, commend, extol their graces;
   Though ne'er so black, say they have angels' faces.
   That man that hath a tongue, I say, is no man,
   If with his tongue he cannot win a woman.   *105*

Duke. But she I mean is promised by her friends
   Unto a youthful gentleman of worth,
   And kept severely from resort of men,
   That no man hath access by day to her.

Valentine. Why, then, I would resort to her by night. *110*

Duke. Ay, but the doors be locked, and keys kept safe,
   That no man hath recourse to her by night.

---

81 *in Verona here* (some editors emend *in* to "of," but probably
Shakespeare forgot his characters are now in Milan)   82 *nice* fastidious   87 *bestow* conduct   90 *kind* nature

Valentine. What lets° but one may enter at her window?

Duke. Her chamber is aloft, far from the ground,
115   And built so shelving° that one cannot climb it
Without apparent hazard of his life.

Valentine. Why, then, a ladder, quaintly made of cords,
To cast up, with a pair of anchoring hooks,
Would serve to scale another Hero's tow'r,
120   So bold Leander would adventure it.

Duke. Now, as thou art a gentleman of blood,°
Advise me where I may have such a ladder.

Valentine. When would you use it? Pray, sir, tell me that.

Duke. This very night; for Love is like a child,
125   That longs for everything that he can come by.

Valentine. By seven o'clock I'll get you such a ladder.

Duke. But, hark thee; I will go to her alone.
How shall I best convey the ladder thither?

Valentine. It will be light, my lord, that you may bear it
130   Under a cloak that is of any length.

Duke. A cloak as long as thine will serve the turn?

Valentine. Ay, my good lord.

Duke.   Then let me see thy cloak.
I'll get me one of such another length.

Valentine. Why, any cloak will serve the turn, my lord.

135 *Duke*. How shall I fashion me to wear a cloak?
I pray thee, let me feel thy cloak upon me.
                         [*Opens Valentine's cloak.*]
What letter is this same? What's here? "To Silvia"——

113 *lets* prevents   115 *shelving* steeply sloping   121 *of blood* i.e.,
of noble blood

And here an engine° fit for my proceeding.
I'll be so bold to break the seal for once.   [*Reads.*]
"My thoughts do harbor with my Silvia nightly;   140
   And slaves they are to me, that send them flying.
O, could their master come and go as lightly,
   Himself would lodge where senseless they are
      lying!
My herald thoughts in thy pure bosom rest them,
   While I, their king, that thither them importune,   145
Do curse the grace that with such grace hath blessed
      them,
   Because myself do want my servants' fortune.
I curse myself, for they are sent by me,
That they should harbor where their lord should be."
What's here?   150
"Silvia, this night I will enfranchise thee."
'Tis so; and here's the ladder for the purpose.
Why, Phaethon—for thou art Merops' son—
Wilt thou aspire to guide the heavenly car,
And with thy daring folly burn the world?°   155
Wilt thou reach stars, because they shine on thee?
Go, base intruder! Overweening slave!
Bestow thy fawning smiles on equal mates,
And think my patience, more than thy desert,
Is privilege for thy departure hence.   160
Thank me for this more than for all the favors
Which all too much I have bestowed on thee.
But if thou linger in my territories
Longer than swiftest expedition°
Will give thee time to leave our royal court,   165
By heaven, my wrath shall far exceed the love
I ever bore my daughter or thyself.
Be gone! I will not hear thy vain excuse;
But, as thou lov'st thy life, make speed from hence.
                                             [*Exit.*]

138 *engine* contrivance (here, the ladder)   153–55 *Phaethon . . .
the world* (Phaethon's father, Phoebus—not Merops, who was his
mother's husband—let the youth drive the horses of the sun across
the sky, with dire results)   164 *expedition* speed

Valentine. And why not death rather than living tor-
170   ment?
　　To die is to be banished from myself;
　　And Silvia is myself. Banished from her
　　Is self from self: a deadly banishment!
　　What light is light, if Silvia be not seen?
175　　What joy is joy, if Silvia be not by?—
　　Unless it be to think that she is by,
　　And feed upon the shadow° of perfection.
　　Except I be by Silvia in the night,
　　There is no music in the nightingale;
180　　Unless I look on Silvia in the day,
　　There is no day for me to look upon.
　　She is my essence, and I leave° to be,
　　If I be not by her fair influence°
　　Fostered, illumined, cherished, kept alive.
185　　I fly not death, to fly his deadly doom:
　　Tarry I here, I but attend on death;
　　But, fly I hence, I fly away from life.

[Enter Proteus and Launce.]

Proteus. Run, boy, run, run, and seek him out.

Launce. Soho, soho!

190　*Proteus.* What seest thou?

Launce. Him we go to find. There's not a hair° on's
　　head but 'tis a Valentine.°

Proteus. Valentine?

Valentine. No.

195　*Proteus.* Who then? His spirit?

Valentine. Neither.

Proteus. What then?

177 *shadow* mere image　182 *leave* cease　183 *influence* i.e., like
that of the stars (see especially Sonnet 15)　191 *hair* (with pun
on "hare," prepared by preceding *Soho*, a hunting cry)　192 *Valentine* (with pun, as in lines 210–14 below)

Valentine. Nothing.

Launce. Can nothing speak? Master, shall I strike?

Proteus. Who wouldst thou strike?   200

Launce. Nothing.

Proteus. Villain, forbear.

Launce. Why, sir, I'll strike nothing. I pray you—

Proteus. Sirrah, I say, forbear. Friend Valentine, a
   word.

Valentine. My ears are stopped, and cannot hear good
   news,   205
   So much of bad already hath possessed them.

Proteus. Then in dumb silence will I bury mine,
   For they are harsh, untunable, and bad.

Valentine. Is Silvia dead?

Proteus. No, Valentine.   210

Valentine. No Valentine, indeed, for sacred Silvia.
   Hath she forsworn me?

Proteus. No, Valentine.

Valentine. No Valentine, if Silvia have forsworn me.
   What is your news?   215

Launce. Sir, there is a proclamation that you are vanished.

Proteus. That thou art banishèd—O, that's the
   news!—
   From hence, from Silvia, and from me thy friend.

Valentine. O, I have fed upon this woe already,   220
   And now excess of it will make me surfeit.
   Doth Silvia know that I am banishèd?

Proteus. Ay, ay, and she hath offered to the doom—
   Which, unreversed, stands in effectual force—
   A sea of melting pearl, which some call tears: 225
   Those at her father's churlish feet she tendered;

With them, upon her knees, her humble self;
Wringing her hands, whose whiteness so became
    them
As if but now they waxèd pale for woe.
230 But neither bended knees, pure hands held up,
Sad sighs, deep groans, nor silver-shedding tears,
Could penetrate her uncompassionate sire;
But Valentine, if he be ta'en, must die.
Besides, her intercession chafed him so,
235 When she for thy repeal was suppliant,
That to close prison he commanded her,
With many bitter threats of biding° there.

Valentine. No more; unless the next word that thou
    speak'st
Have some malignant power upon my life.
240 If so, I pray thee, breathe it in mine ear,
As ending anthem° of my endless dolor.

Proteus. Cease to lament for that thou canst not help,
And study help for that which thou lament'st.
Time is the nurse and breeder of all good.
245 Here if thou stay, thou canst not see thy love;
Besides, thy staying will abridge thy life.
Hope is a lover's staff; walk hence with that,
And manage it against despairing thoughts.
Thy letters may be here, though thou art hence;
250 Which, being writ to me, shall be delivered
Even in the milk-white bosom of thy love.
The time now serves not to expostulate.
Come, I'll convey thee through the city gate,
And, ere I part with thee, confer at large
255 Of all that may concern thy love affairs.
As thou lov'st Silvia, though not for thyself,
Regard thy danger, and along with me!

Valentine. I pray thee, Launce, and if° thou seest my
    boy,
Bid him make haste, and meet me at the Northgate.

237 *biding* i.e., permanent incarceration   241 *ending anthem* fu-
neral hymn   258 *and if* if

Proteus. Go, sirrah, find him out. Come, Valentine.   *260*

Valentine. O my dear Silvia! Hapless Valentine!
                    [*Exeunt Valentine and Proteus.*]

Launce. I am but a fool, look you, and yet I have the
  wit to think my master is a kind of a knave. But
  that's all one, if he be but one knave. He lives not
  now that knows me to be in love, yet I am in love; *265*
  but a team of horse shall not pluck that from me,
  nor who 'tis I love, and yet 'tis a woman; but what
  woman, I will not tell myself, and yet 'tis a milk-
  maid; yet 'tis not a maid, for she hath had gossips;°
  yet 'tis a maid, for she is her master's maid, and *270*
  serves for wages. She hath more qualities than a
  water spaniel—which is much in a bare Christian.
  [*Pulling out a paper*] Here is the cate-log of her
  condition. "Imprimis:° She can fetch and carry."
  Why, a horse can do no more: nay, a horse cannot *275*
  fetch, but only carry; therefore is she better than a
  jade.° "Item: She can milk"; look you, a sweet virtue in a maid with clean hands.

                    [*Enter Speed.*]

Speed. How now, Signior Launce! What news with
  your mastership?   *280*

Launce. With my master's ship? Why, it is at sea.

Speed. Well, your old vice still; mistake the word.
  What news, then, in your paper?

Launce. The black'st news that ever thou heard'st.

Speed. Why, man, how black?   *285*

Launce. Why, as black as ink.

Speed. Let me read them.

Launce. Fie on thee, jolthead!° Thou canst not read.

---

269 *gossips* godparents (for her own child)   274 *Imprimis* in the
first place   277 *jade* nag   288 *jolthead* blockhead

Speed. Thou liest; I can.

290 *Launce.* I will try thee. Tell me this: who begot thee?

Speed. Marry, the son of my grandfather.

Launce. O illiterate loiterer! It was the son of thy
grandmother. This proves that thou canst not read.

Speed. Come, fool, come; try me in thy paper.

295 *Launce.* There; and Saint Nicholas° be thy speed!°

Speed. [*Reads*] "Imprimis: She can milk."

Launce. Ay, that she can.

Speed. "Item: She brews good ale."

Launce. And thereof comes the proverb: "Blessing of
300   your heart, you brew good ale."

Speed. "Item: She can sew."

Launce. That's as much as to say, Can she so?

Speed. "Item: She can knit."

Launce. What need a man care for a stock° with a
305   wench when she can knit him a stock?

Speed. "Item: She can wash and scour."

Launce. A special virtue; for then she need not be
washed and scoured.

Speed. "Item: She can spin."

310 *Launce.* Then may I set the world on wheels,° when
she can spin for her living.

Speed. "Item: She hath many nameless virtues."

Launce. That's as much as to say, bastard virtues—
that, indeed, know not their fathers, and therefore
315   have no names.

295 *Saint Nicholas* patron saint of scholars (among others)   295
speed aid   304 *stock* dowry (pun follows)   310 *set the world on
wheels* take life easy

Speed. "Here follow her vices."

Launce. Close at the heels of her virtues.

Speed. "Item: She is not to be kissed fasting, in respect of her breath."

Launce. Well, that fault may be mended with a break- 320
fast. Read on.

Speed. "Item: She hath a sweet mouth."°

Launce. That makes amends for her sour breath.

Speed. "Item: She doth talk in her sleep."

Launce. It's no matter for that, so she sleep not in her 325
talk.

Speed. "Item: She is slow in words."

Launce. O villain, that set this down among her vices!
To be slow in words is a woman's only virtue. I
pray thee, out with't, and place it for her chief 330
virtue.

Speed. "Item: She is proud."

Launce. Out with that too; it was Eve's legacy, and
cannot be ta'en from her.

Speed. "Item: She hath no teeth." 335

Launce. I care not for that neither, because I love
crusts.

Speed. "Item: She is curst."°

Launce. Well, the best is, she hath no teeth to bite.

Speed. "Item: She will often praise her liquor." 340

Launce. If her liquor be good, she shall; if she will
not, I will, for good things should be praised.

Speed. "Item: She is too liberal."

Launce. Of her tongue she cannot, for that's writ down

322 *hath a sweet mouth* i.e., likes sweets   338 *curst* shrewish

345   she is slow of; of her purse she shall not, for that
       I'll keep shut. Now, of another thing she may, and
       that cannot I help. Well, proceed.

    Speed. "Item: She hath more hair than wit, and more
       faults than hairs, and more wealth than faults."

350 *Launce.* Stop there; I'll have her. She was mine, and
       not mine, twice or thrice in that last article. Re-
       hearse that once more.

    Speed. "Item: She hath more hair than wit"—

    Launce. More hair than wit? It may be; I'll prove it.
355   The cover of the salt° hides the salt, and therefore
       it is more than the salt; the hair that covers the wit
       is more than the wit, for the greater hides the less.
       What's next?

    Speed. "And more faults than hairs"—

360 *Launce.* That's monstrous. O, that that were out!

    Speed. "And more wealth than faults."

    Launce. Why, that word makes the faults gracious.
       Well, I'll have her; and if it be a match, as nothing
       is impossible—

365 *Speed.* What then?

    Launce. Why, then will I tell thee—that thy master
       stays for thee at the Northgate?

    Speed. For me?

    Launce. For thee! Ay, who art thou? He hath stayed
370   for a better man than thee.

    Speed. And must I go to him?

    Launce. Thou must run to him, for thou hast stayed
       so long that going° will scarce serve the turn.

    Speed. Why didst not tell me sooner? Pox of° your
375   love letters!   [*Exit.*]

355 *salt* saltcellar   373 *going* i.e., merely walking   374 *Pox of*
plague (literally, syphilis) on

Launce. Now will he be swinged for reading my letter
—an unmannerly slave, that will thrust himself into
secrets! I'll after, to rejoice in the boy's correction.
                                              [*Exit.*]

Scene II. [*Milan. The Duke's palace.*]

Enter Duke [and] Thurio.

Duke. Sir Thurio, fear not but that she will love you,
  Now Valentine is banished from her sight.

Thurio. Since his exile she hath despised me most,
  Forsworn my company, and railed at me,
  That I am desperate of obtaining her.   *3*

Duke. This weak impress° of love is as a figure
  Trenchèd in ice, which with an hour's heat
  Dissolves to water, and doth lose his form.
  A little time will melt her frozen thoughts,
  And worthless Valentine shall be forgot.   *10*

[*Enter Proteus.*]

How now, Sir Proteus! Is your countryman,
  According to our proclamation, gone?

Proteus. Gone, my good lord.

Duke. My daughter takes his going grievously.

Proteus. A little time, my lord, will kill that grief. *15*

Duke. So I believe, but Thurio thinks not so.
  Proteus, the good conceit° I hold of thee—
  For thou hast shown some sign of good desert—
  Makes me the better to confer with thee.

III.ii.6 *impress* impression (dent, groove)   17 *conceit* opinion

20 *Proteus.* Longer than I prove loyal to your Grace,
      Let me not live to look upon your Grace.

    Duke. Thou know'st how willingly I would effect
      The match between Sir Thurio and my daughter.

    Proteus. I do, my lord.

25 *Duke.* And also, I think, thou art not ignorant
      How she opposes her against my will.

    Proteus. She did, my lord, when Valentine was here.

    Duke. Ay, and perversely she persevers so.
      What might we do to make the girl forget
30   The love of Valentine, and love Sir Thurio?

    Proteus. The best way is to slander Valentine
      With falsehood, cowardice, and poor descent,
      Three things that women highly hold in hate.

    Duke. Ay, but she'll think that it is spoke in hate.

35 *Proteus.* Ay, if his enemy deliver it;
      Therefore it must with circumstance° be spoken
      By one whom she esteemeth as his friend.

    Duke. Then you must undertake to slander him.

    Proteus. And that, my lord, I shall be loath to do.
40   'Tis an ill office for a gentleman,
      Especially against his very friend.

    Duke. Where your good word cannot advantage him,
      Your slander never can endamage him;
      Therefore the office is indifferent,°
45   Being entreated to it by your friend.

    Proteus. You have prevailed, my lord. If I can do it
      By aught that I can speak in his dispraise,
      She shall not long continue love to him.
      But say this weed her love from Valentine,
50   It follows not that she will love Sir Thurio.

    Thurio. Therefore, as you unwind her love from him,

36 *circumstance* circumstantial detail 44 *indifferent* neutral in
effect

Lest it should ravel and be good to none,
You must provide to bottom° it on me;
Which must be done by praising me as much
As you in worth dispraise Sir Valentine.   55

Duke. And, Proteus, we dare trust you in this kind,°
Because we know, on Valentine's report,
You are already Love's firm votary
And cannot soon revolt and change your mind.
Upon this warrant shall you have access   60
Where you with Silvia may confer at large;
For she is lumpish, heavy, melancholy,
And, for your friend's sake, will be glad of you;
Where you may temper° her by your persuasion
To hate young Valentine and love my friend.   65

Proteus. As much as I can do, I will effect.
But you, Sir Thurio, are not sharp enough;
You must lay lime to tangle° her desires
By wailful sonnets, whose composèd rhymes
Should be full-fraught with serviceable vows.°   70

Duke. Ay,
Much is the force of heaven-bred poesy.

Proteus. Say that upon the altar of her beauty
You sacrifice your tears, your sighs, your heart.
Write till your ink be dry, and with your tears   75
Moist it again, and frame some feeling line
That may discover such integrity.°
For Orpheus' lute was strung with poets' sinews,
Whose golden touch could soften steel and stones,
Make tigers tame, and huge leviathans   80
Forsake unsounded deeps to dance on sands.°
After your dire-lamenting elegies,
Visit by night your lady's chamber window

53 *bottom* anchor, tie (as a weaver's thread)   56 *kind* i.e., an affair of this nature   64 *temper* make pliant, shape   68 *lime to tangle* birdlime to ensnare (birdlime is a sticky substance spread on branches to catch birds)   70 *full-fraught with serviceable vows* loaded with vows to serve faithfully   77 *discover such integrity* exhibit such devotion   78–81 *Orpheus' lute . . . sands* (cf. *Merchant of Venice*, V.i for a simpler tribute to the musician of Thrace)

With some sweet consort;° to their instruments
85 Tune a deploring dump.° The night's dead silence
Will well become such sweet-complaining griev-
    ance.
This, or else nothing, will inherit° her.

Duke. This discipline° shows thou hast been in love.

Thurio. And thy advice this night I'll put in practice.
90 Therefore, sweet Proteus, my direction-giver,
Let us into the city presently
To sort° some gentlemen well skilled in music.
I have a sonnet that will serve the turn
To give the onset° to thy good advice.

95 *Duke.* About it, gentlemen!

Proteus. We'll wait upon your Grace till after supper,
And afterward determine our proceedings.

Duke. Even now about it! I will pardon you.   *Exeunt.*

---

84 *sweet consort* i.e., company of musicians 85 *deploring dump*
doleful ditty 87 *inherit* obtain 88 *discipline* instruction 92 *sort*
sort out, select 94 *give the onset* make a beginning

ACT IV

Scene I. [*A forest.*]

Enter certain Outlaws.

First Outlaw. Fellows, stand fast; I see a passenger.°

Second Outlaw. If there be ten, shrink not, but down
    with 'em.

[*Enter Valentine and Speed.*]

Third Outlaw. Stand, sir, and throw us that° you have
    about ye.
  If not, we'll make you sit, and rifle you.

Speed. Sir, we are undone; these are the villains   5
  That all the travelers do fear so much.

Valentine. My friends—

First Outlaw. That's not so, sir; we are your enemies.

Second Outlaw. Peace! We'll hear him.

Third Outlaw. Ay, by my beard, will we, for he's a
    proper° man.   10

Valentine. Then know that I have little wealth to lose.

IV.i.1 *passenger* pedestrian   3 *that* that which   10 *proper* handsome

99

A man I am crossed with adversity.
My riches are these poor habiliments,
Of which if you should here disfurnish° me,
15 You take the sum and substance that I have.

Second Outlaw. Whiner travel you?

Valentine. To Verona.

First Outlaw. Whence came you?

Valentine. From Milan.

20 *Third Outlaw.* Have you long sojourned there?

Valentine. Some sixteen months, and longer might
      have stayed
    If crooked fortune had not thwarted me.

First Outlaw. What, were you banished thence?

Valentine. I was.

25 *Second Outlaw.* For what offense?

Valentine. For that which now torments me to re-
      hearse:
    I killed a man, whose death I much repent;
    But yet I slew him manfully in fight,
    Without false vantage° or base treachery.

30 *First Outlaw.* Why, ne'er repent it, if it were done so.
    But were you banished for so small a fault?

Valentine. I was, and held me glad of such a doom.°

Second Outlaw. Have you the tongues?°

Valentine. My youthful travel therein made me
      happy,°
35   Or else I often had been miserable.

Third Outlaw. By the bare scalp of Robin Hood's fat
      friar,
    This fellow were a king for our wild faction!

14 *disfurnish* deprive   29 *false vantage* i.e., such advantage as is
gained by deceit   32 *doom* sentence   33 *Have you the tongues*
do you know foreign languages   34 *happy* fortunate

First Outlaw. We'll have him. Sirs, a word.

Speed. Master, be one of them; it's an honorable kind
   of thievery.   40

Valentine. Peace, villain!

Second Outlaw. Tell us this: have you anything to
   take to?°

Valentine. Nothing but my fortune.

Third Outlaw. Know, then, that some of us are gen-
   tlemen,
   Such as the fury of ungoverned youth   45
   Thrust from the company of awful° men:
   Myself was from Verona banishèd
   For practicing° to steal away a lady,
   An heir, and near allied unto the Duke.

Second Outlaw. And I from Mantua, for a gentleman   50
   Who, in my mood, I stabbed unto the heart.

First Outlaw. And I for suchlike petty crimes as these.
   But to the purpose—for we cite our faults,
   That they may hold excused our lawless lives;
   And partly, seeing you are beautified   55
   With goodly shape, and by your own report
   A linguist, and a man of such perfection
   As we do in our quality much want°—

Second Outlaw. Indeed, because you are a banished
   man,
   Therefore, above the rest, we parley to you.   60
   Are you content to be our general,
   To make a virtue of necessity,
   And live, as we do, in this wilderness?

Third Outlaw. What say'st thou? Wilt thou be of our
   consort?
   Say ay, and be the captain of us all.   65

---

42 *anything to take to* any trade to take up   46 *awful* deeply
respectful (but possibly a printer's slip for "lawful")   48 *prac-
ticing* plotting   58 *in our quality much want* much lack in our profession

We'll do thee homage and be ruled by thee,
Love thee as our commander and our king.

First Outlaw. But if thou scorn our courtesy, thou
diest.

Second Outlaw. Thou shalt not live to brag what we
have offered.

70   *Valentine.* I take your offer, and will live with you,
Provided that you do no outrages
On silly° women or poor passengers.

Third Outlaw. No, we detest such vile base practices.
Come, go with us; we'll bring thee to our crews
75   And show thee all the treasure we have got,
Which, with ourselves, all rest at thy dispose.

Exeunt.

Scene II. [*Milan. Beneath Silvia's window.*]

Enter Proteus.

Proteus. Already have I been false to Valentine,
And now I must be as unjust to Thurio.
Under the color° of commending him,
I have access my own love to prefer.°
5   But Silvia is too fair, too true, too holy
To be corrupted with my worthless gifts.
When I protest true loyalty to her,
She twits me with my falsehood to my friend;
When to her beauty I commend my vows,
10   She bids me think how I have been forsworn
In breaking faith with Julia whom I loved.
And notwithstanding all her sudden quips,
The least whereof would quell a lover's hope,
Yet, spaniel-like, the more she spurns my love,

72 *silly* defenseless   IV.ii.3 *color* pretense   4 *prefer* advance

The more it grows, and fawneth on her still.   15
But here comes Thurio; now must we to her window
And give some evening music to her ear.

[*Enter Thurio and Musicians.*]

Thurio. How now, Sir Proteus, are you crept before
   us?

Proteus. Ay, gentle Thurio, for you know that love
   Will creep in service where it cannot go.°   20

Thurio. Ay, but I hope, sir, that you love not here.

Proteus. Sir, but I do; or else I would be hence.

Thurio. Who? Silvia?

Proteus.   Ay, Silvia, for your sake.

Thurio. I thank you for your own. Now, gentlemen,
   Let's tune, and to it lustily awhile.   25

[*Enter, at a distance, Host, and Julia in boy's
clothes.*]

Host. Now, my young guest, methinks you're allycholly.° I pray you, why is it?

Julia. Marry, mine host, because I cannot be merry.

Host. Come, we'll have you merry. I'll bring you where
   you shall hear music, and see the gentleman that   30
   you asked for.

Julia. But shall I hear him speak?

Host. Ay, that you shall.

Julia. That will be music.   [*Music plays.*]

Host. Hark, hark!   35

Julia. Is he among these?

Host. Ay, but, peace! Let's hear 'em.

20 *go* walk upright   26–27 *allycholly* i.e., melancholy

Song.

 Who is Silvia, what is she,
  That all our swains commend her?
 Holy, fair, and wise is she;
  The heaven such grace did lend her,
 That she might admirèd be.

 Is she kind as she is fair?
  For beauty lives with kindness.
 Love doth to her eyes repair,
  To help him of his blindness,
 And, being helped, inhabits there.

 Then to Silvia let us sing,
  That Silvia is excelling;
 She excels each mortal thing
  Upon the dull earth dwelling.
 To her let us garlands bring.

Host. How now! Are you sadder than you were before? How do you, man? The music likes° you not.

Julia. You mistake; the musician likes me not.

Host. Why, my pretty youth?

Julia. He plays false, father.

Host. How? Out of tune on the strings?

Julia. Not so; but yet so false that he grieves my very heartstrings.

Host. You have a quick ear.

Julia. Ay, I would I were deaf; it makes me have a slow° heart.

Host. I perceive you delight not in music.

Julia. Not a whit, when it jars so.

54 *likes* pleases 63 *slow* i.e., heavy

Host. Hark, what fine change° is in the music!

Julia. Ay, that change is the spite.

Host. You would have them always play but one thing?

Julia. I would always have one play but one thing.
But, host, doth this Sir Proteus that we talk on   70
Often resort unto this gentlewoman?

Host. I tell you what Launce, his man, told me—he
loved her out of all nick.°

Julia. Where is Launce?

Host. Gone to seek his dog, which tomorrow, by his   75
master's command, he must carry for a present to
his lady.

Julia. Peace! Stand aside. The company parts.

Proteus. Sir Thurio, fear not you. I will so plead
That you shall say my cunning drift excels.   80

Thurio. Where meet we?

Proteus.   At Saint Gregory's well.

Thurio.   Farewell.
[*Exeunt Thurio and Musicians.*]

[*Enter Silvia above.*]

Proteus. Madam, good even to your ladyship.

Silvia. I thank you for your music, gentlemen.
Who is that that spake?

Proteus. One, lady, if you knew his pure heart's truth,   85
You would quickly learn to know him by his voice.

Silvia. Sir Proteus, as I take it.

Proteus. Sir Proteus, gentle lady, and your servant.

---

66 *change* modulation (in the next line Julia puns, alluding to
the change in Proteus' affections)   73 *out of all nick* beyond
measure

Silvia. What's your will?

Proteus.   That I may compass yours.

90 *Silvia.* You have your wish; my will is even this:
        That presently you hie you home to bed.
        Thou subtle, perjured, false, disloyal man!
        Think'st thou I am so shallow, so conceitless,°
        To be seducèd by thy flattery,
95   That hast deceived so many with thy vows?
        Return, return, and make thy love amends.
        For me, by this pale queen of night I swear,
        I am so far from granting thy request
        That I despise thee for thy wrongful suit,
100   And by and by intend to chide myself
        Even for this time I spend in talking to thee.

    Proteus. I grant, sweet love, that I did love a lady;
        But she is dead.

    Julia. [*Aside*] 'Twere false, if I should speak it,
105   For I am sure she is not burièd.

    Silvia. Say that she be; yet Valentine thy friend
        Survives, to whom, thyself art witness,
        I am betrothed. And art thou not ashamed
        To wrong him with thy importunacy?

110 *Proteus.* I likewise hear that Valentine is dead.

    Silvia. And so suppose am I, for in his grave
        Assure thyself my love is burièd.

    Proteus. Sweet lady, let me rake it from the earth.

    Silvia. Go to thy lady's grave, and call hers thence;
115   Or, at the least, in hers sepulcher thine.

    Julia. [*Aside*] He heard not that.

    Proteus. Madam, if your heart be so obdurate,
        Vouchsafe° me yet your picture for my love,
        The picture that is hanging in your chamber.
120   To that I'll speak, to that I'll sigh and weep;
        For since the substance of your perfect self

93 *conceitless* witless   118 *Vouchsafe* grant

　　　Is else devoted,° I am but a shadow,
　　　And to your shadow° will I make true love.

Julia. [*Aside*] If 'twere a substance, you would, sure,
　　　deceive it,
　　　And make it but a shadow, as I am.   *125*

Silvia. I am very loath to be your idol, sir;
　　　But since your falsehood shall become you well
　　　To worship shadows and adore false shapes,
　　　Send to me in the morning, and I'll send it.
　　　And so, good rest.

Proteus.　　　　　　As wretches have o'ernight   *130*
　　　That wait for execution in the morn.
　　　　　　　　[*Exeunt Proteus and Silvia severally.*]

Julia. Host, will you go?

Host. By my halidom,° I was fast asleep.

Julia. Pray you, where lies° Sir Proteus?

Host. Marry, at my house. Trust me, I think 'tis almost   *135*
　　　day.

Julia. Not so; but it hath been the longest night
　　　That e'er I watched, and the most heaviest.
　　　　　　　　　　　　　　　　[*Exeunt.*]

Scene III. [*Milan. Beneath Silvia's window.*]

Enter Eglamour.

Eglamour. This is the hour that Madam Silvia
　　　Entreated me to call and know her mind.
　　　There's some great matter she'd employ me in.
　　─Madam, madam!

122 *else devoted* vowed to someone else   123 *shadow* portrait
133 *halidom* sacred relic (a mild oath)   134 *lies* lodges

[*Enter Silvia above.*]

Silvia. Who calls?

5 *Eglamour.*   Your servant and your friend,
  One that attends your ladyship's command.

Silvia. Sir Eglamour, a thousand times good morrow.

Eglamour. As many, worthy lady, to yourself.
  According to your ladyship's impose,°
10 I am thus early come to know what service
  It is your pleasure to command me in.

Silvia. O Eglamour, thou art a gentleman—
  Think not I flatter, for I swear I do not—
  Valiant, wise, remorseful,° well accomplished.
15 Thou art not ignorant what dear good will
  I bear unto the banished Valentine,
  Nor how my father would enforce me marry
  Vain Thurio, whom my very soul abhors.
  Thyself hast loved, and I have heard thee say
20 No grief did ever come so near thy heart
  As when thy lady and thy true love died,
  Upon whose grave thou vow'dst pure chastity.
  Sir Eglamour, I would to Valentine,
  To Mantua, where I hear he makes abode;
25 And, for the ways are dangerous to pass,
  I do desire thy worthy company,
  Upon whose faith and honor I repose.
  Urge not my father's anger, Eglamour,
  But think upon my grief, a lady's grief,
30 And on the justice of my flying hence
  To keep me from a most unholy match,
  Which heaven and fortune still rewards with plagues.
  I do desire thee, even from a heart
  As full of sorrows as the sea of sands,
35 To bear me company, and go with me:
  If not, to hide what I have said to thee,
  That I may venture to depart alone.

Eglamour. Madam, I pity much your grievances,

IV.iii.9 *impose* command   14 *remorseful* compassionate

Which since I know they virtuously are placed,
I give consent to go along with you,   *40*
Recking as little what betideth me
As much I wish all good befortune you.
When will you go?

Silvia.   This evening coming.

Eglamour. Where shall I meet you?

Silvia.   At Friar Patrick's cell,
Where I intend holy confession.   *45*

Eglamour. I will not fail your ladyship. Good morrow,
gentle lady.

Silvia. Good morrow, kind Sir Eglamour.
                                Exeunt [severally].

Scene IV. [*Milan. Beneath Silvia's window.*]

Enter Launce, [with his dog].

Launce. When a man's servant shall play the cur with
him, look you, it goes hard: one that I brought up
of° a puppy; one that I saved from drowning, when
three or four of his blind brothers and sisters went
to it! I have taught him, even as one would say pre-   *5*
cisely, "thus I would teach a dog." I was sent to
deliver him as a present to Mistress Silvia from my
master, and I came no sooner into the dining chamber, but he steps me to her trencher° and steals her
capon's leg. O, 'tis a foul thing when a cur cannot   *10*
keep° himself in all companies! I would have, as
one should say, one that takes upon him to be a
dog indeed, to be as it were, a dog at all things. If
I had not had more wit than he, to take a fault upon
me that he did, I think verily he had been hanged   *15*

IV.iv.3 *of* from   9 *trencher* wooden plate   11 *keep* control

for't; sure as I live, he had suffered for't. You shall
judge. He thrusts me himself into the company of
three or four gentlemanlike dogs under the Duke's
table; he had not been there—bless the mark!—a
pissing while, but all the chamber smelt him. "Out
with the dog!" says one. "What cur is that?" says
another. "Whip him out," says the third. "Hang him
up," says the Duke. I, having been acquainted with
the smell before, knew it was Crab, and goes me to
the fellow that whips the dogs. "Friend," quoth I,
"you mean to whip the dog?" "Ay, marry, do I,"
quoth he. "You do him the more wrong," quoth I;
" 'twas I did the thing you wot° of." He makes me
no more ado, but whips me out of the chamber.
How many masters would do this for his servant?
Nay, I'll be sworn, I have sat in the stocks for pud-
dings° he hath stol'n; otherwise he had been executed. I have stood on the pillory for geese he hath
killed; otherwise he had suffered for't. Thou think'st
not of this now. Nay, I remember the trick you
served me when I took my leave of Madam Silvia.
Did not I bid thee still mark me, and do as I do?
When didst thou see me heave up my leg, and make
water against a gentlewoman's farthingale? Didst
thou ever see me do such a trick?

[*Enter Proteus and Julia.*]

Proteus. Sebastian is thy name? I like thee well.
And will employ thee in some service presently.

Julia. In what you please. I'll do what I can.

Proteus. I hope thou wilt. [*To Launce*] How now, you
whoreson peasant!
Where have you been these two days loitering?

Launce. Marry, sir, I carried Mistress Silvia the dog
you bade me.

Proteus. And what says she to my little jewel?

28 *wot* know   31–32 *puddings* sausages

Launce. Marry, she says your dog was a cur, and tells
  you currish thanks is good enough for such a present.   50

Proteus. But she received my dog?

Launce. No, indeed, did she not. Here have I brought
  him back again.

Proteus. What, didst thou offer her this from me?

Launce. Ay, sir. The other squirrel° was stol'n from   55
  me by the hangman's boys° in the market place, and
  then I offered her mine own, who is a dog as big
  as ten of yours, and therefore the gift the greater.

Proteus. Go get thee hence and find my dog again,
  Or ne'er return again into my sight.   60
  Away, I say! Stayest thou to vex me here?
                [*Exit Launce.*]
  A slave, that still an end° turns me to shame!
  Sebastian, I have entertainèd° thee
  Partly that° I have need of such a youth
  That can with some discretion do my business,   65
  For 'tis no trusting to yond foolish lout;
  But chiefly for thy face and thy behavior,
  Which, if my augury deceive me not,
  Witness good bringing up, fortune, and truth.
  Therefore, know thou, for this I entertain thee.   70
  Go presently, and take this ring with thee;
  Deliver it to Madam Silvia.
  She loved me well delivered it to me.

Julia. It seems you loved not her, to leave her token.
  She is dead, belike?

Proteus.   Not so; I think she lives.   75

Julia. Alas!

Proteus. Why dost thou cry "Alas"?

---

55 *squirrel* i.e., little dog 56 *hangman's boys* i.e., boys who
will surely belong to the hangman (hang) at last 62 *still an end*
forevermore 63 *entertainèd* retained 64 *Partly that* in part
because

Julia.   I cannot choose
　　But pity her.

Proteus.   Wherefore shouldst thou pity her?

Julia. Because methinks that she loved you as well
80　　As you do love your lady Silvia.
　　She dreams on him that has forgot her love;
　　You dote on her that cares not for your love.
　　'Tis pity love should be so contrary;
　　And thinking on it makes me cry "Alas!"

85　*Proteus.* Well, give her that ring, and therewithal
　　This letter. That's her chamber. Tell my lady
　　I claim the promise for her heavenly picture.
　　Your message done, hie home unto my chamber,
　　Where thou shalt find me, sad and solitary. [*Exit.*]

90　*Julia.* How many women would do such a message?
　　Alas, poor Proteus! Thou hast entertained
　　A fox to be the shepherd of thy lambs.
　　Alas, poor fool! Why do I pity him
　　That with his very heart despiseth me?
95　　Because he loves her, he despiseth me;
　　Because I love him, I must pity him.
　　This ring I gave him when he parted from me,
　　To bind him to remember my good will;
　　And now am I, unhappy messenger,
100　　To plead for that which I would not obtain,
　　To carry that which I would have refused,
　　To praise his faith which I would have dispraised.
　　I am my master's true-confirmèd love,
　　But cannot be true servant to my master
105　　Unless I prove false traitor to myself.
　　Yet will I woo for him, but yet so coldly
　　As, heaven it knows, I would not have him speed.°

[*Enter Silvia, attended.*]

　　Gentlewoman, good day! I pray you, be my mean
　　To bring me where to speak with Madam Silvia.

107 *speed* prosper, succeed

Silvia. What would you with her, if that I be she?   110

Julia. If you be she, I do entreat your patience
  To hear me speak the message I am sent on.

Silvia. From whom?

Julia. From my master, Sir Proteus, madam.

Silvia. O, he sends you for a picture.   115

Julia. Ay, madam.

Silvia. Ursula, bring my picture there.
  Go give your master this. Tell him, from me,
  One Julia, that his changing thoughts forget,
  Would better fit his chamber than this shadow.   120

Julia. Madam, please you peruse this letter—
  Pardon me, madam; I have unadvised°
  Delivered you a paper that I should not.
  This is the letter to your ladyship.

Silvia. I pray thee, let me look on that again.   125

Julia. It may not be; good madam, pardon me.

Silvia. There, hold!
  I will not look upon your master's lines.
  I know they are stuffed with protestations,
  And full of new-found oaths which he will break   130
  As easily as I do tear his paper.

Julia. Madam, he sends your ladyship this ring.

Silvia. The more shame for him that he sends it me,
  For I have heard him say a thousand times
  His Julia gave it him at his departure.   135
  Though his false finger have profaned the ring,
  Mine shall not do his Julia so much wrong.

Julia. She thanks you.

Silvia. What say'st thou?

Julia. I thank you, madam, that you tender her.°   140

122 *unadvised* unintentionally   140 *tender her* i.e., have a care for
her interest

Poor gentlewoman! My master wrongs her much.

Silvia. Dost thou know her?

Julia. Almost as well as I do know myself.
To think upon her woes, I do protest
145   That I have wept a hundred several° times.

Silvia. Belike she thinks that Proteus hath forsook her.

Julia. I think she doth; and that's her cause of sorrow.

Silvia. Is she not passing° fair?

Julia. She hath been fairer, madam, than she is.
150   When she did think my master loved her well,
She, in my judgment, was as fair as you.
But since she did neglect her looking glass,
And threw her sun-expelling mask away,
The air hath starved the roses in her cheeks
155   And pinched the lily-tincture of her face,
That now she is become as black° as I.

Silvia. How tall was she?

Julia. About my stature: for, at Pentecost,°
When all our pageants of delight were played,
160   Our youth got me to play the woman's part,
And I was trimmed in Madam Julia's gown,
Which servèd me as fit, by all men's judgments,
As if the garment had been made for me.
Therefore I know she is about my height.
165   And at that time I made her weep agood,°
For I did play a lamentable part.
Madam, 'twas Ariadne° passioning
For Theseus' perjury and unjust flight,
Which I so lively acted with my tears
170   That my poor mistress, movèd therewithal,
Wept bitterly; and would I might be dead

145 *several* separate   148 *passing* surpassingly   156 *black* i.e.,
from the sun   158 *Pentecost* (Whitsunday [seventh Sunday after
Easter], an occasion for morris dances, "pageants of delight," and
such outdoor festivities)   165 *agood* aplenty   167 *Ariadne* (daughter of King Minos, who aided Theseus' flight from the Cretan laby-
rinth, only to be abandoned on the isle of Naxos)

If I in thought felt not her very sorrow!

Silvia. She is beholding° to thee, gentle youth.
Alas, poor lady, desolate and left!
I weep myself to think upon thy words.   *175*
Here, youth, there is my purse. I give thee this
For thy sweet mistress' sake, because thou lov'st her.
Farewell.   [*Exit Silvia, with attendants.*]

Julia. And she shall thank you for't, if e'er you know
    her.
A virtuous gentlewoman, mild and beautiful!   *180*
I hope my master's suit will be but cold,
Since she respects my mistress' love so much.
Alas, how love can trifle with itself!
Here is her picture: let me see; I think,
If I had such a tire,° this face of mine   *185*
Were full as lovely as is this of hers.
And yet the painter flattered her a little,
Unless I flatter with myself too much.
Her hair is auburn, mine is perfect yellow:
If that be all the difference in his love,   *190*
I'll get me such a colored periwig.
Her eyes are gray as glass, and so are mine:
Ay, but her forehead's low, and mine's as high.
What should it be that he respects in her,
But I can make respective° in myself,   *195*
If this fond Love° were not a blinded god?
Come, shadow, come, and take this shadow up,°
For 'tis thy rival. O thou senseless form,
Thou shalt be worshiped, kissed, loved, and adored!
And, were there sense in his idolatry,   *200*
My substance should be statue in thy stead.
I'll use thee kindly for thy mistress' sake,
That used me so; or else, by Jove I vow,
I should have scratched out your unseeing eyes,
To make my master out of love with thee!   *Exit.*   *205*

173 *beholding* indebted   185 *tire* headdress   195 *respective* worthy
of respect   196 *fond Love* i.e., foolish Cupid   197 *Come . . .
shadow up* come, shadow (of my former self), and "take on" this
other shadow (Silvia's portrait)

ACT V

Scene I. [*Milan. An abbey.*]

Enter Eglamour.

Eglamour. The sun begins to gild the western sky,
    And now it is about the very hour
    That Silvia, at Friar Patrick's cell, should meet me.
    She will not fail, for lovers break not hours,
5   Unless it be to come before their time,
    So much they spur their expedition.
    See where she comes.

             [*Enter Silvia.*]

                Lady, a happy evening!

Silvia. Amen, amen! Go on, good Eglamour,
    Out at the postern° by the abbey wall.
10   I fear I am attended° by some spies.

Eglamour. Fear not; the forest is not three leagues off.
    If we recover° that, we are sure enough.   *Exeunt.*

V.i.9 *postern* small door at side or rear   10 *attended* followed
12 *recover* reach

116

Scene II. [*Milan. The Duke's palace.*]

Enter Thurio, Proteus, [and] Julia.

Thurio. Sir Proteus, what says Silvia to my suit?

Proteus. O, sir, I find her milder than she was;
    And yet she takes exceptions at your person.

Thurio. What, that my leg is too long?

Proteus. No; that it is too little.   5

Thurio. I'll wear a boot, to make it somewhat rounder.

Julia. [*Aside*] But love will not be spurred° to what
    it loathes.

Thurio. What says she to my face?

Proteus. She says it is a fair one.

Thurio. Nay then, the wanton lies; my face is black.   10

Proteus. But pearls are fair; and the old saying is,
    Black men are pearls in beauteous ladies' eyes.

Julia. [*Aside*] 'Tis true, such pearls as put out ladies'
    eyes;
    For I had rather wink than look on them.

Thurio. How likes she my discourse?°   15

Proteus. Ill, when you talk of war.

Thurio. But well, when I discourse of love and peace?

Julia. [*Aside*] But better, indeed, when you hold your
    peace.

V.ii.7 *spurred* (with reference to preceding "boot")   15 *discourse*
conversational ability

Thurio. What says she to my valor?

20 *Proteus.* O, sir, she makes no doubt of that.

Julia. [*Aside*] She needs not, when she knows it cowardice.

Thurio. What says she to my birth?

Proteus. That you are well derived.

Julia. [*Aside*] True, from a gentleman to a fool.

25 *Thurio.* Considers she my possessions?

Proteus. O, ay, and pities them.

Thurio. Wherefore?

Julia. [*Aside*] That such an ass should owe° them.

Proteus. That they are out by lease.°

30 *Julia.* Here comes the Duke.

[*Enter Duke.*]

Duke. How now, Sir Proteus! How now, Thurio!
　　Which of you saw Sir Eglamour of late?

Thurio. Not I.

Proteus.　　　Nor I.

Duke.　　　　　Saw you my daughter?

Proteus.　　　　　　　　　Neither.

Duke. Why then,
35　　She's fled unto that peasant Valentine,
　　And Eglamour is in her company.
　　'Tis true; for Friar Laurence met them both
　　As he in penance wandered through the forest.
　　Him he knew well, and guessed that it was she,
40　　But, being masked, he was not sure of it;
　　Besides, she did intend confession
　　At Patrick's cell this even, and there she was not.

---

28 *owe* own   29 *out by lease* i.e., because Thurio is such a fool,
he will surely hold onto his possessions only temporarily

These likelihoods confirm her flight from hence.
Therefore, I pray you, stand not to discourse,
But mount you presently, and meet with me   45
Upon the rising of the mountain foot°
That leads toward Mantua, whither they are fled.
Dispatch, sweet gentlemen, and follow me.   [*Exit.*]

Thurio. Why, this it is to be a peevish girl
That flies her fortune when it follows her.   50
I'll after, more to be revenged on Eglamour
Than for the love of reckless Silvia.   [*Exit.*]

Proteus. And I will follow, more for Silvia's love
Than hate of Eglamour, that goes with her.   [*Exit.*]

Julia. And I will follow, more to cross that love   55
Than hate for Silvia, that is gone for love.   [*Exit.*]

Scene III. [*A forest.*]

[*Enter*] *Silvia* [*and*] *Outlaws.*

First Outlaw. Come, come,
Be patient; we must bring you to our captain.

Silvia. A thousand more mischances than this one
Have learned me how to brook° this patiently.

Second Outlaw. Come, bring her away.   5

First Outlaw. Where is the gentleman that was with
her?

Third Outlaw. Being nimble footed, he hath outrun us,
But Moyses and Valerius follow him.
Go thou with her to the west end of the wood;
There is our captain. We'll follow him that's fled;   10
The thicket is beset;° he cannot 'scape.

46 *rising of the mountain foot* i.e., foothill   V.iii.4 *learned me how
to brook* taught me how to endure   11 *beset* surrounded

First Outlaw. Come, I must bring you to our captain's
cave.
Fear not; he bears an honorable mind,
And will not use a woman lawlessly.

15 *Silvia.* O Valentine, this I endure for thee!   *Exeunt.*

Scene IV. [*Another part of the forest.*]

Enter Valentine.

Valentine. How use° doth breed a habit in a man!
This shadowy desert,° unfrequented woods,
I better brook than flourishing peopled towns.
Here can I sit alone, unseen of any,
5   And to the nightingale's complaining notes
Tune my distresses and record my woes.
O thou that dost inhabit in my breast,
Leave not the mansion so long tenantless,
Lest, growing ruinous, the building fall,
10   And leave no memory of what it was!
Repair me with thy presence, Silvia;
Thou gentle nymph, cherish thy forlorn swain!
                              [*Noise within.*]
What halloing and what stir is this today?
These are my mates, that make their wills their law,
15   Have° some unhappy passenger in chase.
They love me well; yet I have much to do
To keep them from uncivil outrages.
Withdraw thee, Valentine. Who's this comes here?
                              [*Retires.*]

[*Enter Proteus, Silvia, and Julia.*]

Proteus. Madam, this service I have done for you—
20   Though you respect not aught your servant doth—

V.iv.1 *use* custom   2 *shadowy desert* wild place inhabited only with
shadows (of trees)   15 *Have* who have

To hazard life, and rescue you from him
That would have forced your honor and your love.
Vouchsafe me, for my meed, but one fair look;
A smaller boon than this I cannot beg,
And less than this, I am sure, you cannot give.   25

Valentine. [*Aside*] How like a dream is this I see and
    hear!
Love, lend me patience to forbear awhile.

Silvia. O miserable, unhappy that I am!

Proteus. Unhappy were you, madam, ere I came;
But by my coming I have made you happy.   30

Silvia. By thy approach thou mak'st me most unhappy.

Julia. [*Aside*] And me, when he approacheth to your
    presence.

Silvia. Had I been seizèd by a hungry lion,
I would have been a breakfast to the beast
Rather than have false Proteus rescue me.   35
O, Heaven be judge how I love Valentine
Whose life's as tender° to me as my soul!
And full as much, for more there cannot be,
I do detest false perjured Proteus.
Therefore be gone; solicit me no more.   40

Proteus. What dangerous action, stood it next to death,
Would I not undergo for one calm look!
O' tis the curse in love, and still approved,°
When women cannot love where they're beloved!

Silvia. When Proteus cannot love where he's beloved!   45
Read over Julia's heart, thy first, best love,
For whose dear sake thou didst then rend thy faith
Into a thousand oaths; and all those oaths
Descended into perjury, to love me.
Thou hast no faith left now, unless thou'dst two,   50
And that's far worse than none; better have none
Than plural faith, which is too much by one.
Thou counterfeit to thy true friend!

37 *tender* precious   43 *still approved* perennially proved true

Proteus.   In love,
Who respects friend?

Silvia.   All men but Proteus.

35   *Proteus.* Nay, if the gentle spirit of moving words
Can no way change you to a milder form,
I'll woo you like a soldier, at arms' end,
And love you 'gainst the nature of love—force ye.

Silvia. O heaven!

Proteus.   I'll force thee yield to my desire.

Valentine. [*Advancing*] Ruffian, let go that rude uncivil
60   touch,
Thou friend of an ill fashion!°

Proteus.   Valentine!

Valentine. Thou common° friend, that's without faith
or love—
For such is a friend now; treacherous man!
Thou hast beguiled my hopes; nought but mine eye
65   Could have persuaded me. Now I dare not say
I have one friend alive; thou wouldst disprove me.
Who should be trusted, when one's right hand
Is perjured to the bosom? Proteus,
I am sorry I must never trust thee more,
70   But count the world a stranger for thy sake.
The private° wound is deepest. O time most accurst,
'Mongst all foes that a friend should be the worst!

Proteus. My shame and guilt confounds° me.
Forgive me, Valentine. If hearty sorrow
73   Be a sufficient ransom for offense,
I tender't here; I do as truly suffer
As e'er I did commit.°

Valentine.   Then I am paid;°

61 *friend of an ill fashion* i.e., false friend   62 *common* i.e.,
no better than the ordinary   71 *private* intimate (here, given by
a friend)   73 *confounds* destroys   76–77 *I do . . . did commit* i.e.,
I do indeed suffer, as truly as I did commit the fault   77 *paid*
satisfied

And once again I do receive thee honest.°
Who by repentance is not satisfied
Is nor of heaven nor earth, for these are pleased.   80
By penitence th' Eternal's wrath's appeased;
And, that my love may appear plain and free,
All that was mine in Silvia I give thee.

Julia. O me unhappy!   [*Swoons.*]

Proteus. Look to the boy.   85

Valentine. Why, boy! Why, wag! How now! What's
  the matter? Look up; speak.

Julia. O good sir, my master charged me to deliver a
  ring to Madam Silvia, which, out of my neglect, was
  never done.   90

Proteus. Where is that ring, boy?

Julia.   Here 'tis; this is it.

Proteus. How! Let me see.
  Why, this is the ring I gave to Julia.

Julia. O, cry you mercy,° sir, I have mistook.
  This is the ring you sent to Silvia.   95

Proteus. But how cam'st thou by this ring? At my
  depart I gave this unto Julia.

Julia. And Julia herself did give it me;
  And Julia herself hath brought it hither.

Proteus. How! Julia!   100

Julia. Behold her that gave aim to° all thy oaths,
  And entertained 'em deeply in her heart.
  How oft hast thou with perjury cleft the root!
  O Proteus, let this habit° make thee blush!
  Be thou ashamed that I have took upon me   105
  Such an immodest raiment, if shame live
  In a disguise of love.°

78 *receive thee honest* accept you as being honorable   94 *cry you
mercy* I beg your pardon   101 *gave aim to* was the object (target)
of   104 *habit* i.e., her boy's garb   106–07 *if shame ... of love*
if it can be shameful to disguise oneself for the sake of love

It is the lesser blot, modesty finds,
Women to change their shapes than men their
minds.

Proteus. Than men their minds! 'Tis true. O heaven,
110   were man
But constant, he were perfect! That one error
Fills him with faults, makes him run through all th'
sins:
Inconstancy falls off ere it begins.°
What is in Silvia's face, but I may spy
115   More fresh in Julia's with a constant eye?

Valentine. Come, come, a hand from either.
Let me be blest to make this happy close;°
'Twere pity two such friends should be long foes.

Proteus. Bear witness, Heaven, I have my wish forever.

120   *Julia.* And I mine.

[*Enter Outlaws, with Duke and Thurio.*]

Outlaws. A prize, a prize, a prize!

Valentine. Forbear, forbear, I say! It is my lord the
Duke.
Your Grace is welcome to a man disgraced,
Banished Valentine.

Duke.   Sir Valentine!

125   *Thurio.* Yonder is Silvia, and Silvia's mine.

Valentine. Thurio, give back,° or else embrace thy
death.
Come not within the measure° of my wrath.
Do not name Silvia thine; if once again,
Verona° shall not hold thee. Here she stands.
130   Take but possession of her with a touch:
I dare thee but to breathe upon my love.

113 *Inconstancy . . . begins* i.e., the inconstant man proves false
even before he begins to love   117 *close* joining of hands   126
give back back off   127 *measure* range, reach   129 *Verona* (i.e.,
Milan; see III.i.81,n.)

Thurio. Sir Valentine, I care not for her, I.
 I hold him but a fool that will endanger
 His body for a girl that loves him not.
 I claim her not, and therefore she is thine.   135

Duke. The more degenerate and base art thou,
 To make such means for° her as thou hast done,
 And leave her on such slight conditions.
 Now, by the honor of my ancestry,
 I do applaud thy spirit, Valentine,   140
 And think thee worthy of an empress' love.
 Know, then, I here forget all former griefs,
 Cancel all grudge, repeal° thee home again,
 Plead a new state in thy unrivaled merit,°
 To which I thus subscribe: Sir Valentine,   145
 Thou art a gentleman, and well derived;
 Take thou thy Silvia, for thou hast deserved her.

Valentine. I thank your Grace; the gift hath made me
     happy.
 I now beseech you, for your daughter's sake,
 To grant one boon that I shall ask of you.   150

Duke. I grant it, for thine own, whate'er it be.

Valentine. These banished men that I have kept withal°
 Are men endued° with worthy qualities.
 Forgive them what they have committed here,
 And let them be recalled from their exile: 155
 They are reformèd, civil, full of good,
 And fit for great employment, worthy lord.

Duke. Thou hast prevailed; I pardon them and thee.
 Dispose of them as thou know'st their deserts.
 Come, let us go. We will include all jars°   160
 With triumphs, mirth, and rare solemnity.°

137 *means for* efforts to win   143 *repeal* recall (from banishment)   144 *plead ... merit* (the general sense appears to be one of the following: (1) plead to be restored to your good graces, having formerly misjudged them (2) proclaim that you are elevated to a new place in my favor, earned by your unrivaled merit)   152 *kept withal* lived with   153 *endued* endowed   160 *include all jars* conclude all discords   161 *triumphs ... solemnity* celebrations ... festivity

Valentine. And, as we walk along, I dare be bold
  With our discourse to make your Grace to smile.
  What think you of this page, my lord?

163 *Duke.* I think the boy hath grace in him; he blushes.

Valentine. I warrant you, my lord, more grace than
  boy.

Duke. What mean you by that saying?

Valentine. Please you, I'll tell you as we pass along,
  That you will wonder what hath fortunèd.°
170 Come, Proteus; 'tis your penance but° to hear
  The story of your loves discoverèd.°
  That done, our day of marriage shall be yours;
  One feast, one house, one mutual happiness.

                                        Exeunt.

                    FINIS

---

169 *fortunèd* chanced   170 *'tis your penance but* your only penance
is   171 *discoverèd* revealed

Textual Note

The Two Gentlemen of Verona was first printed in the
First Folio of 1623, which is the authority for the present
text. In the Folio it is the second play, standing between
The Tempest and The Merry Wives of Windsor, the title
of the latter play mistakenly appearing at the top of the
final two pages. Names of characters who participate in
each scene are grouped at the head of the scene, without
notice made of the point of their entrance. The present
edition deletes these names, and provides them, in square
brackets, at the appropriate places later in the scenes. The
Folio gives "Protheus" for "Proteus" and places the drama-
tis personae at the end of the text. Certain irregularities
occur in place names, as though Shakespeare had changed
his mind or become confused about principal locations;
thus in II.v Padua rather than Milan is identified as the
place of action by Speed, and in III.i the Duke of Milan
speaks of a lady "in Verona here." In the present edition,
speech prefixes have been regularized, spelling and punctuation have been modernized, and obvious typographical
errors have been corrected. Added material (stage directions, etc.) is set in brackets. Act and scene divisions are
those of the Folio, translated from Latin into English. The
relatively few emendations of the Folio text are indicated
below: the present reading is given in italics, followed by
the Folio reading in roman.

I.i.65 *leave* loue   77 *a sheep* Sheepe   144–45 *testerned* cestern'd

I.ii.88 *your* you

I.iii.91 *Exeunt* Exeunt. Finis

II.iii.29 *wood* would

II.iv.49 *father's in* father is in   107 *mistress* a Mistresse   165 *makes* make   195 *Is it mine eye* It is mine   213 *Exit* Exeunt

II.v.38 *that my* that that my

III.i.281 *master's ship* Mastership   318 *kissed fasting* fasting 378 s.d. *Exit* Exeunt

IV.i.10 *he's* he is   35 *miserable* often miserable   49 *An* And 49 *near* Neece

IV.ii.111 *his* her

IV.iii.18 *abhors* abhor'd

IV.iv.70 *thou* thee   74 *to leave* not leaue   205 *Exit* Exeunt

V.ii.18 *your peace* you peace   32 *Sir Eglamour* Eglamoure   56 *Exit* Exeunt

The Source of
The Two Gentlemen of Verona

Both because its plot is filled with well-known romance elements and because its poetic style is laden with rhetorical devices fashionable at the time it was written, *The Two Gentlemen of Verona* appears inevitably to owe an unusual number of debts to a wide variety of materials. In its conventions as well as in its basic materials and their manner of use, it is as deeply embedded in the literary life of its time as any work of Shakespeare's.

The central theme of the play—conflict between the duties of friendship and love—had been used by Boccaccio in *La Teseide*, by Chaucer in *The Knight's Tale*, and by Lyly in *Euphues: The Anatomy of Wit* and *Endimion;* but, indeed, this theme is ancient and widespread, and Shakespeare would have encountered it in any event. Specific incidents and motifs in the play, such as Julia's disguise as a boy, may have been suggested by Sidney's pastoral romance of *Arcadia;* the abrupt election of Valentine as captain of the outlaws may derive from the same source. Many echoes of Brooke's *Romeus and Juliet,* the narrative poem which Shakespeare followed in *Romeo and Juliet,* occur in the play, perhaps the most notable being the device of the rope ladder which figures prominently in both plays.

In poetic manner and attitude, the play shows the pervasive influence of Lyly, the fashionable stylist of courtly language and the master of dramatic artifice in dialogue, scene, and character. Long stretches of wit duels between servant and servant, servant and master, lady and attendant, filled with quips and quirks and turns of phrase, mark the play as Lylyan in its most basic conception. In *The Two Gentlemen of Verona* the artifices of Lyly are more than superficial ornamentation; they are organic.

For the core of the play, however, which is the love story of Julia and Proteus, Shakespeare went to a prose romance originally written in Spanish, the *Diana Enamorada,* by the Portuguese Jorge de Montemayor, published in 1542. How Shakespeare came to know this work is uncertain, for though it was translated into English by Bartholomew Yonge about 1582, the translation was not published until 1598—some four to six years after the play was written. It has been suggested that Shakespeare could have become acquainted with the *Diana* through a French translation made before 1590; that he may have seen Yonge's manuscript before it was published; or that the story was represented in a play now lost.

In any event, it is now generally accepted that Montemayor's romance somehow came to serve as Shakespeare's principal source, and, accordingly, an abridged version of the story follows. Inserted references to acts and scenes mark incidents of special interest.

Jorge de Montemayor

from *Diana Enamorada*

You shall therefore know, fair nymphs, that great Vandalia is my native country, a province not far hence, where I was born, in a city called Soldina, my mother called Delia, my father Andronius, for lineage and possessions the chiefest of all that province. It fell out that as my

Translated by Bartholomew Yonge, 1598

mother was married many years and had no children (by reason whereof she lived so sad and malcontent that she enjoyed not one merry day), with tears and sighs she daily importuned the heavens, and with a thousand vows and devout offerings besought God to grant her the sum of her desire: whose omnipotency it pleased, beholding from his imperial throne her continual orisons, to make her barren body (the greater part of her age being now spent and gone) to become fruitful. What infinite joy she conceived thereof, let her judge, that after a long desire of anything, fortune at last doth put it into her hands. Of which content my father Andronius being no less partaker, showed such tokens of inward joy as are impossible to be expressed. My mother Delia was so much given to reading of ancient histories that if, by reason of sickness or any important business, she had not been hindered, she would never (by her will) have passed the time away in any other delight; who (as I said) being now with child and finding herself on a night ill at ease, entreated my father to read something unto her, that her mind being occupied in contemplation thereof, she might the better pass her grief away. My father, who studied for nothing else but to please her in all he might, began to read unto her the history of Paris, when the three ladies referred their proud contention for the golden apple to his conclusion and judgment. But as my mother held it for an infallible opinion that Paris had partially given that sentence (persuaded thereunto by a blind passion of beauty), so she said, that without all doubt he did not with due reason and wisdom consider the goddess of battles; for, as martial and heroical feats (said she) excelled all other qualities, so with equity and justice the apple should have been given to her. My father answered that since the apple was to be given to the fairest, and that Venus was fairer than any of the rest, Paris had rightly given his judgment, if that harm had not ensued thereof, which afterwards did. To this my mother replied that, though it was written in the apple that it should be given to the fairest, it was not to be understood of corporal beauty, but of the intellectual beauty of the mind. And therefore since fortitude was a thing that made one most beautiful, and the exercise of arms an exterior act of this virtue, she affirmed that to the goddess of battles this apple should be given, if Paris had judged like a prudent and unappassionate judge. So that, fair nymphs, they spent a great part of the night in this controversy, both of them alleging the most reasons they could to confirm their own purpose. They persisting in this point, sleep began to overcome her whom the reasons and arguments of her husband could not once move; so that being very deep in her disputations, she fell into as deep a sleep, to whom (my father being now gone to his chamber) appeared the goddess Venus, with as frowning a countenance as fair, and said, "I marvel, Delia, who hath moved thee to be so contrary to her that was never opposite to thee? If thou hadst but called to mind the time when thou wert so overcome in love for Andronius, thou wouldest not have paid me the debt thou owest me with so ill coin. But thou shalt not escape free from my due anger; for thou shalt bring forth a son and a daughter, whose birth shall cost thee no less than thy life, and them their contentment, for uttering so much in disgrace of my honor and beauty: both which shall be as unfortunate in their love as any were ever in all their lives, or to the age wherein, with remediless sighs, they shall breathe forth the sum of their ceaseless sorrows." And having said thus, she vanished away: when, likewise, it seemed to my mother that the goddess Pallas came to her in a vision, and with a merry countenance said thus unto her: "With what sufficient rewards may I be able to requite the due regard, most happy and discreet Delia, which thou hast alleged in my favor against thy husband's obstinate opinion, except it be by making thee understand that thou shalt bring forth a son and a daughter, the most fortunate in arms that have been to their times." Having thus said, she vanished out of her sight, and my mother, through exceeding fear, awaked immediately. Who, within a month after, at one birth was delivered of me and of a brother of mine, and died in childbed, leaving my father the most sorrowful man in the world for her sudden death; for grief whereof, within a little while after, he also died. And because you may know, fair nymphs, in what great extremities love hath put me, you must understand that (being a woman of that quality and disposition as you have heard) I have been forced by my cruel destiny to leave my natural habit and liberty, and the due respect of mine honor, to follow him who thinks (perhaps) that I do but lose it by loving him so extremely. Behold how bootless and unseemly it is for a woman to be so dextrous in arms, as if it were her proper nature and kind, wherewith, fair nymphs, I had never been indued, but that, by means thereof, I should come to do you this little service against these villainies; which I account no less than if fortune had begun to satisfy in part some of those infinite wrongs that she hath continually done me. The nymphs were so amazed at her words that they could neither ask nor answer anything to that the fair shepherdess told them, who, prosecuting her history, said:

My brother and I were brought up in a nunnery, where an aunt of ours was abbess, until we had accomplished twelve years of age, at what time we were taken from thence again, and my brother was carried to the mighty and invincible King of Portugal his court (whose noble fame and princely liberality was bruited over all the world) where, being grown to years able to manage arms, he achieved as valiant and almost incredible enterprises by them as he suffered unfortunate disgraces and foils by love. And with all this he was so highly favored of that magnificent king that he would never suffer him to depart from his court. Unfortunate I, reserved by my sinister destinies to greater mishaps, was carried to a grandmother of mine, which place I would I had never seen, since it was an occasion of such a sorrowful life as never any woman suffered the like. And because there is not anything, fair nymphs, which I am not forced to tell you, as well for the great virtue and deserts which your excellent beauties do testify, as also for that for my mind doth give me, that you shall be no small part and means of my comfort, know that as I was in my grandmother's house, and almost seventeen years old, a certain young gentleman fell in love with me, who dwelt no further from our house than the length of a garden terrace, so that he might see me every summer's night when I walked in the garden. Whenas therefore ingrateful Felix had beheld in that place the unfortunate Felismena (for this is the name of the woeful woman that tells you her mishaps) he was extremely enamored of me, or else did cunningly dissemble it, I not knowing then whether of these two I might believe, but am now assured that whosoever believes least, or nothing at all in these affairs, shall be most at ease. Many days Don Felix spent in endeavoring to make me know the pains which he suffered for me, and many more did I spend in making the matter strange, and that he did not suffer them for my sake. And I know not why love delayed the time so long by forcing me to love him, but only that (when he came indeed) he might enter into my heart at once, and with greater force and violence. [I.i] When he had, therefore, by sundry signs, as by tilt and tourneys, and by prancing up and down upon his proud jennet before my windows, made it manifest that he was in love with me (for at the first I did not so well perceive it) he determined in the end to write a letter unto me; and having practiced divers times before with a maid of mine, and at length, with many gifts and fair promises, gotten her good will and furtherance, he gave her the letter to deliver to me. [I.ii] But to see the means that Rosina made unto me (for so was she called), the dutiful services and unwonted circumstances, before she did deliver it, the oaths that she sware unto me, and the subtle words and serious protestations she used, it was a pleasant thing, and worthy the noting. To whom (nevertheless) with an angry countenance I turned again, saying, "If I had not regard of mine own estate, and what hereafter might be said, I would make this shameless face of thine be known ever after for a mark of an impudent and bold minion: but because it is the first time, let this suffice that I have said and give thee warning to take heed of the second."

Methinks I see now the crafty wench, how she held her peace, dissembling very cunningly the sorrow that she conceived by my angry answer; for she feigned a counterfeit smiling, saying, "Jesus, Mistress! I gave it you, because you might laugh at it, and not to move your patience with it in this sort; for if I had any thought that it would have provoked you to anger, I pray God He may show His wrath as great towards me as ever He did to the daughter of any mother." And with this she added many words more (as she could do well enough) to pacify the feigned anger and ill opinion that I had conceived of her, and taking her letter with her, she departed from me. This having passed thus, I began to imagine what might ensue thereof, and love (methought) did put a certain desire into my mind to see the letter, though modesty and shame forbade me to ask it of my maid, especially for the words that had passed between us, as you have heard. And so I continued all that day until night, in variety of many thoughts; but when Rosina came to help me to bed, God knows how desirous I was to have her entreat me again to take the letter, but she would never speak unto me about it, nor (as it seemed) did so much as once think thereof. Yet to try, if by giving her some occasion I might prevail, I said unto her: "And is it so, Rosina, that Don Felix, without any regard to mine honor, dares write unto me?" "These are things, mistress," said she demurely to me again, "that are commonly incident to love, wherefore I beseech you pardon me, for if I had thought to have angered you with it, I would have first pulled out the balls of mine eyes." How cold my heart was at that blow, God knows, yet did I dissemble the matter and suffer myself to remain that night only with my desire, and with occasion of little sleep. And so it was, indeed, for that (methought) was the longest and most painful night that ever I passed. But when, with a slower pace (than I desired) the wished day was come, the discreet and subtle Rosina came into my chamber to help me to make me ready, in doing whereof, of purpose she let the letter closely fall, which when I perceived, "What is that that fell down?" said I. "Let me see it." "It is nothing, mistress," said she. "Come, come, let me see it," said I. "What! Move me not, or else tell me what it is." "Good Lord, mistress," said she, "why will you see it: it is the letter I would have given you yesterday." "Nay, that it is

not," said I. "Wherefore show it me, that I may see if
you lie or no." I had no sooner said so but she put it into
my hands, saying, "God never give me good if it be any
other thing"; and although I knew it well indeed, yet I
said, "What, this is not the same, for I know that well
enough, but it is one of thy lover's letters: I will read it,
to see in what need he standeth of thy favor." And opening it, I found it contained this that followeth.

I ever imagined, dear mistress, that your discretion and
wisdom would have taken away the fear I had to write
unto you, the same knowing well enough (without any
letter at all) how much I love you, but the very same hath
so cunningly dissembled that wherein I hoped the only
remedy of my griefs had been, therein consisted my greatest harm. If according to your wisdom you censure my
boldness, I shall not then (I know) enjoy one hour of
life; but if you do consider of it according to love's accustomed effects, then will I not exchange my hope for
it. Be not offended, I beseech you, good lady, with my
letter, and blame me not for writing unto you, until you
see by experience whether I can leave off to write: and
take me besides into the possession of that which is yours,
since all is mine doth wholly consist in your hands, the
which, with all reverence and dutiful affection, a thousand
times I kiss.

When I had now seen my Don Felix his letter, whether
it was for reading it at such a time, when by the same
he showed that he loved me more than himself, or whether
he had disposition and regiment over part of this wearied
soul to imprint that love in it whereof he wrote unto me,
I began to love him too well (and, alas, for my harm!),
since he was the cause of so much sorrow as I have passed
for his sake. Whereupon, asking Rosina forgiveness of
what was past (as a thing needful for that which was to
come) and committing the secrecy of my love to her fidelity, I read the letter once again, pausing a little at every
word (and a very little indeed it was), because I concluded
so soon with myself to do that I did, although in very

truth it lay not otherwise in my power to do. Wherefore, calling for paper and ink, I answered his letter thus.

Esteem not so slightly of mine honor, Don Felix, as with feigned words to think to inveigle it, or with thy vain pretenses to offend it any ways. I know well enough what manner of man thou art, and how great thy desert and presumption is; from whence thy boldness doth arise (I guess), and not from the force (which thing thou wouldst fain persuade me) of thy fervent love. And if it be so (as my suspicion suggesteth) thy labor is as vain as thy imagination presumptuous, by thinking to make me do anything contrary to that which I owe unto mine honor. Consider (I beseech thee) how seldom things commenced under subtlety and dissimulation have good success; and that it is not the part of a gentleman to mean them one way and speak them another. Thou prayest me (amongst other things) to admit thee into possession of that that is mine: but I am of so ill an humor in matters of this quality, that I trust not things experienced, how much less then thy bare words; yet, nevertheless, I make no small account of that which thou hast manifested to me in thy letter; for it is enough that I am incredulous, though not unthankful.

This letter did I send, contrary to that I should have done, because it was the occasion of all my harms and griefs; for after this, he began to wax more bold by un folding his thoughts and seeking out the means to have a parley with me. In the end, fair nymphs, a few days being spent in his demands and my answers, false love did work in me after his wonted fashions, every hour seizing more strongly upon my unfortunate soul. The tourneys were now renewed, the music by night did never cease; amorous letters and verses were recontinued on both sides; and thus passed I away almost a whole year, at the end whereof I felt myself so far in his love that I had no power to retire nor stay myself from disclosing my thoughts unto him, the thing which he desired more than his own life. [I.iii] But my adverse fortune afterwards would, that of these our mutual loves (when as now they were most assured) his father had some intelligence, and whosoever revealed them first persuaded him so cunningly that his father (fearing lest he would have married me out of hand) sent him to the great Princess Augusta Caesarina's court, telling him it was not meet that a young gentleman, and of so noble a house as he was, should spend his youth idly at home, where nothing could be learned but examples of vice, whereof the very same idleness (he said) was the only mistress. He went away so pensive that his great grief would not suffer him to acquaint me with his departure; which when I knew, how sorrowful I remained, she may imagine that hath been at any time tormented with like passion. To tell you now the life that I led in his absence, my sadness, sighs, and tears, which every day I poured out of these wearied eyes, my tongue is far unable: if then my pains were such that I cannot now express them, how could I then suffer them? [II.vii] But being in the midst of my mishaps, and in the depth of those woes which the absence of Don Felix caused me to feel, and it seeming to me that my grief was without remedy, if he were once seen or known of the ladies in that court (more beautiful and gracious than myself), by occasion whereof, as also by absence (a capital enemy to love) I might easily be forgotten, I determined to adventure that which I think never any woman imagined; which was to apparel myself in the habit of a man and to hie me to the court to see him in whose sight all my hope and content remained. Which determination I no sooner thought of than I put in practice, love blinding my eyes and mind with an inconsiderate regard of mine own estate and condition. To the execution of which attempt I wanted no industry; for, being furnished with the help of one of my approved friends and treasuress of my secrets, who bought me such apparel as I willed her, and a good horse for my journey, I went not only out of my country but out of my dear reputation, which (I think) I shall never recover again; and so trotted directly to the court, passing by the way many accidents, which (if time would give me leave to tell them) would not make you laugh a little to hear them. Twenty days I was in going thither, at the end of which, being come to the desired place, I took up mine inn in a street less frequented with concourse of people: and the great desire I had to see the destroyer of my joy did not suffer me to think of any other thing but how or where I might see him. To inquire of him of mine host I durst not, lest my coming might (perhaps) have been discovered; and to seek him forth I though it not best, lest some inopinate mishap might have fallen out, whereby I might have been known. Wherefore I passed all that day in these perplexities while night came on, each hour whereof (methought) was a whole year unto me. [IV.i] But midnight being a little past, mine host called at my chamber door and told me if I was desirous to hear some brave music I should arise quickly and open a window towards the street. The which I did by and by, and making no noise at all, I heard how Don Felix his page, called Fabius (whom I knew by his voice), said to others that came with him, "Now it is time, my masters, because the lady is in the gallery over her garden, taking the fresh air of the cool night." He had no sooner said so but they began to wind three cornets and a sackbut, with such skill and sweetness that it seemed celestial music; and then began a voice to sing, the sweetest (in my opinion) that ever I heard. And though I was in suspense by hearing Fabius speak, whereby a thousand doubts and imaginations (repugnant to my rest) occurred in my mind, yet I neglected not to hear what was sung, because their operations were not of such force that they were able to hinder the desire nor distemper the delight that I conceived by hearing it. That therefore which was sung were these verses:

> Sweet mistress, harken unto me,
>   (If it grieves thee to see me die)
> And hearing though it grieveth thee,
>   To hear me yet, do not deny.
>
> O grant me then this short content,
>   For forced I am to thee to fly:

My sighs do not make thee relent,
　　Nor tears thy heart do mollify.

Nothing of mine doth give thee pain,
　　Nor thou think'st of no remedy:
Mistress, how long shall I sustain
　　Such ill as still thou dost apply?

In death there is no help, be sure,
　　But in thy will, where it doth lie:
For all those ills which death doth cure,
　　Alas, they are but light to try.

My troubles do not trouble thee,
　　Nor hope to touch thy soul so nigh:
O! From a will that is so free,
　　What should I hope when I do cry?

How can I mollify that brave
　　And stony heart, of pity dry?
Yet mistress, turn those eyes (that have
　　No peers) shining like stars in sky;

But turn them not in angry sort,
　　If thou wilt not kill me thereby:
Though yet in anger, or in sport,
　　Thou killest only with thine eye.

　　After they had first, with a concert of music, sung this
song, two played, the one upon a lute, the other upon a
silver-sounding harp, being accompanied with the sweet
voice of my Don Felix. The great joy that I felt in hearing him cannot be imagined, for (methought) I heard
him now as in that happy and passed time of our loves.
But after the deceit of this imagination was discovered,
seeing with mine eyes and hearing with mine ears that
this music was bestowed upon another and not on me,
God knows what a bitter death it was unto my soul: and
with a grievous sigh that carried almost my life away with
it, I asked mine host if he knew what the lady was for

whose sake the music was made? He answered me that he could not imagine on whom it was bestowed, because in that street dwelled many noble and fair ladies. And when I saw he could not satisfy my request, I bent mine ears again to hear my Don Felix, who now, to the tune of a delicate harp, whereon he sweetly played, began to sing this sonnet following:

A SONNET

My painful years impartial Love was spending
  In vain and bootless hopes my life appaying,
  And cruel Fortune to the world bewraying
Strange samples of my tears that have no ending.
Time everything to truth at last commending,
  Leaves of my steps such marks, that now betraying,
  And all deceitful trusts shall be decaying,
And none have cause to 'plain of his offending.
She, whom I loved to my obliged power,
  That in her sweetest love to me discovers
Which never yet I knew (those heavenly pleasures),
And I do say, exclaiming every hour,
  Do not you see what makes you wise, O lovers?
Love, Fortune, Time, and my fair mistress' treasures.

The sonnet being ended, they paused a while, playing on four lutes together, and on a pair of virginals, with such heavenly melody that the whole world (I think) could not afford sweeter music to the ear nor delight to any mind not subject to the pangs of such predominant grief and sorrow as mine was. But then four voices, passing well tuned and set together, began to sing this song following:

A SONG

That sweetest harm I do not blame,
First caused by thy fairest eyes,
But grieve, because too late I came
To know my fault, and to be wise.

I never knew a worser kind of life,
To live in fear, from boldness still to cease:
Nor worse than this, to live in such a strife,
Whether of both, to speak or hold my peace?

And so the harm I do not blame,
Caused by thee or thy fair eyes;
But that to see how late I came
To know my fault, and to be wise.

I ever more did fear that I should know
Some secret things and doubtful in their kind,
Because the surest things do ever go
Most contrary unto my wish and mind.

And yet by knowing of the same
There is no hurt; but it denies
My remedy, since late I came
To know my fault, and to be wise.

When this song was ended, they began to sound divers
sort of instruments and voices most excellently agreeing
together and with such sweetness that they could not
choose but delight any very much who were so far from
it as I. About dawning of the day the music ended, and
I did what I could to espy out my Don Felix, but the darkness of the night was mine enemy therein. And seeing now
that they were gone, I went to bed again, where I bewailed
my great mishap, knowing that he whom most of all I
loved had so unworthily forgotten me, whereof his music
was too manifest a witness. And when it was time I arose
and, without any other consideration, went straight to the
princess her palace, where (I thought) I might see that
which I so greatly desired, determining to call myself
Valerius, if any (perhaps) did ask my name. Coming
therefore to a fair broad court before the palace gate, I
viewed the windows and galleries, where I saw such store
of blazing beauties and gallant ladies that I am not able
now to recount nor then to do any more but wonder at
their graces, their gorgeous attire, their jewels, their brave
fashions of apparel and ornaments wherewith they were

so richly set out. Up and down this place, before the windows, rode many lords and brave gentlemen in rich and sumptuous habits and mounted upon proud jennets, every one casting his eye to that part where his thoughts were secretly placed. God knows how greatly I desired to see Don Felix there, and that his injurious love had been in that famous palace; because I might then have been assured that he should never have got any other guerdon of his suits and services, but only to see and to be seen, and sometimes to speak to his mistress, whom he must serve before a thousand eyes, because the privilege of that place doth not give him any further leave. But it was my ill fortune that he had settled his love in that place where I might not be assured of this poor help. Thus, as I was standing near to the palace gate, I espied Fabius, Don Felix his page, coming in great haste to the palace, where, speaking a word or two with a porter that kept the second entry, he returned the same way he came. I guessed his errand was to know whether it were fit time for Don Felix to come to dispatch certain business that his father had in the court, and that he could not choose but come thither out of hand. And being in this supposed joy which his sight did promise me, I saw him coming along with a great train of followers attending on his person, all of them being bravely apparelled in a livery of watchet silk, guarded with yellow velvet and stitched on either side with threads of twisted silver, wearing likewise blue, yellow, and white feathers in their hats. But my lord Don Felix had on a pair of ash-color hose, embroidered and drawn forth with watchet tissue; his doublet was of white satin, embroidered with knots of gold, and likewise an embroidered jerkin of the same colored velvet; and his short cape cloak was of black velvet, edged with gold lace, and hung full of buttons of pearl and gold and lined with a razed watchet satin: by his side he wore, at a pair of embroidered hangers, a rapier and dagger, with engraven hilts and pommel of beaten gold. On his head, a hat beset full of golden stars, in the midst of every which a rich orient pearl was enchased, and his feather was likewise blue, yellow, and white. Mounted he came upon a fair dapple gray jennet, with a rich furniture of blue, embroidered with gold and seed pearl. When I saw him in this rich equipage, I was so amazed at his sight that how extremely my senses were ravished with sudden joy I am not able, fair nymphs, to tell you. Truth it is that I could not but shed some tears for joy and grief, which his sight did make me feel, but, fearing to be noted by the standers-by, for that time I dried them up. But as Don Felix (being now come to the palace gate) was dismounted, and gone up a pair of stairs into the chamber of presence, I went to his men, where they were attending his return; and seeing Fabius, whom I had seen before amongst them, I took him aside and said unto him, "My friend, I pray you tell me what lord this is, which did but even now alight from his jennet, for (methinks) he is very like one whom I have seen before in another far country." Fabius then answered me thus: "Art thou such a novice in the court that thou knowest not Don Felix? I tell thee there is not any lord, knight, or gentleman better known in it than he." "No doubt of that," said I, "but I will tell thee what a novice I am and how small a time I have been in the court, for yesterday was the first that ever I came to it." "Nay then, I cannot blame thee," said Fabius, "if thou knowest him not. Know, then, that this gentleman is called Don Felix, born in Vandalia, and hath his chiefest house in the ancient city of Soldina, and is remaining in this court about certain affairs of his father's and his own." "But I pray you tell me," said I, "why he gives his liveries of these colors?" "If the cause were not so manifest, I would conceal it," said Fabius, "but since there is not any that knows it not and canst not come to any in this court who cannot tell thee the reason why, I think by telling thee it I do no more than in courtesy I am bound to do. Thou must therefore understand that he loves and serves a lady here in this city named Celia and therefore wears and gives for his livery an azure blue which is the color of the sky, and white and yellow, which are the colors of his lady and mistress." When I heard these words, imagine, fair nymphs, in what a plight I was; but dissembling my mishap and grief, I answered him: "This

lady certes is greatly beholding to him, because he thinks
not enough, by wearing her colors, to show how willing
he is to serve her, unless also he bear her name in his
livery; whereupon I guess she cannot but be very fair and
amiable." "She is no less, indeed," said Fabius, "although
the other whom he loved and served in our own country
in beauty far excelled this and loved and favored him
more than ever this did. But this mischievous absence doth
violate and dissolve those things which men think to be
most strong and firm." At these words, fair nymphs, was
I fain to come to some composition with my tears, which,
if I had not stopped from issuing forth, Fabius could not
have chosen but suspected, by the alteration of my countenance, that all was not well with me. And then the page
did ask me what countryman I was, my name and of
what calling and condition I was: whom I answered that
my country where I was born was Vandalia, my name
Valerius, and till that time served no master. "Then by
this reckoning," said he, "we are both countrymen and
may be both fellows in one house if thou wilt; for Don
Felix my master commanded me long since to seek him
out a page. Therefore if thou wilt serve him, say so. As
for meat, drink, and apparel, and a couple of shillings to
play away, thou shalt never want; besides pretty wenches,
which are not dainty in our street, as fair and amorous
as queens, of which there is not any that will not die for
the love of so proper a youth as thou art. And to tell
thee in secret (because, perhaps, we may be fellows), I
know where an old canon's maid is, a gallant fine girl,
whom if thou canst but find in thy heart to love and serve
as I do, thou shalt never want at her hands fine hand-
kerchers, pieces of bacon, and now and then wine of St.
Martin." When I heard this, I could not choose but laugh
to see how naturally the unhappy page played his part
by depainting forth their properties in their lively colors.
And because I thought nothing more commodious for my
rest, and for the enjoying of my desire, than to follow
Fabius his counsel, I answered him thus: "In truth, I
determined to serve none; but now, since fortune hath
offered me so good a service and at such a time, when I

am constrained to take this course of life, I shall not do amiss if I frame myself to the service of some lord or gentleman in this court, but especially of your master, because he seems to be a worthy gentleman, and such an one that makes more reckoning of his servants than another." "Ha, thou knowest him not so well as I," said Fabius, "for I promise thee, by the faith of a gentleman (for I am one indeed, for my father comes of the Cachopines of Laredo), that my master Don Felix is the best-natured gentleman that ever thou knewest in thy life, and one who useth his pages better than any other. And were it not for those troublesome loves, which makes us run up and down more and sleep less than we would, there were not such a master in the whole world again." [IV.iv] In the end, fair nymphs, Fabius spake to his master Don Felix as soon as he was come forth, in my behalf, who commanded me the same night to come to him at his lodging. Thither I went, and he entertained me for his page, making the most of me in the world; where, being but a few days with him, I saw the messages, letters, and gifts that were brought and carried on both sides, grievous wounds (alas! and corr'sives to my dying heart), which made my soul to fly sometimes out of my body, and every hour in hazard to lose my forced patience before every one. But after one month was past, Don Felix began to like so well of me that he disclosed his whole love unto me from the beginning unto the present estate and forwardness that it was then in, committing the charge thereof to my secrecy and help; telling me that he was favored of her at the beginning and that afterwards she waxed weary of her loving and accustomed entertainment, the cause whereof was a secret report (whosoever it was that buzzed it into her ears) of the love that he did bear to a lady in his own country, and that his present love unto her was but to entertain the time while his business in the court were dispatched. "And there is no doubt," said Don Felix unto me, "but that, indeed, I did once commence that love that she lays to my charge; but God knows if now there be anything in the world that I love and esteem more dear and precious than her." When I heard him say so, you may imagine, fair nymphs, what a mortal dagger pierced my wounded heart. But with dissembling the matter the best I could, I answered him thus: "It were better, sir (methinks), that the gentlewoman should complain with cause, and that it were so indeed; for if the other lady, whom you served before, did not deserve to be forgotten of you, you do her (under correction, my lord) the greatest wrong in the world." "The love," said Don Felix again, "which I bear to my Celia will not let me understand it so; but I have done her (methinks) the greater injury, having placed my love first in another and not in her." "Of these wrongs," said I to myself, "I know who bears the worst away." And (disloyal) he, pulling a letter out of his bosom, which he had received the same hour from his mistress, read it into me, thinking he did me a great favor thereby, the contents whereof were these:

CELIA'S LETTER TO DON FELIX

Never anything that I suspected, touching thy love, hath been so far from the truth that hath not given me occasion to believe more often mine own imagination than thy innocence; wherein, if I do thee any wrong, refer it but to the censure of thine own folly. For well thou mightest have denied or not declared thy passed love, without giving me occasion to condemn thee by thine own confession. Thou sayest I was the cause that made thee forget thy former love. Comfort thyself, for there shall not want another to make thee forget thy second. And assure thyself of this, Lord Don Felix, that there is not anything more unbeseeming a gentleman than to find an occasion in a gentlewoman to lose himself for her love. I will say no more, but that in an ill, where there is no remedy, the best is not to seek out any.

After he had made an end of reading the letter, he said unto me, "What thinkest thou, Valerius, of these words?" "With pardon be it spoken, my lord, that your deeds are showed by them." "Go to," said Don Felix, "and speak no more of that." "Sir," said I, "they must like me well if they like you, because none can judge better of their words that love well than they themselves. But that which I think of the letter is that this gentlewoman would have been the first, and that Fortune had entreated her in such sort that all others might have envied her estate." "But what wouldest thou counsel me?" said Don Felix. "If thy grief doth suffer any counsel," said I, "that thy thoughts be divided into this second passion, since there is so much due to the first." Don Felix answered me again, sighing and knocking me gently on the shoulder, saying, "How wise art thou, Valerius, and what good counsel dost thou give me if I could follow it. Let us now go in to dinner, for when I have dined I will have thee carry me a letter to my lady Celia, and then thou shalt see if any other love is not worthy to be forgotten in lieu of thinking only of her." These were words that grieved Felismena to the heart, but because she had him before her eyes, whom she loved more than herself, the content that she had by only seeing him was a sufficient remedy of the pain that the greatest of these stings did make her feel. After Don Felix had dined, he called me unto him, and giving me a special charge what I should do (because he had imparted his grief unto me, and put his hope and remedy in my hands), he willed me to carry a letter to Celia, which he had already written, and reading it first unto me, it said thus:

DON FELIX HIS LETTER TO CELIA

The thought that seeks an occasion to forget the thing which it doth love and desire, suffers itself so easily to be known that (without troubling the mind much) it may be quickly discerned. And think not, fair lady, that I seek a remedy to excuse you of that wherewith it pleased you to use me, since I never came to be so much in credit with you that in lesser things I would do it. I have confessed unto you that indeed I once loved well, because that true love, without dissimulation, doth not suffer anything to be hid, and you, dear lady, make that an occasion to forget me, which should be rather a motive to love me better. I cannot persuade me that you make so small an account of yourself to think that I can forget you for anything that is, or hath ever been, but rather imagine that you write clean contrary to that which you have tried by my zealous love and faith towards you. Touching all those things that, in prejudice of my good will towards you, it pleaseth you to imagine, my innocent thoughts assure me to the contrary, which shall suffice to be ill recompensed besides being so ill thought of as they are.

After Don Felix had read this letter unto me, he asked me if the answer was correspondent to those words that his lady Celia had sent him in hers, and if there was anything therein that might be amended; whereunto I answered thus: "I think, sir, it is needless to amend this letter, or to make the gentlewoman amends to whom it is sent, but her whom you do injury so much with it. Which under your lordship's pardon I speak, because I am so much affected to the first love in all my life that there is not anything that can make me alter my mind." "Thou hast the greatest reason in the world," said Don Felix, "if I could persuade myself to leave off that which I have begun. But what wilt thou have me do, since absence hath frozen the former love, and the continual presence of a peerless beauty rekindled another more hot and fervent in me?" "Thus may she think herself," said I again, "unjustly deceived, whom first you loved, because that love which is subject to the power of absence cannot be termed love, and none can persuade me that it hath been love." These words did I dissemble the best I could, because I felt so sensible grief to see myself forgotten of him who had so great reason to love me, and whom I did love so much that I did more than any would have thought to make myself still unknown. But taking the letter and mine errand with me, I went to Celia's house, imagining by the way the woeful estate whereunto my hapless love had brought me; since I was forced to make war against mine own self, and to be the intercessor of a thing so contrary to mine own content. But coming to Celia's house, and finding a page standing at the door, I asked him if I might speak with his lady: who being informed of me from whence I came, told Celia how I would speak with her, commending therewithal my beauty and person unto her, and telling her besides that Don Felix had but lately entertained me into his service; which made Celia say unto him, "What, Don Felix so soon disclose his secret loves to a page, but newly entertained? He hath (belike) some great occasion that moves him to do it. Bid him come in, and let us know what he would have." In I came, and to the place where the enemy of my life was, and with great reverence kissing her hands, I delivered Don Felix his letter unto her. Celia took it and, casting her eyes upon me, I might perceive how my sight had made a sudden alteration in her countenance, for she was so far besides herself that for a good while she was not able to speak a word, but remembering herself at last, she said unto me, "What good fortune hath been so favorable to Don Felix to bring thee to this court, to make thee his page?" "Even that, fair lady," said I, "which is better than ever I imagined, because it hath been an occasion to make me behold such singular beauty and perfections as now I see clearly before mine eyes. And if the pains, the tears, the sighs, and the continual disquiets that my lord Don Felix hath suffered have grieved me heretofore, now that I have seen the source from whence they flow and the cause of all his ill, the pity that I had on him is now wholly converted into a certain kind of envy. But if it be true, fair lady, that my coming is welcome unto you, I beseech you by that which you owe to the great love which he bears you, that your answer may import no less unto him." "There is not anything," said Celia, "that I would not do for thee, though I were determined not to love him at all, who for my sake hath forsaken another. For it is no small point of wisdom for me to learn by other women's harms to be more wise and wary in mine own." "Believe not, good lady," said I, "that there is anything in the world that can make Don Felix forget you. And if he hath cast off another for your sake, wonder not thereat, when your beauty and wisdom is so great and the other's so small that there is no reason to think that he will (though he hath worthily forsaken her for your sake) or ever can forget you for any woman else in the world." "Dost thou then know Felismena," said Celia, "the lady whom thy master did once love and serve in his own country?" "I know her," said I, "although not so well as it was needful for me to have prevented so many mishaps" (and this I spake softly to myself). "For my father's house was near to hers; but seeing your great beauty adorned with such perfections and wisdom, Don Felix cannot be blamed if he hath forgotten his first love only to embrace and honor yours." To this did Celia answer, merrily and smiling, "Thou hast learned quickly of thy master to soothe." "Not so, fair lady," said I, "but to serve you would I fain learn: for flattery cannot be where (in the judgment of all) there are so manifest signs and proofs of this due commendation." Celia began in good earnest to ask me what manner of woman Felismena was, whom I answered that, touching her beauty, some thought her to be very fair; but I was never of that opinion, because she hath many days since wanted the chiefest thing that is requisite for it. "What is that?" said Celia. "Content of mind," said I, "because perfect beauty can never be, where the same is not adjoined to it." "Thou hast the greatest reason in the world," said she, "but I have seen some ladies whose lively hue sadness hath not one whit abated, and others whose beauty anger hath increased, which is a strange thing methinks." "Hapless is that beauty," said I, "that hath sorrow and anger the preservers and mistresses of it, but I cannot skill of these impertinent things. And yet that woman that must needs be molested with continual pain and trouble, with grief and care of mind and with other passions to make her look well, cannot be reckoned among the number of fair women, and for mine own part I do not account her so." "Wherein thou hast great reason," said she, "as in all things else that thou hast said, thou hast showed thyself wise and discreet." "Which I have dearly bought," said I again. "But I beseech you, gracious lady, to answer this letter, because my lord Don Felix may also have some contentment, by receiving this first well-employed service at my hands." "I am content," said Celia, "but first thou must tell me if Felismena in matters of discretion be wise and well advised?" "There was never any woman," said I again, "more wise than she, because she hath been long since beaten to it by her great mishaps; but she did never advise herself well, for if she had (as she was accounted wise) she had never come to have been so contrary to herself." "Thou speakest so wisely in all thy answers," said Celia, "that there is not any that would not take great delight to hear them." "Which are not viands," said I, "for such a dainty taste, nor reasons for so ingenious and fine a conceit, fair lady, as you have, but boldly affirming that by the same I mean no harm at all." "There is not anything," said Celia, "whereunto thy wit cannot attain, but because thou shalt not spend thy time so ill in praising me, as thy master doth in praying me, I will read thy letter and tell thee what thou shalt say unto him from me." Whereupon unfolding it, she began to read it to herself, to whose countenance and gestures in reading of the same, which are oftentimes outward signs of the inward disposition and meaning of the heart, I gave a watchful eye. And when she had read it, she said unto me, "Tell thy master that he that can so well by words express what he means, cannot choose but mean as well as he saith," and coming nearer to me, she said softly in mine ear, "and this for the love of thee, Valerius, and not so much for Don Felix thy master his sake, for I see how much thou lovest and tenderest his estate." "And from thence, alas," said I to myself, "did all my woes arise." Whereupon kissing her hands for the great courtesy and favor she showed me, I hied me to Don Felix with this answer, which was no small joy to him to hear it, and another death to me to report it, saying many times to myself (when I did either bring him home some joyful tidings or carry letters or tokens to her), "O thrice unfortunate Felismena, that with thine own weapons art constrained to wound thy ever-dying heart, and to heap up favors for him who made so small account of thine." And so did I pass away my life with so many torments of mind that if by the sight of my Don Felix they had not been tempered, it could not have otherwise been but that I must

needs have lost it. More than two months together did
Celia hide from me the fervent love she bare me, although
not in such sort but that by certain apparent signs I came
to the knowledge thereof, which was no small lighting
and ease of that grief which incessantly haunted my
wearied spirits; for as I thought it a strong occasion, and
the only mean to make her utterly forget Don Felix, so
likewise I imagined that, perhaps, it might befall to him
as it hath done to many that the force of ingratitude and
contempt of his love might have utterly abolished such
thoughts out of his heart. But, alas, it happened not so to
my Don Felix; for the more he perceived that his lady
forgot him, the more was his mind troubled with greater
cares and grief, which made him lead the most sorrowful
life that might be, whereof the least part did not fall to
my lot. For remedy of whose sighs and piteous lamentations, poor Felismena (even by main force) did get favors
from Celia, scoring them up (whensoever she sent them
by me) in the catalogue of my infinite mishaps. For if
by chance he sent her anything by any of his other servants, it was so slenderly accepted that he thought it best
to send none unto her but myself, perceiving what incon-
venience did ensue thereof. But God knows how many
tears my messages cost me, and so many they were that
in Celia's presence I ceased not to pour them forth, ear-
nestly beseeching her with prayers and petitions not to
entreat him so ill who loved her so much, because I would
bind Don Felix to me by the greatest bond as never man
in like was bound to any woman. My tears grieved Celia
to the heart, as well for that I shed them in her presence,
as also for that she saw if I meant to love her, I would
not (for requital of hers to me) have solicited her with
such diligence nor pleaded with such pity to get favors for
another. And thus I lived in the greatest confusion that
might be, amidst a thousand anxieties of mind, for I
imagined with myself that if I made not a show that I
loved her, as she did me, I did put it in hazard lest Celia,
for despite of my simplicity or contempt, would have
loved Don Felix more than before, and by loving him
that mine could not have any good success; and if I feigned

myself, on the other side, to be in love with her, it might have been an occasion to have made her reject my lord Don Felix, so that with the thought of his love neglected and with the force of her contempt, he might have lost his content, and after that, his life, the least of which two mischiefs to prevent I would have given a thousand lives, if I had them. Many days passed away in this sort, wherein I served him as a third between both, to the great cost of my contentment, at the end whereof the success of his love went on worse and worse, because the love that Celia did bear me was so great that the extreme force of her passion made her lose some part of that compassion she should have had of herself. And on a day after that I had carried and recarried many messages and tokens between them, sometimes feigning some myself from her unto him, because I could not see him (whom I loved so dearly) so sad and pensive, with many supplications and earnest prayers I besought Lady Celia with pity to regard the painful life that Don Felix passed for her sake, and to consider that by not favoring him she was repugnant to that which she owed to herself: which thing I entreated, because I saw him in such a case that there was no other thing to be expected of him but death, by reason of the continual and great pain which his grievous thoughts made him feel. But she with swelling tears in her eyes, and with many sighs, answered me thus: "Unfortunate and accursed Celia, that now in the end dost know how thou livest deceived with a false opinion of thy great simplicity (ungrateful Valerius) and of thy small discretion. I did not believe till now that thou didst crave favors of me for thy master, but only for thyself, and to enjoy my sight all that time that thou didst spend in suing to me for them. But now I see thou dost ask them in earnest, and that thou art so content to see me use him well, that thou canst not (without doubt) love me at all. O how ill dost thou acquit the love I bear thee, and that which, for thy sake, I do now forsake? O that time might revenge me of thy proud and foolish mind, since love hath not been the means to do it. For I cannot think that Fortune will be so contrary unto me, but that she will punish thee for con-

temning that great good which she meant to bestow on
thee. And tell thy lord Don Felix that if he will see me
alive, that he see me not at all: and thou, vile traitor,
cruel enemy to my rest, come no more (I charge thee)
before these wearied eyes, since their tears were never of
force to make thee know how much thou art bound unto
them." And with this she suddenly flang out of my sight
with so many tears that mine were not of force to stay
her. For in the greatest haste in the world she got her
into her chamber where, locking the door after her, it
availed me not to call and cry unto her, requesting with
amorous and sweet words to open me the door and to take
such satisfaction on me as it pleased her: nor to tell her
many other things, whereby I declared unto her the small
reason she had to be so angry with me and to shut me
out. But with a strange kind of fury she said unto me,
"Come no more, ungrateful and proud Valerius, in my
sight, and speak no more unto me, for thou art not able
to make satisfaction for such great disdain, and I will
have no other remedy for the harm which thou hast done
me, but death itself, the which with mine own hands I
will take in satisfaction of that which thou deservest."
Which words when I heard, I stayed no longer, but with
a heavy cheer came to my Don Felix his lodging, and,
with more sadness than I was able to dissemble, told him
that I could not speak with Celia, because she was visited
of certain gentlewomen her kinswomen. But the next day
in the morning it was bruited over all the city that a certain trance had taken her that night, wherein she gave
up the ghost, which struck all the court with no small
wonder. But that which Don Felix felt by her sudden
death, and how near it grieved his very soul, as I am not
able to tell, so cannot human intendment conceive it, for
the complaints he made, the tears, the burning sighs, and
heartbreak sobs, were without all measure and number.
But I say nothing of myself, when on the one side the
unlucky death of Celia touched my soul very near, the
tears of Don Felix on the other did cut my heart in two
with grief: and yet this was nothing to that intolerable
pain which afterwards I felt. For Don Felix heard no

sooner of her death, but the same night he was missing in his house, that none of his servants nor anybody else could tell any news of him.

Whereupon you may perceive, fair nymphs, what cruel torments I did then feel: then did I wish a thousand times for death to prevent all these woes and miseries which afterwards befell unto me: for Fortune (it seemed) was but weary of those which she had but till then given me. But as all the care and diligence which I employed in seeking out my Don Felix was but in vain, so I resolved with myself to take this habit upon me as you see, wherein it is more than two years since I have wandered up and down, seeking him in many countries: but my Fortune hath denied me to find him out, although I am not a little now bound unto her by conducting me hither at this time, wherein I did you this small piece of service. Which, fair nymphs, believe me, I account (next after his life in whom I have put all my hope) the greatest content that might have fallen unto me. . . .

[There follows a discussion of the relationship of love to reason.]

The shepherdess having made an end of her sharp answer and Felismena beginning to arbitrate the matter between them, they heard a great noise in the other side of the meadow, like to the sound of blows and smiting of swords upon harness, as if some armed men had fought together, so that all of them with great haste ran to the place where they heard the noise, to see what the matter was. And being come somewhat near, they saw in a little island (which the river with a round turning had made) three knights fighting against one. And although he defended himself valiantly, by showing his approved strength and courage, yet the three knights gave him so much to do that he was fain to help himself by all the force and policy he could. They fought on foot, for their horses were tied to little trees that grew thereabout. And now by this time, the knight that fought all alone and defended himself had laid one of them at his feet with a blow of his good sword, which ended his life. But the other two that were very strong and valiant redoubled their force and blows so thick on him that he looked for no other thing than death. The shepherdess Felismena seeing the knight in so great danger, and if she did not speedily help him, that he could not escape with life, was not afraid to put hers in jeopardy by doing that which in such a case she thought she was bound to perform: wherefore putting a sharp-headed arrow into her bow, she said unto them: "Keep out, knights, for it is not beseeming men that make account of this name and honor, to take advantage of their enemies with so great odds." And aiming at the sight of one of their helmets, she burst it with such force that the arrow running into his eyes came out of the other side of his head so that he fell down dead to the ground. When the distressed knight saw two of his enemies dead, he ran upon the third with such force as if he had but then begun the combat; but Felismena helped him out of more trouble by putting another arrow into her bow, the which transpiercing his armor, she left under his left pap, and so justly smote his heart that this knight also followed his two companions. When the shepherds and the knight beheld what Felismena had done, and how at two shoots she had killed two such valiant knights, they were all in great wonder. The knight therefore, taking off his helmet and coming unto her, said: "How am I able, fair shepherdess, to requite so great a benefit and good turn as I have received at thy hands this day, but by acknowledging this debt forever in my grateful mind?" When Felismena beheld the knight's face and knew him, her senses were so troubled that being in such a trance she could scarce speak, but coming to herself again, she answered him: "Ah, my Don Felix, this is not the first debt wherein thou art bound unto me. And I cannot believe that thou wilt acknowledge this (as thou sayest) no more than thou hast done greater than this before. Behold to what a time and end my fortune and thy forgetness hath brought me, that she what was wont to be served of thee in the city with tilt and tourneys, and honored with many other things, whereby thou didst deceive me (or I suffered myself to be deceived), doth now wander up and down, exiled from her native country and liberty, for using thus thine own. If this brings thee not into the knowledge of that which thou owest me, remember how one whole year I served thee as thy page in the Princess Caesarina's court: and how I was a solicitor against myself, without discovering myself or my thoughts unto thee, but only to procure thy remedy and to help the grief which thine made thee feel. How many times did I get thee favors from thy mistress Celia to the great cost of my tears and griefs: all which account but small, Don Felix, in respect of those dangers (had they been unsufficient) wherein I would have spent my life for redress of thy pains, which thy injurious love afforded thee. And unless thou art weary of the great love that I have borne thee, consider and weigh with thyself the strange effects which the force of love hath caused me to pass. I went out of my native country and came to serve thee, to lament the ill that thou didst suffer, to take upon me the injuries and disgraces that I received therein; and to give thee any content, I cared not to lead the most bitter and painful life that ever woman lived. In the habit of a tender and dainty lady I loved thee more than thou canst imagine, and in the habit of a base page I served thee (a thing more contrary to my rest and reputation than I mean now to rehearse) and yet now in the habit of a poor and simple shepherdess I came to do thee this small service. What remains then more for me to do, but to sacrifice my life to thy loveless soul, if with the same yet I could give thee more content—and if in lieu thereof thou wouldest but remember how much I have loved and do yet love thee! Here hast thou thy sword in thy hand; let none therefore but thy self revenge the offense that I have done thee." When the knight heard Felismena's words and knew them all to be as true as he was disloyal, his heart by this strange and sudden accident recovered some force again to see what great injury he had done her, so that the thought thereof and the plenteous effusion of blood that issued out of his wounds made him like a dead man fall down in a swoon at fair Felismena's feet; who with great care and no less fear, laying his head in her lap, with showers of tears that rained from her eyes upon the knight's pale visage, began thus to lament: "What means this cruel Fortune? Is the period of my life come just with the last end of my Don Felix his days? Ah, my Don Felix (the cause of all my pain), if the plenteous tears, which for thy sake I have now shed, are not sufficient; and these which I now distill upon thy lovely cheeks, too few to make thee come to thyself again, what remedy shall this miserable soul have to prevent that this bitter joy by seeing thee turn not to occasion of utter despair. Ah, my Don Felix, awake my love, if thou dost but sleep or be'st in a trance, although I would not wonder if thou dost not, since never anything that I could do prevailed with thee to frame my least content." And in these and other lamentations was fair Felismena plunged, whom the Portugal shepherdesses with their tears and poor supplies endeavored to encourage, when on the sudden they saw a fair nymph coming over the stony causey that led the way into the island, with a golden bottle in one hand and a silver one in the other, whom Felismena knowing by and by, said unto her: "Ah, Doria, could any come at this time to succor me but thou, fair nymph? Come hither then, and thou shalt see the cause of all my troubles, the substance of my sighs, and the object of my thoughts, lying in the greatest danger of death that may be." "In like occurrents," said Doria, "virtue and a good heart most take place. Recall it then, fair Felismena, and revive thy daunted spirits, trouble not thyself any more, for now is the end of thy sorrows and the beginning of thy contentment come." And speaking these words, she besprinkled his face with a certain odoriferous water which she brought in the silver bottle, whereby he came to his memory again, and then said unto him: "If thou wilt recover thy life, sir knight, and give it her that hath passed such an ill one for thy sake, drink of the water in this bottle." The which Don Felix, taking in his hand, drunk a good draught and, resting upon it a little, found himself so whole of his wounds, which the three knights had given him, and of that which the love of Celia had made in his breast, that now he felt the pain no more which either of them had caused him than if he had never had them. And in this sort he began to rekindle the old love that he bore to Felismena, the which (he thought) was never more zealous than now. Whereupon sitting down upon the green grass, he took his lady and shepherdess by the hands and, kissing them many times, said thus unto her: "How small account would I make of my life, my dearest Felismena, for canceling that great bond wherein (with more than life) I am forever bound unto thee: for since I enjoy it by thy means, I think it no more than right to restore thee that which is thine own. . . . What words are sufficient to excuse the faults that I have committed against thy faith and firmest love and loyalty? . . . Truth is that I loved Celia well and forgot thee, but in such sort that thy wisdom and beauty did ever slide out of my mind. And the best is that I know not wherein to put this fault that may be so justly attributed to me; for if I will impute it to the young age that I was then in, since I had it to love thee, I should not have wanted it to have been firm in the faith that I owed thee. If to Celia's beauty it is clear that thine did far excel hers and all the world's besides. If to the change of time, this should have been the touchstone which should have showed the force and virtue of my firmness. If to injurious and traitorous absence, it serves as little for my excuse, since the desire of seeing thee should not have been absent from supporting thy image in my memory. Behold then, Felismena, what assured trust I put in thy goodness, that (without any other means) I dare put before thee the small reason thou hast to pardon me. But what shall I do to purchase pardon at thy gracious hands, or after thou hast pardoned me, to believe that thou art satisfied: for one thing grieves me more than anything else in the world, and this it is. That, though the love which thou hast borne me, and wherewith thou dost yet bless me, is an occasion (perhaps) to make thee forgive me and forget so many faults: yet I shall never lift up mine eyes to behold thee, but that every injury which I have done thee will be worse than a mortal incision in my guilty heart." The shepherdess Felismena, who saw Don Felix so penitent for his passed misdeeds and so affectionately returned to his first thoughts, with many tears told him that she did pardon him, because the love that she had ever borne him would suffer her to do no less: which if she had not thought to do, she would never have taken so great pains and so many weary journeys to seek him out, and many other things, wherewith Don Felix was confirmed in his former love. . . . And Don Felix wondered not a little to understand how his lady Felismena had served him so many days as his page, and that he was so far gone out of his wits and memory that he knew her not for all that while. And his joy on the other side to see that his lady loved him so well, was so great that by no means he could hide it. Thus therefore, riding on their way, they came to Diana's temple, where the sage Felicia was looking for their coming: and likewise the shepherd Arsileus, and Belisa, Sylvanus, and Selvagia, who were now come thither not many days before. They were welcomed on every side and with great joy entertained; but fair Felismena especially, who for her rare virtues and singular beauty was greatly honored of them all. There they were all married with great joy, feasts, and triumphs, which were made by all the goodly nymphs and by the sage and noble lady Felicia. . . .

Commentaries

SAMUEL JOHNSON

from *The Plays of William Shakespeare*

In this play there is a strange mixture of knowledge and ignorance, of care and negligence. The versification is often excellent, the allusions are learned and just; but the author conveys his heroes by sea from one inland town to another in the same country; he places the Emperor at Milan and sends his young men to attend him, but never mentions him more; he makes Proteus, after an interview with Silvia, say he has only seen her picture; and, if we may credit the old copies, he has, by mistaking places, left his scenery inextricable. The reason of all this confusion seems to be that he took his story from a novel, which he sometimes followed and sometimes forsook, sometimes remembered and sometimes forgot.

From *The Plays of William Shakespeare*, edited by Samuel Johnson. Vol. I. London: Printed for H. Woodfall, etc., 1768.

WILLIAM HAZLITT

from *Characters of Shakespear's Plays*

This is little more than the first outlines of a comedy
loosely sketched in. It is the story of a novel dramatized
with very little labor or pretension; yet there are passages
of high poetical spirit, and of inimitable quaintness of
humor, which are undoubtedly Shakespear's, and there
is throughout the conduct of the fable a careless grace and
felicity which marks it for his. One of the editors (we believe, Mr. Pope) remarks in a marginal note to *The Two
Gentlemen of Verona*: "It is observable (I know not for
what cause) that the style of this comedy is less figurative,
and more natural and unaffected than the greater part of this
author's, though supposed to be one of the first he wrote."
Yet so little does the editor appear to have made up his
mind upon this subject, that we find the following note to
the very next (the second) scene. "This whole scene, like
many others in these plays (some of which I believe were
written by Shakespear, and others interpolated by the
players) is composed of the lowest and most trifling conceits, to be accounted for only by the gross taste of the

From *Characters of Shakespear's Plays* by William Hazlitt. 2nd ed.
London: Taylor & Hessey, 1818.

age he lived in: *Populo ut placerent.* I wish I had authority to leave them out, but I have done all I could, set a mark of reprobation upon them, throughout this edition." It is strange that our fastidious critic should fall so soon from praising to reprobating. The style of the familiar parts of this comedy is indeed made up of conceits—low they may be for what we know, but then they are not poor, but rich ones. The scene of Launce with his dog (not that in the second, but that in the fourth act) is a perfect treat in the way of farcical drollery and invention; nor do we think Speed's manner of proving his master to be in love deficient in wit or sense, though the style may be criticized as not simple enough for the modern taste.

Valentine. Why, how know you that I am in love?

Speed. Marry, by these special marks: first, you have learned, like Sir Protheus, to wreathe your arms like a malcontent, to relish a love song like a robin-red-breast, to walk alone like one that had the pestilence, to sigh like a schoolboy that had lost his A B C, to weep like a young wench that had buried her grandam, to fast like one that takes diet, to watch like one that fears robbing, to speak puling like a beggar at Hallowmas. You were wont, when you laughed, to crow like a cock; when you walked, to walk like one of the lions; when you fasted, it was presently after dinner; when you looked sadly, it was for want of money; and now you are metamorphosed with a mistress, that when I look on you, I can hardly think you my master.

The tender scenes in this play, though not so highly wrought as in some others, have often much sweetness of sentiment and expression. There is something pretty and playful in the conversation of Julia with her maid, when she shows such a disposition to coquetry about receiving the letter from Proteus; and her behavior afterwards and her disappointment, when she finds him faithless to his vows, remind us at a distance of Imogen's tender constancy. Her answer to Lucetta, who advises her against following her lover in disguise, is a beautiful piece of poetry.

Lucetta. I do not seek to quench your love's hot fire,
 But qualify the fire's extremest rage,
 Lest it should burn above the bounds of reason.

Julia. The more thou damm'st it up, the more it burns;
 The current that with gentle murmur glides,
 Thou know'st, being stopp'd, impatiently doth rage;
 But when his fair course is not hindered,
 He makes sweet music with th' enamel'd stones,
 Giving a gentle kiss to every sedge
 He overtaketh in his pilgrimage:
 And so by many winding nooks he strays,
 With willing sport, to the wild ocean.
 Then let me go, and hinder not my course;
 I'll be as patient as a gentle stream,
 And make a pastime of each weary step,
 Till the last step have brought me to my love;
 And there I'll rest, as after much turmoil,
 A blessed soul doth in Elysium.

If Shakespear indeed had written only this and other passages in *The Two Gentlemen of Verona*, he would *almost* have deserved Milton's praise of him—

  And sweetest Shakespeare, Fancy's child,
  Warbles his native wood-notes wild.

But as it is, he deserves rather more praise than this.

GEORGE BERNARD SHAW

from *Our Theatres in the Nineties*

THE TWO GENTLEMEN OF VERONA. Daly's Theatre, 2 July 1895. [6 *July* 1895]

The piece founded by Augustin Daly on Shakespear's *Two Gentlemen of Verona*, to which I looked forward last week, is not exactly a comic opera, though there is plenty of music in it, and not exactly a serpentine dance, though it proceeds under a play of changing colored lights. It is something more old-fashioned than either: to wit, a vaudeville. And let me hasten to admit that it makes a very pleasant entertainment for those who know no better. Even I, who know a great deal better, as I shall presently demonstrate rather severely, enjoyed myself tolerably. I cannot feel harshly towards a gentleman who works so hard as Mr. Daly does to make Shakespear presentable: one feels that he loves the bard, and lets him have his way as far as he thinks it good for him. His rearrangement of the scenes of the first two acts is just like him. Shakespear shews lucidly how Proteus lives with his father (Antonio) in Verona, and loves a lady of that city named Julia. Mr. Daly, by taking the scene in Julia's house between Julia

From *Our Theatres in the Nineties* by George Bernard Shaw. 3 vols. London: Constable & Co., Ltd., 1932. Reprinted by permission of the Public Trustee and the Society of Authors.

and her maid, and the scene in Antonio's house between Antonio and Proteus, and making them into one scene, convinces the unlettered audience that Proteus and Julia live in the same house with their father Antonio. Further, Shakespear shews us how Valentine, the other gentleman of Verona, travels from Verona to Milan, the journey being driven into our heads by a comic scene in Verona, in which Valentine's servant is overwhelmed with grief at leaving his parents, and with indignation at the insensibility of his dog to his sorrow, followed presently by another comic scene in Milan in which the same servant is welcomed to the strange city by a fellow servant. Mr. Daly, however, is ready for Shakespeare on this point too. He just represents the two scenes as occurring in the same place; and immediately the puzzle as to who is who is complicated by a puzzle as to where is where. Thus is the immortal William adapted to the requirements of a nineteenth-century audience.

In preparing the text of his version Mr. Daly has proceeded on the usual principles, altering, transposing, omitting, improving, correcting, and transferring speeches from one character to another. Many of Shakespear's lines are mere poetry, not to the point, not getting the play along, evidently stuck in because the poet liked to spread himself in verse. On all such unbusinesslike superfluities Mr. Daly is down with his blue pencil. For instance, he relieves us of such stuff as the following, which merely conveys that Valentine loves Silvia, a fact already sufficiently established by the previous dialogue:

My thoughts do harbor with my Silvia nightly;
   And slaves they are to me, that send them flying:
Oh, could their master come and go as lightly,
   Himself would lodge where senseless they are lying.
My herald thoughts in thy pure bosom rest them,
   While I, their king, that thither them importune,
Do curse the grace that with such grace hath blessed them,
   Because myself do want my servant's fortune.
I curse myself, for they are sent by me,
   That they should harbor where their lord would be.

Slaves indeed are these lines and their like to Mr. Daly, who "sends them flying" without remorse. But when he comes to passages that a stage manager can understand, his reverence for the bard knows no bounds. The following awkward lines, unnecessary as they are under modern stage conditions, are at any rate not poetic, and are in the nature of police news. Therefore they are piously retained:

> What halloing, and what stir, is this today?
> These are my mates, that make their wills their law,
> Have some unhappy passenger in chase.
> They love me well; yet I have much to do,
> To keep them from uncivil outrages.
> Withdraw thee, Valentine: who's this comes here?

The perfunctory metrical character of such lines only makes them more ridiculous than they would be in prose. I would cut them out without remorse to make room for all the lines that have nothing to justify their existence except their poetry, their humor, their touches of character—in short, the lines for whose sake the play survives, just as it was for their sake it originally came into existence. Mr. Daly, who prefers the lines which only exist for the sake of the play, will doubtless think me as great a fool as Shakespear; but I submit to him, without disputing his judgment, that he is, after all, only a man with a theory of dramatic composition, going with a blue pencil over the work of a great dramatist, and striking out everything that does not fit his theory. Now, as it happens, nobody cares about Mr. Daly's theory; whilst everybody who pays to see what is, after all, advertised as a performance of Shakespear's play entitled *The Two Gentlemen of Verona,* and not as a demonstration of Mr. Daly's theory, does care more or less about the art of Shakespear. Why not give them what they ask for, instead of going to great trouble and expense to give them something else?

In those matters in which Mr. Daly has given the rein to his own taste and fancy: that is to say, in scenery, costumes, and music, he is for the most part disabled by a want of real knowledge of the arts concerned. I say for the most part, because his pretty fifteenth-century dresses, though probably inspired rather by Sir Frederic Leighton than by Benozzo Gozzoli, may pass. But the scenery is insufferable. First, for "a street in Verona" we get a Bath bun colored operatic front cloth with about as much light in it as there is in a studio in Fitzjohn's Avenue in the middle of October. I respectfully invite Mr. Daly to spend his next holiday looking at a real street in Verona, asking his conscience meanwhile whether a manager with eyes in his head and the electric light at his disposal could not advance a step on the Telbin (senior) style. Telbin was an admirable scene painter; but he was limited by the mechanical conditions of gas illumination; and he learnt his technique before the great advance made during the Impressionist movement in the painting of open-air effects, especially of brilliant sunlight. Of that advance Mr. Daly has apparently no conception. The days of Macready and Clarkson Stanfield still exist for him; he would probably prefer a water-color drawing of a foreign street by Samuel Prout to one of Mr. T. M. Rooke; and I daresay every relic of the original tallow candlelight that still clings to the art of scene painting is as dear to him as it is to most old playgoers, including, unhappily, many of the critics.

As to the elaborate set in which Julia makes her first entrance, a glance at it shews how far Mr. Daly prefers the Marble Arch to the loggia of Orcagna. All over the scene we have Renaissance work, in its genteelest stages of decay, held up as the perfection of romantic elegance and beauty. The school that produced the classicism of the First Empire, designed the terraces of Regent's Park and the façades of Fitzroy Square, and conceived the Boboli Gardens and Versailles as places for human beings to be happy in, ramps all over the scenery, and offers as much of its pet colonnades and statues as can be crammed into a single scene, by way of a compendium of everything that is lovely in the city of San Zeno and the tombs of the Scaligers. As to the natural objects depicted, I ask whether any man living has ever seen a pale green cypress in Verona or anywhere else out of a toy Noah's Ark. A man who, having once seen cypresses and felt their presence in a north Italian landscape, paints them lettuce color, must be suffering either from madness, malice, or a theory of how nature should have colored trees, cognate with Mr. Daly's theory of how Shakespear should have written plays.

Of the music let me speak compassionately. After all, it is only very lately that Mr. Arnold Dolmetsch, by playing fifteenth-century music on fifteenth-century instruments, has shewn us that the age of beauty was true to itself in music as in pictures and armor and costumes. But what should Mr. Daly know of this, educated as he no doubt was to believe that the court of Denmark should always enter in the first act of *Hamlet* to the march from *Judas Maccabaeus*? Schubert's setting of "Who Is Silvia?" he knew, but had rashly used up in *Twelfth Night* as "Who's Olivia." He has therefore had to fall back on another modern setting, almost supernaturally devoid of any particular merit. Besides this, all through the drama the most horribly common music repeatedly breaks out on the slightest pretext or on no pretext at all. One dance, set to a crude old English popular tune, sundry eighteenth and nineteenth century musical banalities, and a titivated plantation melody in the first act which produces an indescribably atrocious effect by coming in behind the scenes as a sort of coda to Julia's curtain speech, all turn the play, as I have said, into a vaudeville. Needless to add, the accompaniments are not played on lutes and viols, but by the orchestra and a guitar or two. In the forest scene the outlaws begin the act by a chorus. After their encounter with Valentine they go off the stage singing the refrain exactly in the style of *La Fille de Madame Angot*. The wanton absurdity of introducing this comic opera convention is presently eclipsed by a thunderstorm, immediately after which Valentine enters and delivers his speech sitting down on a bank of moss, as an outlaw in tights naturally would after a terrific shower. Such is the effect of many years of theatrical management on the human brain.

Perhaps the oddest remark I have to make about the performance is that, with all its glaring defects and blunders, it is rather a handsome and elaborate one as such things go. It is many years now since Mr. Ruskin first took the Academicians of his day aback by the obvious remark that Carpaccio and Giovanni Bellini were better painters than Domenichino and Salvator Rosa. Nobody dreams now of assuming that Pope was a greater poet than Chaucer, that Mozart's Twelfth Mass is superior to the masterpieces of Orlandus Lassus and Palestrina, or that our "ecclesiastical Gothic" architecture is more enlightened than Norman axe work. But the theatre is still wallowing in such follies; and until Mr. Comyns Carr and Sir Edward Burne-Jones, Baronet, put King Arthur on the stage more or less in the manner natural to men who know these things, Mr. Daly might have pleaded the unbroken conservatism of the playhouse against me. But after the Lyceum scenery and architecture I decline to accept a relapse without protest. There is no reason why cheap photographs of Italian architecture (sixpence apiece in infinite variety at the bookstall in the South Kensington Museum) should not rescue us from Regent's Park Renaissance colonnades on the stage just as the electric light can rescue us from Telbin's dun-colored sunlight. The opera is the last place in the world where any wise man would look for adequate stage illusion; but the fact is that Mr. Daly, with all his colored lights, has not produced a single Italian scene comparable in illusion to that provided by Sir Augustus Harris at Covent Garden for *Cavalleria Rusticana.*

Of the acting I have not much to say. Miss Rehan provided a strong argument in favor of rational dress by looking much better in her page's costume than in that of her own sex; and in the serenade scene, and that of the wooing of Silvia for Proteus, she stirred some feeling into the part, and reminded us of what she was in *Twelfth Night,* where the same situations are fully worked out. For the rest, she moved and spoke with imposing rhythmic grace. That is as much notice as so cheap a part as Julia is worth from an artist who, being absolute mistress of the situation at Daly's Theatre, might and should have played Imogen for us instead. The two gentlemen were impersonated by Mr. Worthing and Mr. Craig. Mr. Wor-

thing charged himself with feeling without any particular
reference to his lines; and Mr. Craig struck a balance by attending to the meaning of his speeches without taking them
at all to heart. Mr. Clarke, as the Duke, was emphatic, and
worked up every long speech to a climax in the useful old
style; but his tone is harsh, his touch on his consonants
coarse, and his accent ugly, all fatal disqualifications for
the delivery of Shakespearean verse. The scenes between
Launce and his dog brought out the latent silliness and
childishness of the audience as Shakespear's clowning
scenes always do: I laugh at them like a yokel myself.
Mr. Lewis hardly made the most of them. His style has
been formed in modern comedies, where the locutions are
so familiar that their meaning is in no danger of being
lost by the rapidity of his quaint utterance; but Launce's
phraseology is another matter: a few of the funniest lines
missed fire because the audience did not catch them. And
with all possible allowance for Mr. Daly's blue pencil, I
cannot help suspecting that Mr. Lewis's memory was responsible for one or two of his omissions. Still, Mr. Lewis
has always his comic force, whether he makes the most or
the least of it; so that he cannot fail in such a part as
Launce. Miss Maxine Elliot's Silvia was the most considerable performance after Miss Rehan's Julia. The whole
company will gain by the substitution on Tuesday next of
a much better play, *A Midsummer Night's Dream,* as a
basis for Mr. Daly's operations. No doubt he is at this
moment, like Mrs. Todgers, "a dodgin' among the tender
bits with a fork, and an eatin' of 'em"; but there is sure
to be enough of the original left here and there to repay
a visit.

H. B. CHARLTON

from *Shakespearian Comedy*

In its first intention, Elizabethan romantic comedy was an attempt to adapt the world of romance and all its implications to the service of comedy. *The Two Gentlemen of Verona* shows that intention at its crudest. In the story of it, there are all the main marks of the medieval tradition as that tradition had been modified, elaborated, and extended by the idealism of Petrarch and by the speculations of the Platonists. It is yet the same tradition in its essence, corroborated rather than altered by the modifying factors; as, for instance, at the hands of Ficino, Platonism brought a medico-metaphysical theory to explain the love-laden gleam of a beautiful eye. Shakespeare's play embodies a literary manner and a moral code; its actions are conducted according to a conventional etiquette and are determined by a particular creed; and every feature of it, in matter and in sentiment, is traceable to the romantic attitude of man to woman. It presents as its setting a world constituted in such fashion that the obligations and the sanctions of its doctrines could best be realized. The course of the whole play is determined by the values such doctrine attaches to the love of man and woman.

A note struck early in the play recalls one of the few passionate love stories of classical legend—"how young

From *Shakespearian Comedy* by H. B. Charlton. London: Methuen and Co., Ltd.; New York: The Macmillan Company. 1938. Reprinted by permission of Methuen and Co., Ltd.

Leander crossed the Hellespont"—and at another moment,
Ariadne is remembered "passioning for Theseus' perjury."
But the real color of the tale is given unmistakably by the
presence amongst its characters of Sir Eglamour. By his
name is he known and whence he springs. He points
straight back to the source of the religious cult of love:
"servant and friend" of Sylvia, he is ready at call to rush
to any service to which she may command him. His own
lady and his true love died, and on her grave he vowed
pure chastity, dedicating himself to the assistance of lovers
in affliction, recking nothing what danger should betide
him in the venture. His home is in the land of medieval
romance; and his brethren are those consecrated warriors
who will undertake all danger, though it stands next to
death, for one calm look of Love's approval. He comes
to life again in a play where knightly vows are spoken,
where errantry is the normal mode of service, where the
exercise of tilt and tournament is the traditional recreation,
where lovers name themselves habitually the servants of
their ladies, where such service may impose as a duty the
helping of one's lady to a rival, and where the terms of
infamy to which the utmost slander can give voice are
"perjured, false, disloyal." And that is the world in which
Shakespeare makes his Two Gentlemen live.

Throughout the play, "Love's a mighty lord,"

> There is no woe to his correction
> Nor to his service no such joy on earth.

This is the state of the lover as the old *Romaunt of the
Rose* had depicted it:

> The sore of love is merveilous,
> For now is the lover joyous,
> Now can he pleyne, now can he grone,
> Now can he syngen, now maken mone;
> To day he pleyneth for hevynesse,
> To morowe he pleyeth for jolynesse.
> The lyf of love is full contrarie,
> Which stounde-mele can ofte varie.

Heavy penance is visited on unbelievers

> for contemning Love,
> Whose high imperious thoughts will punish him
> With bitter fasts, with penitential groans,
> With nightly tears and daily heartsore sighs.

Sleep is chased from such a rebel's now enthralled eyes, to make them watchers of his own heart's sorrow. From true votaries, nothing less than absolute devotion is required. They must hold no discourse except it be of love. Absent from their lady, they must let no single hour o'erslip without its ceremonial sigh for her sake. The more such languishing fidelity appears to be spurned, the more must it grow and fawn upon its recalcitrant object. Apart from love, nothing in life has the least significance:

> banished from her,
> Is self from self, a deadly banishment.
> What light is light, if Sylvia be not seen?
> What joy is joy, if Sylvia be not by?
> Except I be by Sylvia in the night,
> There is no music in the nightingale.
> Unless I look on Sylvia in the day,
> There is no day for me to look upon.
> She is my essence, and I leave to be,
> If I am not by her fair influence
> Fostered, illumined, cherished, kept alive.

Such is the consecrated desolation of the romantic lover: the medieval sense of a world emptied of its content persists through romantic poetry and is the undertone of the Renaissance sonneteers' woe. Bembo puts it not unlike Valentine in the play:

> Tu m'hai lasciato senza sole i giorni,
> Le notte senza stelle, e grave e egro
> Tutto questo, ond'io parlo, ond'io respiro:
> La terra scossa, e'l ciel turbato e negro;
> Et pien di mille oltraggi e mille scorni
> Me sembra ogni parte, quant'io miro.

> Valor e cortesia si dipartiro
> Nel tuo partire; e'l mondo infermo giacque;
> Et virtu spense i suoi chiari lumi;
> Et le fontane e i fiumi
> Nega la vena antica e l'usate acque:
> Et gli augelletti abandonaro il canto,
> Et l'herbe e i fior lasciar nude le piaggie,
> Ne piu di fronde il bosco si consperse.

But the lover has ample recompense for his sorrow. Setting the world at nought, he gains a heaven in its stead:

> she is mine own,
> And I as rich in having such a jewel
> As twenty seas if all their sand were pearl,
> The water nectar, and the rocks pure gold.

Inevitably, a creed of such ardent devotion has its appropriate liturgy. Stuffed with protestation, and full of new-found oaths, the lover utters his fears in wailful sonnets, whose composed rhymes are fully fraught with serviceable vows:

> . . . and on the altar of her beauty
> You sacrifice your tears, your sighs, your heart:
> Write till your ink be dry, and with your tears
> Moist it again, and frame some feeling line
> That may discover such integrity:
> For Orpheus' lute was strung with poets' sinews,
> Whose golden touch could soften steel and stones,
> Make tigers tame, and huge leviathans
> Forsake unsounded deeps to dance on sands.
> After your dire-lamenting elegies,
> Visit by night your lady's chamber window
> With some sweet concert; to their instruments
> Tune a deploring dump: the night's dead silence
> Will well become such sweet-complaining grievance.
> This, or else nothing, will inherit her.

With oceans of tears, and twenty thousand soul-confirming oaths, the lover excites himself to a fervid bacchanalian orgy, and in his braggardism proclaims his lady "sovereign to all the creatures on the earth," threatening destruction to all who will not at once subscribe, and extermination to any who but dare to breathe upon her. In the intervals of these ecstatic outbursts, the lover stands before the picture of his love, sighing and weeping, wreathing his arms like a malcontent, until at length he walks off alone like one that hath the pestilence.

When cruel circumstance separates him from his lady, etiquette prescribes the proper behavior and the right demeanor. He resorts to the congenial solitude of woods or wilderness. In the earlier days of the cult, his manner on these occasions was more violent than ceremonious. Tristan, as Malory tells us, exiled and separated from his love, goes mad for grief; he would unlace his armor and go into the wilderness, where he "brast down the trees and bowes, and otherwhyle, when he found the harp that the lady sent him, then wold he harpe and playe therupon and wepe togethre." But in the course of time the manners of solitaries became more polite. Chaucer (or the author of the *Romaunt of the Rose*) advises the lover to cultivate a proper solitude:

> For ofte, whan thou bithenkist thee
> Of thy lovyng, where so thou be,
> Fro folk thou must departe in hie,
> That noon perceyve thi maladie.
> But hyde thyne harme thou must aloue,
> And go forthe sole, and make thy mone.

It is only one more stage to the final artistic decorum of the habit. The lover in the French romance *Flamenca* "in the dark of night goes of custom to listen to the nightingale in the wood." Just, in fact, as does Valentine: in the intervals between inspecting the arms or allocating the booty of his bandit band, he takes his laments for Sylvia into the woods for orchestral effects from the nightingales:

> These shadowy, desert, unfrequented woods
> I better brook than flourishing peopled towns:
> Here can I sit alone, unseen of any,

And to the nightingale's complaining notes
Tune my distresses and record my woes.

Such is the way of lovers in romances, and in *The Two
Gentlemen of Verona*. Their state of spiritual ecstasy is
revealed by the progressive etherialization of their sus-
tenance. A collection of the menus of romantic feasts is
more than a gastronomic document. In the beginnings of
romance, eating and drinking was a major occupation.
Owein ate and drank "whilst it was late in the time of the
nones"; and once he was bidden to a feast which took
three months to consume and had taken three years to
prepare. But later, the initiate have so far purged their
mortal grossness that eating and loving begin to appear
incompatible. Again the *Romaunt of the Rose* brings the
evidence:

> Such comyng and such goyng
> Such hevynesse and such wakyng
> Makith lovers, withouten wene,
> Under her clothes pale and lene.
> For love leveth colour ne cleernesse,
> Who loveth trewe hath no fatnesse;
> Thou shalt wel by thy-silf ysee
> That thou must nedis assaied be;
> For men that shape hem other weye
> Falsly her ladyes to bitraye,
> It is no wonder though they be fatt,
> With false othes her loves they gatt.
> For oft I see suche losengours
> Fatter than abbatis or priours.

On occasion, the true lover, like Jehan in *Jehan and
Blonde,* is like to fade away, and can only eat when his
lady serves the dishes to him with her own delicate hands.
Our Valentine had been a good trencherman before he
became a romantic lover; in those days, when he fasted,
it was presently after dinner. But once he becomes a votary, not even ambrosia nor nectar is good enough for his
ethereal table: "now can I break my fast, dine, sup, and
sleep upon the very naked name of love." How he thrives

on this diet will become a primary article of the literary and dramatic criticism of *The Two Gentlemen of Verona*.

So much for the spirit of romance in the play. Now for the world in which it is set—since, taking its religion thence, it must also take the romantic world in which such religion may reveal itself. Not men living dully sluggardized at home, but those bred and tutored in the wider world, seeking preferment out, trying their fortunes in war or discovering islands far away—these are they who have scope to put such religion to the proof. So in *The Two Gentlemen of Verona*, the scene is laid in Italy, the country which to Shakespeare's fellows was the hallowed land of romance. But it is an Italy of romance, not of physiographic authenticity. It has inland waterways unknown to geographers; the journey from Verona to Mantua is a sea voyage; it is indeed a scenario in which all the material trappings of romance may be assembled. Mountain and forest are indispensable, mountains which are brigand-haunted, and forests in the gloom of which are abbeys from whose postern gates friars creep into the encircling woods, so wrapt in penitential mood that lurking lions, prowling hungrily for food, are utterly forgotten. In such a locality, the tale of true love may run its uneven course. The poetically gifted lover meets such obstacles as a rival, at whom he hurls his cartel, and a perverse father whose plans for his daughter are based on such irrelevant considerations as the rivals' bank balances. The father's castle has its upper tower far from the ground, and built so shelving that to climb it is at apparent hazard of one's life. And here is the angelic daughter's chamber wherein she is nightly lodged, within doors securely locked, so that rescue can only be by a corded ladder to her chamber window. Then unexpected difficulties will be expected to intrude: the best-laid plot to carry her away is foiled by the machinations of a villain out of the least suspected quarter. Banishment naturally follows, and at length, with the flight of the heroine and the pursuit of her by the entire court, all will work out well by a series of surprising coincidences, to which rivals, brigands, friars, and lions are all somehow contributory. In this way, romantic love makes its roman-

tic universe; and this in fact is the setting and the story
of *The Two Gentlemen of Verona*.

This, both in matter and in spirit, is the tradition which
the Elizabethan dramatists desired to lift bodily onto their
comic stage. But something somehow went wrong. The
spirit of medieval romance seemed to shrivel in the presence of comedy. Something similar had in fact happened
in the real world outside the theater. The last hero of romance had lived gloriously and had died quite out of his
part. Jacques de Lalaing, le bon chevalier, the mirror of
knighthood who adorned the Burgundian court in the middle of the fifteenth century, had become the pattern of
chivalry for all Europe. To his contemporaries, "fair was
he as Paris, pious as Aeneas, wise as Ulysses, and passionate as Hector": and his exploits in tournament and in
knight-errantry had carried his fame through many lands.
He died an early death in 1453. But he did not die of a
lover's broken heart; nor was he slain in tourney by a
foeman worthy of his steel and of his thirty-two em-
blazoned pennants. He was shot down by a cannon ball
in an expedition against the merchants and shopkeepers
of Ghent. The gross ponderable facts of a very material
world swept the symbol of an outworn ideal from off the
face of the earth. So in *The Two Gentlemen,* a sheer clod
of earth, Launce by name, will, quite unwittingly, expose
the unsubstantiality of the romantic hero with whom the
play throws him into contact. But we are anticipating. The
consequences of Shakespeare's attempt to dramatize romance must be watched in closer detail.

There is little wonder that the Elizabethan dramatists
saw the dramatic possibilities of such material, and did
not at first perceive its dramatic disadvantages. They felt
the dramatic thrill of following these lovers and setting
the world at nought. Nor is it very difficult to set the geo-
graphical world at nought, at least to the extent of making
inland seas in Italy or liberating living lions in its woods.
Yet sometimes the distortions of the physical universe
necessarily ventured by the romanticist entail violent
wrenches of our common consciousness. The dukes of
Shakespeare's Italy, for instance, apparently have magic

power over the flight of time; for whilst a banished man
is speaking but ten lines, the proclamation of his banishment is ratified, promulgated, and has become publicly
known throughout the duchy, and sentinels have already
been posted along the frontiers to prevent a surreptitious
return of the exile to the land which he has not yet had
time to pack his suitcase for leaving. It is a land too where
optical illusions, or perhaps optical delusions, are the normal way of vision. A man seeking a page boy interviews
an applicant for the post; he is just enough of a business-
man to know that some sort of reason must be advanced
for taking on a servant who can show neither character
nor reference from previous employers, and so Proteus,
engaging the disguised Julia, says that the engagement is
specifically on the recommendation of the applicant's face;
but he does not recognize, as he gazes into this face, that
it was the one he was smothering with kisses a few weeks
before when its owner, in her proper dress, was his betrothed. Yet these are really only minor impediments, re-
quiring but a little and a by no means reluctant suspension
of our disbelief. They are altogether insignificant compared
with the reservations involved when romance displays its
peculiar propensity for setting the world of man at nought.
To satisfy its own obligations, it perforce demanded super-
men; at all events, the heroes it puts forward as its votaries
in the play are something either more or less than men.

Romantically speaking, Valentine is the hero, and not
alone in the technical sense. In classical comedy the hero
is simply the protagonist, the central figure who is the
biggest butt of the comic satire. But here the protagonist
is the upholder of the faith on which the play is built, the
man with whom the audience is called upon to rejoice
admiringly, and not the fellow at whom it is derisively to
laugh. He is to play the hero in every sense of the word.
Yet in the event, the prevailing spirit of romance endows
him with sentiments and provides him with occupations
which inevitably frustrate the heroic intention. The story
renders him a fool. Convention may sanctify his sudden
conversion from the mocker to the votary of love, and
may even excuse or palliate his fractious braggardism

when he insults Proteus with ill-mannered comparisons between Silvia and Julia. But his helplessness and his impenetrable stupidity amount to more than the traditional blindness of a lover. Even the clown Speed can see through Silvia's trick, when she makes Valentine write a letter to himself. But Valentine plays out the excellent motion as an exceeding puppet, unenlightened by the faintest gleam of common insight. And despite his vaunt that he knows Proteus as well as he knows himself, he is blind to villainies so palpable that Launce, the other clown of the piece, though he be but a fool, has the wits to recognize them for what they plainly are. The incidents are dramatically very significant, for both Launce and Speed come into the play for no reason whatever but to be unmistakable dolts. One begins to feel that it will be extremely difficult to make a hero of a man who is proved to be duller of wit than the patent idiots of the piece. Even when Valentine might have shone by resource in action, he relapses into conventional laments, and throws himself helplessly into the arms of Proteus for advice and consolation. Heroic opportunity stands begging round him when he encounters the brigands. But besides demonstrating that he can tell a lie— witness his tale of cock and bull about having killed a man —the situation only serves to discredit him still more: for the words of his lie, his crocodile tears for the fictitious man he claims to have slain, and his groundless boast that he slew him manfully in fight without false vantage or base treachery, are in fact nothing but an attempt to make moral capital by means of forgery and perjury. They have not even the recommendation of the Major General's tears for the orphan boy. When at length Valentine is duly installed as captain of the brigands, his chief occupation is to vary highway robbery with sentimental descants on the beauty of nature in her "shadowy, desert, unfrequented woods":

Here can I sit alone, unseen of any—

and we already know his favorite hobby on these saunterings—

And to the nightingale's complaining notes
Tune my distresses and record my woes.

He is own brother to Gilbert's coster, who, when he isn't
jumping on his mother, loves to lie abasking in the sun,
and to the cutthroat, who, when not occupied in crimes,
loves to hear the little brook agurgling and listen to the
merry village chimes. But Valentine's utmost reach of ineptitude comes with what, again romantically speaking, is
meant to be the heroic climax of the play. When he has
just learnt the full tale of the villainy of Proteus, the code
permits him neither resentment nor passion. Like a cashier
addressing a charwoman who has pilfered a penny stamp,
he sums up his rebuke—"I am sorry I must never trust thee
more." And worse follows immediately. With but five lines
of formal apology from the villain, Valentine professes
himself so completely satisfied that he enthusiastically resigns his darling Silvia to the traitor. Even Valentine must
have seen that the gesture was a little odd, because he
quotes the legal sanction. It is the code, a primary article
in the romantic faith—"that my love may appear plain
and free." But it makes a man a nincompoop. Nor does
it help much that after this preposterous episode Valentine
is allowed to spit a little fire in an encounter with another
rival, Thurio. He has already proved himself so true a son
of romance that he can never again be mistaken for a
creature of human nature.

Proteus is less hampered by romantic obligations; because the plot requires him to have just sufficient of salu-
tary villainy to make him throw over their commandments
for his own ends. Yet the villain of romance suffers almost
as much from the pressure of romanticism as does the hero.
The noble fellows whom he, as villain, is called upon to
deceive are such gullible mortals that little positive skill is
necessary. Proteus can fool Thurio and Valentine and the
Duke without exerting himself. But on the one occasion
when he might have shown his wits, he only reveals his
lack of them. Making love to Silvia, he meets her protest
against his disloyalty to Julia by inventing the easy excuse
that Julia is dead. Silvia replies that, even so, he should

be ashamed to wrong Valentine. It is, of course, a tight corner: but the best Proteus can do is to say "I likewise hear that Valentine is dead." He might at least have displayed a little more ingenuity in invention; he fails in precisely such a situation as would have permitted the clown of classical comedy to triumph. Moreover, the main plot requires Proteus to be guilty of incredible duplicity, and of the most facile rapidity in changing morals and mistresses. But he need scarcely have made the change explicit in words so ineptly casual and banal as his remark: *"Methinks* my zeal to Valentine is cold." The phrase is accidentally in keeping with the unintended complacence he displays when, wooing the lady who will have none of him, he begins by informing her that "he has made her happy" by his coming. The trait becomes intolerably ludicrous when, all his sins forgiven him, and Julia restored to his arms, all he can utter in confession is his own fatuous self-conceit:

> O heaven, were man
> But constant, he were perfect.

It is, of course, a fine sentiment; but the audience, having seen Valentine, simply will not believe it.

Even the brigands of romance will scarcely stand the test of the stage. They enter with metaphorical daggers in mouths bristling with black mustachios and with desperate oaths. Callous and bloodthirsty ruffians, spoiling for a fight, their chief regret is that fate is sending only one defenseless traveler to be rifled instead of ten. But when the destined victim turns out to be two, courage perhaps abates a little: at all events, the travelers are warned to keep their distance, and throw over the booty or otherwise to assume a sitting posture, whilst the rifling is safely done by the desperadoes themselves. Perhaps this, and not his customary ineptitude in speech, is what makes Valentine address the villains as "My friends." But, of course, his assumption is, for the trade of brigandage, economically unsound. And so, with apologies for correcting him, Valentine is informed that he is not playing the game—"that's not so,

sir; we are your enemies." But the outlaws are connois-
seurs of masculine beauty, and Valentine's fine figure se-
cures him an opportunity for a hearing: one cannot but
note that this is the first time that any of his romantic attributes has made for his advantage, and that he misuses
it scandalously for his lying brag. Hearing the fiction, however, the bandits feel at once that here is a fellow spirit,
given, like themselves, to "so small a fault" as homicide.
Straightway they implore him to show them his diploma
in the modern languages, promising him the kingship of
the band if it is of good honors' standard. Becoming con-
vivial, they reveal their amiable dispositions in snatches
of their life history. One has amused himself with attempts
at abduction. Another, when the whim takes him, "in his
mood," has the merry trick of stabbing gentlemen unto the
heart; and his gaiety makes us forget that a mood in Shakespeare's English was not quite the casual fancy it now is.
Another acclaims these and other "such like petty crimes"
as congenial peccadilloes in his own repertory. By this
time, the brigands have become so hilarious with their
reminiscences, that they are no longer minded to scrutinize
Valentine's academic credentials. They will take him for
a linguist merely "on his own report," and, mainly because
he "is beautified with goodly shape," they offer him the
leadership, pathetically promising to love him as their commander and their king. Clearly such a thoroughly unbrig-
andlike procedure as this election has almost put them out
of their parts. They must be allowed to recover in a traditional tableau. Daggers are whipped out, threats become
fierce, and Valentine, with steel points at his throat, is
given the choice of being a king or a corpse. Perhaps his
fear is responsible for the odd proviso that "silly women"
shall be exempt from the depredations of the gang over
which he is to rule; but it is of course too much to expect
of better men than Valentine to require them to anticipate
a variation in the meaning of a word. Neither before nor
after *The Two Gentlemen of Verona* has dramatic literature known a band of outlaws like to these—except once:
there are the Pirates of Penzance: but then Gilbert meant
his to be funny.

One begins to suspect that everything which is hallowed by the tradition of romance is made thereby of no avail for the purposes of drama. But there are Julia and Launce to reckon with; and these are figures universally accounted the most substantial beings in the play. So indeed they are. But they owe it entirely to the fact that they are under no obligation whatever to the code of romance. The behavior of Valentine is entirely conditioned by the doctrine of romantic love. But the code allowed to woman no duty but to excite by her beauty the devoted worship of her knight. If England instead of France had performed the final codification of chivalry, its women might have had other and less ladylike propensities, such, for instance, as King Horn's Rimenhild displayed. But when a French romance elaborates its portrait of womanhood, it gives her patience rather than character: women with the forcefulness of a distinct personality might have turned the energies of their knights away from consecrated paths of knighthood, as Chretien's Enide turned her Erec:

> Mes tant l'ama Erec d'amors
> Que d'armes mes ne li chaloit,
> Ne a tornoiemant n'aloit
> N'avoit mes soing de tornoiier.

Wherefore Chretien's romance tells of Erec's regeneration through the discipline by which he reduces his Enide to absolute submission. At the end, she has attained complete self-suppression—

> Ne je tant hardie ne sui
> Que je os regarder vers lui—

and, to the modern eye, has become the perfect pattern of an exquisitely charming nonentity.

When Shakespeare takes over a tradition whose women are like these, so long as he preserves the beauty of their faces, he can endow them with whatever character he may please. His Julia is a creation, not a convention. As she is a woman, acting on a woman's instinct—"I have no other but a woman's reason, I think him so because I think him so"—she is depicted in moods, whimsies, and vagaries which are in fact the stuff of dramatic characterization. Like the heroine of romance, she will cover her first love letter with kisses and press the precious manuscript to her heart. But like the spirited independent young lady of the world, she will not expose herself to the chuckles of her maid by exhibiting the common symptoms of her affections. Hence the pretended contempt, and the struggle to keep up appearances, even at considerable risk to the sacred document. But for what seriously concerns her love, Julia is too levelheaded to overreach herself. As far as may be, she will avoid the disapproval of opinion: but where there is no remedy, she will defy a scandalized world and undertake her pilgrimage of love. She knows the hazards of the road and the many weary steps it will involve. But she also knows her own capacities, and has duly taken note of all material things she will stand in need of. And although Proteus is a poor thing on whom to lavish so much love, Julia knows that love is indeed a blinded god; and in her capable hands even a Proteus may be molded to something worth the having.

Launce is another who insists on remaining in the memory. He has no real right within the play, except that gentlemen must have servants and Elizabethan audiences must have clowns. But coming in thus by a back door, he earns an unexpected importance in the play. Seen side by side with Speed, his origin is clear. Whilst Speed belongs to the purely theatrical family of the Dromios, with their punning and logic-chopping asininities, Launce harks back to the native Costard. And as Costard shows his relationship to Bottom by his skill in village theatricals, so Launce reveals by his wooing his family connection with Touchstone, and Touchstone's Audrey, who was a poor thing, but his own. All the kind of the Launces are thus palpably a mighty stock. Their worth, compared with that of the Speeds and the Dromios, is admirably indicated by Launce's consummate use of Speed's curiosity and of his better schooling. Launce gets his letter deciphered; he gets also an opportunity to display his own superior breeding and to secure condign punishment for the ill-mannered Speed: "now will he be swinged for reading my letter; an unmannerly slave, that will thrust himself into secrets! I'll after, to rejoice in the boy's correction."

Launce is happiest with his dog. Clownage can go no farther than the pantomimic representation, with staff and shoe and dog, of the parting from his home folks. Laughter is hilarious at Launce's bitter grief that his ungrateful cur declined to shed a tear. That Launce should expect it is, of course, the element of preposterous incongruity which makes him a clown. But when he puts his complaint squarely, that his "dog has no more pity in him than a dog," the thrust pierces more than it was meant to. Romance itself has expected no less largely of Valentine, of Proteus, and of the rest. It has demanded that man shall be more than man, and has laid upon him requisitions passing the ability of man to fulfill. At the bidding of romance, Valentine and Proteus have become what they are in the play, and the one thing they are not is men like other men. A further incident in which Launce is concerned takes on a similarly unexpected significance. He has made as great a sacrifice as did Valentine himself: he has given up his own cur in place of the one which Proteus entrusted to him to take to Silvia. But the effect hardly suggests that self-sacrifice is worldly-wise. And so once more it seems to bring into question the worldly worth of the code which sanctifies such deeds. Unintentionally, Launce has become the means by which the incompatibilities and the unrealities of romantic postulates are laid bare. And Launce is palpably the stuff of comedy: awakening our comedy sense, he inevitably sharpens our appreciation of the particular range of incongruities which are the province of comedy—the incongruity between what a thing really is and what it is taken to be.

Romance, and not comedy, has called the tune of *The Two Gentlemen of Verona* and governed the direction of the action of the play. That is why its creatures bear so little resemblance to men of flesh and blood. Lacking this, they are scarcely dramatic figures at all; for every form of drama would appear to seek at least so much of human nature in its characters. But perhaps the characters of the Two Gentlemen are comic in a sense which at first had never entered the mind of their maker. Valentine bids for the sympathy, but not for the laughter of the audience: the ideals by which he lives are assumed to have the world's approbation. But in execution they involve him in most ridiculous plight. He turns the world from its compassionate approval to a mood of skeptical questioning. The hero of romantic comedy appears no better than its clowns. And so topsy-turvy is the world of romance that apparently the one obvious way to be reputed in it for a fool is to show at least a faint sign of discretion and of common sense. Thurio, for instance, was cast for the dotard of the play, and of course he is not without egregious folly. But what was meant in the end to annihilate him with contempt turns out quite otherwise. Threatened by Valentine's sword, he resigns all claim to Silvia, on the ground that he holds him but a fool that will endanger his body for a girl that loves him not. The audience is invited to call Thurio a fool for thus showing himself to be the one person in the play with a modicum of worldly wisdom, a respect for the limitations of human nature, and a recognition of the conditions under which it may survive. Clearly, Shakespeare's first attempt to make romantic comedy had only succeeded so far that it had unexpectedly and inadvertently made romance comic. The real problem was still to be faced.

MARK VAN DOREN

from *Shakespeare*

In its kind *The Two Gentlemen of Verona* is not nearly as good as *The Taming of the Shrew* is in the kind called farce. But Shakespeare will soon do better in the kind he now discovers, and with one exception, *The Merry Wives of Windsor,* he is never to follow any other. *The Two Gentlemen of Verona* is a slight comedy and it minces uncertainly to an implausible conclusion, but it is Shakespeare's own and it sets his course. His problem henceforth is not to keep his fun outside the range of feeling but to keep his feeling within the range of fun; or rather it is to mingle them so that wit and emotion are wedded in an atmosphere which is as grave as it is smiling, as golden as it is bright. This atmosphere, so natural to man's life, so easy to breathe, and so mellow in its hue, is uniquely Shakespeare's, and it will be sufficient for his purposes in comedy; in its amber light he can go anywhere and consider everything, and his people can speak with the richest variety. Its elements are scarcely compounded in *The Two Gentlemen of Verona,* which is only a copy of what is to come; but for that very reason they are separately recognizable, they can be witnessed in the process of creation.

Valentine's opening speech announces the tone as he discourses to his fellow gentleman concerning the advan-

From *Shakespeare* by Mark Van Doren. New York: Henry Holt and Co., 1939; London: George Allen & Unwin, Ltd., 1941. Copyright 1939 by Mark Van Doren. Reprinted by permission of Holt, Rinehart and Winston, Inc.

tages of travel. "Such wind as scatters young men through
the world" will soon blow both the heroes—rather stiff and
humorless figures, newborn in Shakespeare's comic universe—from Verona to Milan, where one of them will
forget his beloved Julia and plot to steal the other's Silvia.
So far they are at peace, and their voices move lightly
through the cadences of a graceful, breeze-haunted music.
Valentine's speech is indeed a poem:

> Cease to persuade, my loving Proteus.
> Home-keeping youth have ever homely wits.
> Were 't not affection chains thy tender days
> To the sweet glances of thy honor'd love,
> I rather would entreat thy company
> To see the wonders of the world abroad
> Than, living dully sluggardiz'd at home,
> Wear out thy youth with shapeless idleness.
> But since thou lov'st, love still and thrive therein,
> Even as I would when I to love begin.
>
> (I.i.1–10)

The rhyme at the end is amateur, but Valentine has caught
the tone which will be heard henceforth in the golden world
of gentlemen where Shakespeare's comedy will occur. It
is a world whose free and graceful movement finds a symbol for itself in the travel of young men:

> Some to the wars, to try their fortune there;
> Some to discover islands far away;
> Some to the studious universities.
>
> (I.iii.8–10)

They are awaited somewhere by ladies of fine and dis-
ciplined feeling; or they will be followed, as Proteus in the
present case is followed by Julia, in brave disguise and be
served as pages by the very sweethearts they have lost.
The ladies will be accustomed to compliment:

Valentine.   Sweet lady, entertain him
To be my fellow servant to your ladyship. . . .

Silvia. Servant, you are welcome to a worthless mistress.

Proteus. I'll die on him that says so but yourself.

Silvia. That you are welcome?

Proteus.   That you are worthless.
                              (II.iv.103–04, 112–14)

In their grace they understand the arts both of bestowing
and of receiving praise. And their ideal might be such a
man as Eglamour, whom Silvia invites to be her escort as
she follows Valentine:

> Thyself hast lov'd; and I have heard thee say
> No grief did ever come so near thy heart
> As when thy lady and thy true love died. . . .
> I do desire thee, even from a heart
> As full of sorrows as the sea of sands,
> To bear me company.

                              (IV.iii.19–21, 33–35)

They are not wailing women; their grief is delicate, well-
taught, tender, and half-concealed. They are at home in
romance: Valentine must climb to Silvia by a corded ladder, Julia must knit up her hair in silken strings with
twenty odd-conceited truelove knots (II.vii. 45–46), and
there will be outlaws in the dangerous forest—hardly dangerous themselves, once a sweet lady adventures among
them. And they live for that love which is both "a mighty
lord" (II.iv. 135) and as tenderly capricious as

> The uncertain glory of an April day   (I.iii.85)

So do their gentlemen live for love of each other. Friendship
is one of the gods here, and he has given laws which
Proteus will find it going against the grain to break, so
that soliloquies will be necessary before he can compre-
hend the depth of his default. He has not heard Valentine
describe him to the Duke of Milan, but the language would
have been familiar:

> I knew him as myself, for from our infancy
> We have convers'd and spent our hours together;
> And though myself have been an idle truant,
> Omitting the sweet benefit of time
> To clothe mine age with angel-like perfection,
> Yet hath Sir Proteus, for that's his name,
> Made use and fair advantage of his days. . . .
> He is complete in feature and in mind
> With all good grace to grace a gentleman.
>
> (II.iv.61–67, 72–73)

It is such a friend that Proteus betrays, and his exclamation at the close, after the reconciliation which no one believes,

> O heaven! Were man
> But constant, he were perfect. That one error
> Fills him with faults,
>
> (V.iv.110–12)

covers his untruth to Valentine no less than his abandonment of Julia.

"Heaven-bred poesy," as the Duke puts it, is natural to the mood of this world. And music is so much so that we cannot be surprised to find an excellent sweet song, Who is Silvia, built into the key scene of the play—laced firmly into it with more than simple irony, for Julia, who hears it sung to her rival, does not know that Proteus is pretending to sing it for Thurio. Nor can we fail to note the balances set up here and there—between Julia's coyness (I.ii) and Silvia's (II.i), between Proteus's concealment of a letter (I.iii) and Valentine's concealment of a ladder (III.i)—as phrases are balanced in music. And the favorite subjects for quibble are note, burden, sharp, flat, bass, string, and change.

Of quibbles there are many in the play; too many, since they are the only device yet known by Shakespeare for securing the effect of wit and he must overwork them. Valentine and Proteus turn directly in the first scene from talk of travel to an exchange of puns; and the servants, Speed and Launce, are soon at it in their own different fashions. Wit belongs of course in such a world, but this early sample of it is dry and curiously spiritless. It is almost purely verbal. "Your old vice still," says Speed to Launce (III.i. 282); "mistake the word." Both masters and men, not to speak of Julia with her maid Lucetta, have caught it like the plague. It does not give them the gaiety which their successors in Shakespearean comedy will have, and which will never depend on puns for its expression, though puns will by no means disappear. There is in fact no gaiety in *The Two Gentlemen of Verona* outside of a few scenes dealing with the sensible Launce and his unwanted dog. Launce looks forward not merely to the Launcelot Gobbo whose name he suggests but to a whole line of clowns whose humor is in their hearts and stomachs rather than on their tongues. Speed looks backward to barrenness and will not thrive.

One of the interesting things about *The Two Gentlemen of Verona* is the studies it contains of things to come in Shakespeare. Julia is something like Portia when she discusses suitors with her maid (I.ii), and something like Viola when she discusses herself in disguise (IV.iv). Proteus tells almost as many lies as Bertram does in *All's Well That Ends Well*. The Friar Patrick at whose cell Silvia can arrange to meet Eglamour is soon, in *Romeo and Juliet*, to change his name to Laurence; and indeed there is already a Friar Laurence here (V.ii.37). And the forest near Mantua which Valentine finds so much more agreeable than "flourishing peopled towns" is a promise of Arden. But *The Two Gentlemen of Verona* is at best half-grown. Its seriousness is not mingled with its mirth. It has done a great deal in that it has set a scene and conceived an atmosphere. It has done no more.

PAULA S. BERGGREN

"More Grace Than Boy":
Male Disguise in *The Two Gentlemen of Verona*

Very few readers come to *The Two Gentlemen of Verona* before having read at least one of Shakespeare's later comedies; thus Julia's conventional decision to put on boy's clothes is likely to be judged by the measure of *As You Like It* or *Twelfth Night*, surely the two plays that exploit the convention most fully. Yet to understand how male disguise works in *The Two Gentlemen of Verona*, one must adjust assumptions drawn from the later comedies. For this play, as its title suggests, takes a male-centered view of the world and consequently, as we shall see, asks for special qualities in its disguised heroine.

In some ways Julia's experience seems typical: like most of the later comic heroines, she announces that she puts on boy's clothes for self-protection, to "prevent / The loose encounters of lascivious men" (II.vii.40–41). In *As You Like It* and *Twelfth Night*, the heroine's initial caution proves unnecessary, with the happy and unexpected result that wearing men's clothing primarily promotes the heroine's fortunes in love. Julia's disguise, by contrast, achieves its original purpose: in a play where "lascivious men" do attack women, she proceeds unmolested.

Julia's disguise fails, on the other hand, to further her

This essay was written for the Signet Classic Shakespeare.

relationship with Proteus. Rosalind has only just met Orlando at the beginning of *As You Like It*, and Viola only heard of Orsino when *Twelfth Night* begins. Their transformed states allow them to know the men they love, who, in turn find themselves drawn to unusually attractive boys. Conversely, Julia and Proteus are in love when *The Two Gentlemen of Verona* begins. Her disguise makes her invisible rather than desirable; unseen by Proteus, she must stand by and hear him blithely declare her dead. When she does present herself to him as a page boy, she may awaken subconscious memories of her female self that lead Proteus to hand her the ring she had herself given him. Yet her "face" and "behavior" (IV.iv.67) recommend her only to serve as a go-between, to deliver her ring to "Madam Silvia." To the page boy Sebastian, Proteus acknowledges that the ring's owner lives, but no sensitivity to the owner's proximity shakes his determination to sue for Silvia's favors.

Not only does Julia's disguise fail to move the man she loves, its original purpose is undercut by the strong presence of Silvia in *The Two Gentlemen of Verona*. All the comic heroines in male disguise share the romantic spotlight with another major heroine, but none is so much in the other's shadow as Julia. For while dressed as a woman, Silvia undertakes to do precisely what Julia felt she needed to disguise herself to manage. Silvia too decides to follow her love, and exceeds Julia in devotion by following him into banishment after contriving to escape from her father's control. She enlists protection, certainly, as did Julia, and in choosing a male escort in place of self-concealment seems at first less courageous than a girl who goes a further distance disguised and on her own. But Silvia from the start is prepared to do without Sir Eglamour if necessary (IV.iii.37), and, of course, Sir Eglamour abandons her at the first sign of danger. Twice outraged by "lascivious men," Silvia nevertheless emerges unharmed and successfully reunited with Valentine, who saves her, while Julia contents herself with Proteus, who betrayed her.

The feckless Sir Eglamour, it may be recalled, is spoken of early in the play as one of Julia's suitors in Verona. His unexplained removal to the court of Milan, often taken as evidence of an unfortunate lack of concentration on Shakespeare's part, may more profitably be interpreted as a sign of an unusual symbiotic relationship between the two heroines of *The Two Gentlemen of Verona*.[1] At first, Silvia threatens to subsume much of the interest originated by Julia. Although we hear Julia pondering the merits of three suitors (among them Sir Eglamour) who "every day with parle encounter" her (I.ii.5), the lady we actually see surrounded by three suitors is Silvia. In the opening scene of the play, Proteus fears and Speed confirms Julia's disdain of his letter: "She's as hard as steel," the messenger reports (I.i.140–41). The men in Verona, it seems, stereotype Julia as the traditional hard-hearted mistress of Petrarchan love poetry. The audience knows better, however, for in the next scene we learn that Speed has mistakenly delivered the letter to Lucetta. As her lady's surrogate, she makes a more convincing Petrarchan mistress than does Julia herself, whom we soon see scrambling on the floor to pick up the pieces of her letter. We must wait for Act II to discover in Silvia a more authentic embodiment of the masculine fantasy of feminine power that Proteus attributes to Julia but relocates the instant he sees the real thing.

By its stage deployment of the two heroines, *The Two Gentlemen of Verona* frequently gives theatrical force to the relative subordination of Julia. Praising Silvia, Valentine deems Julia fit merely to be his lady's handmaid,

> dignified with this high honor—
> To bear my lady's train, lest the base earth
> Should from her vesture chance to steal a kiss.
> (II.iv.157–59)

Girls in doublet and hose forfeit such sartorial compliments; and the implied posture envisaged for Julia here, stooping down to lift up Silvia's garment, is one we have already seen her in as she retrieves Proteus's letter. When the two heroines actually appear on stage together for the first time, Julia in her page boy's outfit lurks in shadow below while Silvia shines down from her tower, above, like the "pale queen of night" (IV.ii.97) by whom she swears.[2]

Even when Julia is the social superior, as in her scenes at home with Lucetta, she plays an oddly subordinate role. Bertrand Evans points out that in *The Merchant of Venice,* where mistress and maid review the lady's suitors in a scene very like Act I, Scene ii of *The Two Gentlemen of Verona*, "Shakespeare knew to give the witty descriptive lines to Portia, not Nerissa."[3] Let us consider, however, that Julia's reticence fits better a young woman who (quite unlike the preening Portia) dwells on her "modesty" (I.ii.41,55), both here and in the momentous scene where, having boldly proposed to follow Proteus in male disguise, she leaves it to Lucetta to work out the details of her physical imposture. Still, she sets careful limits on Lucetta's ingenuity: she must be a "well-reputed page" (II.vii.43), she will not cut her hair (which would be a drastic step, akin to self-mutilation, for a Renaissance woman), and she shrinks even from discussing the sexual indelicacy of an ornamental codpiece. She asks Lucetta to think what will be "meet" and "mannerly" (II.vii.58) and then drops the issue. By the time we see her as a page boy, she has journeyed to Milan and located Proteus. Whatever charm her disguise may initially have held for her has long since passed and goes unremarked.

The pun on "mannerly" and Lucetta's saucy consideration of codpieces should remind us that in the sixteenth and seventeenth centuries, these scenes of boy actors playing girls who dress up as boys had an extra-dramatic dimension difficult for modern audiences to appreciate. Twentieth-century Americans assign one set of meanings to a woman wearing pants, having to do with taking control of, perhaps even displacing, men. We believe the woman in pants empowered, in other words, a belief that (especially) Rosalind's dominant role in *As You Like It* seems to affirm existed even in Shakespeare's day. Having boys successfully play the roles of Rosalind and Portia, female characters who then successfully play boys, must have added a concrete piquancy to the abstract notion of a strong-willed woman's "manliness." Yet since the same boys were equally successful playing shy or unobtrusive women (and since not all men are strong), there is nothing intrinsically assertive about wearing male disguise. In *The Two Gentlemen of Verona*, a play where Proteus's proclivity for change endangers friendship, love, and social harmony, a boy-heroine exulting in deft and tantalizing self-metamorphosis would exacerbate rather than resolve the dramatic crisis.

As You Like It and *Twelfth Night* go on to investigate the process by which the thrice-disguised boys acquire a fluid sexual identity, recognizing that, as potential partners, they seem capable of satisfying any sexual taste. Once conscious of the universal appeal inherent in their multiple selves, the disguised heroines of the later comedies take on almost superhuman powers. Julia does not. But a Rosalind, a Portia, or even a Viola would be an impediment in *The Two Gentlemen of Verona*, where male disguise provides little occasion for erotic dazzle. Although sexually titillating considerations have a place in the critique of male fashion conducted by Lucetta and Julia in II.vii, the early play fails to dramatize them, and with good reason: ultimately it is not the sexual but the social ingredient of Julia's disguise that counts. Julia becomes so faithful a servant to Proteus that, as Sebastian, she perseveres in an errand whose success would be fatal to her deepest desires. In a play focused more on selfishness than on sex, her selflessness restores order.

The Two Gentlemen of Verona explores the virtues of service in a variety of characters. Two of them serve for reward: Valentine, a courtly lover whom Silvia briskly calls "servant" (II.i.97; II.iv.1), wants love; Speed, a witty messenger, wants money. Launce and Julia, as several critics have astutely noted, are set against them and each other.[4] Launce enters the play directly after Julia's

silent farewell to Proteus and leaves it, demoted to a
"slave" (IV.iv.62), just as Sebastian prepares to follow
him into Proteus's service. In his last speech, Launce
shows us that Proteus is like a dog and Julia like Launce,
for both clown and page boy pay for the willful indiscre-
tions perpetrated by creatures whom they love better than
themselves.

The special quality of male disguise in *The Two Gentlemen of Verona* is most evident in the scene where the
messenger Julia approaches Silvia as her rival and discovers instead her staunchest supporter. The symbiotic
blending of the two heroines reaches its apex when Silvia
projects herself empathetically into the plight of a woman
she thinks she has never seen, while speaking directly to
this woman. To cover "his" inadvertent expression of
gratitude on Julia's behalf, "Sebastian" must remember
that he speaks *for* rather than *as* Julia. Julia in male disguise then demonstrates that one best reaches others by
suppressing the self. Although we hear a remote, fictional
Julia described as having wept at the sight of Sebastian
playing Ariadne, the Julia we see does not weep at the raw
truth of her own loss (and in Sebastian's invention we
have no way of knowing whether the weeping Julia is to
be thought of as already abandoned by the Theseus-like
Proteus or not). These are tears of empathy,[5] shed by the
fictive Julia and the "real" Silvia in response to the acting
boy in boy's clothes who projects himself as fully into the
woman's part as he fits perfectly into the heroine's dress.

This invented scene is supposed to have taken place at
Pentecost, the Christian festival that comes fifty days after
Easter and celebrates the descent of the Holy Ghost, a
descent that reenacts the willingness of divinity to take on
an inferior form in order to achieve the salvation of
others. In *The Two Gentlemen of Verona*, taking on male
disguise is to assume inferior status, for it is a world of
"lascivious men," not to be trusted. By becoming a man,
Julia does nothing for herself. She is moved by grace to
give up her own claims in order to move and serve others.

The Petrarchan male fantasy that animates gentlemen

in Verona is dangerous because it falsely imputes power to women and then appeals to that power as a justification for unmannerly, unmanly behavior. If Proteus is the worse offender, neither is Valentine, who would violate the Duke's hospitality, free of blame. Julia and Silvia must work symbiotically, in tandem rather than in opposition, to expose the self-regarding masculine view of the feminine that their lovers' mindless rehearsal of Petrarchan metaphors endorses. Silvia's job is to counter directly the fatuous praise of the false Proteus: "I am very loath to be your idol, sir" (IV.ii.126). But used to flattery, the Duke's daughter does give out her picture, even though she insists that it is an insubstantial "shadow" (IV.iv.120).

Julia's task in the play is to eradicate idolatry completely and to excavate the truth beneath the falsehood; she begins herself in falsehood, refusing a letter that matters more to her than anything except an unconsidered image of propriety. Yet moments later, she falls to the floor to retrieve the essential meaning if not the form of that letter.[6] She closes the play on the same note: again an emotion she would repress but cannot overtakes her and again she falls to the ground, now in a swoon, which reveals her to be the girl Julia and not the boy Sebastian. First and last, Julia reaches down to truth, like Ariadne, prostrate in her grief, and perhaps more tellingly, like the Holy Ghost descending on Pentecost.

The religious note heard in the reference to Pentecost reverberates in the name that the disguised Julia takes— Sebastian. To the extent that her choice evokes the image of a saint whose near-nude posture in martyrdom was a favorite artistic subject combining religious and erotic elements,[7] we recognize a link to Rosalind's taking the name of Ganymede, the Trojan boy loved by Zeus. Rosalind, loved by Phebe and Orlando, and ultimately seconded by the god of marriage in arranging for the ensuing confusion to be put right, revels in her androgynous charms. Sebastian's beauty may be as celebrated as Ganymede's, but Ganymede was not a Christian martyr. No one falls in love with Julia in male disguise; her costume offers her no gratification but the opportunity to serve others. In an age accustomed to see religious content in apparently secular images, Julia in male disguise lightly bodies forth a solemn sacrifice.

Even as it falsifies, then, male disguise is a device that reveals truth. As Sebastian explains to Silvia, the abandoned Julia has given up her Petrarchan affectations in the wake of Proteus's deceit:

> . . . since she did neglect her looking-glass,
> And threw her sun-expelling mask away,
> The air hath starved the roses in her cheeks,
> And pinched the lily-tincture of her face,
> That now she is become as black as I.
>
> (IV.iv.152–56)

The boy actor presumably has scrubbed off his makeup to become a girl in male disguise, and in this very act of calling attention to his adolescent male self, he proclaims the generosity of the girl Julia, "more grace than boy" (V.iv.166). If the page boy Julia misses both the pleasure and the power that male disguise affords the later disguised heroines, paradoxically in the moment when the boy actor shows himself as a boy, Julia proclaims the essence if not the form of Petrarchan spiritual beauty. To demean oneself for love, to throw away the mirror, to give up self-regarding—these central truths give substance to the disguised heroine of The Two Gentlemen of Verona.

ENDNOTES

[1] In "Identity and Representation in Shakespeare," ELH 49 (1982): 339–62, Barry Weller says that Proteus and Valentine "provide patterns for each other's actions and emotions, so that their progress through the play is not so much mirrored as filled with echoes and syncopated repe-

tition" (p. 350). A similar syncopation, it seems to me, may be observed in the relationship of Silvia to Julia.

[2] Silvia's name, of course, links her to the woods, and the goddess of the moon is also the goddess of the hunt. See the discussion of Silvia as "the moon goddess" in W. Thomas MacCary, *Friends and Lovers: The Phenomenology of Desire in Shakespearean Comedy* (New York: Columbia University Press, 1985), pp. 99–108. For a different view of the significance of Silvia's name, cf. Jonathan Goldberg, "Shakespearean characters: the generation of Silvia," in *Voice Terminal Echo: Postmodernism and English Renaissance Texts* (New York: Methuen, 1986), pp. 68–100.

[3] "Introduction," *The Two Gentlemen of Verona,* ed. Bertrand Evans (New York: New American Library, Signet, 1964), p. xxvii.

[4] Most notable is Harold F. Brooks, "Two Clowns in a Comedy (to say nothing of the Dog): Speed, Launce (and Crab) in 'The Two Gentlemen of Verona,'" *Essays and Studies 1963,* ed. S. Gorley Putt (London: John Murray, 1963), pp. 91–100. See too the introduction to the play in the new Arden series by the editor, Clifford Leech (London: Methuen, 1969), pp. lv–lvi, lxi.

[5] Cf. Lisa Jardine, *Still Harping on Daughters* (Brighton: Harvester, 1983), pp. 30–33: Jardine, arguing against the presence of any real emotion on the part of two boys pretending to be women, compares weeping for Ariadne to weeping for Hecuba in *Hamlet.*

[6] See Inga-Stina Ewbank, " 'Were man but constant, he were perfect': Constancy and Consistency in *The Two Gentlemen of Verona,*" in *Shakespearian Comedy,* ed. Malcolm Bradbury and David Palmer (New York: Crane, Russak, 1972), p. 41. This essay offers a brilliant account of the Petrarchan motifs in the play.

[7] Jardine calls Sebastian a "homosexual prototype," p. 19.

FREDERICK KIEFER

The Two Gentlemen of Verona
on Stage and Screen

Anyone who has seen *Two Gentlemen* in performance knows that although the play contains comic speech and stage business, it contains serious matter too: the betrayal of a friend, the betrayer's attempted rape of the woman he desires, and the wronged man's curious offer of his beloved to his rival. The mixture of elements has proved a challenge to directors and actors, who have achieved a balance only with difficulty. Earlier productions accentuated the lighter side of the play by cutting troubling speeches and adding music and spectacle. Some recent productions have had a dark tone, emphasizing the disturbing nature of sexual rivalry and the psychology responsible for it. Whatever the approach, this play has tested the ingenuity of directors and the patience of audiences.

Although no documentary evidence exists, *Two Gentlemen* was apparently first staged ca. 1593. We know virtually nothing of the original production. The staging requirements, however, are quite simple: a stage and a space "above" for Silvia's window. Like many other comedies of the time, the play requires no trapdoor, curtains, or descent machinery. Moreover, there would have been no scenery, no stage properties, and only a few hand properties: a ring, a portrait, a rope ladder, and several letters. The actors would have worn costumes, of course, but most of these would probably have been supplied from the company's wardrobe.

The earliest recorded performance of *Two Gentlemen* was David Garrick's production at the Theatre Royal, Drury Lane, on December 22, 1762. This proved a harbinger of future productions, for instead of using the earliest surviving script—that in the First Folio of 1623—Garrick used an adaptation with "alterations and additions" by Benjamin Victor. The "improvements" included the rearrangement of various scenes so that those situated in Verona were clustered together in the first act, while all of acts II and III were situated in Milan. Although this now seems eccentric, Victor recast the original chiefly because theatrical producers were using painted scenery, and it therefore made sense to minimize changes in the scenes. (We know about the scenery because a report survives from January 25, 1763, saying that one of the actors saved it from destruction during a riot at the theater.) Other of Victor's changes were motivated by a more profound discomfiture with the play. For instance, Victor omitted the offer of Silvia to Proteus in the last act, doubtless owing to the puzzling nature of Valentine's generosity. And in order to enhance the play's comedy, Victor brought Launce and Speed back onstage in the last act. Despite this extensive reworking of the play, Victor seems not to have found the right combination of adaptations to win and hold an audience; this production had only six performances.

When John Philip Kemble became manager of Drury Lane, he decided to stage *Two Gentlemen*, which he rightly saw as neglected. The playbills for his 1790 production announced that the play had not been acted in twenty years, and if this was not strictly accurate (there had been a single performance at Covent Garden in 1784), *Two Gentlemen* was certainly among the least performed of Shakespeare's plays in the eighteenth century. Although he restored the original script, this production failed. Kemble called the play "ineffectual," confessing, "I am sorry I ever took the trouble to revive it." Nevertheless, he tried again, producing the play at Covent Garden in 1808 and playing the role of Valentine himself. This time he used Benjamin Victor's version, though he corrected some errors introduced by Victor (such as Julia's answering Proteus' letter before she receives it!). And Kemble, who had a penchant for naming Shakespeare's unnamed characters, made some changes of his own: he christened the outlaws Ubaldo, Luigi, Carlos, Stephano, Giacomo, and Valerio. None of this tinkering saved the production, which had only three performances.

Instead of presenting *Two Gentlemen* in either of its extant forms, Frederick Reynolds in 1821 decided to recast the play completely, converting it into a musical extravaganza at Covent Garden, where Charles Kemble was manager. Henry Rowley Bishop supplied the music; Shakespeare's other plays and sonnets were ransacked for lyrics. Responding to a growing taste for spectacle, Reynolds sought to delight the eye as well as the ear. The audience saw a ducal palace and the great square of Milan; a procession of actors exotically costumed as the Seasons and the Four Elements; Cleopatra's galley floating down a river; and a carnival featuring masquers, dancing girls, and mountebanks. Reynolds also capitalized on the new sophistication of spectacle that allowed spectators to see, in the Duke's garden, "an artificial mountain reaching to the clouds, the explosion of which discovered a gorgeous temple of Apollo." Although this entertainment departed even further from Shakespeare than Victor's version had, Reynolds at least found an enthusiastic reception: his production ran for twenty-nine performances.

Lavish spectacle alone, however, could not guarantee the success of *Two Gentlemen* in the form that Shakespeare wrote it. William Charles Macready had become manager of Drury Lane when he decided to restore Shakespeare's script in 1841. He prepared playbills that meticulously explained the significance of each set. The opening scene, for example, consisted of "the tombs of the Scaligeri, the former princes of Verona"; and the Duke's palace was adorned with escutcheons of the Sforza and Visconti families. Reviewers acknowledged the "beautiful scenery" but felt that the (apparently drab) costumes were deficient: "the characters were, in truth, rather underdressed (for the comedy in its spirit seems to demand a gay costume)." It was a sign of current taste that one reviewer carefully described the theater's new curtain: "crimson velvet with a broad gold fringe, and ornamented with large gold wreaths of laurel." Once again a respected theatrical manager found only frustration in staging *Two Gentlemen*.

Five years later Charles Kean tried his hand, cutting some scenes and altering the language. He presented *Two Gentlemen* at New York's Park Theater in 1846, playing the role of Valentine himself; his wife, Ellen Tree, played Julia. Neither this nor Benjamin Webster's production in London (with Kean) was a commercial triumph. Nor was the production by Samuel Phelps at Sadler's Wells during the 1856–57 season; although this staging received some critical acclaim, the record of three performances suggests a financial disappointment. Not surprisingly, the play went into eclipse for the next four decades.

Near the end of the nineteenth century, *Two Gentlemen* attracted new interest. The American manager and playwright Augustin Daly presented the comedy, with Ada Rehan as Julia, at his theater in New York during 1895 and, later, at his theater in London. He succeeded in finding some of the play's humor, for George Bernard Shaw wrote: "The scenes between Launce and his dog brought out the latent silliness and childishness of the audience as Shakespeare's clowning scenes always do: I laugh at them like a yokel myself." Shaw, however, found little else to praise. Although Daly was following long-established custom by employing musical embellishment, painted scenery, and special effects (including a thunderstorm in the last act), Shaw objected to Daly's practice of "altering, transposing, omitting, improving, correcting, and transferring speeches from one character to another." At last a thoughtful playgoer was beginning to wonder whether theatrical directors had gone too far in adapting Shakespeare.

Although developments in stagecraft and the new mode of lighting the show by gas and then by electricity drew huge audiences to Victorian theaters, the technical advances moved productions ever further from Elizabethan practice. So did the widespread use of proscenium arch and front curtain, which created a sharp demarcation between audience and stage, inhibiting rapport between actor and spectator. Fortunately, scholarly directors began an effort to recover the theatrical conditions of Shakespeare's time. Prominent among the pioneers was William Poel, who became instructor for the Shakespeare Reading Society in 1887. This group sponsored recital performances: Shakespeare's plays were read aloud without distinct act and scene divisions, thus emulating the continuous action of the Elizabethan public playhouse; the plays were also recited without the cuts that had become commonplace in Victorian England. In 1892 the Society gave a recital of *Two Gentlemen* at St. James's Hall. And in 1896 Poel's Elizabethan Stage Society used the Merchant Taylors' Hall for a production (repeated at the Great Hall of the Charterhouse in 1897). Here Poel sought to break down the invisible barrier separating actors from audience; when Valentine, on his way into exile, left the stage, he moved through the midst of the audience, and the outlaws entered through the same space. Poel tried an even bolder experiment when Herbert Beerbohm Tree invited the Elizabethan Stage Society to present *Two Gentlemen* at a Shakespeare Festival in 1910 (the production was later repeated at the Gaiety Theatre, Manchester). Poel departed from contemporary practice in two important ways: he built an apron stage out over the orchestra pit of His Majesty's Theater, and he eliminated the footlights that had become a theatrical fixture (the lights were instead hung from the balconies). By bringing actors closer to spectators, Poel demonstrated that such Elizabethan conventions as the soliloquy and the aside could be more effective than anyone had realized, and Shakespeare's verse had a new immediacy. A reviewer wrote of this *Two*

Gentlemen: ". . . the lyric beauty of many of its passages came out with unusual freshness."

The first half of the twentieth century witnessed a number of productions, many influenced by Poel's example. These included the work of Harley Granville-Barker at the Court Theatre in 1904, Ben Greet at Stratford-upon-Avon in 1916, W. Bridges-Adams at Stratford in 1925, Robert Atkins in the same year at the Apollo Theatre (with John Gielgud as Valentine), and B. Iden Payne at Stratford in 1938. It was not until after the Second World War, however, that *Two Gentlemen* proved an unqualified hit. Denis Carey achieved this at the Bristol Old Vic in 1952. His production was innovative in its spirit: the play was animated by lyric grace and charm. The comedy of Launce and Speed (played by Michael Aldridge and Newton Blick) delighted audiences by making the word-play, which can seem labored when the play is read in the study, come alive onstage. This production, which surprised people by its very success, was subsequently brought to London to redeem a lackluster season there.

Five years later, in 1957, Michael Langham's production opened at the Old Vic, London. Instead of seeing the play's contrivance and artificiality as impediments, Langham accentuated them. The actors wore costumes of the Regency: frilled shirts, tall hats, swirling cloaks. The unit set, representing Verona, Milan, and the forest by way of changing a backcloth, looked like a Romantic painting: a central fountain flanked by an ivy-covered tower and a ruined building. And the actors in their manner appeared to be imbued with the spirit of Gilbert and Sullivan. The costumes, set, and acting style worked collectively to produce an atmosphere, festive and frivolous, in which the play's potentially troubling action seemed less disturbing. Instead of coming across as a cad, Proteus, played by Keith Michell, emerged as a Byronic hero, overwhelmed by his own youthful passion.

At the same time that *Two Gentlemen* was finding receptive audiences in England, the play was having success in America, too. The challenge was daunting, for relatively few American actors were trained in speaking blank verse, and they had a tendency to emulate the features of British speech. In 1957, however, the Oregon Shakespeare Festival in Ashland presented the play without the affectation that sometimes marred American treatments of Shakespeare; a "relaxed naturalness" marked this production. The actors, directed by James Sandoe, seemed at home in their roles. That same year saw an even more celebrated production at the New York Shakespeare Festival in Central Park. This outdoor performance, directed by Stuart Vaughan, was characterized by vigor, ebullience, and physical action: the actors were literally kept in motion, using stairs on either side of the stage that led to an upper playing area. Jerry Stiller as Launce was singled out for praise, as was Anne Meara as Julia. Harold Clurman wrote: "Here was a consummate ensemble—down to the best cast dog I have ever seen on the stage." The joy of the actors and the directors was reflected in the stage business and sight gags they invented: the Duke was a horticulturist, with pruning shears and watering can at the ready; Eglamour was equipped with a huge sword that he kept tripping over; Silvia inspected purchases from a shopping spree. No longer was there any doubt that Shakespeare's play could, in the right hands, be a huge popular success. What Vaughan discovered, like Carey and Langham before him, was that the key to unlocking the play's humor was a deft touch, a buoyant spirit, and confidence that the potential for brilliant comedy was present in the script.

Curiously, no sooner had *Two Gentlemen* finally proved itself onstage than it suffered a relapse. Peter Hall's Stratford production of 1960 represented a giant step backward. Reviewers complained of awkward pauses and inappropriate emphases in the speeches. Even worse, Hall used a revolving stage to accommodate changes in the scenery; this had the effect of making the action seem choppy and fragmented. Not even good performances by Eric Porter as the Duke and Derek Godfrey as Proteus could save this treatment. Paradoxically, it may have been the very success of productions in the 1950s that led to Hall's debacle, for as Shakespeare festivals proliferated around the globe and as even the most neglected of his plays began to receive their share of attention, directors felt increasing pressure to justify their own particular efforts. In practice this often meant finding an approach different from all those that had already been (successfully) tried. Sometimes the willingness to take risks has breathed life into a production, preventing it from becoming a stale duplication of earlier triumphs. But at times the effort has fallen flat.

Directorial ingenuity has worked best when it has made a Shakespearean play more accessible to an audience, as Robin Phillips demonstrated with his Royal Shakespeare Company production at Stratford-upon-Avon in 1970. He presented the play in modern dress; and Daphne Dare's set evoked the Riviera, with diving board and pool, monogrammed beachwear, and sunglasses. Phillips' purpose was apparent in the opening scene where an athletic Valentine, in swimming attire, exercised with a beach ball. By contrast, Proteus was puny and watched his friend enviously. When Valentine exited, Proteus tested his muscles and found them wanting. By this means the director supplied a psychological explanation for the character's later behavior. Ian Richardson's playboy Proteus suffered from a sense of his own inadequacy, which led to the betrayal of his friend and to the wooing of Silvia. In 1975 Phillips again directed *Two Gentlemen*, this time at the Stratford Shakespeare Festival in Ontario, Canada. This production, codirected by David Toguri, had much in common with Phillips' 1970 endeavor. As earlier, the setting was twentieth century, a world of health salons, cocktail bars, and Mafia chieftains. And again there was a marked physical contrast between Valentine, an amateur boxer, and a less-athletic Proteus.

In 1970 Mel Shapiro and John Guare adapted *Two Gentlemen* as a musical comedy; Guare wrote the lyrics, and Galt MacDermot composed the melodies. They were, in a sense, participating in the same impulse that had led

Frederick Reynolds to set the play to music a century and a half earlier. The watchword of the late sixties and early seventies, however, was "relevance," and the adapters pursued this with a vengeance. The urban flavor of the production reflected its genesis in the New York Shakespeare Festival; the play toured all five boroughs of the city. And when it played at the open-air Delacorte Theater in Central Park, the set consisted of a three-tiered scaffold, suggesting the multistory buildings of the city just beyond the trees. The characters, moreover, made topical remarks (allusions to Vietnam, for instance), and their speeches contained numerous colloquialisms. Befitting the nature of New York, the cast was interracial: Proteus and Julia were Puerto Rican; Valentine and Silvia were black; and Launce had a Yiddish accent. The music reflected this ethnic diversity: Hispanics sang to a Carribean beat, while the blacks performed in Motown style. This was a joyous production, and Joseph Papp moved it to Broadway, where it had 627 performances (and where the play lost the definite article in its title).

In 1981 the Royal Shakespeare Company decided to present *Two Gentlemen* alongside *Titus Andronicus*, both plays to be part of the same evening's entertainment. Necessarily, the two had to undergo major surgery; 850 lines were cut from *Titus*, 515 from *Two Gentlemen*. The point of this cutting and coupling was to enforce differences, thereby heightening the theatrical impact of each play. Although the scheme had a dubious premise—that the tragedy "looks to the past" whereas the comedy looks to "Shakespeare's future"—John Barton managed to intensify the comedy of *Two Gentlemen* both by the sharp contrast in mood between the two plays and by the specific recollection in *Two Gentlemen* of particular moments in the tragedy, still fresh in the minds of the audience. For example, Patrick Stewart's Eglamour, attired in armor, recalled his portrayal of the armed Titus; Sheila Hancock, who played Tamora in the tragedy, played the leader of the outlaws in the comedy; and the forest inhabited by the outlaws consisted of the same prop trees that served as forest in *Titus*. Perhaps never in its theatrical history had *Two Gentlemen* been presented in a stranger context, and the result was controversial; one reviewer called it an abomination. But the yoking of not so mighty opposites had the virtue of demonstrating Shakespeare's diversity at an early point in his career.

Unlike some better-known Shakespearean plays, *Two Gentlemen* has never been made into a movie, but it became part of the BBC television series in 1983. The keynote of this production was its interpretation of Proteus. Tyler Butterworth's character was a troubled man, full of second thoughts and self-doubts. During his soliloquy at the end of II.iv, the camera moved in for a closeup, revealing the face of a man in torment. As Proteus spoke of foresaking Julia and betraying Valentine, thunder was heard in the background; the sky darkened and the wind sprang up. Clearly, the storm without mirrored the storm within. His soliloquy in IV.ii was heartfelt too, and the result was to engender sympathy for the character even as he was pursuing a reprehensible course. There was, however, no glossing over of Proteus' attempted rape of Silvia: he violently ripped off the face mask that she had donned when she entered the forest. And when confronted by Valentine, the guilty Proteus wept, apparently out of shame. In his direction, Don Taylor adopted a tone altogether more serious than those of previous productions. If this TV adaptation sacrificed comic effect, it did so to achieve a psychologically explicable portrait of Proteus.

What we gain from a production like Taylor's is an enhanced appreciation of the pain that lies just beneath and, at times, on the very surface of the action. What we may lose is the sheer delight that a Shakespearean comedy can offer. Directors, of course, do not need to make either-or choices. Indeed, those productions that have accommodated the serious action most successfully have been those that exploited comic effect most exuberantly.

Bibliographic Note: *Shakespeare Quarterly* and *Shakespeare Survey* contain reviews of Shakespeare productions each year. In addition, readers may find short accounts of *Two Gentlemen* productions and references to reviews in the following books: William Babula, *Shakespeare in Production, 1935–1978: A Selective Catalogue* (New York and London: Garland, 1981); Samuel Leiter, ed., *Shakespeare Around the Globe: A Guide to Notable Postwar Revivals* (New York, Westport, Conn., and London: Greenwood Press, 1986). Many university libraries contain the BBC videotaped production of *Two Gentlemen.*

William Shakespeare

THE MERRY WIVES OF WINDSOR

Edited by William Green

Contents

Introduction[*]

What a delightful picture of Elizabethan village life Shakespeare presents in *The Merry Wives of Windsor*. He tickles our palates with hot venison pasty and pippins and cheese. He plunges us into a world where hawking and greyhound racing are matters of concern. He walks us through the town alluding to the nearby Thames, Datchet Mead, Windsor Castle and its chapel. He takes us into the Garter Inn; and, lastly, he leaves us at midnight under Herne's Oak in Windsor Little Park. Yet his intent is not to extol village life for its own sake, for, as always, Shakespeare is interested in people. In this play he gives us a peek into the private lives of his villagers, showing us how love affects as disparate a group of individuals as one would ever expect to encounter in an English village.

There is, of course, the traditional sweet young maiden —Mistress Anne Page, the picture of "pretty virginity." She is in love with a handsome gentleman. He has for his rivals the shy, colorless nephew of a country justice and a choleric French physician who draws his patients from among the gentry and royalty. These are the principals of the subplot. In the main plot we meet a pair of prosperous townsmen—one given to extreme jealousy—whose vivacious wives prove more than a match for a fat, old, lecherous conniver from London. Rounding out this rich

---

[*] Portions of the following are based on concepts developed in extended form in the editor's *Shakespeare's Merry Wives of Windsor*. Princeton: Princeton University Press, 1962. Permission has been granted by the Princeton University Press.

gallery of characters are a Welsh parson more adept at giving a Latin lesson than fighting a duel; a bluff, hearty innkeeper whose equanimity can be shattered only by such a major calamity as the theft of his post horses; a country justice of the peace; a good-hearted housekeeper, skilled as a go-between; and some sharpers parasitically attendant on the lecher.

Shakespeare takes these characters and places them in a fast-paced farce. He blends the two plot lines smoothly, and organically integrates his characters. When the play concludes, the audience may leave in a joyous mood, laughing over the fractured English of Evans and Caius, chuckling at the malapropisms of Mistress Quickly, delighted with the farce escapades, content that Jill got her Jack and that middle-class morality has been upheld.

A major Shakespearean work? Hardly. That audiences have not been disturbed by this question of major or minor is apparent from the long production record the play has had (including a performance before James I in November, 1604) and from the adaptations it has undergone, first in John Dennis' dramatic version of 1702 (*The Comical Gallant*) and later in various operatic treatments.

Yet this play, so much the delight of theatergoers, has proved a bane to scholars. If "To thyself be enough" could be applied to *The Merry Wives,* there would be no problem. But since Shakespeare was a playwright in whom a continual line of development can be traced, the play must be considered in relation to the canon as a whole. And here a host of problems arises.

When examined in the study instead of on the stage, *The Merry Wives* engenders question after question. Why do a set of characters from the history plays *(Henry IV* and *Henry V)* appear in the script? No biographical links can be established between the six characters—Falstaff, Bardolph, Pistol, Nym, Justice Shallow, Mistress Quickly—and their namesakes in the history plays. Why does Shakespeare take such pains to give a historically accurate portrait of Windsor in the 1590's in this his sole play dealing entirely with contemporary English life? Why even select Windsor as the locale for a play about country

life when Shakespeare knew Warwickshire so well? Why
at a time when he had already produced masterful poetry
in *A Midsummer Night's Dream* and *Romeo and Juliet*
does he write a play almost entirely in prose? The little
verse that appears must be classified as inferior. Why
when engrossed in writing romantic comedy—*A Midsummer Night's Dream* and *The Merchant of Venice* show
how far he had come with the genre since *The Two Gentlemen of Verona*—does he suddenly backtrack to the
farcical treatment of love that he successfully presented
in *The Taming of the Shrew*? And what source did he use
for the play? None has been discovered.

A key to the answers to these questions is found in
some allusions to Queen Elizabeth and Windsor Castle
in Act V, Scene v:

> Cricket, to Windsor chimneys shalt thou leap.
> Where fires thou find'st unraked and hearths unswept,
> There pinch the maids as blue as bilberry.
> Our radiant Queen hates sluts and sluttery.

A few lines later the Fairy Queen instructs:

> Search Windsor Castle, elves, within and out.
> Strew good luck, ouphs, on every sacred room,
> That it may stand till the perpetual doom,
> In state as wholesome as in state 'tis fit,
> Worthy the owner, and the owner it.
> The several chairs of Order look you scour
> With juice of ·balm and every precious flow'r.
> Each fair instalment, coat, and several crest,
> With loyal blazon, evermore be blest.
> And nightly, meadow-fairies, look you sing,
> Like to the Garter's compass, in a ring.
> Th' expressure that it bears, green let it be,
> More fertile-fresh than all the field to see;
> And *Honi soit qui mal y pense* write
> In emerald tufts, flow'rs purple, blue, and white—
> Like sapphire, pearl, and rich embroidery,
> Buckled below fair knighthood's bending knee—
> Fairies use flow'rs for their charactery.

Two allusions attract attention in this passage: *Honi soit qui mal y pense*—motto of the Order of the Garter—and the instructions to the fairies to scour "the several chairs of Order." So deliberately does Shakespeare draw attention to the Order that we cannot ignore the references. They stand out even more sharply when we realize that earlier in the play (I.iv) Dr. Caius informed us he was hurrying to court for a "grand affair." Also, in II.ii, Mistress Quickly noted that the town was filling with courtiers. Something concerning the Order of the Garter was happening in Windsor, and that something could only be an installation of Knights-Elect.

Now the Windsor setting makes sense, for if Shakespeare chose to allude to a Garter installation, what more appropriate place to locate the play than in Windsor, home of the Order of the Garter since the fourteenth century? Moreover, what need to state that the preparation of castle and chapel is for this ceremonial? The Elizabethans knew that the only Garter rite celebrated in Windsor was an installation—this by decree of Elizabeth in 1567. And the Elizabethans—at least those in courtly circles during the late 1590's—further knew what Garter installation Shakespeare was referring to—that of May, 1597.

This last statement cannot be verified, but convincing circumstantial evidence has recently been adduced, and generally accepted by scholars, that the sole Garter occasion to which the allusions point is the April 1597 Feast of St. George and its attendant ceremonials. On this occasion five individuals were named to the Order. Two of them have particular bearing on the genesis of *The Merry Wives:* Frederick, Duke of Württemberg (to whom we shall return) and George Carey, the second Lord Hunsdon.

Hunsdon, a favorite cousin of Queen Elizabeth, was patron of Shakespeare's company at this time. His connection with the company becomes particularly significant in light of an old stage tradition concerning the composition of *The Merry Wives*. According to the tradition, first recorded by John Dennis in 1702, Queen Elizabeth

commanded that the play be written and that the task be
completed within fourteen days. Nicholas Rowe, in his
1709 edition of Shakespeare's *Works,* amplified the tradition by stating that the Queen "was so well pleas'd with
that admirable character of *Falstaff,* in the two Parts of
Henry the Fourth, that she commanded him to continue
it for one Play more, and to show him in Love."

Stage traditions, especially one appearing eighty-six
years after Shakespeare's death, must be taken with
skepticism. Yet in the face of no counterevidence, this
tradition deserves respect. Its foundation is based on the
Queen's desire to see Falstaff in love, establishing that
she had already become familiar with old tunbelly. Although no court play lists are extant, we do know that
Shakespeare's company performed before the courtiers
six times during the 1596–97 Christmas play season:
December 26, 27, 1596; January 1, 6, and February 6,
8, 1597. That *1 Henry IV* was among the works presented
is a strong possibility. Recent study of this first Falstaff
play points to the autumn of 1596 as the date for its
completion—a date slightly earlier than the generalized
1597 traditionally assigned.

Allowing for conjecture, we may assume that the Queen
expressed her delight with Falstaff in *1 Henry IV,* wondered aloud how the fat knight would fare in a romantic
entanglement, had her remarks picked up by Lord Hunsdon and transmitted to Shakespeare with a request to
have the play ready for presentation at the April 1597
St. George's Day festivities. Hunsdon had good reason
for making such a request, for not only was he to be
named a Garter knight on that occasion, but he also was
to become Lord Chamberlain of England. Although this
latter event occurred on April 17, Hunsdon knew of the
appointment several weeks in advance, as he did of his
impending Order election. *The Merry Wives* may be
considered his "thank you note" to the Queen.

Now, we need not take Dennis' remarks about finishing
the play in fourteen days literally, especially since Dennis,
in one of his letters, later recorded the time span as ten
days. Rather, they point to a short period of time for

composition. And *The Merry Wives* bears overwhelming marks of hasty composition, perhaps more than any other play of Shakespeare's. The Shallow-Falstaff quarrel of the opening scene is never resolved; the horse-stealing sub-plot of the fourth act with its references to a German duke is not in any way integrated into the main plot lines of the play; the Caius-Evans revenge scheme dies aborning; anachronisms in time sequences are present; the costume colors in the fairy scene are hopelessly confused; and various other errors appear in the text. Since by 1597 Shakespeare had established a reputation as a skilled dramatist—only a year later Francis Meres was to cite him among the English as "most excellent" in comedy and tragedy—so much slipshod workmanship must be attributed to writing against the clock.

Creating a play to order on short notice, one showing Falstaff in love, was a formidable task. Shakespeare simplified it first by trying to adapt material already at hand and then by revamping some old play. In the spring of 1597, he appears to have been at work on *2 Henry IV*. The opening of *The Merry Wives* with Falstaff, Shallow, Bardolph, and Pistol in a country setting reminds us strongly of the Gloucestershire scenes in the *Henry* play. Shakespeare initially attempts to create a new plot situation for these characters, but after about a hundred lines he gives up. Under the pressure of time, instead of starting over, he leaves the Falstaff-Shallow quarrel unresolved and attempts to fit Falstaff and crew into the plot of an old play.

This work, in both its main and subplot, bears traits of Italian comedy, and was probably rooted in a tale or tales from the Italian novellas that had been translated into English in various collections since the 1560's. The main plot deals with the stock situation of a clever lover who attempts to deceive a husband. By reversing the roles and making the lover the duped one, a farce situation results. To this plot is grafted—either by Shakespeare or the source author—the traditional Italian tale of two young lovers who cannot gain parental permission to marry. The girl in these stories often is involved with three suitors, at least one of whom is a grotesque character. She also has her maid as a go-between.

Into these tales Shakespeare marches Falstaff and company. Falstaff, of course, converts easily into the duped lover; but the other characters, with the exception of Dame Quickly, who becomes the go-between, cannot be matched with existing characters in the source. Thus Shakespeare is forced to let Shallow wander in and out of the play with no real function and to make what use he can of Bardolph, Nym, and Pistol before writing them out of the script.

In making Falstaff the duped lover, Shakespeare not only fulfilled the Queen's request, but went one step further, for he knew aesthetically, as Edmund Malone long ago observed, "what the queen, if the story be true, seems not to have known . . . Falstaff could not love, but by ceasing to be Falstaff. He could only counterfeit love, and his professions could be prompted, not by the hope of pleasure, but of money." The Falstaff of *The Merry Wives* must, therefore, be considered a new character with an old name.

At the start of this play the fat knight does bear some resemblances to his counterpart in the *Henry IV* plays in the lusty, blustering manner with which he outfaces Shallow and Slender. And in his soliloquy in Act IV, Scene v, Shakespeare may have allowed him to reminisce over the old days with the mad Prince of Wales when Falstaff says,

> I would all the world might be cozened, for I have been cozened and beaten too. If it should come to the ear of the court how I have been transformed, and how my transformation hath been washed and cudgeled, they would melt me out of my fat drop by drop, and liquor fishermen's boots with me. I warrant they would whip me with their fine wits till I were as crestfall'n as a dried pear.

However, from the beginning of Act I, Scene iii—when the action proper gets under way—we have a different

Falstaff, one who appears to be a reworking of a scholar or pedant from the source story. Thus the Host says to him, "Speak scholarly and wisely"; Ford, in his disguise as Brooke, notes in II.ii, "Sir, I hear you are a scholar," and follows this up several lines later observing, "You are a gentleman of excellent breeding, admirable discourse, of great admittance, authentic in your place and person, generally allowed for your many warlike, courtlike, and learned preparations." Literary allusions and such phraseology as "Mistress Ford . . . I see you are obsequious in your love, and I profess requital to a hair's breadth," crop up in Falstaff's speech and contrast sharply with the racy, oath-laden utterances we have come to associate with the "fat-kidneyed rascal."

This scholar-cum-knight is now a butt, a dupe. He is the farcical target of two delightful Windsor housewives. We must forget the merry rogue who, caught in a pack of lies in describing the Gadshill robbery, is able to wheedle out of the situation by exclaiming, "If reasons were as plentiful as blackberries, I would give no man a reason upon compulsion, I."

In reworking Falstaff's cronies—Pistol, Nym, and Shallow—as well as in handling the new characters Slender, Caius, and Ford, Shakespeare proved himself more than a mechanical adapter. He fashioned these characters according to the mold of "humors comedy," a genre newly introduced to the stage by George Chapman in 1596. Shakespeare first attempted portrayals of humors or temperaments with some of the fringe characters in 2 Henry IV, the play, we will remember, that he probably had been working on when interrupted by the Queen's command; but he did so here on a rather superficial level. Only Pistol of the "irregular humorists" of 2 Henry IV emerges as a full-fledged humors character.

The Pistol of The Merry Wives is basically the same character he is in 2 Henry IV, a blusterer full of sound and fury. His cohort Nym, as the name indicates (Middle English nimen, to take), is a filcher; his deeds proclaim it as he joins with Pistol to part Slender from his purse and Mistress Bridget from the handle of her fan. And his overworked phrase "That's my humor" serves further to betray his generic origin. Their fellow traveler from the history plays, Shallow, remains the talkative, empty-headed country justice of *2 Henry IV*.

Slender and Caius, however, receive fuller treatment, their humors portrayal going beyond the mere use of type names. As the second and third wooer to Anne Page, they function integrally in the plot. They are basically the two grotesques frequently found as suitors to the *amorosa* in Italian comedy; Shakespeare has skillfully retained their grotesque function by casting them as humors figures. Caius is presented as a choleric Frenchman. His medical side is never commented on by Shakespeare. And Slender is portrayed as a country gull. No sooner does he arrive in town than he is robbed by Pistol, Nym, and Bardolph. He is completely passive in the suit to Anne Page. Without his Book of Songs and Sonnets he is unable to woo the lady. Slender of body and slender of mind is he indeed.

The most complete humors portrait in *The Merry Wives* is that of Ford. All Windsor knows, as Quickly relates, that "he's a very jealousy man." Ford even talks of it openly with others. And in private he shows that he is so completely consumed by the flames of jealousy that he would "rather trust a Fleming with my butter, Parson Hugh the Welshman with my cheese, an Irishman with my aqua vitae bottle, or a thief to walk my ambling gelding, than my wife with herself. . . . God be praised for my jealousy." So intense is this emotion that Ford becomes despicable enough to hire another man, Falstaff, to seduce his wife. In this action Shakespeare exploits Ford's humor to increase the plot complications. However, at the proper moment he makes Ford see the foolishness of his ways and repent (IV.iv). The entire handling of Ford's character is one-dimensional and makes an interesting contrast with the deeper study of jealousy found in *Othello*.

What is striking about Shakespeare's treatment of *The Merry Wives* as humors comedy is that nowhere do we see the savage bite of the Jonsonian moralist seeking to strip the mask of hypocrisy from humanity. Nor are follies and vices held up to scorn and ridicule. When Shakespeare exposes the weaknesses of Ford or Caius or Slender, he does so with gentleness—and compassion. Even Nym and Pistol do not meet the fate they deserve. That Shakespeare even was able to graft elements of humors comedy onto the basic farce-comedy plot of *The Merry Wives* is a tribute to his artistry, considering the limited amount of time in which he had to work.

Not only in turning to humors comedy was Shakespeare following the latest dramatic trends, but also in bringing on stage foreign character types. In making Caius a French physician (there is no reason for linking him with the founder of the Cambridge college), Shakespeare may have been mocking the predilection of the upper-class Londoners for foreign physicians. But with Hugh Evans, he was surely capitalizing on the interest in stage Welshmen which started about 1593 and continued unabated for several years. Witness Glendower and Fluellen in Shakespeare's other plays.

Thus far we have seen how Shakespeare, by following popular theatrical trends, reworked his Italianate source and created new interest in what might otherwise have been a dull set of stock characters. Still unaccounted for, however, are the Windsor setting, the Order of the Garter allusions, or the horse-stealing subplot. These are not essential to the action line of the play. In fact, the inferior quarto text excises all references to either the court or the Order of the Garter.

The allusions and setting have already been discussed in establishing the date of the play as 1597. Their presence in the script, however, is more than ornamentation, for Shakespeare does combine them into a logical pattern. Aware of the special occasion for which he was to write the play and the select audience that would see it, Shakespeare apparently decided to include material that would reflect on that occasion and on his patron's own election to the Order.

The initial step was to change the locale of the Italianate original to Windsor, easily done since all this original demanded by way of place was a plausible setting for a group of middle-class characters. Immediately with the Windsor switch a Garter association was set up for an Elizabethan audience. This association is carried still further by depicting activity at Windsor Castle—preparation for a ceremonial that by historical evidence could only be an Order of the Garter installation. Shakespeare then clinched the Garter-Windsor link by penning a tribute to the Order. He also added a compliment to the Queen, knowing that she would be at the special performance.

This type of structuring is not unique for Shakespeare. He was a master at depicting multiple activities in his plays, making his audiences aware that there are worlds within worlds. Using the terms Harry Levin has given us in *The Overreacher*,* the "grand affair" at the castle becomes the overplot; the Falstaff-in-love story, the main plot; and the Anne Page-Fenton romance, which parallels the variation on the "course of true love" in the main plot, the underplot. There is even one character who moves from plot to plot: Dr. Caius. We must not forget that three times in Act I, Scene iv, he informs us that he is on his way to the "grand affair," i.e., the installation.

One problem still remains in this examination of the plot structure: the presence of the horse-stealing subplot of the fourth act. This section is not based on any of the incidents in the story line proper and disappears from the play as mysteriously as it came. The key character in it is a German duke who never appears but whose men make off with three of the Host's post horses. To be understood, this subplot must be seen as an appendage of the Garter overplot, but alas, it is such a weak appendage that it dangles completely unsupported.

The German duke alluded to is most assuredly Frederick, Duke of Württemberg, who, as previously mentioned, was one of the five individuals elected to the Order in 1597. He was, in fact, the only German ruler made a Garter knight between 1579 and 1612. Ever since 1592 when he had made a trip to England while still Count Mompelgard, Frederick had been obsessed with a desire

---

* Levin, Harry. *The Overreacher*, Cambridge, Mass.: Harvard University Press, 1952.

to become a Knight of the Garter. He badgered Elizabeth and her courtiers with letters and with embassages over the next several years in support of this desire. The Queen, for various reasons, paid little heed to his wishes. Finally, in 1597, at a time of serious strain in Anglo-German relations stemming from bitter disagreements over trading policies between the English and the Hanse, Elizabeth sanctioned Frederick's election to the Order. That this was done solely out of political expediency to keep the Duke as a German ally is virtually a certainty. Since Frederick had not been particularly discreet in his campaign for election, a goodly segment of those in court circles were fully aware of this vain duke's interest in the Garter.

Even after his election Frederick continued to be a topical figure, for now he began his campaign for investiture and installation—the two final ceremonies for full-fledged Garter membership. Elizabeth may have delayed in sending an investiture mission to Württemberg because the costs were so great or she may have wanted to have a hold over Frederick, as a friendly German prince, so that he would actively support her in the Hanse dispute. This dispute had become so serious by the summer of 1597 that Emperor Rudolph II barred the English Merchant Adventurers from the German empire. Whatever the reason behind Elizabeth's stalling, the Queen died in 1603 without either an end to the Hanse dispute or investiture for Frederick.

Soon after James I came to the throne, Emperor Rudolph settled the Hanse dispute, and Duke Frederick renewed his pleas for investiture. This time he succeeded, and he received the long-coveted insignia of the Order during the investiture ceremonies in Stuttgart on November 6, 1603. The following April he sent a proxy delegate for installation at Windsor during the annual Feast of St. George celebration. Clearly Duke Frederick and his lobbying activities were known to a great number of those in court circles, and clearly the twelve years that those activities span would have brought Frederick to the attention of even a wider circle of Londoners. There is, therefore, no reason to doubt the recognition of any allusions

to Frederick in the play by the audience at the posited
initial Garter production or at subsequent performances
through 1604.

Moreover, evidence exists in the horse-stealing subplot
to link the "Duke de Jamany" with Frederick. In the corrupt quarto version of the subplot appears the curious
phrase *cosen garmombles*. The Folio text reads *cozen-
Iermans* at the same point. In all probability the Q text
preserves the original reading. (We may attribute the
Folio version to a revision made after the publication of
the quarto text in 1602 when the topicality of a direct
reference to Frederick was either no longer proper or
intelligible.) *Garmombles,* as Leslie Hotson suggests, represents a scrambling of Garter and Mompelgard. That his
suggestion is apt can be supported by the observation that
Shallow's scrambling of *Custos Rotulorum* for *Custalorum*
in the opening scene is similar in technique. The *cosen* of
the phrase is a pun on *cosen* or "cozen," to cheat, and on
the salutatory address used by a ruler at this time when
corresponding with another ruler. This oblique identifica-
tion of Frederick with the German duke of the play is
further established by Dr. Caius' information that "dere
is no duke dat de court is know to come." This exactly
describes the election of Frederick to the Order, for he
was elected *in absentia* (a normal procedure with foreign
rulers) and not informed of this until October, five months
after the installation ceremonies.

Now, neither of the above allusions links Frederick
directly with the theft of the Host's post horses, the action
of the sketchy subplot. Impetus for this incident comes,
probably, from a post-horse scandal which occurred in
September, 1596, when Le Sieur Aymar de Chastes,
Governor of Dieppe, was returning to France from an
embassage to England concerning an Anglo-French defense treaty. De Chastes had been hurrying home to prepare Dieppe for the reciprocating English embassage that
had as one of its charges the investiture of Henry IV into
the Order of the Garter. En route to the coast, de Chastes,
probably through misunderstanding the operations of the
English posting system, abused the authority of a warrant

he had been issued to assist him in procuring post horses, and, with two of his retinue, tried to take by force post horses from an innkeeper in Gravesend. He also got into difficulty with hackneymen from Rochester for attempting to take post horses beyond the stage for which they had been hired. Knowledge of both incidents was widespread.

Only six months later Shakespeare was presumably working on *The Merry Wives* for presentation at the Garter Feast. Intent on reenforcing the Garter overplot to the play, he reworked the de Chastes posting scandal, having recalled that it was connected with a Garter event —the investiture of Henry IV. Since, for diplomatic reasons, he could not lampoon so distinguished a man as de Chastes, Shakespeare turned him into another foreigner, one even more closely bound up with the Order ceremonials and one who could safely be satirized: the Duke of Württemberg. After all, the English Court knew precisely why Frederick had been elected to the Order and how obnoxious he had made himself in lobbying for election. Thus, the three Frenchmen become Germans— a deft stroke at a time when the Hanse troubles would have aroused anti-German sentiment among the normally xenophobic Englishmen; the governor becomes a duke; and the locale shifts from Gravesend and Rochester to Windsor.

Allowing for the conjectural nature of the above account, we see that it does explain the disparate elements of the horse-stealing subplot. The problem is not that this subplot is a fragment of a larger unit, now lost, which developed the Evans-Caius revenge scheme—as some scholars, embarrassed to account for the horse-stealing episode, have hypothesized—but rather that having written the material, Shakespeare could not integrate it into the other plot lines of the play. So he left it alone, an isolated entity mutely joining the fragmentary Shallow-Falstaff quarrel as witnesses to the difficulty of writing against the incessant ticking of a clock.

If history has been dwelled on at length, it is because only through history can we understand the tripartite plot structure of the play. If *The Merry Wives* were written for a special occasion, and here we must realize that the evidence is primarily circumstantial, that occasion must be explored for insight into the peculiar characteristics of the play.

Shakespeare's aim in *The Merry Wives* was to entertain, to counterpoint the serious ceremonials of the 1597 Feast of St. George with mirth. This he does by writing a farce. Thus he tries to make everyone happy: Queen Elizabeth, by fulfilling her wish to see Falstaff in love; Lord Hunsdon, his patron, by prefiguring Hunsdon's own installation at Windsor a month hence; the courtiers at large, by ridiculing the Garter-obsessed Duke of Württemberg; and the general theatrical public, by bringing before them one of the freshest sets of humors characters in Elizabethan comedy as well as upholding on stage the virtue of English women. (Says Mistress Page, "We'll leave a proof by that which we will do,/ Wives may be merry, and yet honest too.") A tall order for a short space of time in which to execute it. Surely Shakespeare deserves some forgiveness for the abundance of loose ends in the play.

WILLIAM GREEN
Queens College of The
City University of New York

The Merry Wives
of Windsor

Sir John Falstaff
Fenton, a young gentleman
Shallow, a country justice
Slender, nephew to Shallow
Ford ⎫
Page ⎬ two citizens of Windsor
William Page, a boy, son to Page
Sir Hugh Evans, a Welsh parson
Doctor Caius, a French physician
Host of the Garter Inn
Bardolph ⎫
Pistol ⎬ followers of Falstaff
Nym ⎭
Robin, page to Falstaff
Simple, servant to Slender
Rugby, servant to Doctor Caius
Mistress Ford
Mistress Page
Anne Page, her daughter
Mistress Quickly, servant to Doctor Caius
Servants to Page, Ford, etc.

Scene: Windsor and the neighborhood]

The Merry Wives of Windsor

ACT I

Scene I. [*Before Page's house.*]

Enter Justice Shallow, Slender, [and] Sir Hugh Evans.

Shallow. Sir°[1] Hugh, persuade me not; I will make a
Star-chamber° matter of it. If he were twenty Sir
John Falstaffs, he shall not abuse Robert Shallow,
Esquire.

Slender. In the county of Gloucester, Justice of Peace,
and Coram.°   5

Shallow. Ay, cousin Slender, and Custalorum.°

Slender. Ay, and Ratolorum° too; and a gentleman
born, Master Parson, who writes himself Armigero,° in any bill, warrant, quittance, or obligation   10
—Armigero.

---

[1] The degree sign (°) indicates a footnote, which is keyed to the
text by line number. Text references are printed in boldface type;
the annotation follows in roman type.   **I.i. 1 Sir** title used before
the first name of ordinary priests   **2 Star-chamber** court having jurisdiction over cases of riot, forgery, and other specific offenses
6 Coram i.e., Quorum (term for justices with special legal qualifica-
tions)   **7 Custalorum** i.e., Custos Rotulorum (a chief justice)   **8
Ratolorum** Slender's garbling of rotulorum   **9–10 Armigero** esquire

Shallow. Ay, that I do, and have done any time these
three hundred years.

Slender. All his successors gone before him hath
15 done't; and all his ancestors that come after him
may. They may give° the dozen white luces° in
their coat.°

Shallow. It is an old coat.

Evans. The dozen white louses do become an old coat
20 well. It agrees well, passant;° it is a familiar beast
to man, and signifies love.

Shallow. The luce is the fresh fish. The salt fish is an
old coat.°

Slender. I may quarter,° coz?°

25 *Shallow.* You may, by marrying.

Evans. It is marring indeed, if he quarter it.

Shallow. Not a whit.

Evans. Yes, py'r lady.° If he has a quarter of your
coat, there is but three skirts for yourself, in my
30 simple conjectures. But that is all one. If Sir John
Falstaff have committed disparagements unto you,
I am of the Church, and will be glad to do my be-
nevolence to make atonements and compromises
between you.

35 *Shallow.* The Council° shall hear it. It is a riot.

---

16 **give** display   16 **luces** pikes (fish)   17 **coat** coat of arms   20 **passant** walking (heraldic)   22–23 **The luce . . . old coat** (obscure line probably containing an involved play on the words "salt" and "saltant" [heraldic term for describing a leaping position for small animals or vermin], "luce" and "louse," "old coat" [as a garment], "coat of arms," and cod [the fish—sometimes pronounced as a homonym of "coat"]. Also, there may be a reference to the coat-of-arms of the Fishmongers Company which is a composite of the arms of the older Saltfishmongers and those of the Freshfishmongers)   24 **quarter** add arms to one's family coat   24 **coz** kinsman   28 **py'r lady** by our Lady (the use of "p" for "b" here is the first of Evans' Welsh pronunciations)   35 **Council** King's Council sitting as the Court of Star-chamber

Evans. It is not meet the Council hear a riot. There is
no fear of Got in a riot. The Council, look you,
shall desire to hear the fear of Got, and not to hear
a riot. Take your vizaments° in that.

Shallow. Ha! O' my life, if I were young again, the   40
sword should end it.

Evans. It is petter that friends is the sword, and end it.
And there is also another device in my prain, which
peradventure prings goot discretions with it. There
is Anne Page, which is daughter to Master George   45
Page, which is pretty virginity.

Slender. Mistress Anne Page? She has brown hair, and
speaks small° like a woman?

Evans. It is that fery person for all the 'orld, as just
as you will desire. And seven hundred pounds of   50
moneys, and gold and silver, is her grandsire, upon
his death's-bed—Got deliver to a joyful resurrec-
tions—give, when she is able to overtake seventeen
years old. It were a goot motion if we leave our
pribbles and prabbles,° and desire a marriage be-   55
tween Master Abraham and Mistress Anne Page.

Shallow. Did her grandsire leave her seven hundred
pound?

Evans. Ay, and her father is make her a petter penny.

Shallow. I know the young gentlewoman. She has   60
good gifts.

Evans. Seven hundred pounds and possibilities° is
goot gifts.

Shallow. Well, let us see honest Master Page. Is Falstaff there?   65

Evans. Shall I tell you a lie? I do despise a liar as I do
despise one that is false, or as I despise one that is

---

39 **vizaments** i.e., advisements   48 **small** gentle   55 **pribbles and
prabbles** petty bickerings   62 **possibilities** prospects of inheritance

not true. The knight Sir John is there; and, I beseech
you, be ruled by your well-willers. I will peat the
70   door for Master Page. [*Knocks.*] What, ho! Got
pless your house here.

Page. [*Within*] Who's there?

Evans. Here is Got's plessing, and your friend, and
Justice Shallow; and here young Master Slender,
75   that peradventures shall tell you another tale, if
matters grow to your likings.

[*Enter*] *Master Page.*

Page. I am glad to see your worships well. I thank you
for my venison, Master Shallow.

Shallow. Master Page, I am glad to see you. Much
80   good do it your good heart! I wished your venison
better—it was ill killed.° How doth good Mistress
Page?—and I thank you always with my heart, la,
with my heart.

Page. Sir, I thank you.

85   *Shallow.* Sir, I thank you; by yea and no, I do.

Page. I am glad to see you, good Master Slender.

Slender. How does your fallow° greyhound, sir? I
heard say he was outrun on Cotsall.°

Page. It could not be judged, sir.

90   *Slender.* You'll not confess, you'll not confess.

Shallow. That he will not. 'Tis your fault,° 'tis your
fault. 'Tis a good dog.

Page. A cur, sir.

Shallow. Sir, he's a good dog, and a fair dog. Can

---

81 **ill killed** (1) improperly killed (?) (2) possibly a reference to Falstaff's doing the killing (see I.i.109–10)   87 **fallow** brownish yellow
88 **Cotsall** the Cotswold hills in Gloucestershire (locale of the
Cotswold Games and center for coursing)   91 **fault** misfortune

there be more said? He is good and fair. Is Sir John 95
Falstaff here?

Page. Sir, he is within. And I would I could do a good
office between you.

Evans. It is spoke as a Christians ought to speak.

Shallow. He hath wronged me, Master Page.   100

Page. Sir, he doth in some sort confess it.

Shallow. If it be confessed, it is not redressed. Is not
that so, Master Page? He hath wronged me; indeed,
he hath. At a word, he hath, believe me. Robert
Shallow, Esquire, saith he is wronged.   105

Page. Here comes Sir John.

[Enter Sir John] Falstaff, Bardolph, Nym, [and] Pistol.

Falstaff. Now, Master Shallow, you'll complain of me
to the King?

Shallow. Knight, you have beaten my men, killed my
deer, and broke open my lodge.   110

Falstaff. But not kissed your keeper's daughter?

Shallow. Tut, a pin!° This shall be answered.

Falstaff. I will answer it straight. I have done all this.
That is now answered.

Shallow. The Council shall know this.   115

Falstaff. 'Twere better for you if it were known in
counsel.° You'll be laughed at.

Evans. Pauca verba;° Sir John, goot worts.

Falstaff. Good worts?° Good cabbage!—Slender, I
broke your head. What matter° have you against 120
me?

112 pin trifle   116–17 in counsel privately   118 pauca verba few
words (Latin)   119 worts (1) words (2) cabbage-like plant   120 matter dispute (but in the next line it has the senses of "brain matter" and
"cause")

Slender. Marry, sir, I have matter in my head against
you, and against your cony-catching° rascals, Bardolph, Nym, and Pistol. They carried me to the
125   tavern and made me drunk, and afterward picked
my pocket.

Bardolph. [*Drawing his sword*] You Banbury cheese!°

Slender. Ay, it is no matter.

Pistol. [*Also draws*] How now, Mephostophilus!°

130   *Slender*. Ay, it is no matter.

Nym. [*Drawing*] Slice, I say! *Pauca, pauca*. Slice!
That's my humor.°

Slender. Where's Simple, my man? Can you tell,
cousin?

135   *Evans*. Peace, I pray you. Now let us understand.
There is three umpires in this matter, as I understand; that is, Master Page, *fidelicet*,° Master Page;
and there is myself, *fidelicet*, myself; and the three
party is, lastly and finally, mine Host of the Garter.°

140   *Page*. We three to hear it and end it between them.

Evans. Fery goot. I will make a prief of it in my notebook, and we will afterwards 'ork upon the cause
with as great discreetly as we can.

Falstaff. Pistol!

145   *Pistol*. He hears with ears.

Evans. The tevil and his tam! What phrase is this, "He
hears with ear"? Why, it is affectations.

Falstaff. Pistol, did you pick Master Slender's purse?

Slender. Ay, by these gloves, did he—or I would I
150   might never come in mine own great chamber again

123 cony-catching cheating   127 Banbury cheese (noted for its thin-
ness, a reference to Slender's build)   129 Mephostophilus i.e., devil
(from Marlowe's *Dr. Faustus*)   132 humor temperament   137 fidelicet i.e., *videlicet*, namely   139 Garter Garter Inn

else—of seven groats° in mill-sixpences,° and two
Edward shovel-boards,° that cost me two shilling
and two pence apiece of Yed° Miller, by these
gloves.

Falstaff. Is this true, Pistol?   155

Evans. No, it is false, if it is a pickpurse.

Pistol. Ha, thou mountain-foreigner!° Sir John and
    master mine,
I combat challenge of this latten bilbo.°
Word of denial in thy *labras*° here!
Word of denial! Froth and scum, thou liest!   160

Slender. By these gloves, then 'twas he.

Nym. Be avised, sir, and pass good humors. I will say
"marry trap"° with you, if you run the nuthook's
humor° on me. That is the very note of it.

Slender. By this hat, then he in the red face had it; for 165
    though I cannot remember what I did when you
    made me drunk, yet I am not altogether an ass.

Falstaff. What say you, Scarlet and John?°

Bardolph. Why, sir, for my part, I say the gentleman
    had drunk himself out of his five sentences.   170

Evans. It is his "five senses." Fie, what the ignorance is!

Bardolph. And being fap,° sir, was, as they say, cash-
    iered;° and so conclusions passed the careers.°

Slender. Ay, you spake in Latin then too. But 'tis no

151 **groats** coins worth fourpence   151 **mill-sixpences** i.e., milled
coins   152 **Edward shovel-boards** shillings from the reign of Edward VI used in the game of shovelboard (rare coins by the 1590's)
153 **Yed** i.e., Ed, Edward   157 **mountain-foreigner** i.e., Welshman
158 **latten bilbo** brass sword   159 **labras** lips   163 **marry trap** (a
term of insult)   163–64 **run the nuthook's humor** i.e., think to involve me with the law (*nuthook* = constable)   168 **Scarlet and John**
Robin Hood's companions (alluding to Bardolph's red face)   172 **fap**
drunk   172–73 **cashiered** robbed   173 **conclusions passed the ca-
reers** (an obscure line possibly meaning "and that brought the matter
to a speedy end" or "he got what he deserved"—from "pass a
careire," a term in horsemanship)

175 matter. I'll ne'er be drunk whilst I live again, but in
honest, civil, godly company, for this trick. If I be
drunk, I'll be drunk with those that have the fear of
God, and not with drunken knaves.

Evans. So Got 'udge me, that is a virtuous mind.

180 *Falstaff.* You hear all these matters denied, gentlemen;
you hear it.

[*Enter*] *Anne Page* [*with wine*], *Mistress Ford* [*and*]
Mistress Page [*following*].

Page. Nay, daughter, carry the wine in; we'll drink
within.   [*Exit Anne Page.*]

Slender. O heaven! This is Mistress Anne Page.

185 *Page.* How now, Mistress Ford!

Falstaff. Mistress Ford, by my troth, you are very well
met. By your leave, good mistress.   [*Kisses her.*]

Page. Wife, bid these gentlemen welcome. Come, we
have a hot venison pasty to dinner. Come, gentle-
190 men, I hope we shall drink down all unkindness.
[*Exeunt all except Shallow, Slender, and Evans.*]

Slender. I had rather than forty shillings I had my
Book of Songs and Sonnets° here.

[*Enter*] *Simple.*

How now, Simple, where have you been? I must
wait on myself, must I? You have not the Book of
195 Riddles about you, have you?

Simple. Book of Riddles? Why, did you not lend it to
Alice Shortcake upon Allhallowmas° last, a fort-
night afore Michaelmas?°

Shallow. Come, coz; come, coz; we stay for you. A
200 word with you, coz. Marry,° this, coz: there is as

192 **Book of Songs and Sonnets** an anthology published by Tottel in
1557, commonly called Tottel's *Miscellany*   197 **Allhallowmas** All
Saint's Day, November 1   198 **Michaelmas** St. Michael's Day, September 29   200 **Marry** (mild oath from "By Mary.")

'twere a tender,° a kind of tender, made afar off°
by Sir Hugh here. Do you understand me?

Slender. Ay, sir, you shall find me reasonable. If it be
so, I shall do that that is reason.

Shallow. Nay, but understand me.   205

Slender. So I do, sir.

Evans. Give ear to his motions.° Master Slender, I will
description the matter to you, if you be capacity
of it.

Slender. Nay, I will do as my cousin Shallow says. I   210
pray you pardon me. He's a Justice of Peace in his
country, simple though° I stand here.

Evans. But that is not the question. The question is
concerning your marriage.

Shallow. Ay, there's the point, sir.   215

Evans. Marry, is it, the very point of it—to Mistress
Anne Page.

Slender. Why, if it be so, I will marry her upon any
reasonable demands.

Evans. But can you affection the 'oman? Let us com-   220
mand to know that of your mouth, or of your lips;
for divers° philosophers hold that the lips is parcel°
of the mouth. Therefore, precisely, can you carry
your goot will to the maid?

Shallow. Cousin Abraham Slender, can you love her?   225

Slender. I hope, sir, I will do as it shall become one
that would do reason.

Evans. Nay, Got's lords and his ladies! You must
speak possitable,° if you can carry her your desires
towards her.   230

201 **tender** offer   201 **afar off** indirectly   207 **motions** proposals
212 **simple though** as sure as   222 **divers** various   222 **parcel** part
229 **possitable** positively

Shallow. That you must. Will you, upon good dowry, marry her?

Slender. I will do a greater thing than that, upon your request, cousin, in any reason.

235 *Shallow*. Nay, conceive me,° conceive me, sweet coz. What I do is to pleasure you, coz. Can you love the maid?

Slender. I will marry her, sir, at your request; but if there be no great love in the beginning, yet heaven
240 may decrease it upon better acquaintance when we are married and have more occasion to know one another. I hope upon familiarity will grow more contempt. But if you say, "Marry her," I will marry her; that I am freely dissolved, and dissolutely.

243 *Evans*. It is a fery discretion answer, save the faul'° is in the 'ort "dissolutely." The 'ort is, according to our meaning, "resolutely." His meaning is goot.

Shallow. Ay, I think my cousin meant well.

Slender. Ay, or else I would I might be hanged, la.

[*Enter Anne Page.*]

250 *Shallow*. Here comes fair Mistress Anne.—Would I were young for your sake, Mistress Anne.

Anne. The dinner is on the table. My father desires your worships' company.

Shallow. I will wait on him, fair Mistress Anne.

255 *Evans*. Od's° plessed will! I will not be absence at the grace.   [*Exeunt Shallow and Evans.*]

Anne. Will't please your worship to come in, sir?

Slender. No, I thank you, forsooth, heartily; I am very well.

260 *Anne*. The dinner attends you, sir.

Slender. I am not a-hungry, I thank you, forsooth.
235 conceive me understand me   245 faul' fault   255 Od's God's

[*To Simple*] Go, sirrah,° for all you are my man, go wait upon my cousin Shallow. [*Exit Simple.*] A justice of peace sometime may be beholding to his friend for a man. I keep but three men and a boy 265 yet, till my mother be dead. But what though? Yet I live like a poor gentleman born.

Anne. I may not go in without your worship; they will not sit till you come.

Slender. I' faith, I'll eat nothing. I thank you as much 270 as though I did.

Anne. I pray you, sir, walk in.

Slender. I had rather walk here, I thank you. I bruised my shin th' other day with playing at sword and dagger with a master of fence—three veneys° for 275 a dish of stewed prunes—and, by my troth, I cannot abide the smell of hot meat since. Why do your dogs bark so? Be there bears i' th' town?

Anne. I think there are, sir; I heard them talked of.

Slender. I love the sport° well, but I shall as soon 280 quarrel at it as any man in England. You are afraid if you see the bear loose, are you not?

Anne. Ay, indeed, sir.

Slender. That's meat and drink to me now. I have seen Sackerson° loose twenty times, and have taken him 285 by the chain; but, I warrant you, the women have so cried and shrieked at it, that it passed. But women, indeed, cannot abide 'em; they are very ill-favored rough things.

[*Enter Page.*]

Page. Come, gentle Master Slender, come. We stay for 290 you.

Slender. I'll eat nothing; I thank you, sir.

---

262 **sirrah** (term of address used to inferiors) 275 **veneys** bouts
280 **the sport** i.e., bearbaiting 285 **Sackerson** (a famous bear)

Page. By cock and pie,° you shall not choose, sir!
   Come, come.

295 *Slender*. Nay, pray you, lead the way.

Page. Come on, sir.

Slender. Mistress Anne, yourself shall go first.

Anne. Not I, sir; pray you keep on.

Slender. Truly, I will not go first; truly, la! I will not
300   do you that wrong.

Anne. I pray you, sir.

Slender. I'll rather be unmannerly than troublesome.
   You do yourself wrong, indeed, la!   *Exeunt*.

Scene II. [*Before Page's house*.]

Enter Evans and Simple.

Evans. Go your ways, and ask of Doctor Caius' house,
   which is the way; and there dwells one Mistress
   Quickly, which is in the manner of his nurse, or
   his dry nurse,° or his cook, or his laundry, his
5   washer, and his wringer.

Simple. Well, sir.

Evans. Nay, it is petter yet. Give her this letter, for it
   is a 'oman that altogether's acquaintance with Mistress Anne Page; and the letter is to desire and re-
10   quire her to solicit your master's desires to Mistress
   Anne Page. I pray you be gone. I will make an end
   of my dinner; there's pippins and seese° to come.
                                          Exeunt.

293 **cock and pie** (an oath)   I.ii.4 **dry nurse** i.e., housekeeper   12
pippins and seese apples and cheese

Scene III. [*Falstaff's room in the Garter Inn.*]

Enter Falstaff, Host, Bardolph, Nym, Pistol,
[*and Robin, the*] *Page.*

Falstaff. Mine Host of the Garter!

Host. What says my bully rook?° Speak scholarly and
wisely.

Falstaff. Truly, mine Host, I must turn away some of
my followers.   *3*

Host. Discard, bully Hercules, cashier. Let them wag;°
trot, trot.

Falstaff. I sit at° ten pounds a week.

Host. Thou'rt an emperor—Caesar, Keisar,° and Pheazar.° I will entertain° Bardolph: he shall draw,°   *10*
he shall tap.° Said I well, bully Hector?

Falstaff. Do so, good mine Host.

Host. I have spoke; let him follow. [*To Bardolph*] Let
me see thee froth and lime.° I am at a word;° fol-
low.   [*Exit.*]   *15*

Falstaff. Bardolph, follow him. A tapster is a good
trade. An old cloak makes a new jerkin; a withered
servingman, a fresh tapster. Go, adieu.

Bardolph. It is a life that I have desired. I will thrive.

I.iii. 2 **bully rook** (friendly term of address used by the Host)   6 **wag**
depart   8 **I sit at** my expenses run   9 **Keisar** Kaiser   9–10 **Pheazar**
vizier   10 **entertain** employ   10 **draw** draw liquor   11 **tap** serve as
tapster   14 **froth and lime** i.e., cheat the customers by putting a big
head of foam on the beer or by adulterating wine with lime   14 **I
am at a word** i.e., I speak briefly

20 *Pistol.* O base Hungarian wight!° Wilt thou the spigot
wield?   [*Exit Bardolph.*]

Nym. He was gotten° in drink. Is not the humor conceited?°

Falstaff. I am glad I am so acquit° of this tinderbox.
25   His thefts were too open. His filching was like an
unskillful singer: he kept not time.

Nym. The good humor is to steal at a minute's rest.°

Pistol. "Convey," the wise it call. "Steal?" Foh, a fico°
for the phrase!

30 *Falstaff.* Well, sirs, I am almost out at heels.°

Pistol. Why then, let kibes° ensue.

Falstaff. There is no remedy. I must cony-catch, I
must shift.°

Pistol. Young ravens must have food.

35 *Falstaff.* Which of you know Ford of this town?

Pistol. I ken° the wight. He is of substance good.

Falstaff. My honest lads, I will tell you what I am
about.

Pistol. Two yards, and more.

40 *Falstaff.* No quips now, Pistol. Indeed, I am in the
waist two yards about. But I am now about no
waste; I am about thrift. Briefly, I do mean to make
love to Ford's wife. I spy entertainment in her: she
discourses, she carves,° she gives the leer of invi-
45   tation. I can construe the action of her familiar
style; and the hardest voice of her behavior, to be
Englished rightly, is, "I am Sir John Falstaff's."

---

20 **base Hungarian wight** i.e., beggarly fellow 22 **gotten** begotten
22–23 **conceited** ingenious 24 **acquit** rid 27 **minute's rest** i.e., in
the shortest possible interval 28 **fico** fig 30 **out at heels** penniless
31 **kibes** chilblains 33 **shift** devise some stratagem 36 **ken** know
44 **carves** shows courtesy

Pistol. He hath studied her well, and translated her will, out of honesty° into English.°

Nym. The anchor is deep.° Will that humor pass?　*50*

Falstaff. Now, the report goes she has all the rule of her husband's purse. He hath a legion of angels.°

Pistol. As many devils entertain. And "To her, boy," say I.

Nym. The humor rises; it is good. Humor me the angels.　*55*

Falstaff. I have writ me here a letter to her; and here another to Page's wife, who even now gave me good eyes too, examined my parts with most judicious oeillades.° Sometimes the beam of her view gilded my foot, sometimes my portly belly.　*60*

Pistol. [*Aside*] Then did the sun on dunghill shine.

Nym. [*Aside*] I thank thee for that humor.

Falstaff. O, she did so course o'er my exteriors with such a greedy intention that the appetite of her eye did seem to scorch me up like a burning-glass. Here's another letter to her. She bears the purse too. She is a region in Guiana, all gold and bounty. I will be cheater° to them both, and they shall be exchequers to me. They shall be my East and West Indies, and I will trade to them both. [*To Pistol*] Go, bear thou this letter to Mistress Page; [*To Nym*] and thou this to Mistress Ford. We will thrive, lads, we will thrive.　*65*　*70*

Pistol. Shall I Sir Pandarus° of Troy become, And by my side wear steel? Then Lucifer take all!　*75*

49 **honesty** chastity　49 **English** (probably with a pun on *ingle* = paramour)　50 **The anchor is deep** (an obscure line possibly meaning [1] it is a deeply thought-out scheme or [2] That wine keg [i.e., Falstaff] is a deep thinker [from "anker," a wine keg])　52 **angels** gold coins worth about ten shillings　60 **oeillades** amorous glances　69 **cheater** (1) escheator, official who looked after the king's escheats (2) one who defrauds　75 **Sir Pandarus** (the go-between in Chaucer's *Troilus and Criseyde,* from whose name the word "pander" comes)

Nym. I will run no base humor. Here, take the humor-
    letter. I will keep the havior of reputation.

Falstaff. [*To Robin*] Hold, sirrah, bear you these let-
    ters tightly.°
80   Sail like my pinnace to these golden shores.
    Rogues, hence, avaunt! Vanish like hailstones, go!
    Trudge, plod away o' th' hoof; seek shelter, pack!°
    Falstaff will learn the humor of the age:
    French thrift,° you rogues—myself and skirted
      page.   [*Exeunt Falstaff and Robin.*]

Pistol. Let vultures gripe thy guts! For gourd and
85   fullam° holds,
    And high and low° beguiles the rich and poor.
    Tester° I'll have in pouch when thou shalt lack,
    Base Phrygian Turk!°

Nym. I have operations which be humors of revenge.

90 *Pistol.* Wilt thou revenge?

Nym. By welkin° and her star!

Pistol. With wit or steel?

Nym. With both the humors, I.
    I will discuss° the humor of this love to Page.

95 *Pistol.* And I to Ford shall eke unfold
        How Falstaff, varlet vile,
      His dove will prove, his gold will hold,
        And his soft couch defile.

Nym. My humor shall not cool. I will incense Page to
100   deal with poison. I will possess him with yellow-
    ness,° for the revolt of mind is dangerous. That is
    my true humor.

---

79 **tightly** well   82 **pack** be off   84 **French thrift** (an allusion to the
French custom then current to use one page instead of many serv-
ing men)   85 **gourd and fullam** kinds of false dice   86 **high and
low** numbers on the dice   87 **Tester** sixpence   88 **Base Phrygian
Turk** (term of insult)   91 **welkin** sky   94 **discuss** declare   100-01
yellowness i.e., jealousy

Pistol. Thou art the Mars of malcontents. I second
   thee; troop on.   *Exeunt.*

Scene IV: [*A room in Dr. Caius' house.*]

Enter Mistress Quickly [and] Simple.

Quickly. [*Calling*] What, John Rugby! ([*Enter*] John
   Rugby.) I pray thee, go to the casement and see if
   you can see my master, Master Doctor Caius, coming. If he do, i' faith, and find anybody in the house,
   here will be an old° abusing of God's patience and   *5*
   the King's English.

Rugby. I'll go watch.

Quickly. Go, and we'll have a posset° for't soon at
   night, in faith, at the latter end of a sea-coal° fire.
   [*Exit Rugby.*] An honest, willing, kind fellow, as   *10*
   ever servant shall come in house withal;° and, I
   warrant you, no telltale, nor no breedbate.° His
   worst fault is that he is given to prayer; he is something peevish° that way, but nobody but has his
   fault. But let that pass.——Peter Simple you say your   *15*
   name is?

Simple. Ay, for fault of a better.

Quickly. And Master Slender's your master?

Simple. Ay, forsooth.

Quickly. Does he not wear a great round beard like a   *20*
   glover's paring knife?

I.iv.5 **old** great, plenty of   8 **posset** hot milk curdled with ale or
wine   9 **sea-coal** coal brought by sea   11 **withal** with   12 **breedbate** mischiefmaker   14 **peevish** silly

Simple. No, forsooth. He hath but a little whey° face,
with a little yellow beard—a Cain-colored° beard.

Quickly. A softly-sprighted° man, is he not?

25 *Simple.* Ay, forsooth. But he is as tall a man of his
hands° as any is between this and his head. He hath
fought with a warrener.°

Quickly. How say you? O, I should remember him.
Does he not hold up his head, as it were, and strut
30 in his gait?

Simple. Yes, indeed does he.

Quickly. Well, heaven send Anne Page no worse
fortune. Tell Master Parson Evans I will do what I
can for your master. Anne is a good girl, and I
35 wish—

[*Enter Rugby.*]

Rugby. Out, alas! Here comes my master!

Quickly. We shall all be shent.° Run in here, good
young man; go into this closet.° He will not stay
long. [*Shuts Simple in the chamber.*] What, John
40 Rugby! John, what, John, I say! Go, John, go inquire for my master. I doubt° he be not well, that
he comes not home.   [*Exit Rugby.*]

[*Sings.*] "And down, down, adown-a," &c.

[*Enter*] Doctor Caius.

Caius. Vat is you sing? I do not like dese toys.° Pray
45 you go and vetch me in my closset *un boitier vert*—
a box, a green-a box. Do intend° vat I speak? A
green-a box.

Quickly. Ay, forsooth, I'll fetch it you. [*Aside*] I am

---

22 **whey** i.e., pale (the Folio gives "wee," perhaps a dialectal pronunciation)   23 **Cain-colored** i.e., reddish-yellow (traditional color of
Cain's beard in tapestries)   24 **softly-sprighted** gentle-spirited   25–
26 **tall a man of his hands** i.e., valiant   27 **warrener** gamekeeper
37 **shent** scolded   38 **closet** private room   41 **doubt** fear   44 **toys**
foolish nonsense   46 **intend** hear (Fr. *entendre*)

glad he went not in himself. If he had found the
young man, he would have been horn-mad.° [*Exit.*]   *50*

Caius. Fe, fe, fe, fe! *Ma foi, il fait fort chaud. Je m'en
vais à la Cour—la grande affaire.*°

Quickly. [*Returning with the box*] Is it this, sir?

Caius. Oui; mette le au mon pocket; dépêche,° quickly.
Vere is dat knave Rugby?   *55*

Quickly. What, John Rugby! John!

[*Enter Rugby.*]

Rugby. Here, sir.

Caius. You are John Rugby, and you are Jack Rugby.
Come, take-a your rapier and come after my heel
to de court.   *60*

Rugby. 'Tis ready, sir, here in the porch.

Caius. By my trot,° I tarry too long. Od's me! *Qu'ai
j'oublié?*° Dere is some simples° in my closset dat
I vill not for de varld I shall leave behind.
[*Crosses to the chamber.*]

Quickly. [*Aside*] Ay me, he'll find the young man   *65*
there, and be mad.

Caius. O diable, diable! Vat is in my closset? Villainy!
Larron!°[*Pulls Simple out.*] Rugby, my rapier!

Quickly. Good master, be content.

Caius. Verefore shall I be content-a?   *70*

Quickly. The young man is an honest man.

Caius. Vat shall de honest man do in my closset? Dere
is no honest man dat shall come in my closset.

---

50 **horn-mad** enraged   51-52 **Ma foi . . . grande affaire** faith, it is
very hot. I am going to the Court—the grand affair.   54 **Oui . . .
dépêche** yes; put it in my pocket; be quick   62 **trot** i.e., troth
62-63 **Qu'ai j'oublié** what have I forgotten   63 **simples** medicinal
herbs   68 **Larron** thief

Quickly. I beseech you, be not so phlegmatic.° Hear
75   the truth of it. He came of an errand to me from
Parson Hugh.

Caius. Vell?

Simple. Ay, forsooth, to desire her to—

Quickly. Peace, I pray you.

80   *Caius.* Peace-a your tongue.—Speak-a your tale.

Simple. To desire this honest gentlewoman, your maid,
to speak a good word to Mistress Anne Page for
my master in the way of marriage.

Quickly. This is all, indeed, la! But I'll ne'er put my
85   finger in the fire, and need not.

Caius. Sir Hugh send-a you?—Rugby, *baille*° me some
paper. Tarry you a little-a while.   [*Writes.*]

Quickly. [*Aside to Simple*] I am glad he is so quiet. If
he had been throughly moved, you should have
90   heard him so loud, and so melancholy. But notwithstanding, man, I'll do you your master what good
I can; and the very yea and the no is, the French
doctor, my master—I may call him my master, look
you, for I keep his house; and I wash, wring, brew,
95   bake, scour, dress meat and drink, make the beds,
and do all myself—

Simple. [*Aside to Quickly*] 'Tis a great charge° to
come under one body's hand.

Quickly [*Aside to Simple*] Are you avised o' that? You
100 shall find it a great charge. And to be up early and
down late; but notwithstanding—to tell you in your
ear, I would have no words of it—my master himself is in love with Mistress Anne Page. But notwithstanding that, I know Anne's mind. That's
105 neither here nor there.

---

74 phlegmatic (Quickly's error for "choleric")   86 baille fetch   97
charge burden

Caius. You jack'nape,° give-a dis letter to Sir Hugh.
By gar, it is a shallenge. I vill cut his troat in de
Park; and I vill teach a scurvy jackanape priest to
meddle or make. You may be gone; it is not good
you tarry here. [*Exit Simple.*] By gar, I vill cut all   *110*
his two stones;° by gar, he shall not have a stone to
trow at his dog.

Quickly. Alas, he speaks but for his friend.

Caius. It is no matter-a ver dat. Do not you tell-a me
dat I shall have Anne Page for myself? By gar, I   *115*
vill kill de Jack° priest; and I have appointed mine
Host of de Jarteer to measure our weapon.° By gar,
I vill myself have Anne Page.

Quickly. Sir, the maid loves you, and all shall be well.
We must give folks leave to prate. What the good-   *120*
year!°

Caius. Rugby, come to the court vit me. [*To Quickly*]
By gar, if I have not Anne Page, I shall turn your
head out of my door. Follow my heels, Rugby.
                                      [*Exeunt Caius and Rugby.*]

Quickly. [*Calling after Caius*] You shall have An°—   *125*
fool's-head of your own. No, I know Anne's mind
for that. Never a woman in Windsor knows more
of Anne's mind than I do, nor can do more than I
do with her, I thank heaven.

Fenton. [*Offstage*] Who's within there, ho?   *130*

Quickly. Who's there, I trow?° Come near° the house,
I pray you.

                      [*Enter*] *Fenton.*

Fenton. How now, good woman. How dost thou?

---

106 **jack'nape** coxcomb   111 **stones** testicles   116 **Jack** (term of
contempt)   117 **measure our weapon** i.e., umpire the duel   120–21
good-year (a meaningless expletive)   125 **An** (1) Anne (2) an
131 **trow** wonder   131 **Come near** i.e., enter

Quickly. The better that it pleases your good worship
135   to ask.

Fenton. What news? How does pretty Mistress Anne?

Quickly. In truth, sir, and she is pretty, and honest,° and gentle—and one that is your friend. I can tell you that by the way, I praise heaven for it.

140   *Fenton.* Shall I do any good, think'st thou? Shall I not lose my suit?

Quickly. Troth, sir, all is in His hands above. But notwithstanding, Master Fenton, I'll be sworn on a book she loves you. Have not your worship a wart
145   above your eye?

Fenton. Yes, marry, have I. What of that?

Quickly. Well, thereby hangs a tale. Good faith, it is such another Nan;° but, I detest,° an honest maid as ever broke bread. We had an hour's talk of that
150   wart. I shall never laugh but in that maid's company. But, indeed, she is given too much to allicholy° and musing. But for you—well, go to.

Fenton. Well, I shall see her today. Hold, there's money for thee; let me have thy voice in my behalf.
155   If thou seest her before me, commend me—

Quickly. Will I? I' faith, that we will. And I will tell your worship more of the wart the next time we have confidence, and of other wooers.

Fenton. Well, farewell. I am in great haste now.

160   *Quickly.* Farewell to your worship. [*Exit Fenton.*] Truly, an honest gentleman. But Anne loves him not, for I know Anne's mind as well as another does. Out upon't, what have I forgot?   *Exit.*

---

137 **honest** chaste   148 **such another Nan** i.e., charming female
148 **detest** (Quickly's error for "protest")   151–52 **allicholy** melancholy

ACT II

Scene I. [*Before Page's house.*]

Enter Mistress Page [with a letter].

Mrs. Page. What, have 'scaped love letters in the holiday time° of my beauty, and am I now a subject
for them? Let me see.   [*Reads.*]

"Ask me no reason why I love you, for though Love
use Reason for his precisian,° he admits him not for   *5*
his counselor. You are not young, no more am I.
Go to then, there's sympathy. You are merry, so
am I. Ha, ha, then there's more sympathy. You
love sack,° and so do I. Would you desire better
sympathy? Let it suffice thee, Mistress Page—at   *10*
the least, if the love of soldier can suffice—that I
love thee. I will not say, pity me—'tis not a soldier-
like phrase; but I say, love me. By me,
              Thine own true knight,
              By day or night,   *15*
              Or any kind of light,
              With all his might
              For thee to fight,
                        John Falstaff."

What a Herod of Jewry° is this! O wicked, wicked   *20*
world. One that is well-nigh worn to pieces with
age to show himself a young gallant! What an un-

II.i.1-2 **in the holiday time** i.e., in my youth   5 **precisian** inflexible
spiritual adviser 9 **sack** Spanish white wine   20 **Herod of Jewry**
(portrayed as a ranting villain in the miracle plays)

63

weighed° behavior hath this Flemish drunkard°
picked—with the devil's name!—out of my con-
25 versation° that he dares in this manner assay me?
Why, he hath not been thrice in my company.
What should I say to him? I was then frugal of my
mirth—Heaven forgive me! Why, I'll exhibit° a
bill in the parliament for the putting down° of men.
30 How shall I be revenged on him? For revenged I
will be, as sure as his guts are made of puddings.°

[Enter] Mistress Ford.

Mrs. Ford. Mistress Page! Trust me, I was going to
your house.

Mrs. Page. And, trust me, I was coming to you. You
35 look very ill.

Mrs. Ford. Nay, I'll ne'er believe that. I have to show
to the contrary.

Mrs. Page. Faith, but you do, in my mind.

Mrs. Ford. Well, I do then; yet I say I could show you
40 to the contrary. O Mistress Page, give me some
counsel.

Mrs. Page. What's the matter, woman?

Mrs. Ford. O woman, if it were not for one trifling
respect, I could come to such honor.

45 *Mrs. Page.* Hang the trifle, woman; take the honor.
What is it? Dispense with trifles. What is it?

Mrs. Ford. If I would but go to hell for an eternal
moment or so, I could be knighted.

Mrs. Page. What? Thou liest. Sir Alice Ford? These
50 knights will hack;° and so thou shouldst not alter
the article of thy gentry.°

22–23 **unweighed** inconsiderate   23 **Flemish drunkard** (the Flemish
were notorious for heavy drinking)   24–25 **conversation** behavior
28 **exhibit** submit   29 **putting down** suppressing   31 **puddings** sausages   50 **hack** (meaning not clear in this context; a double entendre
on giving indiscriminate blows with a sword is possible)   51 **article
of thy gentry** character of your rank

Mrs. Ford. We burn daylight.° [*Giving her a letter*]
Here, read, read! Perceive how I might be knighted.
I shall think the worse of fat men as long as I have
an eye to make difference of° men's liking.° And   55
yet he would not swear; praised women's modesty;
and gave such orderly and well-behaved reproof to
all uncomeliness° that I would have sworn his disposition would have gone to the truth of his words.°
But they do no more adhere and keep place to-   60
gether than the Hundredth Psalm to the tune of
"Greensleeves."° What tempest, I trow, threw this
whale, with so many tuns of oil in his belly, ashore
at Windsor? How shall I be revenged on him? I
think the best way were to entertain him with hope   65
till the wicked fire of lust have melted him in his
own grease. Did you ever hear the like?

Mrs. Page. [*Comparing the two letters*] Letter for letter, but that the name of Page and Ford differs.—
To thy great comfort in this mystery of ill opin-   70
ions,° here's the twin brother of thy letter. But let
thine inherit first, for I protest mine never shall. I
warrant he hath a thousand of these letters, writ
with blank space for different names—sure, more—
and these are of the second edition. He will print   75
them, out of doubt; for he cares not what he puts
into the press, when he would put us two. I had
rather be a giantess and lie under Mount Pelion.°
Well, I will find you twenty lascivious turtles° ere
one chaste man. [*Gives both letters to Mrs. Ford.*]   80

Mrs. Ford. Why, this is the very same: the very hand,
the very words. What doth he think of us?

52 **burn daylight** waste time   55 **make difference of** discriminate
between   55 **liking** looks   58 **uncomeliness** improper behavior
58-59 **his disposition . . . words** i.e., appearances are deceiving
62 **Greensleeves** popular love ballad   70-71 **ill opinions** i.e., sullied
reputations   78 **Mount Pelion** (mountain in Thessaly noted in
mythology for the attempt of the giants to reach heaven by piling
Mount Ossa on Pelion)   79 **turtles** turtledoves (noted for their fidelity to their mates)

Mrs. Page. Nay, I know not. It makes me almost ready
to wrangle with mine own honesty.° I'll entertain
85   myself like one that I am not acquainted withal; for
sure, unless he know some strain in me that I know
not myself, he would never have boarded° me in
this fury.

Mrs. Ford. "Boarding" call you it? I'll be sure to keep
90   him above deck.

Mrs. Page. So will I. If he come under my hatches,
I'll never to sea again. Let's be revenged on him.
Let's appoint him a meeting, give him a show of
comfort in his suit, and lead him on with a fine-
95   baited° delay till he hath pawned his horses to mine
Host of the Garter.

Mrs. Ford. Nay, I will consent to act any villainy
against him that may not sully the chariness° of our
honesty. O that my husband saw this letter! It
100   would give eternal food to his jealousy.

Mrs. Page. Why, look where he comes, and my good-
man° too. He's as far from jealousy as I am from
giving him cause. And that, I hope, is an unmea-
surable distance.

105 *Mrs. Ford.* You are the happier woman.

Mrs. Page. Let's consult together against this greasy
knight. Come hither.   *[They retire.]*

   *[Enter] Master Page [with] Nym, [and] Master
          Ford [with] Pistol.*

Ford. Well, I hope it be not so.

Pistol. Hope is a curtal° dog in some affairs.
110   Sir John affects° thy wife.

Ford. Why, sir, my wife is not young.

84 honesty chastity 87 boarded made advances to 94-95 fine-
baited subtly alluring 98 chariness scrupulous integrity 101-02
goodman husband 109 curtal with a docked tail 110 affects loves

Pistol. He woos both high and low, both rich and poor,
Both young and old, one with another, Ford.
He loves the gallimaufry.° Ford, perpend.°

Ford. Love my wife?   115

Pistol. With liver° burning hot. Prevent, or go thou,
Like Sir Actaeon° he, with Ringwood° at thy heels.
O, odious is the name!°

Ford. What name, sir?

Pistol. The horn, I say. Farewell.   120
Take heed, have open eye, for thieves do foot by
night.
Take heed, ere summer comes or cuckoo birds° do
sing.
Away, Sir Corporal Nym!
Believe it, Page; he speaks sense.   [*Exit.*]

Ford. [*Aside*] I will be patient; I will find out this.   125

Nym. [*To Page*] And this is true; I like not the humor
of lying. He hath wronged me in some humors. I
should have borne the humored letter to her, but I
have a sword and it shall bite upon my necessity.
He loves your wife. There's the short and the long. 130
My name is Corporal Nym; I speak, and I avouch
'tis true. My name is Nym, and Falstaff loves your
wife. Adieu. I love not the humor of bread and
cheese.° And there's the humor of it. Adieu. [*Exit.*]

Page. "The humor of it," quoth 'a? Here's a fellow 135
frights English out of his wits.

Ford. I will seek out Falstaff.

114 **gallimaufry** i.e., medley   114 **perpend** consider   116 **liver** (supposed seat of love)   117 **Sir Actaeon** (accidentally coming upon Diana bathing, Actaeon was turned into a stag for punishment and then killed by his own hounds)   117 **Ringwood** (common Elizabethan name for a hound)   118 **odious is the name** (allusion to Actaeon as a horned beast, i.e., a cuckold)   122 **cuckoo birds** (allusion to cuckoldom from the cuckoo's habit of laying its eggs in the nests of other birds)   133–34 **bread and cheese** (possible allusion to the cuckoo-bread flower, i.e., feeding cuckoldry)

Page. I never heard such a drawling, affecting° rogue.

Ford. If I do find it—well.

140 *Page.* I will not believe such a Cataian,° though the
priest o' th' town commended him for a true man.

Ford. 'Twas a good sensible fellow—well.

[*Mrs. Page and Mrs. Ford come forward.*]

Page. How now, Meg.

Mrs. Page. Whither go you, George? Hark you.
[*They speak aside.*]

145 *Mrs. Ford.* How now, sweet Frank. Why art thou melancholy?

Ford. I melancholy? I am not melancholy. Get you
home, go.

Mrs. Ford. Faith, thou hast some crotchets° in thy
150 head now. Will you go, Mistress Page?

Mrs. Page. Have with you.°—You'll come to dinner,
George?

[*Enter*] *Mistress Quickly.*

[*Aside to Mrs. Ford*] Look who comes yonder. She
shall be our messenger to this paltry knight.

155 *Mrs. Ford.* [*Aside to Mrs. Page*] Trust me, I thought
on her. She'll fit it.

Mrs. Page. You are come to see my daughter Anne?

Quickly. Ay, forsooth; and, I pray, how does good
Mistress Anne?

160 *Mrs. Page.* Go in with us and see. We have an hour's
talk with you.
[*Exeunt Mistress Page, Mistress Ford,
and Mistress Quickly.*]

138 **affecting** affected   140 **Cataian** Cathaian (i.e., Chinese; not considered trustworthy by the Elizabethans)   149 **crotchets** peculiar no-
tions   151 **Have with you** I'll go along with you

Page. How now, Master Ford.

Ford. You heard what this knave told me, did you
    not?

Page. Yes, and you heard what the other told me?   165

Ford. Do you think there is truth in them?

Page. Hang 'em, slaves! I do not think the knight
    would offer° it. But these that accuse him in his in-
    tent towards our wives are a yoke° of his discarded
    men—very rogues, now they be out of service.   170

Ford. Were they his men?

Page. Marry were they.

Ford. I like it never the better for that. Does he lie at
    the Garter?

Page. Ay, marry does he. If he should intend this voy-   175
    age toward my wife, I would turn her loose to him;
    and what he gets more of her than sharp words, let
    it lie on my head.°

Ford. I do not misdoubt my wife, but I would be loath
    to turn them together. A man may be too confident.   180
    I would have nothing lie on my head. I cannot be
    thus satisfied.

[*Enter*] *Host.*

Page. Look where my ranting Host of the Garter
    comes. There is either liquor in his pate or money
    in his purse when he looks so merrily.—How now,   185
    mine Host.

Host. How now, bully rook, thou'rt a gentleman.
    [*Calling behind him*] Cavaliero° Justice, I say!

[*Enter*] *Shallow.*

Shallow. I follow, mine Host, I follow. Good even

---

168 offer try   169 yoke pair   177–78 let it lie on my head (1) it's
my responsibility (2) I would be cuckolded   188 Cavaliero (Spanish
title for a gentleman trained in arms)

190   and twenty,° good Master Page. Master Page, will
         you go with us? We have sport in hand.

Host. Tell him, Cavaliero Justice; tell him, bully rook.

Shallow. Sir, there is a fray to be fought between Sir
   Hugh the Welsh priest and Caius the French doctor.

195 *Ford.* Good mine Host o' th' Garter, a word with you.
                                    [*Draws him aside.*]

Host. What sayest thou, my bully rook?

Shallow. [*To Page*] Will you go with us to behold it?
   My merry Host hath had the measuring of their
   weapons, and, I think, hath appointed them con-
200   trary° places; for, believe me, I hear the Parson is
   no jester. Hark, I will tell you what our sport shall
   be.   [*They converse apart.*]

Host. Hast thou no suit against my knight, my Guest
   Cavaliero?

205 *Ford.* None, I protest. But I'll give you a pottle° of
   burnt° sack to give me recourse to him and tell him
   my name is Brooke—only for a jest.

Host. My hand, bully. Thou shalt have egress and
   regress—said I well?—and thy name shall be
210   Brooke. It is a merry knight. Will you go, mynheers?°

Shallow. Have with you, mine Host.

Page. I have heard the Frenchman hath good skill in
   his rapier.

215 *Shallow.* Tut, sir, I could have told you more. In these
   times you stand on distance,° your passes,° stoccadoes,° and I know not what. 'Tis the heart, Master Page; 'tis here, 'tis here. I have seen the time

189–90 **Good even and twenty** good evening twenty times over
(there is an error in time here, for it is morning.)   199–200 **contrary**
different   205 **pottle** two-quart tankard   206 **burnt** heated   210–
11 **mynheers** gentlemen   216 **distance** i.e., space between fencers
216 **passes** lunges   216–17 **stoccadoes** thrusts

with my long sword I would have made you four
tall fellows skip like rats.　　　　　　　　220

Host. Here, boys, here, here! Shall we wag?°

Page. Have with you. I had rather hear them scold
than fight.　　　　*Exeunt [Host, Shallow, and Page].*

Ford. Though Page be a secure fool and stands so
firmly on his wife's frailty, yet I cannot put off my　225
opinion so easily. She was in his company at Page's
house, and what they made there, I know not. Well,
I will look further into't; and I have a disguise to
sound Falstaff. If I find her honest, I lose not my
labor. If she be otherwise, 'tis labor well bestowed.　230
　　　　　　　　　　　　　　　　　　[Exit.]

Scene II. *[Falstaff's room in the Garter Inn.]*

Enter Falstaff [and] Pistol.

Falstaff. I will not lend thee a penny.

Pistol. Why, then the world's mine oyster,
Which I with sword will open.

Falstaff. Not a penny. I have been content, sir, you
should lay my countenance° to pawn. I have grated　5
upon° my good friends for three reprieves for you
and your coach-fellow Nym; or else you had
looked through the grate, like a geminy° of ba-
boons. I am damned in hell for swearing to gentlemen my friends you were good soldiers and tall　10
fellows. And when Mistress Bridget lost the handle
of her fan,° I took't° upon mine honor thou hadst
it not.

221 **wag** go　II.ii.5 **countenance** reputation　5–6 **grated upon** pes-
tered　8 **geminy** pair　11–12 **handle of her fan** (often made of gold
or silver)　12 **took't** swore

Pistol. Didst not thou share? Hadst thou not fifteen
15   pence?

Falstaff. Reason, you rogue, reason. Think'st thou I'll
endanger my soul gratis? At a word, hang no more
about me; I am no gibbet for you. Go! A short
knife° and a throng!° To your manor of Pickt-hatch,°
20   go! You'll not bear a letter for me, you rogue? You
stand upon your honor! Why, thou unconfinable
baseness, it is as much as I can do to keep the terms
of my honor precise. I, I, I myself sometimes, leaving the fear of God on the left hand and hiding
mine honor in my necessity, am fain to shuffle,° to
25   hedge,° and to lurch;° and yet you, rogue, will
ensconce your rags, your cat-a-mountain° looks,
your red-lattice° phrases, and your bold-beating°
oaths, under the shelter of your honor! You will not
30   do it? You!

Pistol. I do relent. What would thou more of man?

                    [*Enter*] *Robin.*

Robin. Sir, here's a woman would speak with you.

Falstaff. Let her approach.

                [*Enter Mistress*] *Quickly.*

Quickly. Give your worship good morrow.

35   *Falstaff.* Good morrow, good wife.

Quickly. Not so, and't please your worship.

Falstaff. Good maid then.

Quickly. I'll be sworn, as my mother was the first hour
I was born.

40   *Falstaff.* I do believe the swearer. What with me?

18–19 **short knife** (for cutting purses) 19 **throng** i.e., crowd
of victims 19 **Pickt-hatch** (a notorious district of London)
25 **shuffle** act underhandedly 26 **hedge** cheat 26 **lurch** pilfer 27
cat-a-mountain wildcat 28 **red-lattice** i.e., alehouse 28 **bold-beat-
ing** blustering

Quickly. Shall I vouchsafe your worship a word or two?

Falstaff. Two thousand, fair woman, and I'll vouchsafe thee the hearing.

Quickly. There is one Mistress Ford—[*glancing at* 45 *Pistol and Robin*] sir, I pray, come a little nearer this ways. I myself dwell with Master Doctor Caius.

Falstaff. Well, on; Mistress Ford, you say—

Quickly. Your worship says very true. I pray your worship, come a little nearer this ways.   50

Falstaff. I warrant thee, nobody hears. Mine own people, mine own people.

Quickly. Are they so? God bless them and make them his servants!

Falstaff. Well, Mistress Ford, what of her?   55

Quickly. Why, sir, she's a good creature. Lord, Lord, your worship's a wanton! Well, heaven forgive you, and all of us, I pray—

Falstaff. Mistress Ford—come, Mistress Ford.

Quickly. Marry, this is the short and the long of it. 60
You have brought her into such a canaries° as 'tis
wonderful. The best courtier of them all, when the
court lay at Windsor, could never have brought her
to such a canary. Yet there has been knights, and
lords, and gentlemen, with their coaches. I warrant 65
you, coach after coach, letter after letter, gift after
gift; smelling so sweetly—all musk—and so rushling,° I warrant you, in silk and gold; and in such
alligant° terms, and in such wine and sugar of the
best and the fairest that would have won any   70
woman's heart; and I warrant you, they could never

61 **canaries** i.e., quandaries (?) mentally intoxicated, as with canary
wine (?)   67–68 **rushling** i.e., rustling   69 **alligant** elegant (?) elo-
quent (?)

get an eye-wink of her. I had myself twenty angels
given me this morning; but I defy all angels—in any
such sort, as they say—but in the way of honesty;
75   and I warrant you, they could never get her so much
as sip on a cup with the proudest of them all; and
yet there has been earls—nay, which is more, pensioners;° but, I warrant you, all is one with her.

Falstaff. But what says she to me? Be brief, my good
80   she-Mercury.°

Quickly. Marry, she hath received your letter; for the
which she thanks you a thousand times; and she
gives you to notify that her husband will be absence
from his house between ten and eleven.

85   *Falstaff.* Ten and eleven.

Quickly. Ay, forsooth; and then you may come and
see the p᷀ ᷀ure, she says, that you wot° of. Master
Ford, her husband, will be from home. Alas, the
sweet woman leads an ill life with him; he's a very
90   jealousy man; she leads a very frampold° life with
him, good heart.

Falstaff. Ten and eleven.—Woman, commend me to
her; I will not fail her.

Quickly. Why, you say well. But I have another mes-
95   senger to your worship. Mistress Page hath her
hearty commendations to you too; and let me tell
you in your ear, she's as fartuous° a civil modest
wife, and one, I tell you, that will not miss you
morning nor evening prayer, as any is in Windsor,
100   whoe'er be the other. And she bade me tell your
worship that her husband is seldom from home, but
she hopes there will come a time. I never knew a
woman so dote upon a man. Surely I think you
have charms, la; yes, in truth.

77–78 **pensioners** members of the royal bodyguard   80 **she-Mercury**
i.e., messenger   87 **wot** know   90 **frampold** disagreeable   97 **fartu-
ous** i.e., virtuous

Falstaff. Not I, I assure thee. Setting the attraction of 105
my good parts° aside, I have no other charms.

Quickly. Blessing on your heart for't!

Falstaff. But, I pray thee, tell me this: has Ford's wife
and Page's wife acquainted each other how they
love me?   110

Quickly. That were a jest indeed! They have not so
little grace, I hope; that were a trick indeed! But
Mistress Page would desire you to send her your
little page, of all loves;° her husband has a marvelous infection° to the little page; and truly, Master 115
Page is an honest man. Never a wife in Windsor
leads a better life than she does. Do what she will,
say what she will, take all, pay all, go to bed when
she list,° rise when she list, all is as she will. And,
truly, she deserves it; for if there be a kind woman 120
in Windsor, she is one. You must send her your
page; no remedy.

Falstaff. Why, I will.

Quickly. Nay, but do so then; and look you, he may
come and go between you both; and in any case 125
have a nay-word,° that you may know one another's
mind, and the boy never need to understand anything; for 'tis not good that children should know
any wickedness. Old folks, you know, have discretion, as they say, and know the world.   130

Falstaff. Fare thee well, commend me to them both.
There's my purse; I am yet thy debtor.—Boy, go
along with this woman. [*Exeunt Mistress Quickly
and Robin.*] This news distracts me.

Pistol. [*Aside*] This punk° is one of Cupid's carriers.° 135
Clap on more sails; pursue; up with your fights;°

106 parts talents   114 of all loves for love's sake   115 infection i.e.,
affection   119 list   pleases   126 nay-word   password   135 punk
strumpet   135 carriers messengers   136 fights (screens to conceal
and protect crews in naval engagements)

Give fire! She is my prize, or ocean whelm them
all!   [*Exit.*]

Falstaff. Sayest thou so, old Jack? Go thy ways; I'll
make more of thy old body than I have done. Will
140 they yet look after thee? Wilt thou, after the expense of so much money, be now a gainer? Good
body, I thank thee. Let them say 'tis grossly done;
so it be fairly done, no matter.

[*Enter*] *Bardolph.*

Bardolph. Sir John, there's one Master Brooke below
145 would fain speak with you, and be acquainted with
you; and hath sent your worship a morning's
draught of sack.

Falstaff. Brooke is his name?

Bardolph. Ay, sir.

150 *Falstaff.* Call him in. [*Exit Bardolph.*] Such Brookes
are welcome to me, that o'erflows such liquor. Aha!
Mistress Ford and Mistress Page, have I encom-
passed° you? Go to; *via!*°

[*Enter Bardolph, with*] *Ford* [*disguised*].

Ford. Bless you, sir.

155 *Falstaff.* And you, sir; would you speak with me?

Ford. I make bold to press with so little preparation
upon you.

Falstaff. You're welcome. What's your will?—Give us
leave, drawer.   [*Exit Bardolph.*]

160 *Ford.* Sir, I am a gentleman that have spent much. My
name is Brooke.

Falstaff. Good Master Brooke, I desire more acquaintance of you.

Ford. Good Sir John, I sue for yours, not to charge°

152–53 **encompassed** outwitted 153 **via** go on 164 **charge** cause
expense to

you; for I must let you understand I think myself in 165
better plight for a lender than you are, the which
hath something embold'ned me to this unseasoned°
intrusion; for they say if money go before, all ways
do lie open.

Falstaff. Money is a good soldier, sir, and will on. 170

Ford. Troth, and I have a bag of money here troubles
me. If you will help to bear it, Sir John, take all, or
half, for easing me of the carriage.

Falstaff. Sir, I know not how I may deserve to be your
porter. 175

Ford. I will tell you, sir, if you will give me the hearing.

Falstaff. Speak, good Master Brooke. I shall be glad
to be your servant.

Ford. Sir, I hear you are a scholar—I will be brief 180
with you—and you have been a man long known
to me, though I had never so good means as desire
to make myself acquainted with you. I shall dis-
cover° a thing to you wherein I must very much lay
open mine own imperfection; but, good Sir John, 185
as you have one eye upon my follies, as you hear
them unfolded, turn another into the register of
your own, that I may pass with a reproof the easier,
sith° you yourself know how easy it is to be such
an offender. 190

Falstaff. Very well, sir. Proceed.

Ford. There is a gentlewoman in this town, her husband's name is Ford.

Falstaff. Well, sir.

Ford. I have long loved her, and, I protest to you, be- 195
stowed much on her, followed her with a doting

---

167 **unseasoned** unseasonable   183–84 **discover** reveal   189 **sith**
since

observance, engrossed opportunities° to meet her,
fee'd° every slight occasion that could but niggardly
give me sight of her, not only bought many presents
200 to give her but have given largely to many to know
what she would have given. Briefly, I have pursued
her as love hath pursued me, which hath been on
the wing of all occasions. But whatsoever I have
merited—either in my mind or in my means—
205 meed,° I am sure, I have received none, unless experience be a jewel. That I have purchased at an
infinite rate, and that hath taught me to say this,
"Love like a shadow flies when substance Love
    pursues;
Pursuing that that flies, and flying what pursues."

210 *Falstaff.* Have you received no promise of satisfaction
at her hands?

Ford. Never.

Falstaff. Have you importuned her to such a purpose?

Ford. Never.

215 *Falstaff.* Of what quality was your love then?

Ford. Like a fair house built on another man's ground,
so that I have lost my edifice by mistaking the place
where I erected it.

Falstaff. To what purpose have you unfolded this to
220 me?

Ford. When I have told you that, I have told you all.
Some say that though she appear honest to me, yet
in other places she enlargeth her mirth so far that
there is shrewd construction made of her.° Now,
225 Sir John, here is the heart of my purpose: you are
a gentleman of excellent breeding, admirable discourse, of great admittance,° authentic° in your

---

197 **engrossed opportunities** i.e., manufactured as many opportunities as possible   198 **fee'd** employed   205 **meed** reward   223–24 **she
enlargeth . . . of her** i.e., she is so free in her merriment that she has
a bad reputation   227 **great admittance** high social prestige   227 **authentic** duly qualified

place and person, generally allowed° for your many
warlike, courtlike, and learned preparations.°

Falstaff. O sir!   230

Ford. Believe it, for you know it. There is money.
Spend it, spend it; spend more; spend all I have.
Only give me so much of your time in exchange
of it as to lay an amiable siege to the honesty of
this Ford's wife. Use your art of wooing; win her   235
to consent to you. If any man may, you may as
soon as any.

Falstaff. Would it apply well to the vehemency of your
affection that I should win what you would enjoy?
Methinks you prescribe to yourself very preposter-   240
ously.

Ford. O, understand my drift. She dwells so securely
on the excellency of her honor that the folly of my
soul dares not present itself. She is too bright to be
looked against. Now, could I come to her with any   245
detection in my hand, my desires had instance° and
argument to commend themselves. I could drive her
then from the ward° of her purity, her reputation,
her marriage vow, and a thousand other her de-
fenses, which now are too too strongly embattled   250
against me. What say you to't, Sir John?

Falstaff. Master Brooke, I will first make bold with
your money; next, give me your hand; and last, as
I am a gentleman, you shall, if you will, enjoy
Ford's wife.   255

Ford. O good sir!

Falstaff. I say you shall.

Ford. Want no money, Sir John; you shall want none.

Falstaff. Want no Mistress Ford, Master Brooke; you
shall want none. I shall be with her, I may tell you, 260
by her own appointment. Even as you came in to

228 allowed approved   229 preparations accomplishments   246 instance evidence   248 ward defense

me, her assistant, or go-between, parted from me.
I say I shall be with her between ten and eleven,
for at that time the jealous rascally knave her hus-
265 band will be forth. Come you to me at night; you
shall know how I speed.°

Ford. I am blest in your acquaintance. Do you know
Ford, sir?

Falstaff. Hang him, poor cuckoldly knave! I know him
270 not. Yet I wrong him to call him poor. They say
the jealous wittolly° knave hath masses of money,
for the which his wife seems to me well-favored.°
I will use her as the key of the cuckoldly rogue's
coffer, and there's my harvest-home.°

275 *Ford.* I would you knew Ford, sir, that you might
avoid him if you saw him.

Falstaff. Hang him, mechanical° salt-butter° rogue! I
will stare him out of his wits. I will awe him with
my cudgel; it shall hang like a meteor o'er the
280 cuckold's horns. Master Brooke, thou shalt know
I will predominate over the peasant, and thou shalt
lie with his wife. Come to me soon at night. Ford's
a knave, and I will aggravate his style.° Thou, Master Brooke, shalt know him for knave and cuckold.
285 Come to me soon at night.   [*Exit.*]

Ford. What a damned Epicurean° rascal is this! My
heart is ready to crack with impatience. Who says
this is improvident jealousy? My wife hath sent to
him, the hour is fixed, the match is made. Would
290 any man have thought this? See the hell of having
a false woman! My bed shall be abused, my coffers
ransacked, my reputation gnawn at; and I shall not
only receive this villainous wrong, but stand under
the adoption of abominable terms,° and by him

266 speed succeed   271 wittolly cuckoldly   272 well-favored (1)
well chosen (2) good-looking   274 harvest-home i.e., reaped profits
277 mechanical low, vulgar   277 salt-butter (1) possible derogatory
allusion to Ford as a merchant (2) ill-smelling   283 aggravate his
style i.e., add to his title   286 Epicurean i.e., sensual   293-94 stand
under the adoption of abominable terms submit to being called
horrible names

that does me this wrong. Terms! Names! Amaimon   295
sounds well; Lucifer, well; Barbason,° well; yet
they are devils' additions,° the names of fiends. But
Cuckold! Wittol!°—Cuckold! The devil himself
hath not such a name. Page is an ass, a secure° ass.
He will trust his wife; he will not be jealous. I will   300
rather trust a Fleming with my butter, Parson Hugh
the Welshman with my cheese, an Irishman with
my aqua vitae° bottle, or a thief to walk my ambling gelding, than my wife with herself. Then she
plots, then she ruminates, then she devises. And   305
what they think in their hearts they may effect;
they will break their hearts but they will effect.
God be praised for my jealousy. Eleven o'clock the
hour. I will prevent this, detect my wife, be revenged on Falstaff, and laugh at Page. I will about   310
it; better three hours too soon than a minute too
late. Fie, fie, fie! Cuckold! Cuckold! Cuckold! *Exit.*

Scene III. [*A field near Windsor.*]

Enter [Doctor] Caius [and] Rugby.

Caius. Jack Rugby!

Rugby. Sir?

Caius. Vat is de clock, Jack?

Rugby. 'Tis past the hour, sir, that Sir Hugh promised
to meet.   5

Caius. By gar, he has save his soul dat he is no come.
He has pray his Pible vell dat he is no come. By
gar, Jack Rugby, he is dead already if he be come.

295–96 Amaimon . . . Lucifer . . . Barbason (names of devils)
297 additions titles 298 Wittol contented cuckold 299 secure
confident 303 aqua vitae i.e., spirits (brandy, whiskey, etc.)

Rugby. He is wise, sir. He knew your worship would
10   kill him if he came.

Caius. By gar, de herring is no dead so as I vill kill
  him. Take your rapier, Jack. I vill tell you how I
  vill kill him.

Rugby. Alas, sir, I cannot fence.

15 *Caius.* Villainy, take your rapier.

Rugby. Forbear; here's company.

  [*Enter*] *Page, Shallow, Slender,* [*and*] *Host.*

Host. Bless thee, bully doctor.

Shallow. Save you, Master Doctor Caius.

Page. Now, good Master Doctor.

20 *Slender.* Give you good morrow, sir.

Caius. Vat be all you, one, two, tree, four, come for?

Host. To see thee fight, to see thee foin,° to see thee
  traverse;° to see thee here, to see thee there; to
  see thee pass thy punto, thy stock, thy reverse, thy
25   distance, thy montant.° Is he dead, my Ethiopian?°
  Is he dead, my Francisco?° Ha, bully? What says
  my Aesculapius?° My Galen?° My heart of elder?°
  Ha, is he dead, bully stale?° Is he dead?

Caius. By gar, he is de coward Jack-priest of de vorld.
30   He is not show his face.

Host. Thou art a Castilian King-Urinal!° Hector of
  Greece,° my boy!

II.iii.22 **foin** thrust   23 **traverse** move back and forth   24–25 **pass
thy punto . . . thy montant** (in fencing: *punto,* to strike a blow with
the point of the sword; *stock* thrust; *reverse* backhand stroke; *distance* keeping the proper space between combatants; *montant* upward thrust)   25 **Ethiopian** i.e., dark-bearded or dark complexioned
person   26 **Francisco** i.e., Frenchman   27 **Aesculapius** god of medicine   27 **Galen** Greek physician   27 **heart of elder** i.e., having a
soft pith, coward   28 **stale** (slang term for a physician, from diag-
nosing through urine analysis)   31 **Castilian King-Urinal** i.e., King
of doctors (derogatory allusion to Philip II of Spain)   31–32 **Hector
of Greece** i.e., brave warrior

Caius. I pray you bear vitness dat me have stay six or
seven, two, tree hours for him, and he is no come.

Shallow. He is the wiser man, Master Doctor. He is a   35
curer of souls, and you a curer of bodies. If you
should fight, you go against the hair of your professions. Is it not true, Master Page?

Page. Master Shallow, you have yourself been a great
fighter, though now a man of peace.   40

Shallow. Bodykins,° Master Page, though I now be
old and of the peace, if I see a sword out, my finger
itches to make one.° Though we are justices and
doctors and churchmen, Master Page, we have
some salt° of our youth in us. We are the sons of   45
women, Master Page.

Page. 'Tis true, Master Shallow.

Shallow. It will be found so, Master Page. Master
Doctor Caius, I am come to fetch you home. I am
sworn of the peace. You have showed yourself a   50
wise physician, and Sir Hugh hath shown himself
a wise and patient churchman. You must go with
me, Master Doctor.

Host. Pardon, Guest-Justice.—A word. Monsieur
Mock-water.°   55

Caius. Mock-vater? Vat is dat?

Host. Mock-water, in our English tongue, is valor,
bully.

Caius. By gar, den, I have as much mock-vater as de
Englishman.—Scurvy jack-dog priest! By gar, me   60
vill cut his ears.

Host. He will clapperclaw° thee tightly, bully.

Caius. Clapper-de-claw? Vat is dat?

41 **Bodykins** God's little body (an oath)   43 **make one** join in
45 **salt** liveliness   55 **Mock-water** i.e., physician (precise meaning
unclear; possible corruption of muck-water or make-water, with an
allusion to urine analysis)   62 **clapperclaw** thrash

Host. That is, he will make thee amends.

65 *Caius*. By gar, me do look he shall clapper-de-claw
me; for, by gar, me vill have it.

Host. And I will provoke him to't, or let him wag.

Caius. Me tank you for dat.

Host. And moreover, bully—But first, Master Guest,
70   and Master Page, and eke Cavaliero Slender [*aside
to them*] go you through the town to Frogmore.°

Page. Sir Hugh is there, is he?

Host. He is there. See what humor he is in. And I will
bring the doctor about by the fields. Will it do well?

75 *Shallow*. We will do it.

Page, Shallow, and Slender. Adieu, good Master Doctor.   [*Exeunt Page, Shallow, and Slender*.]

Caius. By gar, me vill kill de priest, for he speak for
a jackanape to Anne Page.

80 *Host*. Let him die. Sheathe thy impatience; throw cold
water on thy choler. Go about the fields with me
through Frogmore. I will bring thee where Mistress
Anne Page is, at a farmhouse a-feasting; and thou
shalt woo her. Cried game;° said I well?

85 *Caius*. By gar, me dank you vor dat. By gar, I love
you; and I shall procure-a you de good guest: de
earl, de knight, de lords, de gentlemen, my patients.

Host. For the which I will be thy adversary toward
Anne Page. Said I well?

90 *Caius*. By gar, 'tis good; vell said.

Host. Let us wag then.

Caius. Come at my heels, Jack Rugby.   *Exeunt*.

71 **Frogmore** (village southeast of Windsor; Caius had been waiting
on the north side of the town)   84 **Cried game** (a puzzling expression, possibly from Elizabethan sporting slang, conjecturally meaning the game is under way)

ACT III

Scene I. [*A field near Frogmore.*]

Enter Evans [and] Simple. [Evans is in doublet and hose and carries a sword. Simple carries Evans' gown and a book.]

Evans. I pray you now, good Master Slender's servingman, and friend Simple by your name, which
way have you looked for Master Caius, that calls
himself Doctor of Physic?

Simple. Marry, sir, the pittie-ward,° the park-ward,°   *5*
every way; Old Windsor° way, and every way but
the town way.

Evans. I most fehemently desire you, you will also
look that way.

Simple. I will, sir.   [*Exit.*]   *10*

Evans. Pless my soul, how full of cholers° I am, and
trempling of mind. I shall be glad if he have deceived me.—How melancholies I am.—I will knog
his urinals° about his knave's costard° when I have
goot opportunities for the 'ork. Pless my soul!   *15*

III.i.5 **the pittie-ward** i.e., towards Windsor Little Park   5 **the park-
ward** i.e., towards Windsor Great Park   6 **Old Windsor** a village
south of Frogmore   11 **cholers** i.e., choler, anger   13–14 **knog his
urinals** i.e., knot his testicles   14 **costard** i.e., head (literally, a type
of large apple)

85

[*Sings.*] To shallow rivers, to whose falls
    Melodious birds sings madrigals;
    There will we make our peds of roses,
    And a thousand fragrant posies.°
20   To shallow—

Mercy on me, I have a great dispositions to cry.

[*Sings.*] Melodious birds sing madrigals—
    When as I sat in Pabylon°—
    And a thousand vagram° posies.
25   To shallow, etc.

[*Enter Simple.*]

Simple. Yonder he is coming, this way, Sir Hugh.

Evans. He's welcome.

[*Sings.*] To shallow rivers, to whose falls—

Heaven prosper the right! What weapons is he?

30 *Simple.* No weapons, sir. There comes my master,
Master Shallow, and another gentleman, from Frogmore, over the stile, this way.

Evans. Pray you, give me my gown—or else keep it
in your arms.   [*Takes the book and reads.*]

[*Enter*] Page, Shallow, [*and*] Slender.

35 *Shallow.* How now, Master Parson. Good morrow,
good Sir Hugh. Keep a gamester from the dice, and
a good student from his book, and it is wonderful.

Slender. [*Aside*] Ah, sweet Anne Page!

Page. Save you, good Sir Hugh.

40 *Evans.* Pless you from His mercy sake, all of you.

Shallow. What, the sword and the word?° Do you
study them both, Master Parson?

16–19 **To shallow rivers . . . fragrant posies** (garbled lines from
Marlowe's "The Passionate Shepherd to his Love")   23 **When as I
sat in Pabylon** (from Psalm 137)   24 **vagram** i.e., fragrant   41 **word**
i.e., the Bible

Page. And youthful still—in your doublet and hose this raw rheumatic day.

Evans. There is reasons and causes for it.   45

Page. We are come to you to do a good office, Master Parson.

Evans. Fery well; what is it?

Page. Yonder is a most reverend gentleman who, be-like having received wrong by some person, is at   50
most odds with his own gravity and patience that ever you saw.

Shallow. I have lived fourscore years and upward; I never heard a man of his place, gravity, and learn-ing so wide of his own respect.°   55

Evans. What is he?

Page. I think you know him: Master Doctor Caius, the renowned French physician.

Evans. Got's will, and his passion of my heart! I had as lief you would tell me of a mess of porridge.   60

Page. Why?

Evans. He has no more knowledge in Hibocrates° and Galen—and he is a knave besides, a cowardly knave as you would desires to be acquainted withal.

Page. I warrant you, he's the man should fight with   65
him.

Slender. [*Aside*] O sweet Anne Page!

Shallow. It appears so by his weapons.

[*Enter*] *Host, Caius,* [*and*] *Rugby.*

Keep them asunder; here comes Doctor Caius.

Page. Nay, good Master Parson, keep in your weapon.   70

Shallow. So do you, good Master Doctor.

55 **wide of his own respect** indifferent to his reputation   62 **Hibo-crates** i.e., Hippocrates (fifth century B.C. Greek physician)

Host. Disarm them, and let them question.° Let them
keep their limbs whole and hack our English.

Caius. I pray you let-a me speak a word with your ear.
75   Verefore vill you not meet-a me?

Evans. [*Aside to Caius*] Pray you, use your patience.
[*Aloud*] In good time.

Caius. By gar, you are de coward, de Jack dog, John
ape.

80   *Evans.* [*Aside to Caius*] Pray you, let us not be laugh-
ing-stogs° to other men's humors. I desire you in
friendship, and I will one way or other make you
amends. [*Aloud*] I will· knog your urinals about
your knave's cogscomb for missing your meetings
85   and appointments.

Caius. Diable! Jack Rugby, mine Host de Jarteer,
have I not stay for him to kill him? Have I not, at
de place I did appoint?

Evans. As I am a Christians soul, now look you, this
90   is the place appointed. I'll be judgment by mine
Host of the Garter.

Host. Peace, I say, Gallia and Gaul,° French and
Welsh, soul-curer and body-curer.

Caius. Ay, dat is very good, excellent.

95   *Host.* Peace, I say. Hear mine Host of the Garter. Am
I politic? Am I subtle? Am I a Machiavel?° Shall
I lose my doctor? No; he gives me the potions and
the motions.° Shall I lose my parson, my priest, my
Sir Hugh? No; he gives me the proverbs and the
100 no-verbs. Give me thy hand, terrestrial; so. Give
me thy hand, celestial; so. Boys of art,° I have deceived you both; I have directed you to wrong

72 **question** i.e., dispute verbally   80–81 **laughing-stogs** i.e., laughing
stocks   92 **Gallia and Gaul** Wales and France   96 a **Machiavel** i.e.,
an intriguer (from Niccolò Machiavelli, regarded by the Elizabethans
as the archintriguer)   98 **motions** bowel movements   101 **art** learning

places. Your hearts are mighty, your skins are
whole, and let burnt sack be the issue.° Come, lay
their swords to pawn. Follow me, lad of peace; fol-   *105*
low, follow, follow.

Shallow. Trust me, a mad Host.—Follow, gentlemen,
follow.

Slender. [*Aside*] O sweet Anne Page!
            [*Exeunt Shallow, Slender, Page, and Host.*]

Caius. Ha, do I perceive dat? Have you make-a de   *110*
sot° of us, ha, ha?

Evans. This is well! He has made us his vlouting-
stog.° I desire you that we may be friends, and let
us knog our prains together to be revenge on this
same scall,° scurvy, cogging companion,° the Host   *115*
of the Garter.

Caius. By gar, with all my heart. He promise to bring
me where is Anne Page. By gar, he deceive me too.

Evans. Well, I will smite his noddles. Pray you follow.
                                    [*Exeunt.*]

Scene II. [*Windsor. A street.*]

[*Enter*] *Mistress Page* [*and*] *Robin.*

Mrs. Page. Nay, keep your way, little gallant. You
were wont to be a follower, but now you are a
leader. Whether° had you rather lead mine eyes,
or eye your master's heels?

---

104 **issue** conclusion   111 **sot** fool   112–13 **vlouting-stog** i.e., flout-
ing-stock, laughing stock   115 **scall** i.e., scald, scurvy   115 **cogging
companion** cheating rascal   III.ii.3 **Whether** i.e., I wonder whether

5 *Robin.* I had rather, forsooth, go before you like a
man than follow him like a dwarf.

Mrs. Page. O, you are a flattering boy. Now I see
you'll be a courtier.

[*Enter*] *Ford.*

Ford. Well met, Mistress Page. Whither go you?

10 *Mrs. Page.* Truly, sir, to see your wife. Is she at home?

Ford. Ay, and as idle as she may hang together,° for
want of company. I think if your husbands were
dead, you two would marry.

Mrs. Page. Be sure of that—two other husbands.

15 *Ford.* Where had you this pretty weathercock?°

Mrs. Page. I cannot tell what the dickens his name is
my husband had him of. What do you call your
knight's name, sirrah?

Robin. Sir John Falstaff.

20 *Ford.* Sir John Falstaff!

Mrs. Page. He, he; I can never hit on's name. There
is such a league° between my goodman and he. Is
your wife at home indeed?

Ford. Indeed she is.

25 *Mrs. Page.* By your leave, sir. I am sick till I see her.
[*Exeunt Mistress Page and Robin.*]

Ford. Has Page any brains? Hath he any eyes? Hath
he any thinking? Sure, they sleep; he hath no use
of them. Why, this boy will carry a letter twenty
mile as easy as a cannon will shoot pointblank
30 twelve score.° He pieces out° his wife's inclination;
he gives her folly motion° and advantage. And now

11 **as idle as she may hang together** i.e., as idle as she can be without
going to pieces   15 **weathercock** (an allusion to Robin's gaudy
clothes)   22 **league** friendship   30 **twelve score** i.e., at twelve score
paces   30 **pieces out** i.e., assists   31 **motion** prompting

she's going to my wife, and Falstaff's boy with her.
A man may hear this shower sing in the wind. And
Falstaff's boy with her.—Good plots! They are laid,
and our revolted wives share damnation together.   35
Well, I will take him, then torture my wife, pluck
the borrowed veil of modesty from the so-seeming
Mistress Page, divulge Page himself for a secure
and willful Actaeon;° and to these violent proceedings all my neighbors shall cry aim.° [*Clock strikes.*]   40
The clock gives me my cue, and my assurance bids
me search. There I shall find Falstaff. I shall be
rather praised for this than mocked, for it is as
positive as the earth is firm that Falstaff is there. I
will go.   45

> [*Enter*] *Page, Shallow, Slender, Host, Evans,*
>   *Caius, [and Rugby].*

Shallow, Page, &c. Well met, Master Ford.

Ford. Trust me, a good knot.° I have good cheer at
home, and I pray you all go with me.

Shallow. I must excuse myself, Master Ford.

Slender. And so must I, sir. We have appointed to dine   50
with Mistress Anne, and I would not break with
her for more money than I'll speak of.

Shallow. We have lingered about a match between
Anne Page and my cousin Slender, and this day
we shall have our answer.   55

Slender. I hope I have your good will, father Page.

Page. You have, Master Slender. I stand wholly for
you. But my wife, Master Doctor, is for you altogether.

Caius. Ay, be-gar, and de maid is love-a me; my   60
nursh-a Quickly tell me so mush.

Host. What say you to young Master Fenton? He

---

39 **Actaeon** i.e., cuckold   40 **cry aim** i.e., applaud (from archery)
47 **knot** company

capers, he dances, he has eyes of youth, he writes
verses, he speaks holiday,° he smells April and
65 May. He will carry't,° he will carry't; 'tis in his buttons;° he will carry't.

Page. Not by my consent, I promise you. The gentleman is of no having.° He kept company with the
wild Prince and Poins;° he is of too high a region;
70 he knows too much. No, he shall not knit a knot in
his fortunes with the finger of my substance. If he
take her, let him take her simply.° The wealth I
have waits on my consent, and my consent goes
not that way.

75 *Ford.* I beseech you heartily, some of you go home
with me to dinner. Besides your cheer, you shall
have sport. I will show you a monster. Master Doctor, you shall go. So shall you, Master Page, and
you, Sir Hugh.

80 *Shallow.* Well, fare you well. We shall have the freer
wooing at Master Page's.
                    [*Exeunt Shallow and Slender.*]

Caius. Go home, John Rugby. I come anon.
                                    [*Exit Rugby.*]

Host. Farewell, my hearts. I will to my honest knight
Falstaff, and drink canary° with him.   [*Exit.*]

85 *Ford* [*Aside*] I think I shall drink in pipe-wine° first
with him; I'll make him dance.—Will you go,
gentles?

All. Have with you to see this monster.   *Exeunt.*

---

64 **speaks holiday** uses choice language   65 **carry't** win   65–66 **'tis
in his buttons** i.e., he has it in him   68 **having** property   69 **wild
Prince and Poins** (Prince Hal and Poins, characters from *1 & 2
Henry IV*)   72 **simply** by herself without any dowry   84 **canary** a
sweet wine   85 **pipe-wine** wine from the cask; involved punning on
pipe (1) a cask (2) a musical instrument, and on *canary* (1) a type of
wine (2) a lively dance

Scene III. [*A room in Ford's house.*]

Enter Mistress Ford [and] Mistress Page.

Mrs. Ford. What, John! What, Robert!

Mrs. Page. Quickly, quickly. Is the buck basket°—

Mrs. Ford. I warrant. What, Robert, I say!

[*Enter*] *Servants* [*with a basket*].

Mrs. Page. Come, come, come!

Mrs. Ford. Here, set it down.   5

Mrs. Page. Give your men the charge. We must be
    brief.

Mrs. Ford. Marry, as I told you before, John and
    Robert, be ready here hard by in the brewhouse;
    and when I suddenly call you, come forth, and   10
    without any pause or staggering, take this basket on
    your shoulders. That done, trudge with it in all
    haste, and carry it among the whitsters° in Datchet
    Mead,° and there empty it in the muddy ditch close
    by the Thames side.   15

Mrs. Page. You will do it?

Mrs. Ford. I ha' told them over and over; they lack
    no direction. Begone, and come when you are
    called.   [*Exeunt Servants.*]

[*Enter*] *Robin.*

Mrs. Page. Here comes little Robin.   20

III.iii.2 **buck basket** basket for soiled linen   13 **whitsters** bleachers
of linen   13–14 **Datchet Mead** (meadow between Windsor Little
Park and the Thames)

Mrs. Ford. How now, my eyas-musket.° What news
with you?

Robin. My master, Sir John, is come in at your back
door, Mistress Ford, and requests your company.

25 *Mrs. Page.* You little Jack-a-Lent,° have you been
true to us?

Robin. Ay, I'll be sworn. My master knows not of
your being here, and hath threat'ned to put me into
everlasting liberty if I tell you of it; for he swears
30 he'll turn me away.

Mrs. Page. Thou'rt a good boy. This secrecy of thine
shall be a tailor to thee and shall make thee a new
doublet and hose. I'll go hide me.

Mrs. Ford. Do so. [*To Robin*] Go tell thy master I
35 am alone. [*Exit Robin.*] Mistress Page, remember
you your cue.

Mrs. Page. I warrant thee; if I do not act it, hiss me.
[*Exit.*]

Mrs. Ford. Go to, then. We'll use this unwholesome
humidity, this gross wat'ry pumpion.° We'll teach
40 him to know turtles from jays.°

[Enter] Falstaff.

Falstaff. "Have I caught thee, my heavenly jewel?"°
Why, now let me die, for I have lived long enough.
This is the period° of my ambition. O this blessed
hour!

45 *Mrs. Ford.* O sweet Sir John!

Falstaff. Mistress Ford, I cannot cog,° I cannot prate,
Mistress Ford. Now shall I sin in my wish: I would

---

21 **eyas-musket** young male sparrow hawk; i.e., a sprightly lad
25 **Jack-a-Lent** (an allusion to Robin's gaudy clothes, from the
decorated puppet used in Lenten games)   39 **pumpion** pumpkin
40 **turtles from jays** i.e., faithful women from unfaithful ones
41 **"Have I . . . heavenly jewel?"** (from Sir Philip Sidney's collection
of sonnets, *Astrophel and Stella*)   43 **period** end   46 **cog** fawn

thy husband were dead. I'll speak it before the best
lord; I would make thee my lady.

Mrs. Ford. I your lady, Sir John? Alas, I should be a   50
pitiful lady.

Falstaff. Let the court of France show me such
another. I see how thine eye would emulate the
diamond. Thou hast the right arched beauty of the
brow that becomes the ship-tire,° the tire-valiant,°   55
or any tire of Venetian admittance.°

Mrs. Ford. A plain kerchief, Sir John. My brows become nothing else, nor that well neither.

Falstaff. Thou art a tyrant to say so. Thou wouldst
make an absolute° courtier, and the firm fixture of   60
thy foot would give an excellent motion to thy gait
in a semicircled farthingale.° I see what thou wert
if Fortune, thy foe, were—not Nature—thy friend.°
Come, thou canst not hide it.

Mrs. Ford. Believe me, there's no such thing in me.   65

Falstaff. What made me love thee? Let that persuade
thee there's something extraordinary in thee. Come,
I cannot cog and say thou art this and that, like a
many of these lisping hawthorn buds° that come
like women in men's apparel and smell like Buck-   70
lersbury° in simple-time.° I cannot. But I love
thee, none but thee; and thou deserv'st it.

Mrs. Ford. Do not betray me, sir. I fear you love
Mistress Page.

Falstaff. Thou mightst as well say I love to walk by   75

55 **ship-tire** headdress shaped like a ship   55 **tire-valiant** fanciful
headdress   56 **tire of Venetian admittance** i.e., Venetian-style headdress   60 **absolute** perfect   62 **semicircled farthingale** half-hooped
petticoat   62–63 **I see . . . friend** i.e., since you are already naturally
pretty, I can imagine what you would look like dressed for the world
of high society if Fortune had not made you a member of the
bourgeois class ("Fortune thy foe" is the title of an Elizabethan
popular ballad)   69 **hawthorn buds** i.e., dandies   70–71 **Bucklers-
bury** (a street in London where herbs were sold)   71 **simple-time** herb-
selling season

the Counter-gate,° which is as hateful to me as the
reek of a limekiln.

Mrs. Ford. Well, heaven knows how I love you, and
you shall one day find it.

80 *Falstaff.* Keep in that mind; I'll deserve it.

Mrs. Ford. Nay, I must tell you, so you do, or else I
could not be in that mind.

[*Enter Robin.*]

Robin. Mistress Ford, Mistress Ford! Here's Mistress
Page at the door—sweating and blowing and look-
85   ing wildly, and would needs speak with you
presently.°

Falstaff. She shall not see me; I will ensconce me behind the arras.°

· *Mrs. Ford.* Pray you, do so; she's a very tattling
90   woman.   [*Falstaff hides.*]

[*Enter Mistress Page.*]

What's the matter? How now!

Mrs. Page. O Mistress Ford, what have you done?
You're shamed, y'are overthrown, y'are undone forever!

95 *Mrs. Ford.* What's the matter, good Mistress Page?

Mrs. Page. O well-a-day, Mistress Ford! Having an
honest man to your husband, to give him such
cause of suspicion!

Mrs. Ford. What cause of suspicion?

100 *Mrs. Page.* What cause of suspicion! Out upon you;
how am I mistook in you!

Mrs. Ford. Why, alas, what's the matter?

Mrs. Page. Your husband's coming hither, woman,

76 **Counter-gate** (gate of the debtors' prison, known as an area of
foul odors)   86 **presently** immediately   88 **arras** hanging tapestry
used for wall decoration

with all the officers in Windsor, to search for a
gentleman that he says is here now in the house— *105*
by your consent—to take an ill advantage of his
absence. You are undone.

Mrs. Ford. 'Tis not so, I hope.

Mrs. Page. Pray heaven it be not so that you have
such a man here! But 'tis most certain your hus- *110*
band's coming, with half Windsor at his heels, to
search for such a one. I come before to tell you.
If you know yourself clear,° why, I am glad of it;
but if you have a friend° here, convey, convey him
out. Be not amazed; call all your senses to you; *115*
defend your reputation, or bid farewell to your
good life forever.

Mrs. Ford. What shall I do? There is a gentleman, my
dear friend; and I fear not mine own shame so
much as his peril. I had rather than a thousand *120*
pound he were out of the house.

Mrs. Page. For shame! Never stand° "you had rather"
and "you had rather." Your husband's here at
hand; bethink you of some conveyance. In the
house you cannot hide him.—O, how have you de- *125*
ceived me!—Look, here is a basket. If he be of
any reasonable stature, he may creep in here; and
throw foul linen upon him, as if it were going to
bucking.° Or—it is whiting time°—send him by
your two men to Datchet Mead. *130*

Mrs. Ford. He's too big to go in there. What shall I
do?

Falstaff. [*Rushing forward*] Let me see't, let me see't.
O let me see't! I'll in, I'll in! Follow your friend's
counsel. I'll in! *135*

Mrs. Page. What, Sir John Falstaff! [*Aside to Falstaff*]
Are these your letters, knight?

---

113 **clear** innocent   114 **friend** paramour   122 **stand** lose time over
129 **bucking** washing   129 **whiting time** bleaching time

Falstaff [*Aside to Mistress Page*] I love thee. Help me
    away.—Let me creep in here. I'll never—
[*Climbs into the basket; they cover him with foul
                                        linen.*]

140 *Mrs. Page* [*To Robin*] Help to cover your master, boy.
    Call your men, Mistress Ford. [*Aside to Falstaff*]
    You dissembling knight!

    Mrs. Ford. What, John! Robert! John!   [*Exit Robin.*]

                    [*Enter Servants.*]

    Go, take up these clothes here quickly. Where's
145 the cowlstaff?° Look how you drumble!° Carry
    them to the laundress in Datchet Mead. Quickly,
    come!

            [*Enter*] Ford, Page, Caius, [*and*] Evans.

    Ford. [*To his companions*] Pray you, come near. If I
    suspect without cause, why then make sport at me;
150 then let me be your jest; I deserve it. How now,
    who goes here? Whither bear you this?

    Servants. To the laundress, forsooth.

    Mrs. Ford. Why, what have you to do whither they
    bear it? You were best meddle with buck-washing!

155 *Ford.* Buck? I would I could wash myself of the
    buck!° Buck, buck, buck! Ay, buck; I warrant you,
    buck—and of the season° too, it shall appear.
    [*Exeunt Servants with the basket.*] Gentlemen, I
    have dreamed tonight.° I'll tell you my dream.
160 Here, here, here be my keys. Ascend my chambers;
    search, seek, find out. I'll warrant we'll unkennel°
    the fox. Let me stop this way first. [*Locks the door.*]
    So, now uncope.°

    Page. Good Master Ford, be contented. You wrong
165 yourself too much.

    145 cowlstaff pole for carrying a basket between two persons
    145 drumble dawdle   156 buck i.e., horned beast, cuckold   157 of
    the season in season   159 tonight last night   161 unkennel dislodge
    163 uncope i.e., flush him out (hunting)

Ford. True, Master Page. Up, gentlemen; you shall
see sport anon. Follow me, gentlemen.   [*Exit.*]

Evans. This is fery fantastical humors and jealousies.

Caius. By gar, 'tis no de fashion of France; it is not
jealous in France.   170

Page. Nay, follow him, gentlemen. See the issue of his
search.   [*Exeunt Page, Caius, and Evans.*]

Mrs. Page. Is there not a double excellency in this?

Mrs. Ford. I know not which pleases me better—that
my husband is deceived, or Sir John.   175

Mrs. Page. What a taking° was he in when your husband asked who was in the basket!

Mrs. Ford. I am half afraid he will have need of washing; so throwing him into the water will do him a
benefit.   180

Mrs. Page. Hang him, dishonest rascal! I would all of
the same strain were in the same distress.

Mrs. Ford. I think my husband hath some special suspicion of Falstaff's being here, for I never saw him
so gross in his jealousy till now.   185

Mrs. Page. I will lay a plot to try that, and we will yet
have more tricks with Falstaff. His dissolute disease
will scarce obey this medicine.

Mrs. Ford. Shall we send that foolish carrion° Mistress Quickly to him, and excuse his throwing into   190
the water, and give him another hope to betray him
to another punishment?

Mrs. Page. We will *do* it. Let him be sent for tomorrow, eight o'clock, to have amends.

        [*Enter Ford, Page, Caius, and Evans.*]

Ford. I cannot find him. May be the knave bragged   195
of that he could not compass.

176 **taking** fright   189 **carrion** i.e., body of corrupting flesh

Mrs. Page [*Aside to Mrs. Ford*] Heard you that?

Mrs. Ford. You use me well, Master Ford, do you?

Ford. Ay, I do so.

200 *Mrs. Ford.* Heaven make you better than your thoughts!

Ford. Amen.

Mrs. Page. You do yourself mighty wrong, Master Ford.

205 *Ford.* Ay, ay, I must bear it.

Evans. If there be any pody in the house, and in the chambers, and in the coffers, and in the presses,° heaven forgive my sins at the day of judgment!

Caius. Be-gar, nor I too; dere is nobodies.

210 *Page.* Fie, fie, Master Ford, are you not ashamed? What spirit, what devil suggests this imagination? I would not ha' your distemper in this kind for the wealth of Windsor Castle.

Ford. 'Tis my fault,° Master Page. I suffer for it.

215 *Evans.* You suffer for a pad conscience. Your wife is as honest a 'omans as I will desires among five thousand, and five hundred too.

Caius. By gar, I see 'tis an honest woman.

Ford. Well, I promised you a dinner. Come, come,
220 walk in the Park. I pray you pardon me. I will hereafter make known to you why I have done this.— Come, wife; come, Mistress Page—I pray you pardon me. Pray heartily, pardon me.

Page. Let's go in, gentlemen; but, trust me, we'll mock
225 him. I do invite you tomorrow morning to my house to breakfast. After, we'll a-birding° together. I have a fine hawk for the bush.° Shall it be so?

207 **presses** cupboards   214 **fault** i.e., weakness   226 **a-birding** hawking   227 **fine hawk for the bush** (a hawk especially trained to fly at small birds sheltered in bushes)

Ford. Anything.

Evans. If there is one, I shall make two in the company.   230

Caius. If dere be one, or two, I shall make-a de turd.

Ford. Pray you, go, Master Page.

Evans. [*Aside to Caius*] I pray you now, remembrance tomorrow on the lousy knave, mine Host.

Caius. [*Aside to Evans*] Dat is good, by gar; with all   235
my heart.

Evans. [*Aside to Caius*] A lousy knave, to have his gibes and his mockeries!   *Exeunt.*

Scene IV. [*Before Page's house.*]

Enter Fenton [*and*] *Anne Page.*

Fenton. I see I cannot get thy father's love;
    Therefore no more turn me to him, sweet Nan.

Anne. Alas, how then?

Fenton.   Why, thou must be thyself.
    He doth object I am too great of birth,
    And that my state° being galled with my expense,°   5
    I seek to heal it only by his wealth.
    Besides these, other bars he lays before me:
    My riots past, my wild societies;
    And tells me 'tis a thing impossible
    I should love thee but as a property.   10

Anne. May be he tells you true.

Fenton. No, heaven so speed° me in my time to come!

III.iv.5 **state** estate   5 **galled with my expense** i.e., squandered away
12 **speed** prosper

Albeit I will confess thy father's wealth
Was the first motive that I wooed thee, Anne.
15 Yet, wooing thee, I found thee of more value
Than stamps° in gold or sums in sealèd bags;
And 'tis the very riches of thyself
That now I aim at.

Anne.   Gentle Master Fenton,
Yet seek my father's love; still seek it, sir.
20 If opportunity and humblest suit
Cannot attain it, why, then—

[*Enter*] *Shallow, Slender,* [*and Mistress*] *Quickly.*

Hark you hither.
[*Takes Fenton aside.*]

Shallow. Break their talk, Mistress Quickly. My kinsman shall speak for himself.

Slender. I'll make a shaft or a bolt on't.° 'Slid,° 'tis
25 but venturing.

Shallow. Be not dismayed.

Slender. No, she shall not dismay me. I care not for
that, but that I am afeard.

Quickly. [*To Anne*] Hark ye, Master Slender would
30 speak a word with you.

Anne. I come to him. [*Aside*] This is my father's
choice.
O, what a world of vile ill-favored faults
Looks handsome in three hundred pounds a year.

Quickly. And how does good Master Fenton? Pray
35 you, a word with you.   [*They converse together*.]

Shallow. She's coming; to her, coz. O boy, thou hadst
a father!

Slender. I had a father, Mistress Anne; my uncle can
tell you good jests of him. Pray you, uncle, tell Mis-

16 stamps coins   24 make a shaft or a bolt on't i.e., do it one way
or another (literally, use a slender arrow or a thick one)   24 'Slid
God's eyelid (mild oath)

tress Anne the jest how my father stole two geese   40
out of a pen, good uncle.

Shallow. Mistress Anne, my cousin° loves you.

Slender. Ay, that I do, as well as I love any woman in
Gloucestershire.

Shallow. He will maintain you like a gentlewoman.   45

Slender. Ay, that I will, come cut and long-tail, under
the degree of a squire.°

Shallow. He will make you a hundred and fifty pounds
jointure.

Anne. Good Master Shallow, let him woo for himself.   50

Shallow. Marry, I thank you for it; I thank you for
that good comfort. She calls you, coz. I'll leave you.

Anne. Now, Master Slender—

Slender. Now, good Mistress Anne—

Anne. What is your will?   55

Slender. My will? 'Od's heartlings,° that's a pretty jest
indeed! I ne'er made my will yet, I thank God. I am
not such a sickly creature, I give heaven praise.

Anne. I mean, Master Slender, what would you with
me?   60

Slender. Truly, for mine own part, I would little or
nothing with you. Your father and my uncle have
made motions.° If it be my luck, so; if not, happy
man be his dole.° They can tell you how things go
better than I can. You may ask your father; here   65
he comes.

---

42 **cousin** kinsman   46–47 **cut . . . a squire** i.e., all kinds so long as
they are not too high-ranking   56 **'Od's heartlings** God's little heart
(an oath)   63 **motions** suggestions   63–64 **happy man be his dole**
happiness be his portion

[Enter] Page [and] Mistress Page.

Page. Now, Master Slender. Love him, daughter
    Anne.—
Why, how now! What does Master Fenton here?
You wrong me, sir, thus still to haunt my house.
70   I told you, sir, my daughter is disposed of.

Fenton. Nay, Master Page, be not impatient.

Mrs. Page. Good Master Fenton, come not to my
    child.

Page. She is no match for you.

Fenton. Sir, will you hear me?

Page.   No, good Master Fenton.
75   Come, Master Shallow; come, son Slender, in.
Knowing my mind, you wrong me, Master Fenton.
    [Page, Shallow, and Slender enter the house.]

Quickly. Speak to Mistress Page.

Fenton. Good Mistress Page, for that I love your
    daughter
In such a righteous fashion as I do,
80   Perforce, against all checks,° rebukes, and manners,
I must advance the colors° of my love
And not retire. Let me have your good will.

Anne. Good mother, do not marry me to yond fool.

Mrs. Page. I mean it not. I seek you a better husband.

85 *Quickly.* *[To Anne]* That's my master, Master Doctor.

Anne. Alas, I had rather be set quick° i' th' earth,
And bowled to death with turnips.

Mrs. Page. Come, trouble not yourself. Good Master
    Fenton,
I will not be your friend, nor enemy.
90   My daughter will I question how she loves you,
And as I find her, so am I affected.

80 **checks** reproofs   81 **colors** banners   86 **quick** living

Till then, farewell, sir. She must needs go in.
Her father will be angry.
          [*Mistress Page and Anne enter the house.*]

Fenton. Farewell, gentle mistress. Farewell, Nan.

Quickly. This is my doing now. "Nay," said I, "will   *95*
you cast away your child on a fool, and a physician?
Look on Master Fenton." This is my doing.

Fenton. I thank thee, and I pray thee, once° tonight
Give my sweet Nan this ring. There's for thy pains.
          [*Gives the ring and some money to Quickly
                        and then departs.*]

Quickly. Now heaven send thee good fortune! A kind   *100*
heart he hath. A woman would run through fire
and water for such a kind heart. But yet, I would
my master had Mistress Anne; or I would Master
Slender had her; or, in sooth, I would Master Fenton had her. I will do what I can for them all three,   *105*
for so I have promised, and I'll be as good as my
word—but speciously° for Master Fenton. Well, I
must of another errand to Sir John Falstaff from
my two mistresses. What a beast am I to slack it!°
                                        Exit.

---

98 once sometime   107 speciously i.e., especially   109 slack it be
remiss about it

Scene V. [*Falstaff's room in the Garter Inn.*]

Enter Falstaff.

Falstaff. Bardolph, I say!

[*Enter*] *Bardolph.*

Bardolph. Here, sir.

Falstaff. Go fetch me a quart of sack—put a toast°
in't. [*Exit Bardolph.*] Have I lived to be carried in
5 a basket like a barrow of butcher's offal, and to be
thrown in the Thames? Well, if I be served such
another trick, I'll have my brains ta'en out and
buttered, and give them to a dog for a New-Year's
gift. The rogues slighted° me into the river with as
10 little remorse as they would have drowned a blind
bitch's puppies, fifteen i' th' litter. And you may
know by my size that I have a kind of alacrity in
sinking; if the bottom were as deep as hell, I should
down. I had been drowned but that the shore was
15 shelvy and shallow—a death that I abhor, for the
water swells a man; and what a thing should I have
been when I had been swelled. I should have been
a mountain of mummy.°

[*Enter Bardolph with two cups of wine.*]

Bardolph. Here's Mistress Quickly, sir, to speak with
20 you.

Falstaff. Come, let me pour in some sack to the
Thames water, for my belly's as cold as if I had
swallowed snowballs for pills to cool the reins.° Call
her in.

III.v.3 **a toast** a piece of toast   9 **slighted** tossed contemptuously
18 **mummy** dead flesh   23 **reins** kidneys

Bardolph. Come in, woman.   25

[*Enter Mistress*] *Quickly.*

Quickly. By your leave; I cry you mercy.° Give your
worship good morrow.

Falstaff. Take away these chalices.° Go brew me a
pottle of sack finely.

Bardolph. With eggs, sir?   30

Falstaff. Simple of itself; I'll no pullet-sperm in my
brewage. [*Exit Bardolph.*] How now.

Quickly. Marry, sir, I come to your worship from
Mistress Ford.

Falstaff. Mistress Ford? I have had ford enough; I   35
was thrown into the ford; I have my belly full of
ford.

Quickly. Alas the day, good heart, that was not her
fault. She does so take on with her men; they mistook their erection.°   40

Falstaff. So did I mine, to build upon a foolish
woman's promise.

Quickly. Well, she laments, sir, for it that it would
yearn° your heart to see it. Her husband goes this
morning a-birding. She desires you once more to   45
come to her between eight and nine. I must carry
her word quickly. She'll make you amends, I warrant you.

Falstaff. Well, I will visit her. Tell her so, and bid
her think what a man is. Let her consider his frailty,   50
and then judge of my merit.

Quickly. I will tell her.

Falstaff. Do so.—Between nine and ten, sayest thou?

Quickly. Eight and nine, sir.

26 **cry you mercy** beg your pardon   28 **chalices** drinking cups
40 **erection** i.e., direction   44 **yearn** grieve

55 *Falstaff.* Well, begone. I will not miss her.

Quickly. Peace be with you, sir.

> [*Exit, leaving the door open.*]

Falstaff. I marvel I hear not of Master Brooke. He
sent me word to stay within. I like his money well.
—O, here he comes.

> [*Enter*] *Ford.*

60 *Ford.* Bless you, sir.

Falstaff. Now, Master Brooke, you come to know
what hath passed between me and Ford's wife?

Ford. That, indeed, Sir John, is my business.

Falstaff. Master Brooke, I will not lie to you. I was at
65 her house the hour she appointed me.

Ford. And sped you,° sir?

Falstaff. Very ill-favoredly, Master Brooke.

Ford. How so, sir? Did she change her determination?

Falstaff. No, Master Brooke, but the peaking cornuto°
70 her husband, Master Brooke, dwelling in a continual 'larum of jealousy, comes me in the instant
of our encounter, after we had embraced, kissed,
protested, and, as it were, spoke the prologue of
our comedy; and at his heels a rabble° of his com-
75 panions, thither provoked and instigated by his distemper,° and, forsooth, to search his house for his
wife's love.

Ford. What, while you were there?

Falstaff. While I was there.

80 *Ford.* And did he search for you, and could not find
you?

---

66 **sped you** did you succeed   69 **peaking cornuto** prying cuckold
(with a pun on "peak" as the tip of the horn)   74 **rabble** pack
75–76 **distemper** ill temper

Falstaff. You shall hear. As good luck would have it,
comes in one Mistress Page, gives intelligence of
Ford's approach; and in her invention and Ford's
wife's distraction, they conveyed me into a buck   85
basket.

Ford. A buck basket?

Falstaff. By the Lord, a buck basket! Rammed me in
with foul shirts and smocks, socks, foul stockings,
greasy napkins, that,° Master Brooke, there was   90
the rankest compound of villainous smell that ever
offended nostril.

Ford. And how long lay you there?

Falstaff. Nay, you shall hear, Master Brooke, what I
have suffered to bring this woman to evil for your   95
good. Being thus crammed in the basket, a couple
of Ford's knaves, his hinds,° were called forth by
their mistress to carry me in the name of foul
clothes to Datchet Lane. They took me on their
shoulders; met the jealous knave their master in   100
the door, who asked them once or twice what they
had in their basket. I quaked for fear lest the lunatic knave would have searched it; but Fate, ordain-
ing he should be a cuckold, held his hand. Well,
on went he for a search, and away went I for foul   105
clothes. But mark the sequel, Master Brooke. I suffered the pangs of three several deaths: first, an
intolerable fright to be detected with° a jealous
rotten bellwether;° next, to be compassed like a
good bilbo° in the circumference of a peck, hilt to   110
point, heel to head; and then, to be stopped in,
like a strong distillation, with stinking clothes that
fretted° in their own grease. Think of that, a man
of my kidney°—think of that—that am as subject

90 that so that   97 hinds servants   108 with by   109 bellwether
ram with a bell around his neck who led the flock (with an implied
reference to a horned beast or cuckold)   109–10 compassed like a
good bilbo bent around like a well-tempered sword blade (a test for
ascertaining the quality of a good blade)   113 fretted decayed
114 kidney temperament

115 to heat as butter; a man of continual dissolution°
and thaw. It was a miracle to 'scape suffocation.
And in the height of this bath, when I was more
than half stewed in grease, like a Dutch dish, to be
thrown into the Thames, and cooled, glowing hot,
120 in that surge, like a horseshoe. Think of that—hissing hot—think of that, Master Brooke!

Ford. In good sadness,° sir, I am sorry that for my
sake you have suffered all this. My suit then is desperate. You'll undertake her no more?

125 *Falstaff.* Master Brooke, I will be thrown into Etna, as
I have been into Thames, ere I will leave her thus.
Her husband is this morning gone a-birding. I have
received from her another embassy° of meeting.
'Twixt eight and nine is the hour, Master Brooke.

130 *Ford.* 'Tis past eight already, sir.

Falstaff. Is it? I will then address me° to my appointment. Come to me at your convenient leisure, and
you shall know how I speed; and the conclusion
shall be crowned with your enjoying her. Adieu.
135 You shall have her, Master Brooke; Master Brooke,
you shall cuckold Ford.   [*Exit.*]

Ford. Hum! Ha! Is this a vision? Is this a dream? Do
I sleep? Master Ford, awake; awake, Master Ford!
There's a hole made in your best coat, Master
140 Ford. This 'tis to be married; this 'tis to have linen
and buck baskets! Well, I will proclaim myself
what I am. I will now take the lecher; he is at my
house; he cannot 'scape me; 'tis impossible he
should. He cannot creep into a halfpenny purse,
145 nor into a pepperbox. But, lest the devil that guides
him should aid him, I will search impossible places.
Though what I am I cannot avoid, yet to be what
I would not shall not make me tame. If I have
horns to make one mad, let the proverb go with
150 me—I'll be horn-mad.   *Exit.*

115 **dissolution** liquefaction   122 **sadness** seriousness   128 **embassy**
message   131 **address me** i.e., go

ACT IV

Scene I. [*A street.*]

*Enter Mistress Page, [Mistress] Quickly,
[and] William.*

Mrs. Page. Is he at Master Ford's already, think'st
thou?

Quickly. Sure he is by this, or will be presently. But,
truly, he is very courageous° mad about his throwing into the water. Mistress Ford desires you to   5
come suddenly.°

Mrs. Page. I'll be with her by and by.° I'll but bring
my young man here to school. Look where his master comes; 'tis a playing-day, I see.

[Enter] Evans.

How now, Sir Hugh! No school today?   10

Evans. No. Master Slender is let the boys leave to play.

Quickly. Blessing of his heart.

Mrs. Page. Sir Hugh, my husband says my son profits
nothing in the world at his book. I pray you, ask
him some questions in his accidence.°   15

Evans. Come hither, William. Hold up your head;
come.

IV.i.4 **courageous** i.e., outrageous   6 **suddenly** immediately   7 **by
and by** quickly   15 **accidence** i.e., knowledge of grammatical inflections

Mrs. Page. Come on, sirrah; hold up your head; answer your master; be not afraid.

20   *Evans.* William, how many numbers is in nouns?

William. Two.

Quickly. Truly, I thought there had been one number more, because they say, "Od's nouns."°

Evans. Peace your tattlings. What is "fair," William?

25   *William.* "*Pulcher.*"

Quickly. Polecats!° There are fairer things than polecats, sure.

Evans. You are a very simplicity 'oman. I pray you peace. What is "*lapis,*" William?

30   *William.* A stone.

Evans. And what is "a stone," William?

William. A pebble.

Evans. No, it is "*lapis.*" I pray you remember in your prain.

35   *William.* "*Lapis.*"

Evans. That is a good William. What is he, William, that does lend articles?

William. Articles are borrowed of the pronoun, and be thus declined: *Singulariter, nominativo, hic,*
40   *haec, hoc.*

Evans. Nominativo, hig, hag, hog. Pray you, mark: *genitivo, hujus.* Well, what is your accusative case?

William. Accusativo, hinc.

Evans. I pray you, have your remembrance, child:
45   *accusativo, hung, hang, hog.*

---

23 Od's nouns i.e., God's wounds (an oath)   26 Polecats (1) wild-cats (2) prostitutes

Quickly. "Hang-hog"° is Latin for bacon, I warrant
  you.

Evans. Leave your prabbles, 'oman. What is the focative case, William?

William. O—*vocativo, O.*   50

Evans. Remember, William; focative is *caret.*°

Quickly. And that's a good root.

Evans. 'Oman, forbear.

Mrs. Page. Peace.

Evans. What is your genitive case plural, William?   55

William. Genitive case?

Evans. Ay.

William. Genitive—*horum, harum, horum.*

Quickly. Vengeance of Jenny's case!° Fie on her!
  Never name her, child, if she be a whore.   60

Evans. For shame, 'oman.

Quickly. You do ill to teach the child such words. He
  teaches him to hick and to hack,° which they'll do
  fast enough of themselves, and to call "horum."
  Fie upon you!   65

Evans. 'Oman, art thou lunatics? Hast thou no under-
  standings for thy cases and the numbers of the
  genders? Thou art as foolish Christian creatures as
  I would desires.

Mrs. Page. Prithee, hold thy peace.   70

Evans. Show me now, William, some declensions of
  your pronouns.

46 Hang-hog (an allusion to a famous story of the jurist Sir Nicholas
Bacon who told a prisoner named Hog who tried to have his death
sentence commuted on grounds of kindred that "you and I cannot
be of kindred unless you are hanged; for Hog is not Bacon till it be
well hanged")   51 caret is lacking (Latin)   59 case pudendum
(Mistress Quickly associates Latin *horum* with whore, and *harum*
with hare, a slang term for a prostitute)   63 to hick and to hack hic-
cup (?) and go wenching (?; precise meaning unknown, but dissolute-
ness is implied)

William. Forsooth, I have forgot.

Evans. It is *qui, quae, quod.* If you forget your *qui's,*
75   your *quae's,* and your *quod's,*° you must be
preeches.° Go your ways and play; go.

Mrs. Page. He is a better scholar than I thought he
was.

Evans. He is a good sprag° memory. Farewell, Mis-
80   tress Page.

Mrs. Page. Adieu, good Sir Hugh. [*Exit Evans.*] Get
you home, boy. Come, we stay too long.   *Exeunt.*

Scene II. [*A room in Ford's house.*]

Enter Falstaff [*and*] *Mistress Ford.*

Falstaff. Mistress Ford, your sorrow hath eaten up my
sufferance.° I see you are obsequious° in your love,
and I profess requital to a hair's breadth, not only,
Mistress Ford, in the simple office of love, but in
5   all the accoutrement, complement, and ceremony
of it. But are you sure of your husband now?

Mrs. Ford. He's a-birding, sweet Sir John.

Mrs. Page. [*Within*] What ho, gossip° Ford. What ho!

Mrs. Ford. Step into th' chamber, Sir John.
[*Exit Falstaff.*]

[*Enter*] *Mistress Page.*

10   *Mrs. Page.* How now, sweetheart! Who's at home besides yourself?

74–75 qui's, quae's, quod's (Latin *qu* was pronounced k, giving rise
to bawdy puns on *keys* = penises, *case* = pudendum, *cods* = testicles)
76 preeches i.e., breeched, flogged   79 sprag sprack, alert   IV.ii.2
sufferance suffering   2 obsequious devoted   8 gossip friend

Mrs. Ford. Why, none but mine own people.

Mrs. Page. Indeed?

Mrs. Ford. No, certainly. [*Aside to her*] Speak louder.

Mrs. Page. Truly, I am so glad you have nobody here.   15

Mrs. Ford. Why?

Mrs. Page. Why, woman, your husband is in his old
   lunes° again. He so takes on yonder with my husband, so rails against all married mankind, so curses
   all Eve's daughters—of what complexion soever,   20
   and so buffets himself on the forehead, crying,
   "Peer out,° peer out!" that any madness I ever yet
   beheld seemed but tameness, civility, and patience
   to this his distemper he is in now. I am glad the
   fat knight is not here.   25

Mrs. Ford. Why, does he talk of him?

Mrs. Page. Of none but him; and swears he was carried out, the last time he searched for him, in a
   basket; protests to my husband he is now here, and
   hath drawn him and the rest of their company from   30
   their sport to make another experiment of his suspicion. But I am glad the knight is not here. Now
   he shall see his own foolery.

Mrs. Ford. How near is he, Mistress Page?

Mrs. Page. Hard by, at street end; he will be here   35
   anon.

Mrs. Ford. I am undone! The knight is here.

Mrs. Page. Why then you are utterly shamed, and
   he's but a dead man. What a woman are you! Away
   with him, away with him. Better shame than   40
   murder.

Mrs. Ford. Which way should he go? How should I
   bestow him? Shall I put him into the basket again?

18 lunes lunacies   22 Peer out (alluding to the cuckold's horns)

[*Enter Falstaff.*]

Falstaff. No, I'll come no more i' th' basket. May I
45   not go out ere he come?

Mrs. Page. Alas, three of Master Ford's brothers
watch the door with pistols that none shall issue
out; otherwise you might slip away ere he came.
But what make you here?

50   *Falstaff.* What shall I do? I'll creep up into the chim-
ney.

Mrs. Ford. There they always use to discharge their
birding pieces.

Mrs. Page. Creep into the kilnhole.°

55   *Falstaff.* Where is it?

Mrs. Ford. He will seek there, on my word. Neither
press, coffer, chest, trunk, well, vault, but he hath
an abstract° for the remembrance of such places,
and goes to them by his note. There is no hiding
60   you in the house.

Falstaff. I'll go out then.

Mrs. Page. If you go out in your own semblance, you
die, Sir John. Unless you go out disguised—

Mrs. Ford. How might we disguise him?

65   *Mrs. Page.* Alas the day, I know not. There is no
woman's gown big enough for him; otherwise, he
might put on a hat, a muffler, and a kerchief, and
so escape.

Falstaff. Good hearts, devise something. Any extrem-
70   ity rather than a mischief.

Mrs. Ford. My maid's aunt, the fat woman of Brainford,° has a gown above.

---

54 kilnhole oven   58 abstract list   71–72 fat woman of Brainford
(an actual personage who kept a tavern in Brentford, a town on the
Thames twelve miles east of Windsor)

Mrs. Page. On my word, it will serve him; she's as big
   as he is. And there's her thrummed° hat and her
   muffler too. Run up, Sir John.   *75*

Mrs. Ford. Go, go, sweet Sir John. Mistress Page and
   I will look some linen for your head.

Mrs. Page. Quick, quick! We'll come dress you
   straight; put on the gown the while. [*Exit Falstaff.*]

Mrs. Ford. I would my husband would meet him in   *80*
   this shape. He cannot abide the old woman of
   Brainford; he swears she's a witch, forbade her my
   house, and hath threat'ned to beat her.

Mrs. Page. Heaven guide him to thy husband's cudgel,
   and the devil guide his cudgel afterwards!   *85*

Mrs. Ford. But is my husband coming?

Mrs. Page. Ay, in good sadness, is he; and talks of
   the basket too, howsoever he hath had intelligence.

Mrs. Ford. We'll try that; for I'll appoint my men to
   carry the basket again, to meet him at the door with   *90*
   it, as they did last time.

Mrs. Page. Nay, but he'll be here presently. Let's go
   dress him like the witch of Brainford.

Mrs. Ford. I'll first direct my men what they shall do
   with the basket. Go up; I'll bring linen for him   *95*
   straight.   [*Exit.*]

Mrs. Page. Hang him, dishonest° varlet, we cannot
   misuse him enough.
   We'll leave a proof by that which we will do,
   Wives may be merry, and yet honest too.   *100*
   We do not act that often jest and laugh;
   'Tis old but true, "Still swine eats all the draff."°
                                                  [*Exit.*]

[*Enter Mistress Ford with two*] *Servants.*

Mrs. Ford. Go, sirs, take the basket again on your

74 **thrummed** fringed   97 **dishonest** unchaste   102 **draff** swill

shoulders. Your master is hard at door; if he bid
105 you set it down, obey him. Quickly, dispatch. [*Exit.*]

First Servant. Come, come, take it up.

Second Servant. Pray heaven, it be not full of knight
again.

First Servant. I hope not; I had lief as bear so much
110 lead.   [*They lift the basket.*]

[*Enter*] Ford, Page, Caius, Evans, [*and*] Shallow.

Ford. Ay, but if it prove true, Master Page, have you
any way then to unfool me again? Set down the
basket, villain. Somebody call my wife. Youth in
a basket!° O you panderly rascals! There's a knot,°
115 a ging,° a pack, a conspiracy against me. Now shall
the devil be shamed.° What, wife, I say! Come,
come forth! Behold what honest clothes you send
forth to bleaching!

Page. Why, this passes,° Master Ford! You are not
120 to go loose any longer; you must be pinioned.

Evans. Why, this is lunatics, this is mad as a mad
dog.

Shallow. Indeed, Master Ford, this is not well, indeed.

125 *Ford.* So say I too, sir.

[*Enter Mistress Ford.*]

Come hither, Mistress Ford; Mistress Ford, the honest woman, the modest wife, the virtuous creature
that hath the jealous fool to her husband! I suspect
without cause, mistress, do I?

130 *Mrs. Ford.* Heaven be my witness you do, if you suspect me in any dishonesty.

113–14 **Youth in a basket** (a contemporary phrase apparently con-
noting a "fortunate lover")   114 **knot** band   115 **ging** gang   115–
16 **Now shall the devil be shamed** ("Speak the truth and shame the
devil"—proverbial)   119 **passes** exceeds everything

Ford. Well said, brazen-face; hold it out.—Come
   forth, sirrah!   [*Pulling clothes out of the basket.*]

Page. This passes!

Mrs. Ford. Are you not ashamed? Let the clothes   135
   alone.

Ford. I shall find you anon.

Evans. 'Tis unreasonable. Will you take up your wife's
   clothes? Come away.

Ford. Empty the basket, I say!   140

Mrs. Ford. Why, man, why?

Ford. Master Page, as I am a man, there was one
   conveyed out of my house yesterday in this basket.
   Why may not he be there again? In my house I
   am sure he is. My intelligence° is true; my jealousy   145
   is reasonable. Pluck me out all the linen.
        [*Ford and Page pull out more clothes.*]

Mrs. Ford. If you find a man there, he shall die a
   flea's death.

Page. Here's no man.

Shallow. By my fidelity, this is not well, Master Ford;   150
   this wrongs you.

Evans. Master Ford, you must pray, and not follow
   the imaginations of your own heart. This is jealousies.

Ford. Well, he's not here I seek for.   155

Page. No, nor nowhere else but in your brain.

Ford. Help to search my house this one time. If I find
   not what I seek, show no color for my extremity.°
   Let me forever be your table-sport.° Let them say
   of me, "As jealous as Ford that searched a hollow   160

145 **intelligence** information   158 **show no color for my extremity**
suggest no excuse for my extravagance   159 **table-sport** i.e., laugh-
ingstock

walnut for his wife's leman."° Satisfy me once more; once more search with me.

Mrs. Ford. What ho, Mistress Page, come you and the old woman down. My husband will come into
165   the chamber.

Ford. Old woman? What old woman's that?

Mrs. Ford. Why, it is my maid's aunt of Brainford.

Ford. A witch, a quean,° an old cozening° quean! Have I not forbid her my house? She comes of er-
170   rands, does she? We are simple men; we do not know what's brought to pass under the profession of fortune-telling. She works by charms, by spells, by th' figure,° and such daubery° as this is, beyond our element; we know nothing. Come down, you
175   witch, you hag, you; come down, I say!

Mrs. Ford. Nay, good, sweet husband! Good gentle-men, let him not strike the old woman.

[*Enter Falstaff in woman's clothes, and Mistress Page.*]

Mrs. Page. Come, Mother Prat, come, give me your hand.

180   *Ford.* I'll "prat"° her. [*Beats him.*] Out of my door, you witch, you rag, you baggage, you polecat, you runnion!° Out, out! I'll conjure you, I'll fortune-tell you!   [*Exit Falstaff, running.*]

Mrs. Page. Are you not ashamed? I think you have
185   killed the poor woman.

Mrs. Ford. Nay, he will do it. 'Tis a goodly credit for you.

Ford. Hang her, witch!

Evans. By Jeshu, I think the 'oman is a witch indeed.

161 **leman** lover   168 **quean** hussy   168 **cozening** cheating, deceiv-ing   173 **by th' figure** by making wax effigies for enchantments   173 **daubery** false show   180 **prat** beat on the buttocks   182 **run-nion** (abusive term for a woman)

I like not when a 'oman has a great peard; I spy   *190*
a great peard under his muffler.

Ford. Will you follow, gentlemen? I beseech you, follow. See but the issue of my jealousy. If I cry out
thus upon no trail,° never trust me when I open°
again.   *195*

Page. Let's obey his humor a little further. Come,
gentlemen.
    [*Exeunt Ford, Page, Shallow, Caius, and Evans.*]

Mrs. Page. Trust me, he beat him most pitifully.

Mrs. Ford. Nay, by th' mass, that he did not; he beat
him most unpitifully, methought.   *200*

Mrs. Page. I'll have the cudgel hallowed and hung o'er
the altar; it hath done meritorious service.

Mrs. Ford. What think you? May we, with the warrant of womanhood and the witness of a good conscience, pursue him with any further revenge?   *205*

Mrs. Page. The spirit of wantonness is, sure, scared
out of him. If the devil have him not in fee-simple,°
with fine and recovery,° he will never, I think, in
the way of waste,° attempt us again.

Mrs. Ford. Shall we tell our husbands how we have   *210*
served him?

Mrs. Page. Yes, by all means, if it be but to scrape
the figures° out of your husband's brains. If they
can find in their hearts the poor unvirtuous fat
knight shall be any further afflicted, we two will   *215*
still be the ministers.°

Mrs. Ford. I'll warrant they'll have him publicly
shamed, and methinks there would be no period to
the jest, should he not be publicly shamed.

194 **upon no trail** i.e., where there is no scent   194 **open** cry out
from picking up a scent (used of hounds)   207 **fee-simple** absolute
possession   208 **fine and recovery** (legal procedure for transferring
an entailed estate into a fee-simple)   209 **waste** spoliation   213 **figures** phantasms   216 **ministers** agents

220 *Mrs. Page.* Come, to the forge with it; then shape it.
I would not have things cool.   *Exeunt.*

Scene III. [*A room in the Garter Inn.*]

Enter Host and Bardolph.

Bardolph. Sir, the Germans desire to have three of
your horses. The Duke himself will be tomorrow
at court, and they are going to meet him.

Host. What duke should that be comes so secretly?
5   I hear not of him in the court. Let me speak with
the gentlemen. They speak English?

Bardolph. Ay, sir; I'll call them to you.

Host. They shall have my horses, but I'll make them
pay; I'll sauce them.° They have had my house a
10   week at command.° I have turned away my other
guests. They must come off.° I'll sauce them. Come.
Exeunt.

Scene IV. [*A room in Ford's house.*]

*Enter Page, Ford, Mistress Page, Mistress Ford,
and Evans.*

Evans. 'Tis one of the best discretions of a 'oman° as
ever I did look upon.

IV.iii.9 **sauce them** make them pay dearly   10 **at command** reserved   11 **come off** pay   IV.iv.1 **best discretions of a 'oman** most
discreet woman

Page. And did he send you both these letters at an
  instant?

Mrs. Page. Within a quarter of an hour.   *5*

Ford. Pardon me, wife. Henceforth do what thou wilt.
  I rather will suspect the sun with cold
  Than thee with wantonness. Now doth thy honor
    stand,
  In him that was of late an heretic,
  As firm as faith.

Page.   'Tis well, 'tis well; no more.   *10*
  Be not as extreme in submission as in offense.
  But let our plot go forward. Let our wives
  Yet once again, to make us public sport,
  Appoint a meeting with this old fat fellow,
  Where we may take him and disgrace him for it. *15*

Ford. There is no better way than that they spoke of.

Page. How? To send him word they'll meet him in the
  Park at midnight? Fie, fie, he'll never come.

Evans. You say he has been thrown in the rivers, and
  has been grievously peaten as an old 'oman. Me- *20*
  thinks there should be terrors in him that he should
  not come. Methinks his flesh is punished; he shall
  have no desires.

Page. So think I too.

Mrs. Ford. Devise but how you'll use him when he
  comes,   *25*
  And let us two devise to bring him thither.

Mrs. Page. There is an old tale goes that Herne the
  Hunter,
  Sometime° a keeper here in Windsor Forest,
  Doth all the wintertime, at still midnight,
  Walk round about an oak, with great ragg'd horns; *30*
  And there he blasts° the tree, and takes° the cattle,

28 **Sometime** formerly   31 **blasts** blights   31 **takes** bewitches

And makes milch-kine yield blood, and shakes a
    chain
In a most hideous and dreadful manner.
You have heard of such a spirit, and well you know
35   The superstitious idle-headed eld°
Received, and did deliver to our age,
This tale of Herne the Hunter for a truth.

Page. Why, yet there want not many that do fear
In deep of night to walk by this Herne's Oak.
But what of this?

40   *Mrs. Ford.*   Marry, this is our device:°
That Falstaff at that oak shall meet with us,
Disguised like Herne, with huge horns on his head.

Page. Well, let it not be doubted but he'll come,
And in this shape. When you have brought him
    thither,
45   What shall be done with him? What is your plot?

Mrs. Page. That likewise have we thought upon, and
    thus:
Nan Page my daughter, and my little son,
And three or four more of their growth, we'll dress
Like urchins,° ouphs,° and fairies, green and white,
50   With rounds of waxen tapers on their heads,
And rattles in their hands. Upon a sudden,
As Falstaff, she, and I are newly met,
Let them from forth a sawpit rush at once
With some diffusèd° song. Upon their sight,
55   We two in great amazedness will fly.
Then let them all encircle him about,
And, fairy-like, to pinch the unclean knight,
And ask him why, that hour of fairy revel,
In their so sacred paths he dares to tread
In shape profane.

60   *Mrs. Ford.*   And till he tell the truth,

35 eld elders   40 device plan   49 urchins goblins   49 ouphs elves
54 diffusèd i.e., cacophonous

. Let the supposèd fairies pinch him sound°
And burn him with their tapers.

Mrs. Page.   The truth being known,
We'll all present ourselves, dis-horn the spirit,
And mock him home to Windsor.

Ford.   The children must
Be practiced well to this, or they'll ne'er do't.   *65*

Evans. I will teach the children their behaviors; and I
will be like a jackanapes° also, to burn the knight
with my taber.

Ford. That will be excellent. I'll go buy them vizards.°   *4*

Mrs. Page. My Nan shall be the Queen of all the
Fairies,   *70*
Finely attirèd in a robe of white.

Page. That silk will I go buy. [*Aside*] And in that tire°
Shall Master Slender steal my Nan away,
And marry her at Eton.°—Go, send to Falstaff
straight.

Ford. Nay, I'll to him again in name of Brooke.   *75*
He'll tell me all his purpose. Sure, he'll come.

Mrs. Page. Fear not you that. Go, get us properties°
And tricking° for our fairies.

Evans. Let us about it. It is admirable pleasures and
fery honest knaveries.   *80*
                  [*Exeunt Page, Ford, and Evans.*]

Mrs. Page. Go, Mistress Ford,
Send Quickly to Sir John, to know his mind.
                  [*Exit Mistress Ford.*]
I'll to the Doctor. He hath my good will,
And none but he, to marry with Nan Page.
That Slender, though well landed, is an idiot;   *85*
And he my husband best of all affects.

61 **sound** soundly   67 **jackanapes** monkey   69 **vizards** masks   72
tire attire   74 **Eton** (across the river from Windsor)   77 **properties**
stage properties   78 **tricking** adornment, costumes

The Doctor is well moneyed, and his friends
Potent at court. He, none but he, shall have her,
Though twenty thousand worthier come to crave
her.   [*Exit.*]

Scene V. [*The room in the Garter Inn.*]

Enter Host [*and*] *Simple.*

Host. What wouldst thou have, boor? What, thick-
skin? Speak, breathe, discuss; brief, short, quick,
snap.

Simple. Marry, sir, I come to speak with Sir John Fal-
5   staff from Master Slender.

Host. There's his chamber, his house, his castle, his
standing-bed and truckle bed.° 'Tis painted about
with the story of the Prodigal,° fresh and new. Go,
knock and call. He'll speak like an Anthropophagi-
10   nian° unto thee. Knock, I say.

Simple. There's an old woman, a fat woman, gone up
into his chamber. I'll be so bold as stay, sir, till
she come down. I come to speak with her, indeed.

Host. Ha, a fat woman? The knight may be robbed.
15   I'll call. Bully knight, bully Sir John! Speak from
thy lungs military. Art thou there? It is thine Host,
thine Ephesian,° calls.

Falstaff. [*Above*] How now, mine Host?

Host. Here's a Bohemian-Tartar° tarries the coming
20   down of thy fat woman. Let her descend, bully, let

IV.v.7 **truckle bed** trundle bed   8 **Prodigal** i.e., the Prodigal Son
9–10 **Anthropophaginian** cannibal   17 **Ephesian** boon companion
19 **Bohemian-Tartar** i.e., wild man

her descend. My chambers are honorable. Fie, pri-
vacy, fie!

[Enter] Falstaff.

Falstaff. There was, mine Host, an old fat woman
even now with me, but she's gone.

Simple. Pray you, sir, was't not the wise woman of   25
Brainford?

Falstaff. Ay, marry, was it, mussel-shell.° What would
you with her?

Simple. My master, sir, my Master Slender, sent to
her, seeing her go thorough the streets, to know, sir,   30
whether one Nym, sir, that beguiled him of a chain,
had the chain or no.

Falstaff. I spake with the old woman about it.

Simple. And what says she, I pray, sir?

Falstaff. Marry, she says that the very same man that   35
beguiled Master Slender of his chain cozened him
of it.

Simple. I would I could have spoken with the woman
herself. I had other things to have spoken with her
too from him.   40

Falstaff. What are they? Let us know.

Host. Ay, come; quick!

Simple. I may not conceal° them, sir.

Host. Conceal them, or thou diest.

Simple. Why, sir, they were nothing but about Mis-   45
tress Anne Page; to know if it were my master's fortune to have her, or no.

Falstaff. 'Tis, 'tis his fortune.

Simple. What, sir?

27 mussel-shell i.e., one who gapes   43 conceal i.e., reveal

50 *Falstaff.* To have her, or no. Go; say the woman told
me so.

Simple. May I be bold to say so, sir?

Falstaff. Ay, Sir Tyke;° who more bold?

Simple. I thank your worship: I shall make my master
55 glad with these tidings.   [*Exit.*]

Host. Thou art clerkly, thou art clerkly,° Sir John.
Was there a wise woman with thee?

Falstaff. Ay, that there was, mine Host; one that hath
taught me more wit than ever I learned before in
60 my life; and I paid nothing for it neither, but was
paid for my learning.

[*Enter*] *Bardolph.*

Bardolph. Out, alas, sir, cozenage, mere° cozenage!

Host. Where be my horses? Speak well of them, varletto.°

65 *Bardolph.* Run away with the cozeners; for so soon
as I came beyond Eton, they threw me off from
behind one of them, in a slough of mire; and set
spurs and away, like three German devils, three
Doctor Faustuses.°

70 *Host.* They are gone but to meet the Duke, villain.°
Do not say they be fled: Germans are honest men.

[*Enter*] *Evans.*

Evans. Where is mine Host?

Host. What is the matter, sir?

---

53 Sir Tyke i.e., Master Cur   56 clerkly scholarly   62 mere pure
63-64 varletto rascal   69 Doctor Faustuses (Faustus was a German scholar who allegedly obtained magical powers by making a
compact with Lucifer; known to the Elizabethans primarily through
Marlowe's play)   70 villain base fellow

Evans. Have a care of your entertainments.° There is
a friend of mine come to town tells me there is three   *75*
cozen-germans° that has cozened all the hosts of
Readins,° of Maidenhead, of Colebrook, of horses
and money. I tell you for good will, look you. You
are wise and full of gibes and vlouting-stogs, and
'tis not convenient you should be cozened. Fare   *80*
you well.   [*Exit.*]

[*Enter*] *Caius.*

Caius. Vere is mine Host de Jarteer?

Host. Here, Master Doctor, in perplexity and doubt-
ful° dilemma.

Caius. I cannot tell vat is dat; but it is tell-a me dat   *85*
you make grand preparation for a Duke de Jamany.
By my trot, dere is no duke dat de court is know
to come. I tell you for good vill. Adieu.   [*Exit.*]

Host. Hue and cry, villain, go! [*To Falstaff*] Assist me,
knight. I am undone. [*To Bardolph*] Fly, run, hue   *90*
and cry, villain! I am undone!
                      [*Exeunt Host and Bardolph.*]

Falstaff. I would all the world might be cozened, for
I have been cozened and beaten too. If it should
come to the ear of the court how I have been transformed, and how my transformation hath been   *95*
washed and cudgeled, they would melt me out of
my fat drop by drop, and liquor° fishermen's boots
with me. I warrant they would whip me with their
fine wits till I were as crestfall'n° as a dried pear.
I never prospered since I forswore myself at pri-   *100*
mero.° Well, if my wind were but long enough to
say my prayers, I would repent.

74 **entertainments** i.e., total supplies for running an inn   76 **cozen-
germans** (1) cousin-germans, relatives (2) cheating Germans
77 **Readins** Reading   83–84 **doubtful** fearful   97 **liquor** grease
99 **crestfall'n** i.e., undistinguished   100–01 **primero** (a card game)

[Enter Mistress] Quickly.

Now, whence come you?

Quickly. From the two parties, forsooth.

105 *Falstaff.* The devil take one party and his dam the
other! And so they shall be both bestowed. I have
suffered more for their sakes, more than the villainous inconstancy of man's disposition is able to bear.

Quickly. And have not they suffered? Yes, I warrant
110 —speciously° one of them. Mistress Ford, good
heart, is beaten black and blue that you cannot see
a white spot about her.

Falstaff. What tell'st thou me of black and blue? I was
beaten myself into all the colors of the rainbow;
115 and I was like to be apprehended for the Witch of
Brainford. But that my admirable dexterity of wit,
my counterfeiting the action of an old woman, delivered me, the knave constable had set me i' th'
stocks, i' th' common stocks, for a witch.

120 *Quickly.* Sir, let me speak with you in your chamber.
You shall hear how things go, and, I warrant, to
your content. Here is a letter will say somewhat.
Good hearts, what ado here is to bring you together. Sure, one of you does not serve heaven well
125 that you are so crossed.°

Falstaff. Come up into my chamber.   *Exeunt.*

---

110 speciously i.e., especially   125 crossed thwarted

Scene VI. [*The Garter Inn.*]

Enter Fenton [and] Host.

Host. Master Fenton, talk not to me. My mind is
　heavy; I will give over all.

Fenton. Yet hear me speak. Assist me in my purpose,
　And, as I am a gentleman, I'll give thee
　A hundred pound in gold more than your loss.　　　　5

Host. I will hear you, Master Fenton, and I will, at
　the least, keep your counsel.

Fenton. From time to time I have acquainted you
　With the dear love I bear to fair Anne Page,
　Who mutually hath answered my affection,　　　　10
　(So far forth as herself might be her chooser)
　Even to my wish. I have a letter from her
　Of such contents as you will wonder at,
　The mirth whereof so larded° with my matter°
　That neither singly can be manifested　　　　15
　Without the show of both. Fat Falstaff
　Hath a great scene. The image° of the jest
　I'll show you here at large.　　[*Takes out a letter.*]
　　　　　　　　　Hark, good mine Host:
　Tonight at Herne's Oak, just 'twixt twelve and one,
　Must my sweet Nan present° the Fairy Queen—　　20
　The purpose why, is here—in which disguise,
　While other jests are something rank° on foot,
　Her father hath commanded her to slip
　Away with Slender, and with him at Eton
　Immediately to marry. She hath consented.　　　　25
　Now, sir,

IV.vi.14 **larded** intermixed　14 **matter** i.e., courtship problems
17 **image** form　20 **present** represent　22 **something rank** rather
abundantly

Her mother (ever strong against that match
And firm for Doctor Caius) hath appointed
That he shall likewise shuffle° her away,
30 While other sports are tasking of their minds,
And at the dean'ry, where a priest attends,
Straight marry her. To this her mother's plot
She, seemingly obedient, likewise hath
Made promise to the Doctor. Now, thus it rests:
35 Her father means she shall be all in white,
And in that habit, when Slender sees his time
To take her by the hand and bid her go,
She shall go with him. Her mother hath intended—
The better to denote her to the Doctor,
40 For they must all be masked and vizarded—
That quaint° in green she shall be loose enrobed,
With ribands pendent, flaring 'bout her head;
And when the Doctor spies his vantage ripe,
To pinch her by the hand, and on that token°
45 The maid hath given consent to go with him.

Host. Which means she to deceive, father or mother?

Fenton. Both, my good Host, to go along with me.
And here it rests, that you'll procure the Vicar
To stay for me at church 'twixt twelve and one,
50 And, in the lawful name of marrying,
To give our hearts united ceremony.°

Host. Well, husband your device;° I'll to the Vicar.
Bring you the maid, you shall not lack a priest.

Fenton. So shall I evermore be bound to thee;
55 Besides, I'll make a present recompense.   *Exeunt.*

29 shuffle spirit 41 quaint elegantly 44 token signal 51 united
ceremony union through the marriage rite   52 husband your device
i.e., manage your plan prudently

ACT V

Scene I. [*The Garter Inn.*]

Enter Falstaff [and Mistress] Quickly.

Falstaff. Prithee, no more prattling. Go. I'll hold.°
This is the third time; I hope good luck lies in odd
numbers. Away; go. They say there is divinity° in
odd numbers, either in nativity, chance, or death.
Away!   5

Quickly. I'll provide you a chain, and I'll do what I
can to get you a pair of horns.

Falstaff. Away, I say; time wears. Hold up your head,
and mince.°   [*Exit Mistress Quickly.*]

[Enter] Ford.

How now, Master Brooke. Master Brooke, the mat-   10
ter will be known tonight, or never. Be you in the
Park about midnight, at Herne's Oak, and you shall
see wonders.

Ford. Went you not to her yesterday,° sir, as you told
me you had appointed?   15

Falstaff. I went to her, Master Brooke, as you see, like

V.i.1 **hold** keep the engagement   3 **divinity** divination   9 **mince**
trip off   14 **yesterday** (a slip; should be "this morning")

a poor old man; but I came from her, Master
Brooke, like a poor old woman. That same knave
Ford, her husband, hath the finest mad devil of
20   jealousy in him, Master Brooke, that ever governed
frenzy. I will tell you: he beat me grievously, in
the shape of a woman; for in the shape of man,
Master Brooke, I fear not Goliath with a weaver's
beam,° because I know also life is a shuttle.° I am
25   in haste. Go along with me; I'll tell you all, Master
Brooke. Since I plucked geese, played truant, and
whipped top, I knew not what 'twas to be beaten
till lately. Follow me. I'll tell you strange things of
this knave Ford, on whom tonight I will be re-
30   venged, and I will deliver his wife into your hand.
Follow. Strange things in hand, Master Brooke!
Follow.   *Exeunt.*

Scene II. [*Windsor Little Park.*]

Enter Page, Shallow, [and] Slender.

Page. Come, come; we'll couch° i' th' Castle ditch°
till we see the light of our fairies. Remember, son
Slender, my daughter.

Slender. Ay, forsooth; I have spoke with her and we
5   have a nay-word° how to know one another. I come
to her in white, and cry, "mum"; she cries,
"budget";° and by that we know one another.

23–24 **Goliath with a weaver's beam** (an allusion to Goliath's staff
from 1 Samuel 17:7 and 2 Samuel 21:19)   24 **life is a shuttle** (para-
phrased from Job 7:6: "My days are swifter than a weaver's shuttle")
V.ii.1 **couch** hide   1 **Castle ditch** (a ditch running along the east
side of Windsor Castle)   5 **nay-word** password   6–7 **mum . . . budget** (mumbudget, a game in which the player pretended to be
tongue-tied)

Shallow. That's good too. But what needs either your "mum," or her "budget"? The white will decipher her well enough.—It hath struck ten o'clock. 10

Page. The night is dark; light and spirits will become it well. Heaven prosper our sport. No man means evil but the devil, and we shall know him by his horns. Let's away; follow me. *Exeunt.*

Scene III. [*Outside the Park.*]

Enter Mistress Page, Mistress Ford,
[*and Doctor*] *Caius.*

Mrs. Page. Master Doctor, my daughter is in green. When you see your time, take her by the hand, away with her to the deanery, and dispatch it quickly. Go before into the Park. We two must go together. 5

Caius. I know vat I have to do. Adieu.

Mrs. Page. Fare you well, sir. [*Exit Caius.*] My husband will not rejoice so much at the abuse of Falstaff as he will chafe at the Doctor's marrying my daughter. But 'tis no matter; better a little chiding 10 than a great deal of heartbreak.

Mrs. Ford. Where is Nan now and her troop of fairies, and the Welsh devil, Hugh?

Mrs. Page. They are all couched in a pit hard by Herne's Oak, with obscured lights which at the 15 very instant of Falstaff's and our meeting they will at once display to the night.

Mrs. Ford. That cannot choose but amaze° him.

V.iii.18 **amaze** frighten

Mrs. Page. If he be not amazed, he will be mocked;
20   if he be amazed, he will every way be mocked.

Mrs. Ford. We'll betray him finely.

Mrs. Page. Against such lewdsters° and their lechery,
Those that betray them do no treachery.

Mrs. Ford. The hour draws on. To the Oak, to the
25   Oak!   *Exeunt.*

Scene IV. [*Outside the Park.*]

Enter Evans [disguised as a Satyr] and [others as]
Fairies.

Evans. Trib,° trib, fairies. Come, and remember your
parts. Be pold, I pray you. Follow me into the pit,
and when I give the watch-'ords, do as I pid you.
Come, come; trib, trib.   *Exeunt.*

Scene V. [*Herne's Oak in Windsor Little Park.*]

Enter Falstaff [disguised as Herne,] with a buck's head
upon him.

Falstaff. The Windsor bell hath struck twelve; the
minute draws on. Now, the hot-blooded gods assist
me! Remember, Jove, thou wast a bull for thy
Europa;° love set on thy horns. O powerful love,
that in some respects makes a beast a man; in some

22 lewdsters lechers   V.iv.1 **Trib** i.e., trip   V.v.3–4 **bull for thy
Europa** (disguise adopted by Jove for his abduction of Europa)

other, a man a beast. You were also, Jupiter, a
swan for the love of Leda.° O omnipotent love, how
near the god drew to the complexion° of a goose!
A fault done first in the form of a beast. O Jove, a
beastly fault! And then another fault in the sem-   10
blance of a fowl; think on't, Jove; a foul fault!
When gods have hot backs, what shall poor men
do? For me, I am here a Windsor stag; and the fat-
test, I think, i' th' forest. Send me a cool rut-time,°
Jove, or who can blame me to piss my tallow?°   15
Who comes here? My doe?

[Enter] Mistress Page [and] Mistress Ford.

Mrs. Ford. Sir John? Art thou there, my deer, my
male deer?

Falstaff. My doe with the black scut!° Let the sky rain
potatoes;° let it thunder to the tune of "Green-   20
sleeves," hail kissing-comfits,° and snow eringoes.°
Let there come a tempest of provocation,° I will
shelter me here.   *[Hugs her.]*

Mrs. Ford. Mistress Page is come with me, sweetheart.   25

Falstaff. Divide me like a bribed° buck, each a
haunch. I will keep my sides to myself, my shoulders for the fellow of this walk,° and my horns I
bequeath your husbands. Am I a woodman,° ha?
Speak I like Herne the Hunter? Why, now is Cupid   30
a child of conscience;° he makes restitution. As I
am a true spirit, welcome!   *[Noise within.]*

6–7 a swan for the love of Leda (another animal disguise adopted by
Jove in an amorous adventure)   8 complexion temperament
14 rut-time (annual period of sexual excitement for the male deer)
15 piss my tallow (during rut-time the main food for the hart was the
red mushroom which supposedly brought on urination)   19 scut
(1) tail (2) pudendum   20 potatoes i.e., sweet potatoes, formerly
considered aphrodisiacs   21 kissing-comfits perfumed sweetmeats
21 eringoes candied seaholly (considered an aphrodisiac)   22 provocation lustful stimulation   26 bribed stolen   28 fellow of this
walk forester on this beat   29 woodman hunter (here, of women)
31 of conscience conscientious

Mrs. Page. Alas, what noise?

Mrs. Ford. Heaven forgive our sins!

35 *Falstaff.* What should this be?

Mrs. Ford.
        } Away, away!   [*They run off.*]
Mrs. Page.

Falstaff. I think the devil will not have me damned,
lest the oil that's in me should set hell on fire. He
would never else cross me thus.

*Enter Sir Hugh [Evans] like a satyr, [Anne Page] and
boys dressed like fairies, Mistress Quickly like the
Queen of Fairies, [Pistol as Hobgoblin. They carry
tapers].*

40 *Quickly.* Fairies, black, gray, green, and white,
    You moonshine revelers, and shades of night,
    You orphan° heirs of fixèd destiny,
    Attend your office° and your quality.°
    Crier Hobgoblin, make the fairy oyes.°

45 *Pistol.* Elves, list your names; silence, you airy toys!
    Cricket, to Windsor chimneys shalt thou leap.
    Where fires thou find'st unraked° and hearths un-
        swept,
    There pinch the maids as blue as bilberry.°
    Our radiant Queen hates sluts° and sluttery.

Falstaff. They are fairies; he that speaks to them shall
50   die.
    I'll wink° and couch; no man their works must eye.
               [*Lies down upon his face.*]

---

42 orphan (possible allusion to the folklore belief that fairies were
born spontaneously and thus had no parents)   43 office duty   43
quality profession   44 oyes hear ye (public crier's call)   47 unraked
not properly covered with coals   48 bilberry blueberry   49 sluts
untidy kitchen-maids   51 wink close my eyes

Evans. Where's Bead? Go you, and where you find a
   maid
  That ere she sleep has thrice her prayers said,
  Raise up the organs of her fantasy,°
  Sleep she as sound as careless infancy.   *55*
  But those as sleep and think not on their sins,
  Pinch them, arms, legs, backs, shoulders, sides, and
   shins.

Quickly. About, about.
  Search Windsor Castle, elves, within and out.
  Strew good luck, ouphs,° on every sacred room,   *60*
  That it may stand till the perpetual doom,°
  In state as wholesome as in state 'tis fit,
  Worthy the owner, and the owner it.
  The several chairs of Order° look you scour
  With juice of balm and every precious flow'r.   *65*
  Each fair instalment,° coat,° and several crest,°
  With loyal blazon,° evermore be blest.
  And nightly, meadow-fairies, look you sing,
  Like to the Garter's compass,° in a ring.
  Th' expressure° that it bears, green let it be,   *70*
  More fertile-fresh than all the field to see;
  And *Honi soit qui mal y pense*° write
  In emerald tufts, flow'rs purple, blue, and white—
  Like sapphire, pearl, and rich embroidery,
  Buckled below fair knighthood's bending knee—   *75*
  Fairies use flow'rs for their charactery.°
  Away, disperse! But till 'tis one o'clock,
  Our dance of custom round about the Oak
  Of Herne the Hunter, let us not forget.

Evans. Pray you, lock hand in hand; yourselves in
   order set;   *80*

54 **Raise up the organs of her fantasy** i.e., cause her to have pleasant
dreams 60 **ouphs** elves 61 **perpetual doom** Day of Judgment 64
chairs of Order stalls of the knights of the Order of the Garter in
St. George's Chapel 66 **instalment** stall 66 **coat** coat of arms 66
crest helmet (affixed above the stall) 67 **blazon** armorial bearings
69 **compass** circle 70 **expressure** image, picture 72 **Honi soit qui
mal y pense** Ill be to him who evil thinks (motto of the Order of the
Garter) 76 **charactery** writing (accent on second syllable)

And twenty glowworms shall our lanterns be,
To guide our measure round about the tree.
But, stay—I smell a man of middle earth.°

Falstaff. Heavens defend me from that Welsh fairy,
85   lest he transform me to a piece of cheese!°

Pistol. Vile worm, thou wast o'erlooked° even in thy
birth.

Quickly. With trial-fire touch me his finger end.
If he be chaste, the flame will back descend
And turn him to no pain; but if he start,
90   It is the flesh of a corrupted heart.

Pistol. A trial, come.

Evans.   Come, will this wood take fire?
    They put the tapers to his fingers, and he starts.

Falstaff. O, O, O!

Quickly. Corrupt, corrupt, and tainted in desire!
About him, fairies, sing a scornful rhyme;
95   And, as you trip, still pinch him to your time.

The Song.

Fie on sinful fantasy!
Fie on lust and luxury!°
Lust is but a bloody fire,°
Kindled with unchaste desire,
100   Fed in heart, whose flames aspire,
As thoughts do blow them, higher and higher.
Pinch him, fairies, mutually;°
Pinch him for his villainy;
Pinch him, and burn him, and turn him about,
105   Till candles and starlight and moonshine be out.

83 **middle earth** i.e., that section of the universe between heaven and
hell, realm of mortals   84–85 **Heavens . . . cheese** (cheese was the
favorite food of Welshmen. Since Evans smells Falstaff, the latter
fears he will be turned into cheese and then devoured)   86 **o'erlooked** bewitched   97 **luxury** lasciviousness   98 **bloody fire** fire in
the blood   102 **mutually** jointly

Here they pinch him, and sing about him, and [Caius]
the Doctor comes one way and steals away a boy in
green. And Slender another way; he takes a boy in
white. And Fenton steals Mistress Anne. And a noise
of hunting is made within, and all the Fairies run
away. Falstaff pulls off his buck's head and rises up.

[Enter] Page, Ford, [Mistress Page, Mistress Ford,
and Evans°].

Page. Nay, do not fly. I think we have watched you°
  now.
  Will none but Herne the Hunter serve your turn?

Mrs. Page. [*To Page*] I pray you, come, hold up the
  jest no higher.°
  [*To Falstaff*] Now, good Sir John, how like you
  Windsor wives?
  See you these, husband? [*Points to Falstaff's horns.*]
  Do not these fair yokes   *110*
  Become the forest better than the town?

Ford. Now sir, who's a cuckold now? Master Brooke,
  Falstaff's a knave, a cuckoldly knave; here are his
  horns, Master Brooke. And, Master Brooke, he
  hath enjoyed nothing of Ford's but his buck basket,   *115*
  his cudgel, and twenty pounds of money, which
  must be paid to Master Brooke; his horses are
  arrested° for it, Master Brooke.

Mrs. Ford. Sir John, we have had ill luck; we could
  never meet.° I will never take you for my love   *120*
  again, but I will always count you my deer.

Falstaff. I do begin to perceive that I am made an ass.

---

105 s.d. **Evans** (Q1 brings in Evans and Shallow with the others.
Evans presumably left the stage at the previous direction, when "all
the Fairies run away." He must reenter because he speaks later.
Shallow speaks no lines, but he may well belong to this group
scene)   106 **watched you** i.e., caught you in the act   108 **hold up**
the jest no higher i.e., put an end to the jest   118 **arrested** seized by
warrant   120 **meet** (possible aural pun on *mate*)

Ford. Ay, and an ox° too: both the proofs° are extant.

Falstaff. And these are not fairies? I was three or four
125   times in the thought they were not fairies; and yet
      the guiltiness of my mind, the sudden surprise of
      my powers,° drove the grossness of the foppery°
      into a received belief, in despite of the teeth of all
      rhyme and reason, that they were fairies. See now
130   how wit may be made a Jack-a-Lent, when 'tis upon
      ill employment.

Evans. Sir John Falstaff, serve Got and leave your
      desires, and fairies will not pinse you.

Ford. Well said, fairy Hugh.

135 *Evans.* [*To Ford*] And leave you your jealousies too,
      I pray you.

Ford. I will never mistrust my wife again, till thou art
      able to woo her in good English.

Falstaff. Have I laid my brain in the sun and dried it,
140   that it wants° matter to prevent so gross o'erreach-
      ing as this? Am I ridden with a Welsh goat too?
      Shall I have a coxcomb of frieze?° 'Tis time I were
      choked with a piece of toasted cheese.

Evans. Seese is not goot to give putter; your belly is
145   all putter.

Falstaff. "Seese" and "putter"? Have I lived to stand
      at the taunt of one that makes fritters of English?
      This is enough to be the decay of lust and late-walk-
      ing° through the realm.

150 *Mrs. Page.* Why, Sir John, do you think though we
      would have thrust virtue out of our hearts by the
      head and shoulders, and have given ourselves with-

---

123 **ox** i.e., fool (from the expression "to make an ox of someone")
123 **proofs** i.e., the long horns   127 **powers** faculties   127 **foppery**
deceit   140 **wants** lacks   142 **coxcomb of frieze** fool's cap of coarse
Welsh woolen cloth   148–49 **late-walking** staying out late

out scruple to hell, that ever the devil could have made you our delight?

Ford. What, a hodge-pudding?° A bag of flax?   155

Mrs. Page. A puffed man?

Page. Old, cold, withered, and of intolerable entrails?

Ford. And one that is as slanderous as Satan?

Page. And as poor as Job?

Ford. And as wicked as his wife?   160

Evans. And given to fornications, and to taverns, and sack and wine and metheglins,° and to drinkings and swearings and starings,° pribbles and prabbles?

Falstaff. Well, I am your theme. You have the start of   165 me; I am dejected;° I am not able to answer the Welsh flannel.° Ignorance itself is a plummet° o'er me. Use me as you will.

Ford. Marry, sir, we'll bring you to Windsor, to one Master Brooke, that you have cozened of money, to whom you should have been a pander. Over and   170 above that you have suffered, I think to repay that money will be a biting affliction.

Page. Yet be cheerful, knight. Thou shalt eat a posset tonight at my house, where I will desire thee to laugh at my wife that now laughs at thee. Tell her   175 Master Slender hath married her daughter.

Mrs. Page. [*Aside*] Doctors doubt that.° If Anne Page be my daughter, she is, by this, Doctor Caius' wife.

[*Enter Slender.*]

Slender. Whoa, ho, ho, father Page!

155 **hodge-pudding** large sausage of many ingredients   162 **metheg-lins** spiced Welsh mead   163 **starings** swaggerings   165 **dejected** cast down   166 **Welsh flannel** (teasing name for a Welshman)   166 **plummet** (1) garment (from "plumbet," a woolen fabric) (2) line for sounding   177 **Doctors doubt that** (expression of disbelief)

180   *Page.* Son, how now; how now, son! Have you dis-
         patched?°

       Slender. Dispatched? I'll make the best in Gloucester-
         shire know on't; would I were hanged, la, else.

       Page. Of what, son?

185   *Slender.* I came yonder at Eton to marry Mistress
         Anne Page, and she's a great lubberly boy. If it had
         not been i' th' church, I would have swinged° him,
         or he should have swinged me. If I did not think
         it had been Anne Page, would I might never stir—
190   and 'tis a postmaster's° boy!

       Page. Upon my life, then, you took the wrong.

       Slender. What need you tell me that? I think so, when
         I took a boy for a girl. If I had been married to him,
         for all he was in woman's apparel, I would not have
195   had him.

       Page. Why, this is your own folly. Did not I tell you
         how you should know my daughter by her gar-
         ments?

       Slender. I went to her in white, and cried, "mum,"
200   and she cried, "budget," as Anne and I had ap-
         pointed; and yet it was not Anne, but a postmaster's
         boy.

       Mrs. Page. Good George, be not angry. I knew of your
         purpose; turned my daughter into green; and indeed
205   she is now with the Doctor at the dean'ry, and there
         married.

                    [*Enter Doctor Caius.*]

       Caius. Vere is Mistress Page? By gar, I am cozened!
         I ha' married *un garçon,* a boy; *un* peasant, by gar,
         a boy; it is not Anne Page. By gar, I am cozened!

210   *Mrs. Page.* Why? Did you take her in green?

       180–81 dispatched settled the business   187 swinged beaten   190
       postmaster master of post horses

Caius. Ay, be-gar, and 'tis a boy. Be-gar, I'll raise all
  Windsor.   [*Exit*]

Ford. This is strange. Who hath got the right Anne?

Page. My heart misgives me. Here comes Master
  Fenton.   *215*

     [*Enter Fenton and Anne Page.*]

  How now, Master Fenton!

Anne. Pardon, good father! Good my mother, pardon!

Page. Now, mistress, how chance you went not with
  Master Slender?

Mrs. Page. Why went you not with Master Doctor,
  maid?   *220*

Fenton. You do amaze° her. Hear the truth of it.
  You would have married her most shamefully,
  Where there was no proportion held in love.
  The truth is, she and I, have since contracted,°
  Are now so sure° that nothing can dissolve us.   *225*
  Th' offense is holy that she hath committed,
  And this deceit loses the name of craft,
  Of disobedience, or unduteous title,
  Since therein she doth evitate° and shun
  A thousand irreligious cursèd hours   *230*
  Which forcèd marriage would have brought upon
    her.

Ford. Stand not amazed. Here is no remedy.
  In love the heavens themselves do guide the state;
  Money buys lands, and wives are sold by fate.

Falstaff. I am glad, though you have ta'en a special   *235*
  stand° to strike at me, that your arrow hath
  glanced.

---

221 amaze perplex   224 contracted   betrothed   225 sure firmly
bound in wedlock   229 evitate avoid   236 stand hunter's place for
shooting

Page. Well, what remedy? Fenton, heaven give thee
    joy!
    What cannot be eschewed must be embraced.

Falstaff. When night dogs run, all sorts of deer are
240   chased.

Mrs. Page. Well, I will muse° no further. Master
    Fenton,
    Heaven give you many, many merry days!
    Good husband, let us every one go home,
    And laugh this sport o'er by a country fire;
    Sir John and all.

245 *Ford.*   Let it be so. Sir John,
    To Master Brooke you yet shall hold your word;
    For he tonight shall lie with Mistress Ford. *Exeunt.*

FINIS

241 **muse** grumble

Textual Note

Two texts of *The Merry Wives of Windsor* exist: that of the 1602 Quarto and that of the 1623 Folio. The play had been entered in the Stationers' Register on January 18, 1602, for publication by John Busby, but Busby immediately transferred his rights to Arthur Johnson. Johnson brought out Q1 later that year with Thomas Creede as his printer. In 1619, Thomas Pavier issued a second quarto that basically reprints Q1 and is therefore without textual authority. The last early quarto of the play, that of 1630, except for some changes in spelling and punctuation, was printed from the Folio. Thus Q1 and F stand as the only texts of editorial importance.

There are significant differences between these two texts. Not only is Q1 some twelve hundred lines shorter, but it omits and transposes scenes, cuts speaking parts for William and Robin, excises all references to the court and Order of the Garter, and makes a jumble of many individual passages. In sum, although coherent, the Quarto text is inferior to the Folio version. Yet the Quarto contains certain passages and readings—notably Brooke as the alias for Ford, and *cosen garmombles* in place of *cozen-germans*—which appear to be genuinely Shakespeare's.

Various theories have been advanced over the years to account for the two versions of the play. Scholarly consensus marks the Folio text as the authentic version. However, according to a strong current theory, F rests upon a 1597 mother text that had undergone minor modifica-

tions between the original production and publication of
the Folio in 1623.

The Quarto version, it is posited, represents an abridg-
ment of that mother text, illegitimately made through memorial reconstruction for a provincial acting company
around 1601. The pirate was most certainly a "hired
man" who played the Host in the original Lord Chamberlain's Men productions of the play. While making his
memorial reconstruction, this traitor actor seems to have
restored to the text the Brooke reading that had been
altered to Broome in 1597. This was done to avoid conflict with the family of William Brooke, Lord Cobham,
who had taken umbrage at Shakespeare's original name
for Falstaff in *1 Henry IV*—Oldcastle, a Brooke family
ancestor. At the same time, the pirate-actor, through his
playing knowledge of the original script, corrected other
anomalies, such as the confusion over the costume colors
in the fairy scene, which hasty composition had let creep
into the mother text. Thus, while Q1 must be regarded
as a corrupt text, it has helped to get us closer to Shakespeare's original version.

Trying to recapture that original version, we are further
handicapped by certain peculiarities in the Folio text. The
only stage directions indicate entries and exits; character
names are massed at the head of each scene; the play is
fully divided into acts and scenes; and there are idiosyncrasies in punctuation. These oddities, considered collectively, are now taken as an indication that the Folio
Merry Wives is a literary transcription of either the
author's manuscript or a prompt copy—it is impossible
to tell which—made by Ralph Crane, distinguished scriv-
ener of the King's Men. Since *The Merry Wives* shares
these scribal characteristics with the three other plays
opening the Folio, it appears as if the original plan was to
have Crane make a set of literary transcriptions for all the
plays in the Folio, but the plan never was completely
executed.

The present edition is based on the Folio text. The
massed entries have been changed from the scene heads to
the appropriate places within the scene. The Latin of the

Folio's act and scene divisions has been translated into
English. The French of Dr. Caius is modernized, and the
Welsh pronunciations of Sir Hugh Evans are indicated a
little more consistently than in the Folio. For example, at
I.i.246, where the Folio in a single speech gives both
"ord" and "ort," the Signet edition alters the first to agree
with the second. Prose passages set as verse in the Folio
appear here as prose. Added stage directions and indications of locale are in brackets. The name "Broome," which
appears regularly in F, is here given as "Brooke," speech
prefixes and abbreviations are expanded, spelling and
punctuation are modernized, and obvious typographical
errors are corrected. Other departures from F are listed
below, the adopted reading first, in italic type, followed by
the Folio reading in roman. Adopted readings from Q1
are indicated by a bracketed Q. Readings from later
quartos, folios, or those by editors appear unbracketed.

I.i.45 *George* Thomas   57, 60 *Shallow* Slender   124–26 *They carried . . . pocket* [Q; F omits]   243 *contempt* content

I.ii.12 *seese* cheese

I.iii.14 *lime* [Q] liue   48 *well* [Q] will   52 *legion* [Q: legians] legend
60 *oeillades* illiads   69 *cheater* Cheaters   82 *o' th'* ith'   83 *humor*
honor   94 *Page* [Q] Ford   95 *Ford* [Q] Page   99 *Page* Ford   101
mind mine

I.iv.22 *whey face* [Q: whay coloured] wee-face   45 *boitier vert* boy-
teene verd

II.i.56 *praised* praise   61 *Hundredth Psalm* hundred Psalms   134
and there's the humor of it [Q; F omits]   205 *Ford* Shallow   210–
11 *mynheers* An-heires

II.ii.24, 53, 308 *God* [Q] heauen

II.iii.54 *word* [Q; F omits]   76 *Page, Shallow, and Slender* All

III.i.83 *urinals* [Q] Vrinal   84–85 *for missing your meetings and
appointments* [Q; F omits]   100 *Give me thy hand, terrestrial; so*
[Q; F omits]

III.iii.3 *Robert* Robin   151 *who goes here* [Q; F omits]   163 *un-
cope* uncape   189 *foolish* foolishion

III.iv.12 *Fenton* [F omits]   57 *God* [Q] Heauen   62 *have* hath
109 s.d. *Exit* Exeunt

III.v.88 *By the Lord* [Q] Yes   150 s.d. *Exit* Exeunt

IV.i.45 *hung* hing   66 *lunatics* Lunaties

IV.ii.18 *lunes* lines   54 *Mrs. Page* [F gives the line as part of the previous speech]   62 *Mrs. Page* [Q] Mist. Ford   94 *direct* direct direct   98 *him* [F omits]   177 *not* [F omits]   189 *Jeshu* [Q] yea and no

IV.iii.1 *Germans desire* Germane desires   7 *them* [Q] him   9 *house* [Q] houses

IV.iv.7 *cold* gold   32 *makes* make   42 *Disguised . . . head* [Q, which has "Horne" for "Herne"; F omits]   60 *Mrs. Ford* Ford   72 *tire* time

IV.v.43 *Simple* Fal.   53 Tyke [Q] like   56 *Thou art* [Q] thou are   101–02 *to say my prayers* [Q; F omits]

IV.vi.27 *ever* euen   39 *denote* deuote

V.ii.3 *daughter* [F omits]

V.iii.13 *Hugh* Herne

V.v.s.d. *with a buck's head upon him* [Q; F omits]   2 *hot-blooded* hot-bloodied   39s.d. *Enter . . . of Fairies* [Q] Enter Fairies   71 *More* Mote   91s.d. *They . . . starts* [Q; F omits]   105s.d. *Here . . . rises up* [Q, which gives "red" where we give "green," and "greene" where we give "white," and describes Anne as "being in white"]   199 *white* greene   204,210 *green* white

A Note on the Source of
The Merry Wives of Windsor

The Merry Wives belongs to that small group of Shakespeare's plays which have no known source. But Renaissance Italian novellas afford several duped lovers who, like Falstaff, have three assignations with the wife of a jealous husband. Anne Page, the young maiden sought after by three suitors, finds herself in a situation which is a recurring one in conventional Italian comedy. Thus, there is scholarly consensus that whatever the precise source of *The Merry Wives,* that source was a work based on Italian models.

Italian tales had been known in English translation in the sixteenth century through such collections as Painter's *The Palace of Pleasure* (1566) and Pettie's *A Petite Palace of Pettie his Pleasure* (1576). However, in the face of the stage tradition about hurried composition for *The Merry Wives,* scholars generally believe that Shakespeare, rather than directly having dramatized any of these tales, reworked an old play in the repertory of his company. For convenience, we may term this old play the *Ur-Merry Wives.* That Italianate plays should have been available is not startling; the conventions of Italian comedy had filtered into English drama by the fifteen-seventies (even earlier if we allow for influences from Plautus and Terence) through performances of the School Plays—academic comedies presented at Oxford and Cambridge. These comedies were written in imitation of or translated from the Italian *commedia erudita.* The *commedia dell'arte* also may have provided material; extant *commedia dell'arte* scenari reveal traces of the situations found in both the main and subplot of *The Merry Wives*. And Italian actors appeared in England in the fifteen-seventies in productions from their native repertory.

The dramatic source—if there was one—of *The Merry Wives* is lost, but three tales have been uncovered which contain resemblances to incidents found in Shakespeare's version. That most closely mirroring events of the main plot is a tale published in 1558 in Ser Giovanni Fiorentino's *Il Pecorone* (Day I, Novella 2). It relates how Bucciuolo, upon completing his legal studies in Bologna, goes to his teacher for instruction on the art of falling in love. Following his teacher's advice, he visits a church, where he becomes enamored of a young lady who, unknown to the student, is the wife of the teacher. She encourages Bucciuolo's attentions and soon invites him to visit her. Bucciuolo, as previously requested by the teacher, keeps him apprised of all progress. This teacher, a very jealous man, begins to suspect that his wife is the young woman. When he learns of the meeting, he rushes home at the appointed time. The wife hides Bucciuolo under a pile of newly laundered clothes, and thus he escapes detection. The young man reports the incident to his mentor the next day and adds that he has been invited back for a rendezvous the following night. This time the teacher, in a great rage, follows the student and knocks on the door as soon as Bucciuolo has entered. The lady opens the door and embraces her husband in such a manner that Bucciuolo is able to slip out safely. She then shouts that her husband has gone mad; the neighbors and her brothers arrive, and when the brothers see the teacher pierce the pile of laundry with his sword, they consider him insane. The husband then threatens the brothers, who beat him with cudgels. Word goes through the neighborhood that the teacher indeed has gone mad. Bucciuolo, in sympathy, comes to visit him, discovers that he has been cuckolding his own teacher, tells the wretched man that he grieves for him, and then leaves Bologna.

The tale contains striking similarities with the main plot of *The Merry Wives*. Fiorentino's story revolves around a jealous husband who gets a full report of the assignations between his wife and her lover. The lover is hidden under laundry, which the husband examines on his second attempt to catch the pair. Each time the lover escapes, and at the end he learns the truth of the situation. The duped husband receives a beating after the second visit. Shakespeare's important change is in making the lover rather than the husband the duped male.

Another story of a duped husband that resembles *The Merry Wives* is "The Tale of the Two Lovers of Pisa" from Tarlton's *Newes out of Purgatorie* (1590). The husband, a physician, is a very jealous man who decides to test the virtue of his wife by encouraging a young man to make love to her. The young man, who does not know that the physician and the husband are one, reports daily on the progress of his affair to the physician. Three assignations take place, and each time the young man escapes when the physician arrives to search for him. In the first instance, the young man is concealed in a vat of feathers, in the second he hides between two ceilings, and in the third he is carried from the house in a chest supposedly containing the physician's papers. At the end the lover learns the truth of the situation.

This tale also opens with an account of how the girl came to marry the physician. The details are similar to incidents in the Anne Page story. Margaret, the daughter of a wealthy gentleman, has many suitors, but her father wants her to marry a rich husband. The father finally selects Mutio, a rich but old and jealous physician, and forces Margaret to marry him. It is possible that the germ for the Anne Page subplot lies in this tale. (Or, as Oscar Campbell has theorized, it may come from one of the *commedia erudita*-type plays.)

The third tale with plot parallels is "Of Two Brethren and their Wives" from *Riche his Farewell to Military Profession* (1581) by Barnaby Riche. This tale is of interest because it deals with the intrigues of a married woman who is involved with three suitors. Two of them, the doctor and lawyer, are comic types. Both are duped by the woman. Possibly the author of the *Ur-Merry Wives* switched elements from the main plot to the subplot and vice versa.

What this brief account of possible source materials shows is that all the details of story found in *The Merry Wives* plot lines were known in both narrative and dramatic form by 1590—several years before the composition of *The Merry Wives*. In adapting the to-hand material, Shakespeare added the Falstaff crew from the *Henry* plays and, as discussed in the introduction to this volume, inserted the topical events reflected in the horse-stealing subplot and in the court and Garter allusions.

Commentaries

NORTHROP FRYE

Characterization in Shakespearian Comedy

In drama, characterization depends on function: what a character is follows from what he has to do in the play. Dramatic function in its turn depends on the structure of the play: the character has certain things to do because the play has such and such a shape. Given a sufficiently powerful sense of structure, the characters will be essentially speaking dramatic functions, as they are in Jonson's comedy of humors. The structure of the play in its turn depends on the category of the play; if it is a comedy, its structure will require a comic resolution and a prevailing comic mood.

These sound like simple principles, but it is extraordinary how undeveloped they are in Shakespearian criticism. They have been neglected for a historical approach, which, however useful in itself, is not based squarely on the conventions of the dramatic genre. Of all forms of literary expression, the drama is the least dependent on its historical context. No doubt many in Shakespeare's audience did addle their brains with the theory of mon-

From *Shakespeare Quarterly*, IV (1953). Reprinted by permission of *Shakespeare Quarterly* and Northrop Frye.

archy or Reformation theology or the chain of being or the four humors when they were not being better educated by Shakespeare. But theatrical audiences, as such, hardly change at all from one millennium to another. In the earliest extant European comedy, *The Acharnians* of Aristophanes, we meet the *miles gloriosus* or swaggering soldier who is still going strong in Shaw's *Arms and the Man* and Chaplin's *Great Dictator.* We meet the comic parasite who in the Daly of O'Casey's *Juno and the Paycock* appears practically unchanged in twenty-five centuries. TV audiences are still laughing at the same kind of jokes that were declared to be worn out in the opening dialogue of *The Frogs.* It will therefore not do to explain, say, the rejection of Falstaff in historical terms only, and merely say that the original audience were much more aware than we of the importance of getting France conquered by a strong leader. (One may observe in passing that if any member of Shakespeare's audience did not know that sixty years of unbroken disaster followed the career of Henry V, his ignorance was certainly no fault of Shakespeare's.) We know very little about the contemporary reception of Shakespeare's play, but one of the things we do know is that Falstaff was exactly the same kind of popular favorite then that he is now, and for exactly the same reasons. It is similarly not surprising that Elizabethan audiences could still be amused by Plautus and Terence, or by adaptations of them which differ very little from their models.

The central approach to Shakespeare, therefore, can only lie through a study of dramatic structure, both in the individual play and in the broader structural principles which underlie the categories of tragedy and comedy. Shakespearian comedy is a form in which the same devices are used over and over again. By not paying enough attention to structure, we deprive ourselves of the perfectly legitimate pleasure of appreciating the *scholarly* qualities of Shakespeare, of seeing in the repeated formulas of his comedies a kind of Art of Fugue of comedy.

The most recent dramatic critic to be primarily interested in the structure and the categories of drama appears to be Aristotle, who did not say much about comedy. There does exist, however, a treatise called the *Tractatus Coislinianus,* a dry bald little summary, a page or two in length, of all the essential facts about comedy. Professor Lane Cooper, in his edition of it, suggests that it may summarize Aristotle's own lost work on comedy: it certainly is very close to Aristotelian ideas. And what the *Tractatus* says about characterization in comedy is this: "There are three types of comic characters: the alazon, the eiron, and the bomolochos."

Alazon means impostor, boaster or hypocrite, a man who pretends to be something more than he is. Eiron means a person who deprecates himself, and thereby deflates or exposes the alazon. The proper meaning of bomolochos is buffoon, a word usually restricted to farce in modern English, but which may be extended to the general sense of entertainer, the character who amuses by his mannerisms or powers of rhetoric. This list is closely related to a passage in the fourth book of the *Nicomachean Ethics* where Aristotle contrasts the bragging alazon with the self-deprecating eiron; but Aristotle also contrasts the buffoon with another character whom he calls *agroikos* or churlish, literally "rustic." So we may expand the three types of the *Tractatus* into four. This rustic type may also be extended to cover the whole range of what Elizabethans called gulls and what in vaudeville used to be called the straight man, the solemn or inarticulate character who allows the humor to bounce off him, so to speak. The relation of Sir Toby Belch to Sir Andrew Aguecheek will illustrate the contrast.

We now have four typical characters in comedy, arranged as two opposing pairs. If character depends on dramatic function, it follows that there are four typical functions in comedy, and four cardinal points of comic structure.

It is clear that the buffoon and the churl or rustic polarize, however, not so much the structure of comedy, as the comic mood. What a clown may do in a play is variable: his essential function is to amuse, and the essential function of the rustic is to act as a foil for him. We must therefore look to the opposition of alazon and eiron to find the structural principle of comedy. Such a contest is found in all comic forms: one thinks for instance of the first book of the *Republic,* in which the ironic Socrates, who deprecates his own knowledge, demolishes the boastful Thrasymachus, who says more than he knows. One thinks too of all the hundreds of comic scenes in which some kind of boastful or self-deceived character soliloquizes complacently while another character makes sarcastic asides to the audience. We see at once that the dramatic relation of alazon and eiron is very different from the ethical one. Aristotle disapproves equally of boaster and self-deprecator: to him they are on opposite sides of the golden mean of behavior. But in drama the eiron regularly speaks for or has the sympathy of the audience, and the alazon is his predestined victim.

Now let us apply this idea of a contest of eiron and alazon to the formulas of Terence and Plautus, who were still structural models for the Renaissance dramatists. Their plays are usually based on an erotic intrigue between a young man and a young woman, often a slave or courtesan. The intrigue is opposed either by the young man's father, or by some other kind of rival, often a wandering soldier, often a pimp. At the beginning of the comedy these opponents of the hero have control of the girl, or at least are able to thwart his desire. At the end of the play they are outwitted and the hero has his will. Such comedy turns, then, on a clash between two social groups, who are opposed even when they contain many of the same individuals. The center of one group is the hero and heroine; the center of the other is the father, the rival, or the persecutor of the heroine. We should expect to find our alazon types, then, in the latter group, and the eiron types in the former.

The commonest type of alazon is of course the braggart or *miles gloriosus,* and he runs through Shakespeare from the Thurio of *The Two Gentlemen of Verona* to the Stephano of *The Tempest.* The main reason for his popularity is that he is a man of words rather than deeds, and is consequently far more useful to a dramatist than any

tight-lipped hero could possibly be. Shakespeare gives a
series of subtle and ingenious variations on the theme.
Aguecheek, for example, has, as we have said, many of
Aristotle's *agroikos* characteristics. He is a *miles gloriosus*
gone into reverse: he may be a coward, but he is a completely inarticulate one, a behaviorist's paragon whose
every remark is pure response to stimulus. Slender in *The
Merry Wives* is a similar combination of types. Parolles
is a half-pathetic figure, a compulsive braggart who hates
his own runaway tongue, and is almost relieved to be
unmasked. The kernel of truth in the Morgann conception
of Falstaff seems to me to be that Falstaff is not an uncomplicated bragging coward, like, for instance, Jonson's
Bobadil, but a versatile comic genius who adopts the *miles
gloriosus* as one of his obvious roles.

Another common type of alazon is the pedant or crank,
who is also a man of words without deeds, in the sense
that he is full of ideas that have no relation to reality.
In Renaissance drama such a type is frequently a student
of the occult sciences, like Sir Epicure Mammon or the
astrologer in Congreve's *Love for Love,* though the simple
pedant is common enough from Cinquecento Italian
comedy on. There is a whole nest of comic pedants in
Love's Labor's Lost, including the king himself, with his
academic Utopia, Holofernes, and the metaphysical poet
Armado. Otherwise, Shakespeare seems not greatly interested in the type. The related type of the fop or coxcomb,
who is such a staple of courtly drama, interests Shakespeare even less: the only clear example, Osric, belongs
to a tragedy. The *female* alazon is rare in Elizabethan
drama: Katharina the shrew is the only Shakespearian
example. In later bourgeois comedies the *miles gloriosus*
is often replaced by a female rival to the heroine, a
"menace" or siren, as she would be called now, but this
development is for the most part post-Elizabethan. So is
the comedy of the bluestocking or *précieuse ridicule,*
though the Beatrice of *Much Ado* has a link with the type
in her role as a wit converted to love.

Turning to the eiron characters, we find that the center
of this group are the technical hero and heroine, the

pleasant young man and the pleasant girl he finally gets.
We usually find too that these characters are rather dull
unless they are combined with other types. The young
men (*adulescentes*) of Plautus and Terence are all alike,
as hard to tell apart in the dark as Demetrius and
Lysander. The hero's character has the neutrality that
enables the whole audience to accept him without question, and hence the dramatist plays him down, makes him
quiet and modest, a self-deprecating eiron. In *The Merry
Wives* the technical hero, a man named Fenton, has only
a bit part, and this play has picked up a hint or two from
Plautus' *Casina,* where the hero and heroine are not even
brought on the stage at all.

Far more important, from the point of view of characterization, is the type entrusted with hatching the
schemes which bring about the hero's victory. This character in Roman comedy is almost always a tricky slave
(*dolosus servus*), and in Renaissance comedy he becomes
the scheming valet who is so frequent in Continental
plays, and in Spanish drama is called the *gracioso*. Modern
audiences are most familiar with him in Figaro and in the
Leporello of *Don Giovanni*. Shakespeare starts out full of
enthusiasm for the clever servant in the *Comedy of Errors*
and *The Two Gentlemen of Verona,* but soon reduces
him to the rank of an incidental clown, as in the Lancelot
Gobbo of *The Merchant of Venice*. Elizabethan comedy
however had another type of trickster, represented by the
Matthew Merrygreek of *Ralph Roister Doister,* who is
generally said to be developed from the vice or iniquity
of the morality plays, a complicated question into which
we cannot enter here. The vice, to give him that name, is
very useful to a comic dramatist because he acts from pure
love of mischief, and can set a comic action going without
needing any motivation. The vice may be as lighthearted
as Puck or as malignant as Don John in *Much Ado,* but
as a rule the vice's activity is, in spite of his name,
benevolent, at least from the comic point of view. It is
he who helps the play to end happily, cheats or hood-
winks the stupid old men, and puts the young in one
another's arms. He is in fact the spirit of comedy, and

the two clearest examples of the type in Shakespeare, Puck and Ariel, are both spiritual beings.

The role of the vice includes a great deal of disguising, and the type may usually be recognized by disguise. A typical example is the Brainworm of Jonson's *Every Man in His Humor*, who calls the action of the play the day of his metamorphosis. Similarly Ariel has to surmount the difficult stage direction of "Enter invisible." In tragedy the vice has a counterpart in the type usually called the Machiavellian villain, who also often acts without motivation, from pure love of evil. Edmund in *King Lear* has the role of a tragic vice, and Edmund is contrasted with Edgar. Edgar, with his bewildering variety of disguises, his appearance to blind or mad people in different roles, and his tendency to appear on the third sound of the trumpet and to come pat like the catastrophe of the old comedy, seems to be an experiment in a new type, a kind of tragic "virtue," if I may coin this word by analogy.

The vice is combined with the hero whenever the latter is a cheeky, improvident young man who hatches his own schemes and cheats his rich father or uncle into giving him his patrimony along with the girl. The vice-hero is a favorite of Jonson and Middleton, but not of Shakespeare, though Petruchio is close to the type. The vice can also, however, be combined with the heroine, who usually disguises herself as a boy to forward her schemes. For some reason this is Shakespeare's favorite combination, in which his chief precursor appears to have been Greene.

Another eiron type has been even less noticed. This is a character, generally an older man, who begins the action of the play by withdrawing from it, and ends the play by returning. He is often a father with the motive of seeing what his son will do. The action of *Every Man in His Humor* is set going in this way by Knowell Senior. The disappearance and return of Lovewit, the owner of the house which is the scene of *The Alchemist*, is parallel. The clearest Shakespearian example is the Duke in *Measure for Measure;* but Shakespeare is more addicted to the type than might appear at first glance. One of the tricky slaves in Plautus, in a soliloquy, boasts that he is the *architectus* of the comic action. In Shakespeare the vice is rarely the real architectus: Puck and Ariel both act under orders from an older man, if one may call Oberon a man for the moment. When the heroine takes the vice role, she is often significantly related to her father, even when the father is not in the play at all, like the father of Helena, who gives her his medical knowledge, or the father of Portia, who arranges the scheme of the caskets.

As You Like It and *The Tempest* reverse the usual formula of the retreating eiron, as Duke Senior and Prospero are followed by the whole cast into their retreats. In Prospero the architectus role of this older eiron type is at its clearest. The formula is not confined to comedy: Polonius, who shows so many of the disadvantages of a literary education, attempts the role of a retreating paternal eiron three times, once too often. It also has a tragic counterpart in the returning ghost of the Senecan revenge plays. In other words, the major and minor themes of *Hamlet* are in direct counterpoint, the latter being a stock comic theme adapted to a tragedy. *King Lear* has a very similar structure: there too the minor or Gloucester plot is a tragic adaptation of the common Terentian theme of a stupid old father outwitted by a clever and unprincipled son.

We pass now to the buffoon types, those whose function it is to increase the mood of festivity rather than to contribute to the plot. Renaissance comedy, unlike Roman comedy, has a great variety of such characters, professional fools, clowns, pages, singers, and incidental characters with established comic habits, like the malapropism of Dogberry or the comic accents of Fluellen and Dr. Caius. The oldest buffoon of this incidental nature is the parasite, who may be given something to do, as Jonson gives Mosca the role of a vice in *Volpone,* but who, *qua* parasite, does nothing but entertain the audience by talking about his appetite. He derives chiefly from Greek Middle Comedy, which appears to have been very full of food, and where he was, not unnaturally, closely associated with another established buffoon type, the cook, who breaks into another play of Plautus to bustle and order about and make long speeches about the mysteries of cooking. In the role of cook the buffoon or entertainer appears, not simply as a gratuitous addition, like the parasite, but as something more like a master of ceremonies, a center for the comic mood. There is no cook in Shakespeare, though there is a superb description of one in the *Comedy of Errors,* but a similar role is often attached to a jovial and loquacious host, like the "mad host" of *The Merry Wives* or the Simon Eyre of *The Shoemakers Holiday.* In Middleton's *A Trick to Catch the Old One* the mad host type is combined with the vice. In Falstaff and Sir Toby Belch we can see the affinities of the buffoon or entertainer type both with the parasite and with the master of revels.

Finally, there is a fourth group to which we have assigned the word agroikos, and which usually means either churlish or rustic, depending on the context. We find churls in the miserly, snobbish or priggish characters whose role is that of the refuser of festivity, the killjoy who tries to stop the fun, or, like Malvolio, locks up the food and drink instead of dispensing it. In the sulky and self-centered Bertram of *All's Well* there is a most unusual and ingenious combination of this type with the hero. More often, however, the churl belongs to the alazon group. All miserly old men in comedies are churls, and Shylock has a close affinity with this group. Shakespeare often sets up a churlish or sinister figure at the beginning of his comedy to act as a starting point for the comic action. Examples are Duke Frederick, Leontes and Angelo. In *The Tempest,* Caliban has much the same relation to the churlish type that Ariel has to the vice or tricky slave. But often, where the mood is more lighthearted, we may translate agroikos simply by rustic, as with Shallow, Silence and Slender.

In a very ironic comedy a different type of character may play the role of the refuser of festivity. The more ironic the comedy, the more absurd the society, and an absurd society may be condemned by, or at least contrasted with, a character that we may call the plain dealer, an outspoken advocate of a kind of moral norm who has the sympathy of the audience. A good example is the Cléante of Molière's *Tartuffe*. The plain dealer, however, goes with an implication of moral values, and Shakespeare, with his usual adroitness in keeping out of moral rattraps, avoids the type. His closest approach to one, and it is not very close, is the Lafeu of *All's Well*. In a pastoral comedy, however, the idealized virtues of rural life may be represented by a simple man who speaks for the pastoral ideal. Two social grades of this are exhibited in the Duke Senior and the Corin of *As You Like It*. When the tone deepens from the ironic to the bitter, the plain dealer tends to become the malcontent or railer, like Apemantus, who may be morally superior to his society, as he is to some extent in Marston's play of that name, but who may also be too motivated by envy to be much more than another aspect of his society's evil, like Thersites. Shakespeare makes no attempt to alter the traditional conception of Thersites as an envious railer. But the mood of *Troilus and Cressida* is so sardonic that Thersites steals every scene he is in.

In his characterization, as in everything else, Shakespeare is a better dramatist than his contemporaries, but not a different kind of dramatist. In the writers of humor comedies, Jonson, Marston, Massinger, Middleton, Chapman, dramatic effect is normally predictable in terms of dramatic function. If a braggart is introduced, he will brag until he is unconditionally exposed. Shakespeare uses the same formulas, but in a much more subtle, complex and unpredictable way. Lucio, in *Measure for Measure*, belongs to the alazon group of characters: he is not a *miles gloriosus* like Parolles, but like Parolles he talks too much. The Duke has the eiron role of disguising himself as a simple monk, listening unseen to the action, and then returning as an awful incarnation of omniscient judgment. The stage is set for the utter annihilation of Lucio, and in Jonson it would have been that: the scene is dramatically not unlike the trial of Volpone. But Lucio scores point after point against the Duke; he keeps getting laughs, and any character who gets laughs gets at least some of the audience's sympathy. Horrid doubts arise in our minds: perhaps the Duke after all is only a tiresome and snoopy old bore, who has heard of himself what an eavesdropper deserves to hear. Of course morally and historically sound critics will conclude, no doubt rightly, that the scene represents an impressive triumph of Justice over Slander, and demonstrates the values of personal monarchy to an audience already convinced of them. Those who are morally spineless and historically vague, like myself, will have to take what comfort we can from the incidental victories of impudence over dignity.

But I imagine that Shakespeare had a similar diversity of creatures in mind. Many in his audience doubtless held properly Jacobean views about government and prerogative, and, like some modern critics, thought that the Duke alluded to James I himself. Or there may have been in the audience that Henry Hawkins who asserted that Queen Elizabeth had had five children by Lord Cecil, and went on her progresses in order to be delivered of them. It is because he can get every ounce of dramatic effect out of his situations that Shakespeare's characters seem so wonderfully lifelike. I am not trying to reduce them to stock types, but I am trying to suggest that the notion of an antithesis between the lifelike character and the stock type is a vulgar error. All Shakespeare's characters owe their consistency to the appropriateness of the stock type which belongs to their dramatic function. That stock type is not the character, but it is as necessary to the character as a skeleton is to the actor who plays it.

MARK VAN DOREN

from *Shakespeare*

The Falstaff of *Henry IV* is missing from *The Merry Wives of Windsor,* which is said to have been written for a queen who wanted to see the fat knight in love. The trouble is just there; he is in love with the merry wives—or with the plot to make them think he is—rather than with truth and existence, rather than with the merry lives he had been living when Shakespeare caught him in his comic prime. His ambition for Mistress Ford and Mistress Page, together with the delusions which it requires, fills all his mind; he has a single end in view, and believes he can attain it. He does not lose his belief until the last act, though to every other person in the play he has been a fool from the first. The old man who once had missed nothing now misses everything; he has toppled from his balance, he is unintelligent. Hitherto he had made a large world merry by playing the butt; here he makes a small one sad by being the butt of coarse-grained men and women who drag and buffet him about until the business grows as boring as a practical joke. His dignity was never touched in *Henry IV*; rather it increased with every exposure, for what exposed itself was his understanding. In *The Merry Wives* he has none to lose, being no longer a

From *Shakespeare* by Mark Van Doren. New York: Henry Holt and Co., Inc., 1939; London: George Allen & Unwin, Ltd., 1941. Copyright 1939 by Mark Van Doren. Reprinted by permission of Holt, Rinehart and Winston, Inc.

man of mind but a tub of meat to be bounced downstairs
and thrown in the muddy river. Even the dull senses of
Sir Hugh Evans can smell in him a man of middle-
earth. And it is not until a few minutes from the final
line that Falstaff sees he has been grossly overreached.
Then he utters the incredible sentence:

> I do begin to perceive that I am made an ass.   (V.v.122)

"I do begin to perceive." His perception had once been
without beginning or end; or if there was a beginning it
ran nimbly before that of the quickest eyes about him.
No wonder he has to beg off at the close with three equally
incredible words:

> I am dejected.   (V.v.165)

So will any audience be which remembers the chimes at
midnight, Master Shallow.

Only the husk of Falstaff's voice is here. Shakespeare
has written the part with great talent but without love.
The long speeches, descriptive in most cases of mishaps
by hamper and flood, are certainly very able, and a phrase
in one of them, "I have a kind of alacrity in sinking"
(III.v.12–13), almost restores the man we knew. Nor has
he dropped the habit of spilling his speech in short repeated units: "I warrant thee, nobody hears; mine own
people, mine own people" (II.ii.51–52). The labor of
composition, however, is often apparent in passages where
Falstaff forces his wit. "No quips now, Pistol! Indeed, I
am in the waist two yards about; but I am now about no
waste, I am about thrift"—the pun is poor, and further-
more Falstaff used to get on without puns, just as he
used to manage an effect of verbal felicity without having
to lug in monstrous circumlocutions like "pullet-sperm in
my brewage" for "eggs in my sack" (III.v.31–32). Perhaps his best remark is a reference to the Welshman
Evans as "one who makes fritters of English." But that
is because he retains something of his old interest in language; though it should be pointed out in passing that

Falstaff would have been entertained by the fritters of a vastly better Welshman than Evans if he had lived to hear Fluellen in *Henry V*. So for that matter with Pistol and Bardolph, who do not survive in *Henry V* with all of their old vigor, but who are happier there, along with the laconic Nym, than these poor pieces of them are in *The Merry Wives*. Their betrayal of the fat jester whom once they feared and adored (I.iii) is doubtless the clearest sign of their degradation—not in moral character, for they had none, but in that dramatic character which preserved them in their prime from the indignity of a descent to conventional comic devices. In their prime they lived for no other reason than that they were alive, and loved to come swaggering out of the darkness into lighted taverns. Here they exist simply to keep a comic machinery turning, as Mistress Quickly exists solely in the profession of go-between and talebearer. As for Master Shallow, we have one or two remnants of the well-starved justice: "Come, coz; come, coz; we stay for you. A word with you, coz; marry, this, coz" (I.i.199–200); and "Bodykins, Master Page, . . . we have some salt of our youth in us; we are the sons of women, Master Page" (II.iii.41–46). But the full music of his foolishness is missing too.

The one satisfactory person of the comedy is, perhaps naturally enough, a new one. Mine host of the Garter Inn comes bellowing into the dialogue with something like the primeval force his fellows formerly had. He wields a mad, winy (or is it beery) eloquence. He is a man of few words but he uses them over and over, mounting through repetitions of them to a preposterous peak of self-induced excitement. As his custom is in such cases, Shakespeare has hit upon a single word that will do the trick, and will seem to do it without any further effort on his part. The word is "bully."

Falstaff. Mine host of the Garter!
Host. What says my bully-rook? Speak scholarly and wisely.
Falstaff. Truly, mine host, I must turn away some of my followers.

Host. Discard, bully Hercules; cashier. Let them wag. Trot, trot.

Falstaff. I sit at ten pounds a week.

Host. Thou 'rt an emperor, Caesar, Keisar, and Pheezar. I will entertain Bardolph; he shall draw, he shall tap. Said I well, bully Hector?

Falstaff. Do so, good mine host.

Host. I have spoke; let him follow. Let me see thee froth and lime. I am at a word; follow.   (I.iii.1–15)

The dialogue is clearly mine host's, not Falstaff's. It is he that carries it away, for he is mad about words, he goes into ecstasies of epithet, he boils over into a foam of phrases.

Is he dead, my Ethiopian? Is he dead, my Francisco? Ha, bully! What says my Aesculapius? my Galen? my heart of elder? Ha! is he dead, bully stale? Is he dead?
                                                        (II.iii.25–28)

Let him die; but first sheathe thy impatience, throw cold water on thy choler, go about the fields with me through Frogmore. I will bring thee where Mistress Anne Page is, at a farm-house a-feasting; and thou shalt woo her.
                                                        (II.iii.80–84)

Peace, I say! hear mine host of the Garter. Am I politic? Am I subtle? Am I a Machiavel? Shall I lose my doctor? No; he gives me the potions and the motions. Shall I lose my parson, my priest, my Sir Hugh? No; he gives me the proverbs and the noverbs. Give my thy hand, terrestrial; so. Give me thy hand, celestial; so. Boys of art, I have deceiv'd you both.   (III.i.95–102)

What say you to young Master Fenton? He capers, he dances, he has eyes of youth, he writes verses, he speaks holiday, he smells April and May. He will carry 't, he will carry 't; 't is in his buttons; he will carry 't.
                                                        (III.ii.62–66)

"Trust me," ventures Shallow, "a mad host." Completely

and most comically mad he is; and the only fresh thing in *The Merry Wives*.

Master Fenton has eyes of youth and speaks in verses of the sweet Anne Page whom the action ushers into his arms at the end. But they are meager verses, like those in which she simpers her reciprocated love. It is not a comedy in which poetry would be expected, any more than comedy itself. After *The Comedy of Errors* it is Shakespeare's most heartless farce. And this is too bad, since it is his only citizen play, his one local and contemporary piece. In another mood he might have made much of Ford and Page, and of their wives who to our loss are here so coarse-grained, so monotonous and broad-hipped in their comic dialect.

> *Mrs. Ford.* "Boarding," call you it? I'll be sure to keep him above deck.
> *Mrs. Page.* So will I. If he come under my hatches, I'll never to sea again.   (II.i.89–92)

With craft and talent Shakespeare has supplied what the convention and a queen demanded. But his genius is not here, or his love.

H. B. CHARLTON

from *Falstaff*

Shakespeare, so the story runs, was commanded by his Queen to resuscitate the corpse whose heart had been fracted and corroborate, and to show him in love. Shakespeare obeyed: and there can be no clearer evidence of his own rejection of Falstaff. The boisterous merriment of *The Merry Wives of Windsor* is a cynical revenge which Shakespeare took on the hitherto unsuspecting gaiety of his own creative exuberance. The Falstaff in it bears a name which masks the bitterness of its author's disillusionment. Any competent dramatist after Plautus could have followed the conventions of comedy, and shown a gross, fat, lascivious, old man ludicrously caught in the toils of his own lust. But for Shakespeare to call that old fat man Falstaff, that is the measure of his bitterness. For, as Mr. Bradley has said, the Falstaff of *The Merry Wives* has nothing in common with our Falstaff except his name, a trick or two of inspired speech, and—though Mr. Bradley has not said this—a superficial likeness to Mr. Stoll's pattern of the "comic" character to be found all the way down the ages of theatrical history.

The masquerading figure in *The Merry Wives* is an old fat fellow whom all can gull to make a public sport. He

From *Shakespearian Comedy* by H. B. Charlton. London: Methuen & Co., Ltd.; New York: The Macmillan Company, 1938. Reprinted by permission of Methuen & Co., Ltd.

himself knows how little of the old Sir John survives: it is even time that little were choked with a piece of toasted cheese. "I have been transformed, and how my transformation hath been washed and cudgeled, they [his old associates at court] would melt me out of my fat drop by drop and liquor fisherman's boots with me: I warrant they would whip me with their fine wits till I were as crestfallen as a dried pear." So far is he out at heels that he can only try to provide for himself by shifts and conycatchings which he has no longer the genius to bring successfully off. He is encumbered with new afflictions. He carries his wine now only like a Flemish drunkard. Not only has he quaking fits of sheer fear, but he openly confesses his intolerable fright. His pride has gone: he himself broadcasts the story of his ignominy: "I knew not what 'twas to be beaten till lately." "I suffered the pangs of three several deaths; first, an intolerable fright, to be detected with a jealous rotten bellwether; next, to be compassed, like a good bilbo, in the circumference of a peck, hilt to point, heel to head; and then, to be stopped in, like a strong distillation, with stinking clothes that fretted in their own grease: think of that—a man of my kidney —think of that—that am as subject to heat as butter; a man of continual dissolution and thaw: it was a miracle to 'scape suffocation. And in the height of this bath, when I was more than half stewed in grease, like a Dutch dish, to be thrown into the Thames, and cooled, glowing hot, in that surge, like a horseshoe; think of that—hissing hot —think of that."

Time and again, in *The Merry Wives*, some situation or another recalls by grotesque contrast the extent of Sir John's transformation. Think, for instance, of his impressive nonchalance in planning his own safety at Shrewsbury: "Hal, if thou see me down in the battle, and bestride me, so": and set by its side his frenzy of fear when news of Ford's return renders him witless to plan anything and makes him appeal in a panic to the women to devise any sort of trick by which he may escape: "good hearts, devise something; any extremity rather than a mischief." His counterfeits, too, are different. His *sang-froid*

deceived Douglas into believing that he was dead enough
to need no further killing. But now, he counterfeits by
a ludicrous disguise as an old woman merely to avoid a
jealous husband (think of how Mistress Quickly was rec-
ommended to love *her* husband), and, by so doing, after
heavy thwackings, a mere stroke of luck prevents his being set in the common stocks by a knave constable. How
are the mighty fallen! He cannot indeed fall lower than
he does when, to escape, not now a Douglas, but a band
of children playing fairies, he lies down ostrichwise, with
eyes pressed close to the ground, oblivious altogether of
the receipt of fern seeds he used to carry with him. "I'll
wink and couch."

His wits have lost all their nimbleness. He no longer
has the confidence that they will always be quick enough
to bring him out of his scrapes. Gone is his old art of
creeping into a halfpenny purse, into a pepper box, or
slipping through a keyhole. Difficulties which he would
formerly have welcomed with zest, no longer excite his
exuberance: indeed mere news of them now distracts him.
Worse still, his wit is so dulled that he does not even see
his difficulties. "I do *begin* to perceive," he says—and
that, after he has been fooled egregiously and often—
"I do *begin* to perceive that I am made an ass." Truth is,
they can fool him even as they wish; once, twice, three
times running, he falls into their toils. Anybody can fool
him: neither Mistress Page nor Mistress Ford ever for a
moment imagines that he will be too clever for her—

> Devise but how you'll use him when he comes,
> And let us two devise to bring him thither.

And these are just citizens' wives of Windsor. Even Pistol
knows Mistress Quickly for a punk who is Cupid's car-
rier. But, of all dullards, Mistress Quickly can tell a tale
well enough to gull Falstaff now. When such a go-between
is amply adequate to overreach Sir John, he is indeed
gone beyond recovery. There is scarcely a saving grace.
He who had been a prince's confederate in highway escapades is now a receiver of the petty loot of pocket-picking

and bag-snatching: a fan-handle now, no longer a king's exchequer: and all for fifteen pence. He shuffles, hedges, and lurches amongst a sordid gang of unconfinable baseness. Mean and low as his associates now are, he is on no better than an equal footing with them at best, and as often as not, they round on him and outdo him. With his onetime familiars, he had been Jack Falstaff, John with his brothers and sisters, but Sir John with all Europe. Now he is "bully-rook" even with a provincial innkeeper. He is on entirely new terms with rascals like Pistol and Nym: "my honest lads," he must call them, to ward off their quips. Not only have they the impudence to jibe at him; they have the audacity to defy him openly, and flatly refuse to do his bidding. In the end, two simple bourgeois and their wives, colleagued with a foolish doctor, a comic Welsh parson, and an innkeeper, can trample the once mighty Falstaff in Windsor's mud. "Have I laid my brain in the sun and dried it, that it wants matter to prevent so gross o'erreaching as this? Am I ridden with a Welsh goat too? Shall I have a coxcomb of frize?" "Well, I am your theme: you have the start of me; I am dejected; I am not able to answer the Welsh flannel; ignorance itself is a plummet o'er me: use me as you will." "Use me as you will": that is, in fine, to put a period to the jest.

But why this ruthless exposure, this almost malicious laceration of him who had once rejoiced the hearts of his author and of the rest of the world?

It might be, and has been, claimed that the original Falstaff overgrew his part, and had to be turned out of the cycle at the point when Hal became king. As has been seen, there is matter in the second *Henry IV* to suggest that Shakespeare was leading Falstaff to his dismissal: matter, also, hinting that he did it reluctantly. But if Sir John had necessarily to go, could he not have been allowed a deathbed—a more certain dismissal than a king's rejection—before Hal's coronation? An apoplexy, any affliction to which the body of man is liable might, without stretch of likelihood, have been called in to remove a Falstaff who, on a professional diagnosis, "might have more diseases than he knew for." Moreover, his removal by mere royal edict brought technical troubles with it, the dubieties surrounding the character of Hal. Why then did Shakespeare rest satisfied with Henry's rejection of Falstaff as the expedient by which to get rid of him? Is it indeed Henry, or is it Shakespeare who rejects Falstaff? Throughout the second *Henry IV* Falstaff is falling from Shakespeare's grace; by the end of the play, he has almost forced his author, though reluctantly, to face up to the situation. Falstaff has in fact displayed his inability to be what had seemed to be. He has disqualified himself as a comic hero. He has let Shakespeare down.

The figure which the dramatist's imagination had intuitively compounded, had seemed infinitely better provided than any of his predecessors with the gifts of the comic hero. With such a spirit, such a mind, such intuitions, and such an outlook on life, he appeared to bear within his own nature a complete guarantee of survival and of mastery of circumstance, the pledge of the perfect comic hero. But somehow or other, when the intoxication of creating him is momentarily quieter, hesitancies begin to obtrude and the processes of creation are different. The clogging becomes stronger. Falstaff must be cast off, as he is cast off at the end of the second *Henry IV*. But a pathetic hope persists, and is spoken in the Epilogue: it may still be possible to save Sir John: "our humble author will continue the story with Sir John in it, and make you merry with fair Katherine of France: where, for any thing I know, Falstaff shall die of a sweat, unless already a' be killed with your hard opinions."[1] But before the play with Katherine in it is written, the issue is settled. Falstaff is irrevocably discredited, fit for nothing more but Windsor forest.

This suggestion as to the decline and fall of Falstaff neither requires nor presupposes a conscious purpose in Shakespeare's reason. In the sheer abandon of his imaginative fervor, Falstaff and the circumstances he overcomes are projected by the unthinking zest of the author's imaginative apprehension, and shape themselves into the coherent universe which a play makes for itself. But at

[1] *II Henry IV*. Epilogue.

moments the world of his creation is threatened by the intrusion of circumstances which will have destroyed its validity if they should prove too much for Falstaff. And by no fetch of his imagination can he endow Falstaff with the aptitude to acquire his customary mastery over these intrusions: nor, springing as did Falstaff himself from his imagination, can they be dismissed more readily than can he. In the way in which, without deliberate judgment, an artist's creation of an image of life is satisfying, Falstaff had satisfied Shakespeare. Within the scope of worldly wisdom, which is the philosophy of comedy, Falstaff had seemed to justify entire trust. In this sense, Shakespeare believed in him; and Falstaff proved to be a god with feet of clay. Hence his bitter disillusionment and his willingness to call the contemptible caricature of *The Merry Wives* by the name of Sir John Falstaff.

HERBERT WHITTAKER

Full Shakespeare Texts Return—With Bonuses

The trend in twentieth-century production of Shakespeare has been markedly toward giving the Elizabethan dramatist his full say. More of the original Folio texts are being acted now than at any time since the plays were first produced, it is safe to say. The full-length *Hamlet*, for instance, is no longer the novelty it was in the Thirties.

The return to an Elizabethan type of stage has made this possible. In the more elaborate "scenic" productions, the plays necessarily suffered cuts, to say nothing of other convenient adjustments.

The swing back to full text would seem to have reached its climax in the full-length *Hamlet*, one production of which Maurice Evans staged here in 1940. But this morning we can report that our own Stratford Festival has gone much further.

The audiences who have been seeing *The Merry Wives of Windsor* all this season have actually been seeing more of the play than any other audience ever saw. More than that, they have been seeing more than Shakespeare ever wrote.

On a rough count, Michael Langham's production of *The Merry Wives of Windsor* has added about thirty lines

From *The Globe and Mail* (Toronto), August 11, 1956. Reprinted by permission of *The Globe and Mail*.

to the original. Among those lines, are two or three of the evening's biggest laughs.

Adding to Shakespeare is not unknown in the theater, even at Stratford. It is an open secret that Tyrone Guthrie brought more than his genius to the first year's production of *All's Well That Ends Well*.

Is Michael Langham, Dr. Guthrie's successor, the type of man to pad the plays and throw in extra "gags" in the manner of the infamous Colley Cibber, whose most famous quotation is Richard III's "Off with his head, so much for Buckingham!"? No, Mr. Langham is not. He is one producer with a scholar's deep respect for the playwright.

Those of us who have seen *The Merry Wives of Windsor* in the past have doubtless seen a truncated version, centering on the three hoaxes played on Sir John Falstaff by Mistress Page and Mistress Ford. But if you read the Quarto text you will find a great deal more to the play. Principally, you will find references to an elaborate trick played on Mine Host of the Garter by Dr. Caius and Sir Hugh Evans, in revenge for his misdirection of them when they were to meet for a duel.

The trick concerns the introduction of some spurious Germans into Mine Host's establishment and their departure with his horses, an exit gleefully announced by both Dr. Caius and Sir Hugh. But the actual scene of the deception is missing. As it would have represented the kind of disguise scene Shakespeare was very handy at (and which his audiences delighted in) it is not unlikely that the scene or scenes have been lost.

Proceeding along these lines, Mr. Langham decided to "restore" the business of disguise, as this would allow him to present with more clarity the events leading up to it and the references made after it.

He was also after, he explained when we put the question to him, a better balance between the Falstaff hoaxes and the business with Mine Host. He feels that the inclusion of the extra scenes "greatly assists the structure of the play, from the point of orchestration."

Mr. Langham did not write the extra lines himself. He

called in a member of the Stratford Board of Directors who is also Canada's best-known playwright, Robertson Davies of Peterborough. Mr. Davies accounts *The Merry Wives of Windsor* almost his favorite play of Shakespeare's, but he must have admitted the obscurities because he fell to his task with a gusto which it would not be inappropriate to call Shakespearian.

Mr. Davies wrote more lines than Mr. Langham used —about two-thirds, Mr. Langham estimates. Some of them are almost more Shakespearian than anything Shakespeare wrote, for Mr. Davies is a Welsh-Canadian with a fine ear and a sly sense of humor. In fact, some of the lines are so Shakespearian that they almost defeat the purpose of greater clarity. But there are gems.

Says Mr. Davies' Welsh Dr. Evans to his French confrere: "You have your country's name o' your side, look you, master doctor, for you are all Gaul."

When that French confrere, Dr. Caius, is advancing his hoax on Mine Host there is this exchange:

Caius: "I have tell you, mine host, I bring de lords my patients. These-a shentleman wait upon the Duke of High Germany who come here to da court in two-three days, and desire all de rooms of you Jarteer."

Host: "All my rooms, bully? I have but one."

Caius: "Dey must have all."

Mr. Davies' names for his supposed Germans are certainly Elizabethan, if not Shakespearian. He introduces them as de Hogen-Mogen von Kammerpot, Hogen Mogen von Arsfusstritt and Hogen Mogen von Rumplick!

Contrast this with the lyricism of one of Pistol's lines earlier. Caius questions him: "Vot is your device?"

Pistol:

"Not here, for trees have ears, and meadows, elves

"Pricking our speech in green charactery.

"Thy parlor, honest Cambrian, will be best

"To hear confession of our ripening jest."

The Shakespeare of Peterborough is not above confounding his enemies with a bit of mock-Shakespeare. When Rugby is told to put on vizard and cloak to impersonate one of the Hogen-Mogens, he shudders:

"I like not to play the actor, lest I should fall into naughtiness."

Whereupon the Davies-Caius explodes: "By gar, you are the Puritan-a dog!"

Rugby's line, as delivered by Lloyd Bochner in Mr. Langham's production, incidentally, provides one of the play's greatest laughs.

The ms. of Mr. Davies' additions should be one of Stratford's greatest treasures, especially as he had adorned it with the title: "The 'Lost' Scenes from *The Merry Wives of Windsor,* restored from the 1599 Duodecimo and edited with the notes by the Dark Horse of the Sonnets." The notes are gems of high mock-scholarship.

It is a work which should be prized by all Shakespearian scholars who have seen the Stratford production, but will probably not be—as none of them seem to have spotted Mr. Davies' additions to the text.

MARILYN FRENCH

from *Shakespeare's Division of Experience*

The Merry Wives of Windsor is a farce, an action comedy, with a linear plot, heavy use of disguise, and a male "hero" who is also the villain. The ambivalence of the central character resembles that of Petruchio, who is both hero and villain (for Kate, at least), and the split between the twin Antipholuses, who each unwittingly become the antagonist of the other. The difference between Falstaff and the two other figures is that they win and he does not. Petruchio is able to discard his shrewish side once Kate has subordinated herself to him: both Antipholuses accept happily their given places in the moral-social structure of their world. But Falstaff has set out to violate the core virtue in the Shakespearean value structure; the part of him that willed such an act must be, like Don John, exorcised from the community.

The setting is bourgeois—settled, prosperous, and imbued with a moral complacency lacking even in the puritanical Shylock. Its terms are overwhelmingly "masculine": the play opens with Shallow and Slender listing the former's claim to legitimacy in the form of titles and prerogatives, anciency of house, coats of arms. Because the characters are so foolish, this discussion acts to challenge the notion of legitimacy. Thus, as usual in Shakespeare, the opening of the play sets forth its terms: they seem familiar—legitimacy versus challenges to it. But in this case, the challenge arises (at first) not from outsiders, illegitimates, but in our minds, as a result of the inanity and self-satisfaction of the legitimates. There are further challenges quickly: Falstaff kills Shallow's deer, illegally; his men pick Slender's pockets. And we know by now that Slender is intending a kind of theft: he agrees to marry Anne Page for her money.

The major themes of the play are the cornerstones of bourgeois life: possession of property, possession of women, and fear of theft. There are two plots, each containing a stranger who is a down-at-heels aristocrat (foreigner) who is attempting to "steal" from the propertied men of Windsor. The action concerns the efforts of Falstaff and Fenton to get what they want, and the efforts of the Windsorites to thwart them. The outsiders are perceived as thieves, like the "Germans" who do steal the host's horses.

But in keeping with the suggestion that the legitimates are not any more legitimate than anyone else, the insiders are also busy thieving. The host cheats his customers; Mistress Quickly cheats anyone who will pay for her help; the host intends to cheat the "Germans" who cheat him first. Evans and Caius intend to duel over a piece of property neither of them owns—Anne Page—but are cozened by the host and cozen him in return. Slender and his adherents intend to cheat the Pages by offering a false devotion to Anne in return for her person and her property.

Falstaff, supposedly the major cozener, is cozened into giving money to Mistress Quickly, is cozened by the wives, and is betrayed by his own servants. Ford is cozened by Falstaff into paying for his own cozening. Both Pages cozen each other in their attempts to have Anne stolen away, but she and Fenton cozen them instead. Everyone in the play (except William) cozens, is cozened, or both.

For the most part, the disguises operate similarly—they

fool the person who adopts the disguise. Both Falstaff and Ford become the victims of their own disguises.

Merry Wives is a play about property. . . . Property is *all* it is about. Even the "feminine" elements of the play—chaste constancy in the wives, love in Anne, and Falstaff's outlaw feminine sexual rebellion—become mere counters in a conflict over property.

Falstaff is set up as an example of the outlaw feminine principle (as he is in the *Henry IV* plays). He wishes to undermine or challenge the established order: he has a reputation for drinking, sexual freedom, and petty crime. But very quickly, in this play, a different note enters: his intention in crime and cozening is not primarily the fun of it—it is for survival. He has an edge of desperation in this play that makes him at once more pathetic and less fun—because he is less free—than the Falstaff of the histories.

And here, his opposition to the established order is less a rebellion against its constrictions and hypocrisies, less based in a need to assert other values, than it is an effort, however odd, to win a place within it. He cheats and steals and strives to seduce in order to find a place within the society he is victimizing: he wants money to play the gentleman. Originally, he claims that his intention in attempting to seduce the wives is to get at their husbands' purses; but in his meeting with the wives, particularly that in the last scene, he expresses genuine desire for sexual or perhaps merely affectionate love. In his pathetic longing for esteem and affection, he is a sad scapegoat. He wants what everyone else in the play wants—and however unacceptable his means of attaining it, he is more morally acceptable than Mr. Ford. What keeps Sir John an outsider in Windsor, despite his status, is his lack of wealth.

The pathos built into his character would not preclude him from being a villain—it does not do so for Shylock—if his goal were really what it seems—to destroy chaste constancy, the emblem of the feminine principle. But money values override everything in this world. The wives respond to his letters with an outrage similar to that one would feel at an attempted robbery. Their language and their behavior demonstrate that they, like their husbands, see their bodies and reputations as possessions of which Falstaff is trying to defraud them. Their revenge is motivated by the sense that in writing to them at all, he has stolen something from them, and it is calculated in the same terms: they will lead him on until he is forced to pawn his horses to the host.[1]

The host is jealous and possessive about his property; Caius is jealous and possessive about his house and closets; Ford is jealous and possessive about his wife. Page is jealous and possessive about his daughter, whom he sees as property to be disposed of as he chooses: Caius, Evans, and Slender see Anne the same way. (No wonder she speaks so little in the play.) Even Fenton confesses to her that his original intention in courting her was to gain control of her wealth.

Cuckoldry means something quite different to Mr. Ford than it does to Claudio in *Much Ado About Nothing*, or to Posthumus. For them it is a failure of the pivot on which the rest of human life turns. For Mr. Ford it is theft: "My bed shall be abus'd, my coffers ransack'd, my reputation gnawn at" (II.ii,292–293). He is not concerned with his wife's affections, her relation with him. Nor is he primarily concerned with his reputation—he drags the whole community into his house to witness what he conceives of as *his* degradation. His fear of cuckoldry is a fear of theft.

On the mythic level of this play, a married woman has an affair right under her husband's nose, with the assistance of a woman friend and a village nitwit; and a young woman being courted by two village nitwits defies her parents and elopes. What keeps this underplot from gaining force is that everyone in the community except Anne Page and possibly Fenton perceives all events in terms of money, possession, and theft.

The disguise convention revokes the adultery and operates to punish Falstaff to the point where he can be

---

1 Berry, Ralph, *Comedies*, p. 148, finds revenge the subject of the play.

assimilated in the community. The marriage is irrevocable, but it too seems to be forgiven and accepted by the elders in the conclusion. *Merry Wives* also concentrates on language-as-theme. Like *Love's Labor's Lost*, it is filled with characters who speak idiosyncratically and who criticize the speech of others: Evans, Pistol, Bardolph, Caius, Slender, and Quickly.

The significance of the language theme is indicated by a short scene which is otherwise extraneous.[2] IV.i, is a discussion of language among Evans, William Page, Mrs. Page, and Mrs. Quickly. There is comedy in Evans' pedantry and Quickly's misunderstanding, but that does not seem reason enough for its existence.

The four characters represent four approaches to language, each dictated by the inner world of the speaker. William, whose mind is still flexible, translates *lapis* as *stone* and *stone* as *pebble*, an understandable progression. He has not yet learned to think in circles. Evans has milked all the life out of language: *lapis* is *stone* and *stone* is *lapis*. Mrs. Page has a greater understanding than anyone else of what is going on, but her interest, in keeping with her place in the community, is strictly material: the *profit* her son is obtaining in school. Evans' scolding of Quickly is, like the disguises in the play, self-delusive: with his accent, he is in a poor position to criticize others' lack of comprehension. And Quickly's horror at the drunkenness and lechery Evans seems to be teaching the child is ironic, since it is her own associations that lead her to this conclusion.

The mutual incomprehension of the residents of Windsor is reminiscent of that of the residents of Navarre, but this short scene with its few characters enunciating their attitudes towards language—rigid pedantry and unimaginativeness; learning for profit; and associations with lechery and drunkenness (and food)—underlines the constriction of atmosphere in which this child is growing up.

Despite the difficulty in comprehension of the Windsor-

2 Northrop Frye, *A Natural Perspective* (New York, 1965), p. 36, claims that this scene has been "dragged in merely to fill up time."

ites, despite their mutual censure, hostility, and thievery, there is some sense of community in the town. The two wives are loyal to each other; people dine together; the host prevents the duel between Caius and Evans because the community needs both the "terrestrial" and the "celestial" (III.i.106). Individual idiosyncrasies are overcome in the masque scene, in which all the characters speak "perfect" English in their limited attack on Falstaff.

Fenton, who is in some ways Falstaff's other half, succeeds.[8] He wins Anne Page and proves his love by marrying her even though her father has threatened to cut her off. Falstaff is another case. He is attacked because of his sexual improprieties, mainly, but there is only one value in this town, and Falstaff is no more of a threat to the property of its men than is the host. He is, at the conclusion, accepted as an "insider," but he cannot be an insider because he has no money. Falstaff is an eternal outsider; as a sexual threat he is a poor devil. Neither his defeat nor his acceptance is quite satisfying: a play about property is fun only when the cozeners win.

[8] Frye, *Perspective*, p. 89, writes that Fenton becomes the "technical hero," and that, as part of Prince Hal's world, he merges two societies.

WILLIAM GREEN

The Merry Wives of Windsor
on Stage and Screen

Traditionally, *The Merry Wives* has been performed as
a fast-paced farce centering on Falstaff and the two wives.
Broad comic business has tended to camouflage certain
confusing matters in the script. A particularly vexing production problem has been what to do with the sketchy
Order of the Garter plot and its attendant topical references. Many productions excise this material or tie its
two horse-stealing scenes to the incomplete Evans-Caius
revenge scheme launched at the end of Act III, Scene i.

Luckily, theater audiences do not worry about the
textual problems, and the play has been among the most
popular of the comedies in performance from its own
time to the present. And stage directors have found more
than enough in the admixture of character types, accents,
and rollicking action to compensate for the textual incongruities and elusive references. For instance, the noted
American director Michael Kahn, writing in 1971, commented,

> The characters *are* absolutely wonderful. I don't think
> there is *any* play with such a collection of off-beat,
> marvelous characters. And those people's reality is really
> quite heightened. This is a play where everybody puts on

disguises, everybody plays games and tricks on each other so that kind of particular reality is heightened and there can be funny things happening . . . .

The title page of the 1602 edition of the play, the First Quarto, calls attention to these very features, and gives the earliest evidence of the long and popular stage history of *The Merry Wives*.

A / Most pleasant and / excellent conceited Co- / medie, of Syr *John Falstaffe*, and the / merrie Wius of *Windsor*. / Entermixed with sundrie / variable and pleasing humors, of Syr *Hugh* / the Welch Knight, Iustice *Shallow*, and his / wise Cousin M. *Slender*. / With the swaggering vaine of Auncient / *Pistoll*, and Corporall *Nym*. / By *William Shakespeare*. / As it hath bene diuers times Acted by the right Honorable / my Lord Chamberlaines seruants. Both before her / Maiestie, and else-where. / [*ornament*] / LONDON / Printed by T. C. for Arthur Iohnson, and are to be sold at / his shop in Powles Church-yard, at the signe of the / Flower de Leuse and the Crowne. / 1602.

The allusion to presentation before Her Majesty (Elizabeth I) refers to what is now generally accepted as the probable first performance of the play: April 23, 1597, during the festivities of the Order of the Garter at Whitehall Palace in London. Apparently, from the further reference on this title page to the play's having been acted "diverse times" elsewhere, it quickly went into the repertory of the Lord Chamberlain's Men. However, the earliest reference to a specific performance is to a presentation before King James I at Whitehall Palace in November, 1604. A record of court payment to Shakespeare's company on May 20, 1613, for the performance of fourteen of his plays, may also be relevant, since one of the plays is entitled *Sir John ffalstaffe*. This may refer to *The Merry Wives*, since the following entry in the Chamber accounts of this date lists another Falstaff-related play entitled *The Hotspur*. The next specific record of performance, however, is to one before King Charles I and Queen Henrietta Maria on November 15, 1638, at the Cockpit.

Four years later, in 1642, the theaters were officially closed by an act of Parliament and remained so until 1660. When they reopened in the Restoration era, stage records show that *The Merry Wives* was soon performed. With the London theater companies officially limited to two at this time—those of Sir William Davenant and Thomas Killigrew—Killigrew chose *The Merry Wives* in the division of Shakespeare's plays between them. Samuel Pepys, that inveterate theatergoer and diarist of the period, saw it three times at Killigrew's theater (the King's), but without much joy. On his first visit on December 5, 1660, he found "the humours of the country gentleman and the French doctor done very well, but the rest very poorly, and Sir J. Falstaffe as bad as any." He had a similar negative reaction on September 25, 1661. He tried yet again on August 15, 1667, but recorded that the play "did not please me at all, in no part of it." No records survive to indicate how it was staged by the King's Company, or what the script was like, but it is known that Killigrew stuck fairly closely to Shakespeare's texts, unlike Davenant, who freely adapted the plays. In spite of Pepys's reactions, *The Merry Wives* was occasionally performed in London and Dublin during the late seventeenth century.

In the eighteenth century *The Merry Wives* established itself as one of the most popular of Shakespeare's plays. Hardly a year went by from 1704 to 1798 without several performances in London. From 1720 to 1730 the play was presented exclusively at Lincoln's Inn Fields. Thereafter it was acted frequently at Drury Lane and Covent Garden, with a total of about 336 performances for the century—not an insignificant record for the time.

In 1702 an adaptation by John Dennis appeared, entitled *The Comical Gallant: or The Amours of Sir John Falstaffe*. Dennis tightened the plot structure, amplified the role of Fenton, and made the action center on Fenton, but the adaptation did not find favor, for *The Comical Gallant* received only one performance in May, 1702, at

Drury Lane. Dennis blamed its failure on the actor who played Falstaff. Thereafter, Shakespeare's version returned to the stage.

In April, 1704, it was acted at court with an all-star cast drawn from both theater companies—Thomas Betterton as Falstaff, Anne Bracegirdle as Mistress Ford, and Elizabeth Barry as Mistress Page. On October 22, 1720, James Quin made his first appearance as Falstaff in *The Merry Wives*. Noted for his playing of serious parts, Quin surprised the Lincoln's Inn Fields company with his outstanding performance. Falstaff became one of his most famous roles, both in the comedy and subsequently in the histories. After Quin retired, James Love became a noted Falstaff. Such leading actresses of the eighteenth century as Mrs. Woffington and Mrs. Pope were often seen in the roles of the merry wives.

In America, the earliest professional performance known of *The Merry Wives* is that of the American Company of Comedians, headed by David Douglass, on March 2, 1770, at the Southwark Theatre in Philadelphia. New York had its first *Merry Wives* in 1789 at the John Street Theatre. There were other eighteenth-century productions in Philadelphia in 1790 and 1795, and in Boston in 1796.

The popularity of the play in England continued throughout the nineteenth century, with one leading actor of the time after another playing Falstaff in the comedy. (Sometimes all three Falstaff plays were in the active repertory of a company with the same actor cast as Falstaff, but unless otherwise noted, the Falstaff references herein are to *The Merry Wives*.) In April, 1802, George Frederick Cooke gave his initial performance in the role at Covent Garden. He had already acted Falstaff in *1 Henry IV*, and he had written in his journal, "I have several times repeated it, with the Falstaffs of the second part, and Merry Wives of Windsor [*sic*], but never could please myself, or come up to my own ideas on any of them." In spite of his dissatisfaction with his handling of the role, the London critics found him the best Falstaff of the day. Cooke's fourteen-page partbook for his *Merry Wives* Falstaff, dated 27 April 1802, is at the Folger Shakespeare Library.

Among the great actor-managers of the nineteenth century, John Philip Kemble played Master Ford to Cooke's Falstaff in an 1804 production at Covent Garden. Kemble's younger brother Stephen, noted for being very fat, appeared in the role in both the *Henry IV* plays and *The Merry Wives* at Drury Lane in October, 1816. His girth prompted Hazlitt to comment, "We see no more reason why Mr. Stephen Kemble should play Falstaff, than why Louis XVIII is qualified to fill a throne, because he is fat, and belongs to a particular family. Every fat man cannot represent a great man."

London productions of the comedy took an interesting sidetrack in February, 1824, when Frederick Reynolds transformed *The Merry Wives* into what may loosely be called an opera, with music by Henry Bishop. This version, produced at Drury Lane, included songs from other Shakespearean plays, among them "All that glitters is not gold" placed in Act III and "When daisies pied" in Act V, sung by the merry wives. A prime reason for the popularity of this version was the appearance in the cast of Madame Vestris as Mistress Page. In October of that year she acted in it at her benefit at the Haymarket. At the Lyceum in 1845 she again presented the Reynolds-Bishop version—now casting herself as Mrs. Ford. Seven songs from other plays by Shakespeare still clung to the text. This musicalized *Merry Wives*, the most enduring of the Reynolds and Bishop operatic reworkings of Shakespeare's comedies, lasted almost a century.

While not in the mainstream of productions of the comedy, one worthy of note took place at the Haymarket theatre in London in 1848. Charles Dickens and the illustrator George Cruikshank appeared in a benefit performance for "The Endowment of a Perpetual Curatorship of Shakespeare's House." Cruikshank, incidentally, later executed a series of etchings for Brough's *Life of Sir John Falstaff* (1858).

The hold of the Reynolds-Bishop version was actually broken in November, 1851, when Charles Kean—who had become sole manager of the Princess's Theatre—opened his initial season with the comedy "divested," in the words of J. W. Cole, his eulogist, "of the operatic and textual interpolations by which it had been too long disfigured." (In fact, one song from the Reynolds-Bishop version was retained, using an original lyric from Act V, Scene v, "Fie on sinful fantasy.") The acting was notably strong: Kean and his wife, Ellen Tree, played the Fords, George Bartley played Falstaff—he was considered the best Falstaff of his day—and the outstanding comedian J. P. Harley played Slender. The production had a run of twenty-five nights and made the reputation of the Princess' under Kean.

On December 19, 1874, Samuel Phelps, then principal actor at the Gaiety Theatre, played Falstaff in an outstanding production of the comedy. (He had previously acted the role at Sadler's Wells.) Among the performers was Johnston Forbes-Robertson as Fenton. John Hollingshead, who was producer at the Gaiety at the time, got his friend Arthur Sullivan to compose special music for the production, and Algernon Swinburne wrote the lyrics ("Love laid his sleepless head / On a thorny rosy bed") for a song sung by Miss Furtado, who played Anne Page. The audience, still used to their Reynolds-Bishop favorite, "Fie on sinful fantasy," strongly voiced its displeasure with the substitution. The reception of Sullivan's other music seems to have been more favorable, for, as an example, as Hollingshead has noted in his *Gaiety Chronicles*, "The revels round Herne's Oak were performed by a trained band of singing boys, who did justice to Arthur Sullivan's music, which is now a concert classic."

The closing years of the nineteenth century are marked by two events in the English stage history of *The Merry Wives* which carried over into the twentieth. In 1887, the Shakespeare Memorial Theatre at Stratford-upon-Avon, which had opened in 1879, presented its first of what was to be a long line of productions of the comedy. Under the directorship of Frank Benson the play was performed in twenty of the seasons during the period 1887–1916.

The second event was the Herbert Beerbohm Tree production of the play at the Haymarket Theatre in 1889, in which Tree played Falstaff, with his wife Helen Maud Holt as Anne Page. His presentation was well received, and Tree gained recognition as a leading actor-manager of the day. He revived the play frequently, especially when he took over His Majesty's Theatre in 1897, the house at which he made his great reputation. Tree had both a five-act and a three-act version of the play. He played Falstaff in the comedy to the end of his career. For his merry wives he had in his company in one production or another Ellen Terry, Mrs. Kendal, Lady Tree, and Constance Collier. Oscar Asche, who was soon to gain a reputation as a director, was his Master Ford in several of the revivals. And Tree used Sir Arthur Sullivan's music. While Tree's acting of the role did not bring forth critical acclaim, his make-up and the alteration of his physical appearance from his natural slimness did attract attention. Henry James, who saw him perform Falstaff in London, regarded his portrayal more as scenery than as acting, noting, "a Falstaff all 'make-up' is an opaque substance." When on his first American visit in 1895 Tree presented *The Merry Wives* in New York, the critics treated his interpretation of Falstaff rather harshly, but on a subsequent visit to New York in 1916, as part of the tercentenary celebration of Shakespeare's death, his production was well received, and in fact was considered the best of the three plays he brought with him for the celebration (the other two were *The Merchant of Venice* and *Henry VIII*). Constance Collier and Henrietta Crossman were the merry wives.

A fascinating account of Tree's 1902 revival of the play comes from the pen of Willa Cather, who, while on her first European journey, wrote a review of it for the *Nebraska State Journal* dated Paris, August 8, 1902. This production was part of the festivities for the coronation of Edward VII, who came to the throne in 1901. It was also the production, as Cather notes, that at last brought about a truce between the two most popular women on the English stage—Mrs. Kendal and Ellen Terry. The breach between the two actresses was of some twenty years' standing, and seemed likely to endure until the end of their working days, for Mrs. Kendal is relentlessness itself, and Miss Terry is not overly prone to sue for pardon. But the coronation being an occasion of no little importance, and the King's interest in Mr. Tree's venture being known, the two ladies were got together and the terms of the peace arranged, Miss Terry being cast for the better of the two principal female parts [i.e., Mrs. Page].

Cather was very impressed with the set design, which, in Tree's characteristic manner of filling the stage with elaborate realistic scenery, re-created an Elizabethan Windsor down to cobblestone streets for the village scenes. Cather saw Tree's three-act version of the play, and she was not happy with the pruning that he had done. Nor did she particularly like Tree's interpretation of Falstaff. He "plays the character," she wrote, "with an earnestness which quite robs it of its flavour." Ellen Terry, in contrast, captivated her. "She plays as though she were seventeen yesterday; with an elasticity, a lightness, and a relish" and "that charm."

The successful revivals that *The Merry Wives* had had in England in the nineteenth century carried over to America. President Abraham Lincoln even attended a performance at Ford's Theatre in December, 1863. New York saw productions, for example, at the Park Theatre in 1836, '38, and '44. The actor-manager William E. Burton presented it at Burton's Chambers Street Theatre in 1850, playing the Host; in 1853 again, with himself as Falstaff; and at his benefit performance at Tripler Hall in 1858, also playing.Falstaff. For his 1853 production Burton set the comedy in the reign of Henry IV, with historically accurate scenery and costumes. The production was not well received, nor was Burton's interpretation of Falstaff in which he tried to portray the fat knight as a gentleman. Augustin Daly produced three revivals of *The Merry Wives*, the first at his Fifth Avenue Theatre in November, 1872, and the other two at Daly's Theatre in 1886 and in 1898. Of the 1872 production, *The New York Times* reviewer E. A. Dithmar commented, "It is not likely that the play has ever been as well acted." Daly's 1886 production engendered much debate. Daly used a revised four-act version made by William Winter with a variety of cuts and expurgations of religious and vulgar words. Of this production the *Times* critic Dithmar noted, "The text is shorn of all its vulgarity . . . . Daintiness and gracefulness are the characteristics of performance now, not the boisterous frolic and the hearty animalism of old England, its men and its literature." Not even the brilliant cast received a favorable press. Charles Fisher, who also had performed the role in 1872, played Falstaff as a Santa Claus-like figure; Ada Rehan and John Drew were the Fords; Otis Skinner and Virginia Dreher played the Pages. The actors were considered too young for their roles and their styles of acting too natural. Ada Rehan again played Mrs. Ford in the 1898 production.

Aside from the major revivals mentioned above, *The Merry Wives* in nineteenth-century America is particularly noteworthy for James Henry Hackett's interpretation of Falstaff. Hackett first played the part in *The Merry Wives* in 1838, having already performed Falstaff in *1 Henry IV* in 1828; he added *2 Henry IV* to his repertory in 1841. He became identified with Falstaff for the bulk of his long career, playing him throughout the United States and in London. He adopted a moralizing attitude toward the character, and even subtitled the play in his productions *Falstaff Outwitted by Women*. Hackett's text was basically the Reynolds-Bishop version without the songs, sometimes played in five acts and sometimes in three.

In the twentieth century in England, with the success of the Shakespeare Memorial Theatre, *The Merry Wives* continued as a staple of the Stratford festival under W. Bridges-Adams, who had assumed the directorship of the company in 1919. The play was revived during eight of the Bridges-Adams seasons in the period 1919–31. Thereafter it has been produced regularly but less frequently by the Shakespeare Memorial Theatre, now known as the Royal Shakespeare Company. Some of the company's more noteworthy revivals are alluded to below.

The Old Vic company, which had become a home for Shakespearean production at the start of World War I, between 1914 and 1923 was the first theater in the world to present the complete cycle of Shakespeare's plays. Some of the outstanding Old Vic Falstaffs of that period were Patrick Kerwin (1914), Ben Greet (1917), and Russell Thorndike (1919).

The twentieth century saw the rise of experimental productions of the comedy. The earliest of these is probably Oscar Asche's 1911 "wintry" version at the Garrick, in which he moved the play out of its usually accepted spring season time frame. Asche, a skilled actor who knew *The Merry Wives* well—he acted Falstaff in that 1911 production and earlier had played Pistol in several Benson productions as well as Master Ford with Tree—was not satisfied with an orthodox approach to the text, but his novel production proved unpopular. In 1929 he was even more daring in his modernized production performed in London: Falstaff called for a taxi whenever he left the stage, and Evans (dressed in a speckled straw hat) rode on a bicycle and carried a radio. The production was not well received, and it closed in less than a week. Asche did do a traditional staging of the comedy in 1932 at the Winter Garden for Frank Benson's unofficial London farewell; he played Falstaff, and Benson played Dr. Caius.

A few years later, in 1935, Theodore Komisarjevsky brought nontraditional staging of *The Merry Wives* to the fore with his Viennese-atmosphere production at Stratford-upon-Avon. Set mainly in the 1830s and '40s, the production broke with the traditional stage setting of Elizabethan half-timbered houses. According to one reviewer, Komisarjevsky's Windsor looked like "a series of ice-cream kiosks on a seaside pier." Equally novel was the costuming: Falstaff (Roy Byford), made up to resemble Emperor Franz Josef, wore a scarlet coat and a *jaeger* hat. Komisarjevsky sought to shock the audience into a new aesthetic perception of the play by conceiving of it as a musical farce, a conception which he underscored by employing Viennese-style melodies in the background. Although he puzzled the critics, his approach to this and other plays he directed at Stratford between 1932 and 1939 influenced subsequent Shakespearean staging.

In 1940, during the Battle of Britain, Donald Wolfit included the comedy in his one-hour lunchtime condensed versions of Shakespeare's plays at the Strand Theatre. Wolfit played Falstaff, a role which he repeated in 1942, again at the Strand Theatre, stressing a boyish mischievousness in the character.

Mainly because of the war, the forties were a slack time for *Merry Wives* productions in London and Stratford, with only an occasional revival, but after World War II the Old Vic performed the play in 1951 as part of the Festival of Britain in a production directed by Hugh Hunt. Peggy Ashcroft and Ursula Jeans were the wives, Roger Livesey played Falstaff, and Alec Clunes played Ford. In 1955 the Old Vic again presented the play, staged by Douglas Seale and set in the Restoration era. Wendy Hiller and Margaret Rawlings were the wives, Alex McCowen played Ford, and Paul Rogers acted Falstaff with an air of gentility. In 1959, John Hale directed another Old Vic revival, but it did not attract much attention. Four years later the company disbanded.

Outstanding Stratford-upon-Avon productions of approximately the last thirty years date from Glen Byam Shaw's wintry version of 1955, reminiscent of Oscar Asche's controversial production of 1911. The stage design, by Motley, resembled a Christmas card illustration derived from Breughel paintings. Shaw, like Asche, was attacked by the critics for this winter setting. The cast included Anthony Quayle as Falstaff, Keith Michell as Ford, Angela Baddeley and Joyce Redman as Mistress Page and Mistress Ford, and Rosalind Atkinson as Mistress Quickly. In 1968, Terry Hands directed the first of two revivals he did of the play for the Royal Shakespeare Company. While Hands pushed all the farcical potential of the text, he also stressed a clash between an emerging mercantile society and the world of the court, thereby setting a serious counterpoint to the farce of the play. This theme has influenced many post-World War II directors of *The Merry Wives*. Brewster Mason played Falstaff, with Ian Richardson drawing critical acclaim for his comic interpretation of Ford; Brenda Bruce and Elizabeth Spriggs portrayed Mistress Page and Mistress Ford as the epitome of bourgeois housewives. Hands's second revival, this one in 1975 with basically the same cast, was presented with *1* and *2 Henry IV* and *Henry V* as part of a tetralogy of Falstaff plays, but with no attempt to force *The Merry Wives* into a sequence with the other three. (Any such attempt would be unsuccessful.) But this production of *The Merry Wives* was less favorably received than Hands's earlier one; critics thought it was overacted, and they faulted Ian Richardson for an overuse of farcical tricks. For their 1979 Stratford production, Trevor Nunn and John Caird created a very realistic Tudor Windsor in which, according to the critic Benedict Nightingale, "materialism, greed, and imperviousness to people" were stressed. John Woodvine played Falstaff with Ben Kingsley as Ford.

The most innovative staging *The Merry Wives* has received to date was the 1985 Royal Shakespeare Company's Stratford production of Bill Alexander. With the memory of the successful Terry Hands and Trevor Nunn revivals of 1968 and 1979—set in Elizabethan England—still fresh, Alexander believed that artistically he had to take a different approach to the play. Seeing it, he has said, as dealing with "the new, powerful bourgeois class that was emerging in a time of upward mobility," he found the Harold Macmillan world of 1959 with its slogan "You've never had it so good" as closely paralleling that of the Windsor of the play. Thus, without distorting the text, and with sets and costumes by William Dudley, he created a 1950s suburban Windsor. The merry wives compare their identical letters under hair dryers in the beauty parlor, and Herne's Oak becomes a sawn-off tree stump suggesting that Windsor Great Park has been destroyed for housing development. Falstaff (Peter Jeffrey) wears a yellow waistcoat, plus fours, and golf shoes; Mistress Page (Janet Dale) and Mistress Ford (Lindsay Duncan) are garbed in toreador pants and stiletto heels. The production was well received.

A year before this RSC production, in 1984, an updated revival of the comedy was presented at the Open Air Theatre in London's Regent's Park. It was set in the Victorian era, with the costuming giving the characters a Dickensian quality. While the interpretation of director David Conville was conventional, what made the production particularly attractive was the way the greystone buildings of Regent's Park were used for the Victorian architectural background and the way the park trees were used for the Herne's Oak and Windsor Forest scenes.

In the United States, in the twentieth century, Louis Calvert played Falstaff in a 1910 revival at the New Theatre with Edith Wynne Matthison and Rose Coghlan as Mistress Ford and Mistress Page, but the first significant American production was given in 1916, as part of the tercentenary celebration of Shakespeare's death already alluded to in connection with Herbert Beerbohm Tree's presentation of *The Merry Wives* in New York. James Keteltas Hackett—son of James Henry Hackett and an outstanding actor himself—planned a production at the Criterion Theatre. Henrietta Crossman was cast as Mistress Page and Viola Allen as Mistress Ford, with Hackett as Falstaff. Joseph Urban, the Viennese designer recently arrived in America, did the scenery in the new style of set design hardly then known in the United States. Hackett fell ill and had to withdraw from the production. Tom Wise, a seasoned Broadway comedian who had never played Shakespeare, took over the role and ten days later, on March 20, opened as Falstaff. The critics were not too kind, but the quality of the performances picked up until a couple of months later the comedy was playing to full houses. For contractual reasons it had to close, but it was restaged and reopened in January, 1917, for a successful run at the Park Theatre with Wise again playing Falstaff. The wives now were Constance Collier and Isabel Irving. In March, 1928, in a revival at the Knickerbocker Theatre, Otis Skinner played Falstaff to the Mistress Page of Minnie Maddern Fiske and the Mistress Ford of Henrietta Crossman. Harrison Grey Fiske directed. Charles Coburn, who today is best remembered for his film roles, played Falstaff for the Theatre Guild in 1946.

Slightly out of the mainstream of *Merry Wives* revivals but within the purview of this account is the sketch that the burlesque and vaudeville star Bobby Clark did in Mike Todd's 1942 Broadway burlesque revue *Star and Garter*. Clark, in a sketch entitled "That Merry Wife of Windsor," played a modern-day Falstaff caught in a love encounter by an enraged husband.

The spread of university and regional theater in North America in recent years along with the founding of the great Stratford Festival in Canada and of Shakespeare summer festivals throughout the United States has led, collectively, to frequent revivals of *The Merry Wives*. Only a sampling of the more notable or unusual of these productions can be given here. The comedy was revived twice by the American Shakespeare Festival Theatre in Stratford, Connecticut, in 1959 and 1971. Michael Kahn's 1971 production used black, beige, and white to give a background effect of Elizabethan woodcuts. The linear black and white device was carried through to the costumes. Kahn said that thematically he stressed "the growth of the middle class in Elizabethan England . . . and the emerging Elizabethan woman."

In a production at the San Diego Shakespeare Festival in 1965, the director Mel Shapiro presented a Hogarthian interpretation of the comedy complete with slide projections of boudoirs and breasts to reveal Ford's inner thoughts. Will Geer played Falstaff in what was considered a lively production. Joseph Papp's New York Shakespeare Festival revival of 1974 featured Barnard Hughes as Falstaff in a production which, while visually effective in creating an atmosphere of Elizabethan life through Santo Loquasto's set, was faulted for the weak directorial interpretation of David Margulies. A production at the Shakespeare/Santa Cruz festival in 1983, staged by the Australian director Michael Edwards, transplanted the play to the Plymouth Colony of the 1640s, giving it overtones of an Old World/New World link. Also in the summer of 1983 the Riverside Shakespeare Company in New York presented in various neighborhood city parks a free-wheeling version set in New Orleans after the Civil War. Old-soldier tunes and a ragtime band were added, and the fairy magic was changed into voodoo magic. Falstaff (Joseph Reed) was turned into "a sleazily retired Confederate Colonel," and Mistress Quickly (Anna Deaver Smith) became a voodoo practitioner. The critics liked the broad, farcical treatment, especially the device of having the characters speak with Louisiana inflections.

In Canada the Shakespearean Festival of Stratford, Ontario, presented its first *Merry Wives* in 1956 in a production directed by Michael Langham. It was not well received by either the critics or the public, but Douglas Campbell was praised for the less exuberant, more reflective quality he brought to his portrayal of Falstaff than is usually found. An interesting point about this production is the additions Langham asked the Canadian playwright Robertson Davies to make in the text so that the scenes involving the supposed Germans and the stealing of the post horses in the fourth act became intelligible. The additions were so skillfully done, including the pseudo-Shakespearean dialogue, that they went undetected by the audience. In the 1967 revival, under the direction of David William, Tony van Bridge played Falstaff, with Zoe Caldwell and Francis Hyland as respectively Mistress Page and Mistress Ford. Except for these performers, the cast and production were regarded as dull. The 1978 revival with Peter Moss as director was set in the early Restoration period. William Hutt played Falstaff, and Alan Scarfe as Ford was praised for his interpretation of the role. Moss's attempt to stress class and sexual tensions in society received a mixed reception from the critics. In a 1982 revival, Douglas Campbell returned to the role of Falstaff, playing him in an exaggerated manner to the Ford of Nicholas Pennell. This was a straightforward production of the comedy which stressed the country-town community atmosphere.

The Merry Wives has been transformed into a Broadway-style book musical entitled *I Love Alice*. This version was written by Peter Massey and Victoria Holloway with music and lyrics by John Franceschina. *I Love Alice*, set in suburban Windsor in 1950, was performed by The American Stage Company in St. Petersburg, Florida, in 1985. Chief among the operatic versions are Nicolai's *The Merry Wives of Windsor* (1849), Verdi's *Falstaff* (1893), and Vaughan Williams's *Sir John in Love* (1929).

Film and video treatments of *The Merry Wives* are few and undistinguished. The earliest screen version, a silent film made in 1910 by the Selig Polyscope Company of Chicago, concentrated on Falstaff, and was characterized by a reviewer as "a relatively satisfactory presentation of Falstaff's doings, and markedly appreciated by the audience." In 1911, a silent film entitled *Falstaff* was produced in France by Eclipse. It was imported to the United States, where the *Moving Picture World* commented in its issue of June 24, "The story of Shakespeare's *Merry Wives of Windsor* is well acted in this picture. We have the story plainly enough and it's an amusing one, but very little of the fun that is in the original comes over." Of this one-reel production, Robert Hamilton Ball, the noted historian of the silent film, has commented, "With good acting and photography, *Falstaff* must have been a picture worth seeing in 1911." Falstaff became the unifying feature of Orson Welles's 1965 black and white film *Chimes at Midnight*, a film that can be linked only peripherally with *The Merry Wives*, since Welles—interested chiefly in exploring the relationship between Hal and the fat knight—used only minimal material from *The Merry Wives*.

The BBC presented a television version of the play in 1952 in black and white. Robert Atkins was Falstaff, Betty Huntley-Wright played Mistress Ford, and Mary Kerridge was Mistress Page. In 1955, another BBC black and white version was made with Glen Byam Shaw co-directing with Barrie Edgar. This production was based on Shaw's Shakespeare Memorial Theatre production that season, and used the same company. Anthony Quayle was Falstaff, and Angela Baddeley and Joyce Redman repeated their roles as the merry wives. In the BBC/Time-Life Shakespeare TV series, *The Merry Wives*, in color, was presented in 1982 in a production directed by David Jones. The cast was distinguished (Falstaff was played by Richard Griffiths, Prunella Scales was Mistress Page, Judy Davis acted Mistress Ford, and Ben Kingsley played Ford), but the production was unexciting.

Bibliographic Note: The sources used in preparing this essay range from newspaper and periodical reviews through notes from theater programs to historical studies, calendars culled from performance records, and biographies of theater practitioners. Only a selected list can be given here. For the stage, see William Babula, *Shakespeare in Production, 1935–1978* (1981); Willa Cather, *Willa Cather in Europe* (1956); Richard David, *Shakespeare in the Theatre* (1978); Esther Cloudman Dunn, *Shakespeare in America* (1939); Bernard Grebanier,*Then Came Each Actor* (1975); James Henry Hackett, *Notes, Criticisms and Correspondence upon Shakespeare's Plays and Actors* (1863, rpt. 1968); Charles Beecher Hogan, *Shakespeare in the Theatre 1701–1800*, 2 vols. (1952, 1957); Samuel L. Leiter, *Shakespeare Around the Globe* (1986); George C. D. Odell, *Shakespeare from Betterton through Irving*, 2 vols. (1920, rpt. 1966); Charles H. Shattuck, *Shakespeare on the American Stage*, 2 vols. (1976, 1987); David Wheeler, "Eighteenth-Century Adaptations of Shakespeare and the Example of John Dennis," *Shakespeare Quar-*

terly 36 (1985), 438–49; Don B. Wilmeth, *George Frederick Cooke* (1980); *London Theatre Record*; New Cambridge edition of *The Merry Wives of Windsor* (1921); *The Reader's Encyclopedia of Shakespeare* (1966). For the screen, see Robert Hamilton Ball, *Shakespeare on Silent Film* (1968); Graham Holderness and Christopher McCullough, "A Selective Filmography," *Shakespeare Survey* 39 (1987); Jack J. Jorgens, *Shakespeare on Film* (1977); Roger Manvell, *Shakespeare & the Film* (1971). A special note of thanks for filmography information to Professor Kenneth S. Rothwell (University of Vermont).

Suggested References

The number of possible references is vast and grows alarmingly. (The *Shakespeare Quarterly* devotes one issue each year to a list of the previous year's work, and *Shakespeare Survey*—an annual publication—includes a substantial review of recent scholarship, as well as an occasional essay surveying a few decades of scholarship on a chosen topic.) Though no works are indispensable, those listed below have been found helpful.

1. Shakespeare's Times

Byrne, M. St. Clare. *Elizabethan Life in Town and Country*. Rev. ed. New York: Barnes & Noble, 1961. Chapters on manners, beliefs, education, etc., with illustrations.

Joseph, B. L. *Shakespeare's Eden: The Commonwealth of England 1558–1629*. New York: Barnes & Noble, 1971. An account of the social, political, economic, and cultural life of England.

Schoenbaum, S. *Shakespeare: The Globe and the World*. New York: Oxford University Press, 1979. A readable, handsomely illustrated book on the world of the Elizabethans.

Shakespeare's England. 2 vols. London: Oxford University Press, 1916. A large collection of scholarly essays on a wide variety of topics (e.g. astrology, costume, gardening, horsemanship), with special attention to Shakespeare's references to these topics.

Stone, Lawrence. *The Crisis of the Aristocracy, 1558–1641*, abridged edition. London: Oxford University Press, 1967.

2. Shakespeare

Barnet, Sylvan. *A Short Guide to Shakespeare*. New York: Harcourt Brace Jovanovich, 1974. An introduction to all of the works and to the dramatic traditions behind them.

Bentley, Gerald E. *Shakespeare: A Biographical Handbook.* New Haven, Conn.: Yale University Press, 1961. The facts about Shakespeare, with virtually no conjecture intermingled.

Bush, Geoffrey. *Shakespeare and the Natural Condition.* Cambridge, Mass.: Harvard University Press, 1956. A short, sensitive account of Shakespeare's view of "Nature," touching most of the works.

Chambers, E. K. *William Shakespeare: A Study of Facts and Problems.* 2 vols. London: Oxford University Press, 1930. An invaluable, detailed reference work; not for the casual reader.

Chute, Marchette. *Shakespeare of London.* New York: Dutton, 1949. A readable biography fused with portraits of Stratford and London life.

Clemen, Wolfgang H. *The Development of Shakespeare's Imagery.* Cambridge, Mass.: Harvard University Press, 1951. (Originally published in German, 1936.) A temperate account of a subject often abused.

Granville-Barker, Harley. *Prefaces to Shakespeare.* 2 vols. Princeton, N.J.: Princeton University Press, 1946–47. Essays on ten plays by a scholarly man of the theater.

Harbage, Alfred. *As They Liked It.* New York: Macmillan, 1947. A long, sensitive essay on Shakespeare, morality, and the audience's expectations.

Kernan, Alvin B., ed. *Modern Shakespearean Criticism: Essays on Style, Dramaturgy, and the Major Plays.* New York: Harcourt Brace Jovanovich, 1970. A collection of major formalist criticism.

———. "The Plays and the Playwrights." In *The Revels History of Drama in English,* general editors Clifford Leech and T. W. Craik. Vol. III. London: Methuen, 1975. A book-length essay surveying Elizabethan drama with substantial discussions of Shakespeare's plays.

Schoenbaum, S. *Shakespeare's Lives.* Oxford: Clarendon Press, 1970. A review of the evidence, and an examination of many biographies, including those by Baconians and other heretics.

———. *William Shakespeare: A Compact Documentary Life.* New York: Oxford University Press, 1977. A readable presentation of all that the documents tell us about Shakespeare.

Traversi, D. A. *An Approach to Shakespeare*. 3rd rev. ed. 2 vols. New York: Doubleday, 1968–69. An analysis of the plays, beginning with words, images, and themes, rather than with characters.

Van Doren, Mark. *Shakespeare*. New York: Holt, 1939. Brief, perceptive readings of all of the plays.

3. Shakespeare's Theater

Beckerman, Bernard. *Shakespeare at the Globe, 1599–1609*. New York: Macmillan, 1962. On the playhouse and on Elizabethan dramaturgy, acting, and staging.

Chambers, E. K. *The Elizabethan Stage*. 4 vols. New York: Oxford University Press, 1945. A major reference work on theaters, theatrical companies, and staging at court.

Cook, Ann Jennalie. *The Privileged Playgoers of Shakespeare's London, 1576–1642*. Princeton, N.J.: Princeton University Press, 1981. Sees Shakespeare's audience as more middle-class and more intellectual than Harbage (below) does.

Gurr, Andrew. *The Shakespearean Stage: 1579–1642*. 2nd edition. Cambridge: Cambridge University Press, 1980. On the acting companies, the actors, the playhouses, the stages, and the audiences.

Harbage, Alfred. *Shakespeare's Audience*. New York: Columbia University Press, 1941. A study of the size and nature of the theatrical public, emphasizing its representativeness.

Hodges, C. Walter. *The Globe Restored*. London: Ernest Benn, 1953; New York: Coward-McCann, Inc., 1954. A well-illustrated and readable attempt to reconstruct the Globe Theatre.

Hosley, Richard. "The Playhouses." In *The Revels History of Drama in English*, general editors Clifford Leech and T. W. Craik. Vol. III. London: Methuen, 1975. An essay of one hundred pages on the physical aspects of the playhouses.

Kernodle, George R. *From Art to Theatre: Form and Convention in the Renaissance*. Chicago: University of Chicago Press, 1944. Pioneering and stimulating work on the symbolic and cultural meanings of theater construction.

Nagler, A. M. *Shakespeare's Stage.* Tr. by Ralph Manheim. New Haven, Conn.: Yale University Press, 1958. A very brief introduction to the physical aspect of the playhouse.

Slater, Ann Pasternak. *Shakespeare the Director.* Totowa, N.J.: Barnes & Noble, 1982. An analysis of theatrical effects (e.g., kissing, kneeling) in stage directions and dialogue.

Thomson, Peter. *Shakespeare's Theatre.* London: Routledge & Kegan Paul, 1983. A discussion of how plays were staged in Shakespeare's time.

4. Miscellaneous Reference Works

Abbott, E. A. *A Shakespearean Grammar.* New edition. New York: Macmillan, 1877. An examination of differences between Elizabethan and modern grammar.

Bevington, David. *Shakespeare.* Arlington Heights, Ill.: A. H. M. Publishing, 1978. A short guide to hundreds of important writings on the works.

Bullough, Geoffrey. *Narrative and Dramatic Sources of Shakespeare.* 8 vols. New York: Columbia University Press, 1957–1975. A collection of many of the books Shakespeare drew upon with judicious comments.

Campbell, Oscar James, and Edward G. Quinn. *The Reader's Encyclopedia of Shakespeare.* New York: Crowell, 1966. More than 2,600 entries, from a few sentences to a few pages on everything related to Shakespeare.

Greg, W. W. *The Shakespeare First Folio.* New York: Oxford University Press, 1955. A detailed yet readable history of the first collection (1623) of Shakespeare's plays.

Kökeritz, Helge. *Shakespeare's Names.* New Haven, Conn.: Yale University Press, 1953. Contains much information about puns and rhymes.

Muir, Kenneth. *The Sources of Shakespeare's Plays.* New Haven, Conn.: Yale University Press, 1978. An account of Shakespeare's use of his reading.

The Norton Facsimile: The First Folio of Shakespeare. Prepared by Charlton Hinman. New York: Norton, 1968. A handsome and accurate facsimile of the first collection 1623) of Shakespeare's plays.

Onions, C. T. *A Shakespeare Glossary.* 2d ed., rev., with enlarged addenda. London: Oxford University Press, 1953. Definitions of words (or senses of words) now obsolete.

Partridge, Eric. *Shakespeare's Bawdy.* Rev. ed. New York: Dutton; London: Routledge & Kegan Paul, 1955. A glossary of bawdy words and phrases.

Shakespeare Quarterly. See headnote to Suggested References.

Shakespeare Survey. See headnote to Suggested References.

Shakespeare's Plays in Quarto. A Facsimile Edition. Ed. Michael J. B. Allen and Kenneth Muir. Berkeley, Calif.: University of California Press, 1981. A book of nine hundred pages, containing facsimiles of twenty-two of the quarto editions of Shakespeare's plays. An invaluable complement to *The Norton Facsimile: The First Folio of Shakespeare* (see above).

Smith, Gordon Ross. *A Classified Shakespeare Bibliography 1936–1958.* University Park, Pa.: Pennsylvania State University Press, 1963. A list of some twenty thousand items on Shakespeare.

Spevack, Marvin. *The Harvard Concordance to Shakespeare.* Cambridge, Mass.: Harvard University Press, 1973. An index to Shakespeare's words.

Wells, Stanley, ed. *Shakespeare: Select Bibliographies.* London: Oxford University Press, 1973. Seventeen essays surveying scholarship and criticism of Shakespeare's life, work, and theater.

5. *Love's Labor's Lost*

Arthos, John. *Shakespeare: The Early Writings.* London: Bowes & Bowes, 1972.

Baldwin, T. W. *Shakspere's Five-Act Structure: Shakspere's Early Plays on the Background of Renaissance Theories of Five-Act Structure from 1470.* Urbana, Illinois: University of Illinois Press, 1947.

Barber, C. L. *Shakespeare's Festive Comedy.* Princeton, N.J.: Princeton University Press, 1959.

Bradbrook, M. C. *The School of Night. Study in the Literary Relationship of Sir Walter Raleigh.* Cambridge: Cambridge University Press, 1936.

Carroll, W. C. *The Great Feast of Language in Love's*

Labour's Lost. Princeton, N.J.: Princeton University Press, 1976.

Harvey, N. L., and Carey, A. K. *Love's Labor's Lost, An Annotated Bibliography*. New York and London: Garland Publishers, 1984.

Homans, Sidney. *When the Theater Turns to Itself*. Lewisburg, Pa.: Bucknell University Press, 1981.

Hoy, Cyrus. *The Hyacinth Room*. New York: Knopf, 1964.

Kerrigan, John. "Shakespeare at Work: The Katharine Rosaline Tangle in *Love's Labour's Lost*," *Review of English Studies*, 33 (1982), 129–36.

Lamb, Mary Ellen. "The Nature of Topicality in *Love's Labour's Lost*," *Shakespeare Survey 38* (1985), 49–59.

Montrose, L. A. *"Curious-Knotted Garden": The Form, Themes, and Contexts of Shakespeare's Love's Labour's Lost*. Salzburg: Universität Salzburg, 1977.

Palmer, J. L. *Comic Characters of Shakespeare*. London: Macmillan, 1946.

Parson, Philip. "Shakespeare and the Mask," *Shakespeare Survey 16*, 121–31.

Roesen, Bobbyann, "Love's Labour's Lost," *Shakespeare Quarterly*, 4 (1953), 411–26.

Taylor, Rupert. *The Date of "Love's Labor's Lost."* New York: AMS Press, 1966.

Vyvyan, John. *Shakespeare and the Rose of Love*. New York: Barnes & Noble, 1960; London: Chatto & Windus, 1960.

Wells, Stanley. "The Copy for the Folio Text of *Love's Labour's Lost*," *Review of English Studies*, 33 (1982), 137–47.

Westlund, Joseph. "Fancy and Achievement in *Love's Labour's Lost*," *Shakespeare Quarterly*, 18. (1967), 37–46.

Wilson, J. D. *Shakespeare's Happy Comedies*. London: Faber and Faber, 1962.

Yates, F. A. *A Study of "Love's Labour's Lost."* Cambridge: Cambridge University Press, 1936.

6. *The Two Gentlemen of Verona*

Berry, Ralph. *Shakespeare's Comedies: Explorations in Form*. Princeton, N.J.: Princeton University Press, 1972.

Brooks, Harold F. "Two Clowns in a Comedy (To Say Nothing of the Dog): Speed, Launce (and Crab) in *The Two Gentlemen of Verona*," *Essays and Studies*, New Series 16 (1963), 91–100.

Champion, Larry S. *The Evolution of Shakespeare's Comedy*. Cambridge, Mass.: Harvard University Press, 1970.

Cook, Ann Jennalie. "Shakespeare's Gentlemen," *Deutsche Shakespeare-Gesellschaft Jahrbuch West* 1985, pp. 9–27.

Ewbank, Inga-Stina. " 'Were Man But Constant, He Were Perfect': Constancy and Consistency in *The Two Gentlemen of Verona*." In *Shakespearean Comedy*, ed. Malcolm Bradbury and David Palmer. Stratford-upon-Avon Studies 14. London: Edward Arnold, 1972. Pp. 31–57.

Goldberg, Jonathan. *Voice Terminal Echo: Postmodernism and English Renaissance Texts*. New York: Methuen, 1986.

Holmberg, Arthur. "*The Two Gentlemen of Verona:* Shakespearean Comedy as a Rite of Passage," *Queen's Quarterly*, 90 (1983), 33–44.

Kiefer, Frederick. "Love Letters in *The Two Gentlemen of Verona*," *Shakespeare Studies*, 18 (1986), 65–85.

Leggatt, Alexander. *Shakespeare's Comedy of Love*. New York: Barnes & Noble, 1974.

Lindenbaum, Peter. "Education in *The Two Gentlemen of Verona*," *Studies in English Literature*, 15 (1975), 229–44.

Nevo, Ruth. *Comic Transformations in Shakespeare*. London: Methuen, 1980.

Phialas, Peter G. *Shakespeare's Romantic Comedies*. Chapel Hill: University of North Carolina Press, 1966.

Rossky, William. "*The Two Gentlemen of Verona* as Burlesque," *English Literary Renaissance*, 12 (1982), 210–19.

Slights, Camille Wells. "*The Two Gentlemen of Verona* and the Courtesy Book Tradition," *Shakespeare Studies*, 16 (1983), 13–31.

Weimann, Robert. "Laughing with the Audience: *The Two Gentlemen of Verona* and the Popular Tradition of Comedy," *Shakespeare Survey*, 22 (1969), 35–42.

White, R. S. "Metamorphosis by Love in Elizabethan Romance, Romantic Comedy, and Shakespeare's Early Comedies," *Review of English Studies*, NS 35 (1984), 14–44.

7. *The Merry Wives of Windsor*

Bryant, Jr., J. A. "Falstaff and the Renewal of Windsor," *PMLA*, 89 (1974), 296–301.

Campbell, Oscar James. "The Italianate Background of *The Merry Wives of Windsor*," *Essays and Studies in English and Comparative Literature*, pp. 81–117. University of Michigan Publications in Language and Literature, Ann Arbor: University of Michigan, 1932.

Crofts, John. *Shakespeare and the Post Horses*. Bristol: J. W. Arrowsmith, Ltd., 1937.

Erickson, Peter. "The Order of the Garter, the cult of Elizabeth, and the class-gender tension in *The Merry Wives of Windsor*" in *Shakespeare Reproduced: The Text in History and Ideology*, ed. Jean E. Howard and Marion F. O'Connor (London: Methuen, 1987), pp. 116–40.

Green, William. *Shakespeare's Merry Wives of Windsor*. Princeton, N.J.: Princeton University Press, 1962.

Hinely, Jan Lawson. "Comic Scapegoats and the Falstaff of The Merry Wives of Windsor," *Shakespeare Studies 15* (1982), ed. J. Leeds Barroll III, pp. 37–54.

Hotson, Leslie. *Shakespeare versus Shallow*. Boston: Little, Brown and Co.; London: Nonesuch Press, Ltd., 1931.

Parrott, Thomas Marc. *Shakespearean Comedy*. New York and London: Oxford University Press, 1949.

Roberts, Jeanne Addison. *Shakespeare's English Comedy: "The Merry Wives of Windsor" in Context*. Lincoln: University of Nebraska Press, 1979.

Rosenberg, S. L. Millard. "Duke Friedrich of Württemberg," *Shakespeare Association Bulletin*, 8 (1933), 92–93.

Rye, William Brenchley (ed.). *England as Seen by Foreigners in the Days of Elizabeth and James the First*. London: J. R. Smith, 1865.

Tighe, Robert Richard and James Edward Davis. *Annals of Windsor, being a History of the Castle and Town*. 2 vols. London: Longman, Brown, Green, Longmans, and Robetrs, 1858.